Monstrosities

By Matthew J. Finch

Dedicated to Madison Finch

Contributing Authors:
Andrew Trent ("the Venomous Pao"), Trent Foster, Salvatore Macri ("Skathros"), Scott Wylie Roberts ("Myrystyr"),
Sean Stone ("Stonegiant"), Sean Wills ("Geordie Racer"), Cameron DuBeers, Matt Hoover ("Random"), Mike Davison,
Russell Cone ("Grim"), Mudguard, Old Crawler, Michael Shorten ("Chgowiz"), Mark Ahmed, Scott Casper ("Scottenkainen"),
The Lizard of Oz, James Malizsewski, Michael Kotschi, J.D. Jarvis, John Turcotte, Guy Fullerton, Michael Coté,
Thomas Clark, Tanner Adams, and Matt Finch ("Mythmere").

Editing:
Matt Finch, Aaron Zirkelbach, Matt Hoover, James Redmon

Developmental Editing:
Rob Ragas, Ragnorakk

Cover Art:
Jon Johnson

Interior Art:
Rowena Aitken, Michael Bielaczyc, Paul Bielaczyc. Andrew DeFelice, Chris McFann, MKUltra Studios, Stan Morrison, Jason Sholtis

Layout & Book Design:
Charles A. Wright

FROG GOD GAMES IS

CEO
Bill Webb

V. P. of Marketing & Sales
Rachel Ventura

Creative Director: Swords & Wizardry
Matthew J. Finch

Art Director
Charles A. Wright

Creative Director: Pathfinder
Greg A. Vaughan

Snake Plissken
Skeeter Green

MYTHMERE GAMES™
www.swordsandwizardry.com
www.talesofthefroggod.com

Introduction

Monstrosities was created with the generous help of the Swords & Wizardry internet community, as you can see from the list of unusually brilliant authors whose erudition and eloquence grace these pages. The book's successes are due to them, whilst any errors or failures in the transcription of their noble work are doubtless my own.

This reference book is a resource for the Swords & Wizardry Referee, containing a vast array of monsters for you to use in your campaign. Keep a few things in mind while reading this book. First of all, there aren't any official rules that bind you as the Referee, so if you decide that a monster should have more hit dice, or that it should have better saving throws than the "official" version, make the change! In the same vein, if there is a monster that doesn't really fit into your campaign, this book is only a sourcebook, so feel free to omit that monster entirely.

Reading the Entries and Conversion Notes

The numerical information for each monster is shown as a "stat block" after the description of the monster, in the following format: HD; AC; Atk; Move; Save; AL; CL/XP; Special. Although the abbreviations will be second nature to most readers, they are described here.

HD (HIT DICE): The monster's hit dice. To determine a monster's hit points, roll a d8 once for each hit die, adding the results. If the entry reads something like "4+2," this means you'd roll 4d8 and add 2 to determine the monster's hit points. Bonus hit points are not added to each hit die.

AC (ARMOR CLASS): Each monster has two entries for armor class, one of which is in brackets. The first entry is for games using a "descending" armor class where lower is better. The bracketed number is for games where the Referee chooses to use an "ascending" armor class system where higher is better.

Atk (ATTACK): This entry describes the number, type, and damage of a monster's physical attacks. Sometimes monsters will have special attacks, such as a venomous bite, that are delivered with a physical attack. For this reason, some entries will show damage of (0) or (0 + special) or a similar notation.

Move: This entry gives the monster's Swords & Wizardry movement rate.

Save: This is the monster's target number to make a saving throw of any kind.

AL (ALIGNMENT): This entry contains a default alignment (Law, Neutrality, or Chaos) for the monster. In the first printing of this book we did not include alignments for the monsters, on the theory that they would feel like a limitation on the Referee's ability to change and adapt the monsters to fit the individual campaign. The general reaction, however, is that a default alignment helps the Referee to get the feel of a monster and isn't very constraining. So, feel free to change or adapt the default alignments!

CL/XP (Challenge Level/XP): This is the difficulty level for killing the monster, and the number of experience points gained for killing the monster.

Special: A list of the monster's special powers, with detail given in the text.

Example Encounter: Following the main entry is a short scenario involving a sample encounter with the monster.

Table of Contents

4

Aardvark, Giant

Hit Dice: 9
Armor Class: 5 [14]
Attacks: 1 tongue (swallow), 2 claws (1d8)
Saving Throw: 6
Special: Swallow whole
Move: 6
Alignment: Neutrality
Number Encountered: probably no more than one mated pair of adults, possibly with 1d4 younger ones (half hit dice).
Challenge Level/XP: 11/1,700

Giant aardvarks resemble their smaller cousins, with a long, pig-like snout, rabbit-like ears, and a kangaroo-like tail. Instead of digging for termites like the normal aardvark, giant aardvarks, which can measure as large as twenty feet in length, tend to dig into cottages and subterranean burrows for large prey such as humans, goblins, and ankhegs. The giant aardvark's tongue is ten feet long, and is used to suck prey into the aardvark's mouth. A successful hit with the tongue forces the target to make a saving throw or be yanked into the aardvark's mouth and swallowed. The monster can be attacked from within (at an AC of 9[10]) but only with a short weapon such as a dagger. Anyone inside the aardvark's stomach takes 1d6 points of damage per round as he is digested. Giant aardvarks don't eat more than a couple of people before they lose interest.

— *Author: Matt Finch*

Giant Aardvark: HD 9; AC 5[14]; Atk 1 tongue (swallows), 2 claws (1d8); Move 6; Save 6; CL/XP 11/1700; Special: Swallow whole.

Mud Brothers and the Aardvark

A plume of smoke rises high into the sky. The plume is visible from miles away. The smoke originates from a small, unnatural hill. Fist-sized balls of metallic clay compose the massive 40-foot-tall mound of dirt. Worn tracks wind along the sides and into numerous 4-foot-wide holes that dot the hillside. Crude balls of golden clay lay beside an overturned wheelbarrow at the foot of the path. **Gertsy Borate** and **Custer Feldspar**, two dwarven miners, mine their precious gold clay from the short twisting mine.

While Gertsy slaved away in the mine, a **giant aardvark** launched an attack with its tongue into the holes. The giant aardvark lurks in the brush nearby, biding its time and waiting for its prey to surface. Undiscovered by the giant aardvark, Custer naps in a crude hammock beside the main trail. He is oblivious to Gertsy's predicament. Both dwarves are mud-caked and not the brightest individuals. Gertsy is trapped within the shallow mine. He is burning the pair's supplies, hoping to scare off the aardvark or at least signal Custer for help. The dwarves reward rescuers with a *+2*

ceramic shield that confers complete fire resistance. If an attacker rolls a natural 20, however, the shield shatters into useless fragments.

Aaztar-Ghola

Hit Dice: 6
Armor Class: 3 [16]
Attacks: 2 swords (1d8)
Saving Throw: 11
Special: Spells, magic resistance 25%
Move: 12
Alignment: Chaos
Number Encountered: 1d4
Challenge Level/XP: 9/1,100

Aaztar-gholas are ancient creatures originating from some other dimension, foul things that have established themselves in the prime material plane. They are tall, and attire their hideous bodies in flowing, richly embroidered robes, adorning themselves with strange, baroque jewelry. Aaztar-gholas find human flesh delectable, especially when it is cooked with the strange spices with which they flavor their food. An aaztar-ghola lair often contains cauldrons, skewers, and several more alien and disturbing culinary implements.

Aaztar-gholas have a particular necromantic affinity with ghouls, which for some reason obey their commands without any perceptible reluctance. The lair of an aaztar-ghola is likely (90% chance) to be guarded by a pack of 2d6+6 of these undead. In the presence of an aaztar-ghola, ghouls are highly resistant to being turned; treat them as vampires for this purpose. Ghasts are also willing to serve aaztar-gholas, but they do so for their own purposes; they are unaffected by the strange control that aaztar-gholas have over ordinary ghouls. Aaztar-gholas themselves are not undead and thus cannot be turned, although as creatures not inherently native to the prime material plane they are affected by *protection from evil*.

These horrid creatures are natural adepts of the necromantic arts, and all of them have spellcasting powers. Once per day, an aaztar-ghola can cast the following spells: *cause light wounds* x2 (at a range of 50ft), *fly*, *detect invisibility, dispel magic,* and *finger of death.* They are capable of speaking with any sort of undead creature, even those such as zombies that have no intellect at all. This ability to communicate with the undead does not imply the ability to control; ghouls are the only undead creatures that automatically follow commands given by an aaztar-ghola.

— *Author: Matt Finch*

Aaztar-Ghola: HD 6; AC 3[16]; Atk 2 swords (1d8); Move 12; Save 11; AL C; CL/XP 9/1100; Special: Spells, magic resistance 25%.

wears 10d10x10 gp in jewelry and a magic ring that can cast *phantasmal force* once per day. The spells last for 23 hours. The ring can only mimic the appearance of humans, although the exact details of the manifestation are chosen by the wearer.

Ghouls (8): HD 2; AC 6[13]; Atk 12 claws (1d3), 1 bite (1d4); Move 9; Save 16; AL C; CL/XP 3/60; Special: Immunities, paralysis.

Pauper's Inn

On the outskirts of the metropolis Bard's Gate lies the Pauper's Inn. Nestled on the boundary of an expansive cemetery, the inn serves as a temple and wayward mission. The large decrepit business provides shelter for the homeless and offers free food and lodging if guests tend the surrounding potter's field. The inn serves delectable entrées and fine mead beyond compare. Indeed, the abundant food tastes so delicious that most of the residents tend to have portly frames and jolly spirits. The inn operates under the guise of a temple to Atacharya, the goddess of the downtrodden.

The truth is that the temple priest, **Herbut Tisnyse** is actually an **aaztar-ghola** under a powerful illusion to appear as a jovial friar. **Eight ghouls**, also under the illusion, appear as buxom serving wenches who fulfill their clients' every desire. Herbut, his wenches and even the patrons dress in the finest robes and jewels (taken from those interned in the cemetery). Herbut slowly fattens up patrons in order to cook and serve them as grand feasts for everyone else. He claims the missing patrons simply moved on to a successful life. The stories he weaves serve to instill hope in the remaining destitute patrons. While staying at the Pauper's Inn, patrons live a life full of feasts, elaborate gifts, and delightful favors. The patrons defend their benefactors with their life. Each patron wears 10d10 gp in jewelry and fine clothing. Herbut also

Aboleth

Hit Dice: 9
Armor Class: 3 [16]
Attacks: 4 tentacles (1d6 + slime)
Saving Throw: 6
Special: Charm monster (3/day), Phantasmal force (3/day), Mucus cloud in water (save or cannot breathe air for 3 hours), special disease upon successful hit (save or must be immersed in water every hour).
Move: 9/12 (swimming)
Alignment: Chaos
Number Encountered: 1 (01-90%), 2 (91-98%), 2 +1d4 young (99-00%)
Challenge Level/XP: 12/2,000

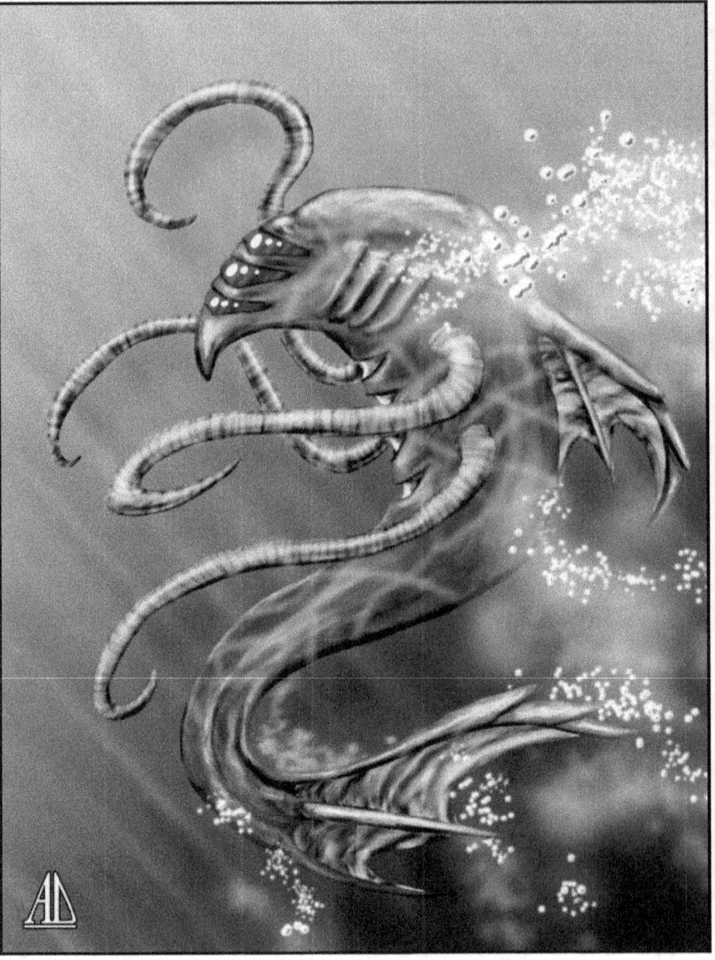

   The aboleth is a revolting fish-like amphibian, primarily subterranean, roughly the size of a killer whale. It vaguely resembles a catfish, but has four long tentacles and four orifices along its belly. The tentacles can be used to drag its bulk across dry land. These horrid abominations are extremely intelligent: an aboleth can cast charm monster three times per day, and create a phantasmal force three times per day. In the water, an aboleth surrounds itself with a cloud of mucus that requires anyone inhaling it to make a saving throw or become unable to breathe air for 3 hours. Finally, the slime on an aboleth's tentacles causes disease if a saving throw fails. Those afflicted suffer a change to their skin, which must be immersed in water every hour, or the victim suffers 1d6 points of damage.

Aboleth: HD 9; AC 3[16]; Atk 4 tentacles (1d6 + slime); Move 9 (swim 12); Save 6; AL C; CL/XP 12/2000; Special: *Charm monster (3/day)*, *phantasmal force (3/day)*, Mucus cloud in water (save or cannot breathe air for 3 hours), special disease upon successful hit (save or must be immersed in water every hour).

Double Trouble, Aboleth in a Bubble

   A rubbery blob of immense proportions bounds down the passage. The viscous jelly-like globule is larger than a whale. Four tentacles extend from the depths of the grotesque ball to pull it along. Five humanoid-shaped figures swim within the opaque bubble near the permeable wall. A dark foreboding shape looms within the bubble's depths.

   An **aboleth** lurks within the watery gel. The aboleth inside has the ability to transform water into a semi-solid coagulation. The gelatinous cloud of mucus acts as water surrounding the aboleth. Cold-based spells slow the aboleth to quarter movement for 2d4 rounds. Electrical attacks effect all within the bubble, and fire-based spells dealing over 25 points of damage dissolve the mucus cloud. The mucus cloud and all those within are immune to fire-based attacks that deal less than 25 points of damage. Those within can see out of the bubble normally. Creatures with aboleth-afflicted skin can pass through the mucus wall freely. Currently, the aboleth has **5 bugbears** under its control within the mucus cloud.

Bugbear: HD 3+1; AC 5[14]; Atk 1 bite (2d4) or weapon (1d8+1); Move 9; Save 14; AL C; CL/XP 3/120; Special: Surprise opponents, 50% chance.

Air Gust

Hit Dice: 3
Armor Class: 4 [15]
Attacks: 1 Wind blast (1d6+1 + Knockdown)
Saving Throw: 14
Special: -2 [+2] to AC vs. missile attacks.
Move: 12/18 (flying)
Alignment: Neutrality
Number Encountered: 1d8
Challenge Level/XP: 4/120

These minor elementals from the plane of Air resemble little whirlwinds. Although no more than a few feet in height and width, these tiny tornadoes can easily send the bulkiest adventurer flying in a range of up to 15ft. The victim of a successful hit by an air gust has a 2 in 6 chance of being knocked down (the referee may wish to modify the roll to take into account exceptional strength).

The violent air gusts that make up this elemental's form (and give it its name) make missile/ranged attacks difficult and afford the elemental a bonus of 2 to AC.

— Author: Skathros

Air Gust: HD 3; AC 4[15]; Atk Wind Blast (1d6+1 + Knockdown - Range up to 15ft.); Move 12 (18 fly); Save 14; AL N; CL/XP 4/120; Special: -2 [+2] to AC vs. missile attacks.

Raiders on the Storm

A wheel-less wagon made of bronze floats along the horizon. The craft billows a dust cloud from its underside. A bronze cage holding **6 normal human slaves** dominates the wagon. **Five uruaks** slavers (scrap gnolls) armed with nets and arquebuses (1d10 damage, backfire and be unusable until repaired on an attack roll of 1) man the floating wagon. **Four air gusts** carry the wagon at the command of a **kzaddich**. These marauding slavers travel the planes in search of the comeliest of humans to sell in otherworldly bazaars. The kzaddich stands atop the cage as the bronze wagon circles its prey. It blows a dragon-shaped bronze trumpet that expels an **air gust** that follows the command of the wielder. The trumpet can only have 10 air gusts at anyone time. Furthermore, the trumpet may implode (1 in 12 chance), releasing a very angry and **large air elemental**. The air gusts gain their freedom once the trumpet implodes as the bronze wagon crashes to the ground.

Uruak (Scrap Gnoll): HD 2; AC 5[14]; Atk 1 weapon (1d10); Move 12; Save 16; AL C; CL/XP 2/30; Special: arquebus.

Kzaddich: HD 1+1; AC −8[27]; Atk 2 weapons (1d8); Move 12; Save 8; AL L; CL/XP 6/400; Special: Haste, improved saving throws, immune to person-affecting spells, immune to time spells, escape into future, mental powers, cannot be surprised, time stop (2/day).

Allip

Hit Dice: 4
Armor Class: 5 [14]
Attacks: 1 strike (no damage, 1d4 points of wisdom lost)
Saving Throw: 13
Special: Drains wisdom, hypnosis
Move: 6 (flying)
Alignment: Chaos
Number Encountered: 1d4
Challenge Level/XP: 7/600

Allips are shadowy, incorporeal undead that mutter and speak with the voice of madness from beyond the grave. The voice acts as a Suggestion spell upon anyone hearing the quiet mutterings: the suggestions of an allip are usually senseless but sinister. The allip's touch does not deal damage, but causes the victim to lose 1d4 points of wisdom. If a victim's wisdom falls to 0, it dies and will become an allip within 2d6 days. Allips can only be hit with magical or silver weapons.

Allip: HD 4; AC 5[14]; Atk 1 strike (no damage, 1d4 points of wisdom lost); Move (fly 6); Save 13; AL C; CL/XP 7/600; Special: drains wisdom, hypnosis.

The Mutterings of an Old Man

Five recently slain, emaciated bodies lie strewn along a five-mile stretch of road. The corpses are dressed in tattered clothing, and their shoes are worn through. They each appear to have walked for days. The bodies, each dressed in funeral attire, lie in grotesque poses. The first man's body appears to have died swallowing and choking on stones. The second corpse of an elderly woman has numerous sticks and twigs inserted under her skin. The next young man appears to have bled to death from hundreds of thorns embedded in his nearly nude body. The forth woman suffocated after burying her head in the dirt. The last victim was repeatedly run over by a wagon. All but the fifth victim appear to have died from self-inflicted wounds.

A small funeral procession rolls along the road one mile past the last body. A man and woman walk behind an ornate funeral carriage. The battered man repeatedly attempts cartwheels down the road despite a dangling and broken arm. The ragged young woman frequently tries to grab the rear wheels of the carriage. Her fingers and hands end in bloody stumps. An old man dressed in black robes drives the carriage. He alternatively whistles, mimics animal noises and jumbles words incoherently. He seems oblivious to the proceedings going on behind him. The dark and heavily shrouded horse-drawn hearse holds an ornate coffin and the corpse of Felgard, a thief of some notoriety. The aged Felgard retired a wealthy man with his family oblivious to his roguish lifestyle and habitual thievery. Despite his easy lifestyle, Felgard still dabbled in his profession by looting local crypts. A few days ago, he was slain by an **allip**. During his funeral parade, Felgard transformed into an allip and currently hides within the shrouded carriage. Its babbling and *suggestion* abilities drove the mourners and driver mad and suicidal.

Amphorons of Yothri

	WORKER	**WARRIOR**	**JUGGERNAUT**
Hit Dice:	2	5	10
Armor Class:	2 [17]	2 [17]	2 [17]
Attacks:	2 pincer-arms (1d6)	2 pincer arms (1d6+2)	2 whirling blades (2d6+2) or crane (special)
Saving Throw:	16	12	5
Special:	Magic resistance 25%, immune to piercing weapons, chance of flickering, chance of electrical belch.	Magic resistance 25%, immune to piercing weapons, chance of flickering, flamethrower.	Magic resistance 25%, crane, chance of flickering.
Move:	9	9	9
Alignment:	Neutrality	Neutrality	Neutrality
Number Encountered:	1d4 workers or 1d4-1 workers, 1d3-1 warriors, and 1d2-1 juggernauts		
Challenge Level/XP:	4/120	8/800	13/2,300

Amphorons of Yothri are mechanisms created by the Artificers of that plane (see, "Artificers of Yothri") using their strange magic-science. Amphorons on the material plane are physical projections of a model that remains on Yothri – the Artificer's mind, possibly using a lens apparatus of some kind, projects the device into the material plane, where it has a physical reality.

These projections can fail, and, moreover, the Artificer's control of more than one Amphoron at a time depends on his mental connection to a single, controlling Amphoron. If the Artificer attempts to switch his mental connection from one Amphoron to another, the process takes 1d6 rounds to complete.

In any given round, any Amphoron has a 1 in 6 chance to "flicker," due to a momentary interruption of the connection across time and space. While flickering, the Amphoron cannot be attacked, and cannot inflict damage. However, it regains 1 hit point when it rematerializes. A flickering Amphoron is visible as a faint, static-shrouded shape. In the following round, the Amphoron reappears (unless it fails a second roll of the d6).

The controlling Amphoron has only a 1 in 20 chance of flickering, but if it does so, all of the Amphorons under its control will flicker. Any Amphoron can be used as the controller, but a single controller cannot control more than six other Amphorons, and an Artificer can only project his mind to one controller at a time. Thus, unless the Artificer has projected some apparatus (the possibilities are many, and left to the Referee's creativity) to allow remote controllers or auto-controls, the maximum number of Amphorons encountered at time is seven (six controlled and one controller). When the Artificer's nefarious schemes on the material plane are complete, he will likely not bother to disintegrate his Amphorons, so their material substance will remain on the material plane, operating randomly, remaining completely inert, or proceeding independently with their rudimentary intelligence.

All Amphorons have a metallic, jointed shell; their insides are filled with wires and a gel-like flesh which allows the mental connection with the distant reality of Yothri, and also gives the creature its basic intelligence. There are three varieties of Amphoron, although the Referee could design others with little effort.

Worker Amphoron

Worker Amphorons are just smaller than a human, and move with crab-like legs (although they can levitate for up to 3 rounds once per day, if need be). As with other Amphorons, they have a 1 in 6 chance of flickering unless used as a controller by the Artificer. In addition to the chance of flickering, a worker Amphoron may randomly belch out arcs of electricity, inflicting 1hp damage to anyone within 10ft (in addition to its other actions).

Worker Amphoron: HD 2; AC 2[17]; Atk 2 pincer-arms (1d6); Move 9; Save 16; AL N; CL/XP 4/120; Special: magic resistance 25%, immune to piercing weapons, chance of flickering, chance of electrical belch.

Warrior Amphoron

Warrior Amphorons are usually used to protect Worker Amphorons, or in situations where the Artificer's schemes involve violence. They have a flamethrower which is in constant operation, allowing the Amphoron to shoot a line of flame at a single target up to 100ft away in addition to its other attacks. The flame inflicts 1d6 damage (saving throw for half damage).

Warrior Amphoron: HD 5; AC 2[17]; Atk 2 pincer arms (1d6+2); Move 9; Save 12; AL N; CL/XP 8/800; Special: magic resistance 25%, immune to piercing weapons, chance of flickering, flamethrower.

Juggernaut Amphoron

The Juggernaut Amphoron is a harvester/processor the size of a semi-attached trailer truck, with a moving crane mounted on its back and two huge circular saws mounted on its articulated arms. If the Juggernaut's crane hits an opponent, the victim is lifted up into the air over the Juggernaut's processing hatch, and dropped automatically in the following round. If the crane hits, a saving throw is permitted to escape the its grasp unless the target is wearing metal armor, in which case no saving throw is allowed (the crane contains a backup magnet). Anyone dropped into the processing hatch is processed within 1d4 rounds into a small brick.

Juggernaut Amphoron: HD 10; AC 2[17]; Atk 2 whirling blades (2d6+2) or crane; Move 9; Save 5; AL C; CL/XP 13/2300; Special: magic resistance 25%, crane, chance of flickering.

— Author: Matt Finch; first appeared in Knockspell Magazine #1

Worker Amphoron — Stairs of Glass

Along the shore stands an impossibly tall spiral staircase. Designed for a creature of gigantic proportions, the staircase reaches a towering 400-foot-tall peak where it abruptly ends. Made of thick, translucent glass embedded with streaks of polished metal, the stair's purpose remains a mystery. Each of the 10-foot-wide steps stands 5 feet tall. The steps spiral around a central column made of a denser opaque black glass.

For the past 50 years, **6 worker amphorons** have worked tirelessly building the staircase. Two of the automatons remain at the top of the tower, painstakingly building the stairs ever upward. The amphorons work around the clock, using their electric arcs to heat, mold and shape the glass and framework. At night, their eclectic sparks are visible for miles. The other amphorons scour the sands and nearby water for pure white silica and veins of metal to use in the spiral stair's creation. The stairs act as a lightning rod, and the entire staircase glows white hot for hours after lightning strikes during severe weather. The amphorons focus their electrical attack on the veins of metal. All living creatures in contact with the stairs suffer the effects of the electrical attack.

Warrior Amphoron — Telluric Turret

Twin, 50-foot-tall towers guard a deeply rutted road leading up a barren mountain. From each, a gleaming metallic turret spews a constant stream of liquid flame in a never-ending circle. All vegetation within a mile of the mountain has been burnt to near ash. Bizarre, insect-like footprints cover the crisp ground in a multitude of crisscrossing paths. **Two warrior amphorons** guard the road up the mountainside to an enormous castle perched on the peak. Although the walls of the towers are as smooth as glass, the large grey bricks swirl as if made of smoke. Upon closer inspection, agonized face can be seen swirling within each block. The blocks resist all form of damage and radiate a harmless feeling of cold and sorrow.

Seven roads lead to the peak of this sole mountain among the plains. Twin towers secure each road. A 30-foot-tall brick wall spans the distance between the towers. At any time, **2d4 worker amphorons** steadily build the walls using more of the gray, misty bricks. In addition there is a 2 in 6 chance that **2d6 worker amphorons** carrying living humans and animals in their claws travel through the gate toward the mountain. The warrior amphorons climb down the towers to attack if the workers are slain.

Juggernaut Amphoron — Telluric Fortress

Atop a mountain peak surrounded by telluric turrets (see warrior amphorons) stands the foundation of a massive fortress. The fortress covers the entire mountain peak and is in the early stages of construction. Judging by the size of the stairs and entry arches, the castle appears made for giant-sized creatures. Normally, **5d6 worker amphorons** work around the clock building the fortress from mysterious gray bricks. In addition there is a 2 in 6 chance that 2d6 worker amphorons carrying living humans and animals in their claws navigate the maze-like foundation toward the fortress's center. Made from impenetrable opaque glass, the bricks appear to trap tormented souls. Peering into the bricks reveals faces of humanoids and animals screaming in silent anguish. Any intrusion into the construction site immediately draws the attention of **3d6 warrior amphorons**. At the heart of the castle stands an **amphoron juggernaut** in what appears to be a throne room of immense proportions. The amphoron juggernaut grasps a human in its crane. It examines the pleading creature before dropping it into its hatch to be processed into a brick. The bricks are then used to build the fortress. Around the juggernaut, 2d6 worker amphorons hold other living creatures waiting their turn with the juggernaut. Four warrior amphorons always accompany the amphoron juggernaut as it processes the hapless creatures. The dreadful castle's purpose remains a mystery beyond mortal ken.

Animated Objects

Animated objects generally do not have minds of their own, being animated by a spell rather than by a spirit of some kind. They may follow programmed instructions, or might follow the orders of a master if the master is actually present. Since there are so many possible types of objects, and so many different ways in which an object might be animated, the exact details of the object are left to the Referee. Two examples are provided, although even with animated chairs and tables the exact details can (and should) occasionally differ.

	ANIMATED CARPET	ANIMATED CHAIR
Hit Dice:	1	1
Armor Class:	9 [10]	8 [11]
Attacks:	1 (entangle)	1 bump (save or fall)
Saving Throw:	17	17
Special:	Entangle	Knock down
Move:	6	12
Alignment:	Neutrality	Neutrality
Number Encountered:	varies	varies
Challenge Level/XP:	1/15	1/15

This version of an animated carpet attacks for no damage, but if the target is hit and fails a saving throw, the carpet holds the character, struggling, until a saving throw is successful.

Animated Carpet: HD 1; AC 9[10]; Atk 1 (no damage); Move 6; Save 17; AL N; CL/XP 1/15; Special: Grab.

This version of an animated chair bumps against its opponents, with a successful hit causing the target to fall to the ground and take 1hp damage.

Animated Chair: HD 1; AC 8[11]; Atk 1 bump (save or fall); Move 12; Save 18; AL N; CL/XP 1/15; Special: Knocks over.

Animated Objects
Patchwork Carpet

Thick, 10-foot-square area rugs cover the entire floor of this 40-foot-wide hall. The hall stretches 100 foot to a center door set against the far wall. Thousands of broken glass beakers and ceramic flasks litter the carpet. Randomly scattered among the normal rugs are **10 animated carpets,** each covering a 10-foot-deep pit. The animated carpets remain stiff and ridged (supporting PCs' weight) until tread upon. The animated carpet then envelops the creature and falls into the pit. A saving throw negates the initial engulfing attack, but the PC must then make a second saving throw to avoid falling into the pit. Each pit is half filled with sludge-like oil. Engulfed creatures that fall into the pit are covered in the viscous oil and run the risk of drowning. Furthermore, the glass and ceramic shards inflict 1 point of damage each round as the animated carpet tightly squeezes the victim and grinds the shards into the PCs' flesh. Opening the door on the far wall causes a shower of sparks to fall from channels in the ceiling. The sparks ignite the oil (on creatures and in pits). The oil pits burn for 1d6 hours or until extinguished. Dense, choking smoke fills the hall and surrounding corridors. PCs covered in oil take 2d6 points of damage for 2d4 rounds or until they wash the oil away.

Festoon Feast of Fervor

A grand banquet hall worthy of nobility stands ready for all. A massive curving table with thirteen table settings sits warm and inviting. Carved in the likeness of two giant crocodiles, the wooden table presents a feast of roast swine, leek and mushroom soup, and honey mead. Each of the large chairs is carved to represent a hoofed animal such as cows, deer, mules and elk. The center throne resembles two gazelles joined at the hindquarters. A massive fireplace sits opposite the curving table, and is ablaze with a warm fire. A bearded gnome sits on the center throne at the table's apex. He jovially welcomes visitors into his chamber, stating he is "a good-natured gnome" on a life quest to bring relief to the weary. He goes by the name

Amikal the Cheery. Amikal, actually a **doppelganger**, has made it his mission to rid the world of hostile, senseless adventurers. Amikal's feast (which he painstakingly prepares with specialty brewed elixirs every night) heals 1d6 hit points and grants a *bless* spell that lasts for 1d6 hours (roll individually). Although he asks for nothing in return for the meal and rest, he expects some token of thanks.

Amikal has a nasty surprise for impolite or impulsive guests. While the table is harmless, the **13 animated chairs** surrounding it are not. Each chair follows Amikal's commands and has straps to secure victims (saving throw to avoid). Amikal commands the chairs to either leap into the fireplace or smash into one another. The gazelle throne has double the movement of normal animated chairs. Amikal uses his throne to escape if the encounter turns against him. Amikal carries a special magical wand that only animates chairs. The wand has 21 charges remaining.

Doppelganger: HD 4; AC 5[14]; Atk 1 claw (1d12); Move 9; Save 13 (5 vs. magic); AL C; CL/XP 5/240; Special: Mimics shape, immune to sleep and charm.

Ankheg

Hit Dice: 3-8
Armor Class: 2 [17]
Attacks: 1 bite (3d6)
Saving Throw: By hit dice
Special: Spits acid
Move: 12/6 (burrowing)
Alignment: Neutrality
Number Encountered: One (or one adult and 1d4 young). Areas might be rife with several such groups, but they would probably be territorial.
Challenge Level/XP: By hit dice

Ankhegs are huge insects, 10 to 20ft long, resembling grasshoppers with vicious mandibles. They burrow through the ground, often in farmlands as well as in caverns. Once per day, an ankheg can squirt digestive acids for 5d6 points of damage (save for half), but this is a defense not used in normal hunting.

Ankheg (3HD): HD 3; AC 2[17] underside 4[15]; Atk 1 bite (3d6); Move 12 (burrow 6); Save 14; AL N; CL/XP 4/120XP; Special: Spits acid 5d6 (1/day, save for half).

Ankheg (4HD): HD 4; AC 2[17] underside 4[15]; Atk 1 bite (3d6); Move 12 (burrow 6); Save 13; AL N; CL/XP 5/240XP; Special: Spits acid 5d6 (1/day, save for half).

Ankheg (5HD): HD 5; AC 2[17] underside 4[15]; Atk 1 bite (3d6); Move 12 (burrow 6); Save 12; AL N; CL/XP 6/400XP; Special: Spits acid 5d6 (1/day, save for half).

Ankheg (6HD): HD 6; AC 2[17] underside 4[15]; Atk 1 bite (3d6); Move 12 (burrow 6); Save 11; AL N; CL/XP 7/600XP; Special: Spits acid 5d6 (1/day, save for half).

Ankheg (7HD): HD: 7; AC: 2[17] underside 4[15]; Atk: 1 bite (3d6); Move: 12 (burrow 6); Save: 9; AL N; CL/XP: 8/800XP; Special: Spits acid 5d6 (1/day, save for half).

Ankheg (8HD): HD: 8; AC: 2[17] underside 4[15]; Atk: 1 bite (3d6); Move: 12 (burrow 6); Save: 8; AL N; CL/XP: 9/1100XP; Special: Spits acid 5d6 (1/day, save for half).

Acid Reflex

At the edge of the forest, a bewildered halfling stands before the scraggly hills. A large, overburdened wagon sits nearby. Odd contraptions and unidentifiable junk lie strewn around it. Ollie Nematoad, an ill-fated inventor, needs help. Ollie wants to harvest acid from a colony of ankhegs lairing in the eroded and dusty hills beyond the forest. Ollie wants the acid from the ankhegs to further research experiments involving acid-resistant suits. Simply killing the beast to harvest the acid may contaminate the samples, however. For this reason, he needs only acid that has been excreted by their acid attack. Ollie has several of his prototype acid resistant suits (made from rubbery and slightly putrid otyugh intestines). He has three human or elf suits, one dwarf and two small (halfling or gnome) sized suits. These cannot be worn over armor. Unfortunately, the suits offer no protection whatsoever, including against acid attacks. Ollie absentmindedly neglects to inform volunteers of this fact; after all he is trying to improve his existing designs and needs to test their resistance qualities. None of the previous employees have returned with acid samples (Ollie also conveniently forgets this). The colony consists of **5d6 ankhegs** of various sizes, although only 1d4+1 will investigate creatures moving into their territory.

Ollie needs a few vats of acid. He currently has 5 large glass vats with cork lids that PCs can use to catch the acid. To do so, PCs must willingly be hit by an acid attack. While facing the acid attack, the PC can counterattack. If the PC's attack roll is higher than the ankheg's, the PC manages to catch enough acid to fill the vat. The acid attack still does half damage to the PC as the acid covers him. The PC takes full damage if his attack is lower than the ankheg's.

Ollie offers 100 gp per filled vat and promises a suit of his perfected, acid-proof suit when it is completed in 2d4 months. Within the ankheg's warrens lie the shredded and partially dissolved former employees Ollie sent into the colony. The corpses have 3d10 gp and wear partially liquefied suits made of oiled fish skins. Among the broken glass vats lay 2 *potions of healing* and a *+2 trident*.

Ant, Giant

	WORKER	WARRIOR	QUEEN
Hit Dice:	2	3	10
Armor Class:	3 [16]	3 [16]	3 [16]
Attacks:	Bite (1d6)	Bite (1d6 + poison)	Bite (1d6)
Saving Throw:	16	14	3
Special:	None	Poison 2d6 (save for 1d4)	None
Move:	18	18	5
Alignment:	Neutrality	Neutrality	Neutrality
Number Encountered:	1d10 (mixed group) or 1d100+20.		
Challenge Level/XP:	2/30	4/120	10/1,400

Giant ants live in vast subterranean hives tunneled through soil and even stone. A hive can hold as many as 100 ants, in a worker-to-warrior ratio of 5:1. The poison of a warrior ant does 2d6 points of damage if a saving throw is failed, 1d4 points of damage if the saving throw succeeds.

Giant Worker Ant: HD 2; AC 3[16]; Atk Bite (1d6); Move 18; Save 16; AL N; CL/XP 2/30; Special: None.

Giant Warrior Ant: HD 3; AC 3[16]; Atk Bite (1d6+ poison); Move 18; Save 14; AL N; CL/XP 4/120; Special: Poison 2d6 (save for 1d4 only).

Giant Queen Ant: HD 10; AC 3[16]; Atk Bite (1d6); Move 3; Save 3; AL N; CL/XP 10/1,400; Special: None.

Wagon Ant Train

Screams of panic bellow down the road from where the ground appears to have swallowed a wagon caravan. Only the top of an enclosed wagon can be seen above a massive sandy area that envelops the road. A second prison wagon buried just past its wheels shudders as some unseen beast pulls it downward. Seven bedraggled humans confined in the wrought-iron barred wagon scream for help as the horrid crunching of splintering wood rises around them as the wagon continues sinking into the sandy soil. Blood, fragments of weapons and the arm of a hobgoblin lie next to the road.

This hobgoblin raiding caravan fell into a giant ant tunnel burrowed too close to the surface. Currently, 6 giant worker ants rip at the lower half of the wagon stuck in the tunnel. The ants burrow upward from below to defend their meal. Once an ant is slain, it releases pheromones that attract warrior ants to the disturbance going on in the tunnel. An additional 2 warrior ants arrive in 2d4 rounds after the death of each ant. The fledgling colony has 20 worker ants, 10 warrior ants and a queen. The queen sits in a central chamber 120 feet down the passage. Two warrior ants (maximum hit points) always accompany the queen. A partial wagon of hobgoblin spoils and a few survivors remain in the chamber. The ants buried survivors in dirt up to their necks to serve as food at a later time. Three humans and two hobgoblins are still alive. The wagon holds a chest secured to the wooden floor. The chest contain 600 gp and a *wand of fireballs* (20 charges)

Ape, Flying

Hit Dice: 5
Armor Class: 6 [13]
Attacks: 2 hands (1d4), 1 bite (1d6)
Saving Throw: 12
Special: Rend or carry airborne
Move: 9/18 (flying)
Alignment: Neutrality (or Chaos)
Number Encountered: One, 1d4, or 1d10+5
Challenge Level/XP: 6/400

Flying apes are somewhat larger and more muscular than gorillas. Most have bat wings, but some have feathered bird-wings. If a flying ape hits with both arms, it can either rend its foe for an additional 1d6 points of damage or gain a good enough hold to carry the foe into the air (to drop later, or deliver the victim to an evil overlord, as applicable). As with gorillas, most flying apes are of far less than human intelligence, but more intelligent (and often chaotic) ones are not uncommon.

Flying Ape: HD 5; AC 6[13]; Atk 2 hands (1d4), 1 bite (1d6); Move 9 (fly 18); Save 12; AL N (or C); CL/XP 6/400; Special: Rend or carry airborne.

The Shrine of Adar Dralg

Thick vines cover this once magnificent settlement. Ruins and vague foundations are all that remain of the once-thriving civilization. A massive 120-foot-high dome rises above the tropical forest floor. Although the columns that once supported the dome have fallen, the dome remains stable and hovers above the jungle floor. Ancient vines entwine the dome as if trying to pull it back to the earth. The vines twirl in massive pillars up to the dome and curtains of lush vegetation cascade down, shrouding the interior from view.

A pedestal under the dome's center holds a multifaceted cluster of lavender crystals. The translucent rock glows slightly under the dome's shadow. Mosaics on the dome depict masculine beasts and apes enslaving more civilized races. Once revered by humans, the deity Adar Dralg represented physical supremacy over the weak. Long ago, humans abandoned his callous doctrine of physical dominance. In his anger, he destroyed their city and filled it with his loyal and chaotic minions. Through years of war and plunder, only a few of his lineage remain to guard the shrine and its treasured centerpiece. Among other dangers that wait in the city, **4 winged apes** of unusual intelligence guard the *Crystal of Adar Dralg*. The apes lounge atop the floating dome. Each is armed with a crude heavy spear and salvaged stone blocks.

The *Crystal of Adar Dralg* imbues the possessor with incredible strength. Unfortunately, the crystal also slowly transforms the possessor over 3d6 days into an ape. Those with more than 6 hit dice turn into a winged ape in service of Adar Dralg.

Ape, Gorilla (and Ape, Carnivorous)

Hit Dice: 4
Armor Class: 6 [13]
Attacks: 2 hands (1d3), 1 bite (1d6)
Saving Throw: 13
Special: Hug and rend
Move: 12
Alignment: Neutrality
Number Encountered: 1d6
Challenge Level/XP: 4/120

If a gorilla hits with both arms, it will crush and rend the victim for an additional 1d6 points of damage. Some gorillas, especially those living near places of eerie magic, might become carnivorous and seek out human prey with abnormal cunning and rudimentary intelligence. Such carnivorous apes would be of chaotic alignment.

Gorilla: HD 4; AC 6[13]; Atk 2 hands (1d3), 1 bite (1d6); Move 12; Save 13; AL N; CL/XP 4/120; Special: Hug and rend.

Palanquin of the Ape King

Deep in the southern jungles lies a treetop kingdom of apes led by a creature that is half man and half ape. Although the apes have rudimentary intelligence, they are a formidable community under the guidance and powers of the Ape King. The apes raid local villages for food and slaves (which are often used in gladiator style battles). The apes are brutal and uncaring, but not chaotic. The ape king is known to have a harem of female apes and captured humans.

The Ape King travels the area leading **8 gorillas**. The gorillas carry the Ape King on a stone palanquin. These ape guards carry heavy spears made of solid iron. These weighty spears require great strength to wield and deal 1d10 points of damage. The apes throw the spears and use their fists in combat.

The Ape King can levitate, create a 10–ft. radius circle of magical darkness, change into a human form, cast sleep and charm monster (apes only), and roar a cone of fear with a range of 60 ft. to a base of 30 ft. (saving throw applies). He carries an overly heavy +1 spear that deals 1d12 points of damage.

The Ape King: HD 6; AC 7[12]; Atk +1 spear (1d12), or special ability, or spell; Save 11; Move 12; AL N; CL/XP 8/800; Special: Spells, Roar.

Aqueous Orb

Hit Dice: 3
Armor Class: 4 [15]
Attacks: Feeding-tail (1d4)
Saving Throw: 14
Special: Sucks blood, luminescence, immune to weapon types.
Move: 3
Alignment: Neutrality
Number Encountered: 1d8
Challenge Level/XP: 5/240

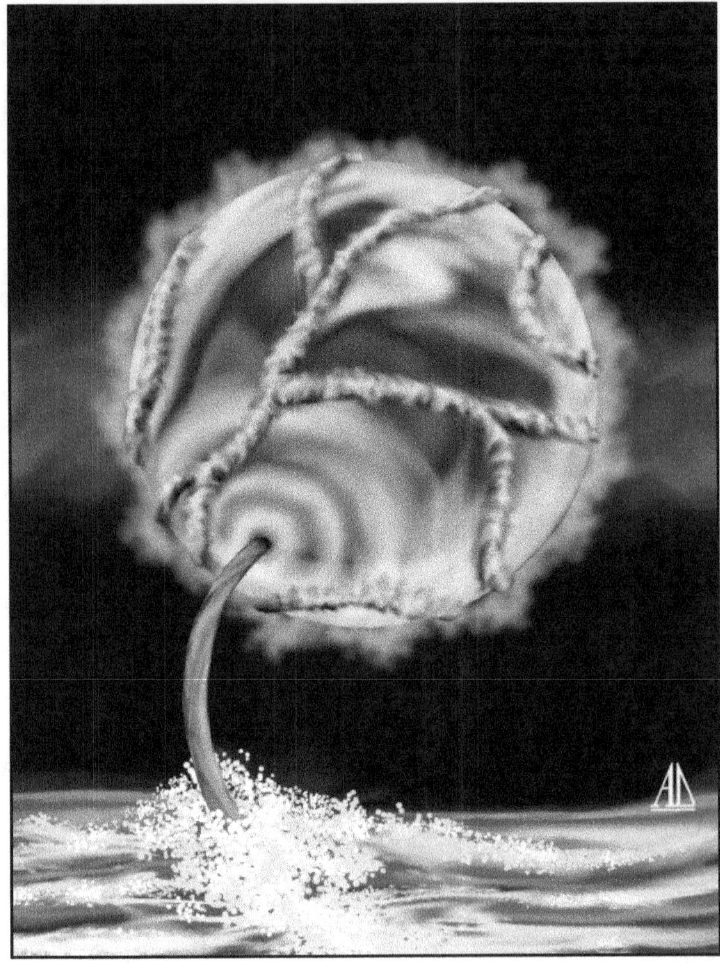

Aqueous orbs are bubble creatures that levitate above the surface of the water, leaving a long, tube-like feeding tail dangling into the water below. Liquid and nutrients are pulled up through the tail to the bubble-like body, which thrives on rotting carrion in the surrounding water. An aqueous orb glows with green luminescence when attacking: those who fail a saving throw will walk toward the orb, enter the water, and most likely drown. The feeding-tail can also be used as a weapon, piercing foes for 1d4 hit points of damage and inflicting 1d4 points of damage automatically thereafter, as it sucks blood from the victim. An aqueous orb is immune to all but piercing weapons; the feeding-tail is immune to all but slashing weapons.

— Author: Matt Finch

Aqueous Orb: HD 3; AC 4[14]; Atk 1 feeding-tail (1d4); Save 15; Move 3; AL N; CL/XP 5/240; Special: Sucks blood, luminescence, immune to weapon types.

A Bridge Too Far

The passage opens into a long wide cavern where a shallow lake covers the floor. The crystal-clear water teems with subterranean life. Calcium dams and natural bridges create traversable paths. Shield-sized oysters sit open along the bottom of the lake, some displaying large pearls. The lake averages five feet deep and its inhabitants are harmless. Semiprecious crystals cover the floors and walls, sparkling from the brilliant luminosity given off by fungi growing along the ceiling. Large spherical mushrooms glow a soft hue and bathe the room in emerald light. Tendrils and spiraling roots dangle from the glowing pods like a radiant jungle reaching for the water below. Near the center of the chamber sits a female statue of a forgotten deity of elvish origin. The statue holds a short sword in one hand and an orb in the other. A crystalline coating of gypsum coats the statue like frost on a cold autumn morning. Among the hanging fungus are **6 aqueous orbs** that feed on the blind fish in the lake. The white stone glaze conceals the true nature of the dark elf statue. The innately evil statute holds a translucent crystal ball with a direct connection to a dark elf priestess. Furthermore, the dark elf priestess can see, hear and cast spells through the crystal ball. Covering or destroying the crystal ball breaks the connection.

Aranea

Hit Dice: 4
Armor Class: 6 [13]
Attacks: 1 bite (1d6 + poison);
Saving Throw: 13
Special: Webs, Spells.
Move: 12
Alignment: Chaos
Number Encountered: one or 1d6+1. If younger ones are in the encounter, they might not be magical, being treated as small giant spiders.
Challenge Level/XP: 7/600

An aranea is an intelligent, shapechanging spider with sorcerous powers. In its natural form, an aranea resembles a big spider, with a humpbacked body a little bigger than a human torso. It has fanged mandibles like a normal spider. Two small arms, each about 2 feet long, lie below the mandibles. Each arm has a hand with four many-jointed fingers and a double-jointed thumb. An aranea weighs about 150 pounds. A hump on its back houses its brain.

Aranea can cast webs at a single opponent at a range up to 40ft (saving throw). The victim is entangled, but can break free within 1d6 rounds. These horrid creatures are spellcasters, able to cast one second level and two first level magic-user spells. Usually, an aranea is prepared with 2 *charm person* spells and a *mirror image* spell; or, alternatively, with 1 *charm person*, 1 *sleep* spell, and *invisibility*.

Aranea: HD 4; AC 6[13]; Atk 1 bite (1d6 + poison); Move 12; Save 13; AL C; CL/XP 7/600; Special: Webs, Spells.

What a Tangled Web She Weaves

Webs cover the ground and surrounding fauna. Millions of normal spiders swarm over the terrain and webs as they flee approaching intruders. The desiccated corpse of a riding horse lies partially cocooned on the path ahead. The once fine horse bears the standard of local nobility. Upon closer inspection, the mummified horse appears to have died months ago. The weakened screams of a human woman carries on the wind from farther down the wooded path. As the webs thicken, the spiders increase in size. Ahead lies a horizontally angled, solid web. The opaque web holds a cocooned human woman. Blood stains the web around her pale body, and she weakly struggles against the strands holding her. A **giant spider (4–ft. diameter)** drops down from the webbed canopy to attack intruders.

The woman is an **aranea** disguised to lure victims into her trap. An additional **2 giant spiders (6–ft. diameter)** hide under the thick white web, ready to defend the aranea once she begins her spell assault. She has a special *wand of web* (18 charges) that carries an electric charge. Those caught in the web suffer 1 point of electrical damage each round until freed. The webs from the wand last 3d6 rounds until it dissipates.

Giant Spider (4ft diameter): HD 2+2; AC 6[13]; Atk 1 bite (1d6 + poison); Move 18; Save 16; AL N; CL/XP 5/240; Special: lethal poison, 5 in 6 chance to surprise prey.

Giant Spider (6ft diameter): HD 4+2; AC 4[15]; Atk 1 bite (1d6+2 + poison); Move 4; Save 13; AL N; CL/XP 7/600; Special: lethal poison, webs.

Arcanix

	MINOR	MAJOR	GREATER
Hit Dice:	3	6	12
Armor Class:	7 [12]	7 [12]	7 [12]
Attacks:	1 weapon, or special ability, or spell	1 weapon, or special ability, or spell	1 weapon, or special ability, or spell
Saving Throw:	14	11	3
Special:	Spells, Spell-Stealing, Teleport	Spells, Spell-Stealing, Teleport	Spells, Spell-Stealing, Teleport
Move:	12	12	12
Alignment:	Neutrality	Neutrality	Neutrality
Number Encountered:	One or 1d4 (mixed group)	One or 1d4 (mixed group)	One or 1d4 (mixed group)
Challenge Level/XP:	5/240	8/800	14/2,600

Arcanixes (also known as Spell-Stealers), resemble tall, gaunt humans with bluish skin and pointed ears. They are extraplanar creatures that foray into the mortal realms in their obsessive search for magic. They prize magical items above all else, but spellbooks and arcane lore (as well as spellcasters themselves) are also sought to take back to their home plane.

There are three types of Arcanix: Arcanix Minor (3HD), Arcanix Major (6HD) and Arcanix Greater (12HD). If an arcanix is encountered bearing a weapon, it is a near certainty that the weapon is magical in nature (the referee should base the weapon in accordance with the type of arcanix).

An arcanix that can successfully touch a spell-caster may steal spell levels up to its own number of hit dice. Example: An Arcanix Minor (3HD) may steal a third level spell from a magic-user, or three 1st level spells, or a 2nd and a 1st level spell. The spell-caster is allowed a saving throw to negate this effect. If the attack is successful (and the save fails) the stolen spells leave the magic-user's memory (until he can re-memorize them again), and the arcanix may use them as if he had memorized them. The number of times per day that an Arcanix may use this ability depends on the type of Arcanix; Minor 1/day, Major 3/day, Greater 6/day.

Arcanixes possess the following spell-like Abilities: Detect Magic 3/day, Read Magic 3/day, Dispel Magic 2/day, Dimension Door 1/day. An arcanix may teleport to or from its home plane once (3HD), twice (6HD), or 3 times (12HD) per week.

— Author: Skathros

Arcanix (Minor): HD 3; AC 7[12]; Atk 1 weapon, or special ability, or spell; Save 14; Move 12; AL N; CL/XP 5/240; Special: Spells, Spell-Stealing, Teleport.

Arcanix (Major): HD 6; AC 7[12]; Atk 1 weapon, or special ability, or spell; Save 11; Move 12; AL N; CL/XP 8/800; Special: Spells, Spell-Stealing, Teleport.

Arcanix (Greater): HD 12; AC 7[12]; Atk 1 weapon, or special ability, or spell; Save 3; Move 12; AL N; CL/XP 14/2600; Special: Spells, Spell-Stealing, Teleport.

Hollow Man

A large armored ogre stands guard outside this sturdy oaken door. Upon closer inspection, the ogre is just a hollowed out corpse. Its fused armor holds the ogre corpse upright. An unknown fire burned from within the ogre, leaving only an empty cavity. Feeble shrieks in the Common tongue can be heard coming from behind the door. The male voice pleads for his life's work between sobs. Behind the locked door lies the wizard Mellum. He is pleading and in obvious mental distress. Mellum spent his entire adult life (98 years) dedicated to recording and accumulating the history of magecraft into massive tomes that fill his library. While a few of the books have magical properties, the vast majority are simply mundane historical references works. The library stands mostly empty. Floating loose leaf papers, dust and debris haphazardly levitate throughout the room. The room has several large wings containing rows of empty bookshelves. Standing above the crumpled old man is an **arcanix**. Books float from the shelves into a

swirling dimensional portal next to the arcanix. The arcanix ignores the pleas of the helpless (and spell-less) wizard as he steals Mellum's life work.

After years of searching and surveillance, the arcanix arrived at Mellum's library to pilfer the knowledge and even Mellum himself. The arcanix has already transported the vast library to its home plane and now plans to kidnap the hapless Mellum as well. The portal is tied to the arcanix and dissipates with his defeat. Currently, the arcanix has stolen *shield* and *mirror image* from Mellum's spell repertoire. (Add more spells for major and greater arcanix as needed.) If rescued, Mellum responds with despair at the irrevocable loss of his life's work. With nothing left, Mellum decides it is time to get on with his life. He immediately sets off to find a suitable bride (starting with any female PCs) to start a family.

Archer Tree

Hit Dice: 7
Armor Class: 6 [13]
Attacks: 1d4 needles (1d6 + paralyze)
Saving Throw: 9
Special: Paralysis
Move: 1
Alignment: Neutrality
Number Encountered: widely-scattered grove of 1d6+2 trees
Challenge Level/XP: 8/800

Archer-trees are a species of walking pine tree. Some of the tree's needles are extremely long, although this is not easy to notice from afar. The tree's animated branches can throw 1d4 of these longer needles per round to a range of 100ft. The needles contain a sedative poison that paralyzes victims for 3d6 turns (saving throw negates).

Archer-Tree: HD 7; AC 6[13]; Atk 1d4 needles (1d6 + paralyze); Move 1; Save 9; AL N; CL/XP 8/800; Special: Paralysis.

Big Prick

The booming logging settlement of Krieger's Pointe has grown since the end of the recent pestilence that plagued the inhabitants. The loggers harvest the timber in the high mountains and send the wood down miles of log flumes to the town of Carson's Mill. Kudan Stoenawl, the owner of Stoenawl Timber has recently experienced some major setbacks. It seems that someone has again vandalized the log flumes a few miles down the mountain. The vandalism makes the flumes inoperable. After an investigation, he sent a repair team to rebuild the flume. Not surprisingly, they did not return. His scouts report the workers were crucified and no other clues were found. Kudan needs mercenaries to escort his laborers down the flume to repair the damage. Kudan offers a seaworthy barge that he needs to unload. The outdated ship (named Log Jammer) is the size of a small galleon (no weapons). It has outlived its purpose in the timber company and Kudan needs to get rid of the well-used vessel.

An **archer tree** recently moved into the area and destroyed part of the flumes in hopes of scaring the loggers away. Once that failed, the archer tree killed the three loggers who arrived to repair the flume. The archer tree impaled the corpses on spear-like pine needles jammed into the ground to serve as a warning. The archer tree currently stands motionless adjacent to the three crucified loggers. While it does not attack scouts, anyone attempting to repair the flume invokes its wrath.

Artificers of Yothri

Hit Dice: 10
Armor Class: 2 [17]
Attacks: 1 claw (1d10+1)
Saving Throw: 5
Special: Magic resistance 50% (80%), psychic powers, magic powers.
Move: 15
Alignment: Chaos
Number Encountered: 1
Challenge Level/XP: 14/2,600

The artificers of Yothri are tall and skeletal, a construction of dark-hued metalloid bones acting as the framework for artificial tubes and organs. They wear hoods and long, black robes – perhaps a necessity of the dead world they inhabit in a distant and eroding reality. Their palaces are of baroque green glass and alien metals, twisting in unnatural shapes, domes, and bubbles. The artificers are mutually hostile, each coveting the others' resources and knowledge. It is remotely possible that player characters might be kidnapped to serve an artificer by attacking the citadel of one of the others in the barren, suppurating wastelands of Yothri itself.

An artificer employs the Science of Yothri, which is a mix of psychic powers, magic, and technology impossible to achieve outside the physical realities of Yothri itself. Rather than manifesting in spells, the Science of Yothri allows the Artificer to use certain powers, some mental, some magical, as follows:

Psychic powers: at will, (in conjunction with a physical attack if desired), the artificer can use telekinesis to lift up to 300 pounds of weight, create or maintain a "double vision" effect similar to a single mirror image per the spell, increase magic resistance to 80%, maintain a mental connection with an amphoron in another plane, or work to establish a connection with an amphoron in another plane (the mental connection with amphorons is described below).

Magical powers: in conjunction with a psychic power (but not with physical attacks), the Artificer may create one of the following effects using the Science of Yothri: (1) once per day, the Artificer can cast charm person in a cone shape 60ft long and reaching 60ft wide at extreme range, (2) three times per day, the Artificer can cast a spell to cause metal poisoning in the target's bloodstream (a saving throw applies), rendering the victim helpless with pain and causing death within 2d6 rounds unless the poison is counteracted.

— *Author: Matt Finch; first appeared in Knockspell Magazine #1*

Artificer of Yothri: HD 10; AC 2[17]; Atk claw (1d10+1); Save 5; Move 15; AL C; CL/XP 14/2600; Special: Magic Resistance 50% (80%), psychic powers, magic powers.

Plague of Erosion

The large town of Alement sits nestled among rolling hills barely under the shadow of the Hollow Spire Mountains. Just over six days ago, a sudden and deafening explosion was heard from the southern woodlands. Scouts reported that a strange blight now covers the area with a rust-like disease. They claim that the plague kills all animals and plant life that it touches.

Indeed, a horrid plague has spread from a massive 10-foot cube of iron lying partially buried in an impact crater. This solid cube radiates a plague that turns all living creatures into rusting iron (saving throw negates). A successful save indicates permanent resistance to the plague regardless of the amount of exposure. The outer cells of living creatures that fail a saving throw begin to rust (just like oxidized iron) and fall to the ground in a fine dust. Creatures affected by the plague remain alive for 1 day for each hit dice they possess (a 4 HD black bear lives for 4 days before oxidizing into a heap of rust). The plague expands in a 10-foot radius every day, emanating from the cube. Currently, the plague has turned everything within a 60-foot-radius to rust-like dust.

An **Artificer of Yothri** is behind the destructive force. The artificer brought the alien plague cube to spread ruin and devastation. She currently hides within the cube, phasing out to greet interlopers. The artificer can freely enter and exit the cube as if it were thin air, although she can not see out of it. The cube is solid iron to all but artificers of Yothri.

Although the rusting plague ravages every living creature and plant, it can be cured by magical means (such as *cure disease*) or a simple covering of oil. Any application of crude oil (or its derivatives) kills the rusting plague on contact. Furthermore, an oil coating over the iron cube stops the plague at its source by turning the cube into nothing more than a solid block of metal (killing the artificer of Yothri if she remains within the cube).

Assassin Vine

Hit Dice: 7
Armor Class: 5 [14]
Attacks: 1 vine (1d6+1)
Saving Throw: 9
Special: Animate plants
Move: 1
Alignment: Neutrality
Number Encountered: 1 (subterranean) or 1d8 (above ground)
Challenge Level/XP: 8/800

The assassin vine is a semi-mobile plant that collects its own grisly fertilizer by grabbing and crushing animals and depositing the carcasses near its roots. A mature plant consists of a main vine, about 20 feet long. Smaller vines, up to 5 feet long, branch off from the main vine about every 6 inches.

An assassin vine can move about, albeit very slowly, but usually stays put unless it needs to seek prey in a new vicinity.

An assassin vine growing underground usually generates enough offal to support a thriving colony of mushrooms and other fungi, which spring up around the plant and help conceal it.

An assassin vine can animate plants in the near vicinity (about 30ft), and these plants will immobilize anyone failing a saving throw.

Assassin Vine: HD 7; AC 5[14]; Atk 1 vine (1d6+1); Move 1; Save 9; AL N; CL/XP 8/800; Special: Animate plants.

Hang in There

An old tower rises from the forest ahead. A crumbled rock wall surrounds the tower's base. Thick vegetation has reclaimed the once manicured grounds. Clinging vines coat the towers, camouflaging the walls. Upon closer inspection, arrow slits can be seen behind the deep foliage covering the tower. The tower does not appear to have any openings on the ground level, but a single large window breaks through the rounded walls near its 40–foot peak. A withered corpse of a maiden hangs partially out the window. Her tattered clothing and desiccated skin attest to her death some months ago. Long golden hair still attached to her skull hangs down from the window and blows in the wind. The thick vines around the tower are harmless and easily climbable.

Just below the window 30 feet from the ground grows an **assassin vine**. The vine actually grows on the inside of the tower but has branched out through a narrow arrow slit. The tower is mostly hollow and the only entrance lies bricked over behind the vines. The wooden floor on the lowest level rotted away long ago. Thick plants and vines (including the assassin vine) now flourish within the moist soil inside the tower. The tower's roof has mostly caved in, allowing sunlight to filter into the structure. The upper (and only remaining level) lies in a state of ruin. Most of the wooden floor and stairs deteriorated to an unstable condition. The wooden floor and stairs can support some weight if carefully tread upon. The assassin vine killed the maiden (once a thief). The vine, either by chance or via some rudimentary intelligence, uses the corpse to attract prey. Its vines grow through the corpse and hold it up near the window. The vines move the corpse like a puppet if it desires. The corpse holds a rope and grappling hook and has a belt pouch containing a sapphire (250 gp), thieves' tools and wears a silver chastity belt (100 gp).

Astral Moth

Hit Dice: 4+2
Armor Class: 4 [15]
Attacks: 1 bite (1d6)
Saving Throw: 13
Special: Dimensional flight
Move: 3/90 (flying)
Alignment: Any (see below)
Number Encountered: 1
Challenge Level/XP: 5/240

Astral moths are large, moth-like creatures with the bizarre ability to carry other creatures between planes of existence, or into other dimensions. The origins of these rare creatures are lost in the sands of time, but three varieties are now known. The dark and the white varieties are both semi-intelligent, the dark-colored moths being Chaotic in alignment and the white ones being aligned with Law. There is also a grey variety which is apparently closer to the original breeding stock, having only animal intelligence and a Neutral alignment. All three varieties are capable of planar travel, taking their instructions by means of a rudimentary mental telepathy. Poorly trained and untrained astral moths may attempt to throw off a rider mid-journey, which is a significant hazard.

Once an astral moth is airborne, it can begin flying into the spaces between realities on the way to other planes of existence or other dimensions. The time required for such travel will vary in accordance with the intended destination.

The creatures themselves are relatively harmless; the threat of an astral moth is whatever strange being might be riding it as a mount. Astral moths have been used by many ancient, non-human civilizations existing in different times, planes, or dimensions. They are, of course, greatly prized by wizards, and the egg of an astral moth is worth 5,000 gp if sold. Capturing a wild adult is possible, but care must be taken in order to keep it from getting airborne: if the creature is able to take wing, it will escape into the unknown dimensions.

— *Author: Matt Finch*

Astral Moth: HD 4+2; AC 4[15]; Atk 1 bite (1d6); Move 3/90 (flying); Save 13; AL (any); CL/XP 5/240; Special: Dimensional flight.

Lunar Moth

A wounded **melgara** lies in a glade, a rusted blade protruding from her chest. Strange blood stains her clothes and the ground around her. The poisoned blade infected her blood, leaving her weak and partially paralyzed. She pleads to adventurers to aid her in her a quest. An **artificer of Yothri** attacked her and stole her crystal wand. Her soul is bound to this particular; no amount of magical healing can save her until the wand is returned. Her immortal nature staved off immediate death from the poison. She knows the artificer came from an iron tower perched on an icy mountain in a dimension stuck in an eternal state of twilight. In addition to the artificer of Yothri, rust monsters and erinyes (demons) exist in the tower.

The melgara has a large moth-shaped flute. If the flute is played under the light of a full moon, **1d4+1 astral moths** arrive to serve the flutist. The astral moths obey the flutist to the best of their ability and remain until the light of day. The powers of the moth flute work once per month. Luckily, the moon rises full on this very night. In reward for the return of her wand, the melgara presents the heroic adventurers with the *lunar flute*. The astral moths automatically know the path to the artificer's dimension.

Athatch

Hit Dice: 11
Armor Class: 3 [16]
Attacks: 1 or 2 weapons (3d6 or 2d6/2d6)/1 bite (1d6+1)
Saving Throw: 4
Special: Poison (nausea) spit, darkness, levitate, phantasmal force, reduced damage from cold, fire, gas, electricity, polymorph into other giant type.
Move: 15
Alignment: Chaos
Number Encountered: 1
Challenge Level/XP: 15/2,900

The offspring of a demon and a giant, an athatch is a monster about 14ft tall, weighing about 2 tons, with 1d3 eyes, 1d3 arms, and 1d3 legs. An odd-numbered eye is located in its forehead, an odd-numbered arm is located in the middle of its chest, and an odd-numbered leg is located behind its haunch. It is ambidextrous (if it has two or more arms) and can wield a weapon in any or all of its hands. They use massive weapons, usually great clubs (2d6 damage). An athatch cannot normally bite opponents man-sized or smaller in melee, but may (if victory seems likely) toy with its victims by grasping and lifting an opponent with a free hand (a to-hit roll is still required) and then biting on the following round. The poisonous spit of the athatch requires a saving throw at -2 or the victim becomes helplessly nauseated for 1d3 turns; the athatch also can spit this poison up to 10ft.

Because of their demonic heritage, athatch have 60ft darkvision and the following spell-like abilities they can use once per hour: darkness (5ft radius), levitate, and phantasmal force. Once per day an athatch can polymorph self into the form of another giant. They subtract 1 point of damage per die from cold, fire, gas, and lightning attacks against them.

— *Author: Scott Casper*

Athatch: HD 11; AC 3 [16]; Atk 1 or 2 weapons (3d6 or 2d6/2d6)/1 bite (1d6+1); Move 15; Save 4; AL C; CL/XP 15/2,900; Special: Poison (nausea) spit, darkness, levitate, phantasmal force, reduced damage from cold, fire, gas, electricity, polymorph into other giant type.

Attack of the Athatch

A brilliant white cloud hovers just a hundred feet above the forest floor. An aura of silver outlines the ever-changing billowing shape. A magnificent castle of enormous proportions majestically stands atop the cloud. A regal giant adorned in golden plate mail armor slowly floats down from the clouds. She wears a kindly smile and wields a two-handed sword shaped like a lightning bolt. She says her name is Thiassi and needs the help of "wee folk" as she calls the PCs. She tells of a gang of ogres that stole her singing harp. The ogres hide in a cave too small for her to enter.

Thiassi (actually a polymorphed **athatch**) lures victims to the ogre den then springs her trap. The illusionary cloud castle disappears after her defeat. The nearby caves hold **6 ogres** loyal to Thiassi. After the ogres pour out of the den to attack, Thiassi attacks spellcasters from the back. The ogres and athatch have accumulated a substantial amount of loot using this ruse. The caves contain the remains of past victims and three chests. The first chest holds 606 gp, 2,108 sp and 6 cp. A massive horn made of dragon bone sits in the second chest and the third chest has a *wand of polymorph other* (5 charges) and a *+2 two–handed sword*.

Ogres (6): HD 4+1; AC 5[14]; Atk 1 spiked club (1d10+1); Move 9; Save 13; AL C; CL/XP 4/120

Azer

Hit Dice: 2
Armor Class: 2 [17]
Attacks: 1 weapon (1d6+1)
Saving Throw: 16
Special: +1 heat damage, immune to fire
Move: 12
Alignment: Law
Number Encountered: 1d4, 1d6+5, or 1d100
Challenge Level/XP: 3/60

Azers are dwarflike beings native to the Elemental Plane of Fire. They wear kilts of brass, bronze, or copper, and bear broad-headed spears or well-crafted hammers in combat. Their attacks deal +1 damage due to their intense heat. They are immune to fire damage. Stats are for the normal azer; sergeants and leaders can be much larger and will have more hit dice.

Azer: HD 2; AC 2[17]; Atk 1 weapon (1d6+1); Move 12; Save 16; AL L; CL/XP 3/60; Special: +1 heat damage, immune to fire.

Tears of Sutur

A grand pool of molten iron sits before a gargantuan statue of a long-bearded fire giant. The statue represents Sutur, the fire giant god. The shrine (oddly not made by fire giants) lies abandoned in this lofty cavern. The giant sits with its legs around the radiant pool, lounging against a two-handed sword. The statue wears gold plate mail (550 gp if peeled from the statue) and a blackened crown of iron. Tears of molten metal fall from his eyes, down the wavy beard, over his portly belly and into the pool. The metal handle of a weapon breaks the surface of the pool. The handle glows brilliant red with heat. The handle belongs to a massive *+1 flaming warhammer* (treat as a two-handed sword). The hammer deals an extra 1d6 points of fire damage and sheds light as a torch. Only those with the strength of an ogre can wield the hammer properly. Once approached, the tears Sutur roll down the beard and transform into **6 azer**. The azer defend the shrine and hammer. The azer throw balls of molten iron (1d6+1 points of damage) before attacking with searing weapons.

Baboon

	NORMAL	ALPHA	GIANT	GIANT ALPHA
Hit Dice:	1	2	3	5
Armor Class:	7 [12]	7 [12]	7 [12]	7 [12]
Attacks:	1 bite (1d4)	1 bite (1d6)	1 bite (1d8)	1 bite (1d8+1)
Saving Throw:	17	16	14	12
Special:	None	None	None	None
Move:	12	12	15	15
Alignment: Neutrality (or possibly Chaos)				
Number Encountered: 1d12+1				
Challenge Level/XP:	1/15	2/30	3/60	5/240

Baboons are vicious pack hunters, usually led by a stronger-than-normal alpha male. They might be susceptible to the influence of ancient and evil powers. Giant baboons stand 8ft tall on two legs, about twice the size of a normal baboon. As with normal baboons, they are susceptible to the influence of ancient and evil powers.

Baboon: HD 1; AC 7[12]; Atk 1 bite (1d4); Move 12; Save 17; AL N; CL/XP 1/15; Special: None.

Baboon alpha male: HD 2; AC 7[12]; Atk 1 bite (1d6); Move 12; Save 16; AL N; CL/XP 2/30; Special: None.

Giant Baboon: HD 3; AC 7[12]; Atk 1 bite (1d8); Move 15; Save 14; AL N; CL/XP 3/60; Special: None.

Giant Baboon alpha male: HD 5; AC 7[12]; Atk 1 bite (1d8+1); Move 15; Save 12; AL N; CL/XP 5/240; Special: None.

Welcome to the Rock

Vines drape down from the dense jungle canopy. The long, twisting strands easily support the weight of anyone swinging from them. A monolithic, 80-foot-tall slab of black stone rises through the fronds of the gnarled and moss-covered trees. More greenish moss covers the stone's exterior, and its sheer surface is riddled with numerous cave-like openings. A pack of **12 baboons** led by an albino **alpha male giant baboon** live inside the stone. The baboons are extremely territorial. They pelt intruders with heavy stones before swinging down on the abundant vines to attack. Inside the giant baboon's cave is an adventurer's pack filled with old clothing, a small hand mirror (broken), and 27 gp

Badger, Giant

Hit Dice: 3
Armor Class: 4 [15]
Attacks: 2 Claws (1d3), bite (1d6)
Saving Throw: 14
Special: None
Move: 6
Alignment: Neutrality
Number Encountered: 1d2 adults (if 2 adults, then add 1d3 young)
Challenge Level/XP: 3/60

These subterranean predators are the size of a full-grown human, and quite aggressive when defending their territory. Young giant badgers have 1HD.

Giant Badger: HD 3; AC 4[15]; Atk 2 Claws (1d3), bite (1d6); Move 6; Save 14; AL N; CL/XP 3/60; Special: None.

Home on the Range

Tall grasses sway in the gentle breezes blowing across the open prairie. Blue asters grow in fragrant clumps, while honey bees buzz noisily around prairie onions. Butterflies waft lazily in the updrafts. Six foot tall mounds of dirt are tossed about in random piles, the fresh loam heavy with clay and peat. An aggressive **giant badger** hunts the plains, digging new dens every couple of days and rotating through past lairs as it patrols its territory. It erupts from the ground to attack anyone walking among the dirt mounds. Its most recent den contains a dwarf corpse. The corpse has a backpack containing three lumps of gold ore (200 gp total), a small silver bell and a parakeet (dead) in a gold cage.

Bag of Teeth

Hit Dice: 1
Armor Class: 9 [10]
Attacks: 1 Bite (1d6+1/round)
Saving Throw: 17
Special: Bites and holds
Move: 0
Alignment: Neutrality
Number Encountered: 1
Challenge Level/XP: 2/30

A bag of teeth is a deceptive-looking little critter. At first glance, the creature looks like a pouch of coins. Its insides, seen when one opens the "pouch", resemble coins of gold. As one inserts his hand within the creature to retrieve the gold within, the critter's razor-sharp teeth spring open around the pouches opening, and clamp down on the victim's wrist. The bite causes 1d6 points of damage and holds on, with 1d6+1 hp being lost automatically each subsequent round until the vicious creature is killed and lets go.

— Author: Skathros

Bag of Teeth: HD 1; AC 9[10]; Atk Bite (1d6+1/round); Move 0; Save 17; AL N; CL/XP 2/30; Special: Bites and holds.

What's in the Bag?

A **hill giant named Ferck** relaxes on a boulder overlooking a mountain pass. He wears the fur of a grizzly bear, and carries a massive club made from the leg bone of some giant beast. Ferck demands gold from anyone trying to go past his boulder, and attacks those who refuse. Ferck is clumsy, and his wild swings with his bone club are made even worse by the fact that he is missing both of his index fingers. Ferck carries a couple of small sacks on his belt. One has six worthless nuggets of fool's gold, 32 silver pieces, a ruby worth (60 gp) and a dead skunk. The other sack is actually a **bag of teeth**. Ferck lost both of his fingers when he poked them into the bag to get to the shiny coins inside.

Banshee

Hit Dice: 7
Armor Class: 0 [19]
Attacks: 1 claw (1d8)
Saving Throw: 9
Special: Magic or silver to hit; magic resistance 49%; shriek of death; immune to enchantments
Move: 12 (flying)
Alignment: Chaos
Number Encountered: 1
Challenge Level/XP: 11/1,700

Banshees are horrid faerie (or undead) creatures that live in swamps and other desolate places. Their shriek (once per day) necessitates a saving throw versus death or the hearer will die in 2d6 rounds. They can travel over water and other terrain as if it were land, but crossing running water causes them to lose their magic resistance for 3d6 hours. They look like gaunt humans (male or female) with long, stringy hair and glowing yellow eyes. They often wear hooded cloaks. At the Referee's discretion, such creatures might be undead rather than faerie-folk, and are considered Type 9 undead for turning purposes.

Banshee: HD 7; AC 0[19]; Atk 1 claw (1d8); Move (fly 12); Save 9; AL C; CL/XP 11/1700; Special: Magic or silver to hit; magic resistance 49%; shriek of death; immune to enchantments.

Screaming Bells

The vacant Seneteal Monastery sits in the high ridges of the Forlorn Crescents, the empty halls open to shrieking winds blowing through the barren peaks. Jutting rock handholds lead up a sheer cliff to the bone-mesh gates and the carved columns supporting the flat-stone roof where six ancient bells hang inside an enclosed belltower. The bells ring once a day, a depressing sound that bounces through the mountain peaks.

Rumors of death magic practiced in the monastery keep most away. Anyone venturing inside finds the bones of the master monks slumped in rotting saffron robes in the main hall. A lone figure still walks the halls, however. The old man wears a black robe and hides his face under a deep cowl. Ellyllon was an elf warrior who visited the monastery to learn the secrets of the world and to achieve his own inner peace. He instead found ancient words carved into the hollow bells. Reciting them turned him into a deadly **banshee**. He rings the bells daily to bring about the end of the world. The bells cause confusion in anyone hearing them if they fail a saving throw. Ellyllon uses his shrieks to set them ringing before tearing into intruders with his claws.

Barracuda

Hit Dice: 1
Armor Class: 6 [13]
Attacks: 1 bite (1d8)
Saving Throw: 17
Special: None
Move: 24 (swimming)
Alignment: Neutrality
Number Encountered: 1 (8hp) or 1d20+3 (random hp)
Challenge Level/XP: 1/15

Barracudas are fast, predatory fish. They are smaller than most sharks, and hunt in groups. The great barracuda can reach lengths of 6ft, but barracuda that hunt in schools are from 3-4ft in length.

Barracuda: HD 1; AC 6[13]; Atk 1 bite (1d8); Move (swim 24); Save 17; AL N; CL/XP 1/15; Special: None.

Blood in the Water

A suspended wooden bridge crosses 30 feet above the surface of a 60-foot-deep pool of cold, clear water filling this cavernous chamber. Small waterfalls drop from the ceiling to create rippling currents in the water below. The bridge is shaky, but supports the weight of those crossing it.

A locked chest sits in the center of the swinging bridge, bolted through the bridge's wooden planks. The chest's locking mechanism is connected via interlocking latches to supports holding the bridge in place. Unlocking the chest simultaneously unlocks both ends of the bridge, dumping the entire structure into the water. The chest contains a *potion of levitation* in a stoppered flask, a ruby ring (100 gp) and an open pot of cow's blood. Rope pulleys automatically hoist the bridge out of the water and re-latch it in 2d6+2 rounds.

The pool is home to **12 barracudas** that swim out of tubes near the bottom of the pool to attack anyone floundering in the water. The cow's blood spreads out of the chest in a murky cloud, driving the barracuda into a frenzy.

Basilisk

Hit Dice: 6
Armor Class: 4 [15]
Attacks: 1 bite (2d6)
Saving Throw: 11
Special: Petrifaction gaze
Move: 6
Alignment: Neutrality
Number Encountered: 1 or 1d4
Challenge Level/XP: 8/800

Basilisks are great multi-legged lizards whose gaze turns to stone anyone meeting its eye (one way of resolving this: fighting without looking incurs a –4 penalty to hit). If the basilisk's own gaze is reflected back at it, it has a 10% chance to force the basilisk into a saving throw against being turned to stone itself.

Basilisk: HD 6; AC 4[15]; Atk 1 bite (2d6); Move 12; Save 11; AL N; CL/XP 8/800; Special: Petrifaction gaze.

Mirror, Mirror

Dark, ruffled curtains cover dozens of full-length mirrors lining this wide hallway. Each mirror has a bronze frame and stands 15 feet tall and 10 feet wide. Sitting on a white pedestal table in the middle of the hall are a silver hand mirror (60 gp), a melted candle, a gold bell (10 gp) and a quill pen. Most of the mirrors are harmless, but one is a portal to an extradimensional space containing a trapped **basilisk** just waiting for the curtain to be pulled aside to release it. The basilisk charges out, trying to turn anyone in the room to stone. The creature was trapped in the mirror by a powerful mage who then placed the glass here to deter intruders. The items on the table belonged to the wizard's wife. He keeps them here to preserve her memory, but they otherwise serve no purpose.

Basilisk, Desert

Hit Dice: 4+4
Armor Class: 3 [16]
Attacks: 1 bite (1d4 + 1d12 poison) or 1 spit (1d12 poison)
Saving Throw: 13
Special: Poisonous gaze (non-lethal), spit poison (non-lethal), poisonous bite (non-lethal)
Move: 9
Alignment: Neutrality
Number Encountered: 1 or 1d6
Challenge Level/XP: 6/400

Desert basilisks appear to be fat cobra snakes, about 20ft long and 2ft in diameter, with four skinny legs that help propel them along the ground and with horns all around the top of the head. These basilisks are extremely poisonous—so much so that even their gaze inflicts 1d6 points of damage unless those meeting its eye make a successful saving throw. Anyone avoiding the basilisk's gaze attacks with a -4 penalty to hit and damage. In addition, a desert basilisk can spit its poison up to 20ft as a missile attack for 1d12 points of poison damage. The desert basilisk's bite inflicts 1d4 points of physical damage and the poison inflicts an additional 1d12 points. A saving throw negates the basilisk's poison, but anyone who purposely comes into physical contact with a basilisk's hide automatically takes 1d6 points of poison damage. Any weapon that strikes a desert basilisk becomes envenomed and does and additional 1d12 points of poison damage to the next target it hits. Desert basilisks are solitary monsters, indigenous to desert regions, but are sometimes transported elsewhere by wizards looking for exotic guardians.

— Author: Scottenkainen

Desert Basilisk: HD 4+4; AC 3 [16]; Atk 1 bite or 1 spit (1d4+1d12 or 1d12); Move 9; Save 13; AL N; CL/XP 6/400; Special: Poisonous gaze (non-lethal), spit poison (non-lethal), poisonous bite (non-lethal).

The Serpent's Drink

The nomads of the Fannuk Desert speak of an oasis in the middle of the shifting sands where the waters of life also bring deadly risk. The massive waterhole is nevertheless an irresistible temptation to those lost in the desert. Anyone nearing the water finds sandy humps of fur from decomposing camels kneeling along the bank. Thick reeds grow around and through their corpses. The body of a nomad lies 20 feet from the water's edge, his face blackened and his throat bloated.

The water is poisoned by a **desert basilisk** hiding under a rush of reeds near the bank. Drinking the liquid has the same risk as touching the basilisk's hide. The basilisk slides through the water with a ripple of curving waves before rising out to attack.

Bat Monster

Hit Dice: 8
Armor Class: 6 [13]
Attacks: 1 bite (2d8), 2 claws (1d6)
Saving Throw: 8
Special: None
Move: 4/18 (flying)
Alignment: Neutrality
Number Encountered: 1 or 1d6
Challenge Level/XP: 9/1,100

These creatures attack with claws as well as a bite. They are twice the size of a man, with a tremendous wingspan. Fearful peasants might even mistake them for small dragons when they fly by night.

— *Author: Matt Finch*

Bat Monster: HD 8; AC 6[13]; Atk 1 bite (2d8), 2 claws (1d6); Move 4 (fly 18); Save 8; AL N; CL/XP 9/1100; Special: None.

A Wing and a Bear

Guttural growls reverberate through the darkness as something large crashes through the pine trees. Tree limbs crack and crash to the ground as a brown furred beast spirals overhead. Massive bat wings extend outward as the monster dips and slides around the tree trunks. Four massive paws claw the air. A moment later, the beast swoops into the PCs' camp and is revealed: a **grizzly bear** with large wings spreading from its back. The grizzly roars in pain as it slams hard into the ground.

The wings separate almost immediately from the grizzly's fur as the angry bear tumbles headlong across the dirt. A **bat monster** swoops upward and away from the injured animal — and then banks for a return pass at its prey. The giant bloodsucker abandons the bear (it was too difficult to lift anyway) in favor of easier meat. The injured bear takes its anger out on anyone nearby.

Bat, Giant

Hit Dice: 4
Armor Class: 7 [12]
Attacks: 1 bite (1d10)
Saving Throw: 13
Special: 10% chance of disease
Move: 4/18 (flying)
Alignment: Neutrality
Number Encountered: 1 or 1d6
Challenge Level/XP: 5/240

Giant bats are massive, man-sized cousins of the bat; they do not suck blood, but their bite is nonetheless deadly. One in ten carries disease.

Giant Bat: HD 4; AC 7[12]; Atk 1 bite (1d10); Move 4 (fly 18); Save 13; AL N; CL/XP 5/240; Special: 10% chance of disease.

Flowers in the Attic

The abandoned manor house is a blight on the hillside, its shutters falling, its doors broken open, its porch sagging. A massive oak tree leans against the side of the house, caving in the roofline and opening the attic to the elements. Flowers grow up the tree and across the roofline. Fragrant purple petals can be seen growing in the open attic.

The house is empty and has been for many years. Nothing of value remains after looters and vandals tore the place apart. The attic is now home to **6 giant bats** that hang from the roof supports during the day. The bats flutter out as the sun goes down in search of prey. A dead mule lies amid the flowers growing wild in the thick bat guano.

Bear, Black

Hit Dice: 4+1
Armor Class: 7 [12]
Attacks: 2 claws (1d3) and 1 bite (1d6)
Saving Throw: 13
Special: Hug for 1d8 additional damage.
Move: 9
Alignment: Neutrality
Number Encountered: 1 or 1d6 (if more than 2, the rest are cubs with 1d2HD)
Challenge Level/XP: 4/120

Black bears are smaller than grizzly bears and polar bears, and have a very broad size range, from 90 pounds (small females) to about 500 pounds (large males). If a black bear hits with both claws, it hugs for an additional 1d8 hit points of damage.

Black Bear: HD 4+1; AC 7[12]; Atk 2 claws (1d3), 1 bite (1d6); Move 9; Save 13; AL N; CL/XP 4/120; Special: Hug (1d8).

Thief in the Night

An industrious **black bear** makes frequent forays into the Silver Plow Tavern. The animal climbs onto the building's flat second-story roof and then pulls open the shutters to get into guests' rooms. The animal has avoided traps set by the owner, and is quite adept at breaking and entering. The shutters are clawed and scratched from its past entries. Once inside, the bear takes the room apart looking for food. It trashes tables, turns over beds, tears open packs, and crunches loudly on anything edible it finds. The bear scampers into the night after its theft unless disturbed. Anyone sleeping in the room gets a violent wake-up indeed. The noise in the hall is loud as wood breaks beneath the bear's assault.

Bear, Grizzly

Hit Dice: 6
Armor Class: 6 [13]
Attacks: 2 claws (1d6), 1 bite (1d10)
Saving Throw: 11
Special: Hug (2d6)
Move: 9
Alignment: Neutrality
Number Encountered: 1 or 1d4 (if more than 2, the rest are cubs with 1d3HD)
Challenge Level/XP: 6/400

Very large brown bears, grizzlies hug for an additional 2d6 points of damage (if hitting with both claw attacks) and can automatically maintain the hold, crushing the victim and continuing attempts to bite as well.

Grizzly Bear: HD 6; AC 6[13]; Atk 2 claws (1d6), 1 bite (1d10); Move 9; Save 11; AL N; CL/XP 6/400; Special: Hug (2d6).

Campfire Terror

A campfire burns brightly in this small clearing, the roaring flames pushing back the inky blackness. Three forms lie around the fire's welcome warmth. But the twisted, contorted bodies will never feel the heat washing over them. Each man is dead, ripped apart in his sleep. Picks and sieve pans lie scattered around their bloody bodies. One appears to have been reaching for a weapon when his head was torn off. Ripped open bags of food lie on the edges of the destroyed camp. Half-eaten loaves of bread and dried figs litter the ground. Four burros lie dead in a small copse of ash trees near the camp. The animals' guide ropes are still tied to the overhanging branches.

The treasure hunters ventured into the woods to pan for gold, but instead found an angry **grizzly bear** waiting for them. The grizzly killed the men and their pack animals, and then tore apart the camp looking for food. It fell into a deep slumber in the warm pile of dead burros to sleep off its meal. It rises to its feet and attacks if disturbed.

Bear, Cave or Polar

Hit Dice: 7
Armor Class: 6 [13]
Attacks: 2 claws (1d6+1), 1 bite (1d10+1)
Saving Throw: 9
Special: Bear hug (3d6)
Move: 12
Alignment: Neutrality
Number Encountered: 1 or 1d4 (if more than 2, the rest are cubs with 1d6HD)
Challenge Level/XP: 7/600

Prehistoric bears and polar bears are even larger than a grizzly bear. When hitting with both claws, they hug for 3d6 points of damage.

Cave Bear/Polar Bear: HD 7; AC 6[13]; Atk 2 claws (1d6+1), 1 bite (1d10+1); Move 12; Save 9; AL N; CL/XP 7/600; Special: Hug (3d6).

Hot Water

An 15-foot-tall ice cave leads into the sheer wall of the Wailing Glacier's sheer cliff. Thick icicles hang from the cavern's mouth, and snow drifts nearly block the icy entrance. The tunnel extends 300 feet into the cold glacier. At the back of the cave is a 15-foot-wide pool of heated water. The well is 40 feet deep. Underwater steam vent keep the water above freezing. At the bottom of the well are several bodies of three snow nomads. Their bodies are ripped and torn. One body still wears a *ring of cold resistance* (wearer receives +5 to saving throws vs. magical cold and is immune to normal cold).

Anyone diving into the warm water finds several smaller passages that split off from the underwater well. These tunnels wind upward to chambers inside the glacier. One cave is home to a **polar bear**. The bear swims up the well and leaps into the room to attack intruders. The bodies in the water are its past meals.

Bee, Giant

Hit Dice: 3
Armor Class: 6 [13]
Attacks: 1 sting (1d3 + poison)
Saving Throw: 14
Special: Poison
Move: 3/24 (fly)
Alignment: Neutral
Number Encountered: 1, 1d4+1, or 1d6 x10
Challenge Level/XP: 5/240

Giant bees may be found in more than one variety: the giant bee addressed here is the hive-building honeybee. Other varieties include the larger giant bumblebees, which make nests rather than hives. The giant honeybee is essentially the same as normal bees, but they are the size of a football. Giant bees are not killed by stinging an opponent, but the sting only carries enough poison for one injection – if the bee continues to fight rather than fleeing, the sting will only inflict the normal damage caused by the stab itself. The honey produced by giant bees is of superlative quality, and the royal jelly produced to feed larvae has powerful medicinal properties.

Giant Bee: HD 3; AC 6[13]; Atk 1 sting (1d3 + poison); Move 3/24 (Fly); Save 14; AL N; CL/XP 5/240; Special: Lethal poison sting.

Angry Bees

A wooden stand supports a bulging scarecrow that stands in the center of a field of poppies and wildflowers. A floppy hat sits askew on the dummy's pumpkin head. The scarecrow's burlap mid-section is filled with more sewn-in ripe pumpkins. The dummy has a squishy feel to anyone prodding it. The entire cloth mannequin is coated with a sticky gel and sprinkled with fragrant pollen. The body of a wizard in pale green robes lies at the feet of the scarecrow. The corpse is bruised and bloated. Large welts raised on the body leak a golden liquid.

The wizard researcher Morlae Reeve placed the scarecrow to gather poison from a nest of giant bees located in the field. His plan didn't work, but the dummy did rile the bees up. They swarmed the poor, allergic man before he could run. Anyone approaching the scarecrow or the body is attacked by **1d4+1 giant bees** that rise from the swaying grasses to attack. The attacking bees draw others from the hive, with **2 more giant bees** arriving every 1d4+2 rounds thereafter.

Beetle, Giant Arcane

Hit Dice: 5
Armor Class: 3 [16]
Attacks: 1 bite (2d6)
Saving Throw: 12
Special: Arcane reflection
Move: 12
Alignment: Neutrality
Number Encountered: 1d2
Challenge Level/XP: 7/600

A gargantuan beetle with a carapace of mirror-like silver. Arcane Beetles are ideally suited as mounts for warring against magic-users and other arcane spellcasters due to their innate abilities. Any spell cast upon an Arcane Beetle, be it from spells or from magic items, is immediately reflected back at the wizard.

— Author: Skathros

Arcane Beetle: HD 5; AC 3[16]; Atk 1 mandibles (2d6); Save 12; Move 12; CL/XP 7/600; Special: Arcane reflection.

Beetle Bane

The burly barbarian Axxhammer Kronk hates wizards. A sorcerous minion of the dark gods killed his favorite pony when he was a child, and Kronk's anger has known no bounds since that evil day. Kronk carries a massive battle axe over his muscular shoulder. He notches the handle each time he slays a mage (or someone he thinks is a mage; Kronk isn't particularly bright). Kronk stands nearly 7 feet tall and has a curly red beard that drops nearly to the wide leather belt he wears. Kronk is missing his left eye. A foul wizard jammed a wand into Kronk's eye socket before the barbarian sliced off the man's head. The wand shoved into his skull didn't do any damage to the dimwitted barbarian's intelligence.

Skittering in front of Kronk are **2 giant arcane beetles**. An iron spike is driven into each beetle's carapace, and a silver chain is attached to each spike. Kronk keeps the other ends wrapped around his massive hand. Kronk yanks the chains occasionally to keep the beetles in check. The beetles learned long ago not to mess with the irritable barbarian. He keeps the beetles between himself and any wizards he encounters until he can get close enough to use his axe.

Axxhammer Kronk: HD 8; hp 52; AC 3[16]; Atk; +1 battle axe (1d8); Save 7; Move 9; AL C; CL/XP 8/800; Equipment +1 battle axe, ring of protection +1, bracers of defense AC 4[15].

Beetle, Giant Fire

Hit Dice: 1+3
Armor Class: 4 [15]
Attacks: 1 bite (1d4+2)
Saving Throw: 17
Special: Light glands
Move: 12
Alignment: Neutrality
Number Encountered: 3d4
Challenge Level/XP: 1/15

A giant fire beetle's oily light-glands glow reddishly, and continue to give off light for 1d6 days after they are removed (shedding light in a 10ft radius).

Giant Fire Beetle: HD 1+3; AC 4[15]; Atk 1 bite (1d4+2); Move 12; Save 17; AL N; CL/XP 1/15; Special: Light glands.

Buyer Beware

Lamp seller Amaz Juventia promises that his lamps last for months (they don't), are unbreakable (they aren't) and bring great adventure to his buyers (they do). Each lamp is little more than a hollow wooden cube with panels on four sides that slide open and shut. A crude brass handle sits on the top of the lamp. Some of the lamps are painted with elaborate scenes (600 gp), but the majority Amaz sells are unadorned wood (10 sp). Each illuminates a 30-foot-radius for up to 3d4 days. They don't require any oil. Amaz claims the lamps are perfect for adventurers going underground. He says the light from the lamp causes jewels to glow in their presence. To prove this, he points to a number of glowing rubies sitting in a locked cage on a table behind the counter. The glowing jewels are fakes, and enchanted with a permanent light spell to produce the glow. The lamps have no special effects. Opening the lamp reveals a squishy lump of glowing organic material. The lamps have a 10% chance of spontaneously catching fire each day.

Amaz recently plowed over a nest of giant fire beetles near his home. His wife wades into the nest each morning wearing a special pheromone to repel the beetles. She harvests the insects' light-glands, which Amaz quickly stuffs into lamps to sell before they go out. Amaz's stall in Bargarsport's bazaar is liberally doused in the pheromone to repel the insects. Anyone who buys one of the lamps attracts **12 giant fire beetles** within 2d4+2 rounds.

Beetle, Giant (Normal)

Hit Dice: 5
Armor Class: 3 [16]
Attacks: 1 bite (5d4)
Saving Throw: 12
Special: None
Move: 9
Alignment: Neutrality
Number Encountered: 1 or 1d10
Challenge Level/XP: 5/240

These stats are for a generic giant beetle about five feet long. Larger or smaller beetles might have different statistics or have unusual abilities; to reflect the vast range of possible sizes, assume one hit die and 1d4 damage per 1ft length of the monster. The common characteristics of giant beetles are a very good armor class (due to the carapace) and a single, strong bite from the mandibles. Uncommon varieties of giant beetle might have unusual characteristics – the giant fire beetle being a good example.

Giant Beetle (5ft): HD 5; AC 3[16]; Atk 1 bite (5d4); Move 9; Save 12; AL N; CL/XP 5/240; Special: None.

Firebugs

Three glowing flames move through the inky dungeon darkness, weaving back and forth, rising and dropping, with a skittering jerkiness. The glowing candles don't illuminate the source of their motion. The candles hover roughly three feet off the ground at all times.

Black candles are affixed to the backs of **3 giant beetles** with melted wax. The beetles move quickly down the hall toward intruders, climbing up the walls and over small furniture to get to their next meal. The insects act as moving light sources and guards for a wizard who dwells in the tower.

Beetle, Giant Huhu

Hit Dice: 1+3
Armor Class: 4 [15]
Attacks: 1 bite (2d6)
Saving Throw: 17
Special: Grab hold
Move: 9/18 (flying)
Alignment: Neutrality
Number Encountered: 1d8+4
Challenge Level/XP: 2/30

This large winged beetle has a brown and yellow-striped carapace, horny black antennae and powerful jaws. Its barbed legs hook relentlessly into the victim's hair, fur or clothing. It is attracted to light sources. The pale yellow HuHu grubs are extremely nutritious and taste like peanut butter.

— Author: Mudguard

Giant HuHu Beetle: HD 1+3; AC 4[15]; Atk Bite (2d6); Move 9 (18 fly); Save 17; AL N; CL/XP: 2/30; Special: Grab hold.

HuHu's There?

A falling down wooden structure sits in the swampy bayou of the Sin Mire. The shack has a locked wooden door. The word "Nok" is carved onto a wooden sign hanging below a brass knocker mounted in the center of the door. The three-room structure is filled with swamp moss that grows up the walls and across the floor. A hole in the ceiling drips stagnant rainwater into the living space. Mosquitoes buzz in swarms. The corpse of a fisherman who made his living in the bayou lies facedown on the wooden floor. Hundreds of white grubs squirm around his bloated body.

A nest of **12 giant huhu beetles** sits on the building's flat roof. The nest looks like a pile of dirt and mud sitting atop one corner of the building. If PCs enter the shack, the aggressive beetles stomp along the roof toward the hole in the ceiling. The beetles' marching steps sound like someone knocking on the wooden structure. The beetles swoop down on intruders in an attempt to drive them away from the young in the nest.

Behir

Hit Dice: 12
Armor Class: 4 [15]
Attacks: 1 bite (1d8)
Saving Throw: 3
Special: Constrict and claw, lightning breath
Move: 15
Alignment: Chaos
Number Encountered: 1d3 (if 3 are encountered, one is young with 1d6+2 hit dice and half damage on all attacks)
Challenge Level/XP: 13/2,300

The behir is a serpentine monster that can slither like a snake or use its dozen legs to move with considerable speed. A behir is about 40 feet long. Most are a deep blue color. Behirs attack by biting, and will swallow prey whole on a natural roll of 20. They also lash their bodies around prey (to hit), and on the first round following this attack they can bring 6 claws into play (6 attacks, 1d6 hit points per attack).

Behirs also have a breath weapon – they can spit a bolt of lightning once per 10 rounds, inflicting 24 points of damage (2 per hit die, for smaller or larger behirs). A successful saving throw indicates half damage.

Behir: HD 12; AC 4[15]; Atk 1 bite (1d8); Move 15; Save 3; AL C; CL/XP 13/2300; Special: Constrict and claw, lightning breath.

Lightning in a Bottle

A glass bottle containing a miniature ship sailing on a wave of blue liquid sits on a marble pedestal in this spacious chamber. Clouds roll above the ship like dark fog, and tiny lightning bolts arc from the sky to the ship's masts. The ship's masts appear to be blue scales of some beast. The ship rises and falls on the waves, and the storm intensifies the longer anyone watches the scene unfold. Swords, shields and polearms sit in wooden racks lining the walls. A gold-colored chandelier supporting hundreds of white candles hangs from the ceiling. The entire room is bathed in an ethereal light. A cork is stuck into the bottle's opening.

The bottle is a portal to an elemental plane. If the cork is removed or the bottle broken, the portal opens as a massive storm cloud above the bottle. The clouds that roiled above the tiny ship billow and clash above the PCs as lightning flashes. Wooden planks drop through the portal to land heavily around PCs. The figurehead of a sailing ship follows, thudding into the ground. In 1d4+1 rounds, a lightning bolt erupts out of the hole to strike the bottle (or its shards). The bolt does 6d6 points of damage (save for half). After the bolt strikes, a shimmering form wavers into existence. A **behir** is unceremoniously dumped into the middle of the room a moment later. The angry creature drops from the air to land heavily on the tiled floor, then immediately attacks those it assumes brought it here.

Birhaakaman (Wild Bird-men)

Hit Dice: 1+3
Armor Class: 6 [13] or 4 [15]
Attacks: 2 claws (1d2) and beak (1d3) or weapon (1d8)
Saving Throw: 17
Special: None
Move: 12/18 (flying)
Alignment: Neutrality (usually)
Number Encountered: 1d4+1 or 3d10+20
Challenge Level/XP: 2/30

Birhaakamen are bird-men, entirely feathered, with beaks and clawed hands at their wing-joints. They live in tribal aeries and are generally not civilized. They carry javelins, and some of the more civilized aeries arm their warriors with spears and shields. These more advanced bird-men may wear scraps of armor, increasing their AC to 4[15].

— Author: Matt Finch

Birhaakaman: HD 1+3; AC 6[13] or 4 [15]; Atk 2 claws (1d2) and beak (1d3) or weapon (1d8); Move 12 (Fly 18); Save 17; AL N; CL/XP 2/30; Special: None.

Bird Men of Aly-Katraz

Stroud Island sits shrouded by mists in the middle of the uncharted Reaping Sea. The island has high, treacherous cliffs that are nearly impossible to climb. Dangerous coral reefs keep ships from easily approaching the sandy beaches. High atop one rocky crag sits the aerie community of Aly-Katraz, a nest-city of birhaakamen who don't look kindly upon unwanted visitors. The bird-men ride the thermal updrafts around their home, sweeping down in waves upon sailors who dare to land upon the white sand beaches. Captives are kept in gilded cages suspended over 300 foot drops for predatory birds to peck apart.

Sitting on a stone pedestal on the south beach is a golden eagle statue. The statue faces outward, staring out at the sea. The idol is worth 300 gp and weighs 600 pounds. The idol grants the owner the ability to take flight as a giant raptor once per day. Flights of **10 birhaakamen** soar on the thermals above the beach, keeping an eagle eye on the precious statue. The birhaakamen believe that if the idol leaves the island, they'll lose their own ability to take to the skies.

Black Pudding

Hit Dice: 10
Armor Class: 6 [13]
Attacks: 1 attack (3d8)
Saving Throw: 5
Special: Acidic surface, immune to cold, divides when hit with lightning
Move: 6
Alignment: Neutrality
Number Encountered: 1 or 1d4
Challenge Level/XP: 12/2,000

Black puddings are amorphous globs with an acidic surface. They are subterranean predators and scavengers. Any weapon or armor contacting a black pudding will be eaten away by the acid as follows: weapon (1 hit by the weapon), chainmail or lesser armor (1 hit by pudding), plate mail (2 hits by pudding). If a weapon or armor is magical, it can take an additional hit per +1 before being dissolved.

Black Pudding: HD 10; AC 6[13]; Atk 1 attack (3d8); Move 6; Save 5; AL N; CL/XP 12/2000; Special: Acidic surface, immune to cold, divides when hit with lightning.

Come Blow Your Horn

Six oversized curving stone trumpets sit on a ledge overlooking a 200-foot-deep pit. The bells of the trumpets point horizontally out over the drop. A plush velvet-lined tray before the stone instruments holds six bronze mouthpieces (20 gp each) that fit into the trumpets. Each mouthpiece has a different-colored gem affixed to it. The trumpets produce clear, clean notes and cause colored lights matching the gemstones on the mouthpieces to glow inside the pit. Blowing multiple trumpets mixes the colors. The lights glow for three rounds before going out. If all of the trumpets are blown in order, the colored lights form a multi-colored staircase circling down inside the pit.

One of the trumpets produces a flat, ugly sound if blown, as if something blocks the interior of the instrument. A **black pudding** fills the curving stone. Anyone blowing the trumpet gets a mouthful of black pudding as the creature oozes up through the instrument to get at the would-be musician.

Blink Dog

Hit Dice: 4
Armor Class: 5 [14]
Attacks: 1 bite (1d6)
Saving Throw: 13
Special: Teleport
Move: 12
Alignment: Lawful
Number Encountered: 1d4+1 or 1d12+4
Challenge Level/XP: 5/240

Blink dogs are pack hunters, intelligent and usually friendly to those who are not of evil intent. They can teleport short distances (without error) and attack in the same turn – in most cases (75%) a blink dog will be able to teleport behind an opponent and attack from the rear (with appropriate bonuses).

Blink Dog: HD 4; AC 5[14]; Atk 1 bite (1d6); Move 12; Save 13; AL L; CL/XP 5/240; Special: Teleport.

Don't Blink

Strobe lights flash throughout this room, the quick pulses throwing off the senses. A five-foot-diameter orb floating in the center of the chamber is the source of the strobing lights. The chamber is home to **4 rabid blink dogs**. The canines blink in and out, their forms flickering from one spot to the next. The incessant strobing makes it seem as if 10 dogs are in the room. A dog is seen in one spot before the light winks out, and then appears across the room when the light returns. Normally friendly to good creatures, the rabies attacks the dogs' brains so that they attack anyone intruding upon their den. The central orb traps the diseased animals and prevents them from leaving the chamber. Shutting it down (by covering it or destroying it) allows the dogs to escape, but doesn't cure the rabies afflicting them. Anyone bitten by the blink dogs must make a saving throw or lose 1 point of Constitution each day thereafter until cured. The person dies when their Constitution reaches zero.

Boar, Wild

Hit Dice: 3+3
Armor Class: 7 [12]
Attacks: 1 gore (3d4)
Saving Throw: 14
Special: Dies hard
Move: 15
Alignment: Neutrality
Number Encountered: 1 boar, 1 sow, or mated pair with 1d6-1 piglets (noncombatant, 1d6hp each).
Challenge Level/XP: 4/120

Boars continue to attack for two rounds after they are actually killed before they drop dead. These stats might also be used for your "blue tusken-hogs of the Ymar Plains," or whatever is appropriate for your campaign. Sows have the same hit dice, but do not have tusks. They bite viciously, however, inflicting 1d6 points of damage.

Wild Boar: HD 3+3; AC 7[12]; Atk 1 gore (3d4); Move 15; Save 14; AL N; CL/XP 4/120; Special: Continue attacks 2 rounds after death.

Pig Skinned

Human skin stretches across seven wooden frames outside this small hut located in the Seething Jungle. The skin was removed from the bodies of men and women in long rolls and then stretched across the frame to cure. Most of the bodies are men and elves, but one is dwarf skin (stretched incredibly thin). A fire pit in the center of the clearing has a boiling pot sitting on the hot coals. Walking around the fire pit are **6 wild boars**. The boars attack anyone approaching the hut. Each pig wears a collar of interlinked finger bones.

The witch doctor who lives in the hut is a vicious necromancer who creates zombies from the stretched skins. The witch doctor is currently away looking for ginseng roots to raise and control the zombies. Inside the hut are **8 zombies** left behind to protect the hut. The zombies have flat black rocks embedded in their faces where their eyes used to be.

Zombie: HD 2; AC 8[11] or with shield 7[12]; Atk 1 weapon or strike (1d8); Move 6; Save 16; AL N; CL/XP 2/30; Special: Immune to sleep and charm.

Bone Mound

Hit Dice: 10
Armor Class: 3 [16]
Attacks: 1d6 claw/kick/bite (1d4 each)
Saving Throw: 5
Special: Animate dead, multiple attacks
Move: 6
Alignment: Chaos
Number Encountered: 1
Challenge Level/XP: 12/2,000

When a nugget of pure chaos ends up in the material plane, the result can be a bone mound, a jelly-like creature that exudes a sticky film from its pores. At first glance, a bone mound appears to be a massive heap of bones and broken skeletal remains, for it picks up osseous material that sticks to the slime-beast's blob-like form, giving it the appearance of a pile of bones. This bone-collecting slime possesses a secondary ability that makes it a truly dangerous foe. In addition to the adhesive film it exudes, the piece of pure chaos at the bone mound's core gives it an innate ability to animate, partially, the bones that stick to it. The effects of this spell-like ability extend up to 2ft away from the creature's body. The bone mound can animate 1d6 of the bony remains that have adhered to it each round. Each of these animated body parts may attack once, inflicting 1d4 damage. A cleric may turn these newly living bits of skeletal remains as if they were Type 1 undead. The bone mound may shift its animate dead power from one set of bones to another at any time.

The chaos nugget inside the mound, which looks like a bit of charcoal, is quite dangerous - it dissolves instantly into anyone who touches it, and the victim must make a saving throw at -2 or the nugget will re-form inside his body and he will become a bone mound himself in 1d6 days.

— *Author: Skathros*

Bone Mound: HD 10; AC 3[16]; Atk 1d6 claw/kick/bite (1d4 each); Move 6; Save 5; AL C; CL/XP 12/2000; Special: Animate dead, multiple attacks.

Death Gnoll

A dying gnoll lies sprawled across a pile of bones in this ossuary. The gnoll's breathing is labored and shallow, and his eyes are rolled into his skull. Sticky sweat gels on his fur. A circle of black scar tissue is burned into his left palm, and the fur of his left arm is burned and blackened. A brazier of coals is overturned on the floor at his feet, the cool chunks scattered over the tile. Skulls sit on stone ledges around the room.

The gnoll discovered a chaos nugget glowing in the brazier of coals and picked it up. The nugget burned its way into his body through his palm and is nearly finished changing its unfortunate victim into a **bone mound**. In 3 rounds, the gnoll's body dissolves into a sticky mass and seeps through the bone mound beneath it. The newly formed bone mound immediately animates the bones to attack.

Borsin (Ape Centaur)

Hit Dice: 4
Armor Class: 6 [13]
Attacks: 2 claws (1d4) and 1 bite (1d3)
Saving Throw: 13
Special: Hug and rend
Move: 15
Alignment: Chaos
Number Encountered: 1d6+1 or 1d100
Challenge Level/XP: 4/120

A borsin is a creature with the head, arms, and upper body of an ape joined to the body and legs of a quadruped. The lower half may be that of a boar, equine, or hound; these may be a race of battle-beasts magically crossbred in antiquity. A borsin has a savage cunning, and is capable of problem-solving and setting crude traps. They do not use weapons or tools, or carry treasure, although pack leaders will drape themselves in the skins and furs of creatures they have killed – including humans and adventurers.

Borsin form packs led by the strongest member. They attack with two claws and a bite, and use pack tactics to drive opponents and prey into traps, kill zones, or natural hazards such as cliffs and ravines. If both its claws hit the same opponent, a borsin can hug and rend for an additional 2d6 points of damage. Borsin packs stake out their territory by making small cairns topped with the skulls of their kills, and patrol their borders regularly. Borsin are omnivorous and hardy, capable of surviving on plant matter, yet enjoying a fresh kill.

— *Author: Scott Wylie Roberts, "Myrystyr"*

Borsin: HD 4; AC 6[13]; Atk 2 claws (1d4) and 1 bite (1d3); Move 15; Save 13; AL C; CL/XP 4/120; Special: Hug and rend.

The Wild Pack

Blood coats the rocks and ground in this dead-end canyon. Parts of various animals are scattered across the rocky ground. PCs find horse heads, cow hooves, stringy pelts and even dog collars amid the carnage. The hoof prints of hundreds of horses are trampled into the blood-soaked ground.

A pack of **7 borsin** hunts the rocky steppes, corralling animals for slaughter. The borsin have the lower bodies of roan stallions and charge easily over the rocky ledges of their hunting ground. The pack sleeps in a cave in another canyon. The creatures post sentries on the hills overlooking the entrance to the box canyon. The animals frequently run wild horse herds into the canyon, then descend and kill as many of the animals as they can. PCs who enter the canyon are targeted for slaughter. The borsin arrive within 3 rounds for the kill.

Brainosaurian

Hit Dice: 10
Armor Class: 5 [14]
Attacks: 2 claws or weapons (1d6) and 1 bite (3d6)
Saving Throw: 5
Special: Control saurians
Move: 15
Alignment: Any
Number Encountered: 1 or 2d6
Challenge Level/XP: 11/1,700

Brainosaurians are highly intelligent dinosaurs, possibly the remnant survivors of some ancient saurian civilization. They are the size of an allosaurus, standing approximately ten feet at the shoulder. A brainosaurian is able to communicate with and control most types of dinosaurs, although this control is not perfect: herbivorous dinosaurs will still instinctively keep their distance from carnivores, for example. Brainosaurians are generally found in areas where dinosaurs are common.

Some rare brainosaurians are shamans, able to cast spells as a 4th to 8th level cleric.

— Author: Matt Finch

Brainosaurian: HD 10; AC 5[14]; Atk 2 claws or weapons (1d6) and 1 bite (3d6); Move 15; Save 5; AL Any; CL/XP 11/1700; Special: Control saurian.

In the Valley of the Ocher God

The rifts of the Beharrel Valley are deep chasms in the Seething Jungle that drop down into a steamy natural hotspot. The massive gouges in the ground contain entire species of dinosaurs that walk freely in the sweltering heat. One deep cavern network is ruled by a **brainosaurian** known as the Ocher God. The intelligent allosaurus uses a **tyrannosaurus** as a guard to protect him from other less-intelligent would-be usurpers. The Ocher God walks the jungle, using his spells and natural abilities to shape and control the jungle and its inhabitants. A race of natives scampers underfoot, desperately staying out of the massive dinosaur's way. They live in underground caves too narrow for the dinosaurs to enter. The Ocher God sleeps on a raised crystal dais surrounded by glowing columns of magical energy that shield him while he slumbers.

Tyrannosaurus Rex: HD 18; AC 4[15]; Atk 1 bite (4d8); Move 18; Save 3; AL N; CL/XP 19/2400; Special: Chews and tears.

Brainstorm

Hit Dice: 5
Armor Class: 4 [15]
Attacks: Special only
Saving Throw: 12
Special: Brainstorm
Move: 9 (flying)
Alignment: Neutrality
Number Encountered: 1
Challenge Level/XP: 7/600

Brainstorms are creatures that reside in the ethereal plane of existence; they are incorporeal, able to move through solid objects and only vulnerable to magic weapons (and spells). The central body of a brainstorm resembles an almost transparent sphere with a ghostly-looking brain at the center. A brainstorm attacks by sending out waves of mental power in a cone shape, extending 100ft from the creature with a 10ft width at the origin and 100ft wide at the end of the cone. Anything caught within the cone must make a saving throw or be affected by one of the following:

1. Charmed (1d6 rounds)
2. Fear (flee for 1d6 turns)
3. Paralysis (1d6 turns)
4. Unbearable headache (2d6 points of damage, lasts only 1 round)
5. Levitated 10ft from ground
6. Rage (attack allies for 1d6 rounds)
7. Healed by 1d6 hit points
8. Teleported (safely) 1d20 x10ft from present location in random direction
9. Drop all items held
10. Headache (1d6 hit points damage)

Characters that are already under the effects of the brainstorm and are hit a second time by the storm will automatically take 1d2 points of headache damage rather than rolling a second result. If anyone is killed by one of the "headache" results, the character's head explodes, a problem that must be addressed before raising the character from the dead.

— Author: Matt Finch

Brainstorm: HD 5; AC 4[15]; Atk Special; Move 9 (flying); Save 12; AL N; CL/XP 7/600; Special: Brainstorm.

Brain Death

A pulsating rift hovers 15 feet in the air over an onyx altar in this blackstone chamber. A high dome ceiling above the opening in the air is decorated with thousands of mirrored tiles. Two winged stone statues stand at the ends of the altar, their hands raised joyously toward the glowing rift. Sixty emeralds (30 gp each) lie on the floor in a circle around the statues. A ceremonial *+1 dagger* lies atop the altar. Lying on the floor outside the gem circle is a freshly killed thief and a skeleton. The thief's head is missing and his clothing is covered in dark-red blood. The skeleton's torso is crushed, his ribs snapped like twigs.

The rift is an opening to the ethereal plane. The dagger is the focal point that summons a **brainstorm** if it touches flesh. The dagger doesn't have to stab someone; merely touching it with a bare hand is enough to bring the brainstorm in 1d4 rounds. One of the statues is a **stone golem** tasked with protecting the sacred dagger. The golem doesn't move unless the dagger is taken, and it ignores the brainstorm when it arrives. The brainstorm caused the thief's head to explode as he dodged the golem; the skeleton was a fighter crushed by the golem years earlier. The thief's corpse still has 67 gp in a pouch on his belt.

Stone Golem: HD 15 (60hp); AC 5[14]; Atk 1 fist (3d8); Move 6; Save 3; AL N; CL/XP 16/3200; Special: +1 or better magic weapon to hit, immune to most magic.

Bugbear

Hit Dice: 3+1
Armor Class: 5 [14]
Attacks: 1 bite (2d4) or weapon (1d8+1)
Saving Throw: 14
Special: Surprise 50%
Move: 9
Alignment: Chaos
Number Encountered: 1d6 or 6d6
Challenge Level/XP: 4/120

These large, hairy, goblin-like humanoids are stealthier than their size would suggest, getting the chance to surprise even alert opponents with a roll of 1-3 on a d6 (50%). Bugbears stand from 7-8ft in height.

Bugbear: HD 3+1; AC 5[14]; Atk 1 bite (2d4) or weapon (1d8+1); Move 9; Save 14; AL C; CL/XP 4/120; Special: Surprise opponents, 50% chance

Wagon Riders of the Purple Plains

A wooden carriage painted garish purple rolls down the dusty road. It weaves from side to side as the driver attempts to control the massive steeds pulling it forward at a full gallop. The vehicle nearly topples once or twice, before miraculously straightening out and staying on its wheels. The horses charge forward, fear in their wide eyes and flecks of foam covering their mouths. Hanging out the carriage's windows are **6 bugbears**. The driver (another **bugbear** wearing a woman's dress and a dirty shawl) guides the animals as best it can toward PCs. The bugbears are armed with swords and bows. This enterprising band of misfits stole the carriage and horses and now terrorizes the plains by riding down travelers. Their treasure (kept inside the carriage with them) includes six bags of molding barley, a keg of ale (mostly empty), a silver serving platter (20 gp), 17 gp and a set of nesting dolls shaped like a chicken.

Bulette

Hit Dice: 7 to 10
Armor Class: -2 [21]
Attacks: Bite (4d12) and 2 Claws (3d6)
Saving Throw: 9 (7HD), 8 (8HD), 6 (9HD), 5 (10HD)
Special: Leaping, surprise
Move: 15/3 (burrowing)
Alignment: Neutrality
Number Encountered: 1 or (seldom) 1d2
Challenge Level/XP: 7 HD (9/1,100), 8 HD (10/1,400), 9 HD (11/1,700), 10 HD (12/2,000)

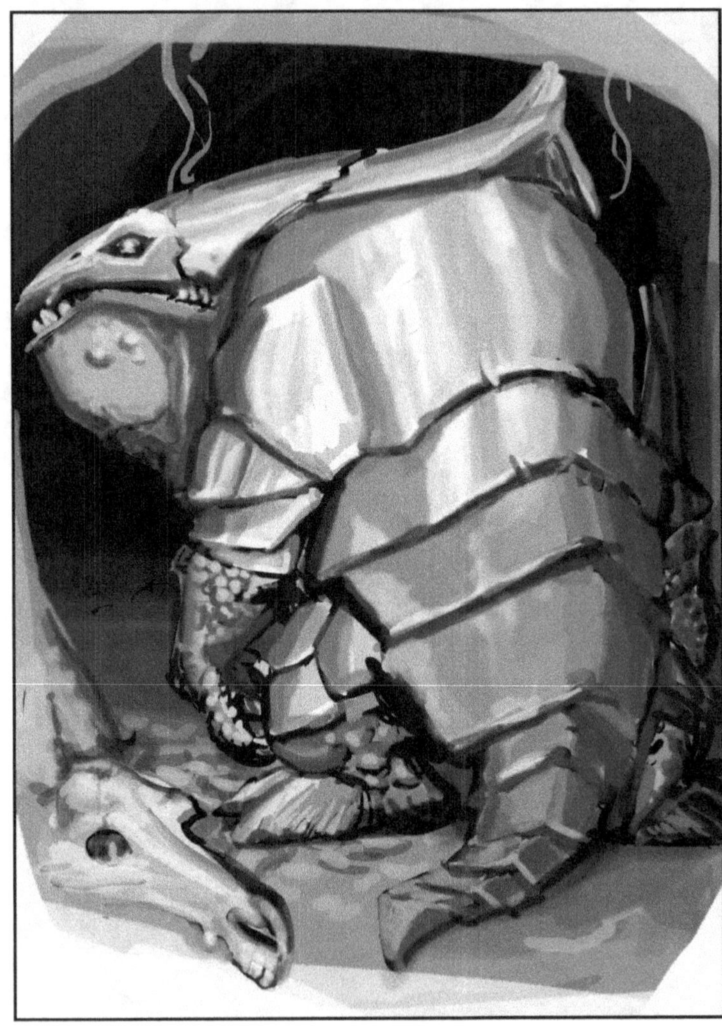

Roughly ten feet in height, a bulette (boo-LAY) is covered in natural armor plating like that of an armadillo, and has a beak-like head that opens to show wicked, serrated teeth. These creatures can leap to the attack; in which case they cannot bite, but may attack with all four claws. Bulettes dig underground to surprise their prey, leaving a furrow in the ground as they go, caused by a dorsal crest in the creature's armor. These voracious hunters eat horses and halflings with gusto, although they will devour anything from badgers to plowshares if their preferred foods are not readily available. Although bulettes burrow, they do not venture further underground, for they are surface predators. When the dorsal crest of the bulette is raised (during combat this is usually only after the thing has been wounded), the area underneath is AC 6 [13], and this vulnerable point can be attacked if the monster is well enough surrounded for its opponents to attack from behind as well as in front.

Bulettes, often called "landsharks," resemble huge armadillos with wide, tooth-filled mouths. They burrow beneath the ground, and surge upward to attack prey. Bulettes can grow to be ten to fifteen feet long. Horses are a favorite food of bulettes.

Bulette (7HD): HD 7; AC –2[21]; Atk Bite (4d12) and 2 Claws (3d6); Move 15 (Burrow 3); Save 9; AL N; CL/XP 9/1100; Special: Leaping, surprise, burrow.

Bulette (8HD): HD 8; AC –2[21]; Atk Bite (4d12) and 2 Claws (3d6); Move 15 (Burrow 3); Save 8; AL N; CL/XP 10/1400; Special: Leaping, surprise, burrow.

Bulette (9HD): HD 9; AC –2[21]; Atk Bite (4d12) and 2 Claws (3d6); Move 15 (Burrow 3); Save 6; AL N; CL/XP 11/1700; Special: Leaping, surprise, burrow.

Bulette (10HD): HD 10; AC –2[21]; Atk Bite (4d12) and 2 Claws (3d6); Move 15 (Burrow 3); Save 5; AL N; CL/XP 12/2000; Special: Leaping, surprise, burrow.

The Ol' Hitching Post

A six-foot-tall wooden hitching post stands on the edge of a field of switchgrass. The slender post has a carved horse's head atop it, with the mouth of the animal forming a slot. A sign hanging around its neck reads "One gold." Any gold piece placed in the horse's mouth rolls down a cleverly concealed twisting strip of wood that winds around inside the post. The coin vanishes at the bottom of the ramp, disappearing into thin air. A moment later, a horse appears beside the post.

The hitching post is a magical summoning item a wizard crafted to rent steeds to needy travelers. The summoned horses are real, and last for 12 hours before vanishing. The post can summon up to 6 normal horses per day. The pole cannot be removed without permanently destroying its magic. The horses are branded and cannot be sold or traded.

Summoning a horse draws the attention of a nearby **bulette**. The creature normally dines on the wild horses that roam the prairie, but won't pass up an easier meal. The bulette craves horseflesh above all other meat.

Camel

Hit Dice: 2
Armor Class: 7 [12]
Attacks: 1 bite (1d2)
Saving Throw: 16
Special: None
Move: 20
Alignment: Neutrality
Number Encountered: 1d10+1
Challenge Level/XP: 2/30

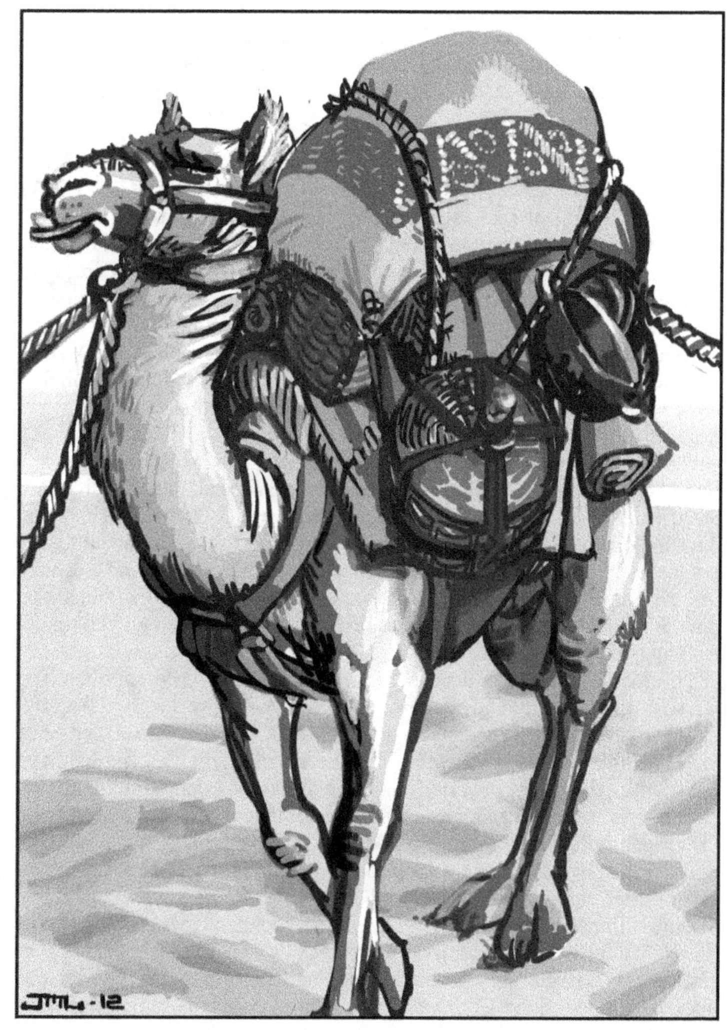

Camels can carry 600 pounds of weight. They often have bad dispositions, and they spit.

Camel: HD 2; AC 7[12]; Atk 1 bite (1d2); Move 20; Save 16; AL N; CL/XP 2/30; Special: None.

Contagious Camel Confusion

Bundles of stained silk and broken kegs of ale line the road. The corpses of robed men holding scimitars lie trampled and broken among the refuse. Hacked and slashed camels and mules from a caravan also lie dead along the path. Jarwal, a rich and plump silk merchant, hides in the wagon as a group of **4 camels** attacks the wagon. The camels batter the enclosed wagon with their hooves and spit. The caravan's pack animals contracted a rabies-like disease. The disease enrages the animals into a violent and deadly rage. The animals turned on the caravan guards and teamsters. Only Jarwal survived the animal uprising. Jarwal rewards his liberators with a few jars of figs and a bolt of silk (50 gp).

The camels spit foamy saliva into opponents' faces before engaging in berserk combat. The disease (saving throw versus poison to avoid) causes confusion in the victim. The disease runs its course and lasts for 1d4 days or until magically cured. During this time, the inflicted individuals continue to act as if under a *confusion* spells.

Each round, the creatures do the following (roll 2d6):

2–5	Attack random creature or object.
6–8	Stand baffled and inactive.
9–10	Attack self.
11–12	Wander away for the duration, oblivious to any dangers or obstacles.

Carrion Fly

Hit Dice: 4
Armor Class: 7 [12]
Attacks: 4 tentacles (paralyze) or 1 spit (2d4)
Saving Throw: 13
Special: Paralyze, acid
Move: 3/18 (flying)
Alignment: Neutrality
Number Encountered: 1 or 1d4+1
Challenge Level/XP: 7/600

A carrion fly is 5 feet long and resembles a large, white grub with wings and no legs. Its head has large black eyes and a small mouth ringed with four long tentacles. It attacks with its tentacles, attempting to paralyze its prey. Once its victim is paralyzed, it will land and begin vomiting digestive acids to melt the victim into a suitable meal of goo. It can also spit these digestive acids at its target from a distance.

— *Author: the Lizard of Oz*

Carrion Fly: HD 4; AC 7[12]; Atk 4 tentacles (paralyze) or 1 spit (2d4); Move 3 (fly 18); Save 13; AL N; CL/XP 7/600; Special: Paralyze, acid

Dragon Flies

A large overhang of rock sits at the base of the White Rock Cliffs. While the ceiling of rock is too shallow to be called a cave, the alcove offers plenty of protection from the elements. The area under the outcropping was the site of a recent and violent battle. Small trees lie splintered and toppled. The ground bears stains, scars and burns worthy of a clash between armies. Deep within the alcove lays the body of a huge red-scaled dragon. Its head, claws and a majority of its scales are missing, assumedly kept as trophies. The dragon is decaying although it remains mostly intact for the moment. A rotting foot of a human juts out from beneath the dragon's decaying body.

Clothing scraps, bits of armor and ruined equipment lie discarded around the battle site. An abandoned campsite is located near the dragon's body, where a party of adventurers stayed to rest, bury their dead and sort their loot. Three shallow graves piled high with rocks sit adjacent to the dragon corpse. The bodies (a human fighter, a human wizard and a dwarf) lie stripped of their usable gear in their final rest. The victors hauled the dragon's hoard off in heavy wagons (evident from the deep wagon tracks leading away from the camp) toward Bard's Gate to the south.

The foot belongs to a dead rogue buried beneath the dragon's mass. He was a member of the dragonslayers who was lost during the fierce battle. He vanished beneath the dragon's bulk when it was killed, and only his limb was revealed as the dragon rotted and shrank. If pulled free, the corpse still wears *boots of leaping* and has a pouch containing two potions (*fire resistance* and *treasure finding*) that survived the weight of the dragon falling on them.

Unfortunately, **3 carrion flies** found the dragon's corpse first. The carrion flies currently crawl across the back of the dragon as they enjoy the rotting meal. They lay their eggs in the abundant carcass. Always in search of a fresh meal, the carrion flies attack PCs approaching the dragon. The carcass is filled with carrion fly maggots. The corpse appears to ripple upon closer inspection as the maggots burrow under the remaining skin. In their current stage, the grubs don't pose a threat. The grubs mature into 5d8 adult carrion flies in under a week.

Cat, Feral Undead

Hit Dice: 1d4 hit points
Armor Class: 8 [11]
Attacks: 2 claws (1 hp)
Saving Throw: 18
Special: Paralyzing scratch (after first 3 hits)
Move: 12
Alignment: Chaos
Number Encountered: 1d3+1 or 3d6+3
Challenge Level/XP: B/10

Feral undead cats look like they were created by zombie-raising magic, but they are actually things quite unlike normal animated undead such as skeletons or zombies. These undead cats are possessed of an animal cunning akin to that of ghouls (although with less intelligence), and they are not slow moving as zombies are. Like ghouls, they tend to form into packs. If a person is scratched more than three times by undead feral cats (not necessarily the same one), he must make a saving throw or be paralyzed for 1d6 turns. After the first set of three scratches, every subsequent scratch requires a saving throw.

— Author: Matt Finch

Feral Undead Cat: HD 1d4 hp; AC 8[11]; Atk 2 claws (1hp); Move 12; Save 18; AL C; CL/XP B/10; Special Paralyzing scratch (after first 3 hits).

Cat Lady

A dilapidated hut of logs, sod and thatch sits surrounded by an unkempt and untidy garden. Dozens of domesticated cats flee into the overgrown brush at the approach of visitors. Pungent, lazy smoke pours from the chimney. A hand-painted sign reads "Auntie Meme; Seer, Mystic and Alchemist." The ancient Auntie Meme (Lawful, female elf, magic-user 5) has led a long and hard life, even for an elf. Perhaps centuries old, Auntie Meme walks hunched over, relying heavily on her ash-stick cane. Perceptive visitors might discover that she wears salvaged metal greaves to protect her ankles and shins under her shredded layers of robes. Auntie Meme has the ability to make uncanny yet vague predictions and to create minor potions with minor side effects.

Auntie Meme has an endearing love of cats. Her cats have been her constant companions and she cares deeply about them. Unfortunately, her beloved cats wandered into a necromancer's garden and were turned into **18 feral undead cats**. The decaying felines now surround the shack and attack anyone trying to leave. Due to her advanced age, poor eyesight and increasing dementia, Auntie Meme does not realize the transformation her beloved pets have undergone. She has noticed that they seem friskier lately, which is why she wears her protective leggings when she goes out to feed them. Her elfish blood makes her immune to the cats' paralyzing attack. If told of the cats' deaths, she grieves the loss of her children. However, PCs might also replace the cats without her noticing a difference to save the old lady any heartache.

Catoblepas

Hit Dice: 6
Armor Class: 7 [12]
Attacks: 1 bite (1d6)
Saving Throw: 11
Special: Lethally ugly
Move: 12
Alignment: Neutrality
Number Encountered: 1 or 1d4
Challenge Level/XP: 8/800

These medieval monsters resemble giant warthogs, but they are so hideous that their appearance can cause death (saving throw). If the first glance doesn't kill, each round of viewing the beast can still stun the viewer into immobility for 1d3 turns.

Catoblepas: HD 6; AC 7[12]; Atk 1 bite (1d6); Move 12; Save 11; AL N; CL/XP 8/800; Special: Lethal appearance.

Silent Farm

The crowd pushes past and ignores a starving blind man lying in the gutter. The beggar grabs at strangers' clothing and pleads for food and assistance. Farmer Earle, the beggar, has fallen on hard times. Once a prosperous farmer, Earle lost his way when his eyesight failed him. He bears a large scar across his face that claimed his ability to see. He also fears his young wife recently left him with his a newly hired farmhand. He wandered away from his farmhouse to the barn to lose himself in his work, only to find that his livestock were missing as well. Scared and alone, he stumbled from the farm to the city hoping to find someone to help.

Indeed hard times have fallen on Earle, but he doesn't know the whole truth. A **catoblepas** from the Sin Mire Swamp wandered onto his property and now lives off the abundant food at Earle's farm. Earle's wife, his new farmhand and the livestock are all dead. Their bodies lie in various spots around the farm. The catoblepas made the barn its lair and hides there during the day. Earle narrowly avoided becoming the creature's next victim when he went out to the barn. Earle has nothing left to offer as reward. No longer able to farm on his own, he has no future. He may offer rescuers his farm at a far reduced price in exchange for safe passage to a shelter or temple where someone will care for him.

Cattle

Hit Dice: 3
Armor Class: 7 [12]
Attacks: 1 gore (1d6)
Saving Throw: 14
Special: None
Move: 18
Alignment: Neutrality
Number Encountered: 1d100 x2
Challenge Level/XP: 3/60

Cattle include oxen and cows. Bulls inflict 1d8 points of damage instead of 1d6.

Cow/Ox: HD 3; AC 7[12]; Atk 1 gore (1d6); Move 18; Save 14; AL N; CL/XP 3/60; Special: None.

Stampede!

From down the road comes a thunderous roar as the ground begins to tremble. Anyone not immediately taking precautions (such as climbing a tree or getting off the road), may be caught up in a stampede of cattle hammering their way down the road. The stampede deals 8d6 points of damage (save for half). Furthermore **2 bulls** stick around after the herd continues down the path to take out their anger on stragglers. The reason for the stampede arrives a few rounds after the herd moves on. A small, animated dog made of metal and wood prances down the path creating a yipping-like bark. The magical bark instills *fear* and/or rage in any cloven-hoofed animal within earshot (saving throw negates), including PCs' horses.

Ollie Nematoad, an eccentric halfling inventor, arrives within a few rounds as he tries to keep up with his newest failed invention. Trying to create an invention to corral animals, Ollie created this animated dog. While the dog worked as far as moving the cattle, Ollie found he had little control over the direction the herd traveled. Ollie rewards adventurers who stop the animated dog with their own prototype version albeit without the *fear* bark. The dog can serve as an ever watchful (and noisy) guard dog with no attack abilities.

Animated dog: HD 1; AC 8[11]; Atk bark *fear* or berserker effects only hoofed animals (save negates); Move 24; Save 18; AL N; CL/XP 1/15.

Cave Eel

Hit Dice: 2
Armor Class: 8 [11]
Attacks: 1 bite (1d6)
Saving Throw: 16
Special: Strike from cave walls
Move: 1
Alignment: Neutrality
Number Encountered: 1d4+1 or 2d10
Challenge Level/XP: 2/30

Cave eels burrow through stone with sharp teeth, but otherwise look like large eels. They usually attack by reaching from their burrows in cave walls to bite. In general, these creatures congregate in groups.

Cave Eel: HD 2; AC 8[11]; Atk 1 bite (1d6); Move 1; Save 16; AL N; CL/XP 2/30; Special: Strike from cave walls.

Holed Up Elemental

The smooth floor of this natural cavern looks like highly polish marble. A small one-foot-tall wall encloses a pool of sparkling water. The pool sinks below the floor level and looks to be around two feet deep. A copper pipe sits in the center of the 10-foot-diameter pool and gently bubbles out fresh water. A drain around the interior edges of the pool keeps the water circulating. Freshwater oysters line the floor of the pool, each open to display a radiant crystalline pearl. A worn path circles the pool where an **earth elemental** slowly walks a continuous and precise path. Holes are carved through the earth elemental like porous cheese. These holes have not weakened the earth elemental despite the numerous openings in the elemental's structure. The holes are the result of **6 cave eels** that lair inside the elemental. The eels and earth elemental have a symbiotic existence and do not seem to impair one another.

The elemental does not deviate from its path if left alone. It attacks when approached or if the pool is disturbed. The eels attack opponents from within the holes once the earth elemental wades into combat. The pool (left over from an ancient dwarf-like race) holds 10d10 pearls worth 100 gp each due to their unique clarity.

Earth Elemental (8HD): HD 8; AC 2[17]; Atk 1 strike (4d8); Move 6; Save 8; AL N; CL/XP 9/1100; Special: Tear down stonework, immune to non-magic weapons.

Centaur

Hit Dice: 4
Armor Class: 5 [14] or 4 [15] with shield
Attacks: 2 kicks (1d6) and weapon
Saving Throw: 13
Special: None
Move: 18
Alignment: Any (usually Neutrality)
Challenge Level/XP: 4/120

Half man, half horse, centaurs are fierce warriors and well-known creatures of mythology. The referee may choose any "version" of the centaur from myth or folklore for his campaign: some are evil, some aloof, and some are soothsayers.

Centaur: HD 4; AC 5[14] or 4[15] with shield; Atk 2 kicks (1d6) and weapon; Move 18; Save 13; AL Any; CL/XP 4/120; Special: None.

Hung Like a Centaur

An odd sight blocks the bridge. A handsome and dark centaur holding a lance stands at the crest of the bridge. The centaur carries a stout bow and a two-handed sword across its flanks. Tattoos of black fire cover his torso and flame patterns are cut into his ebony coat. He wears metallic barding plate mail adorned with the polished skulls of halflings. Riding on his back is a similarly dressed human female. She wields a lance, two-handed sword and wicked bow as well. The pair demands payment for crossing "their bridge." They require a toll of 50 gp for each person wanting to cross. The **centaur Mervel** and Auggie (human female) extort travelers, knowing the bridge provides the only safe passage for miles over the chasm-shored river.

Auggie, once a ranking paladin at Shieldfane, lost her status (and paladin abilities) due to her forbidden love affair with Mervel. Sentenced to hang, Auggie and Mervel fled the walled temple of Muir to pillage and plunder the countryside. The bounty on their return stands at 1,000 gp. Of course they must be brought in alive in order for their sentence to be carried out. Mervel wears magical *+2 barding plate mail*. Auggie wields a *+1 lance* and has *2 potions of speed*. The two work in tandem, using their two lances to devastating effect.

Centipede Nest (Swarm)

Hit Dice: 3
Armor Class: 7 [12]
Attacks: 1 (1hp + non-lethal poison)
Saving Throw: 14
Special: Immune to all but blunt weapons, non-lethal poison
Move: 3
Alignment: Neutrality
Number Encountered: 1d4 swarms in the nest
Challenge Level/XP: 4/120

A nesting of centipedes is a vast collection of normal centipedes, often combined with a few other sorts of bugs that tend to share the same living space: cockroaches and spiders, generally. Such vermin are not appreciably dangerous individually, but when a great number of them are disturbed at once they can present a serious threat. A party will normally encounter a nest of centipedes by accidentally disturbing the nest itself. Moving large wooden beams and prying into ancient masonry entail the risk of arousing one of these huge colonies. The centipedes of the nest are treated, for the sake of convenience, as a single monster. The nesting's hit dice represent the amount of damage required to scatter and kill enough of the swarming vermin so that, as a group, they no longer pose a threat.

If a nest of centipedes manages to swarm over a character (either by landing on him or by moving around him), that character will sustain 1hp of damage per round automatically from the resulting bites. Moreover, even if the character subsequently moves away from the central mass of the nest, he will continue to sustain 1 hp of damage per round until a total of three rounds have been spend picking away and killing the centipedes which remain on him. Other characters may assist with this task, each lessening the time required by one round.

A centipede nest is immune to any damage other than that caused by a bludgeoning weapon such as a mace (although the mere expedient of kicking and stomping can inflict 1d2 hps damage with a successful hit). Any spell which affects an area rather than a single target (such as burning hands) will inflict double damage. For every five hit points of damage inflicted by a nest of centipedes against a single opponent, there is enough poison injected into the victim's body to cause paralysis for 3-12 turns. Fortunately, the poison is relatively weak (+2 on saving throw).
— *Author: Matt Finch (first appeared in Monsters of Myth, published by First Edition Adventure Games)*

Centipede Swarm: HD 3; AC 7 [12]; Atk 1 (1hp + non-lethal poison); Move 3; Save 14; AL N; CL/XP 4/120; Special: Immune to all but blunt weapons, non-lethal poison.

Goblins of Kraza Vako

Deep in the forest lays the corrupted fey king, **Kraza Vako**. Once a faerie king of wonder and serenity; the encroachment of civilization soiled his nurturing soul into one of contempt and paranoia. While most of the good faerie folk fled during his evolution, those who remained became debased and vile. Soon the might and ill repute of Kraza Vako grew, and chaotic followers arrived in droves. Masters of guerilla warfare, his recruits now scour the lands attempting to destroy civilization and law at every opportunity.

Normally dim and unorganized, the goblins of Kraza Vako have developed into a highly effective horde under his leadership. Kraza Vako's elite **10 goblins** (max hit points) set up an ambush along a wooded path atop a hill. Six goblins hide behind small walls and pepper travelers with arrows. They also have small rounded casks filled with powdered manure and ammonia. They light fuses jammed into the casks before rolling them down toward victims. The casks explode in a 10–foot radius for 3d6 points of damage (save for half). In addition, 4 goblins hide above the path near the top of the 150-foot-tall hill. Each is equipped with bladders filled with **4 centipede swarms**. Theses goblins hide on camouflaged tree

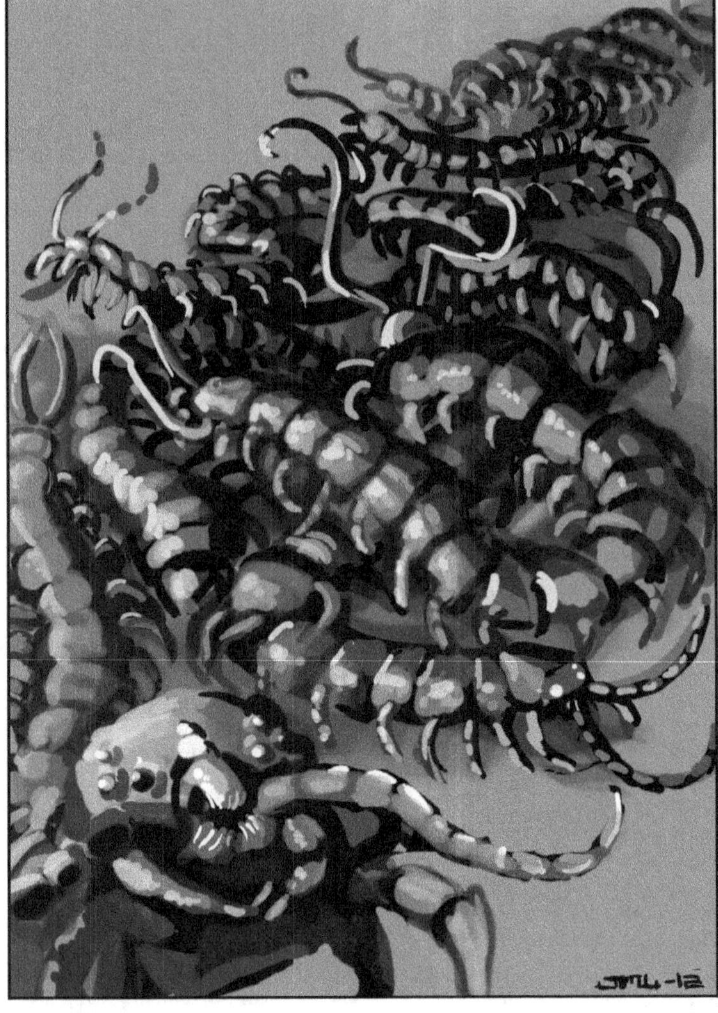

stands 20 feet above the forest floor. The air-filled bladders burst upon impact, spreading the centipede swarm over the area.

Goblin: HD 1d6 hp; AC 6[13]; Atk 1 weapon (1d6); Move 9; Save 18; AL C; CL/XP B/10; Special: –1 to hit in sunlight.

Centipede, Giant

CENTIPEDE, GIANT (SMALL, LETHAL)
Hit Dice: 1d2 hit points
Armor Class: 9 [10]
Attacks: Bite (deals 0 damage)
Saving Throw: 18
Special: Lethal poison, +4 save
Move: 13
Alignment: Neutrality
Number Encountered: 2d12
Challenge Level/XP: 1/15

Lethal giant centipedes of the small size inflict a deadly bite (+4 bonus to saving throw), but cause no damage if the saving throw is successful.

Giant Centipede (small, lethal): HD 1d2 hp; AC 9[10]; Atk 1 bite (0 + poison); Move 13; Save 18; AL N; CL/XP 1/15; Special: poison bite (+4 save or die).

CENTIPEDE, GIANT (SMALL, NON-LETHAL)
Hit Dice: 1d2 hit points
Armor Class: 9 [10]
Attacks: Bite (0 hp damage)
Saving Throw: 18
Special: Non-lethal poison, +4 save
Move: 13
Alignment: Neutrality
Number Encountered: 2d12
Challenge Level/XP: B/10

The non-lethal variety of giant centipede has a painful bits but its poison is only crippling, not lethal. Failing a saving throw (at a +4 bonus) against the poison of this centipede causes 1d4 rounds of crippling pain (the victim is helpless, as when asleep). Additionally, the limb (roll 1d4) is temporarily crippled (treat as a disease) for 2d4 days. A crippled leg reduces movement by 50%; a crippled shield arm cannot wield weapon or shield; a crippled sword arm attacks at -4. A second bite on a leg reduces movement to one quarter normal, and a third bite to the legs reduces movement to 1 foot per minute (prone, dragging oneself by the arms).

— *Author: Matt Finch*

Giant Centipede (small, non-lethal): HD 1d2 hp; AC 9[10]; Atk 1 bite (0 + poison); Move 13; Save 18; AL N; CL/XP B/10; Special: non-lethal poison bite (+4 save).

CENTIPEDE, GIANT (MAN-SIZED)
Hit Dice: 2
Armor Class: 5 [14]
Attacks: Bite (1d8 + poison)
Saving Throw: 16
Special: Lethal poison, +6 save
Move: 15
Alignment: Neutrality
Number Encountered: 1 or 2d6
Challenge Level/XP: 3/60

The man-sized giant centipede is a deadly predator with armored segments, a strong bite, and a lethal (though relatively weak) poison.

Man-sized Giant Centipede (7ft): HD 2; AC 5[14]; Atk 1 bite (1d8 + poison); Move 15; Save 16; AL N; CL/XP 3/60; Special: poison bite (+6 save or die).

CENTIPEDE, GIANT (LARGE, 20 FT LONG)
Hit Dice: 4
Armor Class: 0 [19]
Attacks: Bite (3d8 + poison)
Saving Throw: 13

Special: Lethal poison, +4 save
Move: 18
Alignment: Neutrality
Number Encountered: 1 or 1d4
Challenge Level/XP: 6/400

A twenty-foot long horror of chitin, multiple legs, and clashing pincers dripping with venom.

Large Giant Centipede (20ft): HD 4; AC 0[19]; Atk 1 bite (3d8); Move 18; Save 13; AL N; CL/XP 6/400; Special: poison bite (+4 save or die).

Surf'n Centipedes

The horrible clicking of a multitude of chitin-clad feet against stone signals that a foreboding danger approaches. Four giant centipedes scurry along the floor, walls and even the ceiling. Even more frightening are the riders standing on the mid-backs of the hellacious arthropods. Bugbears wielding battle axes and spears stand unmoving on the centipedes. The bugbears wear special metal boots that are bolted to the centipedes' exoskeleton covered backs. The bugbears cannot remove the boots easily (it takes 1 round). The bugbears barely control the centipedes with chains bolted to sides of the insects' heads. The centipedes attack all others, including the bugbears if they should happen to lose control or dismount.

Chalkeion (Men of Bronze)

Hit Dice: 5 (or more: see below)
Armor Class: 5 [14] (2[17] with armor: see below)
Attacks: 2 (by weapon type)
Saving Throw: 12
Special: None
Move: 12
Alignment: Neutrality (tendency toward Law)
Number Encountered: 6d10
Challenge Level/XP: Hoplite (5HD): 5/240, Sergeant (6HD): 6/400, Lieutenant (7HD): 7/600, Captain (11HD): 11/1,700

The proud Men of Bronze are legendary for their martial prowess and ferocity. They appear as normal men (albeit unusually handsome and well proportioned normal men) with a deep reddish-brown skin tone and are typically armed and dressed in antique fashion. The chalkeions are the last remnants of a former age, and those few who remain make their living as mercenaries, for they crave battle above all things. Their flesh is not literally bronze, but it is exceptionally tough, giving them a natural armor class of 5[14]. In battle, they usually wear leather armor and shields (which improves their AC to 2[17]), carry spears and javelins, and do not typically ride horses. In melee chalkeions function as berserkers, gaining 2 attacks per round and never needing to check morale. Because of their fearlessness and strict discipline they are highly sought after as mercenaries, but it is also well known that the men of bronze place loyalty to their brethren and self preservation above their employers' interests and will not obey orders which they perceive as foolish or suicidal. For every 6 men of bronze encountered there will typically be a sergeant with 6 hit dice, for every 12 a lieutenant with 7 or 8 hit dice, and groups of 30 or more are typically led by a captain with 10-12 hit dice.

— Author: Trent Foster

Man of Bronze (hoplite): HD 5; AC 2[17]; Atk 2 weapon (1d6); Move 12; Save 12; AL N; CL/XP 5/240; Special: None.

Man of Bronze (sergeant): HD 6; AC 2[17]; Atk 2 weapon (1d6); Move 12; Save 11; AL N; CL/XP 6/400; Special: None.

Man of Bronze (lieutenant): HD 7; AC 2[17]; Atk 2 weapon (1d6); Move 12; Save 9; AL N; CL/XP 7/600; Special: None.

Man of Bronze (captain): HD 11; AC 2[17]; Atk 2 weapon (1d6); Move 12; Save 4; AL N; CL/XP 11/1700; Special: None.

Princess on a Pedestal

Music and the sound of marching precede the regal sight of men carrying an exquisite woman resting upon a palanquin. Three men wearing highly polished bronze plate mail play drums, a flute and a lute. Four similar men hoist the palanquin above their heads. The men have elaborate shields, war spears and archaic bows strapped to their backs. The men appear to be perfect in every way with flawless, deeply bronzed skin, finely toned muscles and long, ebon hair. The men are **7 chauklieons** (6 hoplites and a sergeant). A young woman of presumed nobility sits upon a bed of silk pillows. She eats from a gold bowl containing cherries and figs. She is not flawless like the men, but appears rather delicate and petite. The sergeant commands all they meet to clear the road for Princess Ashtie. The soldiers do not move and demand that the road be cleared for the princess's passage.

While Princess Ashtie truly exists, this isn't her. Instead, the persona is a fraud concocted by Tamalyn (human thief 9), a master disguise artist and swindler. Needing to flee Bard's Gate because of a 500 gp bounty on her head, Tamalyn disguised herself and hired the chaulkieons as escorts. They expect a tidy sum for safely delivering the princess. Tamalyn has the men of bronze fully convinced of her royalty, but has no way to pay them when she reaches her destination.

Tamalyn toys with the men. She makes silly demands of peasants, travelers and adventurers she meets. She often demands that the road be cleared of large stones or claims the horse/oxen feces offends her. The chauklieons have even filled wagon ruts and cut weeds from her path. They have standing orders to toss flower petals upon the ground whenever she walks, and to rub her feet rubbed with oil when she returns to the palanquin. The fussy princess might throw strawberries at PCs to anger them. The chauklieons always come to her defense.

Chaos Knight

Hit Dice: 10
Armor Class: 0/19
Attacks: 1 touch (1d6), or sword (1d8+8)
Saving Throw: 5
Special: Special dimension door, wall of ice, spikes of ice, pass through walls, telekinesis, random spell effect, immune to non-magical weapons
Move: 12/4 (flying)
Alignment: Chaos
Number Encountered: 1
Challenge Level/XP: 14/2,600

The Chaos Knight appears to be a faintly glowing, ghostly suit of animated armour. It seems insubstantial, but has a definite physical presence. There are no features to be discerned within its helm, save for a dim blue glow. Intense cold radiates from the Chaos Knight; any fire within 20ft will be dampened or doused, and liquids will cool and turn to ice.

The mere touch of a Chaos Knight is freezing cold, chilling those it touches to the bone. It wields a sword in melee, drawing upon otherworldly might to inflict extra damage.

By concentrating for one round, a Chaos Knight may pass through solid objects such as a wall, leaving an icy outline where it has done so (3/day). It can cast Wall of Ice (3/day), cause shafts of ice to erupt from the ground (3/day), and open a portal similar to a Dimension Door spell (3/day). The portal remains open for up to 10 rounds, and anyone looking at it will see a kaleidoscopic passage of jagged energy bolts and whirling, ever-changing elemental matter. Any being other than the Chaos Knight that passes through the portal suffers 10 points of damage per round. The Chaos Knight may pass back and forth between the two end-points of the portal at will. It may also use Telekinesis once per day, and invoke a random spell effect twice per day. The Chaos Knight is immune to mind-affecting magic, as well as attacks from non-magical weapons. Normal weapons with a Bless spell cast upon them can hit and damage a chaos knight.

— Author: Scott Wylie Roberts, "Myrystyr"

Chaos Knight: HD 10; AC 0[19]; Atk 1 touch (1d6), or sword (1d8+8); Move 12 (Fly 4); Save 5; AL C; CL/XP 14/2600; Special: Special dimension door, wall of ice, spikes of ice, pass through walls, telekinesis, random spell effect, immune to non-magical weapons.

Frozen Fire

The doors of this room radiate heat from a lake of magma that lies beyond them. A 10-foot-wide ledge circles the 80-foot-diameter round room. Several doors line the walls at intervals along the ledge. Despite the close proximity to the pool of molten rock, the room remains survivable and temperate (roughly 100 degrees). The top of the magma lies level with the solid ledge. A small, 20-foot-diameter island sits in the lake's center. A bronze door sits in the island's center. The dimensional door leads to a harem in the palace of an **efreeti** sultan.

A **chaos knight** stands before the door. A slight aura of blue emanates from his suit. Even at a distance, it is apparent that the suit of armor is empty. Despite the lack of a physical body, the hollow helm turns to watch intruders. The knight attacks anyone who attempts to cross the magma or to thwart his sworn duty to guard the harem's door. The magma instantly cools within 20 feet of the knight as he moves toward interlopers. The chaos knight's cold aura ensures that it always walks upon solid land in the magma-filled room. The magma quickly reclaims the stone as the chaos knight strides across the molten surface.

Chimera

Hit Dice: 9
Armor Class: 4 [15]
Attacks: 2 claws (1d3), 2 goat horns (1d4), 1 lion bite (2d4), and 1 dragon bite (3d4)
Saving Throw: 6
Special: Breathes fire
Move: 9/18 (flying)
Alignment: Chaos (sometimes Neutrality)
Challenge Level/XP: 11/1,700

The chimera has three heads; one is the head of a goat, one the head of a lion, and one the head of a dragon. Great wings rise from its lion-like body. The dragon head can breathe fire (3 times per day) with a range of 50ft, causing 3d8 damage to anyone caught within the fiery blast (saving throw for half damage).

Chimera: HD 9; AC 4[15]; Atk 2 claws (1d3), 2 goat horns (1d4), 1 lion bite (2d4), dragon bite (3d4); Move 9 (Fly 18); Save 6; AL C; CL/XP 11/1700; Special: Breathes fire.

Nomengarten

The gnomes of the village of Nomengarten (use halfling stats) live in great peril. A horrifying **chimera** moved into their region to terrorize the hapless community. The young chimera attacks the village at random, tearing open their huge mushroom houses and devouring the gnome families within. These weaponless peace-loving gnomes are at the mercy of the rampaging beast. The eldest gnome summoned a flamingo messenger to seek heroes to do battle with the chimera. The flamingo lands near the party with a pleading message tied around its leg with green twine.

The gnomes dress in earthly colors, but all wear tall, cone-shaped red hats. These gnomes stand only half as tall as a man and often carry shovels or small baby animals. Their village is normally filled with singing and dancing but now remains eerily silent. Despite the occasional burnt patch or demolished mushroom house, the village appears pristine. Lush flowers, carved stone animals and elaborate fountains fill the village and the land around it. The gnomes have a pot of gold (500 gp) and dozens of cherry pastries stashed away to reward heroes.

Clawed Fiend

Hit Dice: 2
Armor Class: 7 [12]
Attacks: 2 claws (1d8)
Saving Throw: 16
Special: -1 to initiative
Move: 3
Alignment: Chaos
Number Encountered: 3d10
Challenge Level/XP: 2/30

Clawed fiends are 5ft tall, pale green humanoids. Their legs are short stumps and their hairless facial features carry a distinctive frog-like cast (large, bulbous eyes, wide mouth). This creature is so named because of its absurdly long arms which end in long, viciously sharp claws. The arms themselves extend to 5ft, with the claws reaching 2 to 3 feet. With such a long range, the clawed fiend isn't limited to attacking foes directly in front of it, but may also attack those up to 8ft away. Although clawed fiends can inflict devastating damage on their foes by way of their vicious claws, they are slow critters, and are penalized with a -1 to initiative rolls. Without the digits required for fine manipulation, clawed fiends are unable to employ weapons of any kind.

— Author: Skathros

Clawed Fiend: HD 2; AC 7[12]; Atk 2 claws (1d8/1d8); Move 3; Save 16; AL C; CL/XP 2/30; Special: -1 to initiative.

Frog Gigging

A teenaged boy sits somberly along the road begging for money. He pleads with stranger to help him out in purchasing a small boat. The bruised and battered youth claims he lost his father's boat in the Sin Mire Swamp. His father beat him for the loss and cast him out of their house until he retrieves the old boat or purchases a new one. The young man, Tobian, claims he was attacked by demonic frog men while frog gigging in the swamp last night. His father didn't believe such a preposterous tale and punished him again for his insolence. Tobian alleges that the frog demons stole the boat. He managed to escape by climbing a cypress tree until they left.

Tobian was indeed attacked while catching frogs. He was set upon by a group of **6 clawed fiends** that needed the boat to transport firewood for a grand ceremony to Tsathogga. The clawed fiends celebrate the upcoming mating season and plan a huge feast of roast meat (of whatever variety they can catch) on a swamp island in the center of the spawning pool. Tobian has little to offer other than his gratitude and a few weeks rations of frog jerky.

Cliessid

Hit Dice: 1d4 hit points
Armor Class: 6 [13]
Attacks: 2 pincers (1hp)
Saving Throw: 18
Special: None
Move: 9/9 (swimming)
Alignment: Neutrality
Number Encountered: 1d100
Challenge Level/XP: A/5

The amphibious Cliessid are small, shelled humanoids with pincers in place of hands, three thick toes on each leg in a Y-shape, and a mass of writhing tentacles in place of a head. They stand no taller than a man's knee. Cliessids live in sluggish rivers, shallow streams, stagnant ponds, and sewer systems, and can move as fast in, or under, the water as on land. Some cities have imported and domesticated these creatures for use in sewer maintenance, but with mixed results, for cliessids are viciously hostile to any who invade their territory.

— *Author: Scott Wylie Roberts, "Myrystyr"*

Cliessid: HD 1d4 hp; AC 6[13]; Atk 2 pincers (1hp); Move 9 (swim 9); Save 18; AL N; CL/XP A/5; Special: None.

Sewer Wars

The city of Bard's Gate has many domestic problems and faces daily challenges to its infrastructure. Sanitation remains a constant issue in order to ward off disease and accumulating filth. Norton Mckiagh, the chief pipe cleaner, and his workers are well paid. But with recent cuts in spending by the High Burgess, Norton has had to take shortcuts and trim the budget. Norton recently bought a pod of **16 trained cliessids** from a traveling entrepreneur, Ollie Nematoad. Ollie claimed the cliessids would cut costs, work for clams (literally) and be able to access smaller pipes. At first, the cliessids worked out well. But soon tensions developed with the pipe cleaners union. Fearful of being replaced, the unionized pipe cleaners began mistreating the cliessids. Open combat soon broke out between the two factions.

Unbeknownst to Norton, the cliessids organized under a **crab man** with minor mental (*charm* mollusks only and *telekinesis*, 50 lbs.) and magical powers (*purify water*, *create water* and *obscuring mist*). Furthermore, Ollie neglected to inform Norton that cliessids notorious breeders. If the cliessids and crab man are not stopped, they overrun the sewers and demand payment from the elected officials.

Cloaker

Hit Dice: 6
Armor Class: 4[15]
Attacks: Tail (1d8), bite (1d6), enfurl
Saving Throw: 11
Special: Moan, mirror image, darkness, enfurl
Move: 6/12 (flying)
Alignment: Chaotic
Challenge Level/XP: 8/800

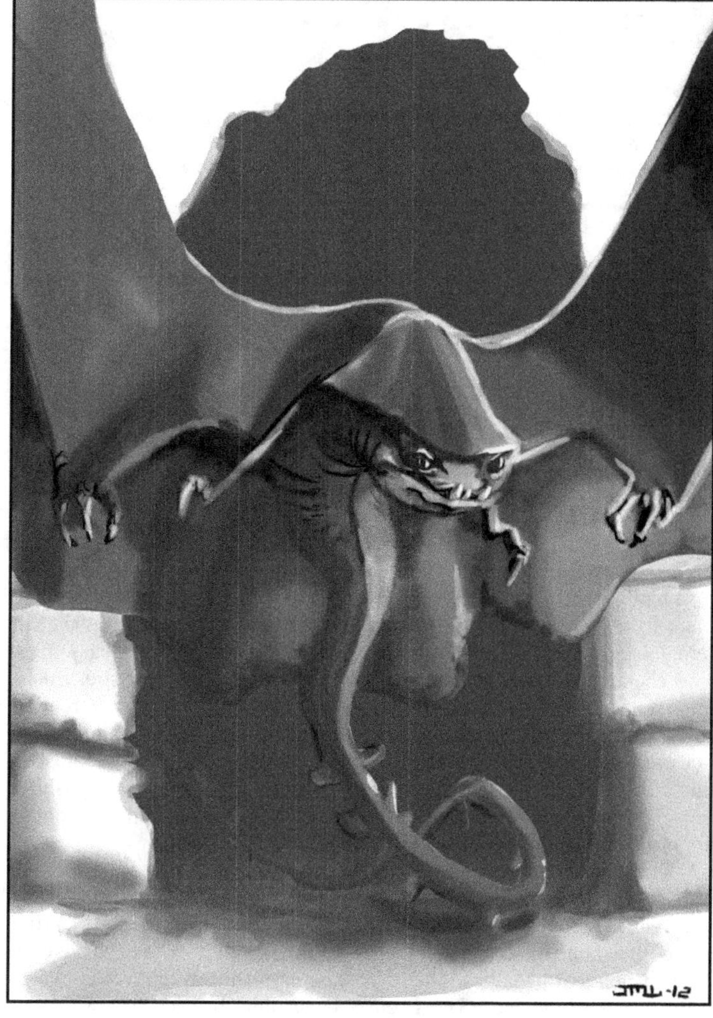

Cloakers are manta-like creatures that resemble a large black cloak – the ivory claws are often even mistaken for a clasp of some kind, as they are kept folded when the cloaker is at rest. Unfurled, the cloaker has a span of about eight feet.

Cloakers can attempt to enfurl their opponents during melee combat, while attacking. If the cloaker hits with its attempt to enfold a target, the victim is clasped in the cloaker's manta-like body (a saving throw allows the victim to escape). The victim is allowed no further saving throws to escape, although it is possible to attack the cloaker with a dagger from within its folds. The cloaker can bite an enfolded opponent with a +4 bonus to hit.

Perhaps more dangerous than the cloaker's ability to enfold an opponent is its ability to moan, for the cloaker's moaning is dire indeed, causing a petrifying fear. Anyone hearing the moan of a cloaker must make a saving throw or do one of two things (50% chance of each): either flee at top speed for 1d6 turns, or be immobilized with fear for 1 turn.

Finally, cloakers have the ability to manipulate darkness and shadows. They can cause *darkness 15ft radius* whenever desired, and as long as shadows or darkness are present, they can create shadowy *mirror images* of themselves (as per the spell) once per day (1d4 images).

Cloaker: HD 6; AC 4[15]; Atk Tail (1d8), bite (1d6), enfurl; Save 11; Move 9 (fly 12); AL N; CL/XP 8/800; Special: Moan, mirror image, darkness, enfurl.

Mood Lighting

This encounter could take place in a large city (as a business) or populated dungeon (as a single room). A continuous red light (*continual light*) beams from a glass globe hanging from a delicate chain outside this door. This dimly lighted chamber boasts of decadence. Crimson and ebon veils drape a large round bed of cushions. Delicate silver chains and manacles droop from the ceiling. Deep draperies hang from the walls casting dark shadows upon the ceiling from red glass oil lamps. Thick incense hangs in the air as a eunuch (non-combatant) plays a harp lightly. A constant and faint moaning echoes throughout the chamber. Within the shrouded curtains lie three maids of ill repute. While the prices of their services are extravagant, the delights they offer are unequaled among mortals.

Two of the ladies of the evening (**thief 3**) legitimately are what they seem. But the head mistress (an **ogre mage** cloaked in illusion) runs the show. She goes by the name Odessa and for the most part operates an honest, yet expensive brothel. The costs far exceed expectations (price is negotiated after services rendered). For those who do not pay, Odessa has a nasty surprise: She hired **2 cloakers** to serve as bodyguards. The cloakers hang above the bed ready to devour those acting out of line or skipping out on paying.

Cockatrice

Hit Dice: 5
Armor Class: 6 [13]
Attacks: Bite (1d6+ turn to stone)
Saving Throw: 12
Special: Bite turns to stone
Move: 6/18 (flying)
Alignment: Neutrality
Number Encountered: 1d6
Challenge Level/XP: 8/800

A cockatrice resembles a bat-winged rooster with a long, serpentine tail. Its bite turns enemies to stone unless a successful saving throw is made.

Cockatrice: HD 5; AC 6[13]; Atk 1 bite (1d6 + turn to stone); Move 6 (Fly 18); Save 12; CL/XP 8/800; Special: bite turns to stone.

Stone Garden

Cries of terror and pleas for help come from a small gnome settlement deep in a primeval forest. The gnomes of the village of Nomengarten (use halfling stats for gnomes) again suffer at the hands of fate. While the majority of the peace-loving gnomes fled into the forest, many of their kin remain trapped. A **cockatrice** moved into the village seeking easy prey. The cockatrice turned a number of gnomes to stone. Their mushroom houses and animal friends suffered similar fates. Trapped gnomes remain safe from the attacks of the cockatrice but are captive inside their now-petrified dwellings. Gnome statues remain eternally frozen in the midst of menial tasks. Stoned gnomes can be found using gardening tools, pushing wheel barrels, cuddling small forest animals, smoking pipes, napping against trees, reading books and holding lanterns.

The cockatrice drank from the gnome's magical fountain and now nests in the tangled roots of a petrified tree. Four eggs in the nest have the magical property of harmlessly turning an imbiber's flesh to partial stone (providing a +2 armor class bonus) for 2d4 days. The eggs have no other benefits or penalties. The eggs remain potent for 2d6 weeks before rotting (unless pickled). The gnomes have little to offer as reward but beg rescuers to take the small stone animals (squirrels, cardinals, rabbits, fawns and mice) from their village. The gnomes see the stone animals as painful reminders of the cockatrice attack.

Coral Clamper

Hit Dice: 6
Armor Class: 2 [17]
Attacks: 4 muscle-tentacles (1d6 + grab)
Saving Throw: 11
Special: Grab victims
Move: 1
Alignment: Neutrality
Number Encountered: 1d4
Challenge Level/XP: 8/800

This mollusk resembles a growth of rock or coral covered with several large (but still normal-looking) clams. When a swimmer nears it, however, the clamper lashes out with long, flexible arms of muscle for which the "clams" are the tips. These appendages encircle and crush prey, with the clam-like tip serving as a viciously biting mouth. A coral clamper normally has four appendages, and these grow to a length of 20ft. The clamper's body is protected by its hard, coral-like shell. If one of the appendages scores a hit, the victim must make a saving throw or be held helpless by the tentacle-like grasp. The clam-mouth at the end of the tentacle can attack while a victim is held, but cannot generally reach a victim other than the one held in the muscle-tentacle.

— Author: Matt Finch

Coral Clamper: HD 6; AC 2[17]; Atk 4 muscle-tentacles (1d6 + grab); Move 1; Save 11; AL N; CL/XP 8/800; Special: Grab victims.

Clamp On, Clamp Off

The all-female crew of the escort ship the Voyager Vixen lies stuck on a reef just offshore of the city of Bargarsport. The maiden crew specializes in the luxury transportation of wealthy merchants and nobility. Although they are somewhat skilled at seamanship, they are by no means professionals which explains the ship's current predicament. The ship is salvageable and safe from sinking, but stuck fast on the reef. All attempts at freeing the ship by the Vixen's crew have failed. Luckily, a small exploration ship (the Arse Biscuit) arrived to assist. Ollie Nematoad, a halfling inventor, created a hand-cranked machine that pumps fresh air though tubes (made of partially sterilized and rubberized sheep intestines). The machine has six tubes available to be used for breathing underwater. The tubes reach a distance of 100 feet from the air-pump. Note that this does not allowed unhindered movement in underwater conditions.

Ollie gladly supplies massive crowbars, weighted boots, and chains to anyone working underwater. He has ropes along with block and tackle to attach to a winch in his boat. With this equipment and a lot of hard work, the Voyager Vixen can be freed in a few hours. Unfortunately a **coral clamper** hides under the waves. Its claws are clamed onto the bottom of the Vixen. The grateful maids of the Voyager Vixen offer free passage (within reason) to any destination along their route with full amenities.

Corpse Tree

Hit Dice: 5+2
Armor Class: 4 [15]
Attacks: 2 fists (1d8)
Saving Throw: 12
Special: Bear hug, Immune to non-magical weapons, ice, electricity, acid, and normal fires.
Move: 0
Alignment: Chaos
Number Encountered: 1
Challenge Level/XP: 7/600

These stunted, gnarled trees look like worn down, time ravaged tree trunks ranging in height from 4 to 8 feet tall, with a corpse-like shape, arms stretched forth, budding from the trunk. Every corpse tree has a tree ghost (see below) that is part of it. Corpse trees are created when a vampire or wraith kills a dryad; the dryad's tree becomes the corpse tree and the dryad herself becomes a tree ghost. At the base of the tree is an opening leading to a strange chamber beneath, where the corpse tree's victims are slowly digested. The "rising corpse" part of the tree animates to keep anyone but the tree ghost and her victims from entering the tree's chamber. A corpse tree can only harmed by magic and silver weapons. Magic fire will affect the tree but ice, electricity, and acid will have no effect, nor will normal fire. The tree ghost instantly knows of any harm coming to the corpse tree, and she can teleport to the tree to defend it against harm. If either the corpse tree or the tree ghost dies, the other will die as well.

— Author: Sean "Stonegiant" Stone

Corpse Tree: HD 5+2; AC 4[15]; Atk 2 fists (1d8); Move 0; Save 12; AL C; CL/XP 7/600; Special: if both fists hit the victim is "bear" hugged for an additional 2d6 damage; immune to to non-magical weapons, ice, electricity, acid, and normal fires.

Snag Hag

An ashen satyr lies dead on the ground, bunched in a crawling position. Claw and fang marks mar his dusty gray skin. The satyr's body instantly turns to ash that blows away in the wind if disturbed. While the satyr was visiting a dryad for some afternoon festivities, a hag-like vampire walked into the glade and interrupted the pair. After being drained nearly to death, the satyr managed to nearly crawl away. The morning sun instantly killed the transitioning satyr, saving it from an eternity of undeath. The satyr's trail can be followed to a glade of death.

Thick mist clings to the ground in the ugly glade. Wet moss covers the soft spongy ground. Limbless trees line the edges of this portion of the Sin Mire. The trees seem to have died quickly and without reason. In the center of mist stands a **corpse tree**. An ancient crone stands atop a decaying stump. She leans heavily upon a gnarled cane. The corpse tree remains motionless while the **crone vampire** stands out of reach. The crone vampire lives deep within the Sin Mire and often ventures onto dry land to spread evil and death. The crone vampire killed the satyr and dryad. Transformed into a **tree ghost**, the dryad hides in one of the many dead trees surrounding the glade. The dryad animates the dead trees to protect her master, the crone vampire. The crone vampire's coffin lies in a root chamber below the corpse tree. The intricate coffin appears to be a dead log. Only upon closer inspection can the lid be found. The coffin contains a *ring of spell storing* (cleric version with *protection from evil 10–foot radius*, *prayer*, and *bless*), a *bronze horn of Valhalla*, and *manual of wisdom*.

Tree Ghost: HD 3; AC 6[13]; Atk: Claws (1d3) or thorns (0); Move 12; Save 14; AL C; CL/XP 9/1,100; Special: Charisma drain, Insect Plague, animate wood, immune to normal

weapons, cold, electricity, acid, and non-magical fire.

Crone Vampire: HD 7; AC 2[17]; Atk: Bite (1d10 + level drain); Move 12/18 (flying); Save 9; AL C; CL/XP: 10/1,400; Special: hit only by magical weapons, regenerate 3/hp each round, gaseous form, turn into domestic cat or toad, can summon horde of crocodiles, looking into eyes causes sleep (saving throw –2), 2 level drain, vampire weaknesses. A crone vampire is consciously surrounded by 30 feet of *obscuring mist* that blocks out the sun. The mist can be dispelled.

Couatl

Hit Dice: 8
Armor Class: 4 [15]
Attacks: 1 bite (2d6 + poison), 1 tail (1d6 constrict)
Saving Throw: 8
Special: Fly, poison (lethal), spells, polymorph
Move: 12 (Fly 24)
Alignment: Law (or, rarely, Chaos)
Number Encountered: 1
Challenge Level/XP: 11/1,700

Intelligent serpents with feathered wings, couatls can be fifteen feet long or more. They can polymorph themselves, constrict victims for 1d6 hit points, and cast spells (3 level 1, 2 level 2, 1 level 3). Generally tropical, some may be servitors of the gods.

Couatl: HD 8; AC 4[15]; Atk 1 bite (2d6 + poison), 1 tail (1d6 constrict); Move 12 (Fly 24); Save 8; AL L or C; CL/XP 11/1700; Special: Fly, poison (lethal), spells, polymorph.

Temple of Kukulcan

A massive cut stone pyramid rises out of the jungle floor. The ancient temple stands in disrepair, but shows signs of frequent use. Sun-faded paint covers the weathered stone blocks. Jaguar-like demon heads adorn the corners of each of the twelve wide tiers. The decaying head of a tribal warrior sits in each of the sculpted jaguar maws. Narrow and acute stairs lead to the pyramid's lofty peak. The flat crest holds a blood-crusted altar. Matted feathers and turquoise jewels lie in dry piles of gore and bone. A ceremonial +3 *flint knife* (1d3 damage) lies atop the altar. The knife is carved in the shape of a feathered serpent. A jade mask with an attached feathered headdress (250 gp) sits adjacent to the altar. If either the mask or the ceremonial knife is removed from the top of the pyramid, the altar statue of Kukulcan comes to life as a **couatl**. Only the sacrifice of a humanoid with the knife can turn the couatl back into stone. As long as the knife remains away from the pyramid, a summoned couatl appears each month to seek the knife's return.

Crab, Giant

Hit Dice: 3
Armor Class: 3 [16]
Attacks: 2 pincers (1d6+2)
Saving Throw: 14
Special: None
Move: 9
Alignment: Neutrality
Number Encountered: 1d12
Challenge Level/XP: 3/60

Larger specimens of giant crabs might move more slowly – these stats are for a crab about 5ft in diameter.

Giant Crab: HD 3; AC 3[16]; Atk 2 pincers (1d6+2); Move 9; Save 14; AL N; CL/XP 3/60; Special: None.

Your Mother Has Crabs

A hut of gigantic proportions sits along the beach. The stout hut is made of entire trees and sits just out of reach of the incoming tide. Tanned whale skins stretched on racks, a massive cauldron of boiling water over a bonfire and wind chimes made of giant clam shells leave little doubt to what creature resides here. **Mable Krumbein** (or Ma' Crum as she prefers) is an enormous human female (about the size – and stats – of a cloud giant, but she does not gain their special abilities). Despite Ma' Crum's appearance, she is nothing more than an elderly commoner who wants to lead a quiet life. Her problems began many years ago when her wayward and estranged son stopped in for a visit. He told her the story of a fish that he had caught. In exchange for its freedom, the fish had granted him three wishes. Her well-meaning but not-too-bright son wished for his most prized treasures to increase.

Soon after, Ma' Crum's son left for other adventures and her growth started. Ostracized from society, she ekes out a living fishing for whales and giant crabs. She trades the meat with the few brave merchants (namely the Boehman Brothers) who accept her stature. Yesterday, Ma' Crum tussled with a 50-foot-long megalodon that took a sizable bite out of her thigh. The shark currently boils in her cauldron. She still needs to collect giant crabs to keep her trade viable and uninterrupted in order to satisfy the merchants (and keep them coming back), but her injury stops her from getting back in the water. Luckily, giant crabs abound in the area. She needs at least 24 live giant crabs to fulfill her next order. Ma' Crum supplies all equipment PCs need, including cages, ropes and nets. In return, Ma' Crum rewards heroes with a head-sized pearl (2,000 gp).

Crab Man

Hit Dice: 2
Armor Class: 4 [15]
Attacks: 2 claws (1d4)
Saving Throw: 16
Special: None
Move: 9/9 (swimming)
Alignment: Neutrality (usually)
Number Encountered: 2d6 or 1d100+10
Challenge Level/XP: 2/30

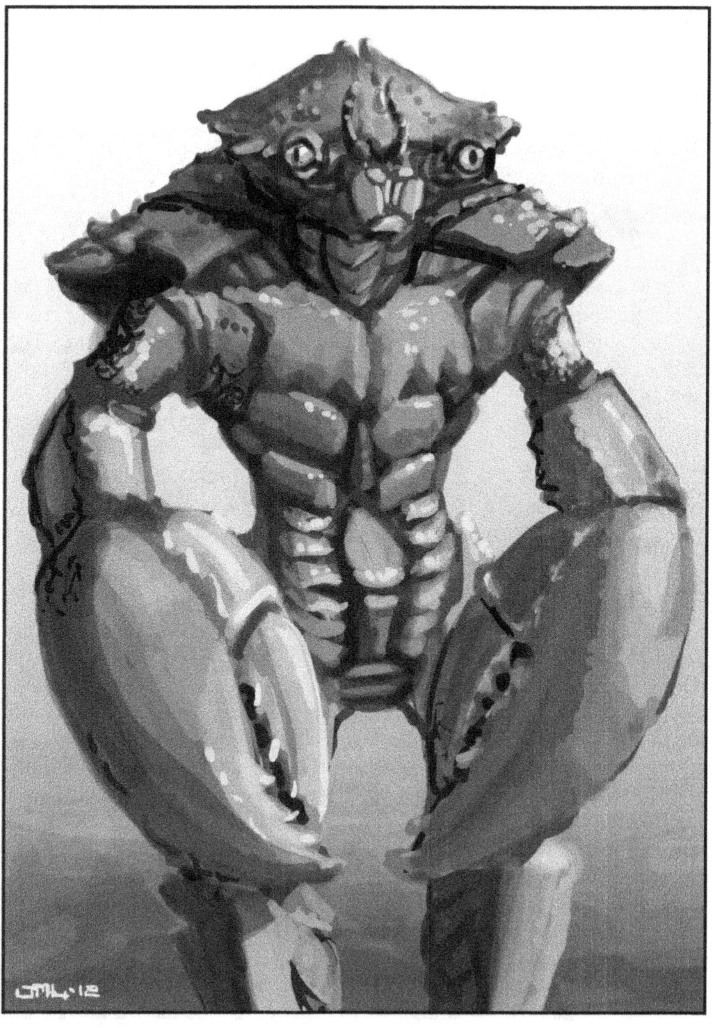

Crab men are bipedal creatures with a crab-like exoskeleton and a pincer at the end of each arm. They are tribal creatures, found living near water (including subterranean lakes and rivers).

Crab men: HD 2; AC 4[15]; Atk 2 claws (1d4); Save 16 Move 9 (swim 9); AL N; CL/XP 2/30; Special: None.

Crab Season

The Boehman Brothers, a merchant company, work out of the city of Stormhaven on the Reaping Sea. The large operation has many ships and specializes in trading unusual merchandise. Recently, the merchants struck gold selling giant crab meat. The unique meat is in high demand with upper-class restaurants and exclusive commercial wholesalers.

The Boehman Brothers recently hit a snag. The Turtlehead, their newest ship, has yet to return from their secret giant crab supplier. The Boehamn Brothers need able-bodied adventurers to accompany the next merchant ship to investigate the Turtlehead's disappearance and protect their goods. They pay their guards handsomely.

The Turtlehead struck a massive reef and foundered along the coast. A tribe of **crab men** built the artificial reef of coral, rocks and salvaged rubbish that nearly sunk the Turtlehead. Once the ship struck the uncharted reef, the crab men swarmed the ship, slaying the crew and setting the captured giant crabs free. While fearful of Ma' Crum (see *giant crab*), the crab men nevertheless declared war on the crab fishermen's fleet.

Crabnipede

Hit Dice: 4
Armor Class: 4 [15]
Attacks: 4 claws (1d4), 1 bite (1d6 + paralysis)
Saving Throw: 13
Special: Paralysis poison (1d6 turns)
Move: 6/12 (swimming)
Alignment: Neutrality
Number Encountered: 1
Challenge Level/XP: 5/240

Crabnipedes are horrible sea creatures resembling man-sized centipedes with 4 pincers. They hunt on sea floors and lake bottoms, and can crawl out from the water for hours, if the hunting seems better on land. The crabnipede's bite is mildly poisonous, causing paralysis for 1d6 turns (saving throw applies).

— Author: Matt Finch

Crabnipede: HD 4; AC 4[15]; Atk 4 claws (1d4), 1 bite (1d6 + paralysis); Move 6 (swim 12); Save 13; AL N; CL/XP 5/240; Special: Paralysis poison (1d6 turns).

Drift Wood

A massive pile of driftwood sits at a bend in the river. Logs, portions of cabins and even several small boats lie in a pile where the rainy season floods piled them. Several rotting carcasses of cattle, deer and other livestock lie tangled in the 20-foot-tall pile of debris. Vultures and rodents scatter at the approach of unwelcomed visitors. The birds squawk angrily at the interruption to their meal. Atop the pile of debris sits a partially buried small chest adorned with a golden eagle icon.

A troop of **4 goblins** tugs and pulls on the chest as they attempt to free the treasure. At the sight of trouble, the goblins pull out small bows and pepper intruders with arrows. The goblins gingerly climbed the debris pile without alerting **2 crabnipedes** that built a lair in a watery tunnel beneath the rubbish pile. The crabnipedes attack anyone nearing the pile before turning on the goblins at the top.

The chest has a magical ability. Just below the golden eagle is inscribed the word "Aubade." Speaking this word under the midday sun cause the golden eagle to animate and fly into the sky, carrying the chest with it. When the eagle (use the stats of a common bird of prey) reaches a height of 250 feet, it plane travels to another dimension where it awaits summoning. The chest may be summoned by the person who sent it away, and only if they stand outside on a sunny day during the noon hour. The command word must be spoken by the current owner of the chest. If the owner dies, the chest automatically appears during the high noon hour as close to the owner's body as possible. If the eagle is slain, the chest and all its contents disintegrate in a cloud of dust. Despite its small size, the chest can hold five cubic feet of matter. The eagle chest currently holds a slingshot, 5 days' worth of rations, a small cask of ale, a drawing of a rather comely young woman, a lurid love letter to someone named "Princess Amina," a bag of 75 gp, and a *cloak of elvenkind*.

Crocodile, Normal

Hit Dice: 3
Armor Class: 4[15]
Attacks: 1 bite (1d6)
Saving Throw: 14
Special: None
Move: 9/12 (swimming)
Alignment: Neutrality
Number Encountered: 3d8
Challenge Level/XP: 3/60

Some normal crocodiles are man-eaters; all are dangerous and can conceal themselves well.

Normal Crocodile: HD 3; AC 4[15]; Atk 1 bite (1d6); Move 9 (Swim 12); Save 14; AL N; CL/XP 3/60; Special: None.

Crocoman

Rumors say that a crazed man lives on the outskirts of the great Sin Mire Swamp, defending the stagnant waters against interlopers and defilers. The man, known only as Crocoman, is a cursed druid bound to the swamp. Crocoman appears as human wearing reptilian hide armor and carrying a bone sword made from the fused jaw of a crocodile. Once Crocoman touches the water of the Sin Mire, he transforms into a human/crocodile hybrid. His skin fuses with his armor, his mouth grows into a toothed maw, and he grows a powerful tail (gaining a swim speed and a bite attack).

Crocoman rides a chariot-like canoe made of bone and reptile skins. A team of **4 crocodiles** pulls the chariot with uncanny precision and intelligence. Crocoman can control crocodiles and alligators in the Sin Mire. These creatures guard him with their lives. If Crocoman is defeated, the spirit of the Sin Mire seeks a replacement. The curse passes to a druid within the swamp. Although the nature of the curse is a mystery, a cure may lie within the boundary of the massive swamp.

Crocoman (Druid 8): HD 8; hp 50, AC 4[15]; Atk 1 toothed-bone sword (1d6 +2) or bite 1d6+2; Move 12 (swim 12); Save 8; AL C; Str 17, Dex 10, Con 15, Int 9, Wis 15, Cha 9; CL/XP 8/800; Special: *charm crocodile/ alligators, spells*; spells 1st-*farie fire, locate animals, predict weather, purify water*; 2nd-*heat metal, obscuring mist, speak with animals*; 3rd-*hold animal, water breathing*; 4th-*animal summoning I*.

Crocodile, Giant

Hit Dice: 6
Armor Class: 3 [16]
Attacks: 1 bite (3d6), 1 tail (1d6)
Saving Throw: 11
Special: None
Move: 9/12 (swimming)
Alignment: Neutrality
Number Encountered: 1 or 3d4
Challenge Level/XP: 6/400

The smallest of giant crocodiles are about 20ft long (normal crocodiles can grow to be as long as 15ft).

Giant Crocodile: HD 6; AC 3[16]; Atk 1 bite (3d6), 1 tail (1d6); Move 9 (swim 12); Save 11; AL N; CL/XP 6/400; Special: None.

Fishing Horror Story

An excursion fishing barge named the Wolf Bair travels in large circles on the water. The barge turns and rapidly moves toward the heroes at their approach. Paddles on both sides help power the barge, but all of the oars are currently still. Although no one paddles the boat, it moves with great speed. The barge owner, Captain Bate, rents the barge to recreational fishermen. He has extensive knowledge of the surrounding waterways and knows the prime fishing spots. Four rich merchant tourists are currently on the barge to enjoy a relaxing evening of fishing. The flat barge holds a plethora of fishing tackle and equipment. Captain Bate keeps live bait in a wooden cage just below the water's surface.

On this particular day, a 25-foot-long **giant crocodile** ate the submerged bait cage and snagged the attached line in it toothy maw. The croc is not aware of the attached barge floating above and swims along looking for its next meal. Captain Bate realizes the barge's precarious predicament. He and his customers stand perfectly still, not wanting to attract the attention of the monstrous beast swimming below. From a distance, the men appear to be frozen in time. Upon closer inspection, the men make slow hand signals and extreme facial expressions of terror (such as looks of wide-eyed horror, biting motions, rigorous shaking of their heads, etc…). The men reward their saviors with several previously caught fish and a large turtle shell.

Crumbler

Hit Dice: 1
Armor Class: 4 [15]
Attacks: 1 thrown rock (1d4) or fist (1d4)
Saving Throw: 17
Special: Immunities
Move: 0
Alignment: Neutrality
Number Encountered: 1d6+1 or 2d6+2
Challenge Level/XP: 3/60

Crumblers are mountain and cavern-dwelling "rock men," who serve as guardians for important things. They are immune to fire, electricity and magical "blasting" attacks. Cutting weapons inflict half damage (and there is a 2 in 6 chance of non-magical weapons breaking against them). Hammers and maces do normal damage. They usually attack in groups, rising up out of the rubble surrounding boulder-laden areas. They cannot pursue, being rooted to the earth.

— *Author: Old Crawler*

Crumbler: HD 1; AC 4[15]; Atk 1 thrown rock (1d4) or fist (1d4); Move 0; Save 17; AL N; CL/XP 3/60; Special: Immunities.

That's the Way the Tower Crumbles

What's left of a tower stands on this rocky mountainside. The tower once belonged to an elemental wizard who vanished decades ago. His own guardians slowly destroyed his proud tower. The low rumble of grinding stone reverberates from within the huge mound of crumbled blocks. At the approach of living creatures, the mounds tremble with unseen pulsations. Dust clouds rise from the ruins with each increasing thump. If PCs approach, **6 crumblers** rise from the ruins. The stationary rock spirits pummel visitors with rocks from atop the mound. The crumblers rise in a circle around the mound's peak.

These beings guard a special *crystal ball* located in the under the rubble. The *crystal ball* resembles a convex disc of green stone. The stone summons one crumbler each week (to a maximum of 6) to guard it. The crumblers attack everything not made of natural stone within their reach (including the *crystal ball's* possessor). The nearly mindless stone elemental spirits pummel everything with fists and rocks. Over the decades they managed to topple the worked stone tower into a huge pile of ruin.

Crystal Growth

Hit Dice: 5
Armor Class: 4 [15]
Attacks: 1 blood drain (1d8)
Saving Throw: 12
Special: Blood drain
Move: 9
Alignment: Neutrality
Number Encountered: Initially 1d2, with up to 1d20 nearby
Challenge Level/XP: 5/240

A strange fungus grown from mineral deposits, the Crystal Growth appears to be a large, multi-faceted, crystalline lump. It may be mistaken for a massive piece of quartz, as it is usually the size of a human head. Crystal growth feeds upon minerals found in the bloodstream of humans, warm-blooded humanoids, and other intelligent mammals. Despite lacking any discernible sense organs, the crystal growth can somehow sense life within 90ft, and anyone touching the crystal growth will suffer an immediate attack. The crystal growth moves by rolling on its facets, and can bounce off walls, rock faces, and other hard objects to leap a few feet into the air. When it comes into contact with bare flesh, it drains blood at the rate of 1d8 hit points per round. Due to its partly mineral structure, it is heavy and can knock creatures off their feet by rolling and leaping at them. Some crystal growths learn the tactic of dropping from above onto the head and shoulders of targets. As the target may be knocked senseless by this tactic, the crystal growth is usually able to get in a few rounds of blood drain before being interrupted by other crystal growths seeking a free meal. A battle over food between crystal growths is a strange sight, with combatants rolling and battering against each other.

Reptilian and avian creatures lack the minerals the crystal growths feed upon, and crystal growths ignore them. Canny reptilians, such as subterranean lizards and cave-dwelling lizard men, have learned to crack open a crystal growth and lick out its salty, milk-like juices. The juice of one crystal growth is sufficient nourishment for one man-sized creature for half a day, or a full day if it contains blood.

— *Author: Scott Wylie Roberts, "Myrystyr"*

Crystal Growth: HD 5; AC 4[15]; Atk 1 blood drain (1d8); Move 9; Save 12; AL N; CL/XP 5/240; Special: Blood drain.

Crystal Bowling

Light refracts into a thousand beams of scintillating colors in this enormous crystalline chamber. Massive quartz crystals grow in droves from the ceiling. After growing too large to support their own weight, the crystals fall to the floor where they shatter into great shard mounds. Hypothermal vents warm a pool of clear water into a steaming haze that drifts through the chamber like a humid fog. Fissures near the water spout columns of steam in a constant hiss that echoes throughout the chamber.

A **giant lizardman** claims this muggy chamber as its lair. The giant lizardman formed a symbiotic relationship with a colony of **6 crystal growths**. It hides behind the largest mound of shards. Once intruders enter his chamber, the lizardman clambers to the top of the mound and launches the crystal growths at his enemies. The crystal growths roll and bounce back to the top of the mound to be thrown again. The lizardman carries a massive axe with a blade of chiselled quartz.

Giant Lizardman: HD 8+8; AC 3[16]; Atk 1 large crystal axe (2d8); Move 12; Save 8; AL C; CL/XP 9/1,100; Special: Hurl boulders

Crystaline

Hit Dice: 3
Armor Class: 3 [16]
Attacks: 1 Weapon ("fist") (1d6)
Saving Throw: 14
Special: Blinding Refracted Light, Explosive Death
Move: 12
Alignment: Neutrality
Number Encountered: 1 or 1d8
Challenge Level/XP: 5/240

The crystalines resemble humanoids whose entire bodies are composed of crystal. When a crystalline dies (reaches 0 hp), its body shatters in an explosion of crystal shards. All within 10ft failing their save suffer 2d6 points of damage (a successful save halves the damage).

Crystalines have learned to use their faceted crystal-like bodies in conjunction with light to temporarily blind their foes. On a failed save the victim is considered blinded and suffers a -4 penalty to hit for the next 1d4 rounds. This ability counts as an action as the crystaline must position it body to capture the light and direct it effectively against a foe.

— Author: Skathros

Crystaline: HD 3; AC 3[16]; Atk Weapon ("fist") (1d6); Move 12; Save 14; AL N; CL/XP 5/240; Special: Blinding Refracted Light, Explosive Light.

Heart of Glass

A maze of towering quartz crystals lines the edges of a boiling lake of water in this seemingly endless chamber. The clusters of transparent quartz reach heights of 20 feet or more. The crystals grow throughout the room, even in the 30 foot depths of the lake. Condensation from the lake collects on the crystalline ceiling only to shower back down in a never-ceasing rain. The cavern rain keeps the crystals clear and gleaming. Paths wind through the crystal forest. Composed of crushed quartz, the paths glisten with water and appear well travelled. Light from several pods of **aqueous orbs** illuminate the chamber in a fluorescent green glow. The orbs usually float above the lake eating the plethora of blind fish.

Two dangers regularly inhabit this spanning crystal forest. A tribe of **12 crystalines** hide throughout the forest, cleverly hiding among the crystals. They stalk interlopers through the forest until enough of them gather to ambush trespassers. Secondly, a **will-o'-the-wisp** shares this chamber. The malign fey creature buzzes through the mineral-forest chamber, darting in and out of the crystal clusters. Radiant beams of light cast harsh shadows across the room as the wisp attempts to corral victims toward the crystalines. The brilliant refraction qualities of the crystals make it nearly impossible to pinpoint the wisp's location.

The largest of the quartz crystals stands 30 feet tall at one end of the room. A translucent faceted stone blue heart sits in the core of the 10-foot-diameter pillar. The heart emanates a cold sapphire radiance that pulses soundlessly. The crystaline tribe worships this heart as their deity although no discernible powers or origin exist. The heart may be the phylactery of a powerful lich or a lost artifact of great power.

Will-o'-the-Wisp: HD 9; AC –8[27]; Atk shock (2d6); Move Fly 18; Save 6; AL C; CL/XP 10/1,400; Special: appearance, lightning.

Darakel

Hit Dice: 10
Armor Class: 6 [13]
Attacks: 1 bite (3d6), 1 tail (2d6)
Saving Throw: 5
Special: Poison breath (3/day)
Move: 12/12 (swimming)
Alignment: Chaos
Number Encountered: 1
Challenge Level/XP: 11/1,700

The Darakel is a gigantic horse-headed eel, forty feet long and highly aggressive. It can attack with a nasty fanged bite and tail slap, and three times per day may exhale a 20-foot radius cloud of poison from its nostrils (5d6 points of damage in addition to normal attacks, saving throw for half damage). The Darakel can slither about on land at its normal movement rate, and enjoys preying upon farmers and livestock. It is immune to poison.

— *Author: Scott Wylie Roberts, "Myrystyr"*

Darakel: HD 10; AC 6[13]; Atk 1 bite (3d6), 1 tail (2d6); Move 12 (swim 12); Save 5; AL C; CL/XP 11/1700; Special: Poison breath (3/day).

When the Levee Breaks

Since Farmer Earle lost his vision, wife and farm, his luck has changed. Shortly after the catoblepas incident, the local church of Atacharya (goddess of the downtrodden) has donated a hefty sum to his well-being. Earle (with his uncanny business sense) hired a caretaker (Big Ted) and expanded his once lifeless farm into a thriving cattle industry. Farmer Earle has expanded his farmland into the Sin Mire Swamp. With his ingenuity and now-considerable wealth, he built levees into the swamp to expand his land. The dams hold the water back and turn once-unusable swamp into fertile soil.

Over the years, Earle's farm has turned into a cattle empire. He has a staff of 50 farmhands and thousands of head of cattle roam the lush dried-out swamp basin. Unfortunately, rumors of larceny and embezzlement forced Earle to fire Big Ted. In his anger, Big Ted vowed revenge and left the cattle ranch. Less than a week later, cattle and farmhands began disappearing. Earle feels this Big Ted is behind it all, but no one has seen nor heard of him since he left. Worse still, Earle learned the latest dike built to further expand his farm is failing – likely sabotaged by the angry Big Ted.

The truth of Earle's misfortune lies with the newest levee built farther into the swamp. The encroaching land crossed the territory of a **darakel**. While attempting to sabotage the levee, Big Ted met his fate in the darakel's jaws. The creature normally hides beneath the swamp scum and algae waits as it waits for prey to investigate the new dike.

82

Dark Creeper

Hit Dice: 1+1
Armor Class: 7[12]; 0[19] in darkness
Attacks: dagger (1d4+poison)
Saving Throw: 17
Special: create special darkness, death-flash, level 4 thief.
Move: 9
Alignment: Chaos
Number Encountered: 1d100
Challenge Level/XP: 3/60

Dark creepers are humanoids that stand just under 4 feet tall, always swathed in heavy, dark cloaks and wrappings. Their flesh is pale and moist, and their eyes are milky white. Dark creepers exude a foul stench of sweat and spoiled food, owing primarily to the fact that they never take off their clothing—instead piling on new layers when the outermost one grows too ragged.

Dark creepers lurk in the black places deep below the surface of the world, venturing forth at night or into neighboring societies when the urge to steal and cause mayhem grows too great to resist. Endless layers of filthy, moldering black cloth shroud these small creatures, leading some to believe that the creature inside is smaller still. Usually encountered in groups, dark creepers flee from bright light, but are quite brave in the dark.

For all the mayhem and trouble a pack of dark creepers can cause, this is nothing compared to the dangers a tribe led by the taller, even more sinister dark stalkers represents. Dark creepers treat their tall, lithe masters almost like gods, presenting them with offerings and obeying their every whim. Invariably, several dark stalkers serve as leaders to dark creeper tribes, with all of the tribe's heavy work and labor falling on the diminutive shoulders of the creepers, freeing the dark stalkers for their own decadent pleasures. Yet the dark creepers themselves see no inherent imbalance in this arrangement—to a dark creeper, a life in the servitude of a dark stalker is a life fulfilled.

Dark creepers use daggers in combat, coating them with the poison called black smear. Black smear poison (unless a saving throw is made) reduces the victim's strength by 1d2 points per round for 2d6-1 rounds. If the victim's strength is reduced to 0, the victim dies. If the victim survives, the points of strength will return in 1d6 hours. The poison on a blade is used up when the weapon hits.

Dark creepers (and dark stalkers) are able to employ magic to create a very deep darkness, much more potent than ordinary darkness/light spells. This deeper darkness has a radius of 50ft, and several effects: (1) all normal light sources in the radius of effect are not only extinguished, but cannot be relit for a period of one hour; (2) all magical light sources must make a saving throw or be extinguished for a period of one hour; (3) darkvision will not penetrate the 50ft radius area around the object upon which the deeper darkness has been cast. Magical light sources that are not extinguished by the spell are able to function within the deeper darkness, but convey a range of vision no greater than 30ft.

When a dark creeper is slain, its body combusts in a flash of bright white light, leaving its gear in a heap on the ground. All creatures within a 10-foot burst must make a saving throw or be blinded for 1d6 rounds. Other dark creepers within 10 feet are automatically blinded for at least 1 round.

Dark Creeper: HD 1+1; AC 7[12] or 0[19] in darkness; Atk 1 dagger (1d4 + special poison); Move 9; Save 17; AL C; CL/XP 3/60; Special: create special darkness, death-flash, level 4 thief.

Night of the Creepers

Imhale Mansion stands on a hillside overlooking the village of Greenbriar, its shutters closed tight and its paint peeling. Villagers fear the house and stay away from the overgrown fields surrounding the structure. The villagers whisper of the horrid experiments a necromancer and his grotesque son performed there in the dark of the night. The blood-stained basement still reeks of decay from the night of horrors the pair wrought on the town's residents. The villagers would burn the place to the ground if they didn't fear releasing the evil the old-timers say is trapped within its walls. The villagers fear that the recent disappearances of household pets and the schoolmarm are signs the house's evil legacy is re-awakening.

The house is indeed home to ancient evil, but not the restless spirits the villagers fear. A group of **9 murderous black hunters** broke through the rock wall into the basement and set up their lair. The black hunters travel in groups of three as they skulk around Greenbriar looking for lone travelers, pets out after dark or drunk villagers. The darklings scamper through the walls of the old house, moving quickly and quietly to attack anyone entering their domain. Thick black curtains leave the manor's interior in perpetual darkness, perfect for the night-loving cannibals.

Dark Stalker

Hit Dice: 6+2
Armor Class: 7[12]; 0[19] in darkness
Attacks: short sword (1d6 + poison)
Saving Throw: 11
Special: create special darkness, death-flash, level 4 thief.
Move: 12
Alignment: Chaos
Number Encountered: 1
Challenge Level/XP: 8/800

The strange and mysterious dark stalkers are apparently a noble sub-race of the dark creepers. The stalkers dwell in strange villages (some rumors suggest entire cities) built of stone and fungus, in remote underground caverns where they are served and worshiped by their coarser, diminutive kin, the dark creepers. Dark stalkers come to the surface rarely, but when they do it is on a mission, and with a force of creatures such that it never ends well for those they seek to rob or torment. Dark stalkers are tall, frail humanoids with incredibly pale skin. They always wear multiple layers of dark cloth and black leather armor, yet unlike their lesser kin, a dark stalker's garb is always clean and spotless. Each dark stalker carries a pair of short swords— they prefer these weapons to all others, and coat them with the poison called black smear. Black smear poison (unless a saving throw is made) reduces the victim's strength by 1d2 points per round for 2d6-1 rounds. If the victim's strength is reduced to 0, the victim dies. If the victim survives, the points of strength will return in 1d6 hours. The poison on a blade is used up when the weapon hits.

Dark stalkers are 6 feet tall and weigh 100 pounds.

Dark stalkers have the ability to create a very powerful form of *darkness* magic 3 times per day (see dark creeper). All dark stalkers have the abilities of a level 4 thief. When a dark stalker is killed, its body explodes in a flash of illumination that causes 3d6 points of damage to anyone within 40ft (save for half damage).

In a fight, dark stalkers are not above sacrificing lesser creatures, including dark creepers, to win the day or cover their retreat if things go poorly. They hate well-lit areas and always prefer to fight under the cover of magical darkness. Dark stalkers rarely fight to the death if it can be avoided, preferring to slip away if things begin to look grim. The origins of the dark stalkers and the dark creepers are shrouded in mystery, made more difficult to decipher by the fact that the dark stalkers do not keep records of their history. Many scholars believe that, just as the drow descended from elves, so too must the dark folk have descended from humanity, their eerie powers and spell-like abilities the result of generation upon generation of devotion to profane and sinister magic.

Dark Stalker: HD 6+2; AC 7[12] or 0[19] in darkness; Atk 1 short sword (1d6 + special poison); Move 12; Save 11; AL C; CL/XP 8/800; Special: create special darkness, death-flash, level 4 thief.

Cult Leader

In a vast cavern, approximately 200 feet in diameter, with a high ceiling you discover numerous piles of junk. The piles contain all manner of refuse - rusted armor, broken weapons, candle stubs, bits of cord and rope - as well as a few good, even valuable items. The junkyard is the abode of 1d4 x 10 dark creepers and their leader, a dark stalker.

The darklings have been collecting bits and pieces for ages, and there is a 1% chance that any useful item resides in the yard, and a 1 in 1000 chance that a minor magic item is present. The items in question are buried in the piles of junk and thus take days to locate. The dark creepers have burrows in the piles of junk, and can find the item in question in mere moments if they have a mind to. The dark stalker dwells in a tent made of cast off cloaks over a wire frame atop the tallest pile in the yard.

Darkmantle

Hit Dice: 1+2
Armor Class: 4 [15]
Attacks: 1 Grab (1d4)
Saving Throw: 17
Special: Suffocation, darkness
Move: 3/3 (flying)
Alignment: Neutrality
Number Encountered: 1d4 or 3d6+3
Challenge Level/XP: 2/30

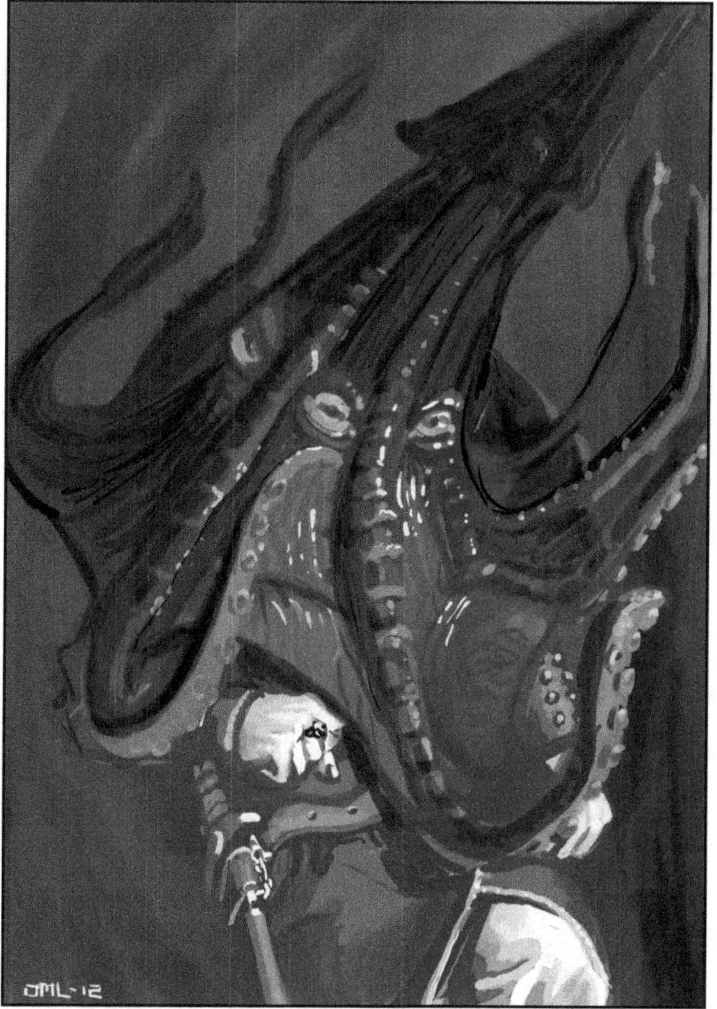

Darkmantles are flying, octopus-like creatures with skin textured and colored to resemble limestone. They ambush prey by sticking to cavern ceilings, and dropping to the attack (they are clumsy fliers). If a darkmantle hits, it attempts to suffocate its prey by folding its tentacles (and the webbing between the tentacles) around the victim's head. If a darkmantle misses its attack, it will flap heavily into the air to make another attempt. When a darkmantle hits, the victim makes a saving throw to avoid having his head enfolded in the darkmantle's octopoid clutches. If the saving throw succeeds, no damage is inflicted. If the saving throw fails, the darkmantle has attached and inflicts 1d4 points of damage, continuing to constrict for an automatic 1d4 points each round thereafter. Darkmantles have the ability to create darkness in a radius of 15ft.

Darkmantle: HD 1+2; AC 4[15]; Atk 1 grab (1d4); Move 3 (Fly 3); Save 17; AL N; CL/XP 2/30; Special: Suffocation, darkness.

Darkness Descending . . . err . . . Ascending

The walls and ceiling of this hall end abruptly. The passage continues on as a bridge arching out across a pit of impenetrable darkness. The bridge stretches 50 feet to the hallway on the other side. The walls of this black, rectangular chamber extend 25 feet from the either side of the bridge. A blast of air rising from the depths of the pit whips loose items around. A magical wind blasts upward from the floor straight up to the ceiling. The wind is strong enough to lift a human-sized creature. Smaller creatures are tossed to the 20-foot-high ceiling and pinned against the torrent of wind. Creatures larger than a man are not bothered by the wind.

The floor is actually only 20 feet below, but a clutch of **8 darkmantles** nests at the bottom of the chamber. The darkmantles learned to control their flight in the windy room, giving them incredible precision and a flight speed of 12. The alien creatures keep the floor under magical darkness and shoot into the air to make diving attacks (at a +1 bonus) against PCs on the bridge or tossed about by the wind. A number of items are pinned to the ceiling by the hurricane-force winds. Among the numerous bones, rocks, scraps of cloth and other refuse are 6 torches, 2 lanterns, 2 ropes (50 feet), a grappling hook, 23 arrows, a short sword, 36 gp, 127 sp, 16 cp and an *arrow of direction*.

Deasic (Ice Creeper)

Hit Dice: 9
Armor Class: 3 [16]
Attacks: 1 smother (2d6) or 3 ice daggers (1d4)
Saving Throw: 6
Special: Smothers, explosion of shards, immunities
Move: 6
Alignment: Neutrality
Number Encountered: 1 or 4d6+4
Challenge Level/XP: 11/1,700

The Deasic, or Ice Creeper, is a creature of living ice, resembling a long, branching, crystal-like structure. The deasic attacks by stealth, creeping up to living creatures in their sleep, smothering their air passages and draining their life heat. Anyone slain in this manner becomes frozen solid, as the warmth of life is sucked out of them. If discovered before it can complete its attack, the deasic will defend itself with dagger-like shafts of ice. It is immune to fire and cold based attacks, and can cause a burst of icy shards to erupt from its body, three times per day, causing 6d6 damage to all within 20ft. Deasic apparently have a rudimentary intelligence and society, as they have occasionally been observed gathering in large numbers to form gigantic snowflake-shaped structures under the aurora of polar skies in winter.

— Author: Scott Wylie Roberts, "Myrystyr"

Deasic (Ice Creeper): HD 9; AC 3 [16]; Atk 1 smother (2d6) or 3 ice daggers (1d4); Move 6; Save 6; CL/XP 11/1700; Special: Smothers, explosion of shards, immunities.

No More Mr. Ice Guy

A lonely, two-story cabin sits at the tree line high in the snowy Hollow Spire Mountains. A warm glow radiates from the windows at all hours, day and night. Several barns stocked with firewood, frozen meat and dried fruits sit adjacent to the house. Mounds of snow lie banked against the back of the house and barns. Dozens of frozen corpses are hidden within the heaps of discolored snow. Most of the corpses froze while sleeping. Some appear to have awakened — and died instantly — with expressions of undying terror.

The house belongs to Erlenmeyer, an elderly, senile man. Erlenmeyer spent his life as a scout, huntsman, trapper and explorer in the vast Hollow Spire Mountains. He lived and raised a family here with his wife, Myrtle. Their children are long gone from the homestead, but Erlenmeyer and Myrtle had one another. A year ago, however, a **deasic** robbed Myrtle of her life force. Her death was too much for Erlenmeyer, who is suffering an advanced state of dementia. In his confused mind, he truly believes she still lives. He keeps her frozen body in her rocking chair in front of the cold fireplace. Myrtle's body is draped in knitted shawls in an eternal sleep. Her killer, the icy deasic, still sleeps upstairs.

Erlenmeyer welcomes visitors and attempts to be a gracious host. He offers visitors his home to escape the weather, to rest and to share a warm meal in exchange for their company. His emotional instability makes for an awkward visit, as he descends into fits of sorrow and rage at inanimate objects and long-forgotten memories.

Why the deasic hasn't slain Erlenmeyer is a mystery. In fact, the deasic seems to have adopted him. The creature raids caravans, neighbors and hapless travelers, and then hauls supplies back to Erlenmeyer's residence. It buries victims in the snow and stores the supplies in the barns for Erlenmeyer to use. With his mind slipping away, Erlenmeyer doesn't realize an alien creature is caring for him. The deasic enters through an open upstairs window via the mound of snow in back. It has no qualms about slaying Erlenmeyer's guests.

DEMONS

Demons are creatures of the lower planes of existence, but they are occasionally encountered in places where they have been enslaved to serve as guardians by powerful magic-users or evil priests. The more intelligent varieties might also be interrupted while carrying out plots of their own. *Swords & Wizardry* makes no game distinction between demons and devils, for the convenience of those using only a three-alignment system; all are simply creatures of the lower planes, to be used as desired with the Referee's own campaign.

Demon, Achaierai

Hit Dice: 6
Armor Class: 3[16]
Attacks: 1 bite (2d6), 2 claws (1d6)
Saving Throw: 11
Special: Magic resistance (25%), breath of confusion, immune to fire
Move: 12
Alignment: Chaos
Number Encountered: 1d2 or 1d8+1
Challenge Level/XP: 9/1,100

Achaierai resemble hellish birds standing fifteen feet tall on four stilt-like legs with cruel talons. Three times per day an achaierai can breathe a black cloud of gas, inflicting 1d6 points of damage and requiring a saving throw to prevent being affected as if by a Confusion spell. As demons, they are immune to fire.

Achaierai Demon: HD 6; AC 3[16]; Atk 2 claws (1d6), 1 bite (2d6); Move 12; Save 11; AL C; CL/XP 9/1100; Special: Magic resistance (25%), breath of confusion, immune to fire.

Angry Bird

A golden birdcage sits alone on a marble pedestal in this dark, empty chamber. The well-crafted cage gleams in the light. Jewels adorn the intricate lace bars. The magical cage is always clean and filled with fresh provisions fit for a small songbird with brilliant yellow plumage sitting on a perch inside the cage. The bird sings delightful melodies and hops about as it playfully mimics sounds in whimsical chirps and tweets.

The stand and cage belie their true nature. The cage is a prison for an **achaierai** summoned and forgotten by a wizard ages ago. The cage forcibly changed the achaierai into a songbird as long as the cage remains intact and in contact with its stand. The achaierai retains its intelligence but looses all powers while trapped within songbird form. Once the delicate cage is removed, opened or damaged, the enchantment breaks, transforming the achaierai back into its true form. Once the curse is broke, the achaierai breathes a cloud of confusion as the hellish bird bursts from the dinky cage.

Demon, Arauk (First-Category Demon)

Hit Dice: 8
Armor Class: 0 [19]
Attacks: 4 weapons (by weapon)
Saving Throw: 8
Special: See below
Move: 12/12 (flying)
Alignment: Chaos
Number Encountered: 1d3 or 1d6
Challenge Level/XP: 11/1,700

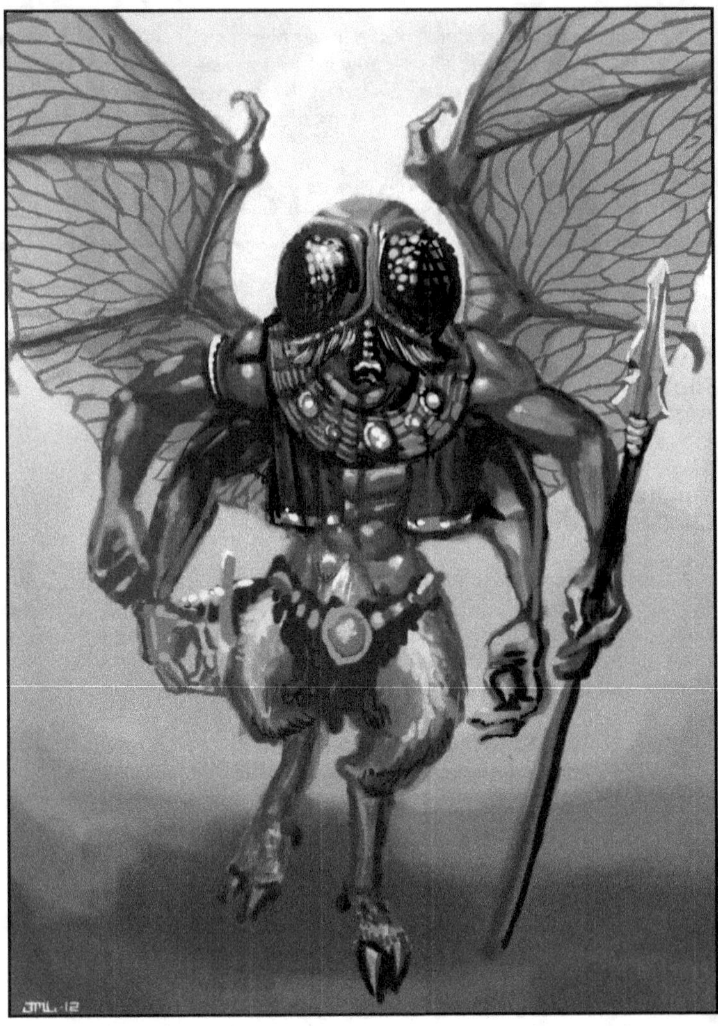

Arauks are a somewhat lesser-known first-category demon, unrelated to the Vrock type but roughly equal in strength to the other type. Arauk demons have heads resembling that of a horsefly and legs like a goat's; the demon's hair-covered torso is human, but with four arms. They have bat-like wings, but they are slow and clumsy fliers.

Arauks take only half damage from electricity, cold, fire, and poison gas. They are able to cast *darkness* in a radius of 5ft at will, and to *teleport* once per day. In addition, they have the ability to *detect invisibility*, cause *fear* (as per a wand), and to *telekinese* 100 pounds of weight, each usable at will. In addition to the weapons they carry, Arauk demons can breathe a small cloud of fire (10ft in diameter) in addition to their normal attacks, causing 1d6 hit points of damage unless the target(s) make a saving throw against the breath weapon.

Arauk demons can be hit by normal weapons. They can *gate* in another Arauk (10% chance of success).

— Author: Matt Finch

Arauk Demon: HD 8; AC 0[19]; Atk 4 weapons (by weapon); Move 12 (Fly 12); Save 8; AL C; CL/XP 11/1700; Special: Demonic immunities, magical abilities, breathe fire, gate (10%).

Garbage Island

Down the Stoneheart River, a massive bend collects refuse, sewage and other indescribable waste from the city of Bard's Gate. The swirl waters pile the garbage into a plodding island reaching a height of 12 feet and spanning 75 feet in diameter. Scraps of wood, rotting vegetation and occasional corpses of animals and humanoids make up the island. The semi-solid island spins slowly in the flowing river. Traversing the pile is dangerous but not impossible. The island reeks of an indescribable stench that sickens all but the hardiest of trolls. Clouds of flies move in great masses that cloak the sun. Despite the amount of carrion, larger scavengers are mysteriously absent.

A gondola and three rotting passengers lie wrecked and partially buried atop the rubbish heap. The well-dressed cadavers appear to have been well dressed aristocrats at one time. The putrid carcass of an enormous otyugh lies near the center of the island, just below the gondola. Numerous (and harmless) maggots infest the heap, some of them reaching lengths of 4 feet or more. The trash hides **12 giant flies** that busily mate and lay eggs within the sludgy portions. An **aruak demon** feasts within the otyugh. The flies crawl out of the moldering mass of refuse and attack those interrupting their ghastly orgy. While the flies distract front-line warriors, the aruak teleports to attack spellcasters. The aruak attacks with two paddles (1d6, as mace), an anchor and chain (1d8, as two-handed flail) and a logging cant hook (1d8+1, as polearm).

Giant Flies (12): HD 3; AC 5[14]; Atk 1 bite (1d6); Move 12/24 (flying); Save 14; AL N; CL/XP 4/120.

Demon, Baalroch (Balor), (Sixth-Category Demon)

Hit Dice: 10
Armor Class: 2 [17]
Attacks: Sword (1d12+2) and whip (see below)
Saving Throw: 5
Special: Magic resistance (75%), surrounded by flame (3d6), magic weapon required to hit, unaggected by spells from casters lower than 6th level.
Move: 6/15 (flying)
Alignment: Chaos
Number Encountered: 1, 1d3, or 1d6
Challenge Level/XP: 17/3,500

The Baalroch's name means, roughly, the Bull of Baal: the Baal-aurochs (the aurochs was a bull that stood twelve feet tall at the shoulder, and Baal is an ancient and evil pagan deity). These powerful demons somewhat resemble vast minotaurs with great, spreading bat-wings; they burn with the fires of hell and are wreathed in flame. Spells from casters below 6th level do not affect them, and against higher-level spell casters they are yet 75% immune to all spells. In combat, a baalroch uses whip and sword; the whip can be used to reach great distances – on a successful hit the victim is pulled close to the baalroch and burned by the fires of the demon's body (3d6 hit points). Baalrochs are sometimes referred to in ancient texts as Balor or Baalor, which may be the name of a single demon rather than a term for all of them. A baalroch could be forced or tricked into the service of a powerful wizard, but the risk would be immense.

Baalrochs may attempt to gate in an ally with a 70% chance of success. The responding demon will usually be a third-category demon (01-80 on 1d100) but an unusually successful summoning might call a fourth-category demon (81-00 on 1d100).

Baalroch Demon: HD 10; AC 2[17]; Atk 1 sword (1d12+2) and 1 whip (entangles); Move 6 (Fly 15); Save 5; AL C; CL/XP 17/3500; Special: Magic Resistance (75%), surrounded by flame (3d6), magic weapon required to hit, unaffected by spells from casters lower than 6th level.

Eternal Fire Prison

A dome of shimmering glass dominates this chamber. The 15-foot-high translucent dome traps a woman amid a floor of refuse. The woman appears to be starving and feeble. Her clothing is tattered, and her skin is pale. Her hair lies in long, greasy tangles. A 20-foot-tall whirlwind of fire dances a ring around the dome. The floor has a burnt ring signifying the fire's countless circles around the dome.

Dirt and grime cover the woman, hiding her true beauty. Arcane symbols and incantations drawn in feces and stains cover the dome's floor. The woman is a young and stunningly beautiful magic-user named **Francesca the Alluring**. In the midst of negotiating terms of services, a **baalroch demon** broke free from her entrapment ward. She fled into the dome, a permanent ward that protects her from the demon. The dome only keeps the demons at bay and has no other special abilities. Exhausted of spells, she survives with a magical spoon that provides her with an endless supply of food and water. Bordering on madness, Francesca has survived in the dome for nearly two years. The demon waits patiently for her to attempt to escape or for insanity to take its hold.

The flame tornado quickly winds downs to reveal the demon. This particular demon has the ability to transform into a whirlwind of fire. In this form, it can sweep away any creature with one or fewer HD. In addition, the mere touch of the whirlwind deals 3d6 points of fire damage and sets creatures on fire (1d6 points of fire damage per round, save each round to extinguish the flames). The whirlwind's diameter is 5 feet.

Francesca, Magic-user Level 12: HP 31; AC 9 [10]; Atk 1 weapon; Move 12; Save 5 (3 vs. spells); AL C; CL/XP 11/1700;

Special: Charisma 17, Spells (4/4/4/4/4/1). Equipment: Magical spoon.

Demon, Coral

Hit Dice: 10
Armor Class: -1 [20]
Attacks: 2 pincers (2d6), 4 tentacles (1d4)
Saving Throw: 5
Special: See below
Move: 9/20 (swimming)
Alignment: Chaos
Number Encountered: 1d3 or 1d6
Challenge Level/XP: 15/2,900

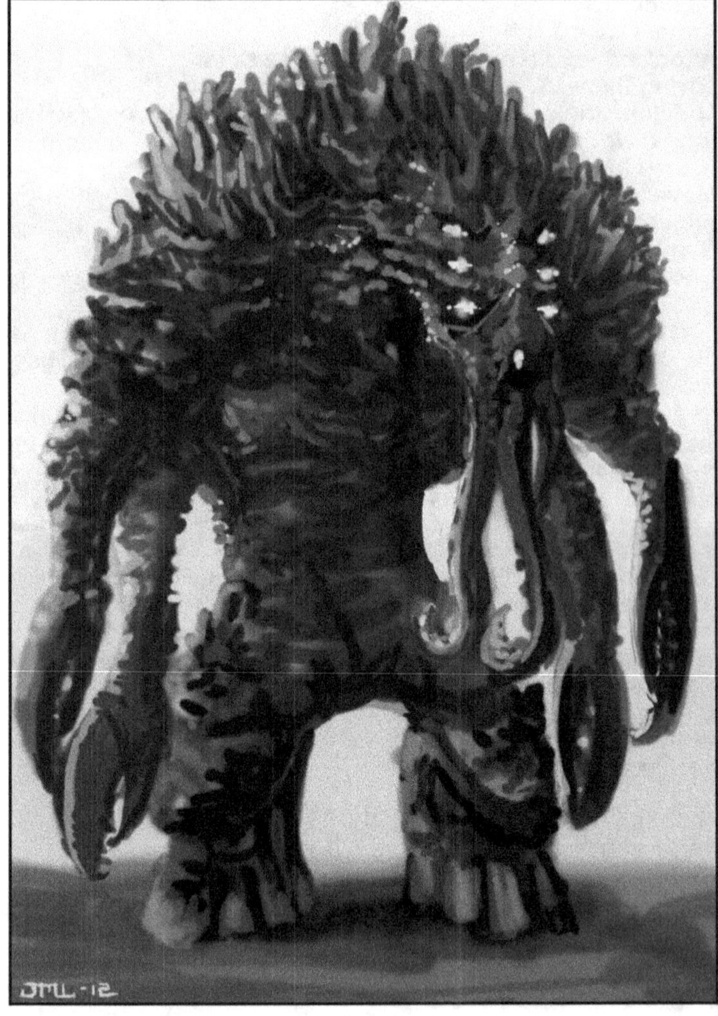

Coral demons are often associated with the Demon-Lord Thalasskoptis, although not all coral demons are in his service. These horrific undersea demons are often found leading large bands of water-ghouls and sea-wights when on the material planes of existence. Such a group will generally be composed of 1d6 sea-wights and 1d10+10 water-ghouls.

A coral demon resembles a mass of coral with a vaguely humanoid shape, but with 4 coral-encrusted tentacles reaching from the body along with a pair of pincers. On land, they give off a stench of brine and rot so strongly that anyone coming within 20ft must make a saving throw or become nauseated for 1d6 rounds.

Coral demons have all the normal powers and resistances of demons, taking half damage from electricity, cold, fire, and poison gas. They can only be hit by magical weapons. They are able to cast *darkness* in a radius of 15ft and to *teleport* once per day. In addition, coral demons have the ability to *detect invisibility*, cause *fear* (as per a wand), and to *telekinese* 200 pounds of weight, each usable at will. If underwater, a coral demon can summon 1d4 giant sharks, and they can also jet forth a cloud of ink 15ft in radius which acts as a *dispel magic* spell (12th level of ability) cast against anyone within the cloud. The cloud persists for 1d3+1 rounds, and anyone remaining inside it for a second round will be treated for each round as if the *dispel magic* had been cast again. They have the ability to *gate* in another coral demon with a chance of 15% on land and 40% if underwater. Finally, all coral demons have magic resistance of 55%.

Clearly, coral demons are considerably weaker on land than under the water, and they seldom venture too far from their natural element. In the dark and dreaded seas of the abyss, coral demons are common, and few other demons venture willingly into the territories they claim as their own.
— *Author: Matt Finch*

Coral Demon: HD 10; AC -1[20]; Atk 2 pincers (2d6), 4 tentacles (1d4); Move 9 (Swim 2); Save 5; AL C; CL/XP 15/2900; Special: Magic resistance (55%), hit only by magic weapons, demonic immunities and magical powers, *gate* (15% or 40%).

Slave Ship Zorgue

Just off the coast in the Reaping Sea grows the massive Bleeding Reef. The reef's jagged coral emits a constant stream of red gametes to propagate into the sea. The crimson clouds give the reef its name as it appears to constantly seep streams of blood. The largest mass of coral juts from the sea, where a partially submerged castle sits on the reef. It is not clear if the coral encased the castle, or if the castle grew from the coral, or who – or what – resides in the barbed palace.

Along the Bleeding Reef lies The Zorgue, a moored merchant slave ship. About three dozen slaves have survived and remain shackled to the ship's deck. They plead to any passing ship for rescue. Swimming in sluggish circles around the ship are **1d4 giant sharks**. The crew of The Zorgue lurk in the bowels of the ship as **1d6 sea-wights** and **1d10+10 water-ghouls**. A **coral demon** lies in hiding, blending into the coral reef adjacent to the boat. The demon uses the survivors to lure victims within its reach. The demon devours a slave survivor every few days, relishing the terror and pain it inflicts. The slaves pledge fealty to their saviors. Slaves could become servants, henchmen or even followers of the heroes.

Ghoul (Aquatic): HD 2; AC 6[13]; Atk 2 claws (1d3), 1 bite (1d4); Move 9 (18, Swim); Save 16; AL C; CL/XP 3/60; Special: Immunities, paralyzing touch.

Giant Shark (7HD): HD 7; AC 6[13]; Atk 1 bite (1d8+4); Move 0 (Swim 24); Save 9; AL C; CL/XP 7/600; Special: Feeding frenzy.

Sea-Wight: HD 4+3; AC 4[15]; Atk 1 claw (1d4 + level drain); Move 9, Swim 12; Save 13; AL C; CL/XP 7/600; Special: Drain 1 level with hit, hit only by magic or silver weapons.

Demon, Darkswimmer

Hit Dice: 9
Armor Class: 4 [15]
Attacks: 2 claws (1d6), 1 bite (2d6)
Saving Throw: 6
Special: See below
Move: 24 (flying)
Alignment: Chaos
Number Encountered: 1d2 or 1d6
Challenge Level/XP: 15/2,900

— Author: Matt Finch

Darkswimmer Demon: HD 9; AC 4[15]; Atk 2 claws (1d6), 1 bite (2d6); Move 24 (Fly 24); Save 6; AL C; CL/XP 15/2900; Special: Magic resistance (90%), hit only by magic weapons, demonic immunities and magical powers, *gate* (25%).

Shrine of the Demon Princess Teratashia

The walls, floors and ceiling of this chamber glimmer with highly polished black granite. Flecks of silver reflect light like a million stars in a night sky within the glossy stone. Eight pillars of the same highly polished stone surround a set of central figures. The 80-foot-tall pillars support a domed ceiling over the center of the 100-foot-diameter-round chamber. A 20-foot-wide colonnade surrounds the dome center between the pillars and outer wall. Each of the 10-foot-diameter pillars seems carved from a single stone. The temperature drops by 30 degrees past the pillars in the center of the room.

Three large humanoid obsidian glass statues surround a central feminine figure. The statues appear hairless, nondescript and physically perfect. The three featureless effigies solemnly stand with arms raised and the tips of their six fingers touching. Each of the masculine forms reaches a height of 12 feet. A single, fist-sized white orb appears to serve as a symbolic eye in the center of their forehead. A dull, pulsating violet light dimly smolders from within each of their chest cavities.

The giant figures stand around a concave depression about 10 feet in diameter. A feminine form of the same smooth glass stands on the tips of her toes in the bowl-shaped depression. The form has two dull crimson eyes (where eyes should be normally located) on an otherwise featureless face. The woman's six-fingered hands clasp one another in prayer between her breasts. She is slightly larger than an average man. The feminine statue always seems to face visitors. It flawlessly shifts despite the location of the viewer regardless of concealment or magic. No matter how many viewers, the female statue appears to stare at each individually. To each viewer, the statue only seems to hold its gaze upon them.

This mysterious shrine to the demon princess Teratashia holds many secrets, none of which are given up easily. Lurking within the pillars are **2 darkswimmer demons**. These alien demons serve as the shrine's guardians. The darkswimmers attack from within the pillars, targeting those alone or near the stone columns first. The shrine may be used to commune or beseech the aid of Teratshia. The shrine may also have the power to open portals to extraterrestrial dimensions or to the abyss itself.

Demon, Dretch

Hit Dice: 4
Armor Class: 2 [17]
Attacks: 2 claws (1d4), 1 bite (1d6)
Saving Throw: 13
Special: Magical abilities
Move: 9
Alignment: Chaos
Number Encountered: 1, 1d8, or 3d6
Challenge Level/XP: 6/400

These creatures are fat, with long, spindly arms and legs. They have rudimentary human heads, with slobbering jaws and folds of fat. Wretch demons have some weak demonic powers. Although they are not particularly intelligent, they can cause a horrible stinking cloud once per day, can teleport once per day, can cause darkness (10ft diameter) once per day, and can summon 1d4 giant rats once per day. The stinking cloud has a radius of 20ft and requires anyone caught within it to make a saving throw or be rendered helpless from nausea for 1d4+1 rounds.

Dretch Demon: HD 4; AC 2[17]; Atk 2 claws (1d4), 1 bite (1d6); Move 9; Save 13; AL C; CL/XP 6/400; Special: Magical abilities.

Bowels of Hell

A ghastly stench emanates from this cavernous chamber. Sinewy excretions cover the surfaces in a sticky tangle of glistening, congealed bile. Cleaned and gnarled bones of rodents and larger creatures lie scattered along the floor. Snarls, grunts and flatulence permeate the humid, disgusting air. Shallow ponds of indescribable ooze and excrement pool in the corners and low areas.

An enormous sludge-like tumor flounders in the room. The growth resembles a grey, pallid, disemboweled stomach. With no obvious sensory organs or even a semblance of a face, the vein-covered lump writhes as if in pain. Surrounding the tuberous cyst are **6 dretch demons**. The gluttonous demons bounce around the swollen bulb in a chaotic ritual. With a great heave, the malignant mass defecates a slime-coated dretch out its long, tube-like tail. Vague faces and appendages of developing dretch stretch its emaciated skin from the inside. The demons claw and pummel within the visceral knob, causing it obvious pain and anguish. The dretch-producing organ has no other attacks other than its repulsive appearance and appalling odor. The entrail-like monster does not have any purpose other than to excrete dretch into this dimension from its sphincter.

Dretch-Pooper Demon: HD 20; AC 9[10]; Atk none; Move 3; Save 5; AL C; CL/XP 11/1,700; Special: continual stinking cloud, 30-foot radius, immune to fire, spawn dretch.

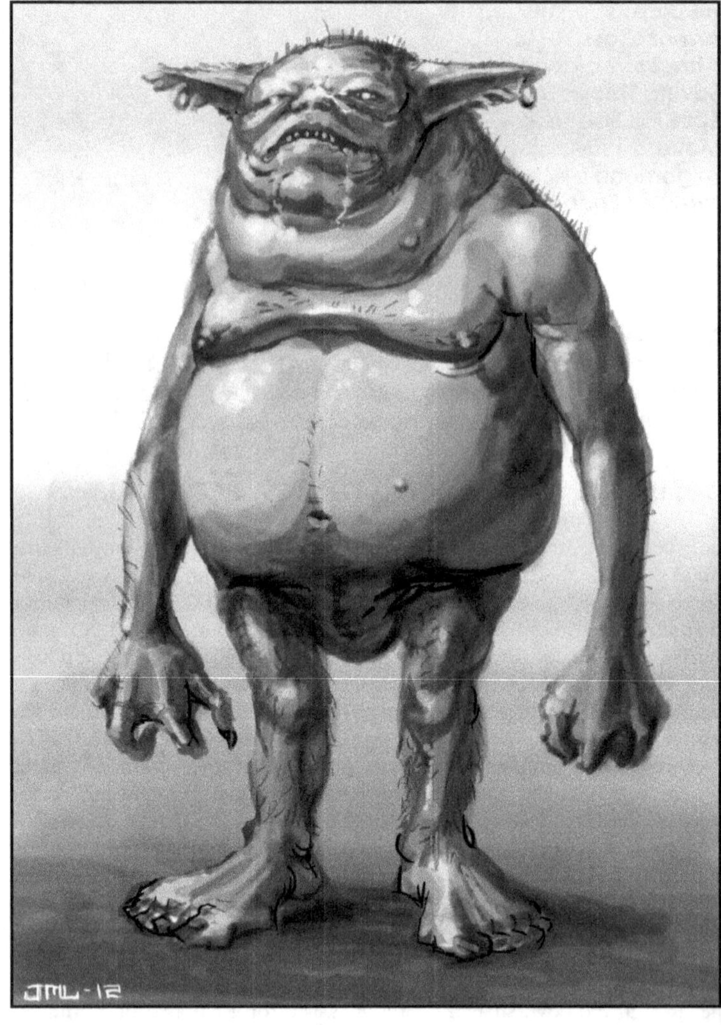

Demon, Erinyes

Hit Dice: 6
Armor Class: 2[17]
Attacks: 1 bronze sword (1d6 + paralysis)
Saving Throw: 11
Special: Magic resistance (25%), magical abilities, immune to fire and cold, entangle, fear
Move: 12/24 (flying)
Alignment: Chaos
Number Encountered: 1d3 or 4d4
Challenge Level/XP: 10/1,400

The erinyes, the "furies" of Ancient Greek mythology, are female demons who pursue those guilty of crimes against the order of the gods. Their appearance is so terrible as to cause *fear* (saving throw). They are impossible to hide from, being able to see invisible things and locate objects at will. The furies carry a whip, which, if it hits, entangles the victim (saving throw) until the fury releases it. The furies are immune to fire and cold, and have a magic resistance of 25%. The blade of a fury's sword causes *paralysis* (saving throw).

Erinyes Demon: HD 6; AC 2[17]; Atk 1 bronze sword (1d6 + paralysis); Move 12 (Fly 24); Save 11; AL C; CL/XP 10/1400; Special: Magic resistance (25%), magical abilities, fear, immune to fire and cold, entangle.

Tail Spin

A **massive raven** flies high above, casting a huge shadow over the land. The raven has a 65-foot wingspan and clutches an ornate bronze cage. **Two human woman** hang shackled from the cage's exterior. It is unclear from a distance if the humans are unconscious or dead. The women wear silken gowns and tattered flower headpieces. A crossbeam sits across the top of the massive cage and serves as a handle and perch for the raven. The cage contains an unsteady **unicorn** bouncing around on the jarring flight. Battered and exhausted, the unicorn remains proud and glorious. The magnificent beast in the cage bellows in panic to anyone within sight. Two winged women escort the raven. They brandish archaic bronze swords, and barbed whips hang from their belts.

The **2 erinyes** usher the raven and their prize toward a wizard's tower high in the Hollow Spire Mountains. The erinyes used the maidens as bait to lure the unicorn from its enchanted forest. The wizard summoned the eriynes to capture the unicorn for his own nefarious purposes. The giant raven flies in a circle if the erinyes break off to enter combat. The raven drops the cage if it receives 10 or more points of damage from a single attack. The raven flees (possibly with a PC or the cage) if wounded below a quarter of its hit points.

Giant Raven: HD 12; AC 4[15]; Atk 1 bite (3d12), 2 claws (3d6); Move 3 (Fly 30); Save 3; AL N; CL/XP 12/2000; Special: None.

Unicorn: HD 5; AC 2[17]; Atk 2 hoofs (1d8), 1 horn (1d8); Move 24; Save 12; AL L; CL/XP 6/400; Special: double damage for charge, 25% magic resistance, teleport

Demon, Glabrezu (Third-Category Demon)

Hit Dice: 10
Armor Class: −4 [23]
Attacks: 2 pincers (2d6), 2 claws (1d3), 1 bite (1d6)
Saving Throw: 5
Special: Magic resistance (60%), immune to fire, magical abilities
Move: 9
Alignment: Chaos
Number Encountered: 1d3 or 1d6
Challenge Level/XP: 15/2,900

The third-category demons, Glabrezu, are massive and horrible, standing ten feet high or more. They have goat horns and humanoid shape, with no wings. Four arms sprout from the torso: two huge arms with great crab-pincers, and two much shorter arms with claws. Glabrezu can cause darkness in a 10ft radius, are immune to fire, can cause Fear at will, can levitate at will, can polymorph themselves, and are 60% resistant to magic. These demons have a 30% chance to *gate* in an ally (roll 1d4 to determine the category of demon that responds).

Third-Category Demon: HD 10; AC −4[23]; Atk 2 pincers (2d6), 2 claws (1d3), 1 bite (1d6); Move 9; Save 5; AL C; CL/XP 15/2900; Special: Magic resistance (60%),immune to fire, demonic magical powers.

Dead Ringer

Wedged in the crook of a tree branch 20 feet up lies an unmoving, robed humanoid. The figure appears mostly unconscious as it weakly moans in pain. The strangely beautiful androgynous figure wears airy white silk robes stained with spatters of blood. Two vertical openings down the back of the robes reveal jagged and bloody bone protrusions. Aside from not having any discernible sex, the humanoid appears perfect in every way. The angelic creature is weak and disoriented. **Athelstan,** an **angel**, encountered a particularly vicious **glabrezu** named **Galosc** on a dimension bordering the material plane. Athelstan journeyed from its heavenly abode to deliver a message from the gods (possibly to a PC).

Galosc, renowned for its ability to hunt and slay angels, tracked Athelstan down. Whether Galosc attacked Athelstan to prevent the message from reaching its intended target is up to the Referee. Galosc ripped Athelstan's wings from its back, and then began to methodically torture the helpless deva. Mortally wounded, Athelstan managed to escape to the material plane, leaving Galosc to simmer. Athelstan has just enough strength to open a portal once more to the quasi-plane where Galosc lurks. Athelstan perishes soon after the portal opens.

Galosc leaps through the portal to finally butcher the angel. Galosc wears the halos of past prey as bands around his massive upper arms. The halos (now made of dull lead) provide the demon a +1 bonus to attack rolls.

Athelstan: HD 9; AC 2[17]; Atk 1 golden sword (1d10); Move 12 (15 fly); Save 6; CL/XP 13/2300; Special: Magic Resistance (75%), magic weapon required to hit, cast spells as a 9th level cleric, unaffected by spells from casters lower than 3rd level.

Demon, Grimlek

Hit Dice: 5+3
Armor Class: 5 [14]
Attacks: 1 bite (2d6)
Saving Throw: 12
Special: Disease, continuous damage
Move: 24
Alignment: Chaos
Number Encountered: 1d3 or 1d6
Challenge Level/XP: 7/600

Grimleks are large wolf-like demons covered in dark, ratty fur. Their most striking features are over-sized canines that prevent their mouths from closing and their lack of eyes. The absence of eyes does not negatively affect them. They are often used in the service of powerful demons and sorcerers as guards, trackers, or assassins.

A Grimlek may "latch on" to a victim after a successful attack, causing 1d6 points of damage every round until the victim is freed from the bite. Their bites can also cause a lycanthropic-like disease if the victim is not cured before the next new moon, at which point the infected person will become a hybrid similar to a werewolf. At this point even more powerful healing magics are needed to reverse the effects before the following new moon or the person will fully transform into a Grimlek and be lost forever.

— Author: the Lizard of Oz

Grimlek: HD 5+3; AC 5[14]; Atk 1 bite (2d6); Move 24; Save 12; AL C; CL/XP 7/600; Special: Disease, continuous damage.

Wolf Blitzkrieg

The rocky wasteland of the Ghest Caldera presents dangers few live to tell about. Nestled in the Hollow Spire Mountains, this volcanic depression thrives with hostile life. Rivers of lava, boiling lakes and clouds of poisonous gases are only a few of the common natural features. Ruins of past civilizations and fortresses lie scattered among the fantastic natural rock formations.

The Thorax Tower is just one of many inhabited ruins. This 80-foot-tall tower stands near the gorge opening of the caldera. The fluted tower's walls resemble dozens of large vertical backbones connected by corrugated ribs. Windows carved in the likeness of grinning skulls signify each of the four levels. A blind elf stands guard to the side of a gated entrance. With his eye sockets sewn shut, the elf listens for visitors with his acute hearing. He holds a bronze mallet and wears bronze mail resembling snake skin. A bronze gong with the relief of a wolf hangs from a stand beside him. He rings the gong every round as soon as he hears visitors approaching. The gong summons a **grimlek** each round he hammers away at the bronze disk (maximum of 4). Another can materialize once one is slain. The grimleks serve Chaotic beings who sound the gong. The wolf-like demons materialize from the emblazoned wolf image. The grimleks vanish once the gong stops reverberating (usually within 5d4 rounds). They remain as long as the gong sounds.

The elf, **Elucith**, serves as a reluctant guard for the tower's current queen, **Maliza** (a **medusa** with sorceress powers). While not inherently evil, Elucith obeys Maliza to the best of his ability. She holds his wife prisoner (stoned) within the tower.

Maliza (medusa): HD 6; AC 5[14]; Atk 1 dagger (1d4); Move 9; Save 11; AL C; CL/XP 9/1,100; Special: Gaze turns to stone, Spells (invisibility, phantasmal force, suggestion)

Elucith, Elf Fighter Level 3: HP 17; AC 7 [12]; Atk 1 shortsword (1d6) or 1 sling (1d4); Move 12; Save 12; AL N; CL/XP 3/60; Equipment: Leather armor, short sword, sling, 10 bullets.

Demon, Hezrou (Second-Category Demon)

Hit Dice: 9
Armor Class: -2 [21]
Attacks: 2 claws (1d3), 1 bite (4d4)
Saving Throw: 6
Special: Magic resistance 50%, magical abilities
Move: 6/12 (flying)
Alignment: Chaos
Number Encountered: 1d3 or 1d6
Challenge Level/XP: 11/1700

Toad-like demons with bat wings, the Hezrou have magic resistance of 50%. At will, they can cause *fear* (per the spell), *detect invisibility* (per the spell), and cause *darkness 15ft radius*. They are immune to fire. Hezrou have a 20% chance to succeed at summoning another second-category demon to their aid.

Second-Category Demon (Hezrou Type): HD 9; AC -2[21]; Atk 2 claws (1d3), 1 bite (4d4); Move 6 (Fly 12); Save 6; AL C; CL/XP 11/1700; Special: Magic resistance 50%, demonic magical powers.

Mud Island Pyramid

The stench of sulfur rolls from this cavernous chamber. Great blisters of ruddy mud burst, releasing putrid gas across the soupy lake. Narrow rock paths wind through the lake of boiling mud. The paths crisscross throughout the room. They all end at a large flat island near the cavern's center. Blubbery men seemingly made of mud dredge human skulls from the lake. The mud men (actually **12 lemures** covered in mud) bring countless skulls up from the lake's depths and stack them into a 30-foot-tall pyramid. The red mud stains the skulls a pale burgundy. The lemurs use a mash of bile and clay to cement the skulls together.

The lemures are building a shrine to Tsathogga in this mud-ridden caldera. The lemures largely ignore intruders but attack under the orders of their commander. Hiding just under the surface of the mud lake lurks their **hezrou** master. The hezrou explodes out of the mud to attack any magic--users. The hezrou is charged with establishing a new shrine to the demon frog.

Lemure Demon: HD 3; AC 7[12]; Atk 1 claw (1d3); Move 3; Save 14; AL C; CL/XP 4/120; Special: Regenerate (1hp/round).

Demon, Khavorr (Third-Category Demon)

Hit Dice: 10
Armor Class: -3 [22]
Attacks: 2 claws (1d10), 1 bite (3d6)
Saving Throw: 5
Special: See below
Move: 9
Alignment: Chaos
Number Encountered: 1d3 or 1d6
Challenge Level/XP: 13/2,300

Khavorr demons are considered to be a third-category demon, although they are unrelated to the more commonly summoned Glabrezu type. They resemble grossly fat humans, or perhaps giants, for they stand 10ft in height. A Khavorr demon has the head of an alligator, and these powerful jaws are a terrible weapon.

Khavorrs take only half damage from electricity, cold, fire, and poison gas. They are able to cast *darkness* in a radius of 15ft at will, and to *teleport* once per day. In addition, they have the ability to *detect invisibility*, cause *fear* (as per a wand), and to *telekinese* 300 pounds of weight, any of these abilities being employed at will. Khavorrs can *polymorph* themselves into massive alligators or into a human shape, and can cast *charm monster* 3 times per day.

Khavorr demons can be damaged by normal weapons. A Khavorr demon can attempt to *gate* in another demon with a 30% chance of success. The demon appearing may be of Category 1, 2, or 3 (roll 1d3 to determine).

— *Author: Matt Finch*

Third-Category Demon (Khavorr type): HD 10; AC -3[22]; Atk 2 claws (1d10), 1 bite (3d6); Move 9; Save 5; AL C; CL/XP 13/2300; Special: Magic resistance 55%, demonic magical powers.

The Flesh Peddler

In the darkest recesses of the Canal District of Bard's Gate mopes the drunkard, Delmar the Glassblower. Delmar, a very successful glass artist, traveled to city with his beautiful young bride to set up shop. Just a week after their arrival, however, Sonie left him to pursue a life of prostitution. Delmar pleads with anyone with a formidable appearance to help him retrieve his wife. He insists that Sonie would not make such a choice willingly. He believes she is under a spell or perhaps was forced into her sundry occupation. He has little to offer adventurers aside from supplying glassware at wholesale cost.

He tells heroes that Sonie works at Manky Mary's Alehouse. He describes a blubbery man with a wide evil smile who peddles her out like a common trinket. Indeed, Sonie has fallen under the charm of a **khavor demon**. The khavor, known as **Gastro the Greased**, has charmed a dozen comely humans into submission. The demon takes the form of a grotesquely obese human male with exaggerated features. The demon takes great pleasure in despoiling and corrupting societies' chaste. He revels in destroying the bliss of young love. He loiters in the gloomy recesses of the alehouse, surrounded by a charmed entourage. A massive table of food always sits before him. He greedily devours everything Mary feeds him. While she does not care for Gastro, she readily accepts his abundance of coin. She ran out of food long ago and sends her servants into the streets to scrounge for anything to present to Gastro. Currently, she serves putrid goat roast, rat soup (with a touch of lamp oil for flavor) and hash made from the garbage of neighboring taverns.

Demon, Larvaxu (Second-Category Demon)

Hit Dice: 9
Armor Class: -2 [21]
Attacks: 1 bite (2d8)
Saving Throw: 6
Special: Magic resistance (50%), swallow whole, demonic and magical abilities
Move: 9
Alignment: Chaos
Number Encountered: 1d3 or 1d6
Challenge Level/XP: 13/2,300

The Laravaxu are a second form of Type II demon existing in the depths of the abyss in addition to the better-documented Hezrou form. Laravaxu take half damage from electricity, cold, fire, and poison gas. They are able to cast *darkness* in a radius of 15ft at will, and to *teleport* twice per day. In addition, they have the ability to *detect invisibility*, cause *fear* (as per a wand), and to *telekinese* 200 pounds of weight, each usable at will.

Laravaxu have the form of a massive, slimy grub with a huge mouth. They cannot be damaged with blunt weapons, but normal piercing or cutting weapons will damage them. The Laravaxu's only attack is its bite, but if the demon rolls a natural 19 or 20 on its to-hit roll, the opponent has been swallowed whole. Any creature swallowed by the demon will be turned into a demonic larva within 1d3+5 melee rounds unless the Laravaxu is killed.

A Laravaxu demon has the ability to *gate* in another Category 2 demon (20% chance of success). When a Laravaxu successfully *gates* in another demon, there is a 50% chance that the summoned demon will be a Hezrou and a 50% chance that it will be another Laravaxu. If several demons end up being summoned into the battle, if the Hezrou outnumber the Laravaxu by 2:1 or more, the Hezrou will fall upon the Laravaxu and attempt to kill them.

— Author: Matt Finch

Second-Category Demon (Laravaxu type): HD 9; AC -2[21]; Atk 1 bite (2d8); Move 9; Save 6; AL C; CL/XP 13/2300; Special: Magic resistance 50%, swallow whole, demonic magical powers.

The Piper

The Pipe Cleaners Union of Bard's Gate is on strike. Despite the direct request to return to work by **Tunnel Foreman Gorbit Ashenchisel**, the union refuses to comply. The union workers claim that a week ago, they noticed that the sewer rats disappeared entirely. Soon after the rats vanished, workers stopped returning from assignments in the Canal District. The magistrate has offered a 1,000 gp reward for anyone who solves the mystery so the workers can return to their vital tasks.

Exploring the sewers at this time proves a difficult task. Due to the lack of pipe cleaners and scavenging rats, the sewage is backing up. Clogged pipes and fermenting waste fill the sewer drains, backing up the stagnant waters. Standing waste water pools in the tunnels. The system remains eerily quiet without the flowing sewer or the chattering of warm-blooded vermin.

Large maggots and grubs wriggle in the mold-encrusted waste filling the canal. Infesting the island of rancid feces are **2d6 lemure demons** that wriggle slug-like around a central floating block of waste. A gold idol of a bloated demonic figure playing a silver flute (2,100 gp) sits half-buried in the muck. If the flute is cleaned and played, it heals 1d6 points of damage to anyone hearing it once per day.

In a central sewage exchange chamber under the massive blockage, lives a **laravaxu demon**. The demon curls up in a bend in the sewer pipes, and drags its bulk out to attack anyone disturbing the island.

Lemure Demon: HD 3; AC 7[12]; Atk 1 claw (1d3); Move 3; Save 14; AL C; CL/XP 4/120; Special: Regenerate (1hp/round).

Demon, Lemures

Hit Dice: 3
Armor Class: 7 [12]
Attacks: Claw (1d3)
Saving Throw: 14
Special: Regenerate (1 hp/round)
Move: 3
Alignment: Chaos
Number Encountered: 1d6+4 or 6d6
Challenge Level/XP: 4/120

Lemures are vaguely humanoid, but their flesh is mud-like, shifting and soft upon their horrible bodies. (This amorphous form allows them to regenerate 1 hp per round.) Lemures are lower forms of demons, the fleshly manifestations of damned souls. These demons can be permanently destroyed only by sprinkling their disgusting bodies with holy water.

Lemure Demon: HD 3; AC 7[12]; Atk 1 claw (1d3); Move 3; Save 14; AL C; CL/XP 4/120; Special: Regenerate (1hp/round).

Dough Boys

A towering chimney is the most prominent feature of this large brick building. Heavenly aromas of baked pastries, sweet breads and other delicacies fill the air. A large silhouette of a huge cupcake hangs above the door. **Nootbar Tallet** inherited the bakery from generations of Tallets before him. His heart is not quite into baking as a living, however, so he dabbles in black magic. He uses his spell-crafting talents to enhance and create his confectionary masterpieces. His pastries are highly sought after by the wealthy and nobility alike. In his greed, he has relied more on magic than his skill or legendary family recipes.

Nootbar has a problem. In order to cut costs of labor he summoned **2 lemures** to work the ovens and perform menial tasks. Unfortunately, the lemures' evil dispositions and low intelligence make them poor servants. The resulting baked goods do not stand up to the Tallet family's reputation. Sickened clients, foul tastes and unsavory appearance led to a decline in business and income. Now, the flour-covered lemures refuse to leave and Nootbar cannot talk his employees into working alongside the pasty lemures. The lemures continue to bake, wielding giant wooden spatulas and oven forks. The doughy lemures wear chef hats, all the while laughing at the mayhem going on around them.

Nootbar, Magic-user Level 4: HP 10; AC 9 [10]; Atk 1 dagger (1d4); Move 12; Save 12 (10 vs. spells); AL C; CL/XP 4/120; Special: Spells (3/2). Equipment: Dagger, spellbook.

Demon, Manes

Hit Dice: 1
Armor Class: 5[14]
Attacks: 2 claws (1d2), 1 bite (1d4)
Saving Throw: 18
Special: Half damage from non-magic weapons
Move: 5
Alignment: Chaos
Number Encountered: 4d4
Challenge Level/XP: 2/30

Pathetic, damned souls, manes are demons no larger than humans, with gray skin and empty eyes. Non-magical weapons inflict only half normal damage on them.

Manes Demon: HD 1; AC 5[14]; Atk 2 claws (1d2), 1 bite (1d4); Move 5; Save 18; AL C; CL/XP 2/30; Special: Half damage from non-magic weapons.

A Sea of Hands

A smooth rock landing overlooks an unfathomable scene. Several iron, canoe-like boats sit adjacent to the entrance. Iron barbs and rusty blades adorn the boats' exteriors. Whips, tridents and tri-bladed spears lie in the bottom of the boats. The depth of the floor of this massive chamber cannot easily be determined. Thousands of grey hands reach upward from the mass of tightly packed **manes demons** filling the lower reaches of the room. Their grasping hands sit level with the entry floor. Every so often a manes manages to escape from the mass and attempts to flee only to be pulled back down into the grasping horde.

Several exits line the far side of the chamber. A **glabrezu** charges from one of the portals across the lake of hands. The manes' hands meet each step of the glabrezu, supporting its weight as if it were walking on solid ground. Any evil being can walk upon the manes without hindrance. Those of non-evil alignment are pulled under and torn apart by the countless manes. The manes carry any creatures within the boats on command. One simply has to state what direction and speed for the manes to safely carry boat riders. The manes scream in agony as the boats rip through their hands and heads. Regardless of the pain, they obediently move the boats over the mass. The manes can surprisingly pass the boats along above their heads as fast as a horse can run.

Glabrezu, Third-Category Demon: HD 10; AC –3[22]; Atk 2 pincers (2d6), 2 claws (1d3), 1 bite 1d4+1; Move 9; Save 5; AL C; CL/XP 11/1700; Special: Magic resistance (60%), demonic magical powers.

Demon, Marilith (Fifth-Category Demon)

Hit Dice: 7
Armor Class: 7 [12]
Attacks: 6 weapons (1d8), tail (1d8)
Saving Throw: 8
Special: Magic resistance (80%), +1 or better magic weapon required to hit, immune to fire, magical abilities
Move: 12
Alignment: Chaos
Number Encountered: 1d3 or 1d6
Challenge Level/XP: 13/2,300

Mariliths appear as a cruel-eyed beautiful woman with a six-armed torso, but the lower body of a huge constrictor snake. They can wield weapons in all six arms at once, and the tail, if it hits, constricts for automatic damage after the initial hit. Mariliths are among the most feared of demons – as much, even, as the mighty Baalrochs. They can, at will, cast *Charm Person*, *Levitate*, and *Polymorph Self*, and are 80% resistant to magic. Fire does not affect them. They have a 50% chance of success when attempting to gate in allies; if the attempt succeeds, roll 1d12 to determine the result. (1-3) First-category, (4-6) Second-category, (7-8) Third-category, (9-10) Fourth-category, (11) Sixth-category, (12) a demonlord or demon prince.

Fifth-category Demon: HD 7; AC 7[12]; Atk 6 weapons (1d8), tail (1d8); Move 12; Save 8; AL C; CL/XP 13/2,300; Special: Magic resistance (80%), +1 or better magic weapon required to hit, demonic magical powers.

Sphere

This chamber once contained an evil artifact of immense power forged in the bowels of Hell. Its presence on this world acted as a parasite to all that is good and holy. A bulging iron door blocks entry into this chamber. The iron door has melted into a single unmovable sheet of iron welded to the frame. A titanic chamber lies in ruin behind the solid door. Scorched and scared, the room's surfaces tell the story of a horrific battle. Dusty bones, corroded weapons and pieces of armor cover the floor. The remains of men and demons lie mingled in heaps where they perished in battle. Fat pillars uphold the lofty ceiling and obscure vision across the expansive chamber. A harsh light from the depths of the chamber casts deep shadows across the floor. Toward the back of the lightless chamber sits a 20-foot-diameter sphere of iridescent radiance. The scene inside the sphere is drastically different than the room's contents.

Within the sphere, a woman leaps into the air to grasp a ring floating in front of her. Dressed in white leather, the human woman bears an expression of desperation and terror. A man in archaic robes lies on the floor under her. A gigantic iron trident pins him through his chest to the floor. Despite this mortal wound, he shouts something at the woman. Behind the woman stands a **vrock demon** also frozen in time. The vrock appears to chase the woman with a barbed two-handed sword ready to cleave her in two. Amazingly, the creatures with the sphere appear to move in painfully slow motion. The entire scene takes about 10 minutes to play out before the sphere briefly blinks out and repeats the moment. In actuality, the scene only covers about 2 seconds of time. The sphere is a corrupted *time stop* spell that has gone horribly wrong. Those trapped within are bound in a time loop that repeats unendingly. With his last breath, the wizard impaled on the ground finished the spell but the demonic trident tainted the incantation. A perceptive observer may determine that the wizard's last word was "stop."

The woman grasps at a *ring of wishes* (also tainted by the demonic presence). Her wish, which is prevented from fulfillment, was to become powerful enough to stop the demonic horde. Only the vrock survived among the countless demons that once guarded the room. Disturbing any of the sphere's prisoners breaks the *time stop*. Once the spell ends, the

woman in white transforms into a **marilith** complete with six sabers in fulfillment of her wish. As a marilith, her demonic mind takes over and she attacks. Realizing her power, the vrock immediately sides with the marilith. There is one wish remaining on the ring the marilith wears. The dead mage wears magical robes that absorb blows from blunt weapons (AC equal to plate mail versus blunt attacks only). The woman returns to human form if slain or after 24 hours elapse. She is a 12th-level thief.

Vrock Demon: HD 8; AC 1[18]; Atk 1 beak (1d6), 2 foreclaws (1d4), 2 rear claws (1d6); Move 12 (Fly 18); Save 8; AL C; CL/XP 9/1100; Special: Magic resistance (50%), darkness, immune to fire.

Demon, Nalfeshnee (Fourth-Category Demon)

Hit Dice: 7d10
Armor Class: 4 [15]
Attacks: 2 claws (1d4), 1 bite (2d4)
Saving Throw: 9
Special: Magic resistance (65%), +1 or better magic weapon needed to hit, immune to fire, +2 on to-hit rolls, magical abilities
Move: 9/14 (flying)
Alignment: Chaos
Number Encountered: 1d3 or 1d6
Challenge Level/XP: 12/2,000

Nalfeshnee demons have the body of an enormous gorilla, the head of a boar, and cloven hooves. These massive, brutish demons are actually quite intelligent, despite their appearance, an incongruity that has deceived and doomed many who would attempt to control or enslave them. The very size of a nalfeshnee prevents them from being particularly agile flyers, though they do have wings. Nalfeshnee are incredibly powerful (+2 to hit), and have various demonic powers in addition to being immune to fire: they cause fear as per the spell (at will), polymorph self (at will) and dispel magic (at will). They can create a symbol of discord once per day. A nalfeshnee demon has a 60% chance to *gate* in an ally (roll 1d6 to determine which category of demon will respond).

Fourth-category Demon (Nalfeshnee Type): HD 7d10; AC 4[15]; Atk 2 claws (1d4), 1 bite (2d4); Move 9 (Fly 14); Save 9; AL C; CL/XP 12/2000; Special: +1 or better magic weapon needed to hit, magic resistance (65%), +2 on to-hit rolls, immune to fire, magical abilities.

The Forgotten Garden

High in the Hollow Spire Mountains stands a tropical garden surrounded by a low rock wall. Located above the tree line, the garden has a balmy humid environment. Snow piles up along the outside of the wall but not within the garden. No barrier is visible. An unfinished stone arch marks the entrance. A *symbol of discord* etched in stone serves as a keystone. The garden holds unfamiliar giant flowers that grow along the ground amid giant fern-like leaves. A single colorful egg sits in each flower's center. The eggs belong to a race of faerie folk. Long ago, a faerie king defeated a **nalfeshnee demon** in an epic battle. As result of its defeat, the nalfeshnee was forced to serves as guard for 1,000 years.

The nalfeshnee takes the form of a splendid and stunningly female fairy slightly shorter than an elf. The nalfeshnee must stay on the outside of the garden wall and serves to the best of its abilities to protect the garden and faerie folk. Despite its evil nature, the nalfeshnee does not mind serving the fickle faerie folk.

Demon, Quasit

Hit Dice: 3
Armor Class: 2[17]
Attacks: 2 claws (1d2 + non-lethal poison), 1 bite (1d3)
Saving Throw: 14
Special: Magic resistance (25%), regenerate (1 hp/round), non-lethal poison, magical abilities
Move: 14
Alignment: Chaos
Number Encountered: 1 (material plane) or 1d4+1
Challenge Level/XP: 7/600

Quasits are demon familiars, much like imps but without wings and with a less human-like shape. A quasit can polymorph into two other forms (commonly a giant centipede and a bat). These demons are 25% resistant to magic, regenerate at 1hp per round, can become invisible at will, and once per day can cast a Fear spell. Their claws are laden with poison that reduces an opponent's dexterity by 1 point (saving throw applies, lasts for 2d6 rounds).

Quasit: HD 3; AC 2[17]; Atk 2 claws (1d2 + non-lethal poison), 1 bite (1d3); Move 14; Save 14; AL C; CL/XP 7/600; Special: Magic resistance (25%), non-lethal poison, regenerate (1hp/round), magical abilities.

Wild Child

Wild roars of triumph and revelry blast from this small orc settlement. Screams of pain intermingle with the raucous merriment. The **24 orcs** that make up the Black Bone Tribe celebrate around a fire pit. Another 2 dozen orcs lie in tents too sick to move. A young orc girl struggles against chain bindings her to a spit over the fire pit. She screams in terror and pain. The orcish youngling is a recent addition to the tribe (after rescuing her from a local prison wagon). The girl (called Shrawg) is actually a *polymorphed* **quasit**. Its other form is that of a horned lizard. Shrawg wears a *ring of fire resistance* around its tail and feigns agony above the flames.

These downtrodden orcs have had a run of recent bad luck. Their food disappeared, horses ran off, bow strings snapped, etc… With half their tribe immobilized by sickness (quasit poison), the orcs believe themselves to be cursed. They blame (and rightfully so) Shrawg. Shrawg thanks rescuers and promises servitude.

Orc: HD 1; AC 6[13]; Atk 1 by weapon, usually spear (1d6) or scimitar (1d8); Move 9; Save 17; AL C; CL/XP 1/15; Special: None.

Demon, Shaavazi (Fourth-Category Demon)

Hit Dice: 10
Armor Class: -1 [20]
Attacks: 2 claws (1d6)
Saving Throw: 5
Special: Magic resistance (60%), immune to normal weapons, and see below
Move: 12
Alignment: Chaos
Number Encountered: 1d3 or 1d6
Challenge Level/XP: 15/2,900

Shaazavi demons are a fourth-category demon with three vulture-like heads, a human torso, and the legs of a goat.

Shaazavis take only half damage from electricity, cold, fire, and poison gas. They are able to cast *darkness* in a radius of 15ft at will, and to *teleport* once per day. In addition, they have the ability to *detect invisibility*, cause *fear* (as per a wand), and to *telekinese* 300 pounds of weight, any of these abilities being employed at will. Shazavis can *polymorph* themselves, and can cast charm monster 3 times per day.

In addition, each head of a Shaazavi demon can employ a breath weapon, although these cannot all be brought to bear in the same direction at one time, each head "covering" a 120-degree angle around the demon. One of the heads can spit a line of acid similar to that of a black dragon; the second head breathes a cone of fire as a red dragon, and the third head exhales a cloud of gas similar to that of a green dragon. Each breath weapon inflicts 5d6 points of damage, with a successful saving throw indicating half damage.

Shaazavi demons cannot be damaged by normal weapons; magic weapons are required to damage them. A Shaazavi demon can attempt to *gate* in another demon with a 60% chance of success. The demon appearing may be of Category 1, 2, 3, or 4 (roll 1d4 to determine type).

Most Shaazavis have individual names.

— Author: Matt Finch

Shaazavi Demon: HD 10; AC -1[20]; Atk 2 claws (1d6); Move 12; Save 5; AL C; CL/XP 15/2900; Special: Magic resistance (60%), immune to non-magic weapons, demonic and magical abilities.

When the Bell Tolls

In the center of the large brewing community of Alement stands a 20-foot-tall monument carved from granite. On the north face of the obelisk is a large six-foot-tall bronze visage of a satyr. The satyr wears an expression of joy. Its wide grinning mouth is agape. The open mouth extends into the obelisk about an arm's length. A 30-foot-wide band of solid stone flush with the ground surrounds the base. Numbers, algorithms and celestial designs set in bronze adorn the ring of stone. Atop the 8-foot-wide obelisk sits a wide bronze arrow. Glass orbs of varying colors bisect the arrow, allowing light to travel through the exquisite bronze casting. The arrow acts as a sundial to the numeric figures and symbols below. The timepiece also works at night by magically absorbing light from stars and other celestial bodies. Scholars and soothsayers from around the region speculate on the origin and purpose of this relic from ancient times.

During solstices or other astronomical phenomena, the timepiece shimmers with magical light and a resounding gong issues from within the stone. During this time, gold coins (usually 10d10 x10), fine ale, 10d10 random gems (10 gp each) or other blessings pour forth from the satyr's gaping mouth. They place an urn beneath the mouth to collect the blessings.

The citizens of Alement are now joyously gathered to celebrate the upcoming solstice, unaware that a shaavazi demon has spent the past month corrupting the obelisk. As the men and women dance merrily around the stone ring, the mouth begins vomiting forth gallons of bile,

fermented ale and the partially digested remains of a satyr. Anyone near the stone must make a saving throw or be overcome with nausea at the horrible smell that issues from the stone. As the townsfolk are emptying their stomachs, a **shaavazi demon** appears in a massive cloud of putrid smoke and pyrotechnics atop the timepiece. The demon vicious attacks all in the area. The demon remains until the sun rises.

Demon, Vrock (First-Category Demon)

Hit Dice: 8
Armor Class: 0 [19]
Attacks: 1 beak (1d6), 2 foreclaws (1d8), 2 rear claws (1d8)
Saving Throw: 8
Special: Magic resistance (50%), immune to fire, darkness
Move: 12/18 (flying)
Alignment: Chaos
Number Encountered: 1d3 or 1d6
Challenge Level/XP: 11/1,700

These demons are vulture-headed, with feathered but humanoid bodies, and huge dark-feathered wings. All can create darkness in a radius of 5ft and are immune to fire. They use their wings to allow both their arms and legs to be brought into combat, along with their beaked bite. Vrock demons are quite stupid, though like most demons they consider themselves to be tremendously intelligent. A Vrock has a 10% chance to *gate* another first-category demon to its assistance.

Vrock Demon: HD 8; AC 0[19]; Atk 1 beak (1d6), 2 foreclaws (1d8), 2 rear claws (1d6); Move 12 (Fly 18); Save 8; AL C; CL/XP 11/1700; Special: Magic resistance (50%), darkness, immune to fire.

Birds of a Feather

On the rocky cliffs bordering the Hollow Spire Mountains sits a ruined temple of Pazuzu, demon lord of the winds. A harrowing climb leads PCs to the temple sitting atop a thick column of granite. The outer temple is little more than a small ziggurat carved into the top of the column. The only entrance appears to be filled with seamless stone. Paladins ransacked the temple decades ago and filled the entrance with a wall of stone to seal off any evil lingering within the depths.

Winged demons made of the same seamless stone stand atop the temple's crown, each facing one of the Cardinal directions. The effigies surround a 10-foot-diameter hole that descends 50 feet where a magical stone floor seals the pit. Each stone statue points to the horizon with a clawed talon. A whistling scream resonates from each gaping maw as living creatures pass before the statue. While evil lies imprisoned below, cultist and followers of Pazuzu still pay homage to the dark god in the outer temple. Skulking around the ziggurat are **2d4 gargoyles**. In addition, Pazuzu commissioned a large and unusually cunning **vrock** to re-establish the temple. Thus far, the vrock has been able to breach the stone walls. It waits to see if PCs break through the stone, then ambushes them in the temple entrance to keep them from polluting the temple grounds.

Gargoyle: HD 4; AC 5[14]; Atk 2 claws (1d3), 1 bite (1d4), 1 horn (1d6); Move 9 (Fly 15); Save 13; AL C; CL/XP 6/400; Special: Fly, magic weapon required to hit.

Demon, Yildra

Hit Dice: 7
Armor Class: 3 [16]
Attacks: 2 claws (1d6 + slow), 1 bite (1d8), tail (1d4 + poison)
Saving Throw: 9
Special: Disease, poison, magic resistance (10%), demonic immunities
Move: 9
Alignment: Chaos
Number Encountered: 1d4
Challenge Level/XP: 12/2,000

Yildra demons are servitors of Yildraathu, the Demon-Lord of Pestilence, and as such they are not considered to be a general demonic "type." The Yildra take the form of massive rats standing on their hind legs, their fur crawling with vermin and their skin mottled with rot and mange. The demon's long tail bears a wicked barb at the end, and their claws drip with foul ichor.

The claws of a Yildra carry disease, and the barb on the demon's tail carries a lethal poison. The diseased claws have the immediate effect (if a saving throw fails) of causing the diseased victim to move at half speed as if affected by a *slow* spell, and the disease will eventually cause death in 2d6 days if it is not magically cured.

Yildras take only half damage from electricity, cold, fire, and poison gas. They are able to cast *darkness* in a radius of 15ft at will, and to *teleport* once per day. In addition, they have the ability to *detect invisibility*, cause *fear* (as per a wand), and to *telekinese* 300 pounds of weight, any of these abilities being employed at will. Yildras can attempt to summon another Yildra demon, but this can be attempted only once per day and has only a 10% chance of success.

Yildras can be hit with normal weapons, but such weapons have a penalty of -1 to hit and damage against the demon.

— Author: Matt Finch

Yildra Demon: HD 7; AC 3[16]; Atk 2 claws (1d6 + slow), 1 bite (1d8), tail (1d4 + poison); Move 9; Save 9; AL C; CL/XP 12/2000; Special: Disease, poison, magic resistance (50%), darkness, demonic immunities.

Rat Stink

The small prison known as Bastion Evince is known throughout the land as a prison for those committing minor infractions. The prison sits on a rock island in the midst of a large man-made lake. A floating bridge connects the towering prison with the mainland. As a labor camp, prisoners are taken to the adjacent quarries to mine limestone blocks for foundations throughout the land. Prisoners' crimes range from petty theft to tax evasion. The hard labor usually detours repeat offenders.

Endrad arrives every morning to lead prisoners in prayer (to Freya), comfort the dying, and cure the sick. The conditions in Bastion Evince have worsened over the past year. Despite steps taken by the warden, guards and the visiting cleric, prisoners constantly contract diseases. Plague-ridden fleas and rats swarm to the deteriorating jail.

During a recent morning prayer, a **yildra demon** arrived to slay Joandolar and bring death and pestilence to the prison. The yildra manifested inside the temple and began slaughtering prisoners and guards alike as it tried to reach Joandolar. Guards and prisoners alike fled the prison. While some escaped, many others are still chained and shackled together in the main room. The guards have their hands full trying to restore order and can't stop to find missing prisoners.

While the upper prison remains clean, the lower halls and cells are filled with corpses and swarms of rats. Adding to the misery, disease-carrying fleas, skin mites and mosquito swarms buzz throughout the prison. Joandolar locked himself in a cell deep within the compound. He is safe, but the yildra waits patiently for Joandolar to attempt to escape. It

deals violently with any rescuers sent to retrieve the priest.

Endrad, Cleric Level 6: HP 14; AC 9 [10]; Atk 1 mace (1d6); Move 12; Save 10 (8 vs. paralysis and poison); AL C; CL/XP 6/400; Special: Banish undead, spells (2/2/1/1). Mace, unholy symbol

Demon Prince, Isclaadra

DEMON-PRINCE OF MISTS
Hit Dice: 22 (110 hit points)
Armor Class: -6 [25]
Attacks: 1 staff (6d6) or 2 claws (2d6)
Saving Throw: 3
Special: Magic resistance (90%), +2 weapon required to hit, also see below
Move: 12/12 (flying)
Alignment: Chaos
Challenge Level/XP: 30/7,400

Isclaadra is a tall, human-like figure with the horns and legs of a goat, and massive bat wings. He is one of the weakest of the demon princes, and he is uncharacteristically subtle when compared to his peers. He has the spell-casting ability of an 8th level magic-user in addition to the powers described below, and can only be hit by weapons of +2 or greater.

At will, Isclaadra can cast *charm monster, clairvoyance, continual darkness, dispel magic, ESP, fear, read languages, read magic, telekinesis* (1,000 pounds of weight), and *suggestion.*

Isclaadra's Staff of Mist is a powerful magic artifact, allowing the holder to enter gaseous form at will, and capable of summoning forth one of three types of mist (each once per day):

Mist of Magic Absorption: this mist can be streamed forth from the staff up to a distance of 100ft before it expands. Once it blossoms into a cloud, it eats magic in an area 50ft in diameter, temporarily removing all bonuses or other effects from magic items while they are in the mist. The power of the mist does not extend to powerful artifacts, but is enough to suppress magical swords, armor, and miscellaneous items. Spells cannot be cast within the mist, but the effects of a spell that has already been cast (e.g. *invisibility* or *haste*) are unaffected by the mist, and potions will also take effect if imbibed in the mist. The holder of the staff can cause the mist to creep in any direction, but it has a move of only 10ft. Its duration is 5d6 turns

Mist of Confusion: the range, size, move, and duration of the Mist of Confusion are all identical to those of the Mist of Magic Absorption. Its effect is that of a *confusion* spell.

Mist of Striking: The Mist of Striking is a thin ribbon of vapor that extends from the staff up to a length of 100ft. It can attack once per round as a 30HD monster, inflicting 2d6 points of damage. Other than by *dispel magic* against a 12th level caster, the Mist of Striking cannot be killed, although it will disappear after 5d6 turns.

— *Author: Matt Finch*

Demon Prince Isclaadra: HD 22 (110hp); AC –6[25]; Atk 1 staff (6d6) or 2 claws (2d6); Move 12 (Fly 12); Save 3; CL/XP 30/7400; Special: Magic resistance (90%), +2 magic weapon required to hit, spells, staff of mist, magical abilities.

Harbor Mist

The coastal town of Niborlyn recently experienced a handful of misfortunes, but their most recent hardship brought them to the edge of oblivion. A massive fog bank moved over the town, cutting off all visible access to the fishing settlement. The fog severely limits visibility, allowing only a few feet of sight. Even magically enhanced vision falters in the thick, churning fog. The fog bank surrounds the town and stretches about half a mile wide. The fog lightens within the town's boundaries, allows visibility for about 20 feet. Winds don't disperse the cloud, and the fog defies nature. In fact, the winds blowing off the sea can't budge the mist.

All attempts to breach the surrounding fog have failed; **allips, wraiths** and **spectres** lurk within the fog, taking full advantage of the concealment. Each round spent in the fog has a 2 in 6 chance of attracting the undead. In addition, several **gigantic crabs** and hordes of **giant sea spiders** scuttle through the fog. The undead leave the vermin alone. Sensing the impending doom of the community, a **kraken** sits just off the coast,

grabbing those who attempt to escape by water.

The **Demon Prince Isclaadra** floats on a column of billowing vapor above the town's well. Furthermore, a **khryll** hides in the well, ready to protect Isclaadra. The demon prince arrived several days ago and slew the town's militia. Isclaadra demands the willing hand of Ceila Cregzyn in matrimony. Ceila, the virginal, young adult daughter of a single mother, hides within her home. She is the bastard child of Commander Shallatin Green, a paladin in the great northern fortress of Shieldfane. The paladin cross Isclaadra nearly a year ago, and the demon prince spent the time seeking out a way to bring down the haughty warrior. Isclaadra has his own twisted reasons for wanting to marry the girl, but it all leads to destroying the knight. The marriage must have Ceila's compliance and be performed by a righteous priest of sanctity. Ceila's mother screams for aid against the demon.

Allip: HD 4; AC 5[14]; Atk 1 strike (no damage, 1d4 points of wisdom lost); Move (fly 6); Save 13; AL C; CL/XP 7/600; Special: drains wisdom, hypnosis.

Wraith: HD 4; AC 3[16]; Atk 1 touch (1d6+ level drain); Move 9 (Fly 24); Save 13; AL C; CL/XP 6/400; Special: drain 1 level with hit.

Spectre: HD 7; AC 2[17]; Atk 1 spectral weapon or touch (1d8 + level drain); Move 15 (Fly 30); Save 9; AL C; CL/XP 9/1100; Special: Drain 2 levels with hit, immune to non-magical weapons.

Giant Crab: HD 3; AC 3[16]; Atk 2 pincers (1d6+2); Move 9; Save 14; AL N; CL/XP 3/60; Special: None.

Giant Spider (4ft diameter): HD 2+2; AC 6[13]; Atk 1 bite (1d6 + poison); Move 18; Save 16; AL N; CL/XP 5/240; Special: lethal poison, 5 in 6 chance to surprise prey.

Khryll: HD 8; AC 3[16]; Atk 8 tentacles (none); Move 9; Save 8; AL C; CL/XP 9/1,100; Special: Mental blast, liquefy internal organs, magic resistance (80%)

Kraken: HD 20; AC 0[19]; Atk 6 tentacles (2d6), bite (3d6); Move (Swim 3) (Jet 21); Save 3; AL C; CL/XP 24/5600; Special: Ink cloud, constriction, control weather, create lights.

Demon Prince, Kharkazax

DEMON-PRINCE OF CARRION
Hit Dice: 30 (120 hit points)
Armor Class: -6 [25]
Attacks: 2 claws (2d8), 1 bite (4d8)
Saving Throw: 3
Special: Magic resistance (70%), +3 or better weapon to hit, also see below
Move: 9/12 (flying)
Alignment: Chaos
Challenge Level/XP: 38/9,800

Kharkazax resembles a humanoid jackal with the wings and head of a vulture, and he is always accompanied by 6 vrock-type demons of maximum hit points. This demon-lord is known as the Prince of Carrion, for his followers are scavengers and carrion-eaters of all kinds, including, unpleasantly, his human cultists. Although he is brilliant and subtle, Kharkazax is more feral in combat than most demon princes; if he is forced into melee combat he will tear into his foes with beak and claws rather than using weapons. Any creature other than a demon coming within 50ft of him will be affected by his smell, as if by a *slow* spell (no saving throw). His bite is diseased, causing death within 1d4+1 rounds if the rapid course of the disease is not checked (if a saving throw succeeds, the disease merely causes 1d4 points of damage each round, for 1d4+1 rounds, but does not kill).

At will, Kharkazax can cast *charm monster, clairvoyance, continual darkness, dispel magic, ESP, fear, read languages, read magic, telekinesis* (1,000 pounds of weight), and *suggestion*. Once per day, Kharkazax can create a wall of vermin, a mass of roaches and centipedes that rises 40ft in height and 100ft in length, or forms a covered dome thirty feet across and twenty feet in height. The biting creatures in the wall automatically inflict 2d10+20 points of damage against anyone breaking through it, and 1d10 hit points per round against anyone trying to attack it with a melee weapon. The wall is armor class 8, and has 100 hit points. Kharkazax can see through the eyes of his wall-vermin, and cast spells from the wall as if he were standing within it, but for all others the wall blocks vision and cannot be penetrated by spells. Demons take no damage from passing through the wall unless Kharkazax so desires.

This demon-prince cannot be damaged by weapons of less than +3 enchantment.

— *Author: Matt Finch*

Demon Prince Kharkazax: HD 30 (120hp); AC −6[25]; Atk 2 claws (2d8) and 1 bite (4d8); Move 9 (Fly 12); Save 3; CL/XP 38/9800; Special: Magic resistance (70%), +3 magic weapon required to hit, magical abilities.

Carrion Capacity

A horrible stench expands to fill nearly a mile radius. Largely avoided by locals, Carrion Knoll is a haven for vultures. Ancient dead trees litter the hillsides, offering bountiful roosting opportunities for the hundreds of scavenger birds flocking to this area. During the day, a continual spiral of vultures lazily encircles the knoll. The burned ruins of a cathedral of Freya sit atop the knoll's peak. Only the thick walls and buttresses of the massive temple remain. Unlike most scavengers, the vultures bring their decaying meals here to feast. Countless bones and carcasses cover the grounds and hang from dead tree limbs. Jackals and forest hyenas lurk in the shadows, yipping and laughing at the approach of strangers. Clouds of flies swarm the air and hordes of harmless carrion beetles shift under the carcasses. Carrion Knoll started off innocently enough as the local farmers used the yawning well atop the knoll as a dumping grounds for diseased livestock and other refuse. Eventually, the community used the well to dispose of criminals and other unsavory races that encroached on their livelihood. The ruins finally fell into the clutches of the demon lord of carrion, **Kharkazak**, who treats the entire area as a shrine to his putrescence.

Currently, the former temple of Freya on Carrion Knoll serves as a focal point for the degenerate cultists of Kharkazak. While cultists often do not linger on the knoll, there are always **3d6 feral humans** devouring rotting carcasses throughout the wasteland. While the feral humans pose no threat to seasoned adventures, **2d4 cultists** (clerics 2–6 level) maintain and defend the temple grounds. Recently, a **giant vulture** delivered the corpse of a titan child. During a grand ceremony, the carrion lord and **1d4 vrocks** joined in a magnificent feast.

Vrock Demon: HD 8; AC 1[18]; Atk 1 beak (1d6), 2 foreclaws (1d4), 2 rear claws (1d6); Move 12 (Fly 18); Save 8; AL C; CL/XP 9/1100; Special: Magic resistance (50%), darkness, immune to fire.

Giant Vulture: HD 4; AC 7[12]; Atk 2 talons (1d4), 1 bite (1d8); Move 3 (Fly 24); Save 13; CL/XP 4/120; Special: None.

Demon Prince, Orcus

DEMON-PRINCE OF THE UNDEAD
Hit Dice: 30 (125hp)
Armor Class: –6 [25]
Attacks: Wand of Orcus (2d6 or death) or 2 fists (3d6) and tail sting (2d6 plus poison)
Saving Throw: 3
Special: Command undead, spells, summon undead, +3 or better weapon to hit, immunity to electricity and poison, speak with dead, magic resistance (75%), telepathy 100 ft.
Move: 18/24 (flying)
Alignment: Chaos
Challenge Level/XP: 40/10400

Orcus is one of the strongest (if not the strongest) and most powerful of all demon lords. Known as the Prince of the Undead, he fights a never-ending war against rival demon princes that spans several Abyssal layers. From his great bone palace he commands his troops as they wage war across the smoldering and stinking planes of the Abyss. Orcus spends most of his days in his palace, rarely leaving its confines unless he decides to leads his troops into battle (which has happened on more than one occasion). Most of the time though, he is content to let his generals and commanders lead the battles.

Orcus is a squat, bloated humanoid standing 15 feet tall and weighing 3 tons. His goat-like head sports large, spiraling ram-like horns and his legs are covered in thick brown fur and end in hooves. Two large, black, bat-like wings protrude from his back and a long, snake-like tail, tipped with a sharpened barb, trails behind it.

When not warring against rival demon princes, Orcus likes to travel the planes, particularly the Material Plane. Should a foolish spellcaster open a *gate* and speak his name, he is more than likely going to hear the call and step through to the Material Plane. What happens to the spellcaster that called him usually depends on the reason for the summons and the power of the spellcaster. Extremely powerful spellcasters are usually slain after a while and turned into undead soldiers or generals in the demon lord's armies.

Combat

Orcus prefers to fight using his *Wand*. His tail sting delivers a virulent poison (save or die). Orcus can command or banish undead as a 15th-level cleric, controlling up to 150 HD worth of undead at one time. He casts spells as a 15th level Cleric and 12th level Magic-user, and can use the following magical abilities at will: *animate dead, charm monster, darkness, dispel magic, ESP, fear, feeblemind* (1/day), *lightning bolt, speak with dead, symbol (any)* and *wall of fire.*

Orcus radiates a 60-foot-radius aura of fear (as the spell). A creature in the area must succeed at a saving throw or be affected as though by a fear spell.

Three times per day, Orcus can summon one balor, 1d3 nalfeshnees or 1d4 mariliths. As their prince, Orcus can summon up to 100 HD of any type of undead each day.

Wand of Orcus: Mighty Orcus wields a huge, black, skull-tipped rod that functions as a *+3 heavy mace*. It slays any living creature it touches if the target fails a saving throw. Further, the *Wand* has the following magical powers: 3/day—*animate dead, darkness and fear*; 2/day—*unholy word.* Orcus occasionally allows his wand to pass into the Material Plane, usually into the hands of one of his servants.

Orcus: HD 30 (125hp); AC –6[25]; Atk Wand of Orcus (2d6 or death) or 2 fists (3d6) and tail sting (2d6 plus poison); Move 18 (Fly 24); Save 3; AL C; CL/XP 40/10400; Special: Command undead, spells, summon undead, +3 or better weapon to hit, immunity to electricity and poison, speak with dead, magic resistance (75%), telepathy 100 ft.

Orcus and Cake

On the 29th day of the first month, the residents of Covahlam gather to celebrate the birthday of their beloved leader, King Montague I. Every year, the royal baker outdoes himself, creating a masterful cake big enough to feed a kingdom. The 12-foot-tall, tiered cake is nearly 20 feet in diameter. Sugar sculptures celebrating Montague's life decorate its edges. His battle with the dread dragon is a highlight along one cake tier, and his dousing of the elemental fires of Krill is an orange-frosting lover's delight. Each year, a new candle holder is added to the magnificent cake to celebrate the king's latest birthday. An artist is sought out each year to design a magnificent holder to outdo last year's creation.

This year, however, things went horribly wrong. The artist died shortly after completing this year's candle holder. The white-and-black creation is crafted from a dragon's wing bone and looks like a curling finger pointing skyward. It has a natural bone spur on the tip that looks like a grinning skull. When a wax candle is added, the skull's eyes glow red and smoke rolls from its mouth. The effect is horrific, but the royal court doesn't have an option: The king's birthday is tonight, and it is too late to find another candle holder. They hope to hide the candle holder and distract the king and his guests.

What they don't know is that priests of Orcus killed the artist and replaced his creation with this wicked artifact bathed in the blood of hundreds of innocents. The bone candle holder served as the focal point for their sacrifices for 10 years, all time spent preparing it for this very moment. When a candle is placed in the holder and lit, powerful summoning spells poured into the bone over the years are completed. The candle holder immediately opens a portal for the dread **Orcus** to enter the castle's grand ballroom. The demon-prince erupts out of the cake to slay the revelers trapped at the party.

Demon Princess, Teratashia

DEMON-PRINCESS OF DIMENSIONS
Hit Dice: 31 (130 hit points)
Armor Class: -6 [25] or -8 [27]
Attacks: 4 claws (2d6)
Saving Throw: 3
Special: Magic resistance (85%), +2 or better weapon to hit, regeneration in darkness, improved AC (speed) in light, necklace of skulls, demonic powers
Move: 12/24 (flying)
Alignment: Chaos
Challenge Level/XP: 42/11,000

The Demon-Princess Teratashia's dark palace in the depths of the Abyss is a nexus of countless gaps between dimensions, a warren of tunnels worming their way deep into a multitude of other realities. From the center of this web of connections, Teratashia sends her minions creeping and slithering through the planes of existence to do her bidding. Her darkswimmer demons (q.v.) are but one of the many types of servitors employed by this horrid creature.

Teratashia resembles a huge, female-headed cockroach with a feral visage, wearing a necklace of human skulls. This necklace is a powerful artifact (see, "The Necklace of Skulls," below). She is often known as the Mistress of Dimensions, and her servants include many demons and other creatures that hunt and hide in the dark non-places between the true planes of existence.

At will, Teratashia can cast *charm monster, clairvoyance, continual darkness, dimension door, dispel magic, ESP, insect swarm* (3/day), *fear, read languages, read magic, telekinesis* (1,000 pounds of weight), *teleport, suggestion,* and *wall of stone*. In darkness, she regenerates 2 hit points per round, and in the light she moves with preternatural speed, her armor class improving to -8. Only weapons with an enchantment of +2 or more can damage her.

Teratashia's Necklace of Skulls has 25 charges, and recharges itself within 25 hours (one charge per hour). Each round (until the charges are expended) the necklace can perform one of the following actions in addition to Teratashia's other abilities).

Cone of Cold (3 charges)
Cure the wearer of 2d8 hit points of damage (2 charges)
Darkness 30ft radius (1 charge)
Death spell (5 charges)
Fireball (2 charges)
Knock spell (1 charge)
Wizard lock (1 charge)

Teratashia seldom involves herself in the quarrels of the other great demons, being far more interested in controlling the nooks and crannies between dimensions than with her political status in the Abyss.

Demon-Princess Teratashia: HD 25 (130hp); AC –6[25] or -8[27]; Atk 4 claws (2d6); Move 12 (Fly 24); Save 3; AL C; CL/XP 42/11000; Special: Magic resistance (85%), +2 or better weapon to hit, regeneration in darkness, improved AC (speed) in light, necklace of skulls, demonic powers.

Dimensional Dementia

The black reflective door to this alien room melts into a mercury-like substance across the floor as soon as a living creature touches its surface. The door reforms once a living creature enters the camber beyond or after 1 minute elapses. Once inside the room, the door cannot be opened by non-magical means, and is as strong as a 10-inch-thick iron slab.

Small, three- and four-sided pyramids cover the floor of this angular chamber. The 2- to 4-inch-tall shapes seem formed from the floor, making walking difficult, but not impossible. The walls slope up to a pyramid-shaped ceiling. A shaft of light from the apex above illuminates a depthless rectangle spinning impossibly on one corner in the center of the room. One side of the rectangle reflects like a highly polished mirror, while the other absorbs light. The reflected light flashes across the room like an extraterrestrial lighthouse, causing *confusion* (save resists) in any living creature it passes over. The eight-foot-tall rectangle spins more rapidly as living creatures enter the room. As the mirrored surface accelerates, a darkly beautiful woman appears in the spinning light and dark pattern of the stone. The woman stands on a featureless plain and begins to float forward. As she approaches the rectangle (from the other side), the small pyramids sink into the floor. As the light passes over the increasingly smooth floor, the fins of **4 darkswimmer demons** break the surface like water. The floor ripples harmlessly like the wake behind a boat as the fins circle.

This forgotten access point provided a cult of Teratashia access to her nexus. Living creatures in the chamber immediately draw the attention of the **demon princess Teratashia** herself. She arrives in 2d4 rounds to ensure no one enters her nexus via this conduit. The portal leads to nightmarish catacombs that serve as her palace between the layers of the Abyss. If the whirling portal is damaged, it explodes in an explosive blast of fire and sulfur (10d6 points of damage, save for half) releasing Teratashia and an additional **1d4 darkswimmers**. Those entering the portal find themselves trapped with no obvious way to return.

Demon, Darkswimmer: HD 6; AC 0[19]; Atk 2 claws (1d6), 1 bite (2d6); Move 24 Fly; Save 7; AL C; CL/XP 11/1,700; Special: Magic resistance (90%), shift dimensions, resist electricity, cold, fire and poison gas, spell-like abilities.

Demon Prince, Thalasskoptis

THE SEA-DEMON LORD
Hit Dice: 30 (125 hit points)
Armor Class: -6 [25]
Attacks: 8 tentacles (2d8)
Saving Throw: 3
Special: Magic resistance 90%, also see below
Move: 12/24 (swimming)
Alignment: Chaos
Challenge Level/XP: 39/10,100

Thalasskoptis is a mass of writhing tentacles with a feral, boyish face in the center. It is a powerful demon-prince that makes its lair in the deep, dark seas of the Abyss, living in a sprawling palace of coral that dives into deep subterranean tunnels beneath the sea floor. Thalasskoptis is the lord of underwater corruption, the sea-dead, and many horrific beasts of the dark, oceanic deeps. It is an occasional rival with Orcus, given that its rulership of the sea-undead conflicts with the broader claims of the other demon-prince, but the two demons are similar enough that they are allies more frequently than enemies in the grim power struggles of the Abyssal realms. Some rivals of Thalasskoptis even dismiss it as the underwater minion of Orcus, a claim which is likely to incur a terrible vengeance from the sea-demon.

Beyond the realms of the Abyss, Thalasskoptis has scattered followings of human cultists, predominantly in coastal communities, and in the deeps he is served by dark tritons (q.v.). From time to time, his dark ships of drowned, undead sailors will rise from the waters to pillage treasure for their dread lord; one reason why his human cults are not attacked or driven off is the potential for reprisal by these ships. When the black fleets rise from the water, reeking of salt and rot, miles of coastline can be purged of life by hordes of Thalasskoptis's dead men, the inhabitants dragged down beneath the waves to serve the master they dismissed with insufficient fear.

At will, Thalasskoptis can cast *animate dead, charm monster, clairvoyance, continual darkness, dispel magic, ESP, fear, read languages, read magic, telekinesis* (1,000 pounds of weight), *teleport, suggestion,* and *wall of stone*. Three times per day, the demon-prince can also squirt a vast cloud of poisonous ink into the air or water, with twice the dimensions of a fireball. Anyone in the area of the cloud must make a saving throw against this poison or die. Anyone looking directly at the demon must also make a saving throw each round or become entranced for 1d4+3 melee rounds, unable to take any actions until the fascination has ended. Thalasskoptis cannot be damaged by any weapon with less than a +3 enchantment.

— *Author: Matt Finch*

Demon-Prince Thalasskoptis: HD 30 (125hp); AC −6[25]; Atk 8 tentacles (2d8); Move 12 (Swim 24); Save 3; AL C; CL/XP 39/10100; Special: Magic resistance (90%), +3 or better weapon to hit, poison ink, gaze attack, demonic powers.

Death Sea

The smell of death drifts across the Reaping Sea, a horrible stench of decaying bodies rising on the winds blowing over the waves. A Sargasso of gray algae floats in the water. Hundreds of dead and decaying bodies are tangled in the pulp of weeds. A dead sperm whale also floats belly up in the mass, its blubber an ugly ashen color. PCs also find dolphins, a giant seahorse and hundreds of normal crabs. All of the creatures are dead.

Sitting in the center of the floating field of death is a giant clam shell that is propped open with a gleaming silver long sword. A 10-foot-diameter ring of weakened weeds surrounds the clamshell. Anyone stepping on the weeds vanishes as they fall straight through the pulpy mass and into the ocean below the floating isle of death. The weapon is a +2 long sword that does double damage to aquatic creatures on a roll of a natural 20.

Below the island, the **Demon-Prince Thalasskoptis** sleeps in a

300-foot-diameter sphere made of dead humanoid bodies sewn together with seaweed. The sphere of bodies has a single opening that tumbles and spins as the ball of bloated corpses moves with the currents. Clinging weeds from above keep the sphere anchored in one spot beneath the floating Sargasso.

The demon-prince rises out of his corpse lair to attack anyone taking the long sword. He is accompanied by **6 giant sharks**, an **undead kraken** and a pack of **2d6 aquatic ghouls**.

Ghoul (Aquatic): HD 2; AC 6[13]; Atk 2 claws (1d3), 1 bite (1d4); Move 9 (18, Swim); Save 16; AL C; CL/XP 3/60; Special: Immunities, paralyzing touch.

Giant Shark (7HD): HD 7; AC 6[13]; Atk 1 bite (1d8+4); Move 0 (Swim 24); Save 9; AL N; CL/XP 7/600; Special: Feeding frenzy.

Kraken Zombie: HD 12; AC 5[14]; Atk 6 tentacles (2d6), bite (3d6); Move: Swim 3 (15, Jet); Save 3; AL N; CL/XP 12/2,000; Special: Ink cloud, constriction, control weather, create lights.

Demon Prince, Yildraathu

DEMON-LORD OF PESTILENCE
Hit Dice: 32 (160 hit points)
Armor Class: -7 [26]
Attacks: 1d6+4 tentacles (1d8+1+disease)
Saving Throw: 3
Special: Magic resistance (60%), +2 weapon to hit, disease, pestilential breath weapon, demonic and magical powers
Move: 6
Alignment: Chaos
Challenge Level/XP: 40/10,400

Yildraathu is a large, bubbling pool of viscous ichor, with tentacles constantly emerging from and sucking back into the horrid mass of the demon-lord's "body."

At will, Yildraathu can cast *charm monster, clairvoyance, continual darkness, dispel magic, ESP, fear, read languages, read magic, telekinesis* (1,000 pounds of weight), and *suggestion.*

If Yildaathu hits an opponent, the opponent must succeed in a saving throw or be afflicted by a disease. This disease, Yildaathu's Plague, immediately causes the loss of 1d6 hit points in addition to the damage caused by the tentacle itself, and the disease may cause death within 3 rounds (a second saving throw is allowed to avoid death). Even if the victim survives, if a cure disease spell is not used to prevent further infection then death will result in 1d4+3 days. A character who has been hit by a tentacle and succeeds with the initial saving throw is not immune to the disease, but each time that a saving throw is made against the disease a bonus of +1 (cumulative) is gained on saving throws made against infection or death from infection.

Three times per day, Yildraathu can breathe forth a cone-shaped blast of pestilence 100ft long and expanding to 60ft in width. Anything in this cloud must make as saving throw against the poisonous breath or suffer the loss of 6d6 hit points of damage, in addition to paralysis for 3 rounds. Success on the saving throw indicates that only half damage is taken and that the paralysis is avoided.

Yildraathu can only be damaged by weapons with an enchantment of +2 or greater.

The yildra demons (q.v.) are particularly associated with Yildraathu, and are summoned from time to time by Yildraathic cults, but the demon-lord is also served by a number of other demon types.

— *Author: Matt Finch*

Demon-Prince Yildraathu: HD 32 (160hp); AC –7[26]; Atk 1d6+4 tentacles (1d8+1+disease); Move 6; Save 3; AL C; CL/XP 40/10400; Special: Magic resistance (60%), +2 weapon to hit, disease, pestilential breath weapon, demonic and magical powers.

Pestilence

Streams of smoke and spiraling flocks of vultures can be seen from miles away over a war-torn battlefield spreading across the plains as far as the eye can see. The thousands of dead hobgoblins and humans lying on the fields appear weeks old, and no clear victor can be determined in the epic battle. Large fires smolder where the deceased were burned. Roaming the battlefield are 2d4 packs of **3d4 ghouls** that devour the recently fallen. A group of **18 evil highwaymen (bandits)** also pillage the dead. They pile the looted plunder on ox-drawn carts. Packs of rabid dogs, swarms of diseased rats and other loathsome scavengers roam the wasteland of decay.

On the peak of a low hill, a group of **7 diseased Yildraathu cultists** (4 Clerics 5; 2 Clerics 7; 1 cleric 10) hold a vigil around a crude pool of collected gore. The ritual is designed to summon a host of plague zombies from the dead soldiers. Once completed, the **10d10 zombies** rise that can transmit a rapid and deadly disease that turns corpses into zombies. If the ceremony is interrupted, an angered **Yildraathu** rises from the pool of gore to exact his wrath. He gates **4 yildra demons** in when he arrives. The yildra coalesce inside the bloated corpses on nearby horses, then burst forth and attack. The cultists have collected 1d10 x 100 gold pieces in random coins.

Ghoul: HD 2; AC 6[13]; Atk 2 claws (1d3), 1 bite (1d4); Move 9; Save 16; AL C; CL/XP 3/60; Special: Immunities, paralyzing touch.

Bandit: HD 1; AC 7[12]; Atk 1 weapon (1d8); Move 12; Save 17; AL C; CL/XP 1/15; Special: None.

Demon, Yildra: HD 7; AC 3[16]; Atk 2 claws (1d6), 1 bite (1d8), tail (1d4); Move 9; Save 17; AL C; CL/XP 1/15; Special: Poison, magic resistance (10%).

Cultist, Cleric 5: HD 5; AC 5[14]; Atk 1 mace (1d6); Move 12; Save 11; AL C; CL/XP 5/240; Special: Cleric Spells (2/2), disease. Gear: Chain mail, mace

Cultist, Cleric 7: HD 7; AC 5[14]; Atk 1 flail (1d8); Move 12; Save 9; AL C; CL/XP 9/1,100; Special: Cleric Spells (2/2/2/1/1), disease. Gear: Chain mail, flail

Cultist, Cleric 10: HD 10; AC 2[17]; Atk +1 mace (1d6+1); Move 12; Save 6; AL C; CL/XP 10/1,400; Special: Cleric Spells (3/3/3/3/3), disease. Gear: *+1 plate mail, +1 mace*

Zombie: HD 2; AC 8[11] or with shield 7[12]; Atk 1 weapon or strike (1d8); Move 6; Save 16; AL N; CL/XP 2/30; Special: Immune to sleep and charm.

Demon-Stirge

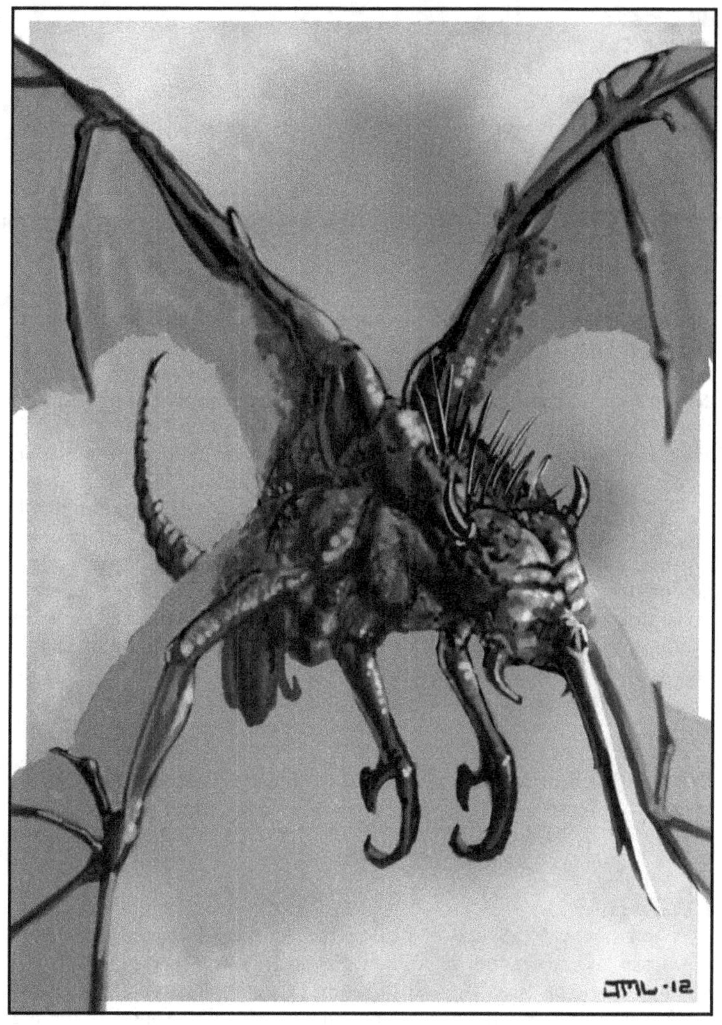

Hit Dice: 2+1
Armor Class: 5[14]
Attacks: 1 proboscis (1d6)
Saving Throw: 16
Special: blood drain (1d6), +2 to hit bonus, disease, darkness.
Move: 3/18 (flying)
Alignment: Chaos
Number Encountered: 3d6
Challenge Level/XP: 3/60

Demon-stirges are the result of magical experimentations with infusing demonic ichor into the bodies of stirges, then breeding the tainted creatures. The result of these experiments, often attributed to the mage Sacavious of the Black Monastery, is a diseased creature more durable and cunning than a natural stirge. A demon-stirge can cast darkness 15ft radius once per day, and there is a 10% chance that with a successful hit, it will infect the character with a disease that will be fatal in 1d4+7 days.

Like a normal stirge, demon-stirges have a proboscis which they jab into their prey to drain blood. After a stirge's first hit, it drains blood automatically at a rate of 1d6 hit points per round. The faster rate of blood-draining is due to barbs and ridges on the proboscis; pulling a dead demon-stirge out of a wound will inflict one last hit point of damage simply from ripping out the barbed tube.

— Originally published in The Black Monastery, by Frog God Games,
adapted to Swords & Wizardry by Matt Finch

Demon-Stirge: HD 2+1; AC 5[14]; Atk 1 proboscis (1d3); Move 3 (Fly 18); Save 16; AL C; CL/XP 3/60; Special: blood drain (1d6), +2 to hit bonus, disease, darkness.

Bats in the Belfry

The ruins of a large cathedral dominate this ruined town. Known on ancient maps as Vaintuel, this large town was founded around the worship of Arden. History does not state what happened to the people or the settlement, but the town now lies devastated. Only the massive stone framework of the bell tower and the partial remains of the church remain intact. A **mongrelman** named **Furgl** lurks in the heights of the bell tower.

Demonic blood runs thick through Furgl's hunched body. In fact, his twisted and diabolical form provides him with immunity to fire and poisons. Furgl's hellish blood has many abilities. It has horribly transformed a swarm of **stirges** living in the bell tower. Furgl has the legs and feet of a goat, the upper torso of an obese human and vestigial horn on his forehead. Furthermore, Furgl has a hump on his upper back. The sentient hump has a twisted but human-like face. Furgl's hump is named Keith. While Keith has no powers other than speech, it constantly belittles and bullies Furgl and anyone it encounters.

While Furgl has good intentions, his low intelligence often countermands his actions.

Furgl begins ringing the church bell to warn visitors of a nest of **6 demon-stirges** that inhabits the tower. The ringing bell awakens the demon-stirges while Keith hurls insults at the approaching heroes. Due to the blood connection, the demon-stirges ally themselves with Furgl and attack all others.

Furgl: HD 3; HP 13; AC 5[14]; Atk 2 horns (1d4); Move 9; Save 14; AL C; CL/XP 7/600; Special: Magic resistance (30%), Immune to blunt damage, fire and poison.

Demon-Wolf of Braazz

Hit Dice: 5
Armor Class: 1 [18]
Attacks: 1 bite (1d10)
Saving Throw: 12
Special: Blink, invisibility, charm, magic weapon required to hit
Move: 15
Alignment: Chaos
Number Encountered: 1d6+3
Challenge Level/XP: 8/800

The demon-wolves of Braazz are creatures from another plane of existence than can be summoned forth by use of forbidden tomes and sorcerous rituals. In their normal shape, they resemble grey-skinned demons with hideous wolf-like faces and the legs and tail of a wolf (the rest of the body being gaunt but human). They are also, however, shape-changers, and can take on the appearance of wolves with twisted human faces.

The Wolves of Braazz can only be hit by a magic weapon, although they do not have any magic resistance to spells. They have certain other supernatural abilities as well: they can blink once per day (teleporting to a random location within 30ft, usually just after attacking or after becoming invisible), they can turn invisible three times per day at will, and they can charm any creature meeting their gaze (although they can maintain this charm over only one creature at a time).

— Originally published in The Black Monastery, by Frog God Games, adapted to Swords & Wizardry by Matt Finch

Demon-Wolf of Braazz: HD 5; AC 1[18]; Atk 1 bite (1d10); Move 15; Save 12; AL C; CL/XP 8/800; Special: Blink, invisibility, charm, magic weapon required to hit.

Huntress

A massive wooden lodge sits on the forested hillside. The lodge resembles more of a fort than a cabin. Skins of cave bear, giant elk and mammoths lie on stretching racks. Giant primeval skulls hang from the roof. A thick coating of rotting animal hair covers the ground. A boiling vat of rendered fat spills a thick sludge into the fire below. The noxious oil smoke clings to everything, leaving a gritty slick residue.

The **hill giant** huntress **Asul Gul** stalks the land searching for prey. Large even for a hill giant, she carries a tree-sized spear and a ballista when she hunts. Asul Gul has trained a pack of **5 worgs** to track quarry. She also adopted a small ugly wolf that leads her pack. The wolf is actually a **demon-wolf of Braazz** that has found this relationship to its liking. In fact, the demon-wolf serves as the brains and true leader of the hunters. Summoned by a wizard long ago (it ate the careless spellcaster), the demon-wolf has terrorized the lands ever since.

Hill Giant: HD 8+2; AC 4[15]; Atk 1 spear (2d8+3) or ballista (3d4); Move 12; Save 8; AL C; CL/XP 9/1100; Special: Throw boulders.

Worg: HD 4; AC 6[13]; Atk 1 bite (1d6+1); Move 18; Save 13; AL C; CL/XP 4/120; Special: None.

Demonvessel

Hit Dice: 6
Armor Class: 2 [17]
Attacks: 2 claws (1d8)
Saving Throw: 11
Special: Magic resistance 10%, +1 or better weapon to hit, immunities
Move: 12
Alignment: Chaos
Number Encountered: 1
Challenge Level/XP: 9/1,100

A demonvessel is a corpse that has been animated by trapping the essence of a demon within the body rather than relying on the more basic necromantic means of animating corpses. Depending upon the exact method used to bind the demon into a dead corpse, these undead creatures usually resemble mummies, but in some cases they will appear to be zombies with strange runes tattooed into the skin. These undead do not have any particularly unusual attacks, but their minor magic resistance, immunity to normal weapons, and demonic immunities (see below) make them dangerous opponents, particularly when they are commanding numbers of lesser undead. A demonvessel is turned as a vampire, and is affected by *protection from evil* spells.

Demonvessels take only half damage from lightning, fire, and cold, and they are unaffected by charm and sleep magic. They have the ability to take permanent control of any non-intelligent undead within speaking distance, and can charm ghouls (although the ghoul would be allowed a saving throw). For this reason, demonvessels are often found leading packs or even small hordes of such lesser undead. Demonvessels are no more intelligent than the demon imprisoned within, so there is a certain amount of variation: many are little more intelligent than ghouls, but some of them are quite crafty and subtle, capable of long range planning and unexpectedly devious thinking.

Most demonvessels will be encountered with a band of 2d4 skeletons, 2d4 zombies, 1d6 ghouls, and 1d2-1 ghasts. These undead are all turned as vampires while under the command of the demonvessel.

— *Author: Matt Finch*

Demonvessel: HD 6; AC 2[17]; Atk 2 claws (1d8); Move 12; Save 11; AL C; CL/XP 9/1100; Special: Magic resistance 10%, +1 or better weapon to hit, immunities.

Wife Resolved

Since his wife's natural death, the successful lamp merchant Garrick has wallowed in self-pity. He offered his vast fortune to anyone who could bring Corliss back to life. Unfortunately, the gods deemed her time had come and resurrection lies beyond mortal magic. A priestess of Orcus (under the guise of a cleric of Freya) named Edlyn (Cleric 8) approached Garrick with empty promises.

Edlyn indeed brought Corliss back from death. Her body, infused with a demonic spirit, became a **demonvessel**. Since her transformation, Garrick's life has spiraled into a horrific nightmare. Blinded by his boundless love for his wife, Garrick truly believes that she can be cured. The elder Garrick has become feral and irrational from the suffering Vorliss has inflicted upon his already weakened mind. Corliss enjoys tormenting the crazed man and has thus far resisted the temptation to turn him into one of her minions. Garrick is prone to violent acts if he feels his wife is threatened.

His unkempt mansion sits atop a small knoll just outside the city. Corliss has turned the household staff into undead. The undead try (unsuccessfully) to maintain their former tasks and job assignments. They try (quite unsuccessfully) to pass themselves off as the living. The house currently holds **15 zombies**, **5 ghouls**, and a **ghast**. Corliss has plans on amassing a horde of undead to attack the city. Thus far from the vantage

point of the knoll, she has managed to pick off a few solitary travelers without drawing too much notice from the city guards.

Zombie: HD 2; AC 8[11] or with shield 7[12]; Atk 1 weapon or strike (1d8); Move 6; Save 16; AL N; CL/XP 2/30; Special: Immune to sleep and charm.

Ghoul: HD 2; AC 6[13]; Atk 2 claws (1d3), 1 bite (1d4); Move 9; Save 16; AL C; CL/XP 3/60; Special: Immunities, paralyzing touch.

Ghast: HD 4; AC 4[15]; Atk 2 claws (1d3), 1 bite (1d6); Move 14; Save 13; AL C; CL/XP 5/240; Special: Stench, paralyzing touch.

Denizen of Leng

Hit Dice: 8
Armor Class: 5 [14]
Attacks: 1 bite (1d3 + lassitude), 2 claws (1d4+1)
Saving Throw: 8
Special: regeneration, lassitude, immune to poison, mirror image, constant ESP
Move: 12
Alignment: Chaos
Number Encountered: 1d6
Challenge Level/XP: 13/2300

The eerie Men of Leng travel the universe from their strange homeland, always disguising themselves as humans in loose-fitting robes, with wrappings about the head and face. They are the same size as humans, but under their disguises they have horned brows, clawed fingers, mouths full of tentacles, and crooked goatish legs with cloven hooves. Many scholars have argued over where the otherworldly realm of Leng lies— some believe it can be found among the Outer Planes, while others are convinced it can only be reached via a dimension of dreams. The denizens of Leng can travel to other planes freely, and often do so in strange, black ships, constantly seeking new breeds of slaves or trading rubies for unusual services or magical treasures. At other times, their visits are much more violent, focusing on abducting victims for use as slaves or worse. On Leng, these denizens have long fought a war against that realm's monstrous spiders, a war that sometimes spills over into other worlds.

A Leng denizen's bite causes lassitude if the victim fails a saving throw (at -2). Any attack rolls, damage rolls, and saving throws are made at -2 thereafter until the victim has slept continuously for 12 hours. If the same victim is bitten (and fails the saving throw) a second time, the victim immediately falls into deep slumber and cannot be awakened for 12 hours. Additionally, a denizen of Leng is constantly able to read the thoughts of nearby creatures (ESP) and once per day can cast a *mirror image* of itself.

The denizens of Leng regenerate naturally if they are not on Leng, at a rate of 5hp per round. The process cannot be arrested by fire as it can, for example, with trolls. However, once a denizen reaches 0 hit points, the body dissolves into slime (and re-forms on Leng). On Leng itself, denizens do not regenerate, and die completely. Not having souls, they cannot be raised from the dead.

— Author: Adapted by Matt Finch

Denizen of Leng: HD 8; AC 5[14]; Atk 1 bite (1d3 + lassitude), 2 claws (1d4+1); Move 12; Save 8; AL C; CL/XP 13/2300; Special: regeneration (5hp), lassitude, immune to poison, mirror image, constant ESP.

Howard's Place

In a small, out of the way back street huddles one of the city's most eclectic and sought-after restaurants, known to the locals as Howard's Place (no one knows its actual name, if it even has one). A dim, eerie interior greets patrons, and the local is popular with the well-to-do youth of the area, who can always be found partaking of the unusual and exotic menu. The area is surprisingly free of panhandlers and thieves, allowing the well-to-do free reign to come to the restaurant frequently.

Serving such delicacies as manticore flank and dire rat wings (try them, they taste like chicken!), "troll-cubes", 1 in. cubes of strange meat that keeps you full for hours, and an exquisite sandwich piled high with very thinly sliced meats, cheeses and fruit, known in the shop as the "Beggars Hoagie", Howard's Place is frequently standing room only. The popular crowd gets here early, often before the 'normal' eating hours just to view the crowd to see who does and does not get in for the evening. The maitre-d, a man named **Tsun**, is exceptionally pleasant, taking care of anything the patrons desire.

One of the biggest secrets of Howard's Place is the chef, Mr. Past, a heavily-garbed **denizen of Leng**. Mr. Past came to the city years ago by dream-travel, enjoyed the available potables here, and set up shop. He is assisted by a gaggle of sous-chefs in the main kitchen, but creates all the exotic meals alone in a separate sub-kitchen. There he is aided by **Mung**, a decidedly thin troll, who butchers meat for him. Mung has been known to get distracted, and occasionally forgets to strain out bits of cloth in his butchering. Tsun is quick to replace any "Beggers Hoagies" that seem underdone, or "stringy" for the clientele.

Mung: HD 6+3; AC 4[15]; Atk 2 claws (1d4), 1 bite (1d8); Move 12; Save 11; CL/XP 8/800; Special: Regenerate 3hp/ round.

Tsun, Human Thief Level 6: HP 17; AC 9 [10]; Atk 1 weapon (1d6); Move 12; Save 11 (9 vs. devices); AL N; CL/XP 5/240; Special: Back stab x3, climb walls 90%, delicate tasks 35%, hear sounds 4 in 6, hide in shadows 30%, move silently 40%, open locks 30%, read languages, read magic writings. Equipment: Excellent suit, assorted jewelry (250 gp value)

Dergenue (Wall Wench)

Hit Dice: 2
Armor Class: 4 [15]
Attacks: 1 strike (1d6)
Saving Throw: 16
Special: Drag into stone, immunities
Move: 12
Alignment: Neutrality
Number Encountered: 1d8+3
Challenge Level/XP: 3/60

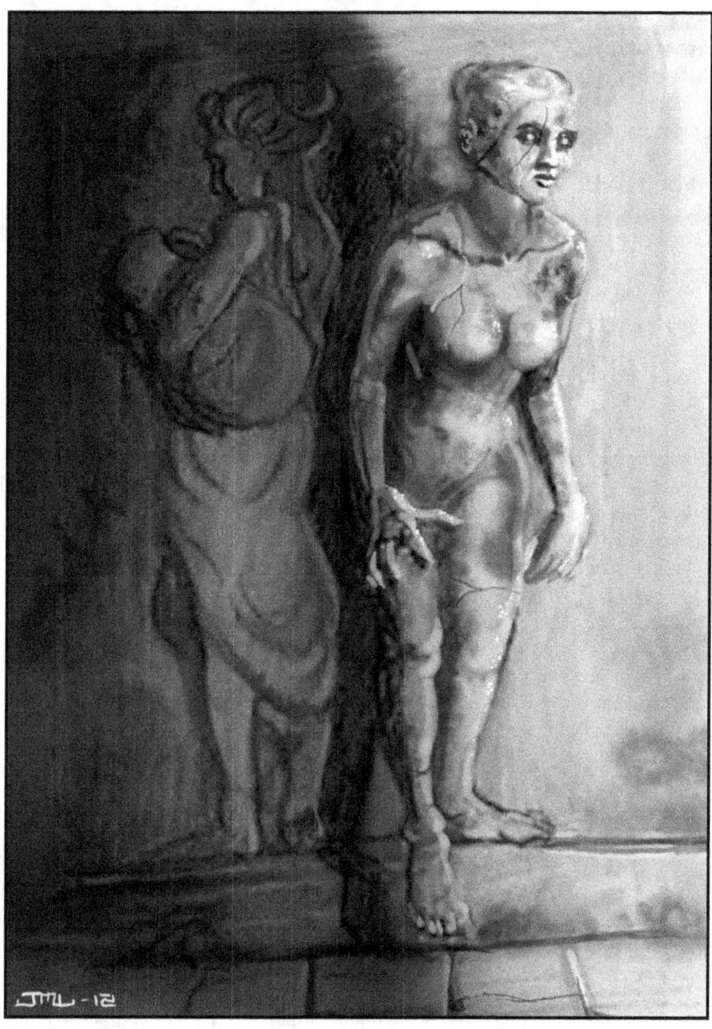

When dungeons and dark temples have bas-reliefs of half-naked women carved into their walls, adventurers should be aware that some of these provocative decorations may be Dergenue, a race of intelligent, mischievous earth elementals. They hide in walls, using their innate ability to phase through earth and stone, and attack by reaching out to grab at unwary passersby (high chance to surprise). Their blows cause 1d6 damage, and they may drag their victims into the wall (to swiftly suffocate and die) if the attack roll succeeds by 4 or more points. Earth-based magic may cause 1d8 damage per spell level to a dergenue, or slay her outright, depending upon the spell. A dergenue takes normal damage from fire, cold, and weapons, but is otherwise immune to almost all other attack forms. If she steps out of a wall, a dergenue must remain in contact with earth or stone or lose 1 HP per turn, and they cannot cross a barrier of fire or water.

— Author: Scott Wylie Roberts, "Myrystyr"

Dergenue: HD 2; AC 4[15]; Atk 1 strike (1d6); Move 12; Save 16; AL N; CL/XP 3/60; Special: Drag into stone, immunities.

Glory Hole

A grand domed covers this round temple dedicated to Aphrodite. Lavishly furnished, this chamber resembles more of a decadent pleasure palace rather than a place of worship. Red satin pillows and white silk sheets cover the floor. Sling-like swings and soft fur-encased manacles hang from the ceiling. Low and wide steps descend in the center of the room to a round lower floor. A candid statue of the beautiful Aphrodite stands in an uninhibited pose amid the depravity. A gold tiara (250 gp) and a pearl necklace (150 gp) adorn the statue.

A scene of seductive debauchery covers the bas-relief wall sculptures. Anatomically correct feminine effigies carved in amorous postures adorn the walls. Some of the figures stand nearly free from the wall. Some of the figures are actually **4 dergenues** waiting patiently for their next victims. One of the pillows acts as a *charm person* spell (saving throw resists) to anyone touching it. If the saving throw fails, the person becomes enamored with the first creature of the opposite sex he sees. The pillow can only charm one creature at a time, but has unlimited uses per day. The charm is permanent until a new creature is charmed. A failed saving throw by a new creature touching the pillow breaks the enchantment on the previously charmed victim.

117

Dertesha

Hit Dice: 6
Armor Class: 6 [13]
Attacks: 1 (special)
Saving Throw: 11
Special: Create tentacles, magic missile, paralysis touch
Move: 12/12/12 (Swimming, flying)
Alignment: Neutrality
Number Encountered: 1d4 (1d10 x10 in lair)
Challenge Level/XP: 9/1100

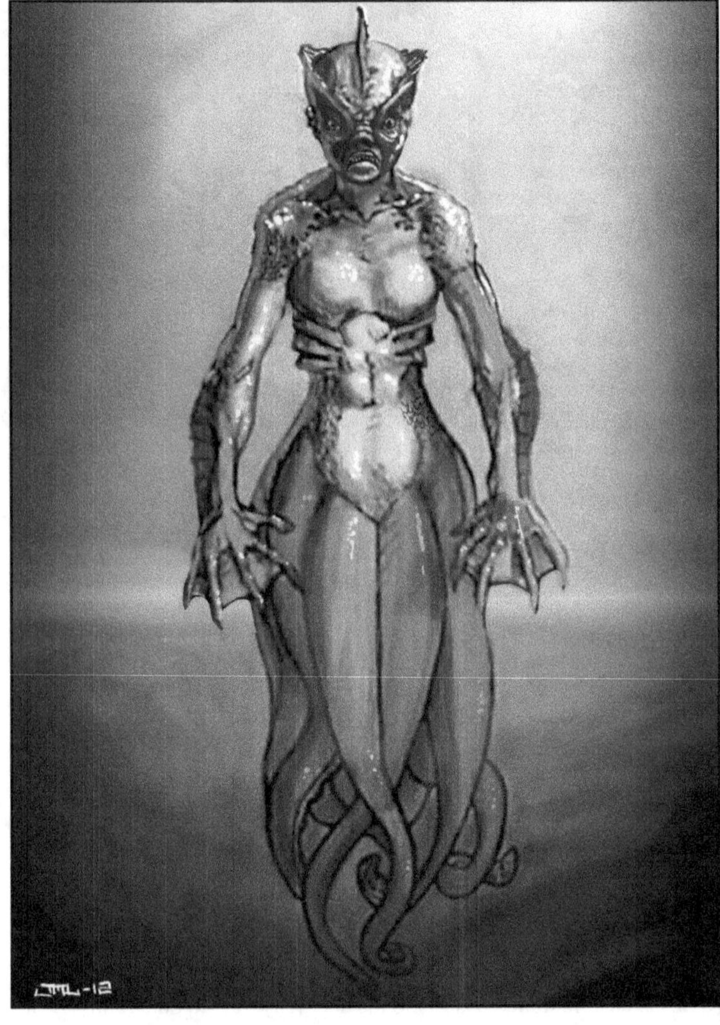

The Dertesha are a race of aquatic humanoids dwelling in rivers and lakes. They appear tall, thin, and human-like, but with long tentacles in place of legs. Some are a mottled greenish-blue in colour, and others are reddish-brown; a few have been reported yellowish-white. Dertesha are able to travel above water – on land and through the air – by magical watery spheres, oily and roiling in appearance. The dertesha are slightly translucent, and their bones are sometimes visible. Dertesha disdain physical conflict, being haughty and convinced of their moral and intellectual superiority over the land-dwelling races. They can cause large tentacles to erupt from any surface within 60ft, one per round, which restrain any target they strike (saving throw if hit negates). They may also cast Magic Missile at will. If pressed into close combat, their touch acts as a paralytic poison that can have hallucinatory after-effects. They may also simply drag air-breathing opponents under the water and hold them there to drown.

Dertesha have a sophisticated culture unseen by land-dwelling races, and they communicate frequently with creatures of elemental air and water.

— Author: Scott Wylie Roberts, "Myrystyr"

Dertesha: HD 6; AC 6[13]; Atk 1 (special); Move 12 (swim or fly 12); Save 11; AL N; CL/XP 9/1100; Special: Create tentacles, magic missile, paralysis touch.

Boon Docks

Screams of terror rise from the dock district where the river meets the sea. The ship *The Incisor* is under attack by a giant tentacle rising from each side of the galley. The Incisor appears to be a merchant vessel transporting barrels and crates of ginger, cinnamon, cassia, turmeric and cardamom. However, hidden under the spices are packages of Black Lotus, Mangan Herb, Dusk Reeds and other forbidden substances. Captain Whitcomb leads the band of buccaneers. Recently the crew slew and pillaged a clan of primitive humans on an island settlement off the coast. The humans worshipped a water goddess (actually a nixie queen). Among the crude gold jewelry and uncut gemstones, Captain Whitcomb stole a large clamshell made of mother of pearl and gold inlay. Unknown to the captain, the clamshell contains an infant nixie princess.

The furious nixie queen has charged a **dertesha** with rescuing the infant and teaching the sailors a lesson. A charmed **first mate** stands guard between the dertesha and the ship. The dertesha conjured large tentacles on the underside of the ship. It stands at the end of the pier commanding the tentacles to drag the smugglers into the water to drown. Captain Whitcomb pleads for anyone to assist him and his crew of sailors at the hands of the so-called water demon. He offers a reward for heroes to become part of his prosperous crew aboard *The Incisor* to take the place of the slain smugglers.

Those returning the nixie princess to her home are rewarded with a *tentacle belt*. This belt can create an 8-foot tentacle on the wearer's body (placement is decided by the wearer). While the tentacle is not dexterous enough to wield a weapon or magical item, it can grab smaller than human-sized opponents, break down doors (1–3), or carry items. It has an effective strength of 16 and can be used to attack as a bludgeoning weapon (1d4). The belt can be used once each day for 1d4 hours, but then must be recharged by submerging it in water for a like amount of time. Once activated, the tentacle remains for the duration and the belt cannot be removed (except by dispel magic or similar magic).

Guards, Human Fighter Level 3: HD 3; AC 7 [12]; Atk 1 spear (1d8); Move 12; Save 13; AL N; CL./XP 3/60; Special: Breathe water. Equipment: Leather armor, spear.

Dhezik

Hit Dice: 4
Armor Class: 7 [12]
Attacks: 1 bite (1d6)
Saving Throw: 13
Special: Entangle, immune to arcane magic.
Move: 12
Alignment: Chaos
Number Encountered: 2d6+10
Challenge Level/XP: 5/240

Dheziks look rather like dwarves with green skin and yellow eyes. However, they are feral, naked savages who paint swirls on their bodies with the blood of their foes. Their long white hair, eyebrows and moustaches are prehensile, enabling the Dhezik to entangle an opponent in close combat (saving throw to avoid), then bite the beard-entwined opponents with their prominent canine fangs. After a fresh kill there is a 1 in 6 chance their bloodlust may cause them to attack each other. Dheziks are completely resistant to arcane magic directed at them, due to strange glyphs branded on their shoulders. They are of low intelligence, are infertile, have a pack mentality, and will viciously attack Dwarves (+1 to hit).

— Author: Sean Wills

Dhezik: HD 4; AC 7[12]; Atk 1 bite (1d6); Move 12; Save 13; AL C; CL/XP 5/240; Special: Entangle, immune to arcane magic.

Dhezik's Midnight Runners

A horn's lone note pierces the midnight darkness. PCs who investigate the sound find 2 elves, a human and a dwarf running toward them through the forested hillside. The figures are each naked, and their hair is long and wild. Leaves and grass are matted in the greasy strands, and dirt and mud cover their bodies. Their eyes are wide with panic. Unless PCs calm them down, the men and women scream and run away from anyone approaching them.

The runners are travellers captured a month ago and kept in the cellar of a nearby manor home. The owner of the manor is an avid hunter who abducts people to make things challenging during his midnight excursions. He doesn't use hounds, however; instead, he releases a pack of **12 dheziks** to chase the game. The dheziks each wear a silver collar that keeps them from turning on the hunter. The dheziks scramble and crash through the woods in pursuit of their prey, seeking to take down anyone they find on the hunter's property.

DINOSAURS

Dinosaurs are particularly useful in time-traveling adventures, for valleys that time forgot, or for the mounts of sword & sorcery barbarians.

Dinosaur, Ankylosaurus

Hit Dice: 9
Armor Class: 0 [19]
Attacks: 1 clubbed tail (3d6)
Saving Throw: 6
Special: None
Move: 6
Alignment: Neutrality
Number Encountered: 1d6
Challenge Level/XP: 9/1,100

An ankylosaurus looks like a turtle with spikes around the edge of its shell and elephant-like legs. It has a tail with a clubbed end. They are herbivores, and travel in small groups.

Ankylosaurus: HD 9; AC 0[19]; Atk 1 clubbed tail (3d6); Move 6; Save 6; AL N; CL/XP 9/1100; Special: None.

Bizarre Barrage in the Bazaar

Ollie Nematoad seems to attract attention, generally unwarranted and destructive. The halfling inventor often needs rescuing from situations he inadvertently creates. This time, Ollie has developed an unconventional device to unclog pipes. The device (which could be used for many purposes) consist of a long string, a thin glass vial with a stopper, and a flammable oily substance that ignites when exposed to air or water. His idea is to lower the vial into a pipe until it hits a clog, then pull the string to burn out the blockage. The vials come in many shapes and sizes to fit the needs of the task and circumstances. He has named his invention "Kablooey Gooey." A potion vial-sized container (a gill) explodes in a five-foot radius dealing 1d6 points of fire damage. His industrial-sized containers (pint) deal 2d6 points of damage in a 10-foot radius.

After several wagon fires, Ollie decided he needed an alternative method of safely transporting his wares. Ollie procured a semi-trained **ankylosaurus** from a far-off land beyond the desert. The slow-moving yet steady animal is the perfect mount for Ollie and his explosive wares (plus, he receives a lot of attention when he arrives into town). Ollie secured the top of a covered wagon atop the dinosaur. Most people clear the way as they gawk at the sight.

On this particular day in the grand bazaar of Bard's Gate, Ollie arrived with the usual fanfare to sell his wares. People throughout the market stop and stare at Ollie's arrival; many drop items and flee in fear. One particular half-orc in the ankylosaurus' path drops his spiked club. The anklyosaurus steps on the spikes (which wedge into its foot). The frightened primeval beast reacts by rampaging through the market, clubbing everything along the way. The harder it runs the more pain the spikes inflict. The jostling and thrashing causes vials of Kablooey Gooey to fly from the wagon and explode. Ollie attempts to regain control, but is powerless until the spike club is removed. The Kablooey Gooey does not land on the ankylosaurus but 1d4–1 vials are flung in random directions every round. On a roll of 1–4 on 6, a gill goes flying; on a 5–6, a pint tumbles out. Ollie has 100 gills and 25 pints on board (he expected to sell a lot). He charges 20 gp for a gill and 50 gp for a pint. Needless to say, the Pipe Cleaners Guild won't be happy at his arrival nor the results of Kablooey Gooey being used to unclog pipes. Ollie rewards rescuers with a discount on purchases.

Dinosaur, Brontosaurus

Hit Dice: 30
Armor Class: 5 [14]
Attacks: 1 stomp (3d6)
Saving Throw: 3
Special: None
Move: 6
Alignment: Neutrality
Number Encountered: 1 or 1d6+4
Challenge Level/XP: 30/7,400

Brontosaurus (Apatosaurus) is a massive, long-necked herbivore. They are encountered in groups or even herds. A brontosaurus stands 20ft tall at the shoulder, and weighs from 35 to 45 tons.

Brontosaurus: HD 30; AC 5[14]; Atk 1 stomp (3d6); Move 6; Save 3; AL N; CL/XP 30/7400; Special: None.

The Walking Dead

Trees crash apart as a monstrous **brontosaurus** stumbles through the corkwood and mangrove trunks. The dinosaur moves slowly, weighed down by a 70-foot-wide wooden platform balanced on its back and supported by struts driven into its sides. The platform supports a small village of two-story houses crowded close together in the narrow space. The homes rock and sway with the movement of the brontosaurus supporting them. Thick vines dangle off the edges of the platform, dragging along the ground alongside the shuffling brontosaurus. Large boulders hang from the corners of the platform to keep the dinosaur from rising up and shaking the village off its back.

The nomadic Walking City of Covalt Green travels where the whim of the brontosaurus takes it. The dinosaur is ancient now, but still a strong beast of burden. Crude trebuchets mounted along the edges of the platform serve to keep the carnivores away from the dinosaur.

Except the normally welcoming lights of the village are dark now, and the sounds of laughter and song are silenced. PCs climbing the vines to the silent village find evidence of violence everywhere: bloodstains soak into the wooden planks, scratches are clawed into the wood, and a few skeletons are tangled in the hanging ivy and vines. The village was overrun by a pack of **15 hungry ghouls** that descended out of the trees to attack the villagers. The ghouls killed everyone in the village who couldn't escape off the edges of the platform. The ghouls now ride comfortably through the jungle, swinging down off the platform in packs to attack creatures on the ground. The brontosaurus keeps walking even if PCs and ghouls are fighting across its back.

Ghoul: HD 2; AC 6[13]; Atk 2 claws (1d3), 1 bite (1d4); Move 9; Save 16; AL C; CL/XP 3/60; Special: Immunities, paralyzing touch.

Dinosaur, Elasmosaurus

Hit Dice: 7
Armor Class: 7[12]
Attacks: 1 bite (4d6)
Saving Throw: 9
Special: None
Move: 1/15 (swimming)
Alignment: Neutrality
Number Encountered: 1 (2 in lair)
Challenge Level/XP: 7/600

Fish-like, 15ft long carnivores, the elasmosaurus has a long neck like a sea serpent, but has a thick, saurian body with fins. This is a good sea monster for use in campaigns where the dark horrors of the far-forgotten past might still survive. These creatures cannot survive more than a few minutes on land.

Elasmosaurus: HD 15; AC 7[12]; Atk 1 bite (4d6); Move 1 (Swim 15); Save 9; AL N; CL/XP 7/600; Special: Aquatic.

Bad Luck Runs Deep

In the middle of the Reaping Sea, a series of stone pillars rise out of the waves to mark the edge of the Laurentian Descent. The boundary of stone columns marks the cliff where the seabed drops off into a miles-deep abyss. Legends say the goddess Muir drove the stone columns into the sea to split the ocean floor so she could descend into the underworld.

A galleon drifts near the pillars, the ship's sail tattered and hanging off the masts. *Luck's Star* went missing nearly a month ago after departing Port Shaw in a search for pirates. The ship is a long way from port, and sailing close reveals obvious damage along its hull. The wood is scratched and scraped. The ship is empty, although PCs who climb aboard and go below decks find a lone sailor sitting dead at the bottom of the steep stairs. His midsection is a gory mess; he looks like he was nearly bitten in two but still managed to fall down the ladder into the hold.

The ship was attacked by **2 elasmosaurus** that rose up on either side of the *Star* to pluck sailors from the deck. The mated dinosaurs swam to the surface from their normal hunting ground within the deep trench below. The elasmosauruses rise out of the deep to attack the ships. They focus on grabbing victims and tossing them into the waves where they can finish them off at their leisure.

Dinosaur, Stegosaurus

Hit Dice: 17
Armor Class: 2 [17]
Attacks: 1 bite (1d4), 1 spiked tail (4d6)
Saving Throw: 3
Special: None
Move: 6
Alignment: Neutrality
Number Encountered: 2d4
Challenge Level/XP: 17/3,500

These dinosaurs have large back-plates standing out from the spine, and a spiked tail. They are herbivores, and travel in small groups.

Stegosaurus: HD 17; AC 2[17]; Atk 1 bite (1d4), 1 spiked tail (4d6); Move 6; Save 3; CL/XP 17/3500; Special: None.

Jurassic Spark

A lighter-than-air gas fills this canyon, the greenish wisps rising from natural vents in the rock-strewn ground. Trapped in the canyon are **2 stegosauruses** that became separated from their herd. Their plaintive cries echo off the flint walls. PCs can breathe the gas, although it makes them a little lightheaded and raises the pitch of their voices.

The dinosaurs are extremely agitated, and the gas makes them unpredictable. They are easily provoked and charge PCs who approach them. They swing their tails wildly to slash and stab at foes. The spikes on their tail chip the rock walls as they advance. Their swinging tails have a 1 in 6 chance of creating a spark as their tail spikes slam into the canyon's flint walls. The spark ignites the flammable gas, setting off a blast that does 4d6 points of damage (save for half) to anyone within a 40-foot radius of the dinosaur.

Dinosaur, Triceratops

Hit Dice: 16
Armor Class: 1 [18] (facing) or 6 [13] (rear)
Attacks: 1 bite (1d8) and 2 horns (1d12)
Saving Throw: 3
Special: Charge
Move: 9
Alignment: Neutrality
Number Encountered: 1 (lone bull), 1d4+1 (small herd), or 3d12 (herd)
Challenge Level/XP: 17/3500

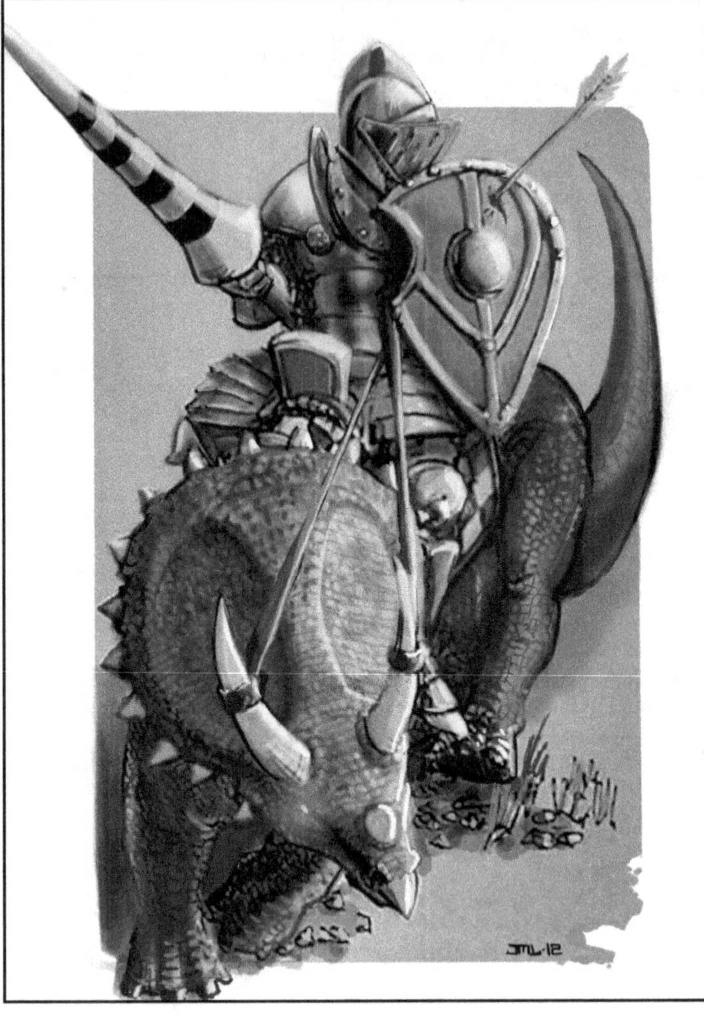

A triceratops has three horns protruding from its face, and a protective plate rising like an armored frill behind its head. They are extremely hard to damage with frontal assaults. The bony plate behind the head would also provide excellent protection for a rider. The horns inflict double damage if the creature charges.

Triceratops: HD 16; AC 1[18] front, 6[13] back; Atk 1 bite (1d8) and 2 gore (1d12); Move 9; Save 3; CL/XP 17/3500; Special: Charge.

Bull Fight

On the edge of the civilized lands stands an ancient coliseum. Hot sand and dust constantly blow in from the rocky wasteland. Low-standing sod block buildings and a tent bazaar surround the stadium during bouts. Spectators seem to appear from nowhere in droves to attend the evening's entertainment. The spectacle consists of clowns, acrobats, minor illusions and dancing girls. The main event is always a massive battle where the crowds wager and legends are made.

Marna and her posse of brigands run the show. She is young, charismatic, stunningly beautiful and utterly ruthless. She does not like to lose. The evening's combat promises 5,000 gp to the winner. Locals know better than to be tempted by the prize. Posters tout a three-round bull fight. Participants are required to wear (provided) red capes into the arena. While Marna tolerates spells, spells that may damage the arena or harm bystanders are not allowed. She and the crowd want to see action, however. A disappointing show may result in a destructive riot or angry mob.

The first round, a large **bull** enters the ring. The second round, bullfighters face a **minotaur** wielding a trident and battleaxe. The last round, Marna releases her newest acquisition: A **triceratops** she brought from beyond the wasteland. She has grown quiet enamored with her expensive pet.

Marna, Human Thief Level 9: HP 27; AC 8 [12]; Atk 1 shortsword (1d6); Move 12; Save 7 (5 vs. devices); AL C; CL/XP 9/1100; Special: Back stab x4, climb walls 93%, delicate tasks 60%, hear sounds 5 in 6, hide in shadows 65%, move silently 70%, open locks 75%, read languages, read magic writings. Equipment: Leather armor, short sword, thieves' tools.

Bull: HD 3; AC 6[13]; Atk 1 gore (2d6); Move 12; Save 14; AL N; CL/XP 3/60; Special: None

Minotaur: HD 6+4; AC 6[13]; Atk Head butt (2d4), 1 bite (1d3) and 1 weapon (1d8); Move 12; Save 11; AL C; CL/XP 6/400; Special: Never get lost in labyrinths.

Dinosaur, Tyrannosaurus

Hit Dice: 18
Armor Class: 5 [14]
Attacks: 1 bite (5d8) and 1 leg (1d10)
Saving Throw: 3
Special: Chew
Move: 15
Alignment: Neutrality
Number Encountered: 1d2
Challenge Level/XP: 19/4,100

Tyrannosaurus is a deadly carnivorous dinosaur, walking on two legs and attacking with a massively powerful bite. When it bites prey, it grabs the victim in its jaws, shaking and chewing for 3d8 points of automatic damage in subsequent rounds. It can inflict such damage even against opponents as large as a brontosaurus. Only creatures with shells, bone frills, or spines can avoid the horrendous tearing damage a tyrannosaur can inflict (e.g., triceratops, stegosaurus, ankylosaurus).

Tyrannosaurus Rex: HD 18; AC 5[14]; Atk 1 bite (5d8); Move 15; Save 3; CL/XP 19/4100; Special: Chew for automatic 3d8 damage after bite.

The Weapon of the Ancients

A ring of roughhewn stone obelisks surround a 50-foot-wide sandy patch of soil. The stones were placed here by an ancient race of primitive people. A stone pedestal stands at one end of the colonnade. Hieroglyphics adorn the sides of the stone. If translated, the glyphs state "Rise, weapon of vengeance and glory. Smite those who bring evil to the mighty Clan of the Axe. Rid the land of infidels and bring peace to our lands." An axe-shaped depression sits atop the pedestal. The bronze head of an ornate battleaxe is embedded in the stone, but the handle is missing. Aside from destroying the pedestal, the axe head cannot be removed by non-magical means.

The desiccated corpse of an elf lies atop one of the larger obelisk. A dozen barbed black orc arrows pierce the body. The elf lies facedown and holds the decorative bronze handle of the axe head below. The elf is difficult to spot without thoroughly searching the area. Once the axe handle is placed in the depression on the pedestal, the weapon created by the Clan of the Axe is complete. Below the center of the colonnade lies a **tyrannosaurus** held in a powerful stasis. Placing the axe handle on the pedestal immediately causes the ground to rumble and pitch as an enormous sooty, opaque sphere rises from the ground. At ground level, the sphere dissipates, leaving a cloud of dust and a rampaging tyrannosaurus. The beast stays within a mile of the colonnade and only follows the commands of the Clan of the Axe chieftain. After six hours, the tyrannosaurus returns to the colonnade where its sinks into the earth. Aside from being impervious to damage or destruction, the bronze axe has no special abilities.

Djinni

Hit Dice: 7+3
Armor Class: 5 [14]
Attacks: Fist or weapon (2d8)
Saving Throw: 9
Special: magical powers, whirlwind
Move: 9/24 (flying)
Alignment: Any
Number Encountered: 1
Challenge Level/XP: 9/1,100

Djinn are one of the genies of folklore, creatures of the air (and possibly of the elemental planes). They can carry 700 pounds of weight, and have a number of magical powers. A djinni can create food and water of high quality, as well as wooden and cloth objects. They can also create objects of metal (including coins), but all such magically created metals disappear in time. Djinn can call up illusions, and although these are quite excellent they disappear when touched. Djinni can turn themselves into gaseous form (cannot attack or be attacked, can enter any area that is not airtight), and can become invisible at will. Finally, a djinni can turn itself into a whirlwind much like an air elemental, sweeping away any creature with one or fewer hit dice (the diameter of the whirlwind is 10ft. More powerful types of djinn might be capable of granting limited wishes or even true wishes.

Djinni: HD 7+3; AC 5[14]; Atk 1 fist or weapon (2d8); Move 9 (Fly 24); Save 9; CL/XP 9/1100; Special: Magical powers, whirlwind.

Junk Yard Dogs

Twisted chunks of metal lie haphazardly over the broken limestone foundations of an ancient temple. Some of the rusted metal shards are nearly 30 feet long and 10 feet wide and twisted into wild, contorted shapes. The tortured pieces of metal weigh tons and can't be moved easily. Fallen statues of defaced gods lie amid the ruins.

Roaming the junkyard of scrap metal and stone are **10 guard dogs** that escaped from a cruel king's kennels. The pack now lives amid the scrap and attacks anyone working their way through the stone and metal debris. Each wears a spiked leather collar.

Dog

	GUARD or WAR	PET or WILD
Hit Dice:	2	1
Armor Class:	7[12]	7 [12]
Attacks:	1 bite (1d6)	1 bite 1d3]
Saving Throw:	16	17
Special:	None	None
Move:	14	15
Alignment:	Neutrality	Neutrality
Number Encountered:	Wild dogs 1 or 1d6+1	
Challenge Level/XP:	2/30	1/15

These are large, trained dogs. Normal dogs would have hit dice 1 or lower, and inflict no more than 1d3 points of damage.

Dog: HD 1; AC 7[12]; Atk 1 bite (1d3); Move 15; Save 17; CL/XP 1/15; Special: None.

Guard/War Dog: HD 2; AC 7[12]; Atk 1 bite (1d6); Move 14; Save 16; CL/XP 2/30; Special: None.

Dynastic Marriage

Small niches line the walls of this 30-foot-tall chamber. Each niche holds an antique oil lamp. This 80-foot-diameter chamber holds nearly 500 oil lamps. The lamps sell for between 1 to 5 gold pieces apiece. The entire collection would sell for about 1,250 gp. A 10-foot-diameter well sits in the center of the domed chamber. Thousands of golden rings fill the shallow, five-foot-deep hole. Each ring is unique and most are worthless. Only 100 of the rings have value, between 5 and 25 gp (950 gp total). Only one lamp and one ring are made of brass. The lamps and rings melt into a pool of molten metal (1d6 points of damage to the holder for each item) if removed from the room. Both the lamps and rings detect as magic.

A brass and baseless statue depicting a large man stands on the opposite side of the room from the entrance. He stands in a brusque pose with arms crossed and a snide grin across his bearded face. The highly polished statue radiates blistering heat.

As the chamber is entered, a small cyclone of rings rises from the center depression. A stunning female **djinni** forms in the pit. Every ring swirls in the torrent that forms her lower half. As the emotionless djinni materializes, she states the means to her freedom. *''Brandish the lamp of father. Don the ring of mother. Wary the betrayed lover. The union shall I answer forever.''*

The bearer of both the brass ring and brass lamp can command the djinni. Finding both of these items in the chamber presents a challenge. After she states the prophecy, the **brass statue** animates and relentlessly attacks those in the chamber. Once defeated, the statue melts into a molten pool of brass for 1d2 rounds. After the time elapses, the statue reforms at full hit points and continues attacking. The statue is slain forever if the ring and lamp are united.

If all the rings and lamps are removed from the chamber, the djinni dies in a blaze of hellfire (similar to *fire storm*). The djinni is **Dysuria**, the daughter of a djinni noble. She was betrothed to an efreeti lord's son to seal a peace pact a millennia ago. Doomed to fail, the arrangement was annulled with the efreeti lord placing a curse upon his son's betrothed.

Brass Statue: HD 50 hp; AC 3[16]; Atk 2 fists 1d6 +1d6 fire; Move 12; Save 3: AL N; CL/XP 16/3,200; Special unaffected by +1 or lesser weapons; immune to most spells, reanimation, fire based spells and attacks heal damage taken.

Dolphin

Hit Dice: 2
Armor Class: 6 [13]
Attacks: 1 bite (1d6)
Saving Throw: 16
Special: None
Move: 0/24 (swimming)
Alignment: Neutrality
Number Encountered: 1d6 or 3d12
Challenge Level/XP: 2/30

Dolphins are unlikely to be opponents in most adventures, but they might be enchanted guardians, or "dark" dolphins of evil temperament.

Dolphin: HD 2; AC 6[13]; Atk 1 bite (1d6); Move 0 (Swim 24); Save 16; CL/XP 2/30; Special: None.

Dastardly Dolphins

A floor-to-ceiling glass wall runs along the length of this 100-foot-long hallway. The glass is thick (nearly 6 inches) and holds back a watery enclosure containing **3 frolicking dolphins**. The animals twirl and spin through the waters, playing as they swim. Green jade panels line the walls of the massive aquarium.

The room is a trap, however, and these decidedly evil dolphins are the central figures in setting it off. Once PCs arrive at the center of the hall, the dolphins stop their cavorting and charge the panels on opposite ends of their enclosure. The dolphins simultaneously press the green panels with their noses, which cause metal doors at either end of the hall to slam shut. Holes in the ceiling immediately open, and water pours into the sealed room. The hall fills with water in 2d4+6 rounds. The dolphins line the window to watch PCs drown.

Doppleganger

Hit Dice: 4
Armor Class: 5 [14]
Attacks: Claw (1d12)
Saving Throw: 13 (5 against any magic)
Special: Mimics shape, immune to sleep and charm spells
Move: 9
Alignment: Chaos
Number Encountered: 1 or 2d6
Challenge Level/XP: 5/240

A doppelganger can change its form to resemble the physical appearance (including clothing and gear) of any person. These creatures are immune to sleep and charm, and are considered magic resistant for purposes such as breaking through *wizard locks* and similar spells. They have a very good saving throw (5) against magic of all kinds.

Doppelganger: HD 4; AC 5[14]; Atk 1 claw (1d12); Move 9; Save 13 (5 vs magic); CL/XP 5/240; Special: Mimics shape, immune to sleep and charm.

Mirror Maze Madness

Mirrors of varying sizes lines the walls of this stone corridor. The mirrors gradually cover the walls as the party moves down the passage. The floor and ceiling also change from common stone to highly polished quartz. The corridor branches off in several directions, each turning and twisting. Lanterns burning with unnaturally bright light hang from the ceilings at regular intervals. Empty mirrored rooms break the corridors from time to time. Eventually, the halls come back together and the corridor returns to normal stone walls.

Some of the mirrors conceal rooms while others are actually secret doors or one-way mirrors. A gang of **4 doppelgangers** hunts these passages. The ingenious creatures mimic prey. Hasty adventurers may perceive the doppelgangers to be their reflections moving alongside them down the hall. The doppelgangers try to separate the party by running off and changing forms. Using confusion and the mirrors to keep opponents guessing, the doppelgangers try to trap single characters in mirror rooms. Once they separate PCs, the doppelgangers take the appearance of the victim and attack. If battle goes against them, they take the form of a medusa (although they lack the petrifying gaze attack) to scare off adversaries.

Dragolem

Hit Dice: 8
Armor Class: 2 [17]
Attacks: 2 claws (1d6), 1 bite (2d10) or breath
Saving Throw: 8
Special: Breath, immunities
Move: 12/24 (flying)
Alignment: Neutrality
Number Encountered: 1
Challenge Level/XP: 12/2.000

Dragolems are golems fashioned in the shape of dragons. These powerful constructs are usually used to guard valuable artifacts or vast treasures. A dragolem is unintelligent and is unaffected by charm spells, hold, sleep or other mind altering spells, as well a gases, cold, and fire. Dragolems are also immune to all spells of up to level 4, and to normal and silver weapons. Dragolems are able to see the invisible and 3 times per day they may breathe a poisonous cloud (20 X 20 X 20ft). The victim of the poisonous cloud must make a successful saving throw or die.

— *Author: Skathros*

Dragolem: HD 8; AC 2[17]; Atk 2 claws (1d6), 1 bite (2d10) or breath; Move 12 (Fly 24); Save 8; CL/XP 12/2000; Special: Breath, immunities.

Spin Cycle

This iron chamber is a 100-foot-diameter circle of steel with a central column. The entire chamber rotates slowly around the pillar. Two doors on opposite sides of the room line up once every 12 rounds so PCs can enter or leave the room. The rest of the time, the doors face cold steel walls scraping past the openings. Millions of steel ingots rise in mounds throughout the chamber. The ingots shift and slide as the room turns. Mixed among the ingots are gleaming gold coins pressed with a king's royal visage on one side and a rising phoenix on the other. The coins are lost among the ingots, but worth 2,560 gp if collected.

A **dragolem** lies curled around the base of the central pillar, hidden under the mounds of metal ingots. The dragolem waits until the PCs enter the room before rising out of the ingots to attack. When the dragolem rises, it steps off a pressure plate on the floor. The plate causes the room to spin faster and faster. After 6 rounds, the room is moving so fast that the ingots and PCs are thrown backward against the walls for 3d6 points of damage (save for half). The good news is that the spinning room separates the ingots and gold and makes the treasure easier to collect. The room spins at high speed for 1d4 rounds before slowing for 2d4 rounds. It repeats the process until the dragolem returns to the pressure plate. The dragolem digs its claws into the metal to stay in one spot, or flies in the middle of the room as PCs whirl around it.

DRAGONS

The size of a dragon is roughly 5 ft of body length per age category, up to the adult size of 20 ft. Dragons have double normal treasure (that is, a gold piece value of four times the dragon's XP value).

Do not roll hit points for dragons as normal. Instead, determine the number of hit dice and the age category of the dragon. The age category indicates both the dragon's hit points per die and how much damage the dragon's breath weapon inflicts, given as points per hit die.

HD	Age Category	Hit Points	Breath Weapon Damage
1	Very young dragon	1 hit point per hit die	1 hit point per die inflicted by breath weapon.
2	Young	2 hit points per hit die	2 hit points per die inflicted by breath weapon.
3	Immature	3 hit points per hit die	3 hit points per die inflicted by breath weapon.
4	Adult	4 hit points per hit die	4 hit points per die inflicted by breath weapon.
5	Old	5 hit points per hit die	5 hit points per die inflicted by breath weapon.
6	Very old (100 years old)	6 hit points per hit die	6 hit points per die inflicted by breath weapon.
7	Aged (101-400 years old)	7 hit points per die	7 hit points per die inflicted by breath weapon.
8	Ancient (401+ years old)	8 hit points per die	8 hit points per die inflicted by breath weapon.

Note that dragons, while they are dangerous opponents, are not by any means invincible. In a medieval-type fantasy world, dragons are a common problem rather than godlike creatures of legend—so the statistics for dragons reflect a deadly but not mythical foe. The Referee is, of course, free to create stats for a more "mythical" conception of dragons. Since dice are not rolled for dragon hit points, it is possible for a truly mythical dragon to have more points per die than it is actually possible to roll on a hit die.

Breath Weapons: All dragons have a breath weapon of some kind, which can be used three times in a day. The Referee chooses when a dragon will use its breath weapon, or may roll a 60% chance in any given round. Damage inflicted by a dragon's breath weapon is indicated under the age category. When used breath weapons appear in three different shapes:

1 — Cloud-shape for gaseous exhalations
2 — A line, for spitting dragons
3 — Cone shape for any others.

The dimensions of a dragon's breath differ according to the dragon's type.

If a dragon is beaten down by subdual damage (see rules for Combat), the dragon will surrender and serve its conquerors, even to the point of allowing itself to be sold. However, subdued dragons are only loyal while they are impressed by and frightened of their masters; signs of weakness may cause the dragon to escape or even attack its master.

A standard-colored dragon generally has a challenge level based on its hit points: CL=(hp/4) +2.

Dragon, Black

Hit Dice: 6–8
Armor Class: 2 [17]
Attacks: 2 claws (1d4), bite (3d6)
Saving Throw: 11, 9, or 8
Special: Spits acid
Move: 9/24 (flying)
Alignment: Chaos
Number Encountered: 1d2, or a nest (2 of age category 4 and 1d4 of age category 1d3)
Challenge Level/XP: Challenge Level = (hit points/4) +2

Black dragons spit a deadly, corrosive acid which covers everything in a line 5 feet wide and 60 feet long. Black dragons have a 45% chance of being able to talk; talking black dragons have a 5% chance of being able to cast 1d4 first-level Magic-User spells.

Adult Black Dragon (6HD): HD 6 (24hp); AC 2[17]; Atk 2 claws (1d4), 1 bite (3d6); Move 9 (Fly 24); Save 11; AL C; CL/XP 8/800; Special: Spits acid.

Adult Black Dragon (7HD): HD 7 (28hp); AC 2[17]; Atk 2 claws (1d4), 1 bite (3d6); Move 9 (Fly 24); Save 9; AL C; CL/XP 9/1100; Special: Spits acid.

Adult Black Dragon (8HD): HD 8 (32hp); AC 2[17]; Atk 2 claws (1d4), 1 bite (3d6); Move 9 (Fly 24); Save 8; AL C; CL/XP 10/1400; Special: Spits acid.

Acid Bath

Dark shadows and black stone columns fill this cavernous stone chamber. Glowing black spots pulse in a strobe-like effect along the walls, causing spots to dance in the vision of PCs looking directly at the non-lights. The granite walls and floor are pitted with thousands of holes that have eaten through the rock. Steam whistles through the porous stone. A black-iron cage hangs from a chain 30 feet off the floor before three large caves that exit the chamber. A steady waterfall of smoking liquid drips from the cage. The liquid pulses and stretches in the strange black lights. A bauxite anvil that weeps acid sits in the cage. The caustic flow falls from the cage and spatters across the stone floor. Anyone touching the liquid takes 3d6 points of damage (save for half).

The cavern is the home of a **black dragon** known to local farmers as Ebon Death. The dragon sleeps in one of the caves. When PCs advance toward the cave or cage, the dragon rises up and flaps its wings to spray the dripping acid throughout the chamber. The dragon continues flapping until PCs get close or start attacking it from a distance. The Ebon Death leaps from the cave to attack. The dragon sleeps on a pile of treasure that includes 2,524 gp, a melted gold stature (274 gp), a collection of cow skulls, and a small silver flask that contains a trapped quasit.

Dragon, Blue

Hit Dice: 8–10
Armor Class: 2 [17]
Attacks: 2 claws (1d6), bite (2d12)
Saving Throw: 8, 6, or 5
Special: Spits lightning
Move: 9/24 (flying)
Alignment: Chaos
Number Encountered: 1d2, or a nest (2 of age category 4 and 1d4 of age category 1d3)
Challenge Level/XP: Challenge Level = (hit points/4) +2

Blue dragons spit a blast of lightning in a line 5 ft wide and 100 ft long, affecting everything in its path. A saving throw indicates half damage. Blue dragons have a 65% chance of being able to talk; talking blue dragons have a 15% chance of being able to cast 1d4 first-level Magic-User spells and 1d3 second-level Magic-User spells.

Adult Blue Dragon (8HD): HD 8 (32hp); AC 2[17]; Atk 2 claws (1d6), 1 bite (3d8); Move 9 (Fly 24); Save 8; AL C; CL/XP 10/1400; Special: spits lightning.

Adult Blue Dragon (9HD): HD 9 (36hp); AC 2[17]; Atk 2 claws (1d6), 1 bite (3d8); Move 9 (Fly 24); Save 6; AL C; CL/XP 11/1700; Special: spits lightning.

Adult Blue Dragon (10HD): HD 10 (40hp); AC 2[17]; Atk 2 claws (1d6), 1 bite (3d8); Move 9 (Fly 24); Save 5; AL C; CL/XP 12/2000; Special: spits lightning.

Blue Harvest

Stalks of corn grow tall in this field, the tassels glowing a faint yellow in the darkness. The field spreads across hundreds of acres. The corn is planted in neat rows that crisscross the low, rolling hills. Scarecrows stand on wooden posts throughout the field. The tops of the scarecrows' heads can barely be seen above the rows of swaying corn. A few of the scarecrows are blackened and burned. Despite the abundance of ripe ears of corn, it appears no one has yet harvested the crop.

A farmer's scorched bones lie scattered across the field he planted last spring. The poor man was killed when he entered the field to gather corn – and came face to face with a **blue dragon** now living among the rows. The dragon broke through the earth in the center of the field when it had to dig a back entrance out of its cave network when an avalanche collapsed the only opening. The dragon slinks through the corn, staying low to the ground as it stalks prey. The dragon injured one of its wings during the cave-in and won't be able to fly for at least another month.

Dragon, Brass

Hit Dice: 6-8
Armor Class: 2[17]
Attacks: 2 claws (1d4), 1 bite (3d6)
Saving Throw: 11 (6HD), 9 (7HD), or 8 (8HD)
Special: Fear or sleep breath
Move: 12/24 (flying)
Alignment: Neutrality (tendency to Law)
Number Encountered: 1d2, or a nest (2 of age category 4 and 1d4 of age category 1d3)
Challenge Level/XP: Challenge Level = (hit points/4) +2

Brass dragons are greedy, but not as inimical to humankind as most of their kin. A brass dragon can breath a cone-shaped blast of sleep gas (70ft long, to a width of 20ft at the end), or a cloud of fear gas 50ft in diameter (20ft from the ground to the top of the cloud). A saving throw is required for anyone caught in a brass dragon's breath weapon, regardless of level. Sleep lasts until the victim is physically awakened; fear causes the victim to flee for 3d6 rounds. Brass dragons have a 50% chance of being able to talk; talking brass dragons have a 5% chance of being able to cast 1d4 first level magic-user spells. Brass dragons range in size from 6 to 8 hit dice.

Adult Brass Dragon (6HD): HD 6 (24hp); AC 2[17]; Atk 2 claws (1d4), 1 bite (3d6); Move 12 (Fly 24); Save 11; AL N; CL/XP 8/800; Special: Fear or sleep breath.

Adult Brass Dragon (7HD): HD 7 (28hp); AC 2[17]; Atk 2 claws (1d4), 1 bite (3d6); Move 12 (Fly 24); Save 9; AL N; CL/XP 9/1100; Special: Fear or sleep breath.

Adult Brass Dragon (8HD): HD 8 (32hp); AC 2[17]; Atk 2 claws (1d4), 1 bite (3d6); Move 12 (Fly 24); Save 8; AL N; CL/XP 10/1400; Special: Fear or sleep breath.

Brass Tacks

A chipped basalt wall rises nearly 30 feet high in the Seething Jungle. Chunks of stone lie at the base of the stone. A screaming man is pinned to the wall about 20 feet in the air via two brass stakes driven through his shoulders and into the stone. His blood drips down the wall that holds him. He doesn't seem to feel the stakes holding him in place, however. He struggles against the pins, but can't pull himself free. Three more men are pinned to the wall in similar ways, but they are asleep, their heads hanging down against their slowly rising and falling chests.

The screaming man is a thief named **Tamme**. He and his adventuring companions (the men asleep on the wall around him) discovered a treasure trove in an ancient ruin deep in the jungle. The men were trying to figure out how to plunder the find when the owner showed up. The brass dragon took offense to the robbers and chased them through the jungle as they made off with what treasure they could carry. The dragon caught each one and pinned them to the wall to teach them a lesson. The men have been pinned to the wall for two days. The dragon routinely breathes clouds of gas over the thieves to cause them to sleep or struggle in fear. The dragon sleeps in a cave concealed by thick vines where it can watch the wall. It attacks anyone trying to free the men.

Dragon, Bronze

Hit Dice: 8-10
Armor Class: 2 [17]
Attacks: 2 claws (1d6), 1 bite (3d8)
Saving Throw: 8 (8HD), 6 (9HD), 5 (10HD)
Special: Spits lightning or misdirection gas
Move: 9/24 (flying)
Alignment: Law
Number Encountered: 1d2, or a nest (2 of age category 4 and 1d4 of age category 1d3)
Challenge Level/XP: Challenge Level = (hit points/4) +2

Bronze dragons are generally quite friendly to humankind. They can spit lightning in a line 100ft long (5ft wide) or exhale a cloud of misdirection gas in a 30ft diameter (20ft from ground to top of cloud). The misdirection gas forces anyone failing a saving throw to retreat away from the dragon for 6 full combat rounds. The lightning bolt causes full damage (age category times dragon's hit dice) on a failed saving throw, half damage with a successful saving throw. Bronze dragons have a 70% chance of being able to talk; talking bronze dragons have a 15% chance of being able to cast 1d4 first level magic-user spells and 1d3 second level magic-user spells. These dragons range in size from 8 to 10 hit dice.

Adult Bronze Dragon (8HD): HD 8 (32hp); AC 2[17]; Atk 2 claws (1d6), 1 bite (3d8); Move 9 (Fly 24); Save 8; AL L; CL/XP 10/1400; Special: Spits lightning or misdirection gas.

Adult Bronze Dragon (9HD): HD 9 (36hp); AC 2[17]; Atk 2 claws (1d6), 1 bite (3d8); Move 9 (Fly 24); Save 6; AL L; CL/XP 11/1700; Special: Spits lightning or misdirection gas.

Adult Bronze Dragon (10HD): HD 10 (40hp); AC 2[17]; Atk 2 claws (1d6), 1 bite (3d8); Move 9 (Fly 24); Save 5; AL L; CL/XP 12/2000; Special: Spits lightning or misdirection gas.

Bronze Age

A series of columns lead down this sloping passage to a circular vault sealed behind a large stone door. Wax is melted along the door's edges, and a three-foot-diameter wax seal sits in the center of the door. Pressed into the wax seal is an image of a man riding a dragon. The wax is old and brittle. Opening the door causes it to disintegrate and releases a poisonous dust mixed into the sealing wax. Anyone within 10 feet of the door must make a saving throw or choke to death as the dust hardens in their lungs.

Opening the door reveals a **bronze dragon** lying curled on the stone floor of the vault. The dragon is ancient, and can barely lift its head. The wyrm was entombed with its friend, the Sage-King Payot Bannon, when the old seer died. **Maelor Gawer** has not moved from this tomb in nearly 300 years. The Sage-King's body lies on a golden platform behind the curled dragon's still form.

Maelor has just a few hours left to live. He's lingered alive in this chamber well past the point he thought would be his end. He believes the Sage-King's life force (even in death) is letting him live on past his days. Maelor is ready for the end, however, but has one final request. He asks PCs to take word of his passing to the Dragon Stone high in the Hollow Spire Mountains and carve his name into the granite monument. If PCs fulfill this last request, Maelor's spirit appears and tells them where the dragon hid its treasure hoard in a sinkhole in Briar Tree Forest.

Dragon, Copper

Hit Dice: 7-9
Armor Class: 2 [17]
Attacks: 2 claws (1d6), 1 bite (2d10)
Saving Throw: 9 (7HD), 8 (8HD), 6 (9HD)
Special: Spit acid or breathe slowing gas
Move: 9/24 (flying)
Alignment: Law
Number Encountered: 1d2, or a nest (2 of age category 4 and 1d4 of age category 1d3)
Challenge Level/XP: Challenge Level = (hit points/4) +2

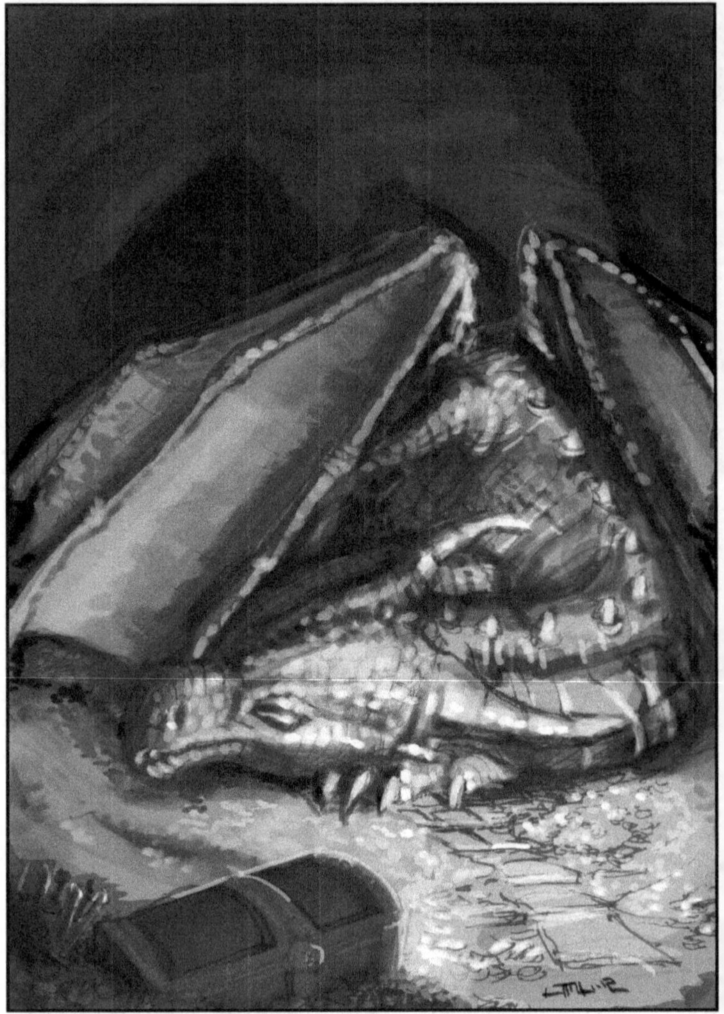

Copper dragons are generally hostile to evil/chaos, although they are not necessarily friendly to humans, either. They are greedy and covet wealth. A copper dragon can choose to spit a line of acid 5ft wide and 60ft long (saving throw for half damage), or to exhale a cloud of gas 30ft in diameter (20ft from top to bottom) that acts as a slow spell for a duration of 6 combat rounds (saving throw negates). Copper dragons have a 60% chance of being able to talk; talking copper dragons have a 10% chance of being able to cast 1d4 first level magic-user spells and 1d2 second level magic-user spells. These dragons range in size from 7 to 9 hit dice.

Adult Copper Dragon (7HD): HD 7 (28hp); AC 2[17]; Atk 2 claws (1d6), 1 bite (2d10); Move 9 (Fly 24); Save 9; AL L; CL/XP 9/1100; Special: Spit acid or breathe slowing gas.

Adult Copper Dragon (8HD): HD 8 (32hp); AC 2[17]; Atk 2 claws (1d6), 1 bite (2d10); Move 9 (Fly 24); Save 8; AL L; CL/XP 10/1400; Special: Spit acid or breathe slowing gas.

Adult Copper Dragon (9HD): HD 9 (36hp); AC 2[17]; Atk 2 claws (1d6), 1 bite (2d10); Move 9 (Fly 24); Save 6; AL L; CL/XP 11/1700; Special: Spit acid or breathe slowing gas.

Copper Wired

Screams sound from the marketplace in Taharath, and farmers run frantically from the clustered stalls set up to sell hand-beaten weapons, fresh produce, rare herbs and roots, and live chickens. Something large crashes through the stalls, ripping and tearing at the boards and cloth curtains. People scream "The beast!" as they grab their children and flee.

A **copper dragon** dropped in on the market. The dragon's mind is crazed and its head and eyes jerk with nervous tics as it rips into the various sellers' stalls. The dragon recently ate a herd of goats that had been munching on a field of hallucinogenic plants. The dragon was coming down off its high when its sensitive nose smelled more of the plants (and fresh goats) in the market. As the creature landed atop a stall, chaos erupted around it. The dragon is wild, attacking stalls, trees and the air. Any PCs who get in front of the dragon may be seen as foes come to harm the delusional, addicted creature.

Dragon, Gold

Hit Dice: 10–12
Armor Class: 2 [17]
Attacks: 2 claws (1d8), bite (3d12)
Saving Throw: 5, 4, or 3
Special: Breathes poisonous gas or fire
Move: 9/24 (flying)
Alignment: Law
Number Encountered: 1d2, or a nest (2 of age category 4 and 1d4 of age category 1d3)
Challenge Level/XP: Challenge Level = (hit points/4) +2

Gold dragons are the noble wyrms of story and song. They can breathe either a cloud of poisonous gas, 50 feet in diameter (a successful saving throw indicates half damage) or they can breathe fire in a cone-shape 90 feet long and roughly 30 feet wide at the base. Gold dragons have a 100% chance of being able to talk and a 25% chance of being able to cast Magic-User spells: 1d4 first-level, 1d3 second-level, 1d2 third-level, and 1 fourth-level spell.

Adult Gold Dragon (10HD): HD 10 (40hp); AC 2[17]; Atk 2 claws (1d6), 1 bite (3d8); Move 12 (Fly 24); Save 5; AL L; CL/XP 13/2300; Special: fire or chlorine breath, magic-user spells.

Adult Gold Dragon (11HD): HD 11 (44hp); AC 2[17]; Atk 2 claws (1d6), 1 bite (3d8); Move 12 (Fly 24); Save 4; AL L; CL/XP 14/2600; Special: fire or chlorine breath, magic-user spells.

Adult Gold Dragon (12HD): HD 12 (48hp); AC 2[17]; Atk 2 claws (1d6), 1 bite (3d8); Move 12 (Fly 24); Save 3; AL L; CL/XP 15/2900; Special: fire or chlorine breath, magic-user spells.

The Gold Bearer

A **gold dragon** shambles across the dirt fields outside Woodburn. The massive wyrm shakes its head angrily and occasionally stops to claw at its skull like a dog scratching a flea. Its skin is covered in old scars and fresh blood. A blood-stained collar with dangling skulls attached to it hangs around the dragon's neck. The skulls rattle with each shake of the dragon's massive head. Its eyes are cloudy gray orbs and it stumbles into fence posts and trees as if blind.

The gold dragon was tricked into putting on the collar, and its mind is now overwhelmed by the enchanted item. The true danger comes from the collar – and the **demi-lich** hanging among the skulls. The demi-lich has some control over the dragon, and can direct its movement. It cannot cause the dragon to attack or defend itself, however. The dragon swings its head toward PCs, allowing the demi-lich to attack. If the demi-lich is destroyed, the dragon stands motionless until the collar is cut off it. It thanks PCs profusely if freed, and grants them a boon.

Demi-Lich: HD 11; 75 hp; AC 0[19]; Atk steal soul; Move 12 (Flying); Save 4; AL C; CL/XP 13/2,300; Special: Immune to most spells, +3 or better magic weapons to hit, immune to acid, electricity, fire, cold and polymorph, rejuvenation, steal souls

Dragon, Green

Hit Dice: 7–9
Armor Class: 2 [17]
Attacks: 2 claws (1d6), bite (2d10)
Saving Throw: 9, 8, or 6
Special: Breathes poisonous gas
Move: 9/24 (flying)
Alignment: Chaos
Number Encountered: 1d2, or a nest (2 of age category 4 and 1d4 of age category 1d3)
Challenge Level/XP: Challenge Level = (hit points/4) +2

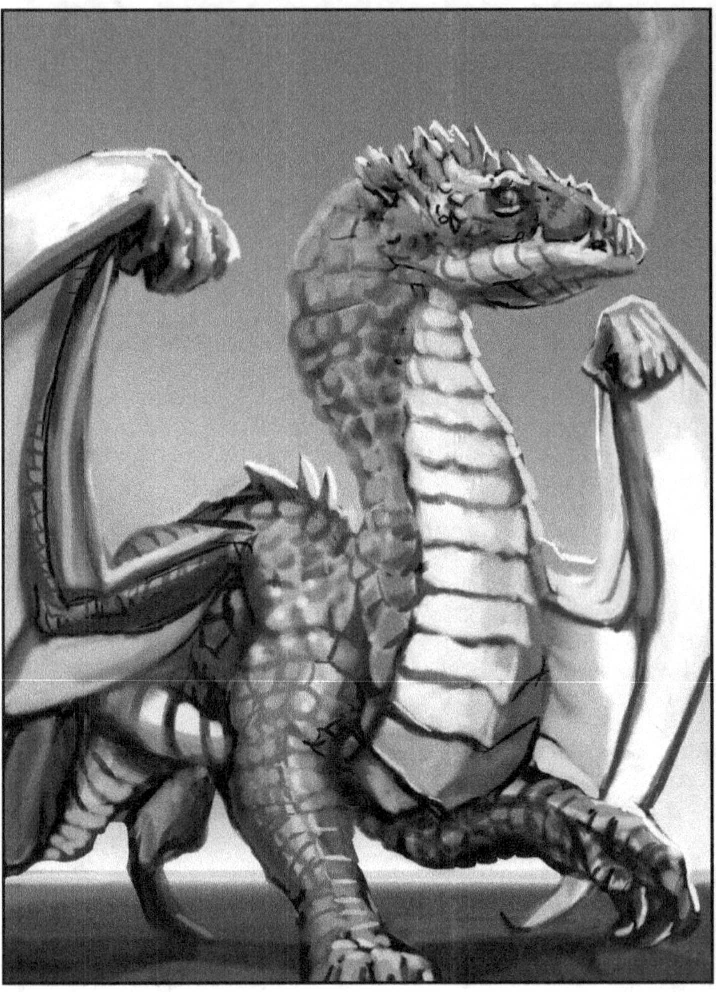

Green dragons breathe a cloud of poisonous gas, 50 ft in diameter. (A successful saving throw indicates half damage.) Green dragons have a 55% chance of being able to talk; talking green dragons have a 10% chance of being able to cast 1d4 first level Magic-User spells and 1d2 second level Magic-User spells.

Adult Green Dragon (7HD): HD 7 (28hp); AC 2[17]; Atk 2 claws (1d6), 1 bite (2d10); Move 9 (Fly 24); Save 9; AL C; CL/XP 9/1100; Special: Breathes poison gas.

Adult Green Dragon (8HD): HD 8 (32hp); AC 2[17]; Atk 2 claws (1d6), 1 bite (2d10); Move 9 (Fly 24); Save 8; AL C; CL/XP 10/1400; Special: Breathes poison gas.

Adult Green Dragon (9HD): HD 9 (36hp); AC 2[17]; Atk 2 claws (1d6), 1 bite (2d10); Move 9 (Fly 24); Save 6; AL C; CL/XP 11/1700; Special: Breathes poison gas.

Swamp Gas

Gouts of green flame rise 20 feet above the Sin Mire Swamp in roiling balls of fire. The flaming geysers erupt from the surface of the mossy peat floating like a wave of thick mud atop the bog. Four black stone pillars rise out of the swamp to support a rock platform. A small temple overrun by thousands of normal frogs sits atop the stone foundation. The rhythmic balls of flame lick the bottom of the platform. Blackened vines hang down from the platform to nearly touch the bog below.

A **green dragon** sleeps in the muck beneath the abandoned temple. The gouts of fire are the result of thick swamp vapors mixing with the dragon's poisonous snores. The mixing gases ignite to form the balls of green flame rising out of the swamp. The green dragon stores its treasure inside the abandoned temple. The creature rises out of the muck to attack anyone wading into the sludge to get to its hoard.

Dragon, Red

Hit Dice: 9–11
Armor Class: 2 [17]
Attacks: 2 claws (1d8), bite (3d10)
Saving Throw: 6, 5, or 4
Special: Breathes fire
Move: 9/24 (flying)
Alignment: Chaos
Number Encountered: 1d2, or a nest (2 of age category 4 and 1d4 of age category 1d3)
Challenge Level/XP: Challenge Level = (hit points/4) +2

Red dragons are the fire-breathing wyrms of legend. They breathe fire in a cone-shape 90 feet long and roughly 30 ft wide at the base. Red dragons have a 75% chance of being able to talk; talking red dragons have a 20% chance of being able to cast 1d4 first level Magic-User spells, 1d3 second level Magic-User spells, and 1d2 third level Magic-User spells.

Adult Red Dragon (9HD): HD 9 (36hp); AC 2[17]; Atk 2 claws (1d8), 1 bite (3d10); Move 9 (Fly 24); Save 6; AL C; CL/XP 11/1700; Special: Breathes fire.

Adult Red Dragon (10HD): HD 10 (40hp); AC 2[17]; Atk 2 claws (1d8), 1 bite (3d10); Move 9 (Fly 24); Save 5; AL C; CL/XP 12/2000; Special: Breathes fire.

Adult Red Dragon (11HD): HD 11 (44hp); AC 2[17]; Atk 2 claws (1d8), 1 bite (3d10); Move 9 (Fly 24); Save 4; AL C; CL/XP 13/2300; Special: Breathes fire.

The Dragon Slayer

A glowing marble bier sits on a grassy knoll rising in the middle of the Fields of Kelt. Gardens of flowers grow in five distinct sections around the slight rise. One triangular patch contains red roses, and another has white lilies. A third has blue asters while the fourth has green hydrangeas. The fifth contains purplish-black tulips. A narrow path of golden stones rises up the incline to the bier. A glass enclosure sits atop the bier, protecting the remains of a skeletal warrior lying on the marble slab.

The skeleton is dressed in a chain mail shirt with a red tunic emblazoned with a rising sun. His armor is burned and blackened in spots, and several large rents are sliced through the chain links. A long sword lies beside the remains. Its pommel has a dragon's head breathing fire on it. An engraved plate at the skeleton's feet reads "Doblut the Brave, Dragon Slayer Extraordinaire." The glass encasing the body shatters easily if anyone strikes it. The sword is a replica of the dragon slayer's real blade. It crumbles into shards of rusty metal if touched.

Disturbing Doblut's bones draws an ancient curse placed on the warrior's bones when he was laid to rest. The curse summons a **red dragon** to protect the bones. The dragon is as surprised as PCs, and immediately attacks. The dragon can appear flying or on the ground, and forgiving Referees might change the color of the dragon based on the PCs' abilities.

The dragon slayer's real sword – a *+3 glowing bastard sword* that kills dragons on a roll of a natural 20 – lies encased in the marble bier supporting Doblut's bones. Destroying the bier is the only way to get the sword. PCs who fail to rebury the dragon slayer's bones may find themselves facing other curses.

Dragon, Silver

Hit Dice: 9-11
Armor Class: 2 [17]
Attacks: 2 claws (1d8), 1 bite (3d10)
Saving Throw: 6 (9HD), 5 (10HD), 4 (11HD)
Special: Breathes frost or paralyzing gas, polymorph
Move: 9/24 (flying)
Alignment: Law
Number Encountered: 1d2, or a nest (2 of age category 4 and 1d4 of age category 1d3)
Challenge Level/XP: Challenge Level = (hit points/4) +2

Silver dragons are active servants of law/good; although they do not necessarily pursue this goal by assisting humankind, most would protect human settlements and civilized regions in the face of serious threats. They have the ability to polymorph themselves into human and animal forms. Silver dragons can either breath a cone of cold (70ft long, to a width of 30ft) or exhale a cloud of paralytic gas 50ft in diameter and 20ft from ground to top (duration 3d6 turns, saving throw negates). Silver dragons have an 80% chance of being able to talk; talking silver dragons have a 20% chance of being able to cast 1d4 first level magic-user spells, 1d3 second level magic-user spells, and 1d2 third level magic-user spells. These dragons range in size from 9 to 11 hit dice.

Adult Silver Dragon (9HD): HD 9 (36hp); AC 2[17]; Atk 2 claws (1d8), 1 bite (3d10); Move 9 (Fly 24); Save 6; AL L; CL/XP 11/1700; Special: Breathes frost or paralyzing gas, polymorph.

Adult Silver Dragon (10HD): HD 10 (40hp); AC 2[17]; Atk 2 claws (1d8), 1 bite (3d10); Move 9 (Fly 24); Save 5; AL L; CL/XP 12/2000; Special: Breathes frost or paralyzing gas, polymorph.

Adult Silver Dragon (11HD): HD 11 (44hp); AC 2[17]; Atk 2 claws (1d8), 1 bite (3d10); Move 9 (Fly 24); Save 4; AL L; CL/XP 13/2300; Special: Breathes frost or paralyzing gas, polymorph.

Tarnished Silver

Twitching bodies lie in the cobblestone streets of the small hamlet of Lilly. Many of the people foam at the mouth, while others jerk spasmodically in the dirt. A fine layer of silver ash coats the street and bodies. The people of Lilly are still alive, although barely. Their eyes are rolled back in their heads and they are unresponsive.

The villagers are victims of a **silver dragon** living among the mountain cliffs overlooking the village. **Argennones the Lustrous** sleeps in a cave overrun in recent years by a creeping moss that causes delusions and incites anger in anyone breathing the red spores. The dragon's mind is clouded by delusions, and he gave up on protecting the villagers and instead turned to gassing them to keep them quiet. The dragon regularly flies over the houses and breathes paralytic gas to subdue the villagers. The dragon's lungs are coated by spores that extend the paralytic poison's effects to 2d6 days instead of hours. The villagers have been paralyzed for less than a day so far, but begin dying of dehydration in another couple of days. PCs can wait for the dragon to find them or seek him out in his mountainside cave.

Dragon, White

Hit Dice: 5–7
Armor Class: 2 [17]
Attacks: 2 claws (1d4), bite (2d8)
Saving Throw: 12, 11, or 9
Special: Breathes cold
Move: 9/24 (flying)
Alignment: Chaos
Number Encountered: 1d2, or a nest (2 of age category 4 and 1d4 of age category 1d3)
Challenge Level/XP: Challenge Level = (hit points/4) +2

White dragons are usually found in cold regions, where they camouflage themselves in ice and snow, lying in wait for prey. They breathe a cone of intensely cold air and frost, with a length of 70 ft and a base of 30 ft. White dragons are not able to talk or cast spells.

Adult White Dragon (5HD): HD 5 (20hp); AC 2[17]; Atk 2 claws (1d4), 1 bite (2d8); Move 9 (Fly 24); Save 12; AL C; CL/XP 7/600; Special: Breathes frost.

Adult White Dragon (6HD): HD 6 (24hp); AC 2[17]; Atk 2 claws (1d4), 1 bite (2d8); Move 9 (Fly 24); Save 11; AL C; CL/XP 8/800; Special: Breathes frost.

Adult White Dragon (7HD): HD 7 (28hp); AC 2[17]; Atk 2 claws (1d4), 1 bite (2d8); Move 9 (Fly 24); Save 9; AL C; CL/XP 9/1100; Special: Breathes frost.

The Whites of His Eyes

A collection of eyeballs dominates this blue-hued room in the Wailing Glacier. Sapphire-colored algae in the ice give the room its color. One large archway cut through the ice leads downward into the depths of the glacier's interior. The eyes are stuck to the 20-foot-tall frozen walls in hundreds of places, and line the floor like misshapen eggs. Other eyes sit in recessed pockets cut into the walls. The eyeballs appear to have been cut from various creatures and range in size from a hummingbird's eye to the size of a person's head.

One of the eyes belongs to **Iciilivennik**, a **white dragon** that hunts the lands around the Wailing Glacier. The dragon stares through a hole that connects with her icy lair on the other side of the wall. Once PCs enter the eye room, she pulls away from the wall and breathes a cone of frost at the wall of her lair. The eyes plug many more holes cut through the ice, and allow the frost to come blasting through in 6 icy torrents. Iciilivennik's treasure hoard lies frozen in clear blocks of ice in her chamber, and includes nearly 2,400 gp and the body of a frozen halfling.

Dragon Turtle

Hit Dice: 11 to 14
Armor Class: 2 [17]
Attacks: 2 claws (1d8), bite (3d10)
Saving Throw: 4 (11HD) or 3
Special: Break ships, breathe steam
Move: 3 (9 swimming)
Alignment: Neutrality or Chaos
Number Encountered: 1
Challenge Level/XP: 11 HD (13/2,300); 12 HD (14/2,600);
13 HD (15/2,900); 14 HD (16/3,200)

These shell-backed monsters breathe scalding steam in a cone-shape 90 feet long and roughly 30 ft wide at the base, inflicting as many hit points of damage as the monster has (when at full hp). Dragon turtles have a 75% chance of being able to talk, and these have a 20% chance of being able to cast 1d4 first level Magic-User spells, 1d3 second level Magic-User spells, and 1d2 third level Magic-User spells. A dragon turtle that rises beneath all but the largest ship can lift it, possibly making it capsize (roughly 50%).

Dragon Turtle (11HD): HD 11; AC 2[17]; Atk 2 claws (1d8), 1 bite (3d10); Move 3 (Swim 9); Save 4; AL N; CL/XP 13/2300; Special: Break ships, breath weapon (steam).

The Turtle King's Retinue

A funeral barge floats slowly down the river, carrying a dead priest-king and his belongings to the afterlife. Four golden statues face inward to hold aloft a brightly decorated sarcophagus in the middle of the 30-foot-wide-by-60-foot-long barge. Piled under the suspended sarcophagus are a bounty of riches, including 600 gp, hundreds of loose gems (1,500 gp total), a silver scepter and a dozen cat statues with emerald eyes (100 gp each). The body in the sarcophagus is wrapped in white linen and wears a golden crown (150 gp) on its head. The crown has a top like a tortoise shell. Hundreds of turtles crawl across the barge.

The body was that of beloved King Nephealin of the Crescent Reaches. The good king took his greatest secret to his grave: He was actually an intelligent turtle transformed into a man. When he finally died of old age, his reptilian brothers came out to accompany his body downriver. The normal turtles are harmless, but the barge is being propelled by a **dragon turtle** swimming underwater. The dragon turtle stops pushing the barge and attacks if PCs try to rob the great king of his treasures.

Dragonne

Hit Dice: 9
Armor Class: 2 [17]
Attacks: 2 claws (1d6), 1 bite (2d6+1)
Saving Throw: 6
Special: Roar
Move: 18/9 (flying)
Alignment: Neutrality
Number Encountered: 1
Challenge Level/XP: 10/1,400

These creatures resemble a cross between a lion and a dragon, for they have a scaled dragon's body (smaller than a dragon's, though) with a great mane of flowing hair. The head is leonine in shape, but has reptilian scales. They do not normally have a breath weapon, but dragonnes have a tremendous roar. Anyone hearing the roar must save or be weakened (-1 to all attacks) for 1 turn.

Dragonne: HD 9; AC 2[17]; Atk 2 claws (1d6), 1 bite (2d6+1); Move 18 (Fly 9); Save 6; AL N; CL/XP 10/1400; Special: Roar.

Cat Wants Your Tongue

Eston Judd's farmhouse sits near a babbling brook in the middle of hundreds of acres of fields. The farmer's cattle roam freely about the fields, kept in by wooden fences that line the property's boundaries. A dirt road leads up to the farmhouse, where chickens peck at the ground and the farmer's six grandchildren get underfoot. Eston sits in a rocking chair on the porch, a well-used scythe at his side and a dour look on his face.

Eston's cows are under attack, and he doesn't know who – or what – to blame. So far, six cows have been killed, their heads ripped clean off their bodies. A monstrous roar in the middle of the night usually means he'll find a cow decapitated the next morning. The farmer needs someone to watch over his cows at night, and he's willing to pay up to 10 gp per person. He fears whatever is stalking the cattle might one day come for him and his grandchildren.

The cattle are under attack by a **dragonne** that has developed a taste for cow tongue. It rips the cows heads off, eats their tongues and leaves the rest of the meat for scavengers. The dragonne has a cave in the hills near Eston's fence line.

Draug (Wolf-Bear Folk)

Hit Dice: 3+3
Armor Class: 7[12] or with shield 6[13]
Attacks: 1 weapon (1d8+2)
Saving Throw: 14
Special: +2 to hit
Move: 12
Alignment: Neutrality (sometimes Law)
Number Encountered: 1d6+3 or 4d10
Challenge Level/XP: 3/60

The Draug are a race of 8ft tall, bear-like humanoids with wolf-like heads and tails. They are brave warriors and strong drinkers, and their shield-lined longhouses resound to boasting and merriment. The "wolf-bear folk" fight with spear, axe, dagger, or broad sword, and gain +2 to hit and damage due to their great strength. Any treasure will be in the form of hack-silver jewelry, weapons and shields of fine craftsmanship and exquisite decoration, and kegs of mead. Suggestions they were created by the same eccentric wizard responsible for the Owl Bear will be met with howls of laughter, and an overflowing tankard of mead.

— Author: Scott Wylie Roberts, "Myrystyr"

Draug: HD 3+3; AC 7[12] or with shield 6[13]; Atk 1 weapon (1d8+2); Move 12; Save 14; AL N or L; CL/XP 3/60; Special: +2 to hit.

Guard Draugs

A girl weeps at the base of a willow tree. She clutches a teddy bear to her side as she sobs. She has yellow hair and big blue eyes. She wears a purple dress that has seen better days. Her knees are dirty from kneeling on the ground. Her cheeks are red from crying. If approached, she shies away from PCs at first before breaking down and telling them that her parents are missing. She claims they were taken by "bear dogs." She says her name is **Hildy**. She asks PCs to rescue her parents, and leads them to where they are being held.

The marble mausoleum is nestled amid the mighty forest oaks. The structure has a peaked roof and a single door. Standing in front of the door are **2 draugs**. Each creature holds the leash of a **winter wolf** that lies at the draug's feet. The draugs laugh at the sound of someone inside the mausoleum screaming. Occasionally, another **draug** steps out of the mausoleums door and shares a joke with the guards. He wipes his bloody hands on his fur before going back inside. The screaming starts anew soon afterward.

The draugs recently stopped **2 doppelgangers** trying to infiltrate their camp. The doppelgangers didn't count on the draugs sniffing out their disguises as they marched into the longhouse. The pair barely escaped with their lives, but lost each other in the forest. One was captured immediately as he hid in the mausoleum. The other assumed the guise of "Hildy" to trick PCs into rescuing her partner. The draugs snarl viciously at PCs if they approach with the doppelganger. Hildy hopes to rescue her mate as the PCs and draug fight.

Doppelganger: HD 4; AC 5[14]; Atk 1 claw (1d12); Move 9; Save 13 (5 vs. magic); AL C; CL/XP 5/240; Special: Mimics shape, immune to sleep and charm.

Winter Wolf: HD 5; AC 5[14]; Atk 1 bite (1d6+1); Move 18; Save 12; AL C; CL/XP 6/400; Special: Breathe frost (1/turn).

Drider

Hit Dice: 7
Armor Class: 3 [16]
Attacks: 1 weapon (1d8)
Saving Throw: 9
Special: Spells, innate magical abilities
Move: 18
Alignment: Chaos
Number Encountered: 1d6
Challenge Level/XP: 9/1,100

Driders are spider-centaurs: the body is that of a massive spider, but the torso is that of a delicate human-like person.

Driders have the following innate magical abilities, usable once per day: create lantern-like lights at a range of 60ft, *darkness 15ft radius, detect magic,* and *levitate.* In addition, driders are spellcasters. Male driders are magic-users (4/3/2/1), and females are clerics (2/2/2/1/1).

Drider: HD 7; AC 3[16]; Atk 1 weapon (1d8); Move 18; Save 9; AL C; CL/XP 9/1100; Special: Spells, magical abilities.

Web of Command

A 100-foot-ball of webs hangs from the high ceiling of this cavernous chamber. Stalactites hang down around the web ball. The ball is suspended from the rocky cave roof by a 20-foot-diameter strand of webbing. A 10-foot-diameter circular hole cut in the side of the globe makes it look like a giant beehive. Crawling across the outer surface of the globe are thousands of normal spiders and **10 giant spiders**. The bones of thousands of creatures are barely visible beneath the sticky strands.

The web ball is the command sphere of a band of driders that terrorizes the land above. **Drider Adjutant General Lierech Voem** wields a *+3 bone staff* topped with a drow skull and is renowned for his ferocity in combat. The staff causes *confusion* (as per the spell) in anyone it hits who fails a saving throw. He is accompanied by **6 drider warriors** who are as loyal as they are bloodthirsty. The interior of the web ball is decorated with the driders' kills. Bodies (some of them still alive) are pressed into the webbing to hold them in place.

Giant Spider (6ft diameter): HD 4+2; AC 4[15]; Atk 1 bite (1d6+2 + poison); Move 4; Save 13; AL N; CL/XP 7/600; Special: lethal poison, webs.

Drow

Hit Dice: 2
Armor Class: 3[16]
Attacks: By weapon
Saving Throw: 16
Special: 50% magic resistance, +2 on all saving throws, spell abilities, 1 in 8 chance to be surprised
Move: 12
Alignment: Chaos
Challenge Level/XP: 5/240

The drow are dark elves, denizens of the Under Realms, dwellers in darkness. They have coal-black skin and white hair. These creatures of chaos despise the surface-dwelling servants of Law, and would certainly choose to eradicate them if the drow themselves did not dislike sunlight. All attacks made by drow in sunlight, or in even magical light, will be made at a penalty of -2.

All drow have the following spell-like powers: *darkness 15ft radius*, ability to limn a target in faint light at a range of 60ft (all have +1 to hit the victim), and the ability to create lantern-like lights at a range of 60ft.

All drow wear +1 chain mail and carry +1 longswords. They wear cloaks and boots that make them difficult to see and hear (75% chance to surprise). All of this equipment will decay in sunlight, becoming useless after 2d6 days of normal exposure. Roughly half of normal drow will also be carrying hand-crossbows that fire poison darts (1d3 damage, sleep poison save at -4).

Drow are capable of advancing in level, and their leaders may be considerably more dangerous than the normal 2HD (Ftr2) drow. Male drow may have magic-user levels up to 12, and fighter levels up to 7. Female drow may have fighter levels up to 9, and magic –user or cleric levels up to 12 or 18 respectively. These higher-level leaders may be carrying swords with greater than a +1 bonus, shields with a magical bonus, and/or wearing chain mail with greater than a +1 bonus.

Drow: HD 2; AC 3[16]; Atk +1 longsword (1d8+1); Move 12; Save 14 (includes +2); AL C; CL/XP 5/240 Special: 50% magic resistance, +2 on all saving throws, lights, darkness 15ft, 1 in 8 to-be-surprised chance.

Ambush!

Travelling along a narrow stretch of cavern, it eventually opens up into a 15 foot passage that allows free movement. A constant dripping can be heard in the lightless environment, although where the sounds is coming form is difficult to determine. The surrounding stone is quite cool to the touch, and a inconsistent breeze issues from somewhere in the vast void of darkness.

Taking a moment to catch your collective breath after squeezing through the rent in the surrounding rock, the party may notice (1 on d6) a slight tapping sound from up ahead, as if metal were hitting stone, oh so softly.

If the party approaches the sound, when their torchlight reaches far enough, they notice a cloaked figure perched atop a boulder, head down and tapping a metal rod of some kind on the stone.

If the party speaks, or after a few minutes of being in the torchlight, the figure raises its head. "You shouldn't be here, surfacers, " it says in Elvish." This wasn't meant for you, but it looks like you scared away our prey. Y ou'll do." The party is attacked by **12 drow warriors** emerging from the darkness as well as their captain, **Mirridon.** Half the drow fire hand crossbows, while the others move to engage the party hand-to-hand.

Mirridon, Drow Fighter 4: HP 20; AC 0[19]; Atk +2 longsword (1d8+2); Move 12; Save 9 (includes +2); AL C; CL/XP 6/400; Special: Dexterity 16, 50% magic resistance, +2 on all saving throws, lights, darkness 15ft, 1 in 8 to-be-surprised chance. Equipment: +1 chainmail, +1 shield, +2 longsword, drow cloak and boots, 2 potions of healing.

Dryad

Hit Dice: 2
Armor Class: 9 [10]
Attacks: Wooden dagger (1d4)
Saving Throw: 16
Special: Charm person (-2 save)
Move: 12
Alignment: Neutrality
Number Encountered: 1
Challenge Level/XP: 3/60

Dryads are beautiful female tree spirits who do not venture far from their home trees. They can cast (as a native magical power) a strong charm that operates as a *Charm Person* spell with a **-2** penalty to the saving throw. Those who are charmed seldom return, or might be kept for a hundred years and a day within the dryad's tree.

Dryad: HD 2; AC 9[10]; Atk 1 wooden dagger (1d4); Move 12; Save 16; AL N; CL/XP 3/60; Special: Charm person (-2 save).

Tear Down That Wall

A 30-foot-tall unfinished stone tower stands atop this small hillock. Sunflowers and lilacs grow abundantly around it, and flowering vines climb the granite blocks. The top of a tree grows out of the tower's open roof. The tree's canopy spreads out above the tower's top, casting deep shadows down the tower's walls. Branches push out through the walls, breaking through the stone. Colorful leaves spread into the sky. A **woman** lounges on a high branch above the tower. A white banner drapes over the limb she rests on. Hanging from a noose tied in the end of the banner is a dead hill giant.

Another **hill giant** works at the base of the tower, fashioning mud into stone blocks. The giant's face is streaked with sweat, mud and tears, and his hands are coated in the thick glop. He is building a new layer of stones around the current tower. The new stone wall rises 15 feet around the current structure. The giant is the brother of the giant hanging in the noose. The dryad tired of her former slave and ordered him to kill himself to torment the brother who kept trying to rescue him. After his death, the giant's twin decided to brick off the tree to slowly kill the dryad. He is immune to the dryad's charm, unlike his brother.

The dryad pleads for help from passing PCs. She uses her charm ability as a last resort, hoping PCs take care of the giant before discovering her true nature. She won't hesitate to charm PCs afterward to destroy the wall for her.

Hill Giant: HD 8+2; AC 4[15]; Atk 1 weapon (2d8); Move 12; Save 8; AL C; CL/XP 9/1100; Special: Throw boulders.

Duergar

Hit Dice: 1+2
Armor Class: 4[15]
Attacks: By weapon
Saving Throw: 18
Special: +4 save vs. magic, immune to illusions, invisibility, enlarge
Move: 9
Alignment: Chaos
Number Encountered: 2d8 or 1d100x2
Challenge Level/XP: 3/60

The duergar, often called the "dark dwarves," are foul-tempered creatures that loathe intruders to their underground realms—but not nearly as much as they do their kinfolk closer to the surface. Duergar dwell in communities deep underground, and appear as darker, more twisted versions of normal dwarves. Their skin is a dull gray, as though rubbed with dust or ash, but this is a natural coloration that better allows them to blend with their underground surroundings. They are a race of slavers, but while non-dwarven prisoners are usually put to backbreaking work, dwarves are generally slain on the spot.

Duergar can turn invisible once per day, and can also double their size once per day (this allows the duergar to attack as a 4HD creature, and heals 50% of any damage the duergar had taken prior to the change). Duergar leaders gain +2 to hit rather than an increase in hit dice.

Duergar: HD 1+2; AC 4[15]; Atk 1 weapon (1d8); Move 9; Save 18; AL C; CL/XP 3/60; Special: +4 save vs. magic, immune to illusions, invisibility, enlarge.

Hi ho!

Following a tunnel that has been going for what seems like miles, it finally opens slightly into a modest natural cavern, 50 feet in diameter. Several tents and a few shabby lean-tos are erected around the perimeter. Barely a scant few feet separate each modest structure.

What room there is between tents is filled with all manner of creatures; drow, humans, orcs, goblins and other less identifiable creatures mingle in what looks to be some kind of underground market place.

Six **duergar merchants** are busy peddling their wares to the highest bidder. Any item could possibly be here (Referee's discretion), but the biggest trade by far is in slaves. Several races are bound in chains; a troll is currently being haggled over. Should the PCs decide to intervene (good characters are almost obliged to, if for no other reason than the deplorable condition of the slaves), they face a myriad of foes drawn from both underground and surface races.

Dwarf

Hit Dice: 1
Armor Class: 4 [15]
Attacks: War hammer (1d4+1)
Saving Throw: 17
Special: Detects attributes of stonework
Move: 6
Alignment: Law
Number Encountered: 1d6, 7, or 4d10
Challenge Level/XP: 1/15

Statistics above are for the common Dwarf with no particular unusual characteristics. A dwarf-at-arms would usually have a full 8 hit points, reflecting skill and general toughness. Stronger Dwarfs (sergeants-at-arms, for example) might have more hit dice or unusual bonuses to hit, or even magical abilities if such is possible (Norse myths are a good example of this.) Do not bother to treat more-powerful NPC dwarfs as Fighters or other character types; just assign the right number of hit dice and abilities (if any) and keep moving along with the fantasy.

Dwarf: HD 1; AC 4[15]; Atk 1 weapon (1d8); Move 6; Save 17; AL L; CL/XP 1/15; Special: Detect attributes of stonework.

Hors' Dwarf

A tree trunk sits over a 10-foot-wide firepit. The bare trunk is held in the air by two large boulders placed across the smoldering pile of ash from one another. A cave opens into the hillside behind the firepit. A mule stands on its hind legs and pushes against the log with its front hooves. The mule doesn't make a sound as it works. A dwarf tied to the trunk with leather straps wriggles angrily but is unable to escape his predicament. The dwarf is tied underneath the log, with straps wrapped around his forehead, legs and body. The straps are tied in crude knots on the other side of the log from the squirming dwarf.

Fuglish Ashenchisel is a **dwarf** prospector who works the Irontrace Hills looking for gold. He stumbled upon a gold vein in the nearby cave, but in his haste he didn't realize he'd stumbled into the lair of **2 ettins**. The ettins returned from a hunting trip and surprised the dwarf. The tired ettins tied the dwarf to the tree to roast him after their nap. Fuglish's highly intelligent mule **Maggard** was smart enough to hide from the creatures. He returned later to free his owner. The ettins charge out of the cave if they hear any loud noises. They each carry clubs and intend to stop anyone trying to take their next snack.

Ettin: HD 10; AC 3[16]; Atk 2 clubs (3d6); Move 12; Save 5; AL C; CL/XP 10/1400; Special: None.

Dwelver

Hit Dice: 4+2
Armor Class: 3 [16]
Attacks: 1 weapon or strike (1d8)
Saving Throw: 13
Special: Collective summoning
Move: 6
Alignment: Chaos
Number Encountered: 1d10+8
Challenge Level/XP: 5/240

Dwelvers were once a race of dwarves that followed their greed to the elemental plane of earth to mine it for its riches. Throughout the millennia they slowly began to change into the very substances they sought. While still resembling dwarves in form, they are made of stone, ores and gems. Dwelvers are malevolent and greedy and will defend their claims against all comers. They now exist only to mine worlds of their mineral resources, which they use to create more of their race. Groups of Dwelvers are able to summon Earth Elementals, which will serve them faithfully. At least eight Dwelvers are needed to summon an 8 hit dice Earth Elemental, twelve for one of 12 hit dice and sixteen to summon one of 16 hit dice. It is also likely Dwelvers are able to employ other earthen magics.

— Author: The Lizard of Oz

Dwelver: HD 4+2; AC 3[16]; Atk 1 weapon or strike (1d8); Move 6; Save 13; AL C; CL/XP 5/240; Special: Collective summoning.

Whistle While You Work

A whistling tune echoes through the granite tunnels of Hopewell Peak, the jaunty sounds bouncing through the mine's stone corridors. The sound comes from **8 dwelvers** walking around a mine cart that tromps slowly forward on four elephantine legs. The whistling comes from holes cut through the dwarf-like bodies of the dwelvers as they move. The dwelvers stop occasionally to dig into the rock walls as they mine gold ore and gems. They toss anything they find into the self-moving cart. The cart currently contains 643 gp worth of ore and 15 gems worth a total of 1,780 gp.

The dwelvers are highly territorial and attack any "claim jumpers" they find in their mine. The dwelvers' whistling tune turns into a tea-kettle scream as they leap into combat. The cart is an **8 HD earth elemental** that rises up into a humanoid form (with the gold and gems it is carrying still embedded in its body) to join the dwelvers in defending their tunnels.

Earth Elemental (8HD): HD 8; AC 2[17]; Atk 1 strike (3d6); Move 6; Save 8; AL N; CL/XP 9/1100; Special: Tear down stonework.

Eagle, Giant

Hit Dice: 4
Armor Class: 7 [12]
Attacks: 2 talons (1d4), 1 bite (1d8)
Saving Throw: 13
Special: None
Move: 3/24 (flying)
Alignment: Neutrality
Number Encountered: 1 (hunting) or 1d20 (aerie)
Challenge Level/XP: 5/240

Giant eagles are just large enough to carry a human rider. Some varieties of the breed may be intelligent, and truly unusual specimens might even be capable of casting spells or using other magical powers. These unusual breeds of giant eagle might be aligned with Law rather than Neutrality. Because giant eagles can be tamed as mounts, their eggs and fledglings are worth considerable amounts of gold (500+gp).

Giant Eagle: HD 4; AC 7[12]; Atk 2 talons (1d4), 1 bite (1d8); Move 3 (Fly 24); Save 13; AL N; CL/XP 5/240; Special: None.

The Eagle's Nest

An eagle's shrieks echo through the high peaks of the Hollow Spire Mountains, but the sound is not majestic and awe-inspiring. Instead, it is filled with pain and terror. A flat rock jutting from the side of the mountain reveals the scene: **3 ogres** have a giant eagle pinned to the ground by its wings. One holds a large club ready to kill the bird. The thrashing bird is fighting back, but on its back it is no match for the stronger ogres. One of the ogres wears a wyvern's skull on its head. It carries a massive spear topped with the stinger of the slain beast.

The ogres discovered the eagle's nest and climbed up to get to the fledglings for a quick meal. They grabbed the mother out of the air when she tried to protect her family. If rescued, the giant eagle remembers the deed and arrives with friends to offer PCs a ride when they require it.

Ogres (3): HD 4+1; HP 15, 18, 20; AC 5[14]; Atk 1 weapon (1d10+1); Move 9; Save 13; AL C; CL/XP 4/120; Special: None.

Ogre Leader: HD 5+1; HP 30; AC 4[15]; Atk 1 Wyvern-tail tipped spear (1d10 + 1 + poison); Move 9; Save 13; AL C; CL/XP 4/120; Special: None.

Eel, Giant

	GIANT ELECTRIC	GIANT MORAY
Hit Dice:	2	4
Armor Class:	8 [11]	7 [12]
Attacks:	1 bite (1d3)	1 bite (2d6)
Saving Throw:	16	13
Special:	Electric shock	None
Move:	0/9 (swimming)	0/9 (swimming)
Alignment:	Neutrality	Neutrality
Number Encountered:	1d4	1d4
Challenge Level/XP:	4/120	4/120

These statistics are for giant eels about ten feet in length. Larger eels would have correspondingly greater hit dice. The electric shock generated by a giant electric eel would cause 3d6 points of damage in the surrounding water, with no saving throw. See also, "Lampreys," which are also eels.

Giant Electric Eel: HD 2; AC 8[11]; Atk 1 bite (1d3); Move 0 (Swim 9); Save 16; AL N; CL/XP 4/120; Special: Electric shock.

Giant Moray Eel: HD 4; AC 7[12]; Atk 1 bite (2d6); Move 0 (Swim 9); Save 13; AL N; CL/XP 4/120; Special: None.

The Foundering Lamprey

The Lamprey is an odd sailing ship captain by a still odder halfling. The ship itself has no oars and no sails, but somehow easily plies the ocean waves. It pushes forward at a fast clip through the rolling swells, barely slowing down. The co-captain, Ollie Nematoad, is a halfling inventor whose creations always seem to get the better of him – or others. This time, however, the Lamprey is exceeding all his expectations.

Until it stopped, that is. The boat now founders in the waves, pushed about by the ocean's swells. A stormy red sky on the horizon promises dangerous weather ahead, and the crew hired on for the Lamprey's maiden voyage look on in fear. Ollie requires someone to jump over the side of the ship and see what's wrong with the propeller. He has special masks (which he invented) that allow a PC to breathe underwater for one hour.

The Lamprey's secret propulsion system lies in an underwater metal cage containing a propeller driven by the static discharges of **4 giant electric eels**. The cage captured the eels' shocks and turned them into electrical charges to drive the ship's propeller. The angry eels bit a hole in the metal cage, however, and now swim freely in the closed hold. A door in the side of the ship allows PCs to enter the side of the ship below the waterline, but the penned-in eels rush anyone doing so.

Efreeti

Hit Dice: 10
Armor Class: 2 [17]
Attacks: Fist or sword (2d8)
Saving Throw: 5
Special: Wall of fire
Move: 9/24 (flying)
Alignment: Chaos
Number Encountered: 1
Challenge Level/XP: 12/2,000

Efreet are a type of genie, associated with fire (in contrast to the djinn, who have powers over the air). Efreet can carry up to 1000 pounds of weight, and under the right circumstances they can be forced to serve as a slave until they figure out how to free themselves. An efreeti can create a wall of fire (per the spell). They appear as giant humans with cruel features, their skin flickering with flames.

Efreeti: HD 10; AC 2[17]; Atk 1 fist or sword (1d8+5); Move 9 (Fly 24); Save 5; AL C; CL/XP 12/2000; Special: Wall of fire.

Hot Spot

Thick snow flies through the air, the forward edge of a freezing wind that slices through clothing to turn skin to ice. Torches flicker in the strong winds, and vision is limited by the driving snow. Drifts move steadily across the deepening snowfield, making it tougher and tougher every moment to slog forward. A flickering red glow in the whiteness is an inviting promise of warmth in this hellish chill. A carved oak staff sticks from the thawing ground in a muddy 20-foot-diameter clearing. Atop the staff, a red ruby flickers and pulses. The gemstone radiates a welcoming heat that melts the snow around it.

The staff was placed here by the natives of the Northern Ice, who trapped an **efreeti** in the ruby's facets. The powerful genie is powerless as long as the gem remains in cold climates. If taken south where snow doesn't cover the ground year-round, the gem shatters in an explosion of fire and heat (3d6 points of damage to any standing within 10 feet, save for half) as the efreeti bursts forth, angry at his years in isolation. The staff has no other magical properties.

ELEMENTALS

Elementals are living manifestations of the basic forms of matter: earth, air, fire, and water. They are usually summoned from their native planes of existence to do the bidding of a powerful wizard. These beings can also be "chained" within objects or structures to give the objects magical properties. Elementals are barely intelligent at all, but they are as powerful as the forces of nature that they actually are.

Elemental, Air

Hit Dice: 8, 12, or 16
Armor Class: 2 [17]
Attacks: Strike (2d8)
Saving Throw: 8, 3, or 3
Special: Whirlwind, immune to non-magic weapons
Move: 36 (flying)
Alignment: Neutrality
Challenge Level/XP: 8 HD (9/1,100), 12 HD (13/2,300), 16 HD (17/3,500)

Air elementals can turn into a whirlwind of air with a diameter of 30 ft, hurling any creature of 1 HD or less for great distances (and almost certainly killing them). These elemental whirlwinds are approximately 100 ft in height.

Air Elemental (8HD): HD 8; AC 2[17]; Atk 1 strike (2d8); Move (Fly 36); Save 8; AL N; CL/XP 9/1100; Special: Whirlwind, immune to non-magic weapons.

Air Elemental (12HD): HD 12; AC 2[17]; Atk 1 strike (2d8); Move (Fly 36); Save 3; AL N; CL/XP 13/2300; Special: Whirlwind, immune to non-magic weapons.

Air Elemental (16HD): HD 16; AC 2[17]; Atk 1 strike (2d8); Move (Fly 36); Save 3; AL N; CL/XP 17/3500; Special: Whirlwind, immune to non-magic weapons.

Daring Young Halfling . . .

A large kite flutters dangerously through the air before a 100-foot-tall column of air twisting across the ground behind it. The tornado slams through the hillsides, tearing trees from their roots and tossing large boulders across the plains like they were toys. Dirt flutters in spasming ribbons around the twister's swirling winds. A halfling strapped to the kite shouts with joy at the wild ride, somehow guiding his flimsy kite out of the way as the tornado slashes at it with arm-like swirls of torrential wind.

The halfling inventor Ollie Nematoad attached a white diamond (2,000 gp) stolen from the plane of air to the kite he rides, hoping it would power his craft. Instead, it drew an angry elemental to retrieve the gem. The air elemental tears across the plains, wreaking havoc as it goes. Whether Ollie sees PCs and glides overhead to "impress" them is left to the GM's discretion …

Elemental, Earth

Hit Dice: 8, 12, or 16
Armor Class: 2 [17]
Attacks: Fist (4d8)
Saving Throw: 8, 3, or 3
Special: Tear down stone, immune to non-magic weapons
Move: 6
Alignment: Neutrality
Number Encountered: 1
Challenge Level/XP: 8 HD (9/1,100), 12 HD (13/2,300), 16 HD (17/3,500)

Earth elementals are hulking man-shapes of rock and earth. They batter opponents with their great fists, although damage is reduced by 1d6 if the opponent is not standing upon earth or rock. Earth elementals can tear apart stone structures, able to rip down even a castle wall in a matter of 1d4+4 rounds (minutes).

Earth Elemental (8HD): HD 8; AC 2[17]; Atk 1 strike (4d8); Move 6; Save 8; AL N; CL/XP 9/1100; Special: Tear down stonework, immune to non-magic weapons.

Earth Elemental (12HD): HD 12; AC 2[17]; Atk 1 strike (4d8); Move 6; Save 3; AL N; CL/XP 13/2300; Special: Tear down stonework, immune to non-magic weapons.

Earth Elemental (16HD): HD 16; AC 2[17]; Atk 1 strike (4d8); Move 6; Save 3; AL N; CL/XP 17/3400; Special: Tear down stonework, immune to non-magic weapons.

The Gem of Tides

Lava rocks surround a dangerous tide pool of crashing waves on the edge of the Reaping Sea. A rock pillar in the middle of the tide pool has a gleaming jewel sitting atop it. The blue agate (1,000 gp) flashes brightly as it beats like a pulse to signal each pounding wave. The waves slam the rocks, then pull back quickly, dragging anything cast into the water into the ocean depths within moments. PCs that fall into the water must make a saving throw to grab a handhold or be pulled outward, taking 4d6 points of damage as he is yanked over the jagged rocks of the tide pool.

The lava rocks around the tide pool are an **earth elemental** tasked with protecting the *Gem of Tides*. The elemental rises up to smash anyone trying to claim the stone. It attempts to throw PCs into the tide pool to let the dangerous waters deal with them. It follows anyone who steals the gem, attacking mercilessly until the gem is returned. The gem can *locate water* (always active), grants the bearer *water breathing* (always active), can *create water* (10/day), can *lower water* (3/day), and allows the bearer to summon and control a water elemental once a month.

Elemental, Fire

Hit Dice: 8, 12, or 16
Armor Class: 2 [17]
Attacks: Strike (3d8)
Saving Throw: 8, 3, or 3
Special: Ignite materials, immune to non-magic weapons
Move: 12
Alignment: Neutrality
Number Encountered: 1
Challenge Level/XP: 8 HD (9/1,100), 12 HD (13/2,300), 16 HD (17/3,500)

Fire elementals are formless masses of flame, perhaps with a vaguely human shape. Their attacks cause flammable materials (including wood) to ignite if the material fails a saving throw (as determined by the Referee).

Fire Elemental (8HD): HD 8; AC 2[17]; Atk 1 strike (3d8); Move 12; Save 8; AL N; CL/XP 9/1100; Special: Ignite materials, immune to non-magic weapons.

Fire Elemental (12HD): HD 12; AC 2[17]; Atk 1 strike (3d8); Move 12; Save 3; AL N; CL/XP 13/2300; Special: Ignite materials, immune to non-magic weapons.

Fire Elemental (16HD): HD 16; AC 2[17]; Atk 1 strike (3d8); Move 12; Save 3; AL N; CL/XP 17/3400; Special: Ignite materials, immune to non-magic weapons.

Flame Eternal

A 50-foot-diameter rocky tunnel slants downward into the earth. Natural gas vents billow nauseating green fumes along its length, filling the cavern with a thick miasma of flammable vapors. The ceiling of the cave is alive with flame from the constant flow of rising gases. The flames roil and hiss across the stone, almost as if speaking in sibilant whispers. The burned corpses of a pair of ogres lie on the floor of the cavern. The air smells of burning hair and flesh. A red ruby (2,000 gp) floats in the burning flames near the ceiling.

The flames have been burning in this cavern for nearly 30 years as the unexhausted supply of gas continues filling the tunnel. The constant fire spontaneously opened a doorway to the plane of fire, allowing creatures of elemental energy a portal into the world. The doorway is currently watched by a fire elemental that leaps through the blazing sheet of flame on top of trespassers in the tunnel. The floating ruby is a stolen treasure taken from an efreet's palace on the plane of fire. The ogres tried to grab the ruby but invoked the wrath of the fire elemental.

Elemental, Water

Hit Dice: 8, 12, or 16
Armor Class: 2 [17]
Attacks: Strike (3d10)
Saving Throw: 8, 3, or 3
Special: Can overturn boats, immune to non-magic weapons
Move: 6/18 (swimming)
Alignment: Neutrality
Number Encountered: 1
Challenge Level/XP: 8 HD (9/1,100), 12 HD (13/2,300), 16 HD (17/3,500)

Water elementals cannot move more than 60 ft from a large body of water, and their damage is reduced by 1d6 if the opponent is not standing in water (or swimming, etc.). These powerful beings can overturn small boats, and can overturn a ship if given 1d4+4 rounds to work at it. On water, they can attack ships, battering them to pieces within 1 hour if not prevented or distracted.

Water Elemental (8HD): HD 8; AC 2[17]; Atk 1 strike (3d10); Move 6/18 (Swim); Save 8; AL N; CL/XP 9/1100; Special: overturn boats, immune to non-magic weapons.

Water Elemental (12HD): HD 12; AC 2[17]; Atk 1 strike (3d10); Move 6/18 (Swim); Save 3; AL N; CL/XP 13/2300; Special: overturn boats, immune to non-magic weapons.

Water Elemental (16HD): HD 16; AC 2[17]; Atk 1 strike (3d10); Move 6/18 (Swim); Save 3; AL N; CL/XP 17/3500; Special: overturn boats, immune to non-magic weapons.

Wasted Effort

A single-person outhouse stands alongside a quickly flowing stream. The well-built privy has double doors and a comfortable cushion situated on a heated marble slab. A washbasin of flowing water stands along the outer wall. The outhouse is the private "getaway" for a young prince with an extremely shy bladder. Unfortunately, the prince isn't very well liked, and a nefarious cousin paid an evil wizard to devise a way to do the poor lad in.

The cousin rigged the seat of the outhouse to drop an enchanted sulfur stone into the water well beneath the privy when someone sat down. The wizard trapped a **water elemental** in the sulfur stone. When the stone hits the water below, it is released. The angry elemental erupts out of the privy's hole in a shower of dirty water and waste, angry at its current environment. The underground stream connects to the river, allowing the elemental to jump from the outhouse to the stream without effort.

Elephant

Hit Dice: 10
Armor Class: 6[13]
Attacks: 1 trunk (1d10), 2 gore (1d10), 2 trample (2d6)
Saving Throw: 5
Special: None
Move: 12
Alignment: Neutrality
Challenge Level/XP: 11/1,700

Trained elephants can carry a howdah upon their backs, with up to six people within. In battle, wounded elephants may become maddened and go on a rampage, ignoring all training.

Elephant: HD 10; AC 6[13]; Atk 1 trunk (1d10), 2 gore (1d10), 2 trample (2d6); Move 12; Save 5; AL N; CL/XP 11/1700; Special: None.

Little White Mice

Borsille's town square is festive and alive with bunting hanging from balconies, rose petals on the ground, and doves flying in white flocks that wheel overhead. The festival celebrates the upcoming union of two houses of elven royalty. Throngs of people fill the streets for the posh wedding, and everyone seems to have worn their brightest and best clothing. The elven families arrive soon after, riding atop **3 trained elephants** carrying ornate howdah's on their backs. The elephants stomp through the streets as the children creep closer and closer to get a good look at the pachyderms.

Suddenly, a scream erupts from the front of the crowd, and the lead elephant trumpets in terror as someone tosses a box of little white mice at its feet. The elephant rises onto its back legs, throwing the bride from the howdah. The enraged animal charges through the crowd in a panic, bowling people out of the way and squashing those who refuse to move. The other elephants follow its lead. The groom and his parents cling to the howdahs. If rescued, they reward PCs with places of honor in the wedding (when it finally begins) and gift bags containing 100 gp, a ruby and diamond ring (50 gp) and an ornate candelabra with scented candles.

Elf

Hit Dice: 1+1
Armor Class: 5 [14]
Attacks: Sword (1d8) or 2 arrows (1d6)
Saving Throw: 17
Special: Darkvision 60ft, 4 in 6 chance to find secret doors, immune to ghoul paralysis.
Move: 12
Alignment: Law (sometimes Neutrality)
Challenge Level/XP: 1/15

The example above is for a typical Elf; trained warriors would likely have the maximum 9 hit points. Obviously, Elves encountered in the course of a party's adventuring will have a variety of powers and different attributes. The Referee will assign such powers as he sees fit, in accordance with the way he envisions elves. They might be the woodland dwellers of Tolkien's *The Hobbit*, or the high Elves of the *Lord of the Rings*, or might be the faerie folk of Irish legend. In any case, the Referee should not bother trying to fit an idea of "advanced" Elves into the constraints of character classes—just assign their attributes to fit the concept. Non-player characters are not subject to the rules that govern building a player character; they are tools for good fantasy.

Elf: HD 1+1; AC 5[14]; Atk 1 sword (1d8) or 2 arrows (1d6); Move 12; Save 17; AL L (or N); CL/XP 1/15; Special: Darkvision 60ft, 4 in 6 chance to find secret doors, immune to ghoul paralysis.

The Hallawstack Brigands

The bodies of six dwarves are tied to the dead trees of the Hallawstack Trees by their black beards. Each dwarf's body is cut and bruised, and arrows protrude from their backs. The arrows have ostrich feather fletching. The dwarven bodies have no treasure. They have been dead for six days. One of the dead dwarves is now a zombie that sits facing tree until PCs approach. Its violent death caused it to awake as one of the undead.

A small band of brigands roams through the scarred oaks known as the Hallawstack Trees. The forest of dead limbs and twisted branches grows where runoff from the dwarven forges of Gortlesnaid killed the once-beautiful forest. The brigands move silently through the trees like black ghosts, wearing the dark colors of the dead forest. The 7 elves are led by Annelise Hallawstack, the daughter of the elven lord who named the dying forest. The elves attack anyone – especially dwarves – who enter the dead trees. They use their bows to drive creatures from the dead forest. The brigands live in hidden treehouses high atop the dead oaks. The dwarves wandered into the woods in search of a lost relic of their god and met the angry forest protectors.

Ethereal Shade

Hit Dice: 8
Armor Class: 1 [18]
Attacks: Icy touch (2d6) or befuddlement
Saving Throw: 8
Special: Hard to see, immune to non-magic weapons.
Move: 9
Alignment: Chaos
Number Encountered: 1
Challenge Level/XP: 10/1,400

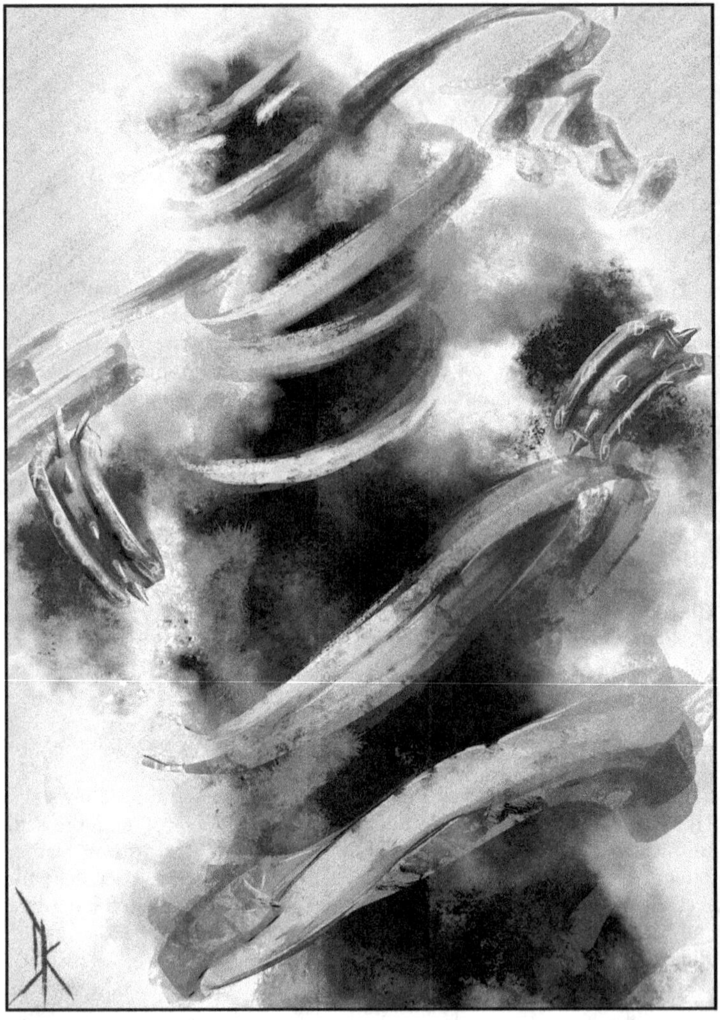

An ethereal shade resembles a mass of black, wispy smoke, which billows and contracts as it floats about. Ethereal Shades are undead and are thus affected by a cleric's Turn Undead ability (treat as a Type 9 undead). At night, or in darkness, it becomes nearly invisible. The referee may require a check or saving throw to spot an ethereal shade in such conditions. Battling an ethereal shade in dimly illuminated environments incurs a -4 penalty to hit. The ethereal shade inflicts damage by use of its icy touch. Ethereal Shades are immune to damage from non-magical weapons.

By wrapping itself around a victim's head, the ethereal shade may momentarily distract and befuddle its foe. The effects are similar to a Confusion spell and last as long as the ethereal shade remains wrapped around the victim's head. Any damage inflicted upon the creature while it is wrapped around a foe will result in the ethereal shade taking half the damage, and its engulfed victim taking the other half.

— Author: Skathros

Ethereal Shade: HD 8; AC 1[18]; Atk Icy touch (2d6) or befuddlement; Move 9; Save 8; AL C; CL/XP 10/1400; Special: Hard to see, immune to non-magic weapons.

Shades of Evil

The Baymoral Estate's haunted past keeps people away from its sprawling grounds. Lady Baymoral slaughtered her family over a dinner slight, then hung the servants and later herself from the rafters in the foyer. The estate fell into disrepair soon after, with no one willing to spend an evening in a place of pure evil.

The dining hall inside the manor is a place of continuing madness. The dark room has heavy velvet tapestries that cover the windows. Dark splotchy bloodstains mar portraits of the Baymoral family still hanging on the walls. A silver serving set (70 gp) and silver knives and forks (100 gp) sit on the table where they were last used. The white lace tablecloth is covered by patches of rust-colored mold. Rotted food sits on porcelain plates. Sitting in the plush chairs are the undead bodies of Lady Baymoral's family. There are **7 zombies** and **2 skeletons** in the seats. Each wears moldy clothing, fresh from the grave. The undead re-enact the last moment of their life each night. PCs disturb them at their peril. The zombies were poisoned by the roast lamb Lady Baymoral cooked, then stabbed to death with their utensils. The skeletons were pushed into the fireplace and burned alive.

Lady Baymoral is the true danger in the room. She became an **ethereal shade** after her death. Her spirit haunts the dining table. She rises from a decorative centerpiece to surround the heads of those she killed in a vain attempt to kill them again. The shade moves to attack PCs who interrupt the last meal. Lady Baymoral assumes anyone in the manor is a lost member of the family whom she failed to kill.

Ettercap

Hit Dice: 5
Armor Class: 6 [13]
Attacks: 2 claws (1d3), 1 bite (1d8 + poison)
Saving Throw: 12
Special: Poison bite, traps
Move: 12
Alignment: Chaos
Number Encountered: 1d2 or 2d4
Challenge Level/XP: 6/400

Ettercaps are a strange race of spindly, long-armed bipeds about seven feet tall. They have spider-like spinnerets, and are often found in the company of giant spiders. Ettercaps are flesh-eating predators who use their spinnerets to create traps of various kinds such as web-filled pits or deadfall traps with silken ropes.

Ettercap: HD 5; AC 6[13]; Atk 2 claws (1d3), 1 bite (1d8 + poison); Move 12; Save 12; AL C; CL/XP 6/400; Special: Poison bite, traps.

Rope Trick

A run-down wooden stall sits just outside the entrance to the empty and abandoned Burgose Mine. Coils of silk rope lie on the stall's wooden tabletop, and rusty picks sit in dirt. An old, rusted lantern lies on its side on the table. Black lamp oil darkens the wooden surface. Just inside the mine entrance hangs the body of an elf. A coil of the silk rope is wrapped around his neck.

The coils of rope on the table are actually lines of incredibly sticky spider-silk that trail down the back of the stall and then up the wall into the mine. The lines inside the mine are smeared with coal dust to hide them against the dirty cave walls. An **ettercap** stands on an overhanging ledge inside the mine entrance with **3 giant spiders**. The giant spiders yank the coils of rope if anyone becomes tangled in them. Anyone failing a saving throw is pulled into the mine and up to the ledge for the spiders to attack. The elf's body is drained of blood. The ettercap hung the corpse to draw people into the mine if they avoided his rope trap.

Ettin

Hit Dice: 10
Armor Class: 3 [16]
Attacks: 2 clubs (3d6)
Saving Throw: 5
Special: None
Move: 12
Alignment: Chaos
Number Encountered: 1d4
Challenge Level/XP: 10/400

Ettins are two-headed giants, twelve to fifteen feet tall. They are difficult to catch by surprise, and make excellent guardians.

Ettin: HD 10; AC 3[16]; Atk 2 clubs (3d6); Move 12; Save 5; AL C; CL/XP 10/1400; Special: None.

Fire Wardens

Blazing walls of fire cut off three of the four archways exiting this temple's square sanctum. The burning flames rise from natural gas vents in the floor, and extend past the ceiling in troughs cut through the stone walls. The ceiling is covered in soot from the billowing smoke and burned black by the intense heat. The only exit is out of the hall through great double doors. Marble statues of fire entities stand in niches along the wall. Illusory flames flicker about the sculptures. The gleaming blue-and-gold checkerboard tile floor is marred by a series of large footprints burned into the tiles. The footprints crisscross the room randomly, making it difficult to determine who or what created them. A gold chandelier hangs from the high-peaked ceiling. A grand staircase rises to a second floor that overlooks the first. A 20-foot-wide basin containing a thick, syrupy liquid sits at the base of the staircase.

The walls of flame are very real, and do 2d6 points of damage each round to anyone touching them. The three rooms behind the flame curtains are home to **3 ettins**. The ettins guard the temple for Ilcevila Blaze, the temple's **azer** priestess. Each chamber contains soft animal furs for a bed, singed animal carcasses and random bones, and a large basin filled with more of the amber liquid found in the sanctum's fountain. The ettins bathe head to toe in the coppery-smelling liquid, which sticks to their bodies and allows them to pass freely through the flaming curtains without being burned. The liquid dries out within a few hours if removed from the basins.

The oily liquid is flammable, and turns the ettins into burning pyres that charge through the curtains of flame to attack intruders. The oil burns off in 10 rounds, but the basin in the main room contains more of the liquid so the ettins can return to their separate rooms. The ettins do an additional 1d6 points of damage with each burning strike. They use the flame curtains to their advantage, tossing foes through the infernos if they can.

Exoskeleton, Giant (Ant)

Hit Dice: 1
Armor Class: 3 [16]
Attacks: Bite (1d6)
Saving Throw: 17
Special: Immune to sleep, hold, and charm spells, half damage from piercing and slashing weapons
Move: 12
Alignment: Neutrality
Number Encountered: 1d4+1 or 3d10
Challenge Level/XP: 2/30

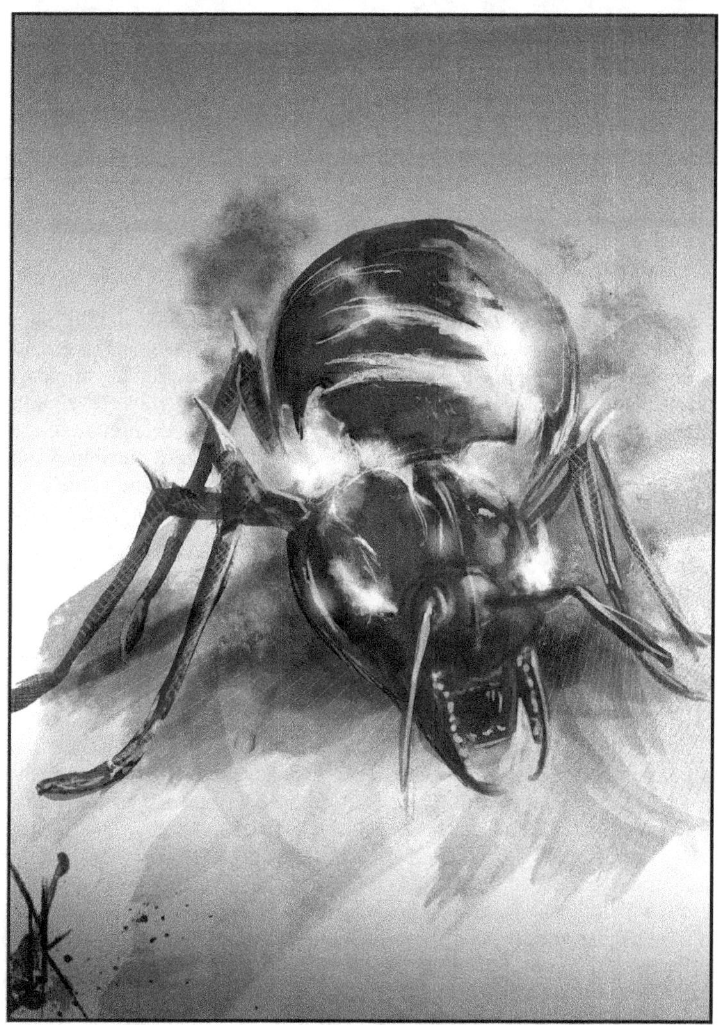

Giant ant exoskeletons can be animated into undead creatures by unusual and rare necromantic magic. They are not poisonous. These dry husks are turned as skeletons.

— *Author: Matt Finch*

Giant Ant Exoskeleton: HD 1; AC 3[16]; Atk Bite (1d6); Move 12; Save 17; AL N; CL/XP 2/30; Special: Immune to sleep, hold, and charm spells, half damage from piercing and slashing weapons.

Dead Ant, Dead Ant

A stone tower on a large sandy hill is draped with the linked bodies of giant ant exoskeletons. The ants' bodies form a chitinous ramp to the top of the squat 60-foot-tall structure. The husks are linked with insect secretions to form a nearly unbreakable ramp to the top. The top of the tower is open to the elements. A stone sarcophagus shaped like a massive beetle sits in the open rotunda.

The sarcophagus contains the body of Ystugrid Flux, a high priest of the Vermin Lord Rachiss. Thousands of millipedes and centipedes fill the coffin, crawling over one another and through the bones of the ancient priest. The cleric's skeletal body clutches a silver staff shaped like a centipede that continually generates the tiny vermin. A long-forgotten command word is the only way to stop the staff from spewing forth the insects. Also lying in the coffin are six pink diamonds (75 gp each), a sealed jar of leathery eyeballs, and a beetle brooch (150 gp).

The tower is protected by **15 giant ant exoskeletons** that rise from the sandy ant hill at the base of the tower to chase anyone climbing the ramp.

Exoskeleton, Giant (Beetle)

Hit Dice: 5
Armor Class: 3 [16]
Attacks: 1 bite (2d6)
Saving Throw: 12
Special: Immune to turning, unaffected by sleep, hold, and charm, immune to non-blunt weapons
Move: 6
Alignment: Neutrality
Number Encountered: 1
Challenge Level/XP: 7/600

Giant beetle exoskeletons are animated by necromantic magic quite different from that used in the Animate Dead spell. Bladed and piercing weapons cannot damage these dry, massive husks. They can be turned as ghasts, but are usually protected from turning by potent glyphs carved into their chitin exteriors. The insides of a giant beetle exoskeleton are quite hollow, and more than one necromancer has carpeted and cushioned the interior of a giant beetle exoskeleton for use as a slow-moving vehicle.

— *Author: Matt Finch*

Giant Beetle Exoskeleton: HD 5; AC 3[16]; Atk 1 bite (2d6); Move 6; Save 12; AL N; CL/XP 7/600; Special: Immune to turning, unaffected by sleep, hold, and charm, immune to non-blunt weapons.

The Burial Beetles

A line of **3 giant beetle exoskeletons** march resolutely down the road, the insect bodies marching in unison as they advance. The front and rear insects are adorned with torn black cloths that hang down over their legs. Poles with faded pennants are driven into the backs of their empty husks. The center beetle has a detailed engraving of a dour-looking man worked into its carapace. The words "In Service of Rachiss, Long May He March" glow with a feeble light along the side of the center insect.

The beetles are the funeral procession of Lord Lucius Caddisfly, a high priest of the Vermin Lord Rachiss. Caddisfly's followers placed his body inside the center beetle exoskeleton upon his death, and set the procession in motion. The exoskeletons have been marching for nearly six years. They turn and fight anyone who tries to stop their progress. Caddisfly's body is nothing more than jumbled bones inside the center beetle. His treasure is carried inside the other exoskeletons and contains 2,000 gp, a silver crown (200 gp) and a staff with a beetle embedded in an amber globe at the top.

Exoskeleton, Giant (Crab)

Hit Dice: 6
Armor Class: 3 [16]
Attacks: 2 pincers (2d6)
Saving Throw: 11
Special: Immune to turning, unaffected by sleep, hold, and charm, immune to non-blunt weapons
Move: 6
Alignment: Neutrality
Number Encountered: 1d3 or 2d6
Challenge Level/XP: 8/800

Giant crab exoskeletons are animated by specific necromantic spells, cast upon the very largest giant crab exoskeletons (10ft in diameter). Bladed and piercing weapons cannot damage these animated empty shells. They can be turned as mummies, but are usually protected from turning by potent glyphs carved into the shell, as are most giant exoskeletons. The insides are hollow, and up to four people can travel inside.

— Author: Matt Finch

Giant Crab Exoskeleton: HD 6; AC 3[16]; Atk 2 pincers (2d6); Move 6; Save 11; AL N; CL/XP 8/800; Special: Immune to turning, unaffected by sleep, hold, and charm, immune to non-blunt weapons.

The Blade Bearer

A 20-foot-diameter **giant crab exoskeleton** walks laboriously through the open gates of Milhaven. The crab's body is covered by swords, daggers and stray bits of armor. The creature attacks randomly, its pincers snapping wildly at anyone approaching it. Runes on the exoskeleton glow with each strike against it. As the creature passes, loose metal flies through the air and sticks to its body. Many of the soldiers who stand before it find themselves weaponless as their swords fly at the creature and become stuck to its sides.

The exoskeleton has a powerful lodestone inside the inner shell that attracts nearby metal. A frail wizard created the monstrosity to precede him into battle, but he didn't expect his first fight to be against a group of monks using wooden staves. Anyone fighting the creature must make a saving throw with each attack or their weapon flies out of their hands and becomes stuck to the exoskeleton. A weapon can be pulled free with another saving throw. Most of the weapons are rusted and worthless, but stuck to the shell are a *+1 long sword*, a *ring of protection +2*, and a *+2 shield*.

Exploding Bones

Hit Dice: 2
Armor Class: 8 [11]
Attacks: 1 weapon (1d8)
Saving Throw: 16
Special: Explode when killed
Move: 12
Alignment: Neutrality
Number Encountered: 1d4+1
Challenge Level/XP: 3/60

Nearly identical to skeletons in appearance, Exploding Bones differ in coloring from their more mundane counterparts. Exploding Bones are a bright pulsating red, their coloring becoming brighter and pulsating faster as they near death and the inevitable explosion which gives them their name.

When these crimson skeletons reach 0 hp their bodies explode sending a shower of jagged bones, which hit all within 20ft. All within this radius suffer 1d6 points of damage from the explosive shower of bony shrapnel. A successful Saving Throw halves this damage. Exploding bones are treated as Type 2 undead for turning purposes.

— Author: Skathros

Exploding Bones: HD 2; AC 8[11]; Atk 1 weapon (1d8); Move 12; Save 16; AL N; CL/XP 3/60; Special: Explode when killed.

Red Bull Bully

A troop of red skeletons march into Lessef, the throng surrounding a silver chariot pulled by a pair of massive red skeletal bulls. Standing in the chariot is necromancer **Anastal Rot**. The wizard demands his daughter be returned to him. The skeletons stand ready to back him up, and the skeletal bulls strike the ground with their hooves. Sparks fly from stones in the rocky soil.

Anastal has been on the move for days, desperately seeking his teenage daughter who fled with a stablehand. The necromancer is attacking villages around the region as he looks for the deceitful boy who absconded with his pride and joy. He orders the **8 exploding bones** to attack, and unleashes the bulls with another command. The bulls are the same a special pair of exploding bones and have a gore attack (1d8) that replaces their normal weapon attack. All of the skeletons – the bulls included – explode when killed.

Anastal Rot: HD 6; hp 20; AC 3[16]; Atk staff (1d6); Save 10; Move 9; AL C; CL/XP 6/400; Equipment: *wand of fear, ring of protection +1, bracers of defense* AC 4[15]. Spells: 1—*charm person, magic missile, sleep*; 2—*invisibility, web*; 3—*fireball, lightning bolt.*

Eyeless Filcher

Hit Dice: 9
Armor Class: 3 [16]
Attacks: 2 claws (1d8)
Saving Throw: 6
Special: Immune to non-magic weapons, strangle, half damage from non-blunt weapons
Move: 12
Alignment: Chaos
Number Encountered: 1
Challenge Level/XP: 12/1,700

An eyeless filcher is the undead body of a criminal maimed or tortured to death in brutal punishment for its crimes; usually these criminals were guilty of particularly heinous crimes during life. These creatures are animated by an extremely powerful undead force, which causes fear and horror in any onlooker: at the sight of an eyeless filcher, anyone failing a saving throw will either flee in terror for 1d12 rounds or be paralyzed until the undead is out of sight (equal chance). The eyeless filcher shares the same resistances and weaknesses of other powerful undead; it is immune to cold-based and mind-affecting spells, magical weapons are required to hit it, it can be turned by a cleric (as a wraith), and suffers harm from holy water (2d8). As there is precious little flesh left on its bones, the eyeless filcher suffers half damage from edged and pointed weapons. It may be distracted by the sight of symbols of law and justice, such as the insignia of the city watch or the holy symbol of a deity of law, and will break off attacking to focus its rage on this image. An eyeless filcher retains any criminal knowledge and thieving skills it had in life, and will use these to its advantage. In combat, if both of its claw attacks hit, it latches on with inhuman strength, strangling for automatic damage (2d6 total) per round thereafter; its deadly grip can only be broken by distracting symbols as above, the death of its victim, or a sincere apology from anyone involved in its own capture, trial, and punishment. If the eyeless filcher manages to kill an officer of the law, whether guard or magistrate or scribe of the court, the unfortunate victim rises from the dead the next day as a double-strength zombie under its control. The eyeless filcher attacks and steals, deliberately causing as much chaos and fear as it can. If a law officer renounces his profession in the creature's presence it will sink to the ground, destroyed, with a mocking laugh.

— *Author: Scott Wylie Roberts, "Myrystyr"*

Eyeless Filcher: HD 9; AC 3[16]; Atk 2 claws (1d8); Move 12; Save 6; AL C; CL/XP 12/1700; Special: Immune to non-magic weapons, strangle, half damage from non-blunt weapons.

The creature wears a blindfold over its eyes (although this doesn't stop it from sensing the living) so that the many badges it surrounds itself with won't distract it. The creature leaves its cave each night to find those who serve the law. Their bodies are stuffed into the coffins in the creature's lair, their badges battered and hung up in shame.

Justice is Blind . . . and Dead

An ocean cave leading into the dark tunnels beneath Kutchaven reeks of rotting fish, seaweed and salt. A thin ledge of rocks leads into the cave. The rocks are wet and smooth from the constant waves battering the stone. The interior of the cavern is humid, the smell of death even worse. The ledge turns into a rocky tunnel about 500 feet into the cave. This tunnel travels nearly a quarter mile into the darkness before it opens into a tomb-like cavern. The forgotten tomb contains coffins that are bolted to the walls. The wooden coffins rise nearly 30 feet above the floor. Bones dangle from many of the oldest coffins, the rotting wood releasing their skeletal occupants. Coins (nearly 200 gp total) lie scattered across the rocks beneath many of the coffins. Dangling from many of the coffins are badges, crowns and other symbols of authority. Most of these badges of office are scratched and deformed, as if they had been hammered against the stone.

The cavern is the home of Jelida Daribe, a vile killer who attacked villages in the dead of night – and left none alive to tell of his foul deeds. Jelida was eventually caught and convicted, but the relatives of his victims tore him apart shortly after his trial. Jelida returned as an **eyeless filcher**.

Falshantog-Yoth (Fal-Yoth, the "Hungering Vine")

Hit Dice: 8
Armor Class: 9 [10]
Attacks: All within 10ft (1d8) or 1 "tail" (4d10)
Saving Throw: 8
Special: Destroys weapons successfully hitting it, generates darkness, partially immune to lightning, causes fear
Move: 13 (0 when planted)
Alignment: Chaos
Number Encountered: 1
Challenge Level/XP: 12/1,200

The Hungering Vines lives in darkness, with a ravenous hunger that can only be satiated by blood and flesh. This creature resembles a writhing mass of vines coming together at a trunk, supported by 4 huge roots. Many eyestalks jut from the trunk, peering about for food; Fal-yoth is almost never surprised. The vines pull fresh carrion under its roots, where there is a huge mouth that consumes the plant's victims. Fal-yoth can move surprisingly fast in a shambling gait, once it pulls its roots from the ground or rock into which it has settled. It takes 1 round for its vines to push it from the earth and allow it to move. Fal-yoth attacks any and all creatures that stray within reach of its vines (10ft) for 1d8 damage, or will twist its vines into a sort of "tail," which can batter a single target for a colossal 4d10 points of damage. Any target hit by the "tail" will be knocked down and backward 1d4x10ft.

If a weapon successfully hits Fal-yoth, the creature's corrosive sap spatters the weapon and destroys it. Magical weapons are permitted a saving throw. Fal-yoth can also generate a sphere of darkness within 30' that lasts 1d4 rounds, every 10 minutes. Fal-yoth is partially immune to lightning attacks, taking half normal damage from such attacks. A saving throw is required each combat round to resist the horror of the hunger radiating from Fal-yoth. If a character fails his save, he is paralyzed by horror and unable to act that round. It may be that more than one of these creatures exist, but only one is known.
— *Author: Chgowiz*

Falshantog-yoth - The Hungering Vines: HD 8, AC 9[10], Atk all within 10ft (1d8) or 1 "tail" (4d10); Move 13 (0 when planted); Save 8; AL C; CL/XP 12/2000; Special: Destroys weapons successfully hitting it, generates darkness, partially immune to lightning, causes fear.

The Walking Hedge

A tall, gaunt man named **Carestru** (fighter 6) stands outside the stone gates of Folsan Downs, a small walled hamlet in the Juniper Forest. He carries a bone-handled scythe, and wears tight-fitting leather that makes him seem even thinner than his gaunt frame should allow. A brown cloak spills off his narrow shoulders, but barely falls to his waist because of his height. He speaks in a deep voice as he tells PCs to declare any plants, shrubs, fruits or vegetables, and wooden weapons (such as staves or maces with wooden handles) that they carry. Iron racks sitting outside the town's wall hold weapons, but he chops up plants and other items with his scythe. Inside the 10-foot-tall stone walls, the villagers live off a diet of meat, fish and grains. No vegetables or fruits are allowed inside the town's borders. The villagers also burned and salted a 300-foot-wide swath of ground around the wall, and keep the area clear of trees and vegetation.

A frantic mother meets PCs once they are allowed to enter the gates. She weeps openly and falls to the ground as she pleads for any information about "Little Stephan." Her son snuck out of the walled community this morning and hasn't come home yet. With dusk fast approaching, the woman screams with anguish at the thought of her child in the woods alone. No one in the village is willing to go into the woods this close to sundown. The villagers fear the Juniper Forest growing abundantly around them, and speak of the dread nights before the wall went up when the "walking hedge" snatched unwary villagers from their homes. The villagers should be scared. A **hungering vine** walks the woods, looking to snare people out after dark. Little Stephan is currently hiding in a lean-to he built in the forest. The scared little boy tries to stay silent, but his noises have already attracted the attention of the dread Falshantog-Yoth.

Felikaur

Hit Dice: 6
Armor Class: 3 [16]
Attacks: 2 claws (1d6), 1 bite (2d6), and tail (1d4+paralysis)
Saving Throw: 11
Special: Spit acid, drop opponents, surprise
Move: 15/18 (flying)
Alignment: Neutrality
Number Encountered: 1d4
Challenge Level/XP: 10/1,400

Felikaur were magically bred from tigers in ancient times, as a battle-beast of the feuding noble houses. Some escaped into the wild and flourished. The felikaur looks like a massive tiger, but with overlapping horn plates instead of fur. They have large bat-like wings sprouting from the shoulders, and a spiky tail. These creatures are intelligent enough to prepare ambushes and use their surroundings to tactical advantage; in the wild, they leap from cover to cover while attacking. In a gladiatorial arena, they are able to take advantage of pit traps, spikes, barriers, or other such tactical obstacles.

A felikaur's tail spikes deal little damage, but secrete a paralysing toxin. They can also pick up a human or smaller foe, carry it into the air for a few rounds, and drop it from a height of 20 to 60 feet. Lastly, the felikaur can spit a glob of corrosive acid to a distance of 20 feet, for 1d6 to 3d6 damage (in any given day, the available stomach acid permits a total of 9 dice of potential damage). This acid will eat through and ruin clothing, non-magical armor, backpack straps, etc, in 1 round. The means by which the ancients controlled and tamed these beasts is unknown - they cannot be trained.

— *Author: Scott Wylie Roberts, "Myrystyr"*

Felikaur: HD 6; AC 3[16]; Atk 2 claws (1d6), 1 bite (2d6), and tail (1d4+paralysis)); Move 15 (Fly 18); Save 11; AL N; CL/XP 10/1400; Special: Spit acid, drop opponents, surprise.

Tunnels Cats

A coliseum of piled black stones rises in the middle of the rocky wastes of the Angern Badlands. The arena was abandoned long ago when the Stark River was rerouted by a magical experiment gone awry. The river slices through the open-air coliseum, splitting it in two. The rushing water flooded the bowl where gladiators once fought, creating a large pond with stone seats rising around it. One of the massive stone walls also fell inward, creating a dangerous path of crumbled stones and shattered debris breaking the water's surface. A body is caught in the rushing water, the corpse pressed against a sharp outcropping of rock in the middle of the flowing river. The body is caught on a rock in the middle of the river and requires four jumps across angled stones to get to it. Anyone trying to jump from stone to stone must make a saving throw with each leap or fall into the water. Anyone swept into the current takes 1d6 points of damage as they are slammed against underwater stones. They can attempt another saving throw to pull themselves out of the water each round.

The body is a dead adventurer placed there by **4 felikaurs** that live in empty tunnels carved into the hillside where gladiators once lived, ate and trained. Empty weapon racks stand against the walls in some rooms, and tables are broken into kindling. The few doors that remain are heavily scratched and have wood peeling away in long, curling ribbons. Several tunnels contain raised portcullises the felikaur can lower to trap and separate creatures. The felikaur take advantage of the darkness within the tunnels to surprise prey. A felikaur sentry always watches the body in the river. The great cats sometimes fly out to attack people standing on the shifting stones.

A partially devoured mule in one tunnel room has a saddle with pouches that contain a map of the desert, 140 gp, a silver badge and a stuffed turkey doll.

Ferec (Foxtaur)

Hit Dice: 6+3
Armor Class: 7 [12]
Attacks: 2 weapons (1d6) and 1 bite (1d4)
Saving Throw: 11
Special: Cannot be surprised
Move: 18
Alignment: Neutrality
Number Encountered: 1d4
Challenge Level/XP: 6/400

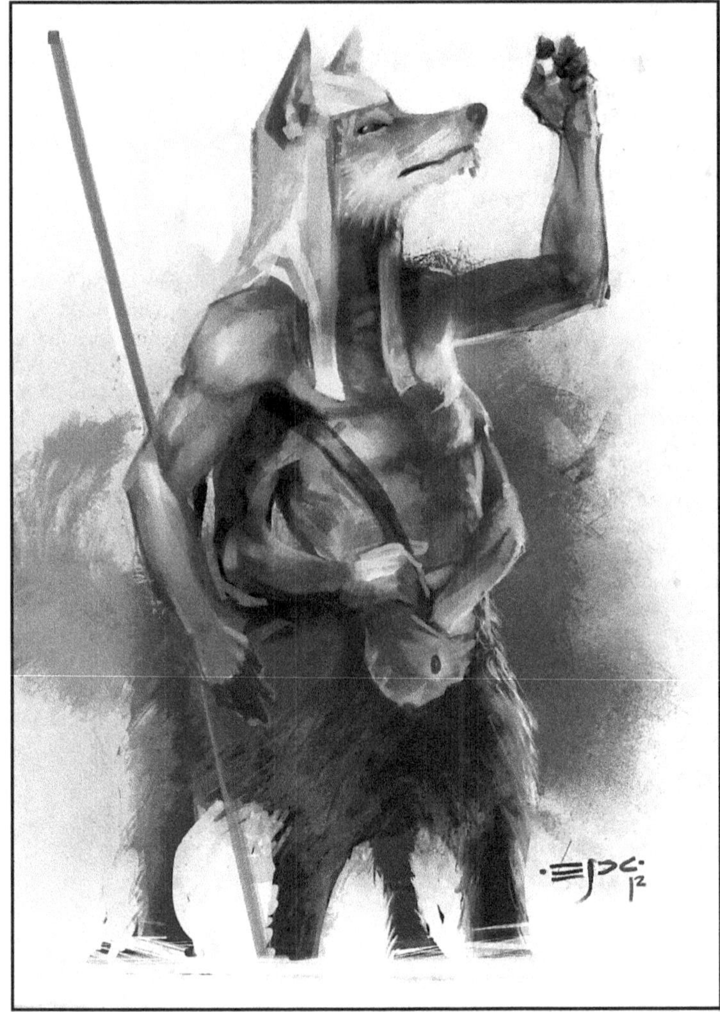

Orange-furred and bushy-tailed with large ears and multiple limbs, the Ferec is a mutated fox. It has a long body, with four pairs of legs, and a centaur-like humanoid torso with two pairs of arms. Despite its creative intelligence and expansive vocabulary, the ferec is excitable, superstitious, and easily distracted. It excels in various forms of craftsmanship, and enjoys puzzling out the workings of traps, puzzle boxes, unusual weapons, or other such contraptions. The heightened senses of a ferec, including superior night vision and heightened hearing, ensure it will never be surprised. They are sensitive to sunlight, and prefer a nocturnal lifestyle.

— Author: Scott Wylie Roberts, "Myrystyr"

Ferec: HD 6+3; AC 7[12]; Atk 2 weapons (1d6) and 1 bite (1d4); Move 18; Save 11; AL N; CL/XP 6/400; Special: Cannot be surprised.

The Unsolvable Solution

A 20-foot-diameter brass plate is inset into the floor of this stark dungeon room. Elaborate sigils are engraved on thousands of movable plates attached to the brass disc's face. Each sigil can be twisted, turned and slid across the flat surface to form larger symbols. The entire disc is hot to the touch. Three iron stakes are driven into the stone floor around the edges of the disc. Chained to the stakes are **3 ferecs**. Each ferec wears a collar linked to a 20-foot-long chain allows the creatures access to the brass plate but not enough room to escape.

The ferecs are prisoners of **Mottle Krackikak, a hezrou demon** who seeks to end the world. The brass plate is known as the Unbound Cyphrica, the puzzle of a thousand solutions. Mottle wants to unlock the puzzle to set about the end of the world, but he couldn't solve the complicated cipher on his own. He captured the ferecs and forced them to solve the riddle for him. The ferecs' paws are badly burned after days working on the hot metal surface as they limp back and forth across the heated metal. The ferecs solved the enigma days ago, but are stalling in the hope rescue arrives soon.

Mottle Krackikak, Second-Category Demon (Hezrou):
HD 9; AC 0[19]; Atk 2 claws (1d3), 1 bite (2d8); Move 9 (Fly 14); Save 6; AL C; CL/XP 11/1700; Special: Magic resistance 50%, demonic magical powers.

Flenser

Hit Dice: 8
Armor Class: 3 [16]
Attacks: 2 claws (1d6) and 1 bite (1d6+2)
Saving Throw: 8
Special: Paralysis
Move: 12
Alignment: Chaos
Number Encountered: 1d3
Challenge Level/XP: 9/1,100

Flensers are undead creatures with the same appearance as ghouls, but wearing cloaks made of rotting skins, mainly those of humans – although if the flenser has not encountered humans or their kin recently, it may have resorted to adorning itself with the skins of animals. Flensers are considerably more intelligent than ghouls, and may be found leading ghoul packs.

Flensers have a 50% chance to be leading a pack of 2d6 ghouls, with a 25% chance that there are also 1d2 ghasts in the group. Like ghouls, the claws and bite of a flenser can induce paralysis, but the flenser's paralysis is extremely powerful – the saving throw against it is made at a penalty of -4 on the saving throw, and elves are not immune to the effects. If a flenser kills a foe, it skins the corpse before eating the flesh, and adds the skin to its hideous cloak.

— *Author: Matt Finch*

Flenser: HD 8; AC 3[16]; Atk 2 claws (1d6) and 1 bite (1d6+2); Move 12; Save 8; AL C; CL/XP 9/1100; Special: Paralysis.

Vrinnor the Skinner

A wooden door sits in a small hillock near the stone foundation of a collapsed home. The wooden door creaks loudly if opened. Rickety stairs lead 30 feet downward to a packed dirt floor. Skeletons lie in and on the dirt, while others are manacled to the cellar's stone walls. Normal rats gnaw the bones, stripping them of flesh and muscle. Mold grows on the bones and across the floor. Tangled tree roots push through the cellar walls. A wooden frame in the corner has a pale sheet of human flesh stretched across it to cure. Various knives and sharp picks hang from sharp hooks on the wall.

The cellar belongs to **Vrinnor**, a **flenser** known to the superstitious villagers of Folsan Downs as "The Skinner" because of the state of his victims when they are found. The undead creature leads **6 ghouls** that roam the Juniper Forest. The ghouls drag travellers back to the cellar and hand them over to Vrinnor to skin. The ghouls get what's left after Vrinnor completes his grisly task. Vrinnor sleeps in a bed of human-skin sheets under the stairs leading down into the cellar. Vrinnor is frequently absent from his abattoir seeking prey on his own. He normally leaves **2 ghouls** to watch the entrance at all times. The ghouls hide in the collapsed ruins and summon Vrinnor when someone enters his killing ground.

Flowerchild

Hit Dice: 5
Armor Class: 8 [11]
Attacks: None (special only)
Saving Throw: 12
Special: Peaceful feelings, pollen, immune to blunt and piercing weapons
Move: 1
Alignment: Neutrality
Number Encountered: 1d2
Challenge Level/XP: 7/600

A flowerchild resembles a mass of flowers that can shape itself in any way it desires, from a carpet to a roughly humanoid form. It does not make any sort of physical attack, but anyone coming within 50ft of one of these plants has walked into considerable danger. The area around the flowerchild has a sweet smell that causes anyone breathing it to become utterly peaceful and uninterested in taking any action other than to sleep (a successful saving throw allows the victim to shake off this effect). The magically-induced lassitude is permanent unless the victim is brought out of the flowerchild's scent. Once it has a helpless victim nearby, the flowerchild will release a cloud of pollen that causes a victim to make a saving throw every three rounds while exposed. If the saving throw fails, the victim becomes a planting-ground for the flowerchild seeds. The victim will begin transforming into a flowerchild, with the transformation becoming complete after 1d3+2 days. A *cure disease* spell will end the infection by killing the pollen.

Flowerchildren are immune to blunt weapons and piercing weapons.

— Author: Matt Finch

Flowerchild: HD 5; AC 8[11]; Atk None; Move 1; Save 12; AL N; CL/XP 7/600; Special: Peaceful feelings, pollen, immune to blunt and piercing weapons.

Orc and Unicorn

A strange sight awaits PCs in this peaceful vale: A **unicorn** kneels amid a carpet of pink flowers, its head down and its eyes closed in sleep. An **orc** wearing animal skins brushes the unicorn's flowing mane with a comb made from a squirrel's rib cage. The orc smiles and hums softly to himself. The flowers sway in the breeze, their fragrant pollen rising in the wind. The orc wears a wreath of lilacs and asters on its head. More flowers decorate the unicorn's golden mane and tail.

The orc and unicorn stumbled separately into a **flowerchild** patch spreading across this peaceful clearing. The flowerchild's pollen overwhelmed both creatures, causing them to sink down among the colorful blooms in tranquil, mindless bliss. The unicorn is near death, with flowers starting to grow from its skin. The orc is holding out, but won't last more than a couple of days. If the flowerchild is killed, the orc and unicorn wake slowly. They flee into the woods once they regain their senses.

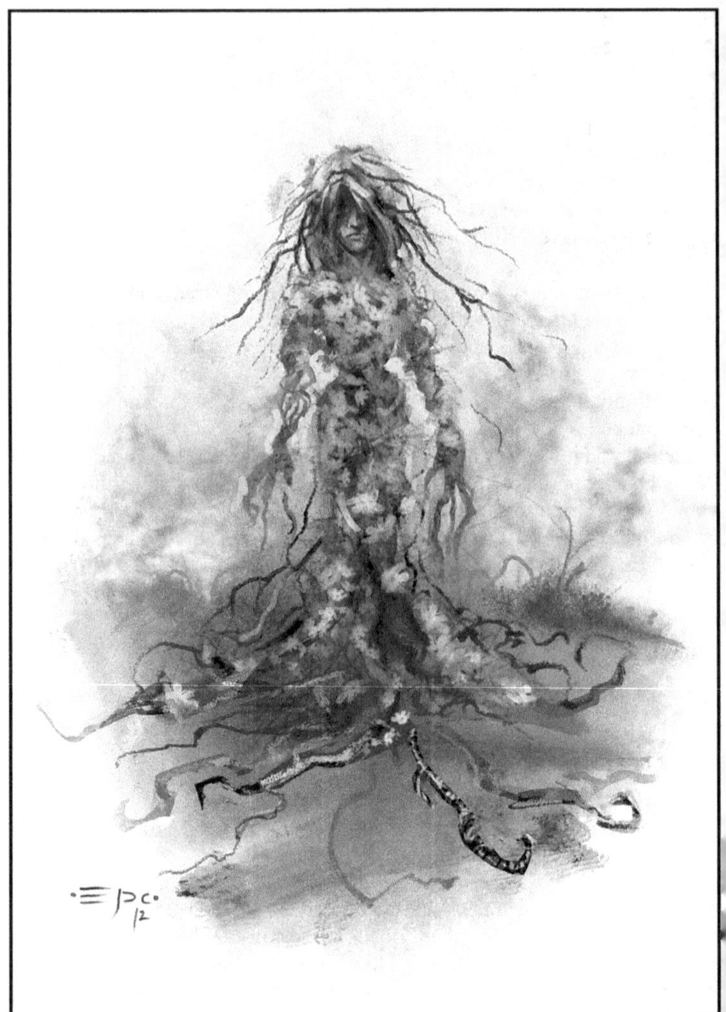

Flowershroud

Hit Dice: 3
Armor Class: 6 [13]
Attacks: 1 thorn-strand (1d4)
Saving Throw: 14
Special: Convulsion poison, immnune to non-cutting weapons
Move: 3
Alignment: Neutrality
Number Encountered: 1
Challenge Level/XP: 4/120

A flowershroud is a carpet-like floral growth, connected by a network of stems and tendrils underneath the blossoms. The tendrils allow the shroud to move slowly from place to place when it is seeking new food, for these are carnivorous plants that hunt down prey. When attacking, a flowershroud lashes out with a strand of thorned blossoms, inflicting 1d4 hit points of damage but also injecting an irritant poison that causes the victim to go into convulsions for 1d6+3 rounds, losing 1 hit point per round until the convulsions cease. Flowershrouds are immune to all but cutting weapons.

— Author: Matt Finch

Flowershroud: HD 3; AC 6[13]; Atk 1 thorn-strand (1d4); Move 3; Save 14; AL N; CL/XP 4/120; Special: Convulsion poison, immnune to non-cutting weapons

Beautiful Evil

A flower-covered marble bier stands in the middle of an idyllic glen. Butterflies fly in colorful formations through the honey-scented air. Rabbits hop innocently through the verdant grass. A statue of a lovely woman wearing flowing robes stands beside the bier. Flowers wrap around the lifelike sculpture, twining about her lithe figure. A plaque at the base of the statue reads "Lady Evellis. May she find peace in nature that eluded her in life." A 15-foot-diameter circle of fragrant flowers surrounds the bier.

The bier is a flat marble slab supported by two round columns. A blanket of colourful flowers completely covers the magical glass bubble protecting Lady Evellis' body. The flowers are magically treated so they never wilt or decay. Lady Evellis' body is similarly preserved. She is a beautiful woman wearing a gold crown (2,000 gp) on her head. Anyone taking the crown suffers horribly as everything seems to go wrong (the PC suffers a −5 penalty to saving throws, straps break on his clothing at inopportune times, people he meets are hostile, etc.).

The wide carpet of blooming flowers growing around the bier is a **flowershroud**. The flowershroud normally exists on forest animals that blunder into it, but it also recently killed the glen's elderly caretaker. His brittle bones lie beneath the shroud, pressed into the soft earth.

Flying Jellyfish, Giant

Hit Dice: 16
Armor Class: 8 [11]
Attacks: Up to 8 tentacles (2d6+paralysis)
Saving Throw: 3
Special: Discharge spell energy, paralysis
Move: 0/9 (flying)
Alignment: Neutrality
Number Encountered: 1
Challenge Level/XP: 19/4,100

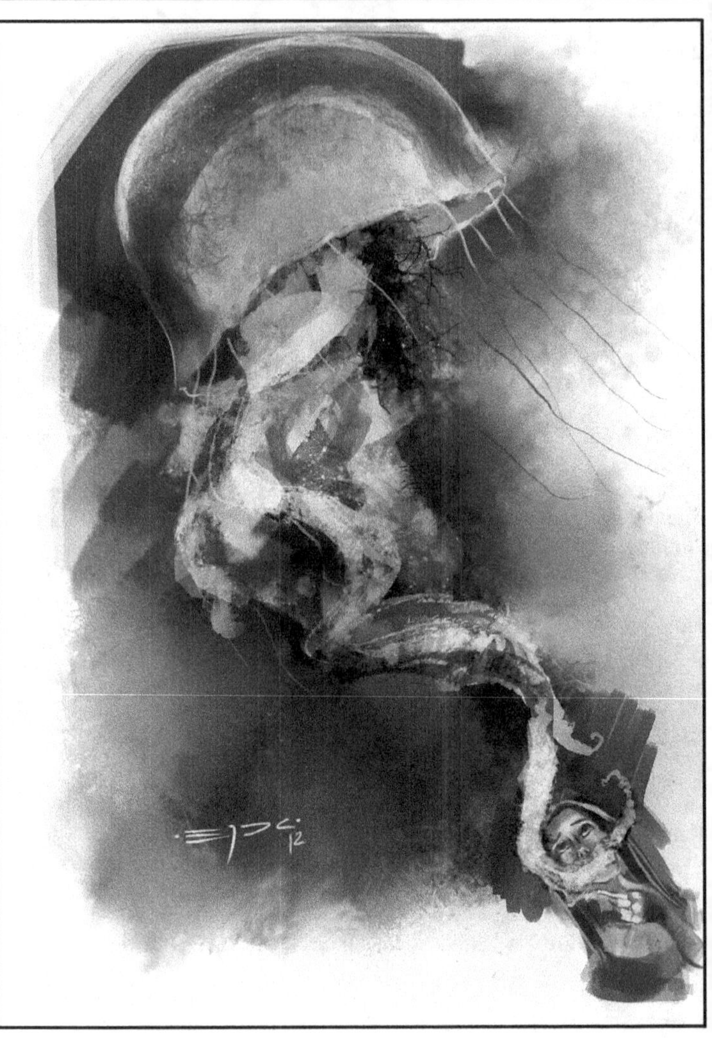

As its name suggests, the Giant Flying Jellyfish is a marine life form that has adapted to existence in the skies. It is a hazard to sky-travelers and flying creatures, as it is almost translucent and is also known to hide in clouds. The giant flying jellyfish is partially gaseous in nature, and flies by means of jetting air. The giant flying jellyfish attacks by trailing its tentacles onto the decks of ships, into the space occupied by flying opponents, or through settlements when it hunts across the ground. It can make up to 2 attacks per 10ft cubic space occupied by opponents, to a maximum of 8 attacks. Each tentacle causes 2d6 damage, and may cause paralysis lasting 1d4 days (saving throw negates). It has also evolved a distinctive defence against magic. Any spell or similar attack against it builds up a charge in the creature, if it makes its saving throw. This charge is equal to 1 point per spell level, to a maximum equal to the jellyfish's hit dice. In any round, in addition to making tentacle attacks, the giant flying jellyfish can discharge from 1 to 4 energy charges with the following effects: (1) All spell-casting beings within 50ft suffer intense mental distress for 1d3 rounds per charge, making it impossible to cast spells during this time. (2) All creatures and vessels flying via magic within 30ft have their movement rate halved for a period of 2 rounds per charge. (3) All creatures within 10ft of the giant flying jellyfish suffer -1 to all die rolls per charge expended for 1d2 turns. If severely threatened, the giant flying jellyfish may expend a blast of 8 charges, with effects as if 4 charges had been expended, but doubling the effective ranges of the blast's effects. This massive expenditure of power also allows the jellyfish to quadruple its flying movement rate for 4 rounds in order to escape. Most specimens are 20-40ft in diameter, with 40-80ft long tentacles. Larger versions, of 24 or even 32 HD, may also exist, particularly in the ethereal realities or in the voids between the moons.

— *Author: Scott Wylie Roberts ("Myrystyr")*

Giant Flying Jellyfish: HD 16; AC 8[11]; Atk up to 8 tentacles (2d6+paralysis); Move 0 (fly 9); Save 3; AL N; CL/XP 19/4100; Special: Discharge spell energy, paralysis.

The Hovering Horde

Screams of terror roll through the streets of Aurellia as people race past the Tavern of the One-Eyed Goat. Elves, humans and dwarves look over their shoulders as they race away in fear. Flying through the air behind the runners are nearly 30 figures that hover at various heights over the city's rooftops. Besides the hovering figures, others slide across the ground, leaving bloody trails as they scoot along. Still more rise and fall ominously, sometimes slamming into roofs face-first before being dragged mercilessly across the sharp stucco tiles. Blood trickles down the slack features of many of the hovering men and women. A few twitch uncontrollably as they float.

A group of three elves facing the oncoming beings twitch and spin, then rise into the air to join the hovering horde. The flying bodies are harmless, and for the most part, quite dead. Each was caught up in the tentacle mass hanging beneath a **giant flying jellyfish**. The floating jellyfish hunts above the rooftops, dragging its long tentacles over anything unfortunate enough to be below it. It recently overturned a sticky honeybee hive owned by an eccentric mage named Fadzien. The mage was testing ways to increase the stickiness of the bee's honey. The jellyfish's tentacles are now coated in the sticky amber liquid. Anyone struck by a tentacle must make a saving throw or become stuck. Any PC stuck to the beast takes automatic damage each round thereafter.

Flying Squirrel, Carnivorous

Hit Dice: 1d4 hit points
Armor Class: 7 [12]
Attacks: 1 bite (1d2)
Saving Throw: 18
Special: Glide silently
Move: 6/12 (gliding)
Alignment: Neutrality
Number Encountered: 1d8+1
Challenge Level/XP: A/5

These squirrels, larger than normal flying squirrels, are carnivorous. They may attack humans if provoked, enchanted, or in sufficient numbers to feel confident of success.

Carnivorous Giant Squirrel: HD 1d4 hp; AC 7[12]; Atk 1 bite (1d2); Move 6 (Glide 12); Save 18; AL N; CL/XP A/5; Special: Glide silently.

Moose and Squirrels

A **moose** charges through the trees of Kilnmass Glen, swinging its wide antlers in pain as it runs. In its panic, it charges over anyone it meets, trampling them into the ground. Blood and sweat streak the beast's flanks and face, further obscuring its vision. Scrambling through the tree branches in pursuit of the moose are **40 carnivorous flying squirrels.** The squirrels glide down to bite the poor moose as it tries to escape. After they attack, the squirrels scamper back into the trees to leap down again. The riled up squirrels attack any creatures that gets in their way of bringing down the angry moose.

Flytrap Shambler

Hit Dice: 3
Armor Class: 4 [15]
Attacks: 1 bite (2d6) and 1 polearm (1d8+1)
Saving Throw: 14
Special: Immune to piercing weapons
Move: 6
Alignment: Neutrality
Challenge Level/XP: 4/120

Flytrap shamblers are mobile plants about the bulk of a horse, but they shuffle along the ground on thick, tentacle-like vines. The body is leafy and sometimes blooms with orchid-like flowers; the head rises on a fibrous stalk topped with the wide mouth of a venus flytrap, which can deliver a powerful bite. It is common for them to carry a polearm or spear in their front vines, for they can use such weapons in tandem with the bite. Despite their appearance, flytrap shamblers are relatively intelligent and often posted as guards by villains with the ability to control plants. Their value in this sort of role is somewhat compromised by the fact that they cannot talk.

Flytrap shamblers are capable of seeding themselves, but are almost always found as a result of direct cultivation by powerful villains who possess the knowledge and skill to breed such vegetation. The creation of a flytrap shambler involves magic, alchemy, and the skillful cultivation of several different flowering plants, some of which are not commonly found. There are manuals and librams describing the process, but these are for the most part forgotten lore.

The leafy body of a flytrap shambler is immune to damage from piercing weapons, but cutting and bludgeoning weapons inflict normal damage.

— Author: Matt Finch

Flytrap Shambler: HD 3; AC 4[15]; Atk 1 bite (2d6) and 1 polearm (1d8+1); Move 6; Save 14; AL N; CL/XP 4/120; Special: Immune to piercing weapons.

Welcome to the Grotto

The Mushroom Grotto is an underground greenhouse ruled by the Fungus Druid Angus Sallow. The greenhouse has a central circular chamber and six 50-foot-long spokes radiating outward into the damp earth. A central pool of clear water is filled with clinging vines of ivy and wet, spongy plants. Moss and mushrooms grow in the side passages. Each hall is lit by blue lichens that glow feebly along the walls and across the ceiling in a cascade of color. Rows of planters sit along the entrances to the tunnels.

The ever-changing Fungus Druid has lived among his plants for so long that he has become what he loves: a **shambling mound**. Sallow lovingly grew **4 flytrap shamblers** that roam freely throughout the complex and do his bidding. Sallow resembles a large lump of peat moss covered in fragrant flowers as he sleeps in a wooden plot of soil. Currently, the heavily decomposed body of a druid wearing blue robes lies half-buried in Sallow's body. The druid has 46 gp and a small soap carving of a dog in a pouch. The flytrap shamblers move to protect their master if Sallow's rest is disturbed.

Shambling Mound (7HD): HD 7; AC 1[18]; Atk 2 fists (2d8); Move 6; Save 9; AL N; CL/XP 10/1400; Special: Damage immunities, enfold and suffocate victims.

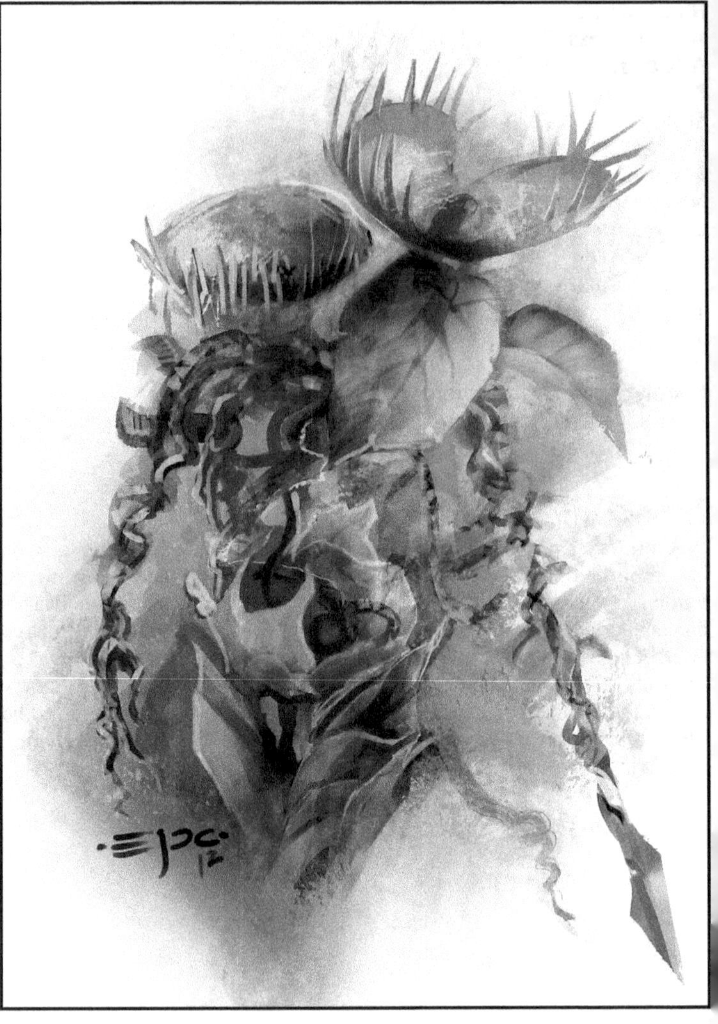

Formian

	WORKER	WARRIOR	TASKMASTER	MALE	QUEEN
Hit Dice:	1	3	7	8	10
Armor Class:	3 [16]	2 [17]	1 [18]	1 [18]	3 [16]
Attacks:	1 bite (1d4)	1 bite (1d6), 2 mandibles (1d4), 1 sting (1 + non-lethal poison)	1 bite (1d6+1), 1 sting (1d2 + non-lethal poison);	1 bite (1d6+1), 1 sting (1d2 + non-lethal poison);	None
Saving Throw:	17	14	9	8	5
Special:	None	Non-lethal poison sting (2d4 damage, save for half)	Non-lethal poison (4d4 damage, save for half)	Non-lethal poison (4d4 damage, save for half)	None
Move:	15	12	12	12	6
Alignment:	Neutrality	Neutrality	Neutrality	Neutrality	Neutrality
Number Encountered:	See below	See below	See below	See below	1
Challenge Level/XP:	1/15	5/240	8/800	9/1,100	noncombatant

Formians are highly intelligent ant-people, walking on their four hind legs but using their specialized fore-claws to hold objects. Their ant-like heads have deadly mandibles, which they use in combat. Formians have a caste society, like ants. The workers are small (about 75 pounds) and fairly stupid. Warriors are as large as a human being, and no more intelligent than the workers. A noble class, the taskmasters, rules formian society and are normally only found in the cities of this strange and alien race. These formians are as large as a horse, and extremely intelligent.

Formian cities are small, containing no more than 500 workers, 50 warriors, and 10 taskmasters, plus a royal retinue. The royal retinue includes a queen, males equal to half the number of taskmasters, and an additional 1d6 taskmasters, 3d6 warriors, and 6d6 workers. Formians also keep humans and members of other races as slaves or trade-goods.

Formian Worker: HD 1; AC 3[16]; Atk 1 bite (1d4); Move 15; Save 17; AL N; CL/XP 1/15; Special: None.

Formian Warrior: HD 3; AC 2[17]; Atk 1 bite (1d6), 2 mandibles (1d4), 1 sting (1 + non-lethal poison); Move 12; Save 14; AL N; CL/XP 5/240; Special: Non-lethal poison sting (2d4 damage, save for half).

Formian Taskmaster: HD 7; AC 1[18]; Atk 1 bite (1d6+1), 1 sting (1d2 + non-lethal poison); Move 12; Save 9; AL N; CL/XP 8/800; Special: Non-lethal poison (4d4 damage, save for half).

Formian Male: HD 8; AC 1[18]; Atk 1 bite (1d6+1), 1 sting (1d2 + non-lethal poison); Move 12; Save 8; AL N; CL/XP 9/1100; Special: Non-lethal poison (4d4 damage, save for half).

Formian Queen (Noncombatant): HD 10, AC 3[16]; Atk None; Move 6; Save 5; AL N; CL/XP noncombatant; Special: None.

Love Slaves

A 300-foot-diameter rock butte topped by a crystal spire rises 180 feet above the Kanderi Desert like an accusatory finger pointing toward the sky. A ramp runs around the butte's outer wall to a series of open caves near its flat top. Formian workers move up and down the ramp in long lines, disappearing into the crystal spire once they reach the top. A formian taskmaster watches the lines of workers, making sure things move smoothly. A formian queen lives inside the crystal spire, protected by her formian warriors. At night, the crystal spire lights from within as the queen cavorts with the consorts that make up her royal retinue. The lights are powered by the sacrifices of intelligent creatures.

At the base of the butte, a large cage sits on the sandy desert in the

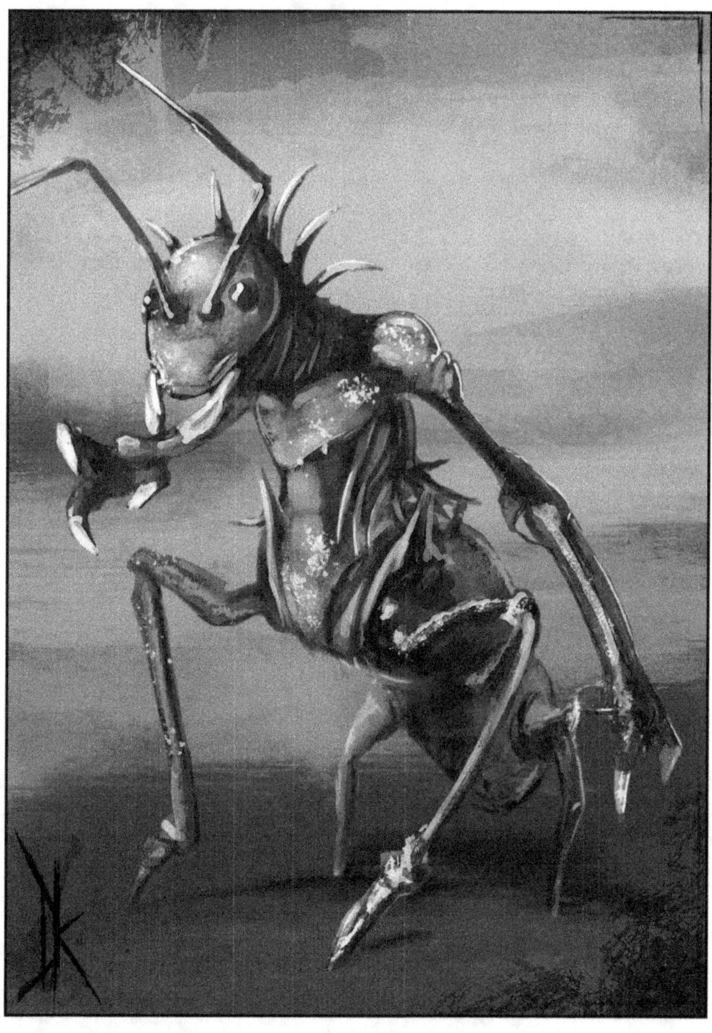

glaring heat of the midday sun. Sitting forlornly in the cage are 12 human men and women, 7 elves and 3 dwarves. All are severely dehydrated and near death. A captive is taken from the pen each day and carried up the rock slopes to the crystal spire to provide the mood lighting each night for the queen's debauchery. The slaves are guarded at all times by **5 formian warriors** armed with spears. At night, the formian sentries are less alert (and largely dejected at missing the festivities going on above them). One of the formians has a horn to bring **2d4 formian warriors** in 1d6 rounds if needed.

Fox Monk

Hit Dice: 2+3
Armor Class: 7 [12]
Attacks: 1 bite (1d4) or 1 strike (1d3 + spasms)
Saving Throw: 16
Special: Spells, monkish strike
Move: 15
Alignment: Law
Number Encountered: 1
Challenge Level/XP: 3/60

The Fox Monk is a short fox-like humanoid, garbed in a shabby, quilted robe and bearing only a begging bowl and walking stick. Fox monks have taken vows of poverty and transience; they rely upon charity for food and somewhere to sleep, never staying in one area for more than a few days. They may defend themselves with a bite (1d4 damage), or in unarmed combat. A fox monk's strike causes the target's nervous system to spasm, causing him to drop any items held and move at half normal speed for 1d4 rounds (saving throw negates). Fox monks may also forego all attacks to perform dodging leaps, causing enemies to attack at -3 to hit. Lastly, a fox monk can cast Protection from Evil and Purify Food and Drink once per day. Despite their vows, these pious beggars are considered troublemakers by most civilized folk.

— Author: Scott Wylie Roberts, "Myrystyr"

Fox Monk: HD 2+3; AC 7[12]; Atk 1 bite (1d4) or 1 strike (1d3 + spasms); Move 15; Save 16; AL N; CL/XP 3/60; Special: Spells, monkish strike.

Sounds, no Silence

The Tainted Mule Tavern in the center of the village of Hoggins is a pleasant place, with low prices, nice rooms and good ale on tap. The owner, Mather Smits, a burly ex-fighter who nurses a noticeable limp, happily serves newcomers piles of food as he regales them with stories of his past exploits and the town's history. Oddly, he throws in wax earplugs to anyone renting a room for the night. Shortly after sunset, a massive iron bell in the bell tower of an abandoned temple to Voard begins chiming the hours. The loud gonging echoes throughout the village, making sleep nearly impossible. The bell chimes until sunrise.

A **fox monk** named **Candric Tuffletail** recently arrived in town, following a dream that told him to head west to the small town. The Voard worshipper climbed into the bell tower and sleeps there during the day. At night, he serves a penance known only to him by ringing the bell to mark the hours of the night. The monk refuses to leave the tower until he has sated the dead god Voard. Anyone trying to physically remove him faces an angry monk very capable of protecting himself.

Frog, Giant

	SMALL	MEDIUM	LARGE
Hit Dice:	1	2	3
Armor Class:	AC 7[12]	AC 7[12]	AC 7[12]
Attacks:	1 bite (1d3)	1 bite (1d6)	1 bite (1d8)
Saving Throw:	17	16	14
Special:	Leap	Leap	Leap, swallow whole
Move:	3 (or 150 ft. leap)	3 (or 150 ft. leap)	3 (or 150 ft. leap)
Alignment:	Neutrality	Neutrality	Neutrality
Number Encountered:	5d8	5d8	5d8
Challenge Level/XP:	1/15	2/30	4/120

Giant frogs range in size from two or three feet long (a "small" giant frog), up to massive specimens of eight feet long (a "large" giant frog). In between are the "medium" giant frogs, five to six feet long. Large giant frogs can swallow opponents whole on a natural attack roll of 20. All giant frogs can make a 100ft leap that reaches a height of 20ft. Small giant frogs increase this length to 150ft. If an opponent is swallowed whole, he dies in three rounds. To escape, the victim cannot attack normally, and must have a bladed weapon to even attempt cutting his way out of the frog. An attack roll of 18 or better, including any modifiers, indicates that the victim cuts his way out of the frog, slaying the beast in the process. Attacks on the giant frog have a chance to damage a swallowed creature. Giant frogs can use their tongues to grab prey and haul them to the frog's mouth; anyone grabbed in this way takes no damage until the frog begins to bite it in the following round, hitting automatically and inflicting maximum damage on that one attack. A group of giant frogs will generally be evenly mixed among the three sizes (roll 1d3 for hit dice on each frog in the encounter).

Giant Frog (small): HD 1; AC 7[12]; Atk 1 bite (1d3); Move 3 (or 150ft leap); Save 17; AL N; CL/XP 1/15; Special: Leap.

Giant Frog (medium): HD 2; AC 7[12]; Atk 1 bite (1d6); Move 3 (or 100ft leap); Save 16; AL N; CL/XP 2/30; Special: Leap.

Giant Frog (large): HD 3; AC 7[12]; Atk 1 bite (1d8); Move 3 (or 100ft leap); Save 14; AL N; CL/XP 4/120; Special: Leap, swallow whole.

Flies to Honey

Golden, syrupy liquid spills out of a half dozen beehives in this 200-foot-wide field of flowers. Sassafras trees surround the open field where the eight-foot-tall hives stand. Clouds of normal bees swarm through the air. A halfling wearing loose robes that puddle at his feet and a net-like helmet over his head stands in the midst of the angry bees. One of the halfling's hands is stuck in the honey dripping out of a hive. He shouts for help, unable to pull himself away.

The halfling is an inventor named **Ollie Nematoad** who ventured out among the hives to try out an idea about insects he plans to test on ankhegs soon. He became stuck in the extra-sticky honey and requires help to pull himself free. The buzzing bees are little more than a nuisance, although anyone running among the nests takes 1 point of damage each round from the multiple stings they receive.

Charging onto the field attracts unwanted attention of a different sort, however. Hiding in the treeline are **6 giant frogs** that leap out to attack anyone trying to help poor Ollie. The frogs easily leap half the distance of the field in a single bound. They land among the PCs and grab them with their tongues before leaping away from the bees with their prize.

Frog, Giant Killer

Hit Dice: 1+4
Armor Class: 7 [12]
Attacks: 2 claws (1d2), 1 bite (1d4+1)
Saving Throw: 17
Special: Leap
Move: 3/15 (leaping)
Alignment: Neutrality
Number Encountered: 3d6
Challenge Level/XP: 2/30

About three feet long, giant killer frogs are the product of mad breeding experiments. They have claws and teeth, and attack relentlessly.

Giant Killer Frog: HD 1+4; AC 7[12]; Atk 2 claws (1d2), 1 bite (1d4+1); Move 3 (leap 15); Save 17; AL N; CL/XP 2/30; Special: Leap.

Red of Tooth and Claw

A collapsed 100-foot-tall tower lies on its side, partially submerged in the Sin Mire Swamp. Bubbles burst around the sunken stones. Brackish water fills half of the empty round tunnel leading into the tower's sideways interior. The collapsed base of the wall has a large, blackened hole blasted through the stone, the obvious reason why it fell. Bullfrogs croak in the reeds growing wildly throughout the swamp. Catfish swim in and out of the collapsed tower. A dead and partially devoured alligator floats belly up atop the murky water. A few bright red teeth are still stuck in the gator's thick hide.

The tower belonged Cornelisa Blent, a mage who experimented with – and on – various unfortunate inhabitants of the ever-expanding swamp. Her last experiment (and the one that spelled doom for her and her tower home) turned an army of giant frogs into deadly killers. As her experiments overwhelmed her, she blasted apart one of the tower's walls in the hope of escaping. The explosion weakened the structure, causing it to topple. Cornelisa died in the fall, but **12 giant killer frogs** escaped unharmed. The amphibians live inside the fallen tower, eating the fish, giant dragonflies and alligators that live in the area. The frogs hop wildly out of the tower toward anyone approaching the opening. Cornelisa's experiment turned all of the frogs' teeth and claws a bright red.

Froglum

Hit Dice: 8
Armor Class: 5 [14]
Attacks: 2 fists (2d6)
Saving Throw: 8
Special: Half damage from fire
Move: 12
Alignment: Neutrality
Number Encountered: 1
Challenge Level/XP: 8/800

In ages past, some mad experimenter created a golem from frog-flesh: the ancestor of all froglums. Some frog genes, however, can switch genders and even produce hermaphrodites. The ancestor of froglums was likely the first (and probably the only) self-breeding golem. Froglums are huge bipeds virtually identical to their shared ancestor: eight feet tall with slimy green skin, webbed feet, and great frog-like eyes. Their legs resemble those of frogs, but are much shorter and allow the froglum to stand upright. These creatures are soulless, having been bred from an unnatural and artificial origin. They have no detectable thoughts. In general, they serve any chaotic master, especially one who resembles a frog or a powerful wizard. They are seldom found acting on their own volition, for it is in their nature to follow a powerful master. A froglum's slimy skin makes it resistant to fire (half damage).

— Author: Matt Finch

Froglum: HD 8; AC 5[14]; Atk 2 fists (2d6); Move 12; Save 8; AL N; CL/XP 8/800; Special: half damage from any fire.

The Frog Prince Bandit

A tall, thin young man with a scraggly yellow beard steps out from behind a stand of cedar trees. He wears a strange green helmet on his head. The helmet has large white eyes painted on the sides, making it look like a squashed frog's head. He demands 200 gp from travelers using the "Frog Prince's Highway." Those who pay are allowed to go on their way. Those who refuse face the prince's protector: an eight-foot-tall **froglum** loyal to the odd-looking young man.

Urdek Longface was a down-on-his-luck, run-of-the-mill bandit until he discovered his odd helmet. When he put it on, he found himself face to face with a froglum willing to do his every command. The froglum is bound to the helmet and willingly serves whoever wears it. Urdek flees combat, and does all he can to protect his precious headgear. He doesn't want to return to nothingness. He carries a belt pouch with 600 gp in it. The gold was taken from travelers too scared to fight the froglum.

Fungal Creeper

Hit Dice: 3
Armor Class: 7 [12]
Attacks: 1 touch (1d6)
Saving Throw: 14
Special: Attaches on 19 or 20
Move: 3
Alignment: Neutrality
Number Encountered: 1d3
Challenge Level/XP: 4/120

The Fungal Creeper is a patch of fungus growing upon a boulder or wall, which often appears weathered and strangely corroded. The name comes from its ability to creep along the wall, moving about to follow living creatures. Fungal creepers draw sustenance from minerals found in rock and stone, but supplement their diets with fresh blood. The fungal creeper can sense the warmth of life within 60ft, and reacts by moving closer. It attacks by sinking tiny root-like appendages into exposed flesh, latching on to cause continuous damage if the attack roll is a 19 or 20. It may be distracted by fresh meat, whether in the form of rations no more than 1 day old or the body of an unconscious combatant. They are scavengers, and will move to feed off carrion as soon as it is detected.

— Author: Scott Wylie Roberts, "Myrystyr"

Fungal Creeper: HD 3; AC 7[12]; Atk 1 touch (1d6); Move 3; Save 14; AL N; CL/XP 4/120; Special: Attaches on 19 or 20.

Nail Fungus

A weathered statue stands beside the entry into this circular room. A round dais in the center of the low-ceilinged chamber is made of marble trimmed with brass. A giant stone hand (with fingers fully six feet long) rises from the center of the dais. It stands on what would be the stump of its wrist. Its nails are pitted and covered with patchy green moss. In its open palm is a mace with a silver head and leather-wrapped handle. A skeleton lies on the floor before the hand, its torso crushed.

The giant hand is a **stone golem** molded into this unique shape. It clamps its fingers down on anyone trying to remove the mace, and then flips over to scuttle about on its fingertips. The golem slams people aside by flicking them out of its way with its long fingers. **A fungal creeper** covers the stone fingers, co-existing with the golem. Anyone hit by the golem is also attacked by the creeper as it latches onto the PC's skin.

The mace is a *+2 mace* with the ability to do an additional 1d6 points of damage to stone creatures when wielded by a Lawful cleric.

Stone Golem: HD 15 (60hp); AC 5[14]; Atk 1 fist (3d8); Move 6; Save 3; AL N; CL/XP 16/3200; Special: +1 or better magic weapon to hit, immune to most magic.

Fungi, Violet

Hit Dice: 3
Armor Class: 7 [12]
Attacks: 4 tendrils (rot)
Saving Throw: 14
Special: Tendrils cause rot
Move: 1
Alignment: Neutrality
Number Encountered: 1d4
Challenge Level/XP: 4/120

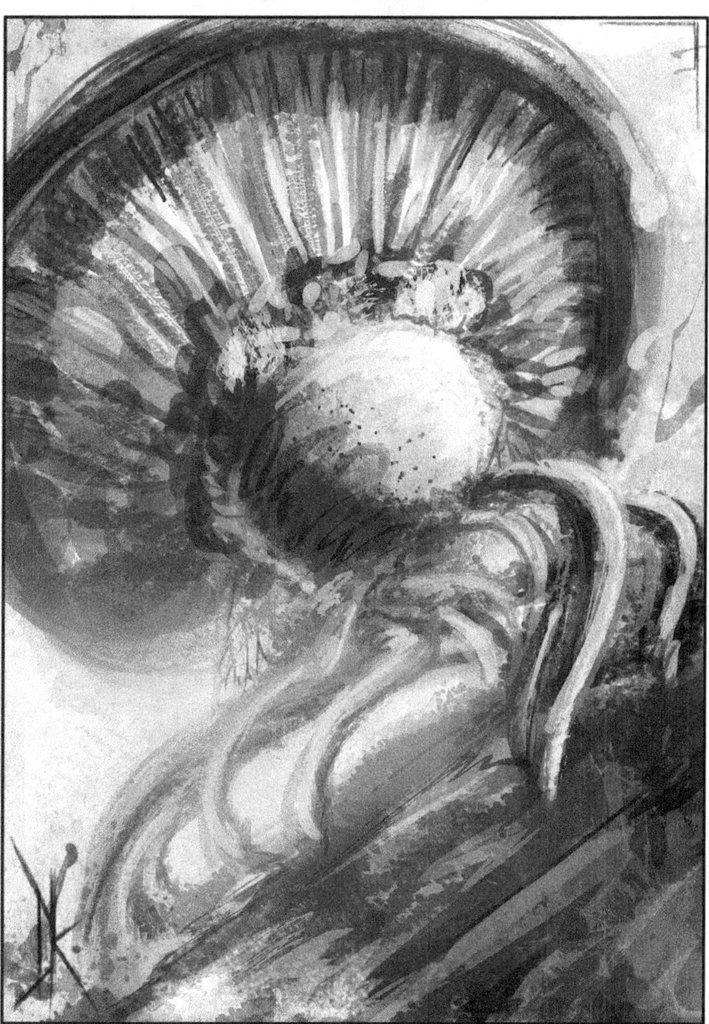

Violet fungi are large mushrooms with tentacle-like growths at the base. The tentacles are not long, averaging about 2-3ft. A hit from a tentacle causes flesh to rot (saving throw applies) unless a cure disease spell is cast upon the afflicted area.

Violet Fungus: HD 3; AC 7[12]; Atk 4 tendrils (rot); Move 1; Save 14; AL N; CL/XP 4/120; Special: Tendrils cause rot.

Dead Bunnies

Dead rabbits lie in the sawgrass around a grove of discolored elm trees. The rabbits' squishy remains are slowly decomposing into the loamy earth. A few of the forest animals are missing ears that appear to have rotted down to their skulls. Others have white and mottled hindquarters. Animal trails crisscross through the thick underbrush, and other dead creatures can be found hidden nearby. PCs find foxes, squirrels and deer. All of them bear discolored spots of decomposition. A path cut by loggers runs parallel to the game trails. It winds around some of the bigger trees.

Growing among the shaded roots of the elm trees are **12 violet fungi**. The fungi grow along the game trails from spores brought aboveground by a diseased mole. The mushrooms lash out creatures using the game trails and paths. The dead animals nourish the soil, allowing the fungi to spread.

Furious Fountain

Hit Dice: 15 (60 hit points)
Armor Class: 5 [14]
Attacks: 1 fist (3d8) or water jet
Saving Throw: 3
Special: Immune to non-magical weapons, immune to most magic, water jet
Move: 6
Alignment: Neutrality
Number Encountered: 1
Challenge Level/XP: 18/3,800

A furious fountain resembles a large anthropomorphic stone fountain, usually spraying a jet of water from its mouth. These creatures are similar to golems, but the animating spirit within is an imprisoned water elemental.

When standing still, a furious fountain is indistinguishable from any ordinary fountain. A furious fountain may attack with its stony fist, or with a jet of water. The animate fountain can spew out a violent stream of water at a range of 200ft, three times per day. The target suffers 3d10 points of damage, and is pushed back the full remaining distance of the jet's range (a successful save halves both the damage and the distance pushed back). A second saving throw allows the victim to remain standing and avoid dropping any items held in hand. Like golems, furious fountains are unaffected by non-magical weapons. These magical creatures can only be affected by spells that specifically target water or stone, with appropriate results to be determined by the referee. As a guideline, the fountain will lose, at most, 4d10 hit points from such spells; Part Water would be an example of a spell that might inflict such damage.

— Author: Skathros

Furious Fountain: HD 60hp (15HD); AC 5[14]; Atk 1 fist (3d8) or water jet; Move 6; Save 3; AL N; CL/XP 18/3800; Special: Immune to non-magical weapons, immune to most magic, water jet.

The Harem's Bath

The comely women of Caliph Anastior's harem lounge around a marble fountain spraying water nearly 20 feet into the air. Water falls like rain on the beautiful women as they relax on plush red cushions and low silver couches about the fountain's wide basin. They eat plump grapes and succulent dates from large ceramic bowls. Each woman wears a thin veil and a thinner gown. Their eyes are rimmed in black, and red rouge brightens their cheeks.

The caliph is a peaceful man, but also very paranoid. His biggest fear is to lose his harem, and the suspicious man fears thieves lurk around every corner and under every flowering plant. He knows they are just waiting to steal away the women with whom he shares his palatial estate. Walking the garden are **6 tigers**, but the true protector is a **furious fountain** hiding in plain sight inside the harem's chamber. The fountain rises from its resting spot to attack any male PCs who enter unbidden into the women's ornate chambers. The fountain is careful to avoid injuring the women as it stands and fights.

Tiger: HD 6; AC 6[13]; Atk 2 claws (1d4+1), 1 bite (1d8); Move 15 (Swim 6); Save 11; AL N; CL/XP 7/600; Special: Rear claws

Gargoyle

Hit Dice: 4
Armor Class: 5 [14]
Attacks: 2 claws (1d3), 1 bite (1d4), 1 horn (1d6)
Saving Throw: 13
Special: Immune to non-magic weapons
Move: 9/15 (flying)
Alignment: Chaos
Number Encountered: 2d8
Challenge Level/XP: 6/400

Gargoyles are winged beings resembling the carven monstrosities that bedeck the walls of cathedrals and many subterranean dungeons. They are terribly vicious predators.

Gargoyle: HD 4; AC 5[14]; Atk 2 claws (1d3), 1 bite (1d4), 1 horn (1d6); Move 9 (Fly 15); Save 13; AL C; CL/XP 6/400; Special: Fly, magic weapon required to hit.

Chasing Waterfalls

As one leaves the tangled woodlands for the scrub-covered foothills of the green mountains, they are drawn toward a narrow defile from which flows a quick, silvery river. The defile is difficult to enter, for the water flows quickly, and there are no ledges upon which one can walk. Over the centuries, adventurers have pounded numerous iron spikes into the walls, using them to secure ropes to make the passage a bit safer.

Once one has breached the defile, ledges appear over the river, which slows a bit. One can see blood red fish, almost eel-like in shape, flittering through the clear waters and gathering in the pools, which are caked with a jade green algae. The river and narrow canyon extend 12 miles into the foothills, the walls of the canyon growing taller and taller, and eventually bathing the canyon in a glorious, ever-present shadow that chills the air.

At the end of this canyon there is a waterfall, about 200 feet tall, and a pool surrounded by mists and caked with that same jade green algae. The waterfall drops into a basin carved from the surrounding green stone. This basin is 30 feet tall and ringed by grotesque gargoyles, from whose mouths pours the waters of the river – from all save one. This gargoyle's mouth is stoppered by a large piece of amber (worth 500 gp) wrapped in a bit of leopard skin and enclosed within a leather sack. One must reach their arm well into the mouth of the gargoyle to reach this parcel, and surely one must wonder if the beast is alive and poised to strike.

The stoppered gargoyle is not alive, but **4 gargoyles** do lurk here, hiding in a cave behind the falling water, about 30 feet above the top of the basin. They are the guardians of the falls, and the mysteries that lie behind them on a tangled plateau of magnolias and tree-ferns reachable through the gargoyle's cave.

Gargoyle, Maggog

Hit Dice: 5+1
Armor Class: 4 [15]
Attacks: 2 claws (1d6) and 1 sting (1d8)
Saving Throw: 12
Special: Spells
Move: 12/18 (flying)
Alignment: Chaos
Number Encountered: 1d4
Challenge Level/XP: 7/600

Maggogs are bat-winged gargoyles. They can utilize magic as a 5th level magic-user (4/2/1). Typically they are found deep in the bowels of the earth. Maggogs are related to demons, but aren't guardians of the underworld. Their terrible claws can inflict damage, along with a barbed tail, which is used as a stinger.

— Author: Old Crawler

Maggog Gargoyle: HD 5+1; AC 4[15]; Atk 2 claws (1d6) and 1 sting (1d8); Move 12 (Fly 18); Save 12; AL C; CL/XP 7/600; Special: Spell use.

Faces in the Crowd

An immense underground cavern here hosts a temple carved from the living rock and hidden behind astounding curtains, 60 feet high, composed of copper wire and the carapaces of giant ants. Behind these curtains, one finds a wall of bas-reliefs – the outer wall of the temple. The lowest portion of the wall is carved with tusked giants, holding aloft platforms while serpents slither about their legs. On these platforms sat grand nymphs swathed in diaphanous silk, fanned by sylphs and served by satyrs. Behind them stand terrible hags with scowling faces, their noses hooked, their eyes leering. Between those leering heads are a number of demons, crouching and holding in their hands vicious hooked spears. A few of the demons are actually **3 maggog gargoyles**, the guardians of the subterranean Temple of Azathoth.

Gas Spore

Hit Dice: 1d4 hit points
Armor Class: 9 [10]
Attacks: 1 touch (disease)
Saving Throw: 18
Special: Disease, explodes, attacks as 3HD monster
Move: 0/3 (flying)
Alignment: Neutrality
Number Encountered: 1d4
Challenge Level/XP: 4/120

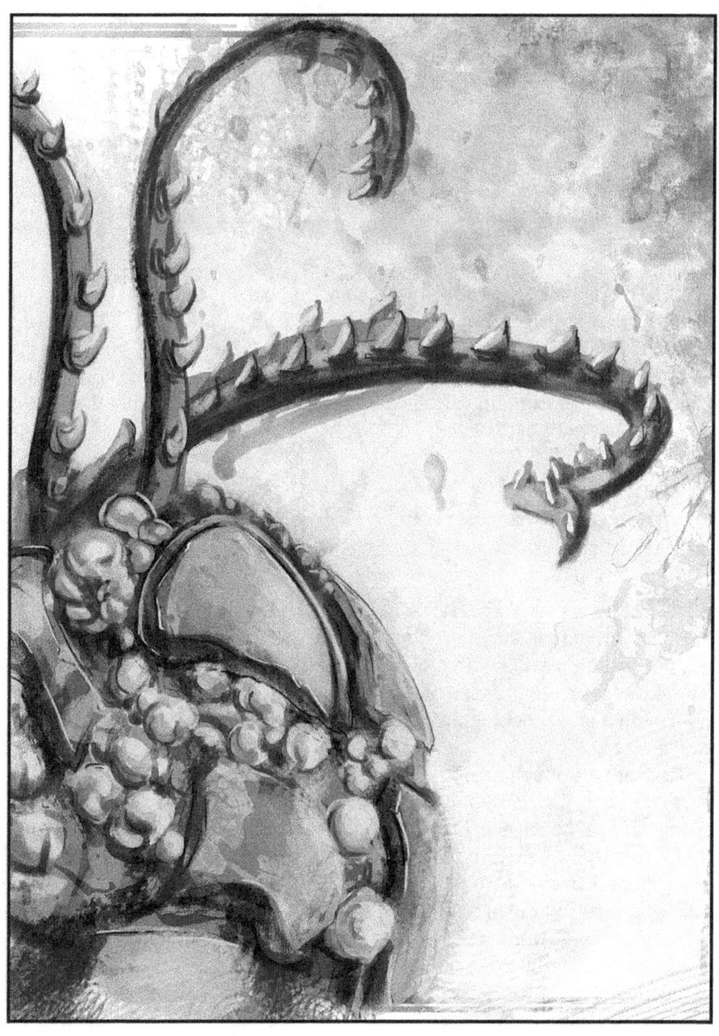

The gas spore is a spherical, chitin-armored sac containing fungus spores, about five feet in diameter, with some moving tendrils growing from the top of the sphere. The sac contains lighter-than-air gases which allow it to float in the air, and it can move by expelling some of these gases in a form of jet-propulsion. When it is near any warm-blooded creatures, it will move toward them by instinct: these creatures are completely non-intelligent.

If a gas spore gets close enough to touch a living creature, it will inject spores into the target with a successful to-hit roll. If the victim fails a saving throw, these spores will bloat and transform the host into 1d6+1 new gas spores within 24 hours unless a *cure disease* spell is used to prevent this (rather disgusting) transformation.

Moreover, when a gas spore is killed (and it is designed by nature to burst easily), it explodes in a radius of 20ft, inflicting 6d6 points of damage in that area (half damage with a successful saving throw). The body of anyone killed by the blast will also begin transforming into new gas spores.

Gas Spore: HD 1d4 hp; AC 9[10]; Atk 1 touch (disease); Move 0 (fly 3); Save 18; AL N; CL/XP 4/120; Special: Causes disease, explodes, attacks as 3HD monster.

Going for a Spin

Adventurers find themselves in a large cavern with smooth walls, floor and ceiling. The cavern is roughly circular, and the only inhabitants are a **12 gas spores**, floating about the place aimlessly. The cavern has two exits, other than the tunnel through which the adventurers enter. Floating in the middle of the cavern is a large sphere, apparently made of white marble swirled with light greys and blues. Touching this sphere reveals the truth, as the temporal stasis that held this rather enraged **air elemental** suddenly ends. The air elemental wastes little time in forming a whirlwind that throws the gas spores around the room. Each person in the room must make a saving throw or be struck by a gas spore as they spin and whirl about the chamber.

Air Elemental (8HD): HD 8; AC 2[17]; Atk 1 strike (2d8); Move (Fly 36); Save 8; AL N; CL/XP 9/1100; Special: Whirlwind.

Gelatinous Cube

Hit Dice: 4
Armor Class: 8 [11]
Attacks: Attack (2d4)
Saving Throw: 13
Special: Paralysis, immune to lightning and cold
Move: 6
Alignment: Neutrality
Number Encountered: 1
Challenge Level/XP: 5/240

Gelatinous cubes are semi-transparent cubes that slosh through subterranean passages, engulfing debris and carrion to digest. Their entire substance is acidic; if the cube hits successfully, the victim must make a saving throw or become paralyzed (6 turns) for the cube to devour. Most gelatinous cubes contain various metallic treasures or gems that they have engulfed but not yet digested.

Gelatinous Cube: HD 4; AC 8[11]; Atk 1 (2d4); Move 6; Save 13; AL N; CL/XP 5/240; Special: Paralysis, immune to lightning and cold.

Getting it Wrong Gets it Right

Somewhere in a forgotten dungeon there is a vault of brass. The walls are brass and covered with clever little decorations of crosses and cubes. The floors are clad in brass tiles. And one wall holds a large, heavy brass door with a large locking mechanism held in what appears to be the head of a dragon.

The locking mechanism is not especially difficult to work, but it is a trap. To open the lock, one must trip what, to any knowledgeable thief, would appear to be the incorrect tumblers. If one succeeds at an open locks roll, they hear a loud *clank!* from within the vault, and feel the floor vibrate and rattle for a moment. A second successful open locks roll causes a metallic moan to sound through the walls and floor and ends in another *clank!* A third successful roll causes the floor tile directly in front of the lock to collapse, sending the thief 20 feet down into the waiting expanse of a **gelatinous cube**. The cube inhabits a network of limestone catacombs, and it is not alone.

Two unsuccessful open lock rolls, on the other hand, cause the vault door to noiselessly swing open. Within, one finds the following treasure: 1,000 silver coins (decorated with crescents and stars), 200 gold coins (bearing the profile of Queen Sarvasti of the Three Eyes), a golden yak worth 50 gp (gold foil around carved bone), a grey-brown cloak (worth 5 sp), a belt of red dragon hide (worth 30 gp) and a rowan lyre that, when the correct tune is played, ejects a vial of basilisk blood.

Ghast

Hit Dice: 4
Armor Class: 4 [15]
Attacks: 2 claws (1d3), 1 bite (1d6)
Saving Throw: 13
Special: Stench, paralyzing touch
Move: 14
Alignment: Chaos
Number Encountered: 1d6
Challenge Level/XP: 5/240

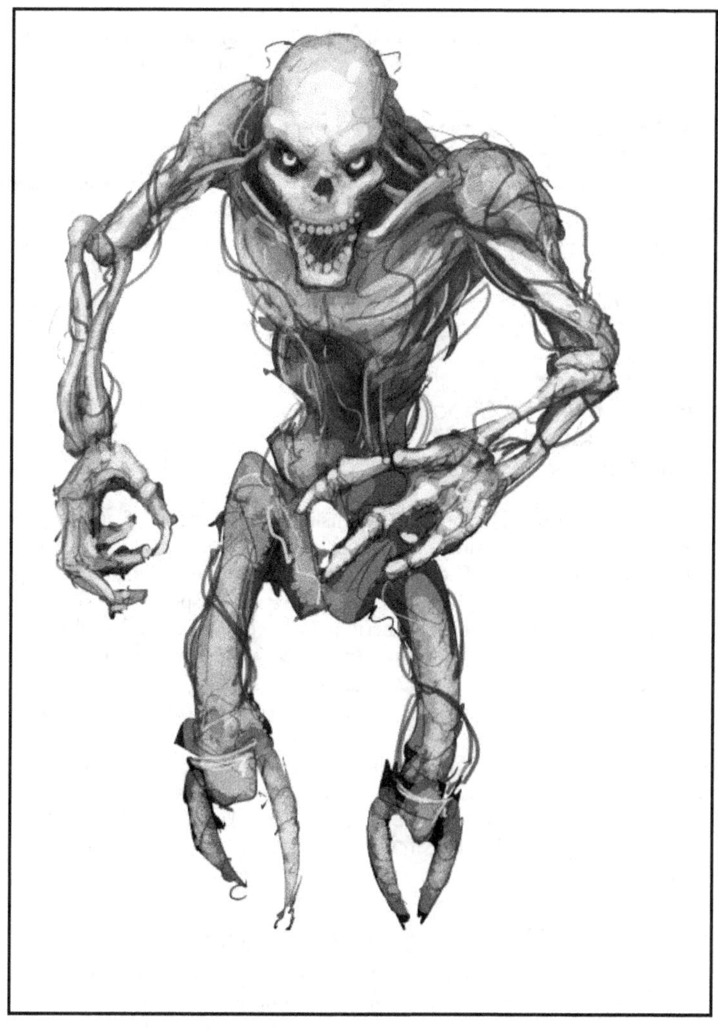

Ghasts are highly intelligent ghouls. Their charnel stench is so powerful that anyone nearby (about 10ft) must make a saving throw or suffer a −2 penalty on attack rolls. As with ghouls, a hit from a ghast causes paralysis if the victim fails a saving throw.

Ghast: HD 4; AC 4[15]; Atk 2 claws (1d3), 1 bite (1d6); Move 15; Save 13; AL C; CL/XP 5/240; Special: Stench, paralyzing touch.

Ghastly Choice

While one is foolishly crawling through the underworld, they might come across a tunnel, the entrance of which is carved to resemble the gaping mouth of a tiger, with eye sockets that hold blue-green orbs of metal. Beyond there is a tunnel, the entire length of which is hung with iron masks on iron chains, the masks representing stoic matrons with full cheeks and empty eyes. At the end of this tunnel lies the grand cavern of the ghasts, an immense void filled with the stench of decay and thousands upon thousands of cast off bones.

Those bones that retain gibbets of flesh are crawling with **rot grubs**. Narrow paths between the bone mounds wind through the cavern, and these paths are crawling with **ghasts**, their cloven hooves clicking on the bare stone of the cavern floor, their vulgar jests filling the noisome air.

A massive column of stone rises from the floor of the cavern and reaches the ceiling. The column looks like two cones that touch at the points, and is 30 feet wide at its most narrow point. The column is 200 feet tall and its base is piled high with bones, for the ghasts appear to avoid the column, never approaching within 30 feet of it. A secret door at the base of the column allows one to enter the column, where they will find a spiral stair that climbs all the way up the column to a more pleasant cavern of slimes that evoke wondrous hallucinations that masquerade as communiqués of the gods.

Rot Grub: HD 1 hp; AC 9[10]; Atk 1 burrow; Move 1; Save 18; AL N; CL/XP 1/15; Special: Burrows to heart.

GHOSTS

There are innumerable types of ghosts with varying qualities, often depending on the nature and circumstances under which the person died. One example follows.

Ghost, Strangling

Hit Dice: 5
Armor Class: 0[19]
Attacks: Insubstantial strangling (see below)
Saving Throw: 12
Special: +1 or silver weapon required to hit; magic resistance 50%
Move: 12 (flying)
Alignment: Usually Chaotic
Number Encountered: 1
Challenge Level/XP: 7/600

These apparitions are similar to banshees, but instead of screeching they can attack only a single opponent at a time, strangling the victim with insubstantial hands. If the attack hits, the victim must make a saving throw or die within 1d4+1 rounds. A *remove curse* spell will break the creature's hold during this time period. *Protection from evil* spells will hold these creatures at bay. Anyone strangled by a strangling ghost will rise as a strangling ghost within 1d6 days.

— *Author: Matt Finch*

Strangling Ghost: HD 5; AC 0[19]; Atk 1 strangulation (save or die in 14+1 rounds); Move (Fly 12); Save 12; AL usually C; CL/XP 7/600; Special: Magic Resistance (50%), magic or silver weapon required to hit, strangles (if hit, save or die in 1d4+1 rounds).

Don't Go Down Strangler's Alley

Local folks will say, time and time again, that you avoid Strangler's Alley at night, no matter what. Despite the rumors about a treasure in the old house at the end of the alley, a treasure one can only find in moonlight, one never enters the alley at night. Prepare for adventurers to ignore this advice.

The alley is ordinary enough. The ground is earth – hard and dry usually, but mucky to a depth of one foot in the rain. It is about 5 feet wide and flanked by two buildings, one an inn composed of red brick (with no windows on this side) and the other a counting house with one story of cut stone and the upper stories composed of wattle-and-daub. Both buildings are four stories tall. At the end of the alley there is a wrought-iron gate and a small courtyard filled with an overgrown garden. A small fountain, now dry, stands there, its playful nymph covered in vines, one of her arms cracked. Beyond the garden there is a manse that wraps around, touching the inn and counting house. It is three stories tall and built of black brick and wood, with a steep roof of copper tile and bronze ornamentation (now green with age) around the windows and doors. At night, the alley is haunted by **3 strangling ghosts**, a trio of assassins who were cut down by mysterious means after leaving the manse one dark and stormy night. They had killed the inhabitant, a sorceress of no little influence in the courts of Hell (where she is said to rule to this day).

Ghoul

Hit Dice: 2
Armor Class: 6 [13]
Attacks: 2 claws (1d3), 1 bite (1d4)
Saving Throw: 16
Special: Immunities, paralysis
Move: 9
Alignment: Chaos
Challenge Level/XP: 3/60

Ghouls are pack-hunting undead corpse eaters. They are immune, like most undead, to charms and sleep spells. The most dangerous feature of these horrid, cunning creatures is their paralyzing touch: any hit from a ghoul requires a saving throw or the victim becomes paralyzed for 3d6 turns.

Ghoul: HD 2; AC 6[13]; Atk 2 claws (1d3), 1 bite (1d4); Move 9; Save 16; AL C; CL/XP 3/60; Special: Immunities, paralyzing touch.

Ghouls' Night Out

In the citadel of the necromancer-king, **ghouls** are kept on short chains and taunted with bits of flesh by the passing acolytes and the children of the grandees of the court who stroll there swathed in their black togas and tunics of silver links, their ebony walking sticks and slippers of volcanic glass tip-tapping along the uneven pavements. At night, when all are secure behind their thick, iron doors, the ghouls are loosed from their chains and roam freely, cleaning the streets of carrion and delving into secret places only they know, to count their hidden treasures and make their secret plans.

Ghoul, Ao-Nyobo (Blue Wife)

Hit Dice: 4
Armor Class: 5 [14]
Attacks: 2 claws (1d4), 1 bite (1d6)
Saving Throw: 13
Special: Paralyzing touch
Move: 14/9 (flying)
Alignment: Chaos
Number Encountered: 1
Challenge Level/XP: 6/400

This female ghoul-creature can be found lurking in the ruins of old castles. They resemble old, courtly ladies with blue skin, blackened teeth, and no eyebrows. As with ghouls and ghasts, a hit from the Ao-nyobo causes paralysis if the victim fails a saving throw. The Ao-nyobo is capable of flight and prefers to ambush victims from above - often hiding in the rafters of half-ruined buildings to swoop down upon the unsuspecting. In the outdoors, an Ao-nyobo will often chase down any escaped prey in a relentless, airborne hunt. Ao-nyobo are turned as ghasts.

— Author: Mike Davison

Ao-nyobo: HD 4; AC 5[14]; Atk 2 claws (1d4), 1 bite (1d6); Move 14 (Fly 9); Save 13; AL C; CL/XP 6/400; Special: Paralyzing touch.

Love/Hate Relationship

The palace of the emperor is enormous, but even the emperor knows not how enormous. Behind the walls covered in gilt plaster and mosaics of tortoise shell and amber there are secret, dank passages haunted by the former empress, a woman called Obomay, who would have ruled the empire from behind the imperial throne had not the emperor took a liking to a dancing girl called Othea who was practiced in the secret art of the of seven venoms. Othea now holds the place of power behind the man-child emperor, and Obomay dwells in the shadows after being unceremoniously dumped into a dry well in the Anemone Garden, her hatred re-awakening her as an **ao-nyobo ghoul**. She still wears her tattered robes of damask, her neck still bears the simple silver chain that was a gift from her mother the duchess royal, but her skin is now a pale blue, her lips as purple as wine and hiding razor-sharp fangs. At night, one can hear her throaty laughter and the scratching of her talons on the stones.

Many knights and knaves have entered the known secret doors in search of her, but none have returned, and now few are willing to take up the quest, despite the promise of a rich, seaside fief. Worse yet, at each full moon she steals into the palace proper and snatches a maiden from the inner circle of the new empress, devouring her body and leaving her head and skeleton elsewhere in the palace to be discovered by the palace's inhabitants.

Ghoul, Crimson

Hit Dice: 4
Armor Class: 6 [13]
Attacks: 2 claws (1d3) and 1 bite (1d6)
Saving Throw: 13
Special: Half damage from non-magic weapons, +1 save vs. spells, paralysis
Move: 9
Alignment: Chaos
Number Encountered: 1d6
Challenge Level/XP: 6/400

Crimson ghouls are created by strange and terrible magical procedures worked by necromancers upon a normal ghoul. They are not ordinarily found in the wild, as regular ghouls are, although from time to time a pack of crimson ghouls might outlive or escape from their masters. In this case, the crimson ghouls will be found in the same sorts of desolate or cursed spots as normal ghouls, even competing with them for the horrid, charnel foods they crave. As with normal ghouls, the touch of a crimson ghoul causes paralysis for 3d6 turns unless the victim makes a saving throw.

As one might expect from the name, crimson ghouls have hides the color of blood. They otherwise resemble normal ghouls, although they are stronger and have a more powerful bite. In addition to the skin color and a more robust physical frame than their ghoulish brethren, crimson ghouls have another signal distinction from a normal ghoul, which is that normal weapons only inflict half damage against them. Magical weapons inflict full damage. Moreover, crimson ghouls are somewhat resistant to spells: they gain a +1 bonus on saving throws against any spell. As with most undead, they are immune to sleep spells, but they can be affected by a charm person or a charm monster spell (although the duration of the charm is extremely short, not lasting more than 1d6 rounds). This strange vulnerability seems to be the result of the necromantic procedures by which they are prepared, a by-product of being created as loyal servants to their necromantic masters.

— Author: Matt Finch

Crimson Ghoul: HD 4; AC 6[13]; Atk 2 claws (1d3), 1 bite (1d6); Move 9; Save 13; AL C; CL/XP 6/400; Special: Half damage from non-magic weapons, +1 save vs. spells, paralysis.

Crimson Guardians

In a dungeon somewhere in the humid south, there is an infamous room of red stone. The room is circular, and decorated with dozens of roiling, flapping tapestries that depict a ghoulish feast, from start to finish. In the room's center there is a strange curtain of wavering, orange light – as one enters, they might first mistake it for flames – that rises from floor to ceiling and encompasses a 30-foot-diameter area. Within, one might catch glimpses of nine figures, as red as newly spilled blood, moving about. The curtains are part of an anti-magic field. Within, there is an iron chest with nine fiendishly clever locks (and traps – each one a poison that robs a thief of dexterity and imposes a –5% to all open locks rolls). The chest is guarded by **9 crimson ghouls** that will not likely have to face magic weapons or spells within the anti-magic field. The chest actually contains a shaft that bypasses the next dungeon level for the one below it.

GIANTS

Giants are a staple of fantasy gaming, huge and dangerous creatures that often have a taste for human flesh. Most are not particularly intelligent.

Giant, Cloud

Hit Dice: 12 + 1d4 hit points
Armor Class: 4 [15]
Attacks: Weapon (6d6)
Saving Throw: 3
Special: Hurl boulders
Move: 15
Alignment: Chaos (sometimes Neutrality)
Number Encountered: 1d6
Challenge Level/XP: 13/2,300

Cloud giants are cunning beasts, often living in cloud-castles in the sky (hence their name). They throw rocks for 6d6 hit points of damage. Cloud giants are famous for their ability to smell out food, enemies, and Englishmen.

Cloud Giant: HD 12 + 1d4hp; AC 4[15]; Atk 1 weapon (6d6); Move 15; Save 3; AL Usually C; CL/XP 13/2300; Special: Hurl boulders.

Castle of the Cloud Bully

An old man in grey robes, a red cloak upon his shoulders, a tall grey hat on his head, gladly offers a circlet of steel to any who offer a few coins of gold. When one looks through this circlet, they see a wondrous vault heaped high with gold and silver and, on a pedestal, a beautiful harp plucked by a golden woman with hair of copper ringlets and eyes as green as emeralds. One can reach through the circlet (it is about 7 inches in diameter), but cannot reach the treasures, which are about 10 feet away.

Should anyone manage to shrink themselves and step through the circlet, they find themselves in the floating castle of the **cloud giant Blunderbore**, who rules over a family of **7 other cloud giants** and a kindly **ogress** called **Alice** who runs the kitchen and tends to the family's pet **griffon, Zmert**. Stepping through the circlet causes it to disappear, so the trip is one way. Blunderbore dresses in the furs of a black bear and wears a necklace of white stones and a red girdle around his waist. His castle sits atop a dingy cloud that never rains, only blotting out the sun over a farmland until his demand for ransom is paid. Blunderbore uses his griffon to collect his ransom (mostly of foodstuffs, but also silver and gold), and sometimes pelts villages with stones to make his point.

Ogre: HD 4+1; AC 5[14]; Atk 1 weapon (1d10+1); Move 9; Save 13; AL C; CL/XP 4/120; Special: None.

Griffon: HD 7; AC 3[16]; Atk 2 claws (1d4), 1 bite (2d8); Move 12 (Fly 27); Save 9; AL N; CL/XP 8/800; Special: None.

Giant, Daimyo

Hit Dice: 12 + 2d6 hit points
Armor Class: 3 [16]
Attacks: 1 sword (5d6)
Saving Throw: 3
Special: +1 to hit with sword, impervious to fire and cold
Move: 12
Alignment: Chaos
Number Encountered: 1 or 1d4+1
Challenge Level/XP: 15/2,900

Daimyo Giants are perhaps improperly named: the term "Daimyo" is ordinarily used as a title, whereas the daimyo giants are a particular sub-race in their own right. However, they are so often found leading groups of other giants (and ogres, as seen below) that the use of the title fits them well. They tend to attract followings of other giant-type creatures, for their charisma – to giant and ogre races only – is always treated as 18 regardless of the giant's true charisma as it would affect members of other races. Storm giants and titans are the exception to this rule; they not only do not find daimyo giants to be more than normally charismatic, but consider them to be irritatingly arrogant. Daimyo giants, for their part, avoid territories claimed by a storm giant or a titan, although with enough followers a daimyo giant might very well attempt to kill a storm giant.

Daimyo giants are slightly shorter but more powerfully muscled than cloud giants. They tend to have blue, yellow, or reddish-orange skin coloration, almost always with long, jet-black hair. They wield 10ft-long two-handed swords, with which they gain a +1 bonus to hit (the swords are not magical, merely well-honed). A daimyo giant will almost always (70%) be found with a small force of giant-retainers (see below), and if the giant does not have such a retinue it will be attended by 1d3+1 hill giants.

01-20: 1d3 cloud giants
21-50: 1d6 frost giants or fire giants (depends on nearest appropriate terrain)
51-60: 1d2 cloud giants and 1d6+1 hill giants
61-70: 1d3 frost or fire giants and 1d6+1 hill giants
71-00: 1d10+2 hill giants

In addition to any giant followers present, a daimyo giant will always have a retinue of ogre types in attendance: 1d3+1 ogre mages, 1d6+1 tusken ogres (q.v.), 1d6+4 ogres.

Daimyo giants are sometimes found occupying ancient ruins in the deep jungle; these will not have retinues of giant followers, but will have twice the normal number of ogre followers (of each type) and their lairs will also be protected by predatory cats and carnivorous apes.

— Author: Matt Finch

Daimyo Giant: HD 12 + 2d6hp; AC 3[16]; Atk 1 sword (5d6); Move 12; Save 3; AL C; CL/XP 15/2900; Special: +1 to hit, impervious to fire and cold.

Race to the Top

At a high mountain pass, where two wide ledges meet, a band of adventurers might come across another band of treasure hunters intent on winning the pass and stopping competitors from reaching the ancient ruin that lies above the tree line. These treasure hunters are **4 frost giants** and **2 ogre magi** under the command of a haughty **daimyo giant** clad from head to toe in white dragon-hide armor. The group has traveled from their lair in a crevasse many miles away to claim the prize that waits in the ruin, a **titaness** with skin the color of newly fallen snow and eyes as icy as a glacier, sleeping under a deific curse to awaken and fall in love with the first giant to kiss her. Of course, the ruin holds many other treasures as well that the daimyo giant's retinue plan to claim.

Frost Giant: HD 10+3; AC 4[15]; Atk 1 weapon (4d6); Move 12; Save 5; AL C; CL/XP 11/1700; Special: Hurl boulders, immune to cold.

Ogre Mage: HD 5+4; AC 4[15]; Atk 1 weapon (1d12); Move 12 (Fly 18); Save 12; AL C; CL/XP 7/600; Special: Magic use.

Giant, Fire

Hit Dice: 11 + 1d4 hit points
Armor Class: 4 [15]
Attacks: Weapon (5d6)
Saving Throw: 4
Special: Hurl boulders, immune to fire
Move: 12
Alignment: Chaos (sometimes Neutrality)
Number Encountered: 1d8
Challenge Level/XP: 12/2,000

Fire giants are usually found near volcanic mountains, in great castles of basalt or even iron. They throw boulders for 5d6 hit points of damage.

Fire Giant: HD 11+ 1d4hp; AC 4[15]; Atk 1 weapon (5d6); Move 12; Save 4; AL C; CL/XP 12/2000; Special: Hurl boulders, immune to fire.

Playing with Fire

As adventurers walk through a dark, secluded wood, they might come across a large mirror propped against a tree. The frame is brass and ornately worked. When a handsome male (charisma 13+) looks into the mirror, two large hands reach through and grab him (surprise on 1-4 on 1d6, saving throw to resist if not surprised), dragging him through the mirror and leaving naught but a cloud of acrid, black smoke in his place. Just as suddenly, the mirror returns to normal, and it will not work as a portal again.

The victim has been carried away to a distant volcano that rumbles and spits in the distance (within sight). Here, a clan of **fire giants** keeps a small fortress. The males are currently away, fighting the frost giants, so the females seek a plaything to entertain them. The man will be wrestled down and chained around the neck (though the chain is a pretty one). His weapons and armor will be removed, of course. The giantesses are gentle and treat their new toy well, offering him spiced wines and exotic viands. In exchange for one year of servitude, they offer him a suit of *+1 chainmail* that is so cunningly crafted as to make the wearer almost immune to fire (50% resistance to damage, +2 to saving throw), or some more suitable reward for characters who cannot wear such armor.

Giant, Frost

Hit Dice: 10 + 1d4 hit points
Armor Class: 4 [15]
Attacks: Weapon (4d6)
Saving Throw: 5
Special: Hurl boulders, immune to cold
Move: 12
Alignment: Chaos (sometimes Neutrality)
Number Encountered: 1d8
Challenge Level/XP: 11/1,700

Frost giants dwell in cold regions, where they build (or conquer) castles in remote places of ice and snow. They throw boulders or great chunks of ice for 4d6 points of damage.

Frost giants dwell in cold regions, where they build (or conquer) castles in remote places of ice and snow. They throw boulders or great chunks of ice for 4d6 points of damage.

Frost Giant: HD 10 + 1d4hp; AC 4[15]; Atk 1 weapon (4d6); Move 12; Save 5; AL C; CL/XP 11/1700; Special: Hurl boulders, immune to cold.

Cold Vengeance

In a frozen wasteland of snow-covered mountains and frozen rivers, the adventurers come across a roaring bonfire in a narrow defile. The defile is not so narrow that one cannot move around the fire, but they find this a moot point as **6 frost giants**, waiting in ambush atop the walls of the defile, suddenly rise and hurl a volley of boulders before leaping down with their axes. They giants are waiting for hated fire giants, and there might be a slim chance they do not attack, but it is more likely they consider the adventurers spies and try to seize them for questioning.

Giant, Hill

Hit Dice: 8
Armor Class: 4 [15]
Attacks: Weapon (2d8)
Saving Throw: 8
Special: Hurl boulders
Move: 12
Alignment: Chaos
Number Encountered: 1d10
Challenge Level/XP: 9/1,100

Hill giants are the least of the giant races; most are brutish cave-dwellers who dress in pelts and uncured hides. They throw rocks for 2d8 points of damage.

Hill Giant: HD 8+2; AC 4[15]; Atk 1 weapon (2d8); Move 12; Save 8; AL C; CL/XP 9/1100; Special: Throw boulders.

House in the Hills

In a cave system within a hillock covered by lilac bushes, a family of **6 hill giants** keeps house. The lady of the cave is brewing a cauldron of treacle while her eldest daughters are tanning cave bear hides in vats of urine. Father and the eldest son are out hunting, but the youngest son has been left behind; he sits about 300 feet away from the cave entrance knapping flint for spears. A swift stream runs beneath the cave, and buckets on ropes are tossed out to retrieve water. The hill giants keep a crude basin carved into the floor filled with the water. Deeper in the cave there is a hearth with a chimney that reaches to the top of the hillock, where it is covered by a grate. A large stone in the hearth is actually a polymorphed magic-user called Cedric. He has been in rock form for more than 200 years.

Giant, Khmornian

Hit Dice: 10+4hp (Female: 9)
Armor Class: 3 [16]
Attacks: 2 weapons (5d6)
Saving Throw: 5 (Female: 6)
Special: Hurl rocks; (females also shapeshift, spells)
Move: 12
Alignment: Chaos
Number Encountered: 1d6
Challenge Level/XP: (Male) 11/1,700, **(Female)** 12/2,000

Khmornian giants are often found living in jungles, but they can be found in virtually any non-arctic terrain. These giants have four arms, and long tusks protruding from wide mouths. Their lairs are often guarded (90% chance) by 1d4 giant pythons.

Khmornian giants can throw rocks at a range up to 200ft, inflicting 2d10 points of damage; if they are not using any of their four arms in melee combat, these giants can hurl two such rocks per round.

The polyandrous female khmornian giants are found in a 1:3 ratio with the males. Females have only 9 hit dice, but they are considerably more dangerous than the males due to their spell casting and shapechanging abilities. All females are shamans with the spell casting ability of a 4th level cleric, and can shapeshift once per day into (and out of) a snakelike hybrid form. The snake hybrid has no significant difference from the normal form of the giantess, still having four arms, but the snake shape has an armor class of 2 and the shapeshift heals 50% of any damage suffered by the giantess prior to the change. Changing back to her normal shape also heals 50% of damage that was incurred while the giantess was in the snake-hybrid form.

Some extremely rare khmornian-giant females are sorceresses with the power of an 11th level magic-user; these individuals reside in well defended castles or ruined temples deep in the jungle.

— Author: Matt Finch

Khmornian Giant (Male): HD 10+4; AC 3[16]; Atk 2 weapons (5d6); Move 12; Save 5; AL C; CL/XP 11/1700; Special: Hurl rocks.

Khmornian Giant (Female): HD 9; AC 3[16]; Atk 2 weapons (5d6); Move 12; Save 6; CL/XP 12/2000; Special: Hurl rocks, shapeshift, spells (Clr4).

The Maidens' Well

A temple hemmed in by the jungle is home to a clan of **20 khmornian giants**, not to mention the **10 giant pythons** they keep as pets and sentries. 1d4 of the giant pythons patrol the grounds around the temple, accessing the subterranean levels inhabited by the giants via a well heavily carved with serpent motifs. The female khmornians often move about the surrounding lands as well, shapeshifted into luminous nymphs, seeking males to lure to the temple with tearful pleas or pleasing songs. Once at the temple, they guide people into what remains of the inner sanctum, where an idol of a four-armed jungle god with a face like a parrot (a **stone golem**) awaits new victims. The giantesses will flee, of course, though the giants below can watch the struggle against the idol via a crystal-ball like pool in the temple's depths.

Constrictor (python): HD 2; AC 6[13]; Atk 1 constriction (1d3); Move 12; Save 16; AL N; CL/XP 2/30; Special: Constriction.

Stone Golem: HD 15 (60hp); AC 5[14]; Atk 1 fist (3d8); Move 6; Save 3; AL N; CL/XP 16/3200; Special: +1 or better magic weapon to hit, immune to most magic.

Giant, Stone

Hit Dice: 9
Armor Class: 0 [19]
Attacks: Club (3d6)
Saving Throw: 6
Special: Hurl boulders
Move: 12
Alignment: Chaos (sometimes Neutrality)
Number Encountered: 1d8
Challenge Level/XP: 10/1,400

Stone giants dwell in caves, isolated in the mountain fastnesses. They throw rocks for 3d6 points of damage, and can be quite crafty in setting up ambushes in their native mountains. Travelers who wander into the territory of stone giants seldom return.

Stone Giant: HD 9+3; AC 0[19]; Atk 1 club (3d6); Move 12; Save 6; AL N; CL/XP 10/1400; Special: Throw boulders.

The Face of God

A dungeon corridor widens into a gallery studded with alcoves holding intricate and disturbing bas-reliefs carved by an artistic tribe of **stone giants**. The corridor curves upward and eventually becomes a set of large, giant-sized stairs that lead to the top of the mountain where the stone giants are carving the face of God (who happens to look like a stone giant – go figure!). A stone giant with the powers of a 9th-level druid oversees the work, aided by his priestesses (**hill giant shamans**) and his **pet cave bear**. The eyes of this godhead hold mystic symbols that, when activated with the proper words, open a tunnel that seems to stretch to the horizon, but which actually leads to the astral plane.

Cave Bear/Polar Bear: HD 7; AC 6[13]; Atk 2 claws (1d6+1), 1 bite (1d10+1); Move 12; Save 9; AL N; CL/XP 8/800; Special: Hug.

Hill Giant Priestesses: HD 8+2; AC 4[15]; Atk 1 weapon (2d8); Move 12; Save 8; AL C; CL/XP 11/1700; Special: Throw boulders, spells as Clr4.

Giant, Storm

Hit Dice: 15
Armor Class: 1 [18]
Attacks: Weapon (7d6)
Saving Throw: 3
Special: Throw boulders, control weather
Move: 15
Alignment: Neutral (sometimes Law or Chaos)
Number Encountered: 1d2
Challenge Level/XP: 16/ 3,200

Storm giants are the largest of giants, the most intelligent, the most magical, and the most likely to talk with humans rather than simply devour them. Storm giants can live in underwater sea-castles as well as on the heights of mountains. They throw boulders for 7d6 points of damage, and have the power to control weather (as per the spell).

Storm Giant: HD 15+5; AC 1[18]; Atk 1 weapon (6d6); Move 15; Save 3; AL Any; CL/XP 16/3200; Special: Throw boulders, control weather.

Lost Love

A forlorn **storm giant** sits on the side of a lonely mountain that rises from a vast desert dotted by ruins. This giant, **Skadamere** by name, lost his lady love to **Plexus of Ghant**, the infamous enchanter, and has not had the will to bring rain to the land for many years. The land is dying — a few hardy shrubs and small trees have persisted on ground water, but the grasses are gone, the herds have left, and the hunters and herdsmen with them. One of the ruins dotting the land holds the ancient manse of Plexus, and Skadamere would give almost anything to have it explored and ransacked for a clue as to where he has fled with the fair **Ulbinia**.

201

Giant Slug of P'Nahk

Hit Dice: 8
Armor Class: 7 [12]
Attacks: 1 bite (2d8)
Saving Throw: 8
Special: Surprise on 1-3, blast of insanity, immune to blunt weapons
Move: 9
Alignment: Chaos
Number Encountered: 1d2
Challenge Level/XP: 11/1,700

P'Nahki slugs are massive, translucent creatures. The only clearly visible part of the slug's anatomy is the disturbingly human-looking brain suspended in the slug's body, appearing at first glance to be floating in the air. These creatures originated in a forgotten place called P'Nahk; whether this was a ruined city, a lost world, or an entirely different dimension is not known.

The giant slugs of P'Nahk are highly intelligent, although this intellect is seldom put to use in a way that can be related to human motivation or logic. All P'Nahki slugs have ESP ability. Three times per day, a giant P'Nahki slug can issue forth a blast of insanity in a cone shape 60ft long, expanding to a width of 60ft at the far end. Anyone within the area of the blast must make a saving throw or be affected as follows:

01-25: frozen by fear for 1d4+1 rounds; the character will (and must) fight back against a direct assault but can take no other action
26-50: insane rage for 1d4+1 rounds; the character attacks any former allies in a frenzy of hatred
51-75: self-hatred for 1d4+1 rounds; the character drops any held items and claws at his/her own body, inflicting 1hp of damage per round.
76-00: adoration for 1d4+1 rounds; the character drops all held items, falls to the floor, and grovels in worship of the slug.

Because of their translucency, giant slugs of P'Nahk surprise opponents with a 1-3 on 1d6. Their rubbery bodies are immune to damage from blunt weapons.

— Author: Matt Finch

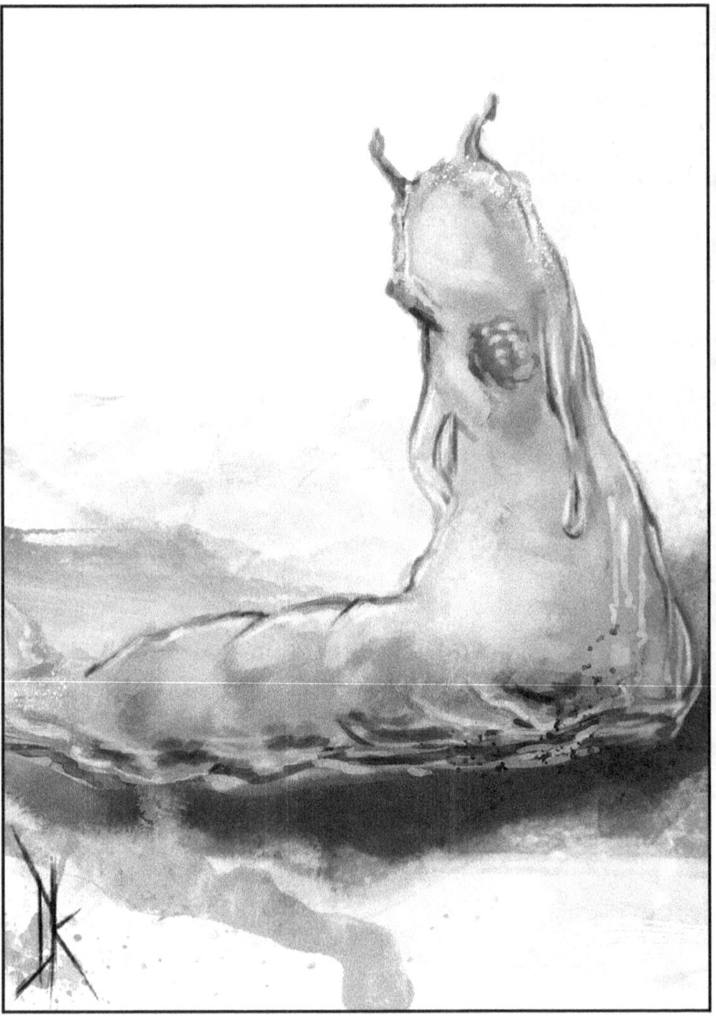

Giant Slug of P'Nahk: HD 8; AC 7[12]; Atk 1 bite (2d8); Move 9; Save 8; AL C; CL/XP 11/1700; Special: Surprise on 1-3, blast of insanity, immune to blunt weapons.

Slug Drug

In one of the deeper caverns of the underworld the adventurers might be unlucky enough to happen upon a convocation of **15 giant slugs of P'nahk** worshipping the slug-god, the spewer of ultimate wisdom. Psychotropic slimes hang about the cavern, and the slaves of the slugs, miserable looking **hobgoblins** (30 of them) with vacant stares and pasty skin, beat drums in time to their wriggling. A deep well in the floor of the cavern erupts in a miasma of slime that delivers strange visions (and possible mutations to non-slugs) and, at the height of the ceremony, provides a portal into P'nahk too small for the slugs to enter. The hobgoblins wear ragged leather armor and are armed with axes and swords, and serve as the first line of defense in case of an assault.

Hobgoblin: HD 1+1; AC 5[14]; Atk 1 weapon (1d8); Move 9; Save 17; AL C; CL/XP 1/15; Special: None.

Gibbering Mouther

Hit Dice: 4+4
Armor Class: 1 [18]
Attacks: 6 mouths (1hp)
Saving Throw: 13
Special: Gibbering, spit, pull prey underneath.
Move: 3
Alignment: Neutrality
Number Encountered: 1
Challenge Level/XP: 6/400

Gibbering mouthers are amorphous blobs of flesh with multiple eyes and mouths appearing and disappearing from the quivering mass of the body as it moves along. The mouths gibber and babble meaningless, speech-like noises; the monster is perpetually accompanied by this disturbing and inhuman sound except when it is waiting to ambush prey, in which case the eyes and mouths are all kept closed, and the monster appears to be nothing more than an oozy pile of earth. When the mouther spots prey, it begins gibbering loudly, causing anyone within 60ft to make a saving throw or become confused (per the spell). Each round spent listening to the mouther requires another saving throw. In any given round, the mouther will have six mouths available either to spit or to bite. The creature's spittle flashes brightly upon impact with most surfaces, causing anyone nearby to make a saving throw or be blinded for one round. The mouther's bites are not particularly deadly in and of themselves, but once a mouth hits it fastens on and continues to do automatic damage thereafter. Also, if a character has 3 or more mouths fastened to him, there is a risk of slipping and being covered by the mouther (which allows the mouther to attack with 12 additional mouths on its underside). The chance of slipping is 5%, and if more than 3 mouths are attached the chance increases by 5% per additional mouth. The ground around a gibbering mouther, in a radius of 5ft, will be soft and mud-like, for the mouther changes the consistency of the ground beneath itself.

Gibbering Mouther: HD 4+4; AC 1[18]; Atk 6 mouths (1hp); Move 3; Save 13; AL N; CL/XP 6/400; Special: Gibbering, spit, pull prey underneath.

What's in the Sphere?

Deep in a dungeon there is a chamber of red brick that holds a well. The well is 7 feet in diameter, and though the first few feet of the well are clad in the same red brick that fills the chamber, the remainder (it is 40 feet deep) are natural, carved granite. Heat rises from the well, and it doesn't take infravision to tell that at the bottom of the well magma sputters and pops. One can also tell that, just above the surface of the magma, there is a tunnel opening.

The chamber of the well measures 20 feet wide and long, with the walls slanting inward to meet at a point 40 feet overhead. From this point, a 10-foot-long chain hangs, a metallic sphere suspended from it. The sphere is about 5 feet in diameter and has an obvious door (which, not coincidentally, is on the proper side of the sphere to allow a person who descended in it to exit on the same side as the tunnel in the well below).

A secret cache in one wall holds a winch that permits one to lower the sphere. Those who do, and who open the sphere's door, discover to their chagrin that it is occupied by a **gibbering mouther** who is not happy to see them.

Gillmonkey

Hit Dice: 1d6 hit points
Armor Class: 6 [13]
Attacks: 1 bite (1d4), 2 claws (1hp)
Saving Throw: 18
Special: Breathe underwater
Move: 6/12 (swimming)
Alignment: Chaos
Number Encountered: 1d100 x2
Challenge Level/XP: B/10

Gillmonkeys are nasty, monkey-like creatures that live in the sea. They have hairless, pinkish-brown skin and short tentacle-like growths on the top of the head. They attack in packs, sometimes swarming over a ship's rail.

Gillmonkey: HD 1d6 hp; AC 6[13]; Atk 1 bite (1d4), 2 claws (1hp); Move 6 (Swim 12); Save 18; AL C; CL/XP B/10; Special: Breathe underwater.

Sea Monkeys

A tribe of **100 gillmonkeys** dwells beneath the waves here in a great mount of coral (long since dead). A heavy iron chain extends from the mount to a merchant cog on the surface above, the cog being used by the gillmonkeys as a lure to treasure hunters. The gillmonkeys hold a treasure trove below consisting of 12,000 cp, 1,700 sp, 120 gp, a rusty greatsword engraved with copper runes of power (no magic, just decorative), a glass bottle sealed with wax and holding a long, narrow scroll containing the *invisibility* spell, and three gold bracelets studded with hematite gems (worth 130 gp each).

Glass Butterfly

Hit Dice: 1d4 hit points
Armor Class: 9 [10]
Attacks: None
Saving Throw: 18
Special: chance of random spell discharge upon death
Move: 20 (flying)
Alignment: Neutrality
Number Encountered: 1d10 x5
Challenge Level/XP: A/5

Glass Butterflies are tiny, wizard-made entities, made of colored glass and resembling butterflies the size of a bird or cat. They were once made as decoration for the noble houses of antiquity, and are usually found in large numbers flitting aimlessly about. Glass Butterflies will usually ignore any creature that comes near them, and simply fly a few feet away if attacked. They are constantly in motion, creating a pleasant play of light and color if there is a light source present, and only touch the ground when destroyed. Being mindless, they are unaffected by spells such as sleep, charm, and hold. They are otherwise extremely susceptible to damage, and can be easily destroyed. However, the magic that animates a Glass Butterfly is too powerful to be contained in such a frail and simple vessel. When slain, there is a burst of energy in a 2ft radius. This does not cause damage, but has a cumulative chance of causing a random spell effect, equal to 5% per Glass Butterfly destroyed in the past turn. Whenever the percentage reaches 100%, it resets to 0%. If caught in an area effect, 1 Glass Butterfly is destroyed per dice of damage, and one damage die is rolled to determine how many additional Glass Butterflies are destroyed. Any Light spell cast upon a Glass Butterfly is increased by 50% in both duration and area of effect.

—*Author: Scott Wylie Roberts, "Myrystyr"*

Glass Butterfly: HD 1d4 hp; AC 9[10]; Atk none; Move 20 (Fly); Save 18; AL N; CL/XP A/5; Special: Chance of random spell discharge upon death.

The Color of Breaking Glass

A tall tower of coral blocks on the seaside is topped by an onion-shaped dome of translucent agate. The tower has a secret entrance , and within is a spiral stair leading up to the dome (and protected by a number of traps). The dome is a wizard's garden, one of the most impressive ever built.

The dome has a floor of limestone tiles. It is filled with pots, large and small, containing a variety of herbs (especially wolfsbane and deadly nightshade) and several wondrous plants, including several mandrake, a barnacle tree allowed to hang over a basin of saltwater, a small bohun upas (bonsai-style), an yggdrasil nut (it will hatch in just three more centuries), a vegetable lamb, still small, but already softly bleating, fern flowers, a patch of hungry grass (under a copper mesh), a vampiric pumpkin that has seen better days, and a Charybdis fig growing up the walls of the dome.

The dome is protected by a vast swarm of **glass butterflies**. When people enter, the butterflies flock to them, with dozens of the pretty things covering each person who enters. Any violent movement taken by a person so covered forces them to make a saving throw to avoid 1d6 of the butterflies breaking and releasing their energies.

Glimmer

Hit Dice: 6
Armor Class: 2 [17]
Attacks: cold blast (2d6)
Saving Throw: 11
Special: Confusion, immune to fire and cold
Move: 9 (flying)
Alignment: Chaos
Number Encountered: 1d3
Challenge Level/XP: 8/800

Glimmers are shapes of greenish or yellowish light, with a slight resemblance to will-o-wisps. They are generally found in dismal swamps and marshes, but can also be found in natural caverns as well. Looking directly at a glimmer requires that the observer make a saving throw or become confused, as per the spell, for 2d6 rounds. Glimmers attack by flashing a blast of magical cold at an opponent, causing 2d6 hit points of damage (saving throw for half damage). Glimmers are immune to both fire and cold.

— Author: Matt Finch

Glimmer: HD 6; AC 2[17]; Atk cold blast (2d6); Move (Fly 9); Save 11; AL C; CL/XP 8/800; Special: Confusion, immune to fire and cold.

Glimmer of Death

While walking through a dismal, misty swamp, a party might come across a corpse frozen against a swamp oak, a golden box clutched in its arms. The box, if chipped out (or if one waits for the ice to melt – it takes about 30 minutes), will be found to contain two platinum earrings (worth 100 gp). The corpse was created by a band of **5 glimmers**, which are still in the area. Their lair, a small, half-submerged cave clad in ice, is about 500 yards away. It was once a dragon's lair, and embedded in the ice is what remains of the dragon's hoard: An elven lyre, a golden brown fez (a bit oversized), three lapis lazuli-encrusted keys (large, stone keys; worth 75 gp each), a blue-steel necklace (worth 15 gp), a dark, blue-violet scale (probably left by the former inhabitant), a *+1 scythe* (treast as *+1 polearm)* and six bronze amulets (each bearing the face of an ancient queen, worth 35 gp each).

Glitterskull

Hit Dice: 8
Armor Class: 2 [17]
Attacks: 1 ram (1d6)
Saving Throw: 8
Special: Spells (as level 8 magic-user), immune to non-magical weapons, immune to poison and gases, half damage from fire
Move: 0/18 (flying)
Alignment: Chaos
Number Encountered: 1
Challenge Level/XP: 13/2,300

The Glitterskull is a gold-plated skull, with large red gems set into the eye sockets. It flies by magical levitation, and is surrounded by a reddish halo. This halo is of magical flame, and causes a roaring sound when the creature is flying about. It also sheds light in a 15ft radius, and at a distance may be mistaken for torchlight. The skull is that of a wizard, usually but not always human. A glitterskull has the spellcasting ability of a level 8 magic-user, and does not require a spellbook to regain its daily spells. Being a former wizard, the glitterskull prefers to attack by casting spells, but it may also fly at opponents, ramming into them for 1d6 damage. Its fiery halo does not cause extra damage, but may ignite flammable objects. Glitterskulls can only be harmed by magical weapons. They can catch a Magic Missile spell within their eyes, and hurl it back at the caster the following round (instead of attacking) or use the spell energy to heal themselves (spell damage adding to HP). Glitterskulls are also immune to poison and gas attacks, and take only half damage from fire-based attacks. The glitterskull is capable of speech, and retains much of the intelligence of its former life. While it may parley with strong parties, the mind trapped inside a glitterskull has been warped by the millennia, and most utter little more than mocking laughter and scornful commentary. The gems and gold plating of a glitterskull may be worth anywhere from 200 to 1,200 GP, in addition to other treasure.

— *Author: Scott Wylie Roberts, "Myrystyr"*

Glitterskull: HD 8; AC 2[17]; Atk 1 ram (1d6); Move 0 (Fly 18); Save 8; AL C; CL/XP 13/2300; Special: Spells (as level 8 magic-user), immune to non-magical weapons, immune to poison and gases, half damage from fire.

Alas, Poor Yorvin

Beneath a ruined monastery hidden in the black hills there is a secret chamber, an ossuary, where the bones of deceased abbots and crusaders are kept. There is a golden reliquary here as well that holds the golden skull of the wizard Yorvin. Yorvin is now a **glitterskull**, and he is the protector of the crypt. Here, he awaits the arrival of a worthy successor to whom he can reveal a *staff of wizardry* (hidden among the bones and made to look like a femur by powerful illusions) and a quest, to end the reign of the Grey Scholars that dwell on the other side of the Green Mountains.

Glurm (Zen Frog)

Hit Dice: 3+2
Armor Class: 4 [15]
Attacks: 1 unarmed strike (1d4) or 1 bamboo staff (1d6+2)
Saving Throw: 14
Special: Martial arts, spells as level 3 cleric (2 level 1 spells)
Move: 12
Alignment: Law
Number Encountered: 1 or 2d6
Challenge Level/XP: 5/240

Intelligent frog-like humanoids, Glurm can usually be found sitting in meditation or study amid scenes of natural beauty. They wear simple loincloths and will have a bamboo staff within arm's reach. Their dwellings are of woven reeds, and contain only a few simple items. If there are several glurm in the area, there will be a "place of harmony" near a stream or river. This will be a cleared expanse of sand, dotted with boulders to sit upon; the glurm come here to discuss philosophy and practice their martial arts.

The spiritual studies of the glurm have given them mystical powers, and they practice martial arts, accounting for their armor class. Glurm are pacifists, and if threatened will attempt to drive off foes with an intimidating display of martial arts. All onlookers within 30ft must make a saving throw or back away for 1 round. If forced into combat, a glurm's unarmed strikes cause 1d4 damage; opponents of equal or smaller size can only act after the glurm in the following round if the glurm inflicts maximum damage. Armed with a bamboo staff, a glurm can focus its spiritual energy for a +2 bonus to damage; in addition, if the attack roll is 4 or more higher than required to hit, the glurm may disarm a foe, trip them up, or perform a similar manuever. In an open area, the glurm may also use its staff to make a pole-vault kick against an opponent up to 10ft away, possibly knocking them down. Lastly, the glurm has the abilities of a level 3 cleric.

Any treasure possessed by the glurm will generally be in the form of scrolls discoursing on obscure philosophical topics, and finely crafted writing materials.

— Author: Scott Wylie Roberts, "Myrystyr"

Glurm (Zen frog): HD 3+2; AC 4 [15]; Atk 1 unarmed strike (1d4) or 1 bamboo staff (1d6+2); Move 12; Save 14; AL L; CL/XP 5/240; Special: Martial arts, spells as level 3 cleric (2 level 1 spells).

The Glurm Lord's Rest

In a tranquil clearing, one might find a stone statue of a glurm sitting atop a giant tortoise set in the middle of a jade-green pond. Paper lanterns hang from surrounding magnolia trees, and stone columns, carved with prayers, protrude from the waters. This is the tomb of a great master of the local glurm, who was actually caught while in meditation with his mentor, the tortoise, and turned into stone by a medusa. The glurms cannot release him from this curse, but reward anyone who can. They allow nobody access to their master, though, until they prove themselves worthy by challenging the **ogre mage** of the far Mountain of Cranes and bringing back from his court a cup of mead brewed from the honey of his giant honeybees.

Ogre Mage: HD 5+4; AC 4[15]; Atk 1 weapon (1d12); Move 12 (Fly 18); Save 12; AL C; CL/XP 7/600; Special: Magic use.

Gnoll

Hit Dice: 2
Armor Class: 5 [14]
Attacks: Bite (2d4) or weapon (1d10)
Saving Throw: 16
Special: None
Move: 9
Alignment: Chaos
Number Encountered: 2d20 x5
Challenge Level/XP: 2/30

Gnolls are tall humanoids with hyena-like heads. They may be found both above ground and in subterranean caverns. They form into loosely organized clans, often ranging far from home in order to steal and kill with rapacious ferocity.

Gnoll: HD 2; AC 5[14]; Atk 1 bite (2d4) or weapon (1d10); Move 9; Save 16; AL C; CL/XP 2/30; Special: None.

Dog Soldiers

On the savannah there is a grand camp of **gnolls**. Three hundred of the foul folk dwell here in tents of tanned antelope hide that are dragged about on wooden sledges pulled by mastodons, which are also used as war elephants by the gnolls. The gnolls also keep packs of hyenas (all owned by the chief and kept by his female slaves), which roam the camp at night, picking off the weak as well as runaway slaves and unwelcome guests. Besides the 200 warriors of the tribe and their females and young, the gnolls keep about 80 human slaves. The males are hobbled and used as servants, while the females are made feral and slightly mad, and are used to handle the hyenas and as hunting dogs in their own right. The gnoll chieftain, Zzagor, dwells in an enormous tent (it takes three mastodons to move it) with his sub-chiefs, harem and servants. He currently holds a princess of the peri captive and in chains, and is entertaining a delegation of elves who are begging for her release.

Goat, Giant

Hit Dice: 3
Armor Class: 7 [12]
Attacks: 1 gore (2d6)
Saving Throw: 14
Special: +4 damage on charge
Move: 18
Alignment: Neutrality
Number Encountered: 1d4 or 1d12
Challenge Level/XP: 3/60

Giant goats include giant mountain goats. These creatures are as large as a pony, and can be ridden.

Giant Goat: HD 3; AC 7[12]; Atk 1 gore (2d6); Move 18; Save 14; AL N; CL/XP 3/60; Special: +4 damage on charge.

Listen to the Plants

A herd of **giant goats** makes a home for itself on the slopes of a mountain. The goats graze on weird, purple, fibrous plants that cover the mountainside like a web. These plants are psychically charged and have a dim intelligence. They have no defense against the teeth of the goats, for the goats are but dumb animals. They do send out a siren call, though, that touches the minds of human beings, placing a powerful suggestion (save at -4) in their minds that they must hunt the goats to extinction. In all, there are 30 of the animals on the mountainside.

Goblin

Hit Dice: 1d6 hit points
Armor Class: 6 [13]
Attacks: Weapon (1d6)
Saving Throw: 18
Special: -1 to hit in sunlight
Move: 9
Alignment: Chaos
Number Encountered: 4d4 or 4d100
Challenge Level/XP: B/10

Goblins are small creatures (4 ft tall or so) that inhabit dark woods, underground caverns, and (possibly) the otherworldly realms of the fey. They attack at -1 in the full sunlight.

Goblin: HD 1d6 hp; AC 6[13]; Atk 1 weapon (1d6); Move 9; Save 18; AL C; CL/XP B/10; Special: -1 to hit in sunlight.

Home Life, Goblin Style

A tribe of **300 goblins** dwell in a grand cavern honeycombed with tiny caves (the living quarters of the goblins). A crude pavilion of stone blocks is set in the midst of the cavern and serves as the fortified house of the chief, **Gobliguk**, and his shaman wife, **Urta**. Gobliguk has a portion of orc blood in his veins, and he uses his larger size and stouter heart to keep the others in line. Around the fortified house there are dozens of natural pits, each one containing a bubbling mass of primordial soup on which the goblins feed when they cannot find meat. They also favor boiling captives in these pits, and allowing their bones to float to the surface. Urta reads the future in the patterns these floating bones form.

Goblin, Belfry

Hit Dice: 1
Armor Class: 6 [13]
Attacks: 2 attacks from claws (1d6), weapons (1d6), and/or 1 bite (1d4)
Saving Throw: 17
Special: Swooping attack, chance of disease
Move: 6/12 (gliding)
Alignment: Chaos
Number Encountered: 1d100 +10
Challenge Level/XP: 2/30

Belfry goblins appear to be related to the other goblinoid species, but they have wing membranes which run from their arms down their sides, quite similar to flying squirrels. These membranes grant the belfry goblin the ability to glide, and in no way inhibit the ability of their hands to manipulate objects. Hanging upside down on the ceiling in dark corners, belfry goblins are all but invisible, waiting for their prey to pass by and then attacking with a deadly swooping attack, a javelin in each hand, doing double damage on a successful hit with the swooping attack. If the swoop attack succeeds on a "to hit" roll of 18 or better, the belfry goblin does additional damage as it passes by, raking with its foot claws for an additional 1d6 damage. A belfry goblin has 2 attacks per round, with any combination of its hand held weapon, claws, or bite. The bite of a belfry goblin is dangerous in much the same way as a rat bite, with a 5% chance per bite the victim will contract a disease. Diseased victims will sicken and die within 1d6 days, unless the victim rolls a saving throw.

For every 20 belfry goblins encountered there will be a leader with the maximum of 9 hit points and who attacks as a 2 HD creature. If a nest of 40 or more individuals is found, there will be a chieftain with 2+2 HD who attacks as a 3 HD monster. The chieftain will have an honor guard of 4 particularly fearsome warriors whose stats are equal to that of the leader type. There is also at least a 15% chance that in any belfry goblin encounter there will be a vampiric variant present. The chance to encounter these special vampiric belfry goblins increases to 30% for standard lairs and 60% for nests of 40 or more.

— *Author: Cameron DuBeers and the Lizard of Oz*

Belfry Goblin: HD 1; AC 6[13]; Atk 2 attacks from claws (1d6), weapons (1d6), and/or 1 bite (1d4); Move 6 (Glide 12); Save 17; AL C; CL/XP 2/30; Special: Swooping attack, chance of disease.

It's a Belfry, but Forget the Bats

The grand metropolis, beset by war, famine and plague (not to mention death), now has many abandoned squares and plazas, where monsters various and sundry hold sway. One square, the Court of Plasterers, had a wonderful bell tower of white brick and porphyry ornaments. Constructed by the Plasterer's Guild in honor of Saint Bartholomew, the bell tower is now occupied by a gang of **10 belfry goblins**. The goblins have rusty weapons, and have hidden a parcel filled with a clutch of petrified red dragon eggs in the bell.

Goblin, Belfry (Vampiric)

Hit Dice: 1-1
Armor Class: 6 [13]
Attacks: 2 attacks from claws (1d6), weapons (1d6), and/or 1 bite (1d4)
Saving Throw: 17
Special: Swooping attack, chance of disease, blood drain
Move: 6/12 (gliding)
Alignment: Chaos
Number Encountered: 1d4
Challenge Level/XP: 4/120

These creatures are physically weaker and lighter in coloration than the standard belfry goblin, having only 1-1 HD, but they are able to gain strength from drinking the blood of their victims. On a successful bite attack, the vampiric belfry goblin sucks blood from its victim for 1d4 points of damage, wrapping its arms and legs around the victim and holding them fast. Each subsequent round, the victim must break the grip or the vampiric belfry goblin automatically drains an additional 1d4 hit points of blood drain; the chance to break the grip is 30%. Vampiric belfry goblins gain temporary bonus hit points from blood they drink, gaining 1 hp for every 1 hit point drained from a victim, up to double its normal number of hit points. Once the vampiric belfry goblin exceeds its normal hit points, it gains +1 to hit and damage.

— *Author: Cameron DuBeers and the Lizard of Oz*

Vampiric Belfry Goblin: HD 1-1; AC 6[13]; Atk 2 attacks from claws (1d6), weapons (1d6), and/or 1 bite (1d4); Move 6 (Glide 12); Save 17; AL C; CL/XP 4/120; Special: Swooping attack, chance of disease, blood drain.

Oh, Here's the Bat!

Beneath the abandoned bell tower, behind a secret door and down a narrow, spiral stair (one of the steps is rigged to collapse, sending people rolling to the bottom of the stairs for 2d6 points of damage), there is a small room. The room is barred by a locked, iron door. Within this room one finds a collection of gears and a large, wooden counterweight banded in iron. The counterweight is actually hollow, and serves as the coffin for a **vampiric belfry goblin**, the master of the goblins who live in the bell tower above. The coffin also holds a small ebony box containing 20 platinum pieces and three pinches of dust of appearance in folded wax paper sealed with the mark of the famed magi Ambrosius of Gax.

Goblin, Oni-Aka (Asian Red Goblin)

Hit Dice: 1
Armor Class: 6 [13]
Attacks: 1 weapon (1d6)
Saving Throw: 17
Special: Resist fire
Move: 9
Alignment: Chaos
Number Encountered: 1d8+2 or 1d100 x2
Challenge Level/XP: 1/15

The Oni-aka (red goblins) are short, scaly humanoids with small horns on their slightly pointed heads. They have coarse black hair, and coal black eyes. These evil beings are known to raid villages to steal slaves and cattle. They are typically armed with clubs and short spears they use for throwing. These goblins are said to have been born of fire in the pits of the earth; and as such they are almost impervious to fire damage, suffering only half normal damage from any fire-based attack. Note that these goblins are from Asian mythology, and might not be related to normal goblins in anything but name. *(Author: MikeD)*

Oni-aka (Red Goblin): HD 1; AC 6[13]; Atk 1 weapon (1d6); Move 9; Save 17; CL/XP 1/15; Special: Fire resistant.

Last Stand of the Oni-Aka

A gang of **12 oni-aka goblins** armed with heavy crossbows and glaives has been trapped in an old, stone tower by **3 human fighting-men** (7th level, 5th level and 4th level) and a small army of peasants. The goblins were part of a larger body of troops that pillaged a farming village a few miles away. The fighters and their men-at-arms were visiting the village on their way to the Caves of Celestial Torments, and managed to thwart the raid, killing many goblins and scattering the others. This particular group of goblins carried away a maiden, and it is for this reason that they were pursued. The stone tower has four levels, though the bottom level is filled with rubble and garbage (and smells awful) and the top level has several large holes in its walls. The goblins are on the third level, using the tower's arrow slits to fire on the humans, who are slowly building up dry brush around the tower that they may set it alight. Beneath the rubble on the bottom floor, there is a secret trapdoor that leads down a long shaft to a crystal cathedral of chaos inhabited by **troglodytes** and an ancient **ophidian priest**.

Troglodyte: HD 2; AC 4[15]; Atk 2 claws (1d3), Bite (1d4+1) or by weapon with shield (1d8); Move 12; Save 16; AL C; CL/XP 3/60; Special: Stench, chameleon skin.

Ophidian Priest: HD3; AC 4[15] or 3[16] with shield; Atk1 two-handed weapon (1d8+1) or weapon with shield (1d8), and bite (0); Move 12; Save 14; CL/XP 6/400; Special: Reproductive bite, cast spells as a 5th-level Cleric.

Goblin, Oni-Kage (Asian Shadow Goblin)

Hit Dice: 1
Armor Class: 7 [12]
Attacks: 1 weapon (1d6)
Saving Throw: 17
Special: -1 penalties in daylight, invisible in darkness
Move: 9
Alignment: Chaos
Number Encountered: 1d100
Challenge Level/XP: 2/30

The Oni-kage (shadow goblins) are short, black-skinned humanoids with large, pale eyes, dwellers of dark caves and deep bamboo thickets. All oni-kage detest bright lights, and they suffer -1 penalties to combat in daylight. They have keen night vision, and their somewhat supernatural nature makes them completely invisible in darkness (visible only by use of spells). Note that these goblins are from Asian mythology, and might not be related to normal goblins in anything but name. *Author: MikeD*

Oni-kage (Shadow Goblin): HD 1; AC 7[12]; Atk 1 weapon (1d6); Move 9; Save 17; AL C; CL/XP 2/30; Special: -1 penalties in daylight, Invisible in darkness.

Beyond the Cavern of Celestial Winds

Beyond the entrance to the Caves of Celestial Torments there is a long gallery strewn with bones and cast-off equipment (some broken, some thrown down by fleeing adventurers). The cavern howls with a strong wind, and after 30 feet becomes completely dark. The cavern widens at that point and continues on another 100 feet. This portion is protected by a tribe of **20 oni-kage goblins**, who take advantage of the dark and the inability to light torches to surprise their foes. At the back of the cave is a bas-relief of The Brazen Beast, a nine-headed horror with gaping, toothy maws from which blows the howling wind. The idol holds an obsidian sphere. If removed, each head of the idol vomits forth a single **shadow** to destroy the interlopers. The sphere, when anointed with unholy water on a moonless night, provides a magic portal into the Shadow Plane.

Shadow: HD 3+3; AC 7[12]; Atk 1 touch (1d4 + strength drain); Move 12; Save 14; AL C; CL/XP 4/120; Special: Drain 1 point str with hit, hit only by magic weapons.

Goblin, Oni-Yama (Asian Mountain Goblin)

Hit Dice: 2
Armor Class: 5 [14]
Attacks: 1 weapon (1d6)
Saving Throw: 16
Special: 50% chance to gain surprise attacks
Move: 12
Alignment: Chaos
Number Encountered: 1d100
Challenge Level/XP: 2/30

The oni-yama are hairless, grey-skinned humanoids with short tusks protruding from their mouths. They are smaller than ogres, but much larger and bulkier than men -- though their distinctively hunched posture makes them appear somewhat smaller than they really are. These big goblins dwell in remote mountain caves and forgotten ruins, often preying upon merchants and travelers passing through their territories. In general, they arm themselves with such weapons as they can take from their victims, for they are not industrious. They wear an assortment of armor, usually misused but still functional. The oni-yama bully, and often enslave, lesser goblins. Despite their size, the oni-yama are extremely stealthy on their great, flat feet, and gain surprise on a roll of 1-3 on a d6. Note that these goblins are from Asian mythology, and might not be related to normal goblins in anything but name.

— Author: MikeD

Oni-yama (Mountain Goblin): HD 2; AC 5[14]; Atk 1 weapon (1d6); Move 12; Save 16; AL C; CL/XP 2/30; Special: 50% chance to gain surprise attacks.

Climbing the Maple Towers

A tribe of **60 oni-yama goblins** dwells in a mountain fastness that overlooks a valley of maples. The fortress has steep walls of grey stone stained with rust that bears a strong resemblance to blood. The upper portions of the castle are made of polished maple. The castle is actually constructed as three separate towers divided by narrow alleys with uneven floors. Narrow stairs lead up to the towers proper, but are barred by locked iron grates. **Giant foxes**, loyal to the goblins, guard these passages from behind the grates. Within the central tower, the largest of the three, there is a shaft that leads down to a giant cavern filled with shallow, warm, salty water and massive crystal growths.

Giant Fox: HD 2+2; AC 7[12]; Atk 1 bite (1d4+1); Move 18; Save 16; AL N; CL/XP 2/30; Special: None.

Goblin, Redcap (Chaos Goblin)

Hit Dice: 1d6 hit points
Armor Class: 6 [13]
Attacks: 1 bite (1d6)
Saving Throw: 17
Special: Vicious healing, -1 to hit in sunlight
Move: 9
Alignment: Chaos
Number Encountered: 4d6
Challenge Level/XP: 1/15

Redcaps (or chaos goblins) are goblins driven mad by the insidious effects of raw Chaos, reducing them to a bestial state. Utterly devoid of empathy with any living creature, including ordinary goblins, redcaps delight in inflicting pain. Indeed, redcaps derive a strange form of sustenance from doing so. Any successful attack a redcap achieves heals it for an amount equal to the amount of damage it deals to its target. Worse yet, a redcap can double its total hit points in this manner. Thus, a undamaged redcap with 5 hit points who manages to deal 3 points of damage on its attack will now have 8 hit points and, assuming it continues to remain undamaged, can be "healed" for another 2 hit points before reaching its maximum potential hit points. Though thoroughly insane, redcaps work well with others of their kind, forming predatory packs that attack any creature they can find. Redcaps often take gruesome souvenirs of their victims, such as fingers, ears, and eyeballs, which they use to adorn themselves. Many also use the blood of their prey to dye their tattered clothing, including their hats, the practice of which gave these foul aberrations their common name.

— *Author: James Malizsewski*

Redcap Goblin (Chaos Goblin): HD 1d6 hp; AC 6[13]; Atk 1 bite (1d6); Move 9; Save 17; AL C; CL/XP 1/15; Special: Vicious healing, -1 to hit in sunlight.

Red Caps, Rotten Attitudes

An old stone castle of reddish stone overlooks a bleak region of moors that crackle with ambient electrical energies left over from the creation of the cosmos. The castle is occupied by a band of brothers: **7 redcap goblins** with red-rimmed eyes, caps soaked in blood, leather breeches and iron-shod boots. Each redcap is armed with a long, iron spear, and they always keep one goblin posted as a guard to look out for travelers on the ancient Blue Road of Kalmakka. The goblins have the normal amount of treasure, but half the value should be in the form of perfectly aged, smoky-flavored whiskey.

GOLEMS

Golems are man-shaped creatures built to serve their masters, usually powerful wizards or high priests. They are often used as guardians. Golems cannot be hit with non-magical weapons, and are immune to the sorts of spells used to create them (iron golems being immune to fire, for instance). You can find the details in the specific monster descriptions.

Golem, Clay

Hit Dice: 10 (45 hit points)
Armor Class: 7 [12]
Attacks: 1 fist (3d10)
Saving Throw: 5
Special: Immune to slashing and piercing weapons, immune to most spells.
Move: 8
Alignment: Neutrality
Number Encountered: 1
Challenge Level/XP: 14/2,600

The "original" golem of folklore, clay golems may be created by Clerics or powerful priests. They are massive clay statues of human beings, imbued with a rudimentary intelligence and the ability to move and follow their masters' commands. For each round of combat, a clay golem has a 1% chance (cumulative) to go berserk, leaving its master's control and attacking enemies and allies alike. Clay golems are not damaged by slashing or piercing weapons. They are immune to all spells other than those affecting earth, and these have very diminished effects – with one exception. An earthquake spell may be used to utterly destroy a clay golem.

Clay Golem: HD 10 (45hp); AC 7[12]; Atk 1 fist (3d10); Move 8; Save 5; AL N; CL/XP; 14/2600; Special: Immune to slashing and piercing weapons, immune to most spells.

The Keeper of the Keys

Those portions of the grand metropolis that are still populated are ramshackle and rough. One large courtyard, ringed by three-story townhouses, bears a crude-looking statue of fired clay – a **clay golem**. The golem was left behind by the religious sect that once occupied these buildings (they have since mostly been displaced by others), a sect of rainbow serpent worshippers. The clay golem holds two keys, both of iron. One is in a clenched fist, while the other is actually inside the golem. When these keys are put together, they open a secret door in the cellar of one of the buildings that ring the courtyard. Behind this door there is an ancient temple dedicated to the Rainbow Serpent and home to a prismatic dragon (treat as an ancient red dragon that can change its color to blue, green, white or black once per round, gaining the abilities of such a dragon when it does so). Besides a gilded idol of the Rainbow Serpent (weighs 300 pounds, worth 600 gp) there is a golden box through which one can commune with the Rainbow Serpent.

Golem, Flesh

Hit Dice: 8 (40 hit points)
Armor Class: 9 [10]
Attacks: 2 fists (2d8)
Saving Throw: 4
Special: Hit only by magic weapons, slowed by fire and cold, immune to most spells, healed by lightning
Move: 8
Alignment: Neutrality
Number Encountered: 1
Challenge Level/XP: 12/2,000

A creation stitched together from human limbs and other parts, a flesh golem is similar to Frankenstein's monster. Only +1 or better magic weapons can harm a flesh golem, and it is slowed by fire and cold spells. Lightning heals the golem for the number of points of damage that it would normally inflict. No other type of spell affects a flesh golem.

Flesh Golem: HD 8 (40hp); AC 9[10]; Atk 2 fists (2d8); Move 8; Save 8; AL N; CL/XP 12/2000; Special: Healed by lightning, hit only by magic weapons, slowed by fire and cold, immune to most spells.

The Thinker

Across a bleak expanse of ancient snow there is a chain of obsidian peaks. In a cave in these peaks, looking out over the snowy plain and a frigid sea, there sits a **flesh golem**, hand on chin, contemplating its painful existence. The cave is stocked with supplies in wooden crates and barrels left by a band of Vikings, who also left a map to their treasure (about 60 miles south on a rocky islet) in the form of cave drawings that look like warriors hunting whales and seals. The flesh golem is not immediately hostile, but it does tend toward violence.

Golem, Glass

Hit Dice: 10 (45HP)
Armor Class: 3 [16]
Attacks: 2 swords (2d8)
Saving Throw: 5
Special: Immunities
Move: 9
Alignment: Neutrality
Number Encountered: 1
Challenge Level/XP: 12/2,000

A glass golem is a human-shaped statue of glass that has been animated by a captured spirit infused into its physical substance. These creatures are immune to all spells other than cold-based magic, which has the effect of a slow spell but does not damage the golem. Blunt weapons inflict double damage against them, and they can be hit by normal weapons. A glass golem glitters brilliantly unless it is in total darkness, capturing and reflecting light by a thousand-fold. Anyone looking upon a glass golem, even through a mirror, must make a saving throw or attack at -2 to hit.

— Conversion by Matt Finch, first appearing in
Black Monastery** by **Frog God Games

Glass Golem: HD 10 (45hp); AC 3[16]; Atk 2 swords (2d8); Move 9; Save 5; AL N; CL/XP 12/2000; Special: Immunities

Gathering Glass

In a desert of glass, most of it ground into a sand-like consistency, some of it solidified into zigzagging canyons, some into jagged towers, there dwells a lich-lord in a grand tower of glass (carnival glass, to be precise, golden-orange and blue-violet), the dread Modrak. Water flows through this desert in narrow channels, but nothing grows here, for the desert is possessed of a weird aura (invisible to the eye, but visible as an aurora with *detect magic*). This aura is quite deadly; travelers must save once per day (at +5) or lose one level and age 1d10 years. Corpses are sometimes found here, corpses that look as though they died while walking or after they simply surrendered to the deadly desert and curled up to die. These corpses are collected from the desert by **glass golems** that serve the lich-lord. They are returned to their master, who animates them as **wights**.

Wight: HD 3; AC 5[14]; Atk 1 claw (1hp + level drain); Move 9; Save 14; AL C; CL/XP 5/240; Special: Drain 1 level with hit, hit only by magic or silver weapons.

Golem, Iron

Hit Dice: 16 (80 hit points)
Armor Class: 3 [16]
Attacks: Weapon or fist (4d10)
Saving Throw: 3
Special: Poison gas, immune to all weapons +2 or less, slowed by lightning, healed by fire, immune to most spells
Move: 6
Alignment: Neutrality
Number Encountered: 1
Challenge Level/XP: 17/3,500

Iron golems are huge moving statues of iron. They can breathe a 10-foot-radius cloud of poison gas as well as attacking with great power. Weapons of +2 or less do not affect iron golems. These hulking statues are slowed by lightning spells, but fire-based spells actually restore hit points to them. No other type of spell affects them.

Iron Golem: HD 16 (80hp); AC 3[16]; Atk 1 weapon or fist (4d10); Move 6; Save 3; AL N; CL/XP 17/3500; Special: Poison gas, immune to all weapons +2 or less, slowed by lightning, healed by fire, immune to most magic.

The War Goddess Waits

Within a dank dungeon there is a perfectly engineered system of canals filled with brackish water and blind eels. The canals all converge on a grand canal that leads to a great cathedral of chaos. Three iron statues of war goddesses stand over this canal, each brandishing a morningstar and round shield. The last of these (they're spaced about 30 feet apart) is an **iron golem**, who has been commanded to protect the temple. One's way along this canal is barred by several iron poles that stick a couple of feet above the water. If any of these are pulled or pushed, they act as levers that open up a trapdoor in the floor of the canal, creating a water slide that deposits them in a vast underground ocean plied by small pirate galleys crewed by such underworld denizens as dark elves, gray dwarves, troglodytes, goblins and orcs.

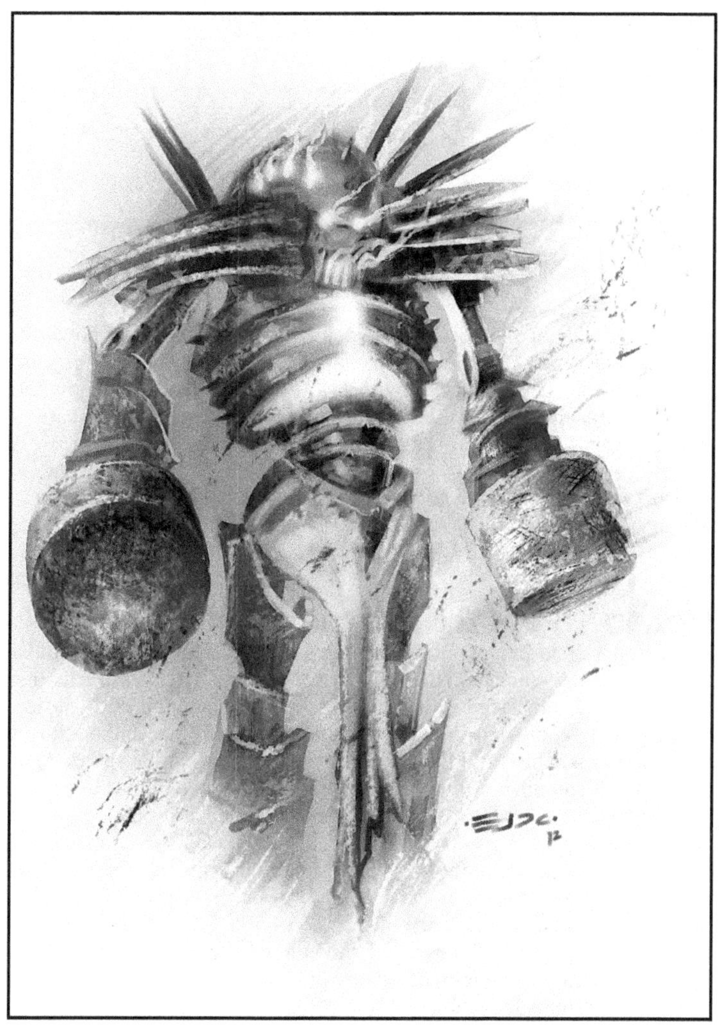

Golem, Stone

Hit Dice: 12 (60 hit points)
Armor Class: 5 [14]
Attacks: Fist (3d8)
Saving Throw: 3
Special: Unaffected by +1 or lesser weapons, immune to most spells
Move: 6
Alignment: Neutrality
Number Encountered: 1
Challenge Level/XP: 16/3,200

Stone golems are massive stone statues animated by very powerful magics (much more than just animate object, in other words). They are slowed by fire spells, damaged by rock-to-mud spells, and healed by the reverse. Spells that affect rock, and fire spells, are the only ones that affect stone golems. They can only be hit by +2 or better weapons.

Stone Golem: HD 12 (60hp); AC 5[14]; Atk 1 fist (3d8); Move 6; Save 3; CL/XP 16/3200; Special: +1 or better magic weapon to hit, immune to most magic.

Honor Always the Sun and Moon

A grand, ruined step pyramid dominates a grassy, rocky plateau amid a landscape of tree-choked valleys and towering, snow-capped mountains. Set into the eastern face of the pyramid is a giant sculpture of a warrior, sitting and clutching his knees, with a sun motif on his face and chest and eagles for arms. The western face of the pyramid has a similar sculpture of a warrior with moon motifs and jaguars for arms. The sun statue has a long, shallow trough before him filled with ever-burning coals. The moon statue has a similar reflecting pool in front of him. One who approaches these statues must take care to throw a handful of gold coins (for the sun god) or silver coins (for the moon god) into their respective sacrificial troughs or the statues animate as **stone golems** and smash the blasphemers. They also animate to protect the pyramid, the entrance being on the top of the pyramid, beneath the sacrificial altar, which slides out of the way easily when one person is lying atop it.

Golem, Wax

Hit Dice: 4 (20 hit points)
Armor Class: 5 [14]
Attacks: 2 fists (1d8+3)
Saving Throw: 13
Special: Resistant to blunt weapons, Magic resistance (25%)
Move: 6
Alignment: Neutrality
Number Encountered: 1
Challenge Level/XP: 6/400

Wax Golems are among the simplest type of golem to create. Their bodies are carved out of tallow or wax and imbued with the same basic level of intelligence as the more powerful Clay Golem. Unlike their stronger kin, Wax Golems have no chance of going berserk, nor are they automatically immune to spells. They do possess magic resistance of 25% and cannot be hit by non-magic weapons. Because of the pliable nature of their bodies, Wax Golems easily absorb the force delivered by blunt weapons and only take half damage from those sources. Slashing and piercing weapons inflict normal damage to Wax Golems. Fire and heat that damage the golem will inflict twice normal damage.

— Author: Andrew Trent

Wax Golem: HD 4 (20 HP); AC 5[14]; Atk 2 fists (1d8+3); Move 6; Save 13; AL N; CL/XP 6/400; Special: Resistant to blunt weapons, Magic resistance (25%).

Waxworks

You enter a circular chamber 30 feet in diameter, the walls of which contain 10 evenly spaced alcoves, with the entrance and exit passages spaced along with them. The chamber slopes downward slightly toward the middle – only by a couple feet, but enough to be noticeable. In each of the alcoves is a wax statue of a famous "bad guy" (use villains from your campaign, or use characters like Dracula, Frankenstein, etc.). Each alcove is lit from below (a *continuous light* effect cast on the stone beneath their feet).

As soon as characters enter the chamber, a *wall of force* springs up to block the entrance and exit (silently, of course; lasts for 24 hours). As adventurers examine the chamber, they notice two things. First, there is a 1-foot-diameter hole in the ceiling above the center of the room. Second, the wax figures begin moving. They are **10 wax golems**, and work toward grappling adventurers and dragging them to the center of the room where hot wax pours from the hole in the ceiling. Those struck by the wax suffer 1d6 points of damage per round. Once per week, orcs loyal to a necromancer in the dungeon come to the room and look for dead, wax-covered bodies.

Gorgon

Hit Dice: 8
Armor Class: 2 [17]
Attacks: Gore (2d6)
Saving Throw: 8
Special: Breath turns creatures to stone
Move: 12
Alignment: Chaos
Number Encountered: 1d4
Challenge Level/XP: 10/1,400

Gorgons are bull-like creatures with scales like dragons. Their breath turns creatures to stone (60-foot range, saving throw applies).

Gorgon: HD 8; AC 2[17]; Atk 1 gore (2d6); Move 12; Save 8; AL C; CL/XP 10/1400; Special: Breath turns to stone.

Watch Your Step

A staircase, about 10 feet long, leads down from one level of a dungeon to another. The lower half of the staircase is an illusion. The first person to step on must make a save or step through it and fall 20 feet into a narrow labyrinth of tunnels beneath the dungeon level the adventurers were trying to reach. This labyrinth is black as night, and roamed by **2 hungry gorgons**. At the center of the labyrinth is a set of spiral stairs that lead up to a dungeon level above the labyrinth.

Gravebird

Hit Dice: 2
Armor Class: 5 [14]
Attacks: 1 bite (1d4) or 2 claws (1d3)
Saving Throw: 16
Special: Disease upon successful hit (save applies), Speak with the Dead
Move: 4/16 (flying)
Alignment: Chaos
Number Encountered: 1d4
Challenge Level/XP: 3/120

Gravebirds are highly intelligent undead birds (usually ravens or crows) that have been brought back to life through foul magic. Any creature wounded by a Gravebird must make a successful saving throw or contract Grave Fever, a disease similar to Mummy Rot, which prevents magical healing and causes wounds to heal at one-tenth of the normal rate. A cure disease spell will remove the fever. Gravebirds can Speak with the Dead (as per the spell) three times daily.

— Author: Andrew Trent

Gravebird: HD 2; AC 5[14]; Atk 1 bite (1d4) or 2 claws (1d3); Move 4 (Fly 16); Save 16; AL C; CL/XP 3/120; Special: Disease upon successful hit (save applies), Speak with the Dead.

Birds on the Battlefield

The adventurers find themselves on a battlefield of greys and browns, with drooping, dying trees, puddles of reddish-brown water and many, many corpses that look to have been dead for at least a week. Three haggard old women in long, mourning gowns (with veils) and baskets are roaming the battlefield collecting bits and bobs from the corpses. Each carries a sickle, and each is an annis hag in service to a powerful necromancer. The hags will not disturb visitors (well, unless they're especially hungry or out of sorts, maybe a 1 in 12 chance). Besides the hags, there are **12 gravebirds** that look like rotting ravens perched on the branches of the wilting trees. They pester the adventurers for gemstones, which they adore, and might be convinced to use their *speak with dead* ability to question corpses. The gravebirds avoid the hags, and if they believe a party is especially weak and carrying treasure, they attack them as well.

Annis Hags: HD 8; AC 1[18]; Atk 2 claws (2d8), 1 bite (1d8); Move 12; Save 8; AL C; CL/XP 10/1400; Special: Hug and rend, polymorph, call mists.

Great Lantern Worm

Hit Dice: 30
Armor Class: 7 [12]
Attacks: Swallow whole
Saving Throw: 3
Special: Acid spray (3d4)
Move: 6
Alignment: Neutrality
Number Encountered: 1
Challenge Level/XP: 30/8,400

Great Lantern Worms are huge megadriles that grow 100ft or more in length, exceeding ten feet in width. They are subterranean, chewing tunnels in rock before swelling to fit the tunnel. Almost their entire length is taken up by the empty stomach, with their organs on the exterior, covered by a tough membrane of earthen hue. At the rear of the worm's long gut is a photophore, a light-emitting organ used as a lure for prey. Once the prey has travelled halfway down the stomach, the worm's mouth will close and acid will be sprayed from various points along the gut wall, requiring a saving throw each round to dodge. Should the entrapped prey try to cut their way out, any weapon that succeeds in hitting the stomach wall has a chance of dissolving. The chance for a non-magic weapon to dissolve is 1 in 8, and for a magic weapon the chance is 1 in 12. Each time a weapon avoids being dissolved, +1 is added to the chance of dissolving upon the next hit. For example, if a magic weapon hits and is not dissolved, the chance of dissolving on the second hit is 2 in 12 rather than 1 in 12. If a victim manages to stay alive long enough to return to the mouth, he can attempt to force it open (1 in 6 chance to succeed, +1 per helper). Victims are digested within hours.

—Author: Sean Wills

Great Lantern Worm: HD 30; AC 7[12]; Atk Acid spray (3d4); Move 6; Save 3; AL N; CL/XP 30/8400 ; Special: Acid spray, swallow whole.

Fool's Choice

Imagine a massive cavern, the ceiling studded with stalactites (and quite a few **piercers**), the floor marked by a myriad puddles (one of them containing a **grey ooze**) and three exits. One of the exits leads into a tunnel smeared with patches of **green slime** (the slime covers only the first 10 feet of the tunnel). From another one can be heard the incessant drumming of goblin drums (actually it is water dripping onto an ancient suit of platemail left to rust by an unlucky adventurer). The third cavern looks promising. It is fairly straight and there is a light at the end of the tunnel. Of course, this tunnel is a **great lantern worm**.

Green Brain

Hit Dice: 5
Armor Class: 3 [16]
Attacks: None
Saving Throw: 12
Special: Mental attacks
Move: 0/15 (flying)
Alignment: Chaos
Number Encountered: 1d2
Challenge Level/XP: 6/400

Green brains are plant-creatures grown by the Shrooms (and possibly by other malevolent races with aptitudes for magically altering and breeding plants). Green brains are relatively intelligent, and are generally used to supervise and oversee the activities of mindless or semi-intelligent creatures using their powers of mental communication. In general, the supervised species will be plant-creatures of some kind, but it is possible for a green brain to act somewhat less effectively as the overseer for brutish humanoids or other non-plant creatures.

Green brains are able to project mental commands and communications at a deep enough level that the brain's demands are clear even to mindless creatures such as oozes or monstrous plants. Indeed, the less intelligent the recipient of the orders, the stronger the green brain's hold over it.

In addition to telepathic communication, a green brain can use its mental powers as a weapon when necessary. A green brain is able to continuously project a cone of mental force 50ft long and widening to 30ft at the end, which has the following effects: (1) any spells being cast are disrupted, although they are not lost from the caster's memory, (2) anyone failing a saving throw within the cone becomes somewhat disoriented, making attacks at a penalty of -2 (duration 1d3 rounds) and having a 1 in 6 chance to drop any item held in the hands. The green brain may also narrow its mental focus to project a beam of concentrated, damaging thought, inflicting 2d6 points of damage to any single individual who fails a saving throw.

— Author: Matt Finch

Green Brain: HD 5; AC 3[16]; Atk None; Move 0/15 (flying); Save 12; AL C; CL/XP 6/400 ; Special: Mental attacks.

Dig that Brain

A **green brain** is working feverishly, on behalf of a tribe of **mushroom men**, to create a summoning chamber for the Great Green Goddess. The room must be precisely shaped, and the workers are **12 black puddings**, who are dissolving the stone slowly. They are about 90% done with the chamber, which is oddly shaped, with multiple pillars of varying diameters and shapes holding up the ceiling. A deep pit is being dug in the center of the chamber, a pit that will be filled with the rotting corpses of 21 elves, the prescribed sacrifice to the Great Green Goddess. The elves are being held elsewhere by the mushroom men.

Black Pudding: HD 10; AC 6[13]; Atk 1 attack (3d8); Move 6; Save 5; AL N; CL/XP 11/1700; Special: Acidic surface, immune to cold, divides when hit with lightning.

Green Slime

Green slime isn't technically a monster, just an extremely dangerous hazard in underground tombs and other such places. Any metal or organic substance it touches begins to turn to green slime (saving throw). It can be killed with fire or extreme cold, and the transformation process can be arrested by the use of a *cure disease* spell.

There's a Catch

The wizard's vault has two massive iron doors with no apparent means of opening them. They are locked, of course, but there are no handles and the lock is within the doors. The only way to open them is via a small mechanical catch hidden behind a false portion of wall. The catch is at the end of a two-foot-long burrow. One can see the catch at the end of this burrow, but what they cannot see is the canister of green slime suspended above the catch. When the catch is worked (this requires an open locks check at −10%), the doors are unlocked and can be pushed open, but the canister is also opened, dropping the green slime on the would-be robber's hand.

Grey Ooze

Hit Dice: 3
Armor Class: 8 [11]
Attacks: Strike (2d6)
Saving Throw: 14
Special: Acid, immune to spells, heat, cold, and blunt weapons.
Move: 1
Alignment: Neutrality
Number Encountered: 1d4
Challenge Level/XP: 5/240

Grey ooze is almost identical in appearance to wet rock, but it is a slimy, formless substance that devours prey and carrion with its acidic secretions, lashing out to strike enemies. Grey ooze is immune to spells, heat, and cold damage. Metal (but not stone or wood) must make a saving throw vs. acid when exposed to grey ooze (even if the contact is as brief as the strike of a sword) or be rotted through. When the grey ooze hits a character in metal armor, the armor must make an item saving throw. Only cutting and piercing damages a grey ooze—it is impervious to blunt or crushing attacks.

Grey Ooze: HD 3; AC 8[11]; Atk 1 strike (2d6); Move 1; Save 14; AL N; CL/XP 5/240; Special: Acid, immune to spells, heat, cold, and blunt weapons.

Caught Up in the Ooze

The hallway the adventurers are traversing is interrupted by a 10-foot-deep pit with spikes at the bottom. The pit is actually an illusion covering up a square, metallic plate, silvery-green in color, that is enchanted with a *reverse gravity* effect. The ceiling above the pit is also an illusion hiding a 10-foot-high shaft. At the top of this shaft is a single grey ooze waiting for its next meal to be tossed up to it. There is also a secret door leading into a tunnel (one walks into the tunnel on the ceiling and then falls to the floor) that leads to a secret vault (see green slime above or invent one of your own).

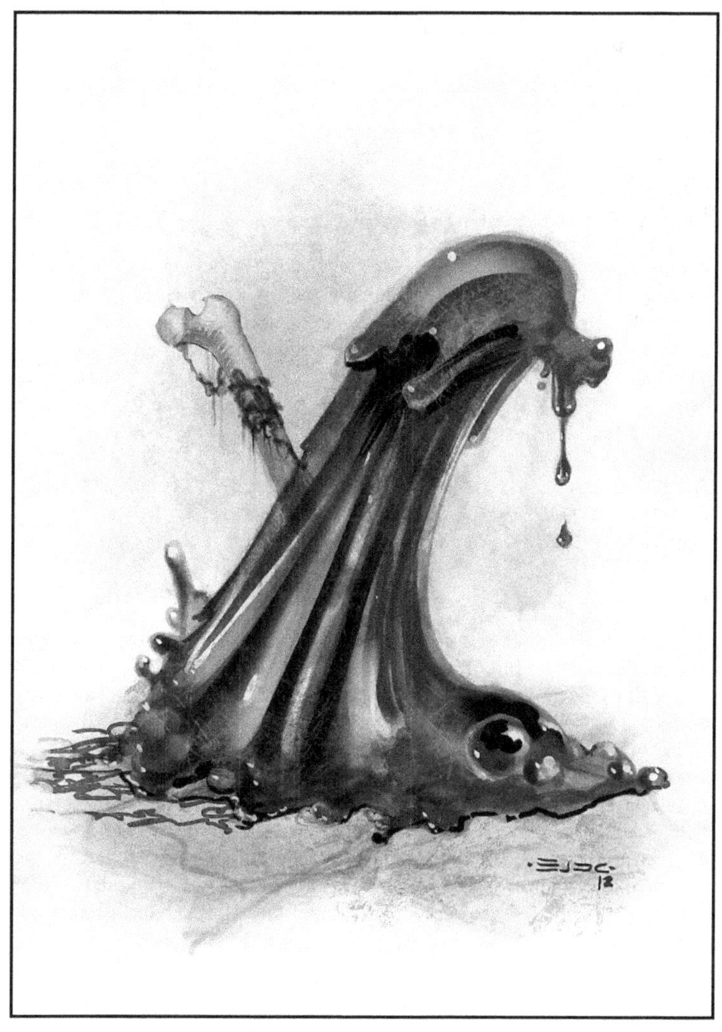

Grick

Hit Dice: 2
Armor Class: 4 [15]
Attacks: 4 tentacles (1d3), 1 beak (1d2)
Saving Throw: 16
Special: Immune to blunt weapons
Move: 6
Alignment: Neutrality
Number Encountered: 1d6
Challenge Level/XP: 4/120

Gricks resemble massive, human-sized worms with 4 tentacles surrounding a beaked mouth. They rear up to attack, focusing on one opponent at a time. They do not immediately try to feed on dying prey, but if given the chance they will drag unconscious or dead bodies into their lairs to feed. Blunt weapons do not harm them, due to their thick hides and resilient flesh.

Grick: HD 2; AC 4[15]; Atk 4 tentacles (1d3), 1 beak (1d2); Move 6; Save 16; AL N; CL/XP 4/120; Special: Immune to blunt weapons.

Toad Pickers

A 60-foot-diameter mound of dirt pushes up through the Sin Mire Swamp like a wart, bursting out of the muck and mire. A wide-mouthed cave delves deep into the dirt, descending 20 feet under the swampy morass. Coral-colored frogs with bright pink eyes and tongues cover the walls of the swampy cave, creating a rippling wave of color that undulates down the passageway. Mixed among the smaller frogs are 6 slightly larger frogs that draw the eye. Three of the amulets are amulets of protection (as a scroll of protection), while the other three are cursed. When worn, they cause one piece of equipment (the most valuable or beloved on the activator) to turn into a full-grown **grick**. If the grick is destroyed, the item collapses into pile of coral-colored sand that turns into a handful of small iridescent frogs.

Griffon

Hit Dice: 7
Armor Class: 3 [16]
Attacks: 2 claws (1d4), 1 bite (2d8)
Saving Throw: 9
Special: None
Move: 12/27 (flying)
Alignment: Neutrality
Number Encountered: 2d6
Challenge Level/XP: 8/800

Griffons have the body of a lion, with the head, fore-claws, and wings of an eagle. These creatures can be tamed and ridden as mounts. They usually nest in high mountain aeries, where they lay their eggs and hunt their prey. Because the fledglings can be tamed, young griffons and griffon eggs command a very high price in the marketplaces of the great cities, or to noble lords and wizards.

Griffon: HD 7; AC 3[16]; Atk 2 claws (1d4), 1 bite (2d8); Move 12 (Fly 27); Save 9; AL N; CL/XP 8/800; Special: None.

Club Griffon

Up a narrow, treacherous mountain trail that starts in an arimaspian village and ends in a yawning cave specked with green garnets. At the end of this cave, which extends back 200 tricky feet, there is a lead door (very heavy). Opening this door reveals a hidden valley studded with cacti, in the middle of which there is a great stone pillar (40 feet in diameter and 100 feet tall) studded with caves and serving as the aerie of **3 griffons** guarding a powerful magical club, reputedly the club of a great barbarian. The club is a *+1 weapon* that can be struck on the ground once per day to activate one of the following powers:

1 – the club becomes a *+2 weapon*
2 – the club becomes a *+1 weapon/+3 vs. dragons and shadows*
3 – the club causes an *earthquake* (as the spell)

Growling Shadow

Hit Dice: 2
Armor Class: 4 [15]
Attacks: 1 bite (1 hit point)
Saving Throw: 16
Special: Automatic damage, vanishing
Move: 12
Alignment: Chaos
Number Encountered: 1d2
Challenge Level/XP: 4/120

Growling shadows are spirit creatures that inhabit darkness and shadow, usually underground but in some cases in dark forests as well. Their presence will immediately be noticed, for they make growling sounds that seem to come from several directions at one time. A growling shadow materializes and vanishes from place to place when attacking, selecting a single victim at a time. Each round, the shadow will appear in front of a randomly determined opponent and attack, disappearing again so swiftly that *only the one character being attacked* has the opportunity to strike back. The shadow's attack automatically deals one hit point of damage without the need to make a to-hit roll; if it is not killed before it has inflicted 10 hit points it will retreat, sated, back into the shadows whence it came.

— Author: Matt Finch

Growling Shadow: HD 2; AC 4[15]; Atk 1 bite (1 hp, automatic); Move 12; Save 16; AL C; CL/XP 4/120; Special: Automatic damage, vanishing.

Angry Shadow

Travelers may one day find themselves crossing a mountain chain through a thickly wooded limestone canyon. The canyon is stained with reds and oranges, and features many small cave complexes inhabited by families of **ogres** (1 in 6 chance per hour of encountering 1d4 of them out fishing). The ogres fish in remarkably deep pools of water, pulling out large, blind tentacle fish. The ogres never leave their caves at night, and actually use great boulders to block the cave entrances, for they know well that a **growling shadow** lurks in this canyon, hunting by night (4 in 6 chance of an encounter). Travelers might, at some point, find a black splotch on a wall that was the growling shadow in life. A sword of adamantine has been plunged into this splotch. If removed, the growling shadow is dispelled, and a passage in the wall opens into a wondrous underworld.

Ogre: HD 4+1; AC 5[14]; Atk 1 weapon (1d10+1); Move 9; Save 13; AL C; CL/XP 4/120; Special: None.

Grue (Type 1)

Hit Dice: 9
Armor Class: 2 [17]
Attacks: 1 bite (2d6)
Saving Throw: 6
Special: Immune to blunt and piercing weapons, extinguish normal lights, swallow whole
Move: 9
Alignment: Chaos
Number Encountered: 1
Challenge Level/XP: 12/2,000

A grue is a nasty, large thing with dark grey or green skin, rather like a half-filled water balloon ten feet long, with a huge mouth. Inside its leathery skin, the grue is mostly gelatinous. Grues cannot coexist with light; if they are exposed to a light source, they instantly recede with the darkness. In the dark, however, they are dangerous. If a grue hits with a natural roll of 20 on its attack die, it swallows the victim whole; which will satisfy the grue, and it will leave if it is permitted to do so (the swallowed victim will suffocate in 2d4 rounds and then be digested). They are non-intelligent, and are immune to blunt and piercing weapons (e.g., clubs, maces, arrows, spears). Swords, axes, and other cutting weapons inflict normal damage. Grues can magically extinguish one normal light source per round at a distance of 100ft.

—Author: Matt Finch

Grue (Type 1): HD 9; AC 2[17]; Atk 1 bite (2d6); Move 9; Save 6; AL C; CL/XP 12/2000; Special: immune to blunt and piercing weapons, extinguish normal lights, swallow whole.

The Sausage King

A grimy placard sits outside this small house on the roadside leading into a ghost town located in the valley below. The sign bears the words "The Sausage King" with an engraving of a smiling sausage link wearing a small gold crown. The crown is a gold piece pressed into the shape of the headgear. Beneath the name, different flavors of sausage are written in chalk with a price for a pound of each. Inside the shop, however, potential patrons are sure to lose their appetites. Gamy meat sits in bushel baskets, surrounded by clouds of flies that buzz angrily around anyone trying to swat them away. Piled links of sausage fill a tub sitting on the floor. Worms, maggots and other insects crawl through the rancid meat. Rat droppings cover the floor.

The shop owner's head lies inside a mound of sausage links lying on the floor. He was killed when he couldn't satisfy the hunger of his "business partner," a deadly grue he trapped in the shop's cellar. The grue looks like a huge deflated sausage lying on the dirt floor at the bottom of the steep stairs leading down from a trapdoor in a backroom behind the counter. When the grue consumes a creature, it soon excretes the victim as a mound of sausage-like links. The Sausage King turned this horrible byproduct into a business the people in the village couldn't get enough of. Even when people started vanishing, they didn't put two and two together. Only when the farmer made a misstep and became a pile of sausage himself did the village truly suffer. The grue leaves its cellar lair each night through a hole in the side of the house and hunts the surrounding land. It returns to the cellar by dawn. It ate the townsfolk fairly quickly, and now subsists on forest animals. PCs coming into the shop are fresh meat for the hungry grue.

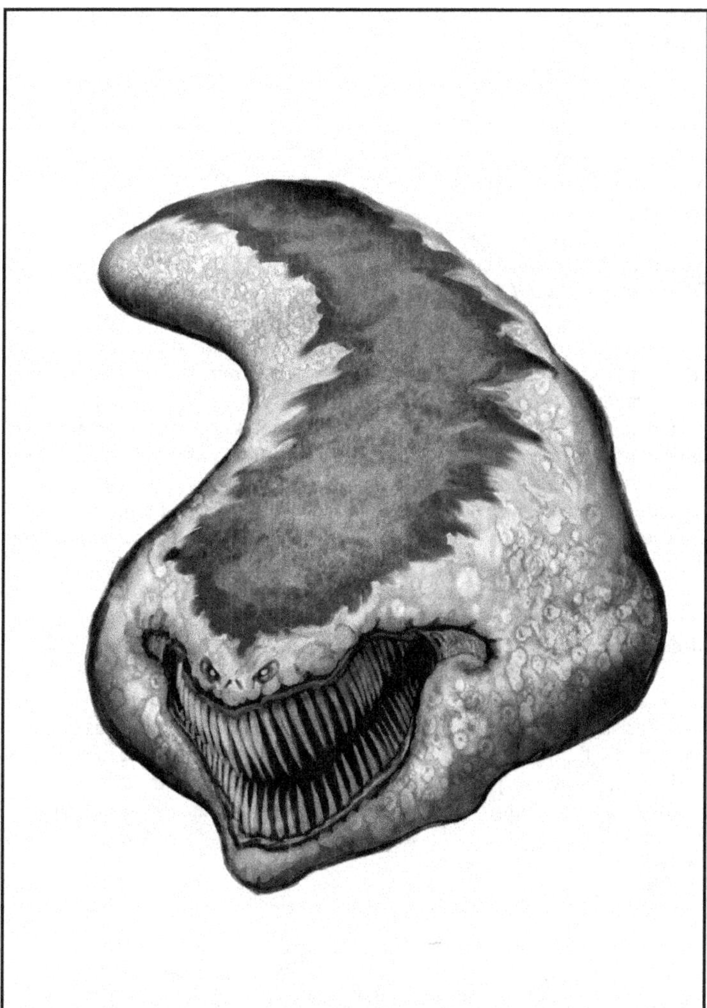

Grue (Type 2)

Hit Dice: 6
Armor Class: 2 [17]
Attacks: 1 bite (2d6)
Saving Throw: 11
Special: Immune to all but magic weapons, and spells with light component/effect, extinguish lights w/in 100ft, healed by damage caused to victims
Move: 12
Alignment: Chaos
Number Encountered: 1
Challenge Level/XP: 11/1,700

Found in the darkest recesses of dungeons or in the deepest corners of attics, grues are the essence of Chaos and Darkness given form by evil and a ravenous appetite for living souls. Grues have no specific shape or form, save for the ravening, slavering jaws that close around the unsuspecting, or those who would venture into the darkness without a torch or match in their inventory. Grues are chaotic spirits that exist in a 10ft x 10ft area of pure darkness. Any light source brought into that same area forces the grue to flee to the nearest dark area. Any creature within the area of darkness is subject to attack by the grue's jaws. For all intents and purposes, grues are invisible to anyone within the area of darkness, but outside of the area, a grue looks like "living darkness." Grues are only affected by magical weapons or weapons that emit light of some kind, including a torch (which would act like a club). They are resistant to all spell attacks, save those that have some sort of light component (a light spell, prismatic spray or even fireball). Grues can magically extinguish one normal light source per round at a distance of 100ft. A grue's attack will replenish its hit points with any hit points "eaten" from its victims. A grue cannot replenish beyond its starting hit points. Anyone killed by a grue will vanish, including all of his equipment. In 1d4 days, he will become a grue.

— Author: Chgowiz

Grue (Type 2): HD 6; AC 2[17]; Atk 1 bite (2d6); Move 12; Save 11; AL C; CL/XP 11/1700; Special: immune to all but light/magic weapons and spells with light component/ effect, can extinguish lights w/in 100ft, restores own HP with damage caused to victims.

Inner Demons

On the first new moon of the year, the people of a curious mountain walk into a wooded valley that hides a great idol of Chaos, the demon of primordial darkness. The idol is a large chunk of black stone that glistens and almost seems to pulse when one looks upon it for more than a moment. It rests in a wide clearing and is surrounded by five smaller black stones. The people of the village walk to this place and disrobe, though it is quite cold. Three chosen villagers are put in voluminous black robes that completely cover their heads and bodies. As the others walk counterclockwise around the idols (at a distance of about 12 feet), the chosen three walk clockwise around the idols at a distance of about 4 feet. After the thirteenth pass, the outer walkers suddenly fall to the ground in a bizarre ecstasy, moaning and writhing. Of the black-garbed three, one is suddenly changed into a **grue** and moves quickly to devour the other two. When this is completed, the grue slinks into the woods and eventually finds its way into the local underworld.

Gump

Hit Dice: 4
Armor Class: 5 [14]
Attacks: 1 weapon (1d6+2)
Saving Throw: 13
Special: Gaze attack paralyzes (+2 save)
Move: 9
Alignment: Chaos
Number Encountered: 1d4
Challenge Level/XP: 5/240

Gumps are large and blubbery humanoids with an overly broad jagged toothed grin and a pair of small, deep-set eyes in an otherwise featureless face. Gumps are motivated by hunger and the deep down joy they feel when murdering a helpless foe. Anyone meeting the gaze of a gump must save vs. paralysis at +2 or be held in place for 2-5 rounds (fighting without looking incurs a -4 penalty to-hit). It is safe to view a gump's reflection in a mirror or other reflective surface. The gump is able to squint in an odd manner which keeps it from paralyzing an ally.

— *Author: JD Jarvis*

Gump: HD 4; AC 5[14]; Atk 1 weapon (1d6+2); Move 9; Save 13; AL C; CL/XP 5/240; Special: Gaze attack paralyzes (+2 save).

Faces in the Crowd

There is an arena here in a grand cavern. The floor is covered with jagged bits of metal and cast-off weapons and shields. About 20 feet above the floor of the arena are several large, circular windows. A gong placed in the center of the arena summons a *magic mouth* directly above. The mouth says "Thy doom is upon thee!" at which point one monstrously huge **giant rat** per adventurer suddenly appears in the arena, rearing its back. More importantly, the sounding of the gong alerts a nearby tribe of **gumps**, who appear in the windows above, pressing their faces against the glass and leering at the adventurers. Of course, the gaze of the gumps has a paralyzing effect, and each round, an adventurer has a 1 in 6 chance per rat attacking them of meeting one of these gazes.

Monstrously Huge Giant Rat: HD 3; AC 6[13]; Atk 2 claws (1d3), 1 bite (1d6); Move 12; Save 14; AL N; CL/XP 3/120; Special: 5% are diseased.

Gwurrum (Mists of Faerie Vengeance)

Hit Dice: 9
Armor Class: 7 [12]
Attacks: 1 per target in 10ft reach (1d8/round)
Saving Throw: 6
Special: Immunities
Move: 6
Alignment: Chaos
Number Encountered: 1
Challenge Level/XP: 12/2,000

An eerie green mist seeps through the trees at twilight, stealing up to the houses of those who have failed to leave an offering to the faerie folk of the woods. It is the gwurrum, monstrous servant of the faerie court, come to pay a visit.

The gwurrum is composed of equal parts choking mist and thirst for blood. It can force its way through the tiniest cracks in any barrier, crawl uphill, and pour down chimneys and throats like cold water. The misty body is roughly 10ft in diameter, and its trailing tendrils can reach up to 10ft from its form. Any and all targets within range will be attacked, though if free to choose, the faerie monster will focus upon children and small animals: those whose loss will cause the greatest sorrow and misery in the punished community. Dim-witted and malicious, it can be distracted by offerings of whiskey, recitations of poetry extolling the virtues of the faerie-folk, and the singing of an unbroken voice. Iron objects cause an additional 1d6 points of damage to the gwurrum (the mere touch of iron causes 1d6 points), but these items will turn to dust within 1 round after contact with the gwurrum. The faerie monster is otherwise immune to fire, electrical, poison, or mind-affecting attacks. Any creature with magical singing abilities, such as a harpy or bard, can keep a gwurrum at bay for 1 round per hit dice or level. A gwurrum is affected by Protection from Evil, and cannot attack anyone who is thoroughly drunk. In the morning, when a gwurrum departs, dead leaves will be found scattered around the dwelling of anyone it attacked. Children who survive the attack of a gwurrum may, upon growing up, pass freely into the faerie realms.

— Author: Scott Wylie Roberts, "Myrystyr"

Gwurrum: HD 9; AC 7[12]; Atk 1 per target in 10ft reach (1d8/round); Move 6; Save 6; AL C; CL/XP 12/2000; Special: Immunities.

The Thing in the Well

Amid the towering trees of a primordial wood, one might come upon the ruins of a castle of the old gods, a ruin of grayish-green walls, majestic arches and delicate towers that disappear into the green canopy above. Beyond the crumbling gatehouse is a courtyard of green marble and cloisters with blue-green roofs supported by fluted ivory columns. The well in the center of the courtyard is the lair of a **gwurrum**. Beyond the cloisters there are locked bronze doors leading into the castle and its maze-like dungeons.

Hag, Annis

Hit Dice: 8
Armor Class: 1 [18]
Attack: 2 claws (2d8), 1 bite (1d8)
Special: Hug and rend, polymorph, call mists
Move: 12
Saving Throw: 8
Alignment: Chaos
Number Encountered: 1
Challenge Level/XP: 10/1,400

Annis Hags are giantesses, horrid looking females as large as ogres. They lust for human flesh to eat, and often polymorph themselves into human form to hunt (an old lady being a common shape), or to lure their prey from places of safety. Strong as a bear, the annis can attack in similar fashion; if she hits with both claws, the victim is held and the annis inflicts automatic damage with all three attacks thereafter. The victim isn't helpless, but cannot break free unless he is as strong as a giant. Annis are somewhat magical; they can summon mists to hide themselves and their rank lairs; some are also witches with the ability to cast spells (such being left to the Referee's determination, if witch-hags are to be encountered).

Annis: HD 8; AC 1[18]; Atk 2 claws (2d8), 1 bite (1d8); Move 12; Save 8; AL C; CL/XP 10/1400; Special: Hug and rend, polymorph, call mists.

Don't Make Mother Angry

On a haunted moor, swathed in summer mists and shaded by an angry sky, there is a shallow lake hemmed in by thick brambles of white rose bushes. The moor is patrolled by worgs, but they are the least of a traveler's problems. In the middle of the lake, reachable by an invisible causeway, there is a gleaming white castle with roofs clad in silver. Inside the castle there dwell **9 nymphs**, the daughters of an **annis hag**. The nymphs lounge and play in their garden, sometimes appearing on the battlements. Those who attempt to reach them find that their mother, **Green Agnes**, does not tolerate their company.

Nymph: HD 3; AC 9[10]; Atk none; Move 12; Save 14; AL N; CL/XP 5/240; Special: Sight causes blindness or death.

Hag, Mountain (Yama-Uba)

Hit Dice: 7
Armor Class: 4 [15]
Attack: 2 claws (1d6), 1 bite (1d8)
Special: None
Move: 12
Saving Throw: 9
Alignment: Chaos
Number Encountered: 1 or 1d3+1
Challenge Level/XP: 7/600

The mountain hags ("Yama-uba" in Asian-type settings) are solitary, horrid looking blue-skinned females as large as ogres. They live in mountainous regions and near passes where they can hunt for food. Mountain hags feast on all manner of flesh; but they prefer humans, attacking with their long claws and wicked mouths that stretch from ear to ear.

— Author: Mike Davison

Mountain Hag/ Yama-uba: HD 7; AC 4[15]; Atk 2 claws (1d6), 1 bite (1d8); Move 12; Save 9; AL C; CL/XP 7/600; Special: None.

Beautiful Dreams Turn Deadly

Above the cherry blossom woods in the mountains teeming with silver foxes there is an infamous tea house. The tea house is home to three beauteous maidens who serve tea of such exquisite quality that it is said to cure diseases and dispel evil magic. The women play their biwas (Japanese lutes) and sing their songs, and as the night wears on, they bring out their rice wine and keep the men enraptured. Invariably, the men find themselves in one of the villages beyond the mountains by the next morning, but missing one of their number. These men have been lured into the cellar, where the **mountain hag** who dreamed these maidens dwells.

Hag, Sea

Hit Dice: 3
Armor Class: 6 [13]
Attack: 1 bite (1d4)
Special: Death gaze, weakness gaze
Move: 6/18 (swimming)
Saving Throw: 14
Alignment: Chaos
Number Encountered: 1d4
Challenge Level/XP: 5/240

The sea hag is a giantess much like the annis, but living in the seas, or in fetid, salt-water marshes. These hags are so hideous that the sight of their faces causes weakness from fright and horror; if the victim fails a saving throw, his strength ability score is reduced by one-half for 1d6 full turns. The hag can also cast an evil eye upon those she chooses to slay; but only three times per day. The range of this deadly gaze is 30ft, and the hag's eye need not be met in order for death to occur (saving throw). Like the annis, sea hags feast with gusto upon human flesh.

Sea Hag: HD 3; AC 6[13]; Atk 1 bite (1d4); Move 6 (Swim 18); Save 14; AL C; CL/XP 5/240; Special: Death gaze, weakness gaze.

The Sea Hag's Secret

Beyond the treacherous reef, but in plain view from the mangrove swamp, there is a windswept island that, under a full moon, gleams as though it were covered by mother-of-pearl. Day and night, the winds howl over this island, making the water choppy and carrying a strange, acrid smell across the water to the swamps. One can also see, sunning themselves on the island, a dozen women, possibly mermaids, with pallid skin and silvery hair. These women are actually **aquatic ghouls**, and they are the servants of the **sea hag Radhna**, who holds a map that shows the secret paths through the swamp to the lost city of Ossgare beyond, wherein dwells the hag queen Morganui and her infamous Silver Legion.

Harpy

Hit Dice: 3
Armor Class: 7 [12]
Attacks: 2 talons (1d3) and weapon (1d6)
Saving Throw: 14
Special: Siren-song
Move: 6/18 (flying)
Alignment: Chaos
Number Encountered: 2d6
Challenge Level/XP: 4/120

Harpies have the upper body of a human female and the lower body and wings of a vulture. Their song is a charm that draws its victims to the harpy (saving throw applies), and the harpy's touch casts the equivalent of a charm person spell (again, saving throw applies).

Harpy: HD 3; AC 7[12]; Atk 2 talons (1d3) and weapon (1d6); Move 6 (Fly 18); Save 14; AL C; CL/XP 4/120; Special: Flight, siren-song.

Bridging the Dead

The only pass through a treacherous mountain chain is, at one point, cut in twain by a curious chasm. The chasm is about 300 feet wide, and spanned by a bridge of ancient manufacture (possibly a specimen of dwarf engineering, though the elves claim it as theirs). The bottom of the chasm is cloaked in a bluish fog in which one can sometimes make out large, bulbous masses moving silently and swiftly. A host of **harpies** (as many as would make a good encounter) perches on the ledges above the bridge, waiting for folk to cross it. They attack as soon as people are midway across, attempting to knock people into the chasm below. The fog hides a sluggish river that flows into the deep, and the shapes are strange boats guided by undead spirits.

Hawktoad

Hit Dice: 2
Armor Class: 7 [12]
Attack: 2 claws (1d2), tongue (strangles)
Special: Strangling tongue
Move: 3/12 (flying)
Saving Throw: 16
Alignment: Neutrality
Number Encountered: 2d6
Challenge Level/XP: 3/60

Hawktoads are levitating amphibians with the body of a very large toad but with long, clawed front legs and no back legs at all. The hind end of a hawktoad is a foot-long tail, like that of a tadpole; the full length of a hawktoad is three feet. These bizarre creatures move by lashing through the air with their tadpole-like tails, and attack by swooping in at opponents, scratching with their tiny claws and lashing out with their long tongues. A hawktoad's tongue does no damage, but if the attack succeeds the tongue has whipped around the character's neck. If this happens, the hawktoad lands at the back of the victim's neck; it holds tight with its tiny claws and begins to strangle the opponent, using its muscular tongue as a garrotte. When a hawktoad is attached in this way, the strangling character will find it difficult to reach around and attack, of course.

Each round thereafter, the character must successfully roll a d20 under his constitution score or fall unconscious; each round a cumulative +1 is added to the d20 roll, making it harder and harder to avoid passing out. Once the character passes out, the toad strangles him to death in three rounds.

— *Author: Matt Finch*

Hawktoad: HD 2; AC 7[12]; Atk 2 claws (1d2), tongue (strangles); Move 3 (Fly 12); Save 16; AL N; CL/XP 3/60; Special: Strangling tongue.

All Hail the Hawktoad!

The barbarians of the Golden Hills are an odd sort. They look as savage as any barbarians you might meet, with unruly beards and mustaches (usually red or reddish-brown), wild eyes of green or gold and golden skin they only barely cover with animal skins. As savage as they look, the barbarians are champions of Law and Good, who plunder the humanoid tribes of the hills and mountains and then sell what they recover to traders who roam the coast. The barbarians dwell in animal hide tents, their warchief holding court in the largest of these tents. There, he sits on a golden stool, flanked by two bodyguards who wear mail hauberks and helms bedecked with bright feathers. To one side, he keeps three **hawktoads**, the mascot of his tribe, in a spherical, wicker cage. These hawktoads are used to judge the righteousness of those brought before him. Prisoners and visitors are stripped naked and brought before the chief, where they are made to kneel. The hawktoads are released on golden chains, and if they fly around the person clockwise, it indicates they are to be trusted; counterclockwise indicates the opposite (the hawktoads don't really know the person's alignment, just toss a coin). If the person attacks the hawktoads, they are set upon by the entire assembly. If the hawktoads attack and blood is drawn, they are pulled away and the people are welcomed into the tribe as blood brothers of the chief.

Head-Stealer

Hit Dice: 3+4
Armor Class: 8 [11]
Attack: 1 weapon (1d6) or strike (1d4)
Special: Immune to sleep and charm
Move: 12
Saving Throw: 14
Alignment: Chaos
Number Encountered: 1 or 1d4
Challenge Level/XP: 3/60

A head-stealer is the headless, undead body of someone who has been decapitated, usually by execution or dungeon trap. The body is animated with a vengeful spirit, and seeks to re-enter society by removing someone else's head and placing it atop its own neck. Although the head-stealer's body remains in a relatively preserved state, its stolen heads continue to decay, and the head-stealer seeks to replace them on a regular basis. Although the head-stealer can animate its substitute heads, the unnatural grafting of dead flesh to undead flesh is highly imperfect. The head does not attach by magic, so the head-stealer is required to use a measure such as rope or nails to affix the new head. Moreover, the head stealer can only imprecisely animate a stolen head, and while it can cause speech to issue forth, the slurring and twitching will tend to raise suspicion. As with all undead creatures, the head stealer is immune to mind-affecting spells and vulnerable to holy water. The head stealer can be immediately destroyed by attaching the head it formerly possessed in life, if the head still exists. Any attack against the head stealer may dislodge the stolen head on a natural roll of 19 or 20, causing the head-stealer to attack at -1 until it can reattach the head or a replacement. If deprived of a head, it may try to rip one from the torso of an attacker.

— *Author: Scott Wylie Roberts, "Myrystyr"*

Head-stealer: HD 3+4; AC 8[11]; Atk 1 weapon (1d6) or strike (1d4); Move 12; Save 14; AL C; CL/XP 3/60; Special: Immune to sleep and charm.

Head Games

The adventurers pass through a secret door and enter a long hallway. The secret door is one way only, and before them is a 100-foot-long hall with blood-caked walls. Midway down the hall there is an intersection, and at the end of the hall is a sealed tomb. About 20 feet down the hall there is a scythe trap, long since sprung and now rusted in place, the blade red with rust and brown with dried blood. As one passes this trap, a **head-stealer** appears at the end of the hall, looking like a headless man wearing mirror armor (treat as plate mail) and wielding a pata (gauntlet sword). This man was once **Rugali**, an anti-paladin of Yama, who lost his head while seeking the tomb of Katimal, a paladin of Krishna (the tomb that lies at the end of this hall). The head-stealer now haunts these passages, defending the tomb from others (if he can't despoil it, then nobody can) and chasing people through the winding corridors of this section of the dungeon until he or they have been destroyed. The only way out of this section of the dungeon is through Katimal's tomb (a sanctified place, provided it is not robbed), where a complex dance (depicted on the walls in bas-relief) can open a portal that allows people to pass to a hidden cavern of delights.

Headless Hound

Hit Dice: 6
Armor Class: 5 [14]
Attack: 1 bite (2d6)
Special: Bite passes through armor, half normal healing rate from wounds, fear, half damage from normal weapons, immune to sleep, charm, hold.
Move: 18/6 (flying)
Saving Throw: 11
Alignment: Chaos
Number Encountered: 2d6
Challenge Level/XP: 8/800

A headless hound appears to be a large black dog, but with an eerie green glow where the head should be. The creature's flanks may be lined with scars or torn open, exposing faintly glowing bones and the absence of innards. The headless hound attacks with a ghostly bite that passes straight through clothing and armor to the flesh. The defender's armor class is modified only by any Dexterity bonus. Bitten flesh heals at half normal rate unless magic is used. If five or more headless hounds are present, their howling requires a saving throw to avoid fleeing in fear (only required once). The headless hound takes half damage from normal weapons. Despite their spectral nature, headless hounds are not undead. However, they are immune to sleep, charm, and hold spells. They are more properly faerie-kin, and according to folklore will cease their haunting and join the wild hunt if it passes nearby. Anyone slain by a headless hound has a chance of returning from the grave as a shadow-like spirit, to be pursued nightly by the headless hound pack.

— *Author: Scott Wylie Roberts, "Myrystyr"*

Headless Hound: HD 6; AC 5[14]; Atk 1 bite (2d6); Move 18 (Fly 6); Save 11; AL C; CL/XP 8/800; Special: Bite passes through armor (only dex bonus modifies AC), half normal healing rate from wounds, fear, half damage from normal weapons, immune to sleep, charm, hold.

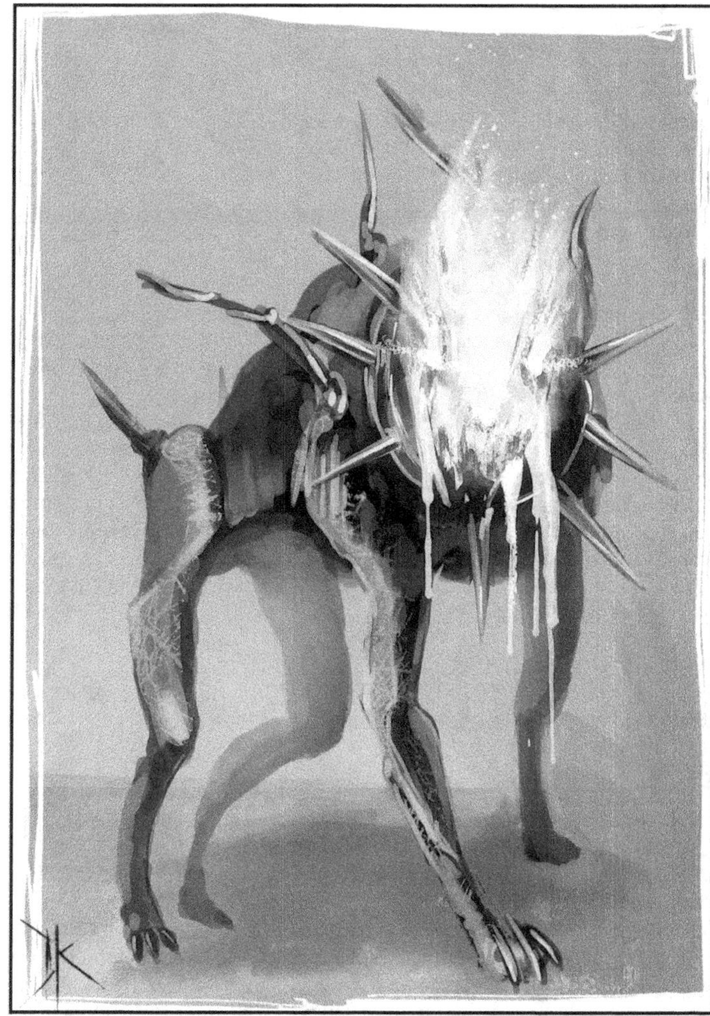

Head for the Hills

In the hills surrounding the great inland sea, there are many quaint villages, remnants of an elder empire that long ago fell into ruin, leaving behind a multitude of peaceful halfling freeholds. An old imperial road of bricks runs around the northern and western shores of the sea, connecting the villages via a network of smaller dirt roads with the old imperial capital, now a ruin save for a single guard tower, controlled by the **halfling sheriff Izbrand** and his merry men, and a large courtyard which serves as a marketplace for the surrounding villages. These market fairs are lively affairs that are well attended. The fairs start early in the morning, but at noon, the revelers and marketers and merchants all pack their goods and head back into the hills. Izbrand and his men retire into their guard tower (they're willing to put people up in the dungeon for a price – think of it as an odd bed and breakfast) and lock the doors securely. No guards are posted outside at night.

This is because of another feature of the ruined capital where stands the old church of St. Althea, halfling saint of home and hearth. The church has long since been forsaken, and now sits in the middle of a great cemetery of small, stone sarcophagi and a few larger crypts. At night, a **headless hound** stalks not only the cemetery, but also makes forays into the ruined streets and as far as the marketplace. It is controlled by the **necromancer Thrush**, who occupies the church cellar along with a band of halfling grave robbers and perhaps a zombie or two.

Hellcat

Hit Dice: 7
Armor Class: 5 [14]
Attacks: 1 bite (2d6) and 2 claws (1d4+1)
Saving Throw: 9
Special: Hit only by magical weapons, 20% magic resistance
Move: 12
Alignment: Chaos
Number Encountered: 1 or 1d4
Challenge Level/XP: 9/1,100

These creatures are demonic felines, often kept as pets by the denizens of the netherworlds. In some cases, they may find their way to the material planes, either by being summoned or by being sent there to serve as the ally (or tempter) of a Chaotic villain who has made a pact with the powers of darkness.

Hellcats cannot be seen in the light, and even in the darkness they are little more than a feline shape limned in strange shadow, the size of a leopard or other great cat. Like most cats of demonic persuasion or not, hellcats can be fickle in their allegiance; a hellcat may change its preferred "master," attaching itself to a particularly Chaotic individual in preference to its original one. Most hellcats encountered on the Material Planes are female; the tomcats are rare, larger, and less capable of traveling from one plane of existence to another.

Hellcats: HD 7; AC 5[14]; Atk 1 bite (2d6) and 2 claws (1d4+1); Move 12; Save 9; AL C; CL/XP 9/1100; Special: Hit only by magical weapons, 20% magic resistance.

Hellcat Valley

In a steamy, godforsaken jungle there is a deep basin called the Demon Land by the natives. The basin has sheer walls, 1d6 x 100 feet high, and the floor is covered in a thick growth of primordial trees and choking swamps. This basin is inhabited by dinosaurs and hunted by a large pride of **hellcats** (3 in 6 chance per day of encountering 1d6 of the monsters). The hellcats make their lairs in small caves, one to a customer. One lair holds a tomb in which is imprisoned a demon princess, **Sxamarya**, interred here along with her guard of hellcats (who went native) by Orcus for failure to pay a secret debt.

Hellhound

Hit Dice: 4–7
Armor Class: 4 [15]
Attacks: Bite (1d6)
Saving Throw: 13, 12, 11, or 9
Special: Breathe fire
Move: 12
Alignment: Chaos
Challenge Level/XP: 4 HD (5/240), 5 HD (6/400), 6 HD (7/600), 7 HD (8/800)

Hell hounds are fire-breathing dogs of the underworlds or lower planes. In addition to biting, they can breathe fire each round, inflicting 2 hp damage per hit die (10 ft range, saving throw for half damage).

Hell Hound (4HD): HD 4; AC 4[15]; Atk 1 bite (1d6); Move 12; Save 13; AL C; CL/XP 5/240; Special: Breathe fire (8hp).

Hell Hound (5HD): HD 5; AC 4[15]; Atk 1 bite (1d6); Move 12; Save 12; AL C; CL/XP 6/400; Special: Breathe fire (10hp).

Hell Hound (6HD): HD 6; AC 4[15]; Atk 1 bite (1d6); Move 12; Save 11; AL C; CL/XP 7/600; Special: Breathe fire (12hp).

Hell Hound (7HD): HD 7; AC 4[15]; Atk 1 bite (1d6); Move 12; Save 9; AL C; CL/XP 8/800; Special: Breathe fire (14hp).

Hounds on the Hunt

While exploring the deeper levels of a dungeon, the adventurers might come upon a second-category demon, mottled pink and green, with drooping yellow eyes, and his pack of **4 hell hounds**. The demon, Pashik, has been sent here to find the thief of a magic sword stolen from his mistress, Marilith. The sword is a *vorpal blade*, and highly value by the demoness. The hell hounds think the demon a fool, and their frustration at his dallying has made them especially keen to get in a fight.

Second-Category Demon: HD 9; AC 0[19]; Atk 2 claws (1d3), 1 bite (2d8); Move 9 (Fly 14); Save 6; AL C; CL/XP 11/1700; Special: Magic resistance 50%, demonic magical powers.

Hieroglyphicroc

Hit Dice: 7
Armor Class: 4 [15]
Attack: 1 bite (2d6)
Special: Swallow whole on natural 20, transform stomach contents into zombie
Move: 9
Saving Throw: 9
Alignment: Chaos
Number Encountered: 1d6
Challenge Level/XP: 8/800

Raised by ancient methods long forgotten or suppressed, hieroglyphicrocs resemble zombie crocodiles, but they are actually more akin to mummies than to zombies, at least in terms of the preservation process. Their eyes glow with a yellow light, and they have rudimentary intelligence - often they are defenders of tombs where mummies are found. These creatures are highly immune to being turned, and attack with a bite that can swallow whole on a natural 20. It takes three rounds to completely swallow a victim, but the victim will turn into a zombie within 1d4+1 rounds after being swallowed. Then the hieroglyphicroc will disgorge it. The bite inflicts 2d6 damage. The dead skin of these creatures is often painted with hieroglyphs.

— Author: Matt Finch

Hieroglyphicroc: HD 7; AC 4[15]; Atk 1 bite (2d6); Move 9; Save 9; AL C; CL/XP 8/800; Special: Swallow whole on natural 20, transform stomach contents into zombie.

Crocodile Fears

Along a slow-moving river one can see, in the distance along the left bank, the ruins of an ancient temple constructed of red sandstone. A canal diverts the river here toward the temple (and possibly beyond), and as one approaches the entrance to the canal they see increasing numbers of **crocodiles** along the banks sunning themselves, or dipping into the water to investigate a boat.

The canal leads to the temple, which, it turns out, is constructed on a manmade island of dark granite set in the middle of a pond ringed by papyrus and blue lotus that grow along the margins, giving the entire pond a heady fragrance. A dozen strange, white crocodiles sun themselves on the granite island, and as adventurers enter the pool, they slide into the water and make their way to the boats. If the adventurers speak the praises of the god of the temple (perhaps Sebek, or another god or goddess that fits better into your cosmology) and throw offerings of silver into the water, the **12 hieroglyphicrocs** escort them to the temple landing and into the outer temple where they may pray and make further sacrifices. If the adventurers make no offerings, the temple guardians attack them on the water, or if they attempt to breach the inner secrets of the temple, they attack them there.

Hippocampus

Hit Dice: 4
Armor Class: 5 [14]
Attack: 1 bite (1d4)
Special: None
Move: 24 (swimming only)
Saving Throw: 13
Alignment: Law
Number Encountered: 1d10
Challenge Level/XP: 4/120

The hippocampus is a mythical sea-horse, with the body, head, and forelegs of a horse, but with the rear part of the body tapering to a fish's tail. They are at least as intelligent as a normal land-horse. Some leaders might be extremely intelligent indeed.

Hippocampus: HD 4; AC 5[14]; Atk 1 bite (1d4); Move (Swim 24); Save 13; AL L; CL/XP 4/120; Special: None.

Daddy's Pets

A herd of rebellious **hippocampi** dwell here in a shallow sea cave – really more a natural amphitheater – in which grows a thick carpet of reddish kelp. The hippocampi feed on the kelp under the watchful eye of a gang of playful **mermaids**, who might be convinced to sell them for a kiss or a pretty bauble. Unfortunately, the mermaids are the adopted daughters of a **gold dragon**, who dwells nearby in an invisible castle. If father awakens and discovers any of his pets missing, he hunts their takers down relentlessly.

Adult Gold Dragon (12HD): HD 12 (48hp); AC 2[17]; Atk 2 claws (1d6), 1 bite (3d8); Move 12 (Fly 24); Save 3; AL L; CL/XP 15/2900; Special: fire or chlorine breath, magic-user spells.

Hippogriff

Hit Dice: 3+1
Armor Class: 5 [14]
Attacks: 2 claws (1d6), 1 bite (1d10)
Saving Throw: 14
Special: None
Move: 18/24 (flying)
Alignment: Neutrality
Number Encountered: 2d8
Challenge Level/XP: 4/120

The hippogriff is similar to a griffon, having the head, foreclaws, and wings of an eagle, but instead of the body of a lion, it has the body of a horse. The poem *Orlando Furioso* (written by the poet Dante in 1516) suggests that the hippogriff is the offspring of a griffon and a horse—but they are apparently an independent breed, for folkloric tradition holds that griffons frequently attack hippogriffs. Hippogriffs are not as hard to train as griffons—again, from *Orlando Furioso*: "Drawn by enchantment from his distant lair, The wizard thought but how to tame the foal; And, in a month, instructed him to bear Saddle and bit, and gallop to the goal; And execute on earth or in mid air, All shifts of manege, course and caracole…"

Hippogriff: HD 3+1; AC 5[14]; Atk 2 claws (1d6), 1 bite (1d10); Move 18 (Fly 24); Save 14; AL N; CL/XP 4/120; Special: None.

Whistleblower

In the chalky foothills of the mountains, where griffon dart among the clouds and snowy peaks, dwell their lesser kin, the hippogriffs. The hippogriffs dine on the lush foliage that grows among the cracks and crevices of the chalk hills, hunting young pegasi that wander away from their herds and all manner of terrestrial creatures. In one crevice, the skeletal body of a magic-user is cradled in the branches of a gnarled pine. In his robe (what remains of it), there is a golden whistle. When blown, the whistle attracts **1d6 hippogriffs**. Mind you – it does not grant the power to control them, only to summon them.

Hippopotamus

Hit Dice: 7
Armor Class: 6 [13]
Attack: 1 bite (2d6)
Special: None
Move: 6/12 (swimming)
Saving Throw: 9
Alignment: Neutrality
Number Encountered: 2d6
Challenge Level/XP: 7/600

Hippopotami are very aggressive and territorial. A herd may be led by a large bull with 8HD, a saving throw of 8, and damage of 3d6 (CL/XP 8/800).

Hippopotamus: HD 7; AC 6[13]; Atk 1 bite (2d6); Move 6 (Swim 12); Save 9; AL N; CL/XP 7/600; Special: None.

Watch Their Ears!

A muddy river flows through the jungle, bounding between soggy lowlands thick with reeds and barren promontories edged by fan palms and assassin vines. One wide bend in the river is the lair of a bloat of **20 hippos**. The hippos are territorial and aggressive (when their ears twitch, you know they're about to attack). They cluster about a granite landing that stands at the end point of an old imperial road of Sulamok, an ancient emperor of the jungles. One of the hippos is actually a cleverly disguised submersible piloted by Ollie Nematoad, a Halfling inventor who is studying the hippos.

Hobgoblin

Hit Dice: 1+1
Armor Class: 5 [14]
Attacks: Weapon (1d8)
Saving Throw: 17
Special: None
Move: 9
Alignment: Chaos
Number Encountered: 2d6 or 20d10
Challenge Level/XP: 1/15

Hobgoblins are simply large goblins, possibly a separate breed living apart from their smaller cousins, or perhaps not, as the Referee decides. As a matter of the campaign's flavoring, the Referee might choose to make hobgoblins the "fey" goblins of Irish legend, while regular goblins are the more Tolkien-style underground-dwellers.

Hobgoblin: HD 1+1; AC 5[14]; Atk 1 weapon (1d8); Move 9; Save 17; AL C; CL/XP 1/15; Special: None.

In the Lair of the Hobgoblin Lord

Beneath the upper regions of a dungeon there is a great fortress of hobgoblins. The fortress appears as a pair of thick, iron doors flanked by bas-reliefs of gorgons that belch steam. The gate is unguarded, and opens onto a stone bridge that spans a boiling moat (it does not run the perimeter of the fortress – rather, it is a naturally heated subterranean river 50 feet wide in a long cavern with a 40-foot-high ceiling). A 20-foot-wide span of the bridge is composed of iron, and can be raised and lowered by **8 hobgoblins** that guard the gatehouse beyond – a tall expanse of granite marred only by a single, iron door (always locked) and eight arrow slits located above it. Beyond this door lies the stronghold of the hobgoblin king Wazzak, a series of tunnels and chambers cut from the earth. They bear the typically Spartan decoration of the hobgoblins, and are full of choke points, covered pits, and rooms with arrow slits and murder holes.

The chambers of the fortress include several feast halls, training halls, armories, foundries, forges, smithies, pantries and butteries. The hobgoblins brew a potent black beer and cultivate fungus for their bread. They also raise plump giant rats, grubs and keep a coterie of **4 carnivorous apes** who have free roam of the place. Wazzak has a bodyguard of **10 rare hybrid hobgoblins** with the paralyzing touch of a ghoul and the regenerative powers of a troll. Besides them, there are 80 warriors and about 120 females and young.

Carnivorous Ape: HD 4; AC 6[13]; Atk 2 hands (1d3), 1 bite (1d6); Move 12; Save 13; AL N; CL/XP 4/120; Special: Hug and rend.

Hobgoblin (hybrid): HD 2+1; AC 5[14]; Atk 1 weapon (1d8); Move 9; Save 16; AL C; CL/XP 4/120; Special: Regenerate 2hp/round, paralyzing touch (save or paralyzed for 2d4 rounds).

Homonculus

Hit Dice: 2
Armor Class: 6[13]
Attack: 1 bite (1d3 + sleep)
Special: Sleep-inducing bite
Move: 6/20 (flying)
Saving Throw: 16
Alignment: Neutrality
Number Encountered: 1
Challenge Level/XP: 3/60

A homunculus is a living, man-like creature created by a powerful magic-user as a servant. The precise abilities of a homunculus depend upon the spells and procedures used in its creation (the details of creating a homunculus are left to the Referee), although virtually all are created with wings of some kind. The most common homunculus has a sleep-inducing bite (saving throw), but others might be created with a poison bite (CL 4/120XP), or might have unusual powers of perception instead (such as the ability to detect magic, evil, spells, etc).

Homunculus: HD 2; AC 6[13]; Atk 1 bite (1d3 + sleep); Move 6 (Fly 20); Save 16; AL N; CL/XP 3/60; Special: Sleep-inducing bite.

Like Looking in a Tiny Mirror

Sigil runes carved deep into the mortar follow a flight of stairs that descends steeply into a deep underground chamber that smells of burning copper. Glyphs, spell notes and even full spells are engraved into the semi-soft walls of the room (anyone copying one of the spells has a 20% chance of making a mistake because of the crumbling letters). A copper vat sits into the stone floor in one corner. The vat is three feet wide and three feet deep. From its wide mouth flows a steady stream of frothy greenish fluid that smells of baked potatoes. The floor is awash in the magical fluid to a depth of two feet. Cracks in the wall and floor allow the mysterious liquid to drain slowly out of the chamber. Four animated suits of plate mail holding longswords guard the room. Any blood spilled during the ensuing battle (any hit from a sword that does 5 or more points of damage) hits the water and begins growing a **homunculus**. It takes the tiny creature 1d4 rounds to fully form, at which time it springs up, a perfect little duplicate of the person who bled, and swims for safety.

Animated Armor: HD 4; AC 5[14]; Atk 1 (1d8); Move 6; Save 16; AL N; CL/XP 4/120; Special: None.

Horses

	RIDING	WAR
Hit Dice:	2	3
Armor Class:	7 [12]	7 [12]
Attack:	1 bite (1d2)	1 bite (1d2), 2 hooves (1d3)
Special:	None	None
Move:	18	18
Saving Throw:	16	14
Alignment:	Neutrality	Neutrality
Number Encountered:	varies	varies
Challenge Level/XP:	2/30	3/60

Riding Horse: HD 2; AC 7[12]; Atk 1 bite (1d2); Move 18; Save 16; AL N; CL/XP 2/30; Special: None.

War Horse: HD 3; AC 7[12]; Atk 1 bite (1d2), 2 hooves (1d3); Move 18; Save 14; AL N; CL/XP 3/60; Special: None.

The Lady of the Meadow

On a high mountain plateau thick with green grass and yellow daffodils, there is a large herd of fine, **white horses** owned by a nymph and tended by a band of elves. The elves are crack archers, armed with longbow and longswords, and wearing ring mail. They dwell in sod houses, and would balk at their servitude were they not all deeply in love with the Lady of the Meadow, and all pledged, as true knights, to her defense and succor. The Lady dwells in a magnificent manse hidden in the mountains, but comes down to the meadow at twilight on warm, summer evenings to pet her horses and bathe in a cool pool on the meadow. The elves allow none to approach the meadow at these times.

Hound of Chronos

Hit Dice: 3
Armor Class: 7 [12]
Attack: 2 claws (1d4), Bite (1d6)
Special: Temporal jump, temporal heal
Move: 18
Saving Throw: 14
Alignment: Neutrality
Number Encountered: 2d4
Challenge Level/XP: 5/240

Hounds of Chronos, also known as Temporal Dogs, are canine creatures from the Plane of Time (or a time-related other dimension). They possess the innate ability to manipulate time in a limited manner. Temporal Dogs hunt in packs that usually consist of 2 to 8 hounds. A Hound of Chronos will always know where, temporally, the other members of his pack are. Hounds of Chronos possess the ability to move forward in time. Twice per day, a Hound of Chronos may "jump" forward in time. This allows the hound to disappear from the present and reappear 1d4 rounds later. The Hounds use this ability in conjunction with surprise to get the drop on their prey. When they re-materialise 1 to 4 rounds into the future, their prey has a chance of being surprised (60%).

Once per day, a Hound of Chronos may shift backward in time to when it was healthier, returning "immediately" with full hit points.

— *Author: Skathros*

Hounds of Chronos: HD 3; AC 7[12]; Atk 2 claws (1d4), Bite (1d6); Move 18; Save 14; AL N; CL/XP 5/240; Special: Temporal jump, Temporal heal.

The Hour of the Hound

Somewhere in the depths of a dungeon, the adventurers come across the inner workings of a complex water clock. The mechanisms lie beneath the laboratory of the archmage Raobin, who now dwells in seclusion on the Plane of Time, elevated to that plane by its strange masters in part because of his wondrous clock, which keeps immaculate time. Raobin used it to track the heavens (which he could not observe, given his seclusion underground), which are depicted above his laboratory on 12 golden dials, each 20 feet in diameter and cut with hundreds of small holes, through which shines a permanent light effect from above when important heavenly concordances are reached.

Within the inner workings, which connect to the laboratory above by a secret (and trapped) door in the ceiling, a spherical polyhedroid (one of the creatures that maintain the cosmic machinery) arrived the day before to make adjustments to the clock and left behind a rather important key to the cosmos. Should adventurers find and take this key (which is made of adamantine, but otherwise quite plain, and was left hanging on a hook) they begin to be tracked in 1d6 days by a pack of **7 hounds of chronos**, who mean to retrieve the key.

HUMANS

Humans are such a versatile race that any number of "monsters" and NPCs can be made from them. Berserker warriors, tribesmen, cavemen, princesses, evil high priests, captains of the guard, foot-soldiers, and tavern-keepers are all different human "monsters."
Don't try to build your non-player characters according to the rules for player characters. Just make up their stats and abilities as you see fit.

Human, Normal

Hit Dice: 1d6 hit points
Armor Class: 9 [10]
Attacks: Weapon (1d6)
Saving Throw: 18
Special: None
Move: 12
Alignment: Any
Number Encountered: Varies
Challenge Level/XP: B/10

Normal humans are untrained peasants or townsfolk.

Normal Human: HD 1d6hp; AC 9[10]; Atk 1 weapon (1d6); Move 12; Save 18; AL Any; CL/XP B/10; Special: None.

Human, Bandits

Hit Dice: 1
Armor Class: 7 [12]
Attacks: Weapon (1d8)
Saving Throw: 17
Special: None
Move: 12
Alignment: Chaos
Number Encountered: 1d8+1 or 20d10
Challenge Level/XP: 1/15

Bandits are roving groups of thieves, sometimes organized into small armies led by more powerful bandit chiefs and captains with higher hit dice.

Bandit: HD 1; AC 7[12]; Atk 1 weapon (1d8); Move 12; Save 17; AL C; CL/XP 1/15; Special: None.

Arrogant and Armed

An abandoned cliff monastery dedicated to the goddess of thieves now serves as the roost of a gang of **40 bandits** led by the charismatic Captain Clive (Fighter 7). They are lusty villains, but not bent on killing, just robbery, and the gang just might be in need of a healer or magician to bolster their ranks. Clive is insulting and arrogant, and he loses no opportunity in tweaking the nose of any warrior in the band, especially a fellow fighter. Weaponry and armor among the rank and file is as follows:

30%: Leather armor, shield, short bow and shortsword
25%: Ringmail, shield, spear and dagger
20%: Ringmail, longsword and 3 javelins
15%: Leather armor, shield, sling and short sword
10%: Chainmail, two-handed sword

Captain Clive wears plate mail and is armed with a morningstar and poisoned dagger.

Human, Berserkers

Hit Dice: 1
Armor Class: 7 [12]
Attacks: Weapon (1d8)
Saving Throw: 17
Special: Berserking
Move: 12
Alignment: Neutrality or Chaos
Number Encountered: 1d6+1 or 10d10
Challenge Level/XP: 2/30

Berserkers are normal humans, but they fight with astounding ferocity. A bonus of +2 is added to their attack rolls. They do not wear armor heavier than leather armor.

Berserker: HD 1; AC 7[12]; Atk 1 weapon (1d8); Move 12; Save 17; AL N or C; CL/XP 2/30; Special: +2 to hit in berserk state.

Her Maddening Song

A longship has run aground on a white beach studded with strange, carved pillars. The boat has a gaping hole in one side, and will surely sink when high tide arrives (in one hour + 1d20 minutes). One can see **30 men** on the boat, large fellows with chests bare save for their long, mucky beards. Many wear fanciful helmets bedecked by bronze boars and leather horns, and one can see they are armed with shields and spears. Instead of escaping their fate, though, the men just sit on the rowing benches, staring straight ahead, gape-mouthed, at a siren perched on the bow of the boat. The siren's song has the men under a spell; she's just waiting for high tide to finish the job that she might pluck out their livers and any treasure that is revealed at the next low tide. Saving the men is a heroic act, no doubt deserving of thanks. Unfortunately, these men are berserkers, and once freed from the spell, there is a very good chance they go on a berserk killing spree. C'est la vie.

Human, Sergeant-at-Arms

Hit Dice: 3
Armor Class: 5 [14]
Attacks: Weapon (1d8)
Saving Throw: 14
Special: None
Move: 12
Alignment: Any
Number Encountered: Varies
Challenge Level/XP: 3/60

Human sergeants are normally found in command of 1d6+5 human soldiers. These are the leaders of city guard units and other small military groups.

Human Sergeant-at-Arms: HD 3; AC 5[14]; Atk 1 weapon (1d8); Move 12; Save 14; AL Any; CL/XP 3/60; Special: None.

Finding Farka

Okay – a lair for a sergeant-at-arms. You'll have to work with me on this one …

When it comes to pass that the adventurers, visiting a town or city, are in need of accessing something important — perhaps a comrade thrown into a drunk tank or weapons that were locked up to keep them from maiming the local populace — let it be known to them that the key is in the possession of the town's **sergeant-at-arms**, **Breen Farka**, a renowned cad. Breen can be found at the Pickled Herring, a local inn known for attracting "the wrong sort."

Finding Farka is a trick. The inn has two common rooms — one serving ale and platters of pickled herring and salted snails to a boisterous crowd of rowdies, the other serving spiced wine and a selection of peppery cheeses and crunchy black bread (heaps of goat butter) in pewter flagons to a more refined crowd of lesser nobles, rakes with fabulous mustachios and mysterious women in velvets and veils. On the second and third floors of the inn there are large common rooms for the poverty ridden (i.e. adventurers) and 20 private rooms per floor for the well-to-do. The fourth floor holds a gambling parlor and brothel, as well as three large suites for noble guests. Somewhere in this maze of rooms is Breen Farka.

Knocking on doors at night is dangerous work, for who knows what one might find in a room (you might use a nighttime encounter chart for settlements; maybe you'll find a cantankerous magic-user trying to sleep one off, a gang of cut-throats planning mischief, or a vampire dining out). Farka is currently on the third floor, in the room reserved for the tavern wenches, tying one on with the wife of Baron Blazengaff, who sits upstairs blissfully unaware, playing trionfi and sipping brandy served by women of modest mores. Farka has **3 guardsmen** keeping watch, and he's quite adept at crawling out windows and finding secret doors. He has several women he is intent on entertaining this night, so catching him in the act will not be easy.

Human guardsmen: HD 1; AC 7[12]; Atk 1 weapon (1d8); Move 12; Save 17; AL N; CL/XP 1/15; Special: None.

Human, Soldier

Hit Dice: 1
Armor Class: 7 [12]
Attacks: Weapon (1d8)
Saving Throw: 17
Special: None
Move: 12
Alignment: Any
Number Encountered: Varies
Challenge Level/XP: 1/15

Human soldiers serve as city guardsmen, mercenaries, and men-at-arms. They are generally armed with leather armor and a mace, sword, or spear.

Human Soldier: HD 1; AC 7[12]; Atk 1 weapon (1d8); Move 12; Save 17; AL Any; CL/XP 1/15; Special: None.

Well Protected

There is a fortress located on a river that flows through a wood that stands as the borderland between civilization and chaos. The fortress is built on a rocky plateau and has tall walls, seven towers, a great gatehouse and a large keep with four towers. The fortress houses **60 men-at-arms** clad in blue tunics over chainmail armor, and mostly armed with spears and light crossbows. The fortress also houses merchants, a cleric and two acolytes (one an agent of Chaos), a jeweler and, at any given time, 1d4 adventurers. The fortress is commanded by a 9th-level fighter, who is assisted by 6 sergeants.

Hydra

Hit Dice: 5-12 (equal to the number of heads)
Armor Class: 5 [14]
Attacks: 5-12 bites (1d6)
Saving Throw: 12, 11, 9, 8, 6, 5, 4, or 3
Special: None
Move: 9
Alignment: Neutrality
Number Encountered: 1 or (rarely) 2
Challenge Level/XP: 5 HD (7/600), 6 HD (8/800),
7 HD (9/1,100), 8 HD (10/1,400), 9 HD (11/1,700),
10 HD (12/2,000), 11 HD (13/2,300), 12 HD (14/2,600)

Hydrae are great lizard-like or snake-like creatures with multiple heads. Each head has one hit die of its own, and when an individual head takes that much damage, that head dies. The body has as many hit dice as the total of the heads, so it is a matter of good strategy for adventurers to focus either on killing heads (when all the heads are dead the body dies) or killing the creature by attacking the body (in which case the heads die, too). Hydrae that breathe fire or regenerate their heads are also known to exist.

Hydra (5 headed): HD 5; AC 5[14]; Atk 5 heads (1d6); Move 9; Save 12; AL N; CL/XP 7/600; Special: None.

Hydra (6 headed): HD 6; AC 5[14]; Atk 6 heads (1d6); Move 9; Save 11; AL N; CL/XP 8/800; Special: None.

Hydra (7 headed): HD 7; AC 5[14]; Atk 7 heads (1d6); Move 9; Save 9; AL N; CL/XP 9/1100; Special: None.

Hydra (8 headed): HD 8; AC 5[14]; Atk 8 heads (1d6); Move 9; Save 8; AL N; CL/XP 10/1400; Special: None.

Hydra (9 headed): HD 9; AC 5[14]; Atk 9 heads (1d6); Move 9; Save 6; AL N; CL/XP 11/1700; Special: None.

Hydra (10 headed): HD 10; AC 5[14]; Atk 10 heads (1d6); Move 9; Save 5; AL N; CL/XP 12/2000; Special: None.

Hydra (11 headed): HD 11; AC 5[14]; Atk 11 heads (1d6); Move 9; Save 4; AL N; CL/XP 13/2300; Special: None.

Hydra (12 headed): HD 12; AC 5[14]; Atk 12 heads (1d6); Move 9; Save 3; AL N; CL/XP 14/2600; Special: None.

Evil to the Core

A river flowing through a rooky wood widens at one point, becoming anywhere from 3 to 6 feet deep. Several trees with golden-brown bark, silver-green leaves and coppery red apples hanging from the boughs rise from the river. These apples hide messages to the gods, which are revealed in the patterns their seeds make when they are cast on a white hot rock. The apple trees are protected by a single **hydra** with twelve heads.

Hyena

Hit Dice: 1
Armor Class: 7 [12]
Attack: 1 bite (1d3)
Special: None
Move: 16
Saving Throw: 17
Alignment: Neutrality
Number Encountered: 1d6+4
Challenge Level/XP: 1/15

Hyenas are pack-hunters and scavengers, known for the eerie laughing sound they make. They are not normally much of a threat, although they may attack weak-looking foes if they have sufficient numbers.

Hyena: HD 1; AC 7[12]; Atk 1 bite (1d3); Move 16; Save 17; AL N; CL/XP 1/15; Special: None.

Hungry, Hungry Hyenas

The thieves' guild in Bargarsport has its headquarters in an ancient underground manor once owned by a furrier who dabbled in the dark arts. The place is grandiose and well-appointed, though each level looks as though it hasn't been occupied for many, many years. The place is rife with secret doors and simple traps. The cellar hides a vault (made of solid steel and protected by three traps – a lethal poison on a needle, an explosive that fills the room with acidic fumes and a magical trap that paralyzes a would-be thief until the curse is removed by a cleric or magic-user of at least 6th level). Before one can get to the vault, though, they must make it by **6 hyenas**, hungry and nearly feral. The hyenas respond only the voice of the guildmaster.

Hyena, Giant

Hit Dice: 5
Armor Class: 6 [13]
Attack: 1 bite (2d6)
Special: None
Move: 18
Saving Throw: 12
Alignment: Neutrality
Number Encountered: 1d6+1
Challenge Level/XP: 5/240

Giant hyenas stand 8ft tall at the shoulder, and are more aggressive than their normal cousins. They might serve as mounts for tribes of gnolls in prehistoric or sword & sorcery campaigns.

Giant Hyena: HD 5; AC 6[13]; Atk 1 bite (2d6); Move 18; Save 12; AL N; CL/XP 5/240; Special: None.

Ride of the Dog Men

As one makes his way across the muggy savannah, he might meet a religious procession moving perpendicularly to his path. The procession is composed of an ancient **gnoll shaman** and his attendants, several lesser gnoll shamans, bodyguards (**12 gnolls** with maximum hit points who fight as bugbears) and about **20 normal gnolls**. The shaman is drawn on a sledge pulled by the normal gnolls, who are seeking cures and omens and paying for it with their labor. The lesser shamans and bodyguards are well armed and mounted on **giant hyenas**, and **2 additional giant hyenas** (albinos with maximum hit points) standing beside him on the sledge.

Gnoll: HD 2; AC 5[14]; Atk 1 bite (2d4) or weapon (1d10); Move 9; Save 16; AL C; CL/XP 2/30; Special: None.

Gnoll Bodyguard: HD 3+1; AC 5[14]; Atk 1 bite (2d4) or weapon (1d10); Move 9; Save 14; AL C; CL/XP 3/60; Special: None.

Gnoll Shaman (lesser): HD 2; AC 5[14]; Atk 1 bite (2d4) or weapon (1d10); Move 9; Save 16; AL C; CL/XP 3/60; Special: Spells.

Gnoll Shaman: HD 4; AC 5[14]; Atk 1 bite (2d4) or weapon (1d10); Move 9; Save 13; AL C; CL/XP 6/400; Special: Spells.

Igniguana

Hit Dice: 4
Armor Class: 4 [15]
Attack: 1 bite (1d6)
Special: Breathe fire, tunnel
Move: 6/12 (tunneling)
Saving Throw: 13
Alignment: Neutrality
Number Encountered: 1d4
Challenge Level/XP: 5/240

Igniguanas are large lizards about six feet long, with reddish hide and glowing eyes. They may be of some sort of elemental origin, coupling attributes of fire and earth, for they crawl directly through solid rock without digging, leaving no tunnel behind to mark their passage. They breathe small but intense blasts of fire, in a cone extending 20ft to a width of 20ft. Anyone within the cone takes 2d6 hit points of damage (save for half).

— Author: Matt Finch

Igniguana: HD 4; AC 4 [15]; Atk 1 bite (1d6); Move 6; Save 13; AL N; CL/XP 5/240; Special: Breathe fire, tunnel

Unwelcome Warmth

While traversing a frozen plain in the northern lands, adventurers might come across a strange plateau illuminated by a blue glow. Atop the plateau, one sees multiple holes in the ground from which shoot blue fire. These holes connect to an underground maze of tunnels, some quite narrow, filled with flaming gas. Within burrows dug into these tunnels live a multitude of **igniguanas**. The igniguanas are aware that the fire holes attract prey, and when one does spend more than a few minutes warming themselves, they suffer an attack by 1d4+1 of the beasts.

Imp

Hit Dice: 2
Armor Class: 2 [17]
Attack: 1 sting (1d4 + poison)
Special: Poison tail, polymorph, regenerate, immune to fire, hit only by magic weapons.
Move: 6/16 (flying)
Saving Throw: 16
Alignment: Chaos
Number Encountered: 1
Challenge Level/XP: 6/400

Imps are demonic creatures sent or summoned into the material plane. They are about a foot tall, and have small but functional wings. An imp can polymorph itself into one or two animal forms: a crow, goat, rat, or dog being common. Imps regenerate 1 hit point per round, and can be hit only by silver or magical weapons (or by animals with 5+ hit dice). In some cases, they may be forced to serve as a familiar to a powerful and evil magic user.

Imp: HD 2; AC 2[17]; Atk 1 sting (1d4 + poison); Move 6 (Fly 16); Save 16; AL C; CL/XP 6/400; Special: Poison tail, polymorph, regenerate, immune to fire, hit only by magic weapons.

Table Games

In a random chamber of some grand dungeon one might find **3 imps**. The imps are playing cards, using a young magic-user on hands and knees as their card table. The magic-user has a blank expression on his face, and is completely under the control of the imps. He borrowed a magic tome from his master and conjured forth the imps, but was unable to control them. A cabinet nearby, carved from walnut and highly polished, holds a ready portal to Hell – one might discern the smell of brimstone coming from the cabinet as they approach it.

Inaed

Hit Dice: 3
Armor Class: 0 [19]
Attack: None
Special: Invisible, spells, immune to all weapons or to normal weapons (depending on state)
Move: 0/18 (flying)
Saving Throw: 14
Alignment: Neutrality
Number Encountered: 1
Challenge Level/XP: 7/600

Inaed are invisible, intangible spirits that inhabit books, scrolls and any other object upon which words are written. They possess no ability to attack directly; however, they can cast each of the following spells twice daily: *sleep, phantasmal force,* and *suggestion.* Inaed inhabiting a book or other object are entirely impervious to physical attacks, for an attack directed at the Inaed only damages the "home." If its host book is completely destroyed, the Inaed will flee in search of a new book to haunt - including spell books. Though they are not undead, Inaed may be cast out of the books they haunt with a successful turning attempt. Treat Inaed as though they were Ghouls for this purpose. Books that have been freed of any Inaed, and books that have been blessed by a Cleric of 9th level or higher, are immune to infestation. "Turned" or otherwise unbound Inaed immediately seek out the nearest book to inhabit. Entering a book takes 2d4 turns, and it is during this time that Inaed are most vulnerable. The creatures are visible during this time -- appearing as ghostly apparitions of adolescent human females -- and can be physically damaged, although only by magical weapons.

— Author: Andrew Trent

Inaed: HD 3; AC 0[19]; Atk none; Move 0 (Fly 18); Save 14; AL N; CL/XP 7/600; Special: Invisible, spells, immune to all weapons or to normal weapons (depending on state).

Love Letter

In the attic of the Manse of the Topaz Magistrate, a wizard of ill repute, there is a small door (about 4 feet high and 2 feet wide) that is *wizard locked.* Behind it, there is an oddly shaped hallway (a bit trapezoidal, the floor slightly slanted to the right and down) that runs about 30 feet and ends in a wall. There are no exits. At the end of the hall there hangs a parchment scroll depicting, in a flowing, colorful style, a woman of exquisite loveliness. There are words on the scroll in an unknown script and language that, if translated with magic, read "Perfect Cycle." The meaning of these words is anyone's guess. On the floor before the poster there is a single chair, padded and upholstered in crushed red velvet, now worn and dusty. The Topaz Magistrate used to come here to gaze on the poster often, but his journeys have left the manse and the chair vacant now for over eight years. His attraction to the place was predicated on the occupant of the scroll, an **inaed** who was once his lady love Argentia, a noble woman turned into an inaed by a jealous rival. She knows many secrets of the Topaz Magistrate, and might divulge them to those who promise to carry her scroll in search of her former lover.

Inner Child

Hit Dice: 3
Armor Class: 3 [16]
Attack: psychic blast (2d6)
Special: ESP, charm person, wall of force
Move: 8
Saving Throw: 14
Alignment: Chaos
Number Encountered: 1
Challenge Level/XP: 5/240

A parasitic organism that lies dormant inside a human host, an inner child can dimensionally shift itself outside of the host's body and return once per day. While outside it can levitate, but remains connected by a 6ft long psychic cord and cannot move further from the host than this. It resembles a smaller version of the host creature, but with a large head, feral features, and an almost vestigial body. The host creature is usually aware that it has an inner child, but (for obvious reasons) usually keeps it a dark secret.

An inner child has strong psionic abilities. It can read minds at will (per the ESP spell), "cast" charm person twice per day, cause a psychic blast at will (2d6 points of damage to all within a cone 60ft long and 60ft wide at the end, saving throw for half damage), and create a wall of mental force once per day (3ft thick, 50ft long and 50ft tall). If the host creature is killed, the inner child dies within 1d6 turns.

— Author: Chad Thorson

Inner Child: HD 3; AC 3[16]; Atk psychic blast (2d6); Move 8; Save 14; AL C; CL/XP: 5/240; Special: ESP and psychic blast at will, charm person (2/day), and wall of mental force (1/day).

Inner Madness

On a run-down street crowded by buildings of a suspicious and vaguely sinister nature, there is one building in particular that even the thugs and rakes avoid. Once a hospice for the demoniacally touched (i.e. the insane), the place was long ago abandoned by the clerics and their lay brethren, all because of a man possessed of an **inner child**. The clerics were minor in ability, and unprepared for the inner child, and so had to quit the place. Several of the inmates were left behind to starve, and now haunt the place as **poltergeists**. Two of the lay brethren were also left behind, and their eventual hunger drove them into **ghoul-hood**. They are now the keepers of the man with the inner child, who still resides in the hospice cellar, awaiting new victims.

Ghoul: HD 2; AC 6[13]; Atk 2 claws (1d3), 1 bite (1d4); Move 9; Save 16; AL C; CL/XP 3/60; Special: Immunities, paralyzing touch.

Invisible Stalker

Hit Dice: 8
Armor Class: 3 [16]
Attacks: "Bite" (4d4)
Saving Throw: 8
Special: Invisible
Move: 12 (fly)
Alignment: Neutrality
Number Encountered: 1
Challenge Level/XP: 9/1,100

Invisible stalkers are generally found only as a result of the spell *Invisible Stalker*. They are invisible flying beings created to follow a single command made by the caster.

Invisible Stalker: HD 8; AC 3[16]; Atk 1 "bite" (4d4); Move 0 (Fly 12); Save 8; AL N; CL/XP 9/1100; Special: Invisible.

Market Stalker

While the adventurers are investigating a local market thronged with hawkish shoppers and lively, colorful merchants selling everything from spicy colognes to camel-hair rugs to walking sticks carved from walrus bone, they witness an extraordinary event. A man walking through the market, hunched, copper-skinned, with aquiline nose and red-rimmed, crazy eyes, suddenly finds himself under attack by an unseen enemy – an **invisible stalker**. The man is a 10th-level magic-user, but his unstable mind has rendered him with only a few prepared spells, and his poor health has left him with just a smattering of hit points. The invisible stalker has been charged with killing the man, that his body and soul may be sucked into the Void wherein dwell powers with which he made foolish bargains. If saved, he introduces himself as Alhazred and reward his saviors with tales of a Cave of Mystery wherein is hidden a very special tome of magic.

Iounifier

Hit Dice: 3
Armor Class: 0 [19]
Attack: None - by projection only
Special: Improved saving throw, immune to electricity, projection beam
Move: 0/25 (fly)
Saving Throw: 5
Alignment: Neutrality
Number Encountered: 1
Challenge Level/XP: varies – see below

The IOUNifier is a small, intricate tangle of wires and filaments with infinitesimal motes of light dancing unpredictably within; they are no more than one inch in diameter. Their small size, coupled with the fact that they move very quickly, makes them difficult to hit with weapons. An IOUNifier projects a beam of bluish light; if any person is caught within the light, the shadow projected by the beam is a solid, material shape that manifests within one round. Once a person is caught within the light beam (requiring a successful to-hit roll by the IOUNifier), the IOUNifier can hold the person in the beam without further effort unless a wall or other very significant obstacle completely obstructs the beam. The projected "shadow" of the target is shaped exactly like the person being projected - it is constructed of wires that look like blood vessels running through and around whirring clockwork internal organs, and with a face-mask of bronze that resembles the face of the target in perfect detail. The shadow wears armor and carries equipment identical to the target's, but these do not duplicate any magical effects of the originals. The shadow has the same number of hit points as the living creature from which it is projected, and regenerates 3hp per round until it is killed. It will attack its original relentlessly until it is killed, whereupon it simply disappears. If the victim is killed by its projection, the projection will instantly fall upon the corpse, envelope it in its wires and filaments, and compress itself and the corpse into an IOUN stone. The IOUN stone will respond to the first person who picks it up, orbiting around that person's head, and granting a bonus to an attribute score for as long as it continues to circle. The attribute affected depends upon the person who is compacted into the stone; if that person was a cleric, the IOUN stone adds +1 to wisdom; if the victim was a magic-user, the stone adds +1 to intelligence; otherwise, the stone adds +1 to strength. These IOUN stones are not permanent, lasting only 1d4+1 days; some other, lost, procedure seems to be needed to make the stones last longer than this. The IOUNifier can only maintain two projections at any given time, and cannot make a second projection of the same person more than once per day. Note: attempts to use IOUNifiers for personal gain, especially by nefarious means, are quite dangerous - whatever programming drives the IOUNifier seems driven to cause ironic and dangerous consequences to those who try to manipulate them. The challenge level of an IOUNifier varies with its targets, and thus can't be calculated ahead of time. The XP value of an IOUNifier should be approximately the same as a monster with the same hit dice as the party has levels.

— Author: Matt Finch

IOUNifier: HD 3; AC 0[19]; Atk none - by projection only; Move 0 (Fly 25); Save 5; AL N; CL/XP varies; Special: Improved saving throw, immune to electricity, projection beam.

Tower of the Frog God

In a bleak, northern land stands a five-sided tower, long abandoned. The tower is composed of five levels, three above ground, and two below. The lowest level holds a shrine to Tsathogga that has been thoroughly defiled, probably by clerics of Law. The middle levels are unremarkable and empty – the tower has been plundered many times, despite its isolated location. The top level, however, is neither empty nor unoccupied.

The top level, like the others, measures about 25 feet long on each side. It contains several pieces of furniture, to whit a bed, two benches, several bookshelves, a table, three wooden chairs and a more comfortable padded chair, all of excellent workmanship. The bed is clad in silk sheets and a woven covering depicting a gang of imps making sport of a nymph, the chair clad in the hide of some reptile, and the bookshelves containing a number of antique volumes (most in poor condition) of a sorcerous nature, as well as several rolls of parchment (of an indeterminate manufacture) containing gruesome paintings depicting the Toad God. The room is decorated with a number of totem poles depicting not only Tsathogga, but also smilodons, mammoths, leopard seals and primitive oxen.

This room is now occupied by an **iounifier**, which apparently was drawn into the room when its former owner opened a rather crude portal that deposited him elsewhere in the cosmos. The iounifier has dwelled here for centuries, hoping beyond hope that the doorway to its own home world would re-open. It is not inherently violent, and might attempt communication with adventurers in the hopes that they can render aid.

Jack-in-the-Box

Hit Dice: 2
Armor Class: 5 [14]
Attack: 1 dagger or other small bladed weapon (1d4)
Special: Surprise
Move: 6
Saving Throw: 16
Alignment: Chaos
Number Encountered: 1
Challenge Level/XP: 2/30

At first glance, this critter appears as a brightly decorated box with a rotating handle at its side. With surprising quickness, a jester-like creature (mounted on a spring, of course!) springs from the box attacking and maiming. If concealed within its "box", a Jack-in-the-Box has a 50% chance of surprising its foes. This chance increases to 70% if the Jack-in-the-Box is released from the box via the rotating handle. When enclosed within its box, the Jack-in-the-Box AC becomes 3[16].

A Jack-in-the-Box may only move by hopping, carrying its cubic abode with him.

— Author: Skathros

Jack-in-the-Box: HD 2; AC 5[14]; Atk Dagger or other small bladed weapon (1d4); Move 6; Save 16; AL C; CL/XP 2/30; Special: Surprise.

Welcome Not Toy Man

While traveling roads on the outskirts of a well-known empire, one might come across the Toy Man. The Toy Man, as he is called in these parts, is a ragged peddler who guides a donkey-pulled cart filled with all manner of toys – mostly rag dolls and toys carved from wood. The toys are high quality, and the man appears to be quite pleasant, but he is quite insistent when it comes to selling. If his pleas fall on deaf ears, he pulls a sort of puzzle box out of his cart and presents it to the youngest member of the party (he often mistakes halflings for children) as a gift, that his skill might be remembered when next they desire to procure an amusement. The puzzle box baffles the wisest of adventurers, and even a knock or open spell does not open it. This is because it is a monster, a **jack-in-the-box**, who waits for its owner to settle down to a good night's sleep before creeping out to kill him or her. If tossed by the wayside, it follows the adventurer until it has had the Toy Man's revenge, and then tries to make its way back to the old peddler.

Jackal

Hit Dice: 1d4 hit points
Armor Class: 7 [12]
Attack: 1 bite (1d2)
Special: None
Move: 14
Saving Throw: 18
Alignment: Neutrality
Number Encountered: 2d6+2
Challenge Level/XP: A/15

Small, dog-like scavengers, jackals present no significant threat to a well-armed party of humans.

Jackal: HD 1d4 hp; AC 7[12]; Atk 1 bite (1d2); Move 14; Save 18; AL N; CL/XP A/15; Special: None.

The Minstrel's Minions

An oasis of lush grass, multiple watering holes, and hundreds of date palms serves as the lair and hunting ground of a pack of **8 to 12 golden jackals**. The monsters are quite bold, but they are also cunning. They inadvertently guard a tent of blue canvas that was abandoned here by a wandering minstrel laboring under a curse. The whereabouts of the minstrel are anybody's guess, but the tent now holds three days of iron rations (one, in a wrapping of reddish-brown paper, has been poisoned), a pot of oil (for polishing his bazuki), a 30-foot coil of rope, two velvet slippers (worth about 15 gp) and a treasure map that supposedly leads to some manner of black pyramid by a lost river about 10 days travel across the desert.

Jackal of Darkness

Hit Dice: 4
Armor Class: 4 [15]
Attack: 1 bite (1d6)
Special: Black fire
Move: 14
Saving Throw: 13
Alignment: Chaos
Number Encountered: 1d10
Challenge Level/XP: 5/240

These creatures resemble jackals with black fur, limned with a dark fire that sheds no light and burns black when the jackal emerges from the darkness. They haunt long-abandoned tombs, possibly being shackled to them as guardians by ancient magics - the relation of the jackals to their tomb-lairs is not known. They seem to be undead, in that they can be turned (as mummies), but do not appear to rot, nor do they seem to be incorporeal in any way. The black fire around the jackal acts almost like an independent creature; when the jackal is in combat, the black fire streams forth and can envelop one opponent (within 50ft of the jackal), causing 1 hit point of damage per round. The jackal can move the black fire where it wishes.

— Author: Matt Finch

Jackal of Darkness: HD 4; AC 4[15]; Atk 1 bite (1d6); Move 14; Save 13; AL C; CL/XP 5/240; Special: Black fire.

The Unseen Pyramid

The golden dunes of a vast desert finally cease at the edge of a strange, black river. The river is slow moving and has a mirror-like quality. Close inspection reveals that it is a sort of winding canal of obsidian! The water is warm, and might contain a hezrou or two if a Referee so desires. At one point of the river, travelers come upon several obsidian statues by the river's edge. Each depicts a jackal-headed man (not necessarily Anubis), the statues carved to represent people in the act of walking with their eyes clamped shut. There are 10 statues in all, and they face the desert. More astounding, though, is that their reflections in the river also show a giant black pyramid! The characters can search the desert shore to their heart's content, but they will find no such pyramid – at least, not unless the proper conditions are met.

The black pyramid does appear, but only when one stands facing the river, waiting for the moon (from crescent to full, it does not matter) to be directly above the pyramid. When this happens, a ripple goes through the river and an obsidian causeway rises from the sand at the river's edge, stretching back to the pyramid. The viewer must not turn around just yet – not until the causeway has risen under her feet. At that point, she may turn around with her eyes closed, and take 10 steps toward the pyramid. At the 10th step, the adventurer finds herself in a demiplane, concordant with the material plane until the sun rises. Within this demiplane of reddish sands and blindingly white sky stands the black pyramid, the tomb of a mummified daemon and his court of **8 jackals-of-darkness**. They need a mortal's blood to allow them to escape back into the material plane.

Jackalwere

Hit Dice: 4
Armor Class: 4 [15]
Attack: 1 bite (2d4)
Special: Sleep gaze, hit by silver or magic weapons only
Move: 12
Saving Throw: 13
Alignment: Chaos
Number Encountered: 1 or 1d4
Challenge Level/XP: 5/240

A jackalwere is an evil spirit with the body of a jackal, but it can also assume a human form. Jackalweres can cause sleep by looking deeply into a human's eyes for a few moments (saving throw). Jackalweres can only be damaged with silver or magical weapons.

Jackalwere: HD 4; AC 4[15]; Atk 1 bite (2d4); Move 12; Save 13; AL C; CL/XP 5/240; Special: Sleep gaze, hit by silver or magic weapons only.

Temple of the Jackal God

The temple of Al-Sakaal is a three-tiered step pyramid deep in the Seething Jungle. Villagers journey daily to the temple, bringing with them prancing goats, baked breads and freshly caught fish. Once a month, the villagers bring a young woman to the temple. The women disappear into the depths of the pyramid, never to be seen again.

A **jackalwere** named **Elip Khaset** rules the pyramid and demands the food and sacrifices. The creature controls the villagers through fear and a pack of **15 jackals** that serve it. Elip has a small treasure hoard (600 gp, 10 rubies worth 245 gp, and a crystal crown worth 75 gp) in a deep room within the pyramid. The gnawed bones of more than 20 women lie scattered across the gold and diamonds. The jackalwere sleeps on a tiger-pelt bed near the treasure pile while the pack curls up on the cool stone.

Jackal: HD 1d4hp; AC 7[12]; Atk 1 bite (1d2); Move 14; Save 18; AL N; CL/XP A/15; Special: None.

Janni

Hit Dice: 6
Armor Class: 3 [16]
Attack: 1 weapon (1d8+4)
Special: Genie powers (see below)
Move: 12/24 (flying)
Saving Throw: 11
Alignment: Usually Neutrality
Number Encountered: 1
Challenge Level/XP: 9/1,100

Jann are genies not tied to any particular element, unlike the efreet and the djinn. Like other genies, they have magical powers: enlarge or shrink themselves, invisibility (5/day), and dimension door (1/day). Jann can travel into the elemental planes, even bringing others with them, but they cannot remain more than an hour and a day in another plane of existence, or they will perish.

Janni: HD 6; AC 3[16]; Atk 1 weapon (1d8+4); Move 12 (Fly 24); Save 11; AL N; CL/XP 9/1100; Special: Genie powers.

Ship of Wonders

One day each year in a great port, a golden dhow appears in the sky, held aloft by a howling wind, its many pennons and its broad, white sails in full array. The dhow passes over the city and lands about a mile away, inland, with crowds rushing to the gates to follow it down. As it lands, a gangplank is lowered and a cavalcade of strange sailors begins unloading the mysterious ship – men with a single eye in their forehead, others with no heads, but with faces on their bare chests, still others with purple or green skin, or with only a single leg and arm. These men unload silk pavilions and barrels and chests full of exotic goods.

The ship belongs to the **janni merchant prince Khaliz**, a wily trader (and sometimes pirate) who scours the elemental and outer planes for rare wonders to sell to noble and peasant alike. From nobles, he demands the finest gems and pearls, the most delicious liquors and the most nubile slave girls. From peasants, he demands tall tales, rowdy dances and oaths of loyalty and friendship (and maybe a few copper or silver pieces to make it legit). He is willing to take on passengers, but they must be sworn members of his crew, and must serve with him for at least one moon before he deposits them on some alien shore.

271

Jellyfish, Hypnotic

Hit Dice: 3
Armor Class: 8 [11]
Attack: 1 sting (1d8 + poison)
Special: Hypnotic colors
Move: 0/3 (swimming)
Saving Throw: 14
Alignment: Neutrality
Number Encountered: 1d4
Challenge Level/XP: 5/240

The colors of a hypnotic jellyfish are so soothing that anyone viewing this undersea predator must make a saving throw or fall into a dreamlike trance for 1d6 turns. The jellyfish is very large, about the size of a man. Its sting carries a lethal poison.

Hypnotic Jellyfish: HD 3; AC 8[11]; Atk 1 sting (1d8 + poison); Move 0 (Swim 3); Save 14; AL N; CL/XP 5/240; Special: Hypnotic colors.

Abyssal Witch

Adventurers in a deep dungeon might enter a chilly room, about 30 feet long, 14 feet wide and 25 feet high. The walls are like slick, black glass. Near the center of the room, there is a dais of snowflake obsidian topped by a solid block of black stone (actually, it is solidified darkness, and it will resist any attempts to pierce it). Within this darkness is the sarcophagus of the **witch-king Hazrepash Fish-Eye**. The dais is ringed by three lamps atop four-foot-tall iron poles. When all three are lit, they descend into the ground, causing first a heavy one-foot-thick bronze door to seal the exit, and second dispelling the block of darkness and revealing the sarcophagus.

While the blackness is dispelling, a soft, persistent light also rises behind the walls, floor and ceiling, revealing them to be transparent. Behind them, there is a vast, still ocean inhabited by dozens of **hypnotic jellyfish**. Though they cannot attack through the glass, they can hold people spellbound. If the sarcophagus is opened without first placing coins on the eyes of the bas-relief of Hazrepash, it sends the waters of the surrounding sea rushing into the chamber to kill the would-be tomb robbers. If opened properly, the sarcophagus contains three magic staves of the Referee's choosing.

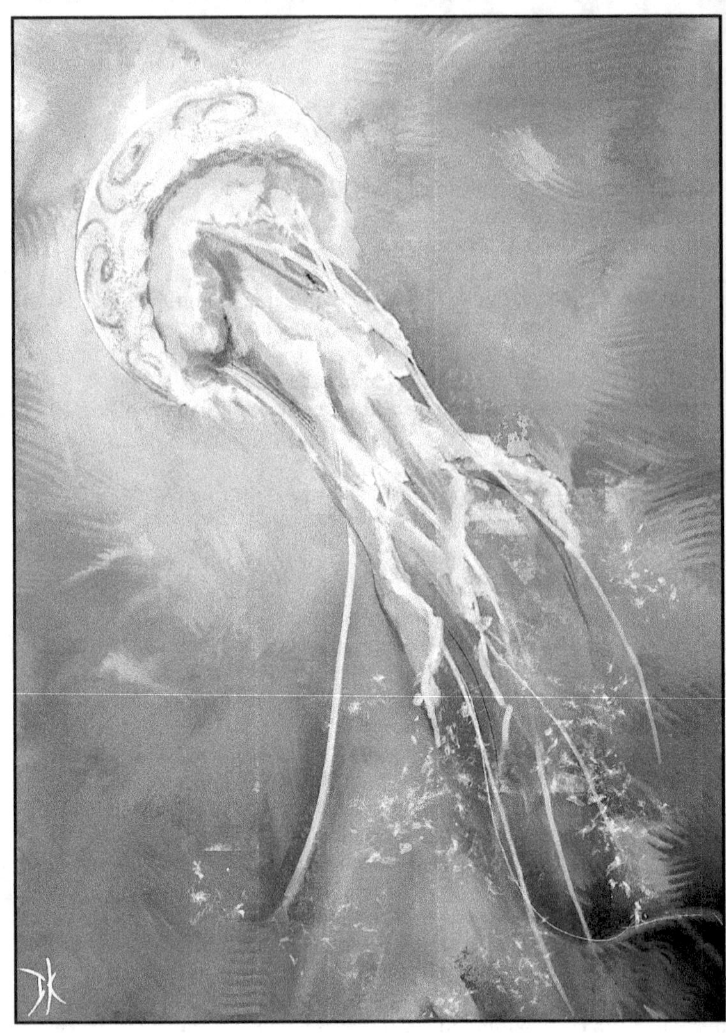

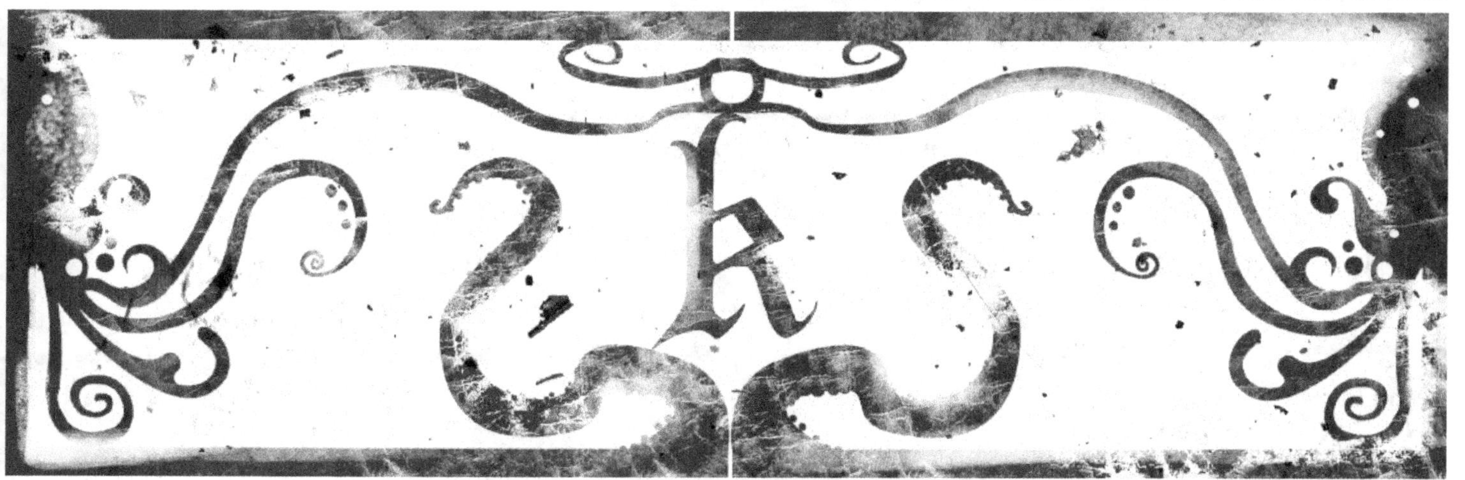

Keeper of the Well

Hit Dice: 9
Armor Class: 2 [17]
Attack: 1 "fist" (2d8)
Special: Fire immunity, magic resistance (75%), water teleport
Move: 0 (see below)
Saving Throw: 6
Alignment: Neutrality
Number Encountered: 1
Challenge Level/XP: 12/2,000

Keepers Of The Well are semi-intelligent water spirits that enter the material world at the behest of a powerful cleric. These spirits willingly enter into a contract with the spiritual leader who brought them forth, agreeing to be bound to a particular well or spring and defend it from all creatures not part of the local village or temple. In return for its service, the Keeper of the Well is freed from the slave-like existence it would normally have on its home place or in the spirit world. A village's Keeper of the Well is often worshipped as a minor deity. A Keeper of the Well appears as a large, snake-like column of water rising out of the opening of the well that it defends. They cannot leave the well, though they can manifest themselves from any opening tied to the local water system, instantly appearing at the desired location. Keepers of the Well are immune to fire and possess magic resistance of 75%. Spells that specifically affect water (such as Part Water) can be used to damage or affect a Keeper of the Well with results that may vary from the spell's normal operation.

— *Author: Andrew Trent*

Keeper Of The Well: HD 9; AC 2[17]; Atk 1 "fist" (2d8); Move 0 (see text for special); Save 6; AL N; CL/XP 12/2000; Special: Fire immunity, magic resistance (75%), water teleport.

Village of the Drowned

Chalky symbols are written in the dirt on the main road leading into the town of Ranoke. If followed, the symbols form a circle that surrounds the entire village. Even standing outside the line, PCs see the bodies of villagers lying motionless in the streets. A **cleric** named **Bodoh** sleeps in a small lean-to in the woods north of town. Every day, the man walks the perimeter of the chalk circle, redrawing the mystic symbols. He claims a great evil in the town must be contained. He refuses to cross into the village.

Anyone entering the town finds bodies inside the homes as well as those in the streets. Many clutch at their throats as if they had died choking. Their clothes are drenched and water fills their mouths and throats. The villagers worshipped a **keeper of the well** that **had access to the entire town through a series of troughs.** Water is evident throughout town. Troughs fill automatically and wooden downspouts open and sprinkle water across beds of blooming flowers. The keeper's stone well has a spinning wheel attached to the side that draws water up through a series of moving buckets to fill the troughs.

An evil cleric angered by the villagers corrupted the peaceful entity, dooming himself and the entire town. The tortured water deity drowned the cleric first, and then turned on the villagers it had protected. The keeper in the well can appear anywhere within town thanks to the ingenious waterway. Destroying the troughs forces the elemental spirit back into the well. It cannot leave the village because the water table doesn't extend that far. The cleric's chalk symbols have no effect on it.

Kheph

	WARRIOR	PRIEST	MAGE	ELDER
Hit Dice:	8	9	10	11
Armor Class:	3 [16]	5 [14]	6 [13]	4 [15]
Attack:	2 scimitars (1d8)	1 scimitar (1d8)	1 scimitar (1d8)	1 scimitar (1d8)
Special:	+2 to hit	Spells as level 9 cleric, symbol of pain, plane shift	Spells as level 10 magic-user, symbol of fear, plane shift	Spells as level 11 magic-user and level 11 cleric, symbol of death, plane shift
Move:	12	12	12	12
Saving Throw:	8	6	5	4
Alignment:	Chaos	Chaos	Chaos	Chaos
Number Encountered:	1d6 (mixed group)			
Challenge Level/XP:	8/800	12/2,000	13/2,300	15/2,900

The Kheph are jackal-headed humanoids with a sleek black covering of body fur. Below the neck, the form of a Kheph's body is very much like that of a muscular and well-proportioned human being, although they are larger (averaging 7 feet tall). The Kheph are an ancient species, older than mankind, and they revere evil gods forgotten or never known by most living races. Their supernatural link to planes of existence beyond material reality is very strong, and Kheph leaders are said to be able to shift between planes of existence with ease.

Warrior kheph have 8HD but no magical abilities. They usually fight with scimitars, attacking twice per round, but may (20%) be armed with bows or (20%) with polearms. Kheph priests cast spells as a cleric of 9th level, and in addition can (as an innate ability) cast *symbol of pain* and *plane shift* once per day. Kheph Magi cast spells as a magic user of 10th level, and in addition can (as an innate ability) cast *symbol of fear* and *plane shift* once per day. Kheph elders have the spell casting abilities of an 11th level cleric and magic user, and in addition can (as an innate ability) cast *symbol of death* and *plane shift* once per day.

— Author: Matt Finch

Kheph Warrior: HD 8; AC 3[16]; Atk 2 scimitars (1d8); Move 12; Save 8; AL C; CL/XP 8/800; Special: +2 to hit.

Kheph Priest: HD 9; AC 5[14]; Atk 1 scimitar (1d8); Move 12; Save 6; AL C; CL/XP 12/2000; Special: Spells as level 9 cleric, symbol of pain, plane shift.

Kheph Mage: HD 10; AC 6[13]; Atk 1 scimitar (1d8); Move 12; Save 5; AL C; CL/XP 13/2300; Special: Spells as level 10 magic-user, symbol of fear, plane shift.

Kheph Elder: HD 11; AC 4[15]; Atk 1 scimitar (1d8); Move 12; Save 4; AL C; CL/XP 15/2900; Special: Spells as level 11 magic-user and level 11 cleric, symbol of death, plane shift.

The Ship of the Air

A ripple in the air expands quickly and the prow of a papyrus boat pushes through the rip in space. The boat smells of cedar and has brown reeds sealing the seams between the boards. The ship glides five feet above the ground on its sickle-shaped hull. The hull is painted with gold and black bands. A gold-colored cloth sail trimmed in black rises above the single deck.

The Kaliph is a floating ship manned by **8 kheph warriors**, and commanded by a **kheph elder**. A **kheph priest** stands at the rail. The raiders fly the ship into towns and cities, attacking from their floating perch. The ship can float as high as 300 feet, although the higher it goes, the less forward momentum it has. At its highest point, the ship becomes a stationary vessel sitting high above the ground. The kheph's treasure is stored in the ship's hull and consists of 2,000 gp, a rack of exotic spices (20 gp), a small golden idol of the god Ra (200 gp) and a bag of diamonds (500 gp). The ship can be made to rise and lower if a spellcaster stands

at the rail and imbues the ship with magical energy. The ship settles to the ground like a feather if the magical energies are interrupted (if the spellcaster is killed or leaves his station).

Khryll

Hit Dice: 8
Armor Class: 3 [16]
Attack: 8 tentacles (see below)
Special: Mental blast, liquefy internal organs, magic resistance (80%)
Move: 9
Saving Throw: 8
Alignment: Chaos
Number Encountered: 1d6 or 3d8
Challenge Level/XP: 13/2,300

Khrylls are bizarre subterranean creatures, possessed of a malevolently genius-level intellect. They have curving, jointed shells like that of a crayfish or lobster, but without claws; rather than legs, the creature has squid-like tentacles emerging from each segment of the armored body. The tentacles of a Khryll permit some kind of limited levitation; a khryll can float and maneuver in the air provided that at least two of its tentacles are in contact with the ground or a wall. They cannot rise higher than the length of the 10ft tentacles.

The origin of these creatures in the deep underworld is unknown, but they are rapacious harvesters of most other intelligent species, even to the extent of breeding slaves to serve as food. They communicate telepathically, and their primary attack is to produce a mental shockwave that necessitates a saving throw by anyone caught in the area of the cone-shaped psychic ripple. The effect of the blast depends upon how many creatures are caught within:

1-2 creatures in area: Natural 1 on saving throw = death,
Failed save = stunned 3d6 turns,
Successful save = panic for 1d10 rounds.

3-4 creatures in area: Natural 1 on saving throw = stunned 3d6 turns,
Failed save = panic for 3d6 turns,
Successful save = confused for 1d10 rounds.

5+ creatures in area: Natural 1 on saving throw = panicked for 3d6 turns,
Failed save = confused for 1d6 turns,
Successful save = confused for 1d6 rounds.

In melee combat (or at leisure if all its foes are incapacitated), Khryll hold prey with their tentacles and insert a mouth-tube into the victim to begin liquefying the internal organs. If an opponent is hit by any two of the khryll's tentacles, the khryll has an opportunity to jab its tube-like tongue down the victim's throat into the body cavity, and begin liquefying organs for ingestion. This inflicts 1d6 points of damage in the first round, 2d6 points of damage in the second round, 3d6 points of damage in the third round, and death in the fourth round (no saving throw). Once the two tentacles have grabbed an opponent with successful hit, no further attacks are necessary to continue holding the victim.

If the Khryll is hungry it will suck the liquefied organs through its mouth-tube as food; otherwise it will lay eggs in the prepared body, and these will hatch into khryll-spawn in 1d3+1 days.

Khryll society is quite complex and byzantine; in general no more than six of them will be encountered together at one time, but in the deepest caverns beneath the earth there are unquestionably much larger populations of them. Their cities are said to be as much vertical as horizontal, with vast schools of khryll floating up the sides of underground cliffs where they have built bizarre structures and tunnels directly into the sides of their great caverns.

— Author: Matt Finch

Khryll: HD 8; AC 3[16]; Atk 8 tentacles (varies by round); Move 9; Save 8; AL C; CL/XP 13/2300; Special: Mental blast, liquefy internal organs, magic resistance (80%).

Blubbery Flesh

A great albino sperm whale lies beached on the shore of an underground ocean filling a massive cavern. The whale's massive bulk is soft and spongy with decay, and the creature as a whole seems to be deflating under its own weight. A four-pronged hook juts from its mouth and a large iron chain trails off across the rocky shore. The chain's links are nearly four feet long. The chain heads up the beach toward a dark cave. Around the whale's body lie the bodies of 8 hill giants. The hill giants' bodies are also soft and pliant. Pinkish goo dribbles from their slack jaws and ears.

A hill giant clan reeled in the whale lying on the beach. During their celebration over landing the beast, they didn't notice **2 khryll** sliding down the cliff. The khryll made short work of the giants, and then laid eggs inside the whale. The khryll wait in the hill giants' cave, their hunger sated for the moment. Inside the dirty cave is the giants' treasure: 14 pretty rocks, a golden rocking horse (200 gp), a side of rotted meat, and a halfling skeleton wearing gray robes and a platinum crown (2,000 gp).

Ki-rin

Hit Dice: 12
Armor Class: -5 [24]
Attack: 1 horn (3d6), 2 hoofs (1d8)
Special: Spells, magical powers, magic resistance (90%)
Move: 18/24 (flying)
Saving Throw: 3
Alignment: Lawful
Number Encountered: 1
Challenge Level/XP: 18/3,800

Ki-rin are wind spirits, looking much like a unicorn, but with dragon-like features such as golden-scaled skin, and having a huge, flowing mane. Most are benevolent in nature, but they seldom interfere in the doings of humankind. A ki-rin can cast spells as an 18th level cleric and as an 18th level magic user.

Cleric spells: 7/7/7/7/7/4/1
Magic-user spells: 6/6/6/6/6/5/2/2/1

A common selection of spells for a ki-rin might be as follows:

Cleric: Level 1: *Cure Light Wounds* (x2), *Detect Evil, Detect Magic, Light, Protection From Evil, Purify Food and Drink,* **Level 2:** *Bless, Find Traps, Hold Person* (x2), *Silence, 15ft Radius, Snake Charm, Speak with Animals,* **Level 3:** *Continual Light, Cure Disease, Locate Object, Prayer, Remove Curse* (x2), *Speak with the Dead,* **Level 4:** *Create Water, Cure Serious Wounds* (x2), *Neutralize Poison, Protection From Evil 10 ft. Radius, Speak With Plants, Sticks to Snakes,* **Level 5:** *Commune, Create Food, Dispel Evil, Finger of Death, Insect Plague, Quest, Raise Dead,* **Level 6:** *Animate Object, Blade Barrier, Speak with Monsters, Word of Recall,* **Level 7:** *Control Weather.*

Magic-user: Level 1: *Charm Person, Detect Magic, Protection From Evil, Read Languages, Read Magic, Sleep,* **Level 2:** *ESP, Invisibility, Locate Object, Mirror Image, Phantasmal Force, Web,* **Level 3:** *Dispel Magic* (x2), *Fireball, Haste, Protection From Normal Missiles, Slow,* **Level 4:** *Confusion* (x2), *Fear, Plant Growth, Polymorph Other, Polymorph Self,* **Level 5:** *Conjure Elemental, Contact Other Plane, Telekinesis* (x2), *Teleport, Wall of Stone,* **Level 6:** *Death Spell, Disintegrate, Flesh to Stone, Legend Lore, Stone to Flesh,* **Level 7:** *Delayed Blast Fireball, Limited Wish,* **Level 8:** *Monster Summoning VI, Power Word Blind,* **Level 9:** *Time Stop.*

Ki-rin: HD 12; AC –5[24]; Atk 1 horn (3d6), 2 hoofs (1d8); Move 18 (Fly 24); Save 3; AL L; CL/XP 18/3800; Special: Spells, magical powers, magic resistance (90%).

Servants of the Flute

An odd silver flute sits on a piece of folded velvet lying atop a crystalline altar in the Forgotten Tomb of the Lich Abomination Ingrilurk. The flute is warm to the touch and has numerous sharp angles and edges that draw blood from those who try to play it. Engraved along its length are images of galloping horses jumping from cloud to wispy cloud. Three 20-foot-long chains wrap around the base of the crystal altar.

The three chains are **animated objects** that attack anyone approaching the altar. Each chain ends in a wicked barbed hook that does 2d4 points of damage with each hit. If a chain hits with a natural 20, it wraps tightly around a victim and deals automatic damage each round thereafter until the victim is freed. Touching the flute summons **Erajellani**, a **marilith demon** tasked with stopping thieves intent on taking Ingrilurk's possession.

Playing the flute summons a **ki-rin** that serves the PC for one day. The flute can be blown once per month in this fashion. Playing the instrument does 1 point of damage to the player that cannot be healed.

Animated Chain: HD 1; AC 7[12]; Atk 1 slam (2d4); Move 12; Save 18; AL N; CL/XP 1/15; Special: Entangle.

Fifth-category Demon: HD 8; AC –3[22]; Atk 6 weapons (1d8), tail (1d8); Move 12; Save 8; AL C; CL/XP 13/2300; Special: Magic resistance (80%), +1 or better magic weapon required to hit, demonic magical powers.

Kobold

Hit Dice: 1d4 hp
Armor Class: 7 [12]
Attacks: Weapon (1d6)
Saving Throw: 18
Special: None
Move: 6
Alignment: Chaos
Number Encountered: 1d4+4 or 1d4 x100
Challenge Level/XP: A/5

Kobolds are subterranean, vaguely goblin-like humanoids. They have a -1 penalty when fighting above ground. Many use slings or short bows, and they fight with short swords or spiked clubs in melee combat.

Kobold: HD 1d4hp; AC 7 [12]; Atk 1 weapon (1d6); Move 6; Save 18; AL C; CL/XP A/15; Special: None.

Sher-myn Tank

A 10-foot-diameter **giant snapping turtle** stomps slowly through the swampy marshgrass of the Sin Mire. Its giant head swings from side to side as it slowly advances. The top of the creature's shell has been sanded down to a five-foot-diameter flat platform. A second flat ring is sanded down around the central area, much like a bull's-eye. Riding atop the shell are **5 kobolds** that sit behind a wooden fence driven into the turtle's shell around the rings. Each kobold is armed with a crossbow and short sword. The kobolds can move quickly around the flat rings to attack people on all sides of the giant turtle.

The kobolds can toss rope ladders down the sides of the turtle to scramble down and attack. They are reluctant to do so until the turtle softens up enemies. The kobolds keep their treasure in a locked box bolted to the turtle's shell. The box contains 114 gp, a silver harp (45 gp), a book about turtles, and a bag of mismatched earrings (15 gp). The kobolds trained the turtle to carry them into battle. They named the creature Sher-myn.

Ko'haai

Hit Dice: 3
Armor Class: 5 [14]
Attack: 1 bite (1d6 + poison) or 1 tongue (1d4 + pinion)
Special: Poison, pinion with tongue
Move: 6
Saving Throw: 14
Alignment: Neutrality
Number Encountered: 1d4
Challenge Level/XP: 4/120

Ko'haai are large, 6-legged lizards covered in scales that coruscate with varying hues of blue. They are normally found in tropical climates where they are used as riding animals and beasts of burden by the local populace. Ko'haai possess long, powerful tongues, used to make a whip-like attack. In addition to suffering damage, the victim of this attack may have his arms pinioned if the tongue wraps around him (saving throw at -2 penalty). The bite of a Ko'haai is mildly poisonous, inflicting 1d3 points of damage (saving throw at +2 negates), and the poison has a very strange property with repeated exposures. The skin of any person who has sustained 3 or more Ko'haai bites within a week takes on a discernible bluish cast, which persists for 3d8 weeks. After six successful saving throws made against Ko'haai poison, the body develops a permanent immunity to the damaging effects of the poison, and begins to treat the poison as a mild amphetamine, providing a +1 to attack rolls and saving throws for 1d4+2 hours after being bitten (the downside to this, of course, is the damage taken from the bite itself).

— Author: Andrew Trent

Ko'haai: HD 3; AC 5[14]; Atk 1 bite (1d6 + poison) or 1 tongue (1d4 + pinion); Move 6; Save 14; AL N; CL/XP 4/120; Special: Poison, pinion with tongue.

Round'Em Up

The village of Ank-Santal sits on the edge of the Seething Jungle. It serves as a waypoint for those looking to mount expeditions into the rainforest's dark heart. Anyone who has made the trek recommends stopping in the village first. The villagers know the secret trails through the dense trees, and mounts and guides can be readily hired. Anyone hiring one of the knowledgeable guides can easily shave days off their trip through the forbidding jungle.

The villagers are friendly and helpful, but every one of them has skin of varying shades of blue. The villagers maintain a stable of **20 ko'haai** just outside of town. They rent the giant lizards for 1 gp per day to those heading into the jungle (as long as they take a village guide). A kapok tree recently fell across the wooden pen. The lizard escaped into the jungle but didn't go far. Each night, the villagers place chunks of meat near the rebuilt fence to lure the lizards back. So far, the lizards have eluded them. They are offering a 10 gp reward to anyone who helps round up a lizard and returns it to the pen. The lizards bite anyone manhandling them into the repaired pen. The villagers have been bitten so many times that their skin is permanently blue.

Koi Folk

Hit Dice: 2+1
Armor Class: 7 [12]
Attack: 1 slap (1d3)
Special: None
Move: 9/12 (swimming)
Saving Throw: 16
Alignment: Law
Number Encountered: 1d100
Challenge Level/XP: 2/30

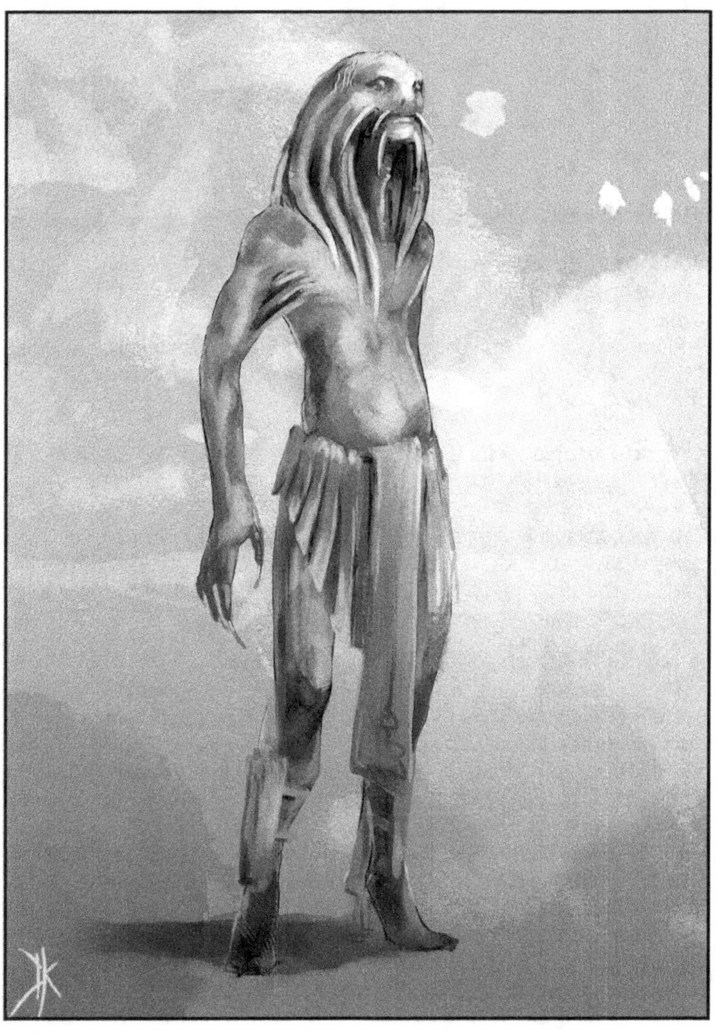

The Koi Folk are brightly colored humanoid goldfish, peaceful and amphibious peasants of Eastern lands, and generally pleasant to be around, if somewhat dull company. They are simple-minded and easily led, often prey to bullies like the Yurmp (see, "Yurmp") or haughty local nobility. Some monks will occasionally attempt to teach the Koi Folk martial arts, and instill the drive to stand up for themselves, only to give up in frustration at these creatures' blank-faced placidity.

— *Author: Scott Wylie Roberts, "Myrystyr"*

Koi Folk: HD 2+1; AC 7[12]; Atk 1 slap (1d3); Move 9 (swim 12); Save 16; AL L; CL/XP 2/30; Special: None.

Catch of the Day

A **hill giant** sits astride a fallen oak tree sitting over a 30-foot-wide gleaming sea inlet. The narrow finger of water pushes inland to form a large saltwater pool. The giant holds a fishing pole and keeps a line dropped into the water below. A second line is attached to a spike driven into the tree. This line also disappears into the water below, where it swings back and forth violently as something in the water struggles to get away. Gold scales flash in the splashing water beneath the rope. Watery voices scream, "Release us!"

The giant discovered that **20 koi folk** swim into the pool each day to spawn. The giant uses large redworms – irresistible bait to the koi folk – to land the fish folk. The giant hooks each fish onto the bait line trailing into the water beside him. He currently has 5 koi folk attached to the line already. If freed, the koi folk reward their rescuers with a golden trident (200 gp) they know rests at the bottom of the pool.

Hill Giant: HD 8+2; AC 4[15]; Atk 1 weapon (2d8); Move 12; Save 8; AL C; CL/XP 9/1100; Special: Throw boulders.

Komodo Dragon

	NORMAL	GIANT
Hit Dice:	2	5
Armor Class:	5 [14]	4 [15]
Attack:	1 bite (1d6 + poison)	1 bite (2d6 + poison)
Special:	Poison bite	Poison bite
Move:	6	9
Saving Throw:	16	12
Alignment:	Neutrality	Neutrality
Number Encountered:	1d4	1d2
Challenge Level/XP:	4/120	7/600

Komodo dragons are very large lizards with a poisonous bite (saving throw). Death from the poison takes place in 1d4 melee rounds after the bite.

Komodo Dragon: HD 2; AC 5[14]; Atk 1 bite (1d6 + poison); Move 6; Save 16; AL N; CL/XP 4/120; Special: Poison bite.

Giant Komodo Dragon: HD 5; AC 4[15]; Atk 1 bite (2d6 + poison); Move 9; Save 12; AL N; CL/XP 7/600; Special: Poison bite.

The Lost Villagers of Varnursal

The small fishing village of Vanursal sits on the shore of the Coral Strain Sea. The 10 huts stand on five-foot-high pillars dug into the sandy beach. Inside each hut, rooms are spacious and comfortable, with plush couches and beds. Various decorations salvaged from the sea and surrounding jungle give the huts an ocean getaway feel. Three huts contain large wooden desks with numerous drawers. Wooden steps lead up to each platform from the beaches. Fishing nets hang from railings around each wooden platform. The huts are empty. Outside the huts, bloody paths in the sand lead into the jungle.

The empty village is now home to **6 komodo dragons** that crawled into the huts in the middle of the night and bit the fishermen. The poisoned men and women staggered from their huts and died on their beloved beach. The lizards dragged the bodies into the jungle to devour. The lizards sleep under the desks and beds inside the huts during the day. They snap at the ankles of anyone walking into the rooms.

Kraken

Hit Dice: 20
Armor Class: 0 [19]
Attack: 6 tentacles (2d6), bite (3d6)
Special: Ink cloud, constriction, control weather, create lights
Move: 0/3/21 (swimming/jet)
Saving Throw: 3
Alignment: Chaos
Number Encountered: 1
Challenge Level/XP: 24/5,600

Kraken are gigantic squid-like monsters of malign, genius-level intelligence, residing in the black depths of the oceans. When kraken strike with their tentacles, they may wrap their prey and constrict them each round for an automatic 2d6 damage, also making the victim defenseless against the kraken's bite. Ships may be constricted in the same way, typically requiring 18 tentacle-rounds to crush the vessel sufficiently to pull below to the kraken's expansive undersea lair. Tentacles may be targeted individually and severed. They each have AC 6[13] and 16 hit points, which are not considered part of the kraken's hit point total. Kraken retreat by jetting backwards, at which point they may release a poisonous 80ft x 80ft x 120ft ink cloud. For a total of four rounds, anyone within the cloud will suffer 1d4 points of damage. It is rumored that kraken possess unnatural powers to control weather and to create false lights in order to ambush or mislead sailors.

— Author: Random

Kraken: HD 20; AC 0[19]; Atk 6 tentacles (2d6), bite (3d6); Move (Swim 3) (Jet 21); Save 3; AL C; CL/XP 24/5600; Special: Ink cloud, constriction, control weather, create lights.

Water Colors

Strange colored lights flash across the waves as the sailing ship Imago plies the waves. A storm dances across the growing waves. The smell of salt hangs heavy in the air as the wind pushes waves across the ship's deck. The sails ripple and fill under the ever-changing elemental assault. Sailors hold holy symbols toward the sky to ward off evil. The balls of light dance and spin across the waters, a trail of colorful spheres that seem to turn and move toward the Imago.

A **kraken** hunts the deeps of the Barrows Abyssal, an undersea cliff dropping into the depths of the Reaping Sea. The beast rises under ships and grabs them in its massive tentacles. The creature tries to crush vessels and drag them into the depths. The creature's massive bulk as it swims under the rolling waves draws multi-colored balls of lightning down atop the waves.

Kurok-Spirit

Hit Dice: 3
Armor Class: 4 [15]
Attack: Bite (1d4 CON)
Special: Drain Constitution, immune to normal weapons
Move: 9
Saving Throw: 14
Alignment: Chaos
Number Encountered: 1 or 1d4+1
Challenge Level/XP: 5/240

A kurok-spirit is a non-human spirit that manifests as a ghostly crocodile, limned with a transparent gray fire. Kuroks can only be damaged by silver or magic weapons (or by spells). Anyone within melee attack range of the creature must make a saving throw or be paralyzed by the ghost-flames around the spirit's crocodile body. When the kurok bites an opponent, the bite causes the temporary loss of 1d4 constitution points (recovered within 1d3 days); if a victim's constitution drops to 0 as the result of a kurok's bite, he dies and the spirit takes his soul to eat.

— Author: Matt Finch

Kurok-Spirit: HD 3; AC 4[15]; Atk Bite (1d4 points of constitution); Move 9; Save 14; AL C; CL/XP 5/240; Special: Drains constitution, immune to normal weapons.

Crocodile Rock

A 15-foot-tall stone carved with leering faces stands on the edge of the Ongsawl River where a wide bend forms a deep pool. Swimming lazily in the river are **10 crocodiles**, their heads barely visible above the waterline. Capirona trees grow wild around the still pool. Monkeys dance in the branches.

At night, a dozen ghostly spirits rise from the rock and dance across the surface of the pool. A **kurok-spirit** that lives under the water killed the beings, but the rock snatched their souls away before the ghost crocodile could devour them. The ghosts' nightly dance taunts the spirit crocodile, drawing it to the water's surface.

The ghosts lead the angry spirit toward living beings. The spirits are trapped in the rock totem until they find a new soul to replace their own. The stone absorbs the souls of those slain by the kurok-spirit. Each new spirit absorbed releases one of the old ones. Killing the kurok-spirit frees all of the spirits trapped in the rock.

Normal Crocodile: HD 3; AC 4[15]; Atk 1 bite (1d6); Move 9 (Swim 12); Save 14; AL N; CL/XP 3/60; Special: None.

Kzaddich

Hit Dice: 1+1
Armor Class: -8 [27]
Attack: 2 weapons (1d8)
Special: Haste, improved saving throws, immune to person-affecting spells, immune to time spells, escape into future, mental powers, cannot be surprised, time stop (2/day)
Move: 12
Saving Throw: 8
Alignment: Law
Number Encountered: 1d4
Challenge Level/XP: 6/400

This weird but benevolent race exists outside of the normal concept of time. They may come from the distant future, but could just as easily hail from the distant past or from an alternate reality altogether. When encountered, they are generally working to defy the plans of their arch-enemies, the Tsalakians (another trans-dimensional race of beings), and to organize resistance against them. The Kzaddich (singular and plural) always appear as man-sized figures, completely covered by cowled cloaks. Their own speech sounds not unlike wind chimes. When dealing with sentient creatures, they use their native telepathy. Their true form defies immediate description; uncloaked, they appear as an amalgamation of shifting, softly glowing spheres in a rough approximation of a bipedal form. The Kzaddich can slip in and out of the time-stream at will, and as a result they are exceedingly difficult to harm. They can anticipate the future actions of their opponents, resulting in their almost unhittable armor class. Moreover, they make saving throws as an 8HD creature and take half or no damage from damage-causing spells that allow saving throws, and are allowed a saving throw against spells that normally do not allow one - whether these spells cause damage or not. They are immune to all person-affecting spells (hold person, charm person, etc.) and cannot be affected by spells that affect time, such as slow or time stop. Indeed, Kzaddich can ignore the effects of these spells and even interrupt and share any beneficial effects of such magics. Kzaddich are loathe to engage in combat, but if forced, they have the innate spell-like ability to haste themselves at will. If faced with certain capture or death, a Kzaddich can, at will, simply slip into the far future or past to avoid the situation. Kzaddich have considerable mental powers. They can mentally alter the density of their bodies from a weight of 0 to 500 pounds at will, heal all damage they have suffered five times per day, levitate at will, communicate telepathically within 100ft with any creature, and read psychic impressions left upon objects. The Kzaddich do not perceive time the way others do; they can perceive the outlines of the future (90% chance to make the most favorable choice between two actions). Kzaddich can never be taken by surprise. Twice per day, a Kzaddich have the ability to create a time stop (as per the spell, with a duration of 2 combat rounds). A Kzaddich can share the time stop with another creature with which it is in physical contact. Almost nothing is known of the Kzaddich culture; they vie against the machinations of the Tsalakians on a scale that mortal creatures cannot comprehend, in a vast war that spans time and dimensions.

— Author: John Turcotte

Kzaddich: HD 1+1; AC -8[27]; Atk 2 weapons (1d8); Move 12; Save 8; AL L; CL/XP 6/400; Special: Haste, improved saving throws, immune to person-affecting spells, immune to time spells, escape into future, mental powers, cannot be surprised, time stop (2/day).

Playing with Time

A bronze sundial stands in the middle of an open plain. The sundial's slanted gnomon is an engraved whale's spine that rises 20 feet above a flat stone disc marked with the hours of the day. Molten brass poured into carvings in the stone set off the hourly markers. Anyone approaching the sundial hears a voice in their head whisper a specific time of day. A cloaked figure appears to anyone standing on the stone at the appointed hour. If the PC fails a saving throw, he is whisked backward in time to the age of dinosaurs to face **3 hungry Tyrannosaurus rexes**. PCs can voluntarily fail the save.

A **kzaddich** is trapped in the sundial's gnomon, but can communicate freely with PCs who travel backward and forward in time to speak with him. If the dinosaurs are defeated, the kzaddich from the past tells PCs a specific position to stand on the gnomon to facilitate his release. The PCs return to the present soon after. If they follow the kzaddich's instructions, they are swept forward to a desolate landscape where **6 Melgara** accompanied by **2 Tsalakians** wait for the sun to explode and consume them. The melgara and tsalakians attack anyone who appears, thinking they have been sent to stop them. If they are defeated, the kzaddich from the past reappears, this time a much older and wiser being. He tells PCs that his present self can be released by casting raise dead on the whale spine. If PCs do so, the spine cracks and releases the imprisoned kzaddich. The odd humanoid gives PCs a golden band that allows them to travel one day into the past or future by destroying one of the 6 gems. Each gem is worth 200 gp.

Tyrannosaurus Rex: HD 18; AC 4[15]; Atk 1 bite (4d8); Move 18; Save 3; AL N; CL/XP 19/2400; Special: Chews and tears.

Melgara: HD 3+2; AC 7[12] or 5[14]; Atk 1 staff (2d4) or wand (1d4 + stun or slow); Save 14; Move 12; AL N; CL/XP 5/240; Special: Spells (1 level 1), mentally augmented attack (hold, sleep, or charm), increase speed.

Tsalakian: HD 2+2; AC −4 [23]; Atk 4 weapon attacks (1d4); Move Infinite; Save 16; AL C; CL/XP: 7/600; Special: Incorporeal/teleport movement, perceive secret and hidden things, immune to spells affecting a "person," saving throw against all magic, reduced damage from spells, immune to restraint, detect good, magic and evil, sense emotions (empathy).

Lamia

Hit Dice: 9
Armor Class: 3 [16]
Attacks: 2 claws (1d6)
Saving Throw: 6
Special: Spells, touch drains WIS
Move: 24
Alignment: Chaos
Number Encountered: 1
Challenge Level/XP: 12/2,000

Lamias are horrid, centaur-like creatures, always female. Below the female human torso is the body of a beast, usually with a lion's forelegs and the hindquarters of a horse – but the beast-like part can vary. A lamia can cast charm person, charm monster, and suggestion once per day, these powers often being used to lure prey into the dismal and abandoned places where the lamia lairs. In addition, the lamia's touch drains a point of wisdom permanently from the victim. Any victim whose wisdom falls to 3 or lower becomes the lamia's slave (one or more such slaves might be used to guard the lair or even participate in luring victims to the place).

Lamia: HD 9; AC 3[16]; Atk 2 claws (1d6); Move 24; Save 6; AL C; CL/XP 12/2000; Special: Spells, touch drains wisdom.

Isle of the Lizard Witch

The Chum Swiller, a three-masted sailing ship lost at sea three weeks ago, lies broken on sharp rocks surrounding Murgato Isle. The hull is split, and the ship's remains rise and fall into the jagged stones holding it in place. One of the mighty masts is broken and lies across the deck. The ship's bedraggled white sail floats like a shroud on the ocean. Jetsom from the ship bobs in the waves. No bodies can be found on or in the ship, however, and its rowboats are missing.

The Chum Swiller's sailors made it ashore, but that's when their troubles started. A squat stone tower on a cliff overlooks the white-sand beach where the empty rowboats sit. A figure atop the tower waves a white banner vigorously to attract attention.

The island is home to **Varanus Karn**, a **lamia witch** with the body of a komodo dragon. Varanus is served by **12 lizardmen**. A lizardman atop the tower waves the white banner to alert his fellow lizardmen that someone has landed on the beach. The lizardmen hunt in the thick jungle leading up to the tower, but drop what they are doing to capture intruders. Varanus resides in a comfortable bedchamber within the tower. Wooden spikes around the tower's base hold the dismembered bodies of the Chum Swillers' sailors.

Lammasu

Hit Dice: 6+2
Armor Class: 6 [13]
Attacks: 2 claws (1d6)
Saving Throw: 11
Special: Invisibility at will, dimension door, protection from evil 10ft radius, spells (CL6)
Move: 12/24 (flying)
Alignment: Law
Number Encountered: 1
Challenge Level/XP: 9/1,100

Lammasu are akin to angels; they are human-headed, winged lions that often serve as temple guardians and agents of divine Law. Lammasu tend to be defenders of Law, temples, and cizilization rather than being active against the forces of Chaos. If the need arises, of course, a lammasu is quite capable of taking the offensive against threats to its wards – but because they are often pledged to guard particular places, people, or objects, they will often engage other servants of Law to pursue such threats. This being the case, a high level party of Lawful characters might very well be contacted by a lammasu with a request for assistance. The lammasu are usually generous with their rewards to those who are effective allies in the battle against Chaos.

Lammasu: HD 6+2; AC 6[13]; Atk 2 claws (1d6); Move 12 (Fly 24); Save 11; AL L; CL/XP 9/1100; Special: Invisibility at will, dimension door, protection from evil 10ft radius, spells (CL6).

The Old Man on the Mountain

Local legend tells of an ancient hermit that, after he discovered all there was to know, decided such depth of knowledge was not meant for others. He left the local village, alone, and ascended the mountain, where only the most dedicated of knowledge seekers would dare to follow.

Occasionally, a traveler seeks out the Old Man, and they to ascend the mountain. These travelers are rarely seen again in the village; it is assumed they either die on the journey or find enlightenment from the Old Man.

The truth of the matter is that the "Old Man" is actually a **lammasu** (the story was pretty vague) that makes its home on a high perch of stone, many miles up the mountain. The few travelers that make it past the stone giant, the giant eagles, and the natural obstacles (landslides, deep crevasses, tangleweeds, etc.) are allowed to ask the lammasu one question. If they desire further knowledge, they are required to climb to the bottom of the mountain and begin the journey again.

Lamprey, Giant

Hit Dice: 4
Armor Class: 6 [13]
Attacks: 1 bite (1d6)
Saving Throw: 13
Special: Sucks blood
Move: 0/9 (swimming)
Alignment: Neutrality
Number Encountered: 1d4
Challenge Level/XP: 5/240

Giant lampreys are slow-moving eels with a toothy, sphincter-like mouth. Once the monster scores a hit, it fastens to the victim and drains blood automatically each round thereafter until the victim is dead. Normal lampreys aren't really dangerous enough to merit a separate entry.

Giant Lamprey: HD 4; AC 6[13]; Atk 1 bite (1d6); Move (Swim 9); Save 13; AL N; CL/XP 5/240; Special: Sucks blood.

Lost at Sea

A haggard **mule** swims in the open ocean as chunks of splintered wood float around it. The bodies of numerous sailors float atop the waves, pushed along by the currents. A few of the men are torn apart, their entrails spilling into the saltwater. Bloody clouds float like dark spots on the ocean. The wild-eyed mule fights to stay afloat. It has a saddle laden with overflowing pouches strapped across its back. The saddle weighs the animal down, but it manages to keep its head just above the surface. Rips in a couple of the pouches allow jewels to spill out into the ocean and sink from sight. The bags contain treasures a sailor tried to save before the ship sank beneath him. The mule made it off the doomed vessel; the sailor wasn't so lucky.

The mule survived, but it found itself thrown into a new fire, so to speak. A school of **6 giant lampreys** are attacking the mule from below. The bloodsuckers attach themselves to the plump pack animal and are quickly draining its blood. The lampreys break free to feast on PCs who jump in to save the doomed mule (or at least the jewels).

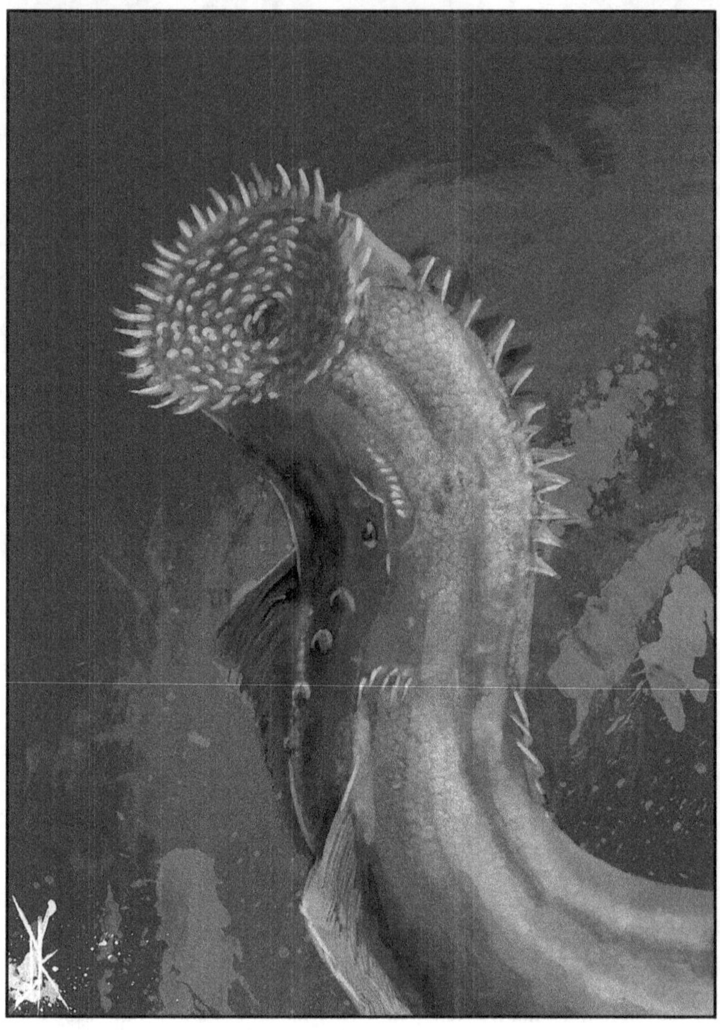

Lamprey, Lightning

Hit Dice: 1
Armor Class: 9 [10]
Attacks: 1 bite (1hp + 1d6 shock)
Saving Throw: 17
Special: Electrical bite
Move: 0/6 (flying)
Alignment: Neutrality
Number Encountered: 2d10
Challenge Level/XP: 1/15

Lightning lampreys are floating creatures about three feet long that feed upon powerful electrical currents and lightning. Schools of them drift along in the wake of storm clouds. They are not normally encountered away from electrical storms (some may sniff their way down from higher altitudes if lightning is actually striking the ground). However, they might be found in unusual magical environments where electrical discharges or lightning is plentiful. Their bite inflicts one point of damage from the sharp teeth, but also delivers an electrical shock of 1d6hp. Their bodies are extremely good electrical conductors.

— Author: Matt Finch, first appeared in Spire of Iron and Crystal

Lightning Lamprey: HD 1; AC 9[10]; Atk 1 bite (1hp + 1d6 shock); Move (Fly 6); Save 17; AL N; CL/XP 1/15; Special: Electrical bite.

All Charged Up

Electricity arcs dangerously through this abandoned laboratory. The bolts of lightning dance at the ends of broken chains dangling from alien machinery. A flat metal table sitting in the middle of the room has links of electrified chains rising from its four corners to the ceiling. A behemoth of a man stands naked amid the arcing energy, basking in the sparking bolts hitting his flesh. Scars cover the man's torso, limbs and face. Metal rods stick out of the man's bare back. They spark and glow like bright embers as each bolt hits the figure. The rods cast a reddish glow throughout the room.

The man is **flesh golem** that raises and lowers the table via a pulley system in the corner of the room. It is programmed to lift the table to the roof three times each day. The golem defends the lab from intruders. The arcing electrical currents are actually **12 lightning lampreys** that entered the lab when the golem last lowered the table. Anyone touching the table or the chains takes 3d6 points of electrical damage (save for half).

Leaping Maw

Hit Dice: 1
Armor Class: 4 [15]
Attacks: 1 bite (1d6)
Saving Throw: 17
Special: Teleport, occupy host, attack vs. unarmored AC.
Move: 0/30 (teleporting)
Alignment: Neutrality
Number Encountered: up to 9
Challenge Level/XP: 2/30

A Leaping Maw is a weird form of parasite that has extra-dimensional properties. It is never encountered alone, as it requires a host of some form. A small creature can support only one Leaping Maw, but a medium-sized creature (such as a human) can support up to four, and a large creature can support nine or more. The Leaping Maw looks like a small, fanged mouth, rather wolf-like, sprouting from a host creature's body. The body is a fist-sized lump, hidden within the host's body, and the host must usually be slain in order to get to it. The Leaping Maw is able to teleport itself directly onto any flesh within 30ft, and if it scores three successful hits it has burrowed into the victim's flesh. It cannot attack anyone who is employing a protection from evil spell. Use of a dimension door within 10ft of a leaping maw kills one leaping maw per 3 levels of the caster. Teleport will drive them out from the host. If a leaping maw remains in a host for a week, the host begins to experience surreal and vivid dreams and hallucinations that cause a permanent loss of 1 Wisdom point per leaping maw per month. When the victim reaches wisdom of 0, he becomes completely controlled by the parasites, a puppet for breeding and transmission.

— Author: Scott Wylie Roberts, "Myrystyr"

Leaping Maw: HD 1; AC 4[15]; Atk 1 bite (1d6); Move 0 (Teleport 30ft); Save 17; AL N; CL/XP 2/30; Special: Teleport, occupy host, attack against unarmored AC.

Words of Wisdom

An elderly cleric dressed in gold robes raises his hands to the sky as he prays to the gods to deliver the land from evil. The man's hands are bone thin, and his face is gaunt, as if he prefers talking to eating. Bowing their heads to the dirty street around him are 10 acolytes. Each one touches his forehead to the earth as their leader rambles on. The people of Crow's Maw stare at the long-winded cleric and his followers, then shake their heads and move on. The cleric doesn't notice the disdain of the magic-worshipping populace. He keeps praying to the gods in a voice that grows louder and stronger with every passing minute.

At the height of his speech, screams erupt among the people passing by. The cleric and his followers are hosts for **24 leaping maws**. The parasites jump from person to person in the crowd, looking for an appropriate host. The cleric and his followers are completely under the control of the leaping maws infecting their bodies. The group travels from city to city, infecting more people every time they stop to espouse their god's wisdom.

Leech, Giant

LEECH, GIANT (Freshwater)
Hit Dice: 1-6 (roll 1d6 for each to determine)
Armor Class: 9 [10]
Attacks: 1 bite (1d4)
Saving Throw: varies by hit dice
Special: Sucks blood (1hp/HD/round)
Move: 3
Alignment: Neutrality
Number Encountered: 3d6
Challenge Level/XP: varies by hit dice

Giant leeches are about one and a half feet long per hit die. After they score a hit, they drain blood automatically at one hit point per hit die of the creature. These are nasty creatures to find inhabiting the murky, muddy waters of a dungeon or swamp.

Giant Freshwater Leech (1HD): HD 1; AC 9[10]; Atk 1 bite (1d4); Move 3; Save 17; AL N; CL/XP 2/30; Special: Sucks blood (1hp/round).

Giant Freshwater Leech (2HD): HD 2; AC 9[10]; Atk 1 bite (1d4); Move 3; Save 16; AL N; CL/XP 3/60; Special: Sucks blood (2hp/round).

Giant Freshwater Leech (3HD): HD 3; AC 9[10]; Atk 1 bite (1d4); Move 3; Save 14; AL N; CL/XP 4/120; Special: Sucks blood (3hp/round).

Giant Freshwater Leech (4HD): HD 4; AC 9[10]; Atk 1 bite (1d4); Move 3; Save 13; AL N; CL/XP 5/240; Special: Sucks blood (4hp/round).

Giant Freshwater Leech (5HD): HD 5; AC 9[10]; Atk 1 bite (1d4); Move 3; Save 12; AL N; CL/XP 6/400; Special: Sucks blood (5hp/round).

Giant Freshwater Leech (6HD): HD 6; AC 9[10]; Atk 1 bite (1d4); Move 3; Save 11; AL N; CL/XP 7/600; Special: Sucks blood (6hp/round).

LEECH, GIANT (Sea)
Hit Dice: 2
Armor Class: 3 [16]
Attacks: 1 bite (2d6)
Saving Throw: 16
Special: Suck blood
Move: 6
Alignment: Neutrality
Number Encountered: 1d6
Challenge Level/XP: 5/240

If a giant leech hits with its attack, it drains a level of experience on the following round. Anyone reduced below a level of 0 will die. Lost levels of experience most likely return at a rate of 1 per day, if the character rests. Freshwater leeches are not as deadly.

Giant Sea Leech: HD 2; AC 3[16]; Atk 1 bite (2d6); Move 6; Save 16; AL N; CL/XP 5/240; Special: Sucks blood (1 level/round).

Swamp Suckers

Gertie Gravelstomper's cows are missing. The dwarf grandmother let the cows out in the morning, but they haven't returned to her farm near the dwarven city of Anvil Plunge. She's upset but can't leave her farm to go searching the Sin Mire for the missing animals. She'll pay 10 gp to anyone willing to take a raft into the swamp to hunt down the wayward cows. She's pretty sure they headed to the east that morning, and fears they might be stuck in a bog and unable to get home.

Gertie's hunch about the missing cows proves correct. The 3 cows trudge through the thick mud of the Sin Mire on their way home. Each animal struggles in the mire as the swamp tries to suck them deeper into its clutches. The cows moo plaintively as they struggle onward. Sludge pushes up around them as kick their way forward. One of the cows wears an iron bell on a rope around its neck. The bell clangs each time the tired bovine shakes its head. Attached to the undersides of the cows are **6 giant leeches**. Two leeches are attached to each cow. The bloodsuckers detach to attack fresh blood if PCs move in to rescue the lost bovines.

Leopard

Hit Dice: 3
Armor Class: 6 [13]
Attacks: 2 claws (1d3), 1 bite (1d6)
Saving Throw: 14
Special: None
Move: 16
Alignment: Neutrality
Number Encountered: 1 or 1d4
Challenge Level/XP: 3/60

Leopards are small, roaring great cats, standing about 2ft tall at the shoulder. They are not quite as fast as the other great cats, but they are stealthy hunters.

Leopard: HD 3; AC 6[13]; Atk 2 claws (1d3), 1 bite (1d6); Move 16; Save 14; AL N; CL/XP 3/60; Special: None.

Night of the Hunter

An old circus wagon sits on the side of the road leading into the small village of Lehane. The colorful wagon is filled with moldy hay. The wagon is clawed and scratched, and the driver's seat is coated in dark stains that might be old blood. A cagy **leopard** tore its way out of the wagon as the circus was leaving the village. The great cat escaped when a "trained" mammoth broke free as it was being led down the dirt road and punched a hole in the wagon. The cat attacked the driver as it escaped its confines, and then fled into the nearby woods.

Lehane is a virtual ghost town now. The wily hunting cat killed or drove out the majority of villagers. The few who stayed fear the great cat that still hunts within their village, but they have no place to go. The leopard sleeps in a rooftop garden where it killed a dwarf tending his roses. The cat climbs across the rooftops at night, hunting anyone unwise enough to be out after dark. The cat is a quiet hunter that stalks prey from above. It leaps down on PCs, clawing and biting, then flees into the village. It repeatedly ambushes people wandering the streets of its territory. During the day, it sleeps in a bower of roses where it hid the body of the dwarf gardener.

Lephane

Hit Dice: 7
Armor Class: 6 [13]
Attacks: 1 trunk (2d4 + constriction), 1 bite (1d6)
Saving Throw: 9
Special: Constriction, pull beneath water
Move: 6
Alignment: Neutrality
Number Encountered: 1d3
Challenge Level/XP: 8/800

The Lephane is a semi-aquatic relative of the Elephant, adapted for dwelling in rivers and lakes. The main body, resembling a boulder, is a shrivelled and shrunken mass, although it is still almost the size of a normal elephant's. The head is barely recognizable as an elephant's, as the ears are atrophied lumps; the trunk is much longer than that of a normal elephant. The lephane attacks by grabbing and constricting with its long, muscular trunk from underwater. Once it has struck, it can apply continuous damage per round and can drag victims underwater. If the lephane manages to drag its prey all the way to its mouth, it can also bite for 1d6 damage. In general, any creature attacking it while it is in the water will suffer a -2 penalty to hit and damage (except with spears or other good underwater weapons). Breaking free from the lephane's trunk can be managed on a roll of 1-2 on a d6.

The lephane is an accomplished swimmer, but lazy. It prefers to walk along a river bottom, poking the tip of its trunk above the water to breathe. Like its land-bound kin, it has ivory tusks that will fetch a fine reward: 100-400gp per tusk. Unlike its land-bound kin, the lephane is omnivorous; it can survive on roots and leaves, but it prefers fresh meat.
— *Author: Scott Wylie Roberts, "Myrystyr"*

Lephane: HD 7; AC 6[13]; Atk 1 trunk (2d4+constriction), 1 bite (1d6); Move 6; Save 9; AL N; CL/XP 8/800; Special: Constriction, pull beneath water.

The River Wild

A wet **monkey** sits atop an overturned canoe in the Quall River. The monkey holds a large gem in its hands. It thumps the jewel on the canoe's overturned hull, and spins it round and round in its hands. It smiles widely at its reflection in the facets. Occasionally, it leaps up and down, causing the floating canoe to bounce in the water. The canoe sits absolutely still in the water, despite the current pushing past it.

A **lephane** walking underwater overturned the canoe, dumping an elderly wizard and his pet monkey and their guide into the deadly river. The wizard was no match for the currents and was washed downstream to his death. The struggling guide died in the lephane's crushing grip. The monkey was able to scramble aboard the overturned canoe. The lephane's trunk currently rises just above the water inside the overturned canoe, anchoring it in place. The gem was in the pouch he was riding in when the lephane attacked. The monkey's name is Mizo. It is written on a red collar around the primate's neck. Mizo befriends anyone who pulls him out of the river and feeds him. The gem is a large ruby worth 1,500 gp.

Leprechaun

Hit Dice: 1
Armor Class: 8 [11]
Attacks: 1 weapon (1d6)
Saving Throw: 15
Special: Magic resistance (10%), magic abilities
Move: 18
Alignment: Neutrality
Number Encountered: 1
Challenge Level/XP: 5/400

Leprechauns are fey creatures, usually portrayed as irrational and possibly quite malevolent (although they have the common fey characteristic of being bound by bargains they make). They are somewhat magic resistant (10%), and are extremely elusive. They can become invisible and dimension door at will. They can also cast phantasmal force once per day.

Leprechaun: HD 1; AC 8[11]; Atk 1 weapon (1d6); Move 18; Save 15; AL N; CL/XP 5/400; Special: Magic resistance (10%), magic abilities.

Flickering Shades

The town of Griffon is empty, although every door stands wide open. PCs that make saving throws see strange flickering shapes just out of the corners of their eyes. These humanoid shapes appear and vanish near all of the town's doorways.

A grumpy **leprechaun** named **Jaffers Kemp** got even with the people of Griffon after the highly intelligent residents tricked him one too many times. Kemp discovered a magical clover (placed by a demon with his own bone to pick with the town) that he used to curse the villagers. The town's doors now tap into the leprechaun's *dimension door* ability and trap anyone using them. Anyone stepping through a portal anywhere in town must make a saving throw or be caught in a magical loop as they flicker from doorway to doorway. The people appear as flickering shades as they progress through the never-ending loop. PCs caught in the loop can make a saving throw each round to exit a doorway somewhere randomly in town.

Kemp dances merrily around the well in the town square. He is fully enjoying the peace and quiet now that the townsfolk are gone. The downside is that that the magical doors prevent him from using his own *dimension door* ability. If he needs to flee, the leprechaun enters a random door and can choose where and when he exits. He doesn't leave the town for fear of being caught without a means to escape.

Leucrota

Hit Dice: 6
Armor Class: 4 [15]
Attacks: 1 bite (3d6)
Saving Throw: 11
Special: None
Move: 18
Alignment: Chaos
Number Encountered: 1
Challenge Level/XP: 6/400

The leucrota has a badger's head and a lion's body, but with cloven hooves instead of claws. Its toothy mouth stretches from ear to ear (and delivers a deadly bite). The original description of a leucrota comes from Pliny the Elder, writing in the first century.

Leucrota: HD 6; AC 4[15]; Atk 1 bite (3d6); Move 18; Save 11; AL C; CL/XP 6/400; Special: None.

Chomp, Chomp

Ash trees along the southern edge of the Dry Stalk Forest are dying. Large bites have been taken out their trunks. The bark appears to have been chewed repeatedly by large teeth. Balls of cud filled with splinters lie on the ground around the trees' roots. Some of the trees are nearly chopped in half from bites ringing the bark. Halves of dead squirrels lie on the ground. Even the rocks sticking out of the ground have visible bite marks along their edges.

The damage is being done by a **leucrota** cursed to eat constantly or die. The creature chomps on everything it encounters, be it animal, mineral or plant. The leucrota moves through the forest, its flanks withered and wasting away. It hungrily attacks anyone it encounters. The creature doesn't stop eating until it is killed. Even then, its mouth continues to bite.

Lich

Hit Dice: 12+
Armor Class: 3 [16]
Attacks: Hand (1d10 + automatic paralysis)
Saving Throw: 3
Special: Appearance causes paralytic fear, touch causes automatic paralysis, spells
Move: 6
Alignment: Chaos
Number Encountered: 1
Challenge Level/XP: 12 HD (15/2,900), 13 HD (16/3,200), 14 HD (17/3,500), 15 HD (18/3,800), 16 HD (19/4,100), 17 HD (20/4,400), 18 HD (21/4,700)

Liches are the undead remnants of wizards, either made undead by their own deliberate acts during life, or as the result of other magical forces (possibly including their own magics gone awry). A lich has the same number of hit dice as the original Magic-User and the same spell-casting powers. A lich's touch causes paralysis with no saving throw, and the very sight of one of these dread creatures causes any being of 4 HD or below to flee in abject terror. Liches are highly intelligent and totally malign.

Lich (12HD): HD 12; AC 0[19]; Atk 1 hand (1d10 + automatic paralysis); Move 6; Save 3; AL C; CL/XP 15/2900; Special: Appearance causes paralytic fear, touch causes automatic paralysis, spells.

Lich (13HD): HD 13; AC 0[19]; Atk 1 hand (1d10 + automatic paralysis); Move 6; Save 3; AL C; CL/XP 16/3200; Special: Appearance causes paralytic fear, touch causes automatic paralysis, spells.

Lich (14HD): HD 14; AC 0[19]; Atk 1 hand (1d10 + automatic paralysis); Move 6; Save 3; AL C; CL/XP 17/3500; Special: Appearance causes paralytic fear, touch causes automatic paralysis, spells.

Lich (15HD): HD 15; AC 0[19]; Atk 1 hand (1d10 + automatic paralysis); Move 6; Save 3; AL C; CL/XP 18/3800; Special: Appearance causes paralytic fear, touch causes automatic paralysis, spells.

Lich (16HD): HD 16; AC 0[19]; Atk 1 hand (1d10 + automatic paralysis); Move 6; Save 3; AL C; CL/XP 19/4100; Special: Appearance causes paralytic fear, touch causes automatic paralysis, spells.

Lich (17HD): HD 17; AC 0[19]; Atk 1 hand (1d10 + automatic paralysis); Move 6; Save 3; AL C; CL/XP 20/4400; Special: Appearance causes paralytic fear, touch causes automatic paralysis, spells.

Lich (18HD): HD 18; AC 0[19]; Atk 1 hand (1d10 + automatic paralysis); Move 6; Save 3; AL C; CL/XP 21/4700; Special: Appearance causes paralytic fear, touch causes automatic paralysis, spells.

Souls for the Forge

Molten metal and burning forges combine to produce incredible heat and oppressive palls of thick black smoke in the Forge-Temple of Kolamax. Silver streams flow slowly down channels cut through stone gears that turn randomly to redirect the molten streams into various vats. A waterfall of molten metal rains down from an upper balcony in the center of the table. A circular table with metal clamps spins through the waterfall, sending splashes of superheated silver flying. Smoldering bodies seared black are clamped into place on the rotating disc. A withered body lies on a stone table far away from the metal and fire.

The **lich Arus Kezanlizil** rules the Forge-Temple, claiming it after an unforeseen accident transferred his undead spirit into the body of the dwarven cleric **Arbor Oakenchisel**. The dwarf's mind was rapidly consumed by the lich, but his memories and abilities remained for the lich to misuse. Kezanlizil believes that he can craft a blade from the spirits of the dead that will separate him from the hated dwarf body he finds himself trapped within. Kezanlizil has full access to his spells and abilities in this new form. The lich has experimented on dozens of hapless victims, but thinks he now how the means to craft the blade. He just needs new bodies to fasten to the wheel to power his next experiment.

Lichenthrope

Hit Dice: 3
Armor Class: 6 [13]
Attacks: 1 bite or weapon (1d6)
Saving Throw: 14
Special: Shapechange, 25% magic resistance (in hound form only), contagion
Move: 12
Alignment: Chaotic
Number Encountered: 1d8
Challenge Level/XP: 5/240

Lichenthropes are human (or similar) creatures that have been infected by a carefully prepared mixture of spores and alchemical ingredients. This infusion causes a condition with effects similar enough to lycanthropy that the infected victims are treated as were-creatures for all purposes except one. Because lichenthropy is an alchemical condition rather than a supernatural one, lichenthropes are not immune to normal weapons, as true were-creatures are. They are, on the other hand, still affected by magic weapons that are especially enchanted against were-creatures.

At will, a lichenthrope can take one of two non-human forms in addition to its human one. The first of these is a noisome agglomeration of fungus-material shaped somewhat like a dog. In this form, the lichenthrope is resistant to magic (25%) and immune to any sort of mental control that would not ordinarily affect a plant. The second non-human form of a lichenthrope is a formless mass of fungus with an air bladder that allows it to fly, provided that it has a full combat round to inhale air.

Lichenthropes can commune with any form of intelligent plant, although they do not exert actual control over such plants.

Any character suffering 50% damage from the attacks of a lichenthrope will begin transforming into a lichenthrope. However, since the process of lichenthropy is alchemical and normally induced directly by a creator of lichenthropes, the transformation does not always proceed in a predictable way. There is a 50% chance that an infected character will simply turn progressively into a mess of disgusting fungus over the course of 1d4 weeks. During this time, whether the transformation is proceeding normally or not, the process can be arrested and cured by the use of a *cure disease* spell.

— *Author: Matt Finch*

Lichenthrope: HD 3; AC 6[13]; Atk 1 weapon (1d8); Move 12; Save 14; AL C; CL/XP 5/240; Special: Shapechange, 25% magic resistance (in hound form only), contagion.

Beware the Moors

The Feisty Harlot Tavern & Inn sits on the edge of the Felderine Moors. The tavern is run by a stooped old woman named Madame Ilista Farnsworth. She wears a dark shawl over her gray hair, and a long dress that hides her turnip-shaped body. She shuffles slowly about her tavern, taking orders, making drinks and chatting with the few people who come into the tavern from the village of Felder nearly a quarter mile down the marsh road. Madame Ilista spits between her fingers often to keep the evils of the moors away. The old woman refuses to go out after dark, and she warns PCs not to do so. Several villagers are still missing after the gray mists rolled across the moors. She wears a silver necklace to ward off spirits.

The moors are alive with nocturnal animals rustling the plants. Numerous small ponds dot the open fields, with bogbean and cinquefoil growing abundantly on the dark waters. Moneywort and clubmoss fill the fields. Nightshade grows in clumps. A **lichenthrope wolf** made entirely of deadly nightshade stalks the moors, attacking and transforming villagers into deadly plant animals. The lichenthrope hunts during the full moon and attacks by rising out of the marshy plants to spring on its victims. It usually waits until the mists cover much of the moors before leaping to

attack stragglers. It controls a pack of former villagers converted into **4 lichenthropes**. The pack waits until the leader attacks before they fly and run in to bring down travelers.

Linnorm

Hit Dice: 7
Armor Class: 3 [16]
Attacks: 1 bite (3d6 + poison) and 1 constrict (3d4)
Saving Throw: 9
Special: Poison, constrict, swallow whole, immune to poison, silence and invisibility, breath weapon
Move: 12/12 (swimming)
Alignment: Chaos
Number Encountered: 1d2
Challenge Level/XP: Challenge Level = (hit points/4) +2

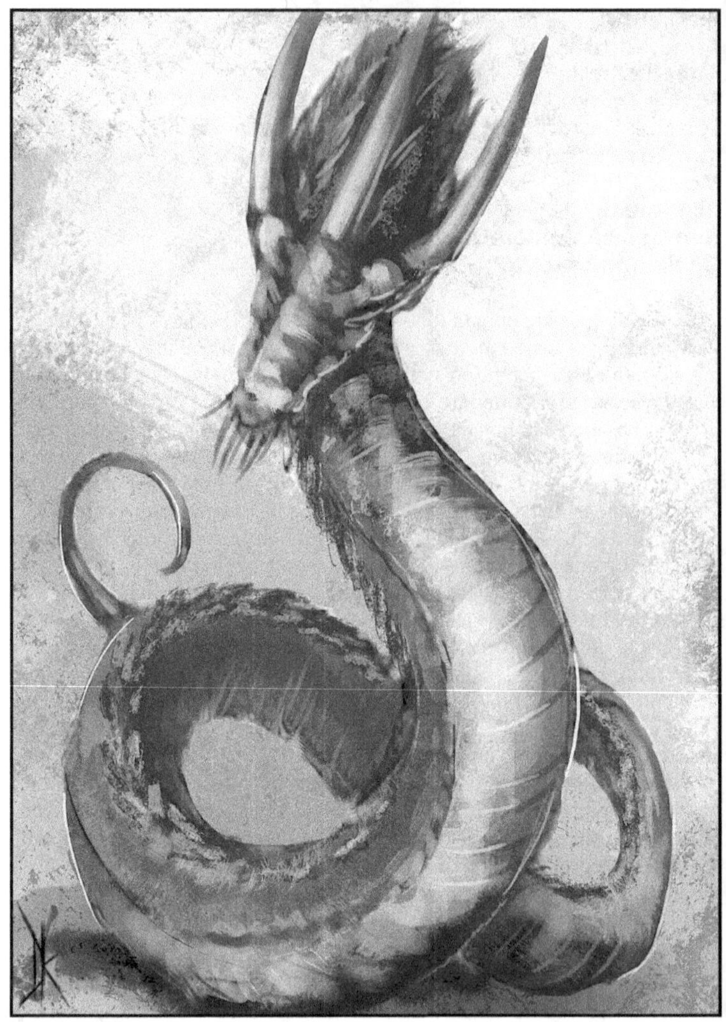

Linnorms look like massive serpents with draconic heads. Linnorms never speak, nor do they have spell-casting ability. Linnorms attack with their bite which deals grievous damage and injects a deadly poison into their opponents (save or die). A linnorm may also constrict an opponent for 3d4 points of damage per round. If a linnorm attacks with its bite and 4 or more than the number needed in rolled on its attack dice, the victim is swallowed whole. Swallowed victims suffer 2d4 hit points of damage per round and may only strike back at the linnorm with short weapons. The inside of a linnorm is considered armor class 8[11].

Linnorms share the size categories and age categories of dragons. They are deaf, detecting heat and vibration, and are therefore unaffected by silence and invisibility. Thrice per day, linnorms may breathe a cloud of poisonous gas 30ft long, 20ft wide, and 10ft high, which deals damage equal to the linnorm's full hit points (save for half damage). Linnorms may not be subdued and are immune to poison. They are excellent swimmers and sometimes lair in or near large bodies of water.

— *Author: John Turcotte, © 2006*

Adult Linnorm (7HD): HD 7; AC 3[16]; Atk 1 bite (3d6 + poison) and 1 constrict (3d4); Move 12 (Swim 12); Save 9; AL C; CL/XP 9/1100; Special: Poison, constrict, swallow whole, immune to poison, silence and invisibility, breath weapon.

Worms on the Waterfront

The halfling inventor Ollie Nematod made a huge mistake. His plan to sail his ship along the waters of Halfordness' north coast to watch the giant linnorms cavorting in the waves and sand instead drew the attention of the massive worm-like creatures. The spawning ground is a deadly spot for anyone to visit given the multitude of linnorms congregating there each year. Ollie's sightseeing expedition was going perfectly as the ship sailed outside the churning waters where the linnorms swam. Ollie watched the great worms using a spyglass of his own creation.

Everything changed when he dropped the metal-and-glass contraption into the ocean. The sound of the spyglass hitting the waves caused a number of the worms to swim out to investigate. The ship's captain set sail immediately, turning the three-master for port in a desperate bid to outrun the approaching worms. It almost worked. But the first sight of the giant linnorms rising near Halfordness' pier caused panic on the waterfront. Soon enough, **3 linnorms** crawled ashore, driving terrified residents before them through the cobblestone streets.

Lion

Hit Dice: 5+2
Armor Class: 6 [13]
Attacks: 2 claws (1d4), 1 bite (1d8)
Saving Throw: 12
Special: None
Move: 12
Alignment: Neutrality
Number Encountered: 1d6
Challenge Level/XP: 5/240

A lioness has an AC of 7[12], but is otherwise similar to the male lion. The first lion encountered will be male; all the rest in the encounter will be lionesses.

Lion: HD 5+2; AC 6[13]; Atk 2 claws (1d4), 1 bite (1d8); Move 12; Save 12; AL N; CL/XP 5/240; Special: None.

Leaping Lions

The streets of Bards Bottom are empty, and the doors and windows of the small cottages are shut and locked tight. People move inside their homes, but no one opens their doors to strangers. A few brave souls crack their shutters to warn PCs to get off the road before the cats see them. They tell PCs to steer clear of the tavern on the hill.

The Bard's Call tavern sits empty. Its door is splintered, and giant claw marks mar the wooden posts holding up the covered porch. A pride of **5 lions** that escaped from a magic-user's zoo now lives inside the tavern. The animals wear collars that let them dimension door forward with each leap, essentially doubling their movement. Residents are trapped in their homes, unable to escape without attracting the lions' attention. Visitors find themselves flanked by the lions as they hunt new prey.

Lithonnite

Hit Dice: 8
Armor Class: 2[17] (frontal shell) or 6[13] (body)
Attacks: 2 tentacles (2d6)
Saving Throw: 8
Special: Body (not shell) immune to blunt weapons
Move: 9
Alignment: Neutrality
Number Encountered: 1 or 1d2
Challenge Level/XP: 9/1,100

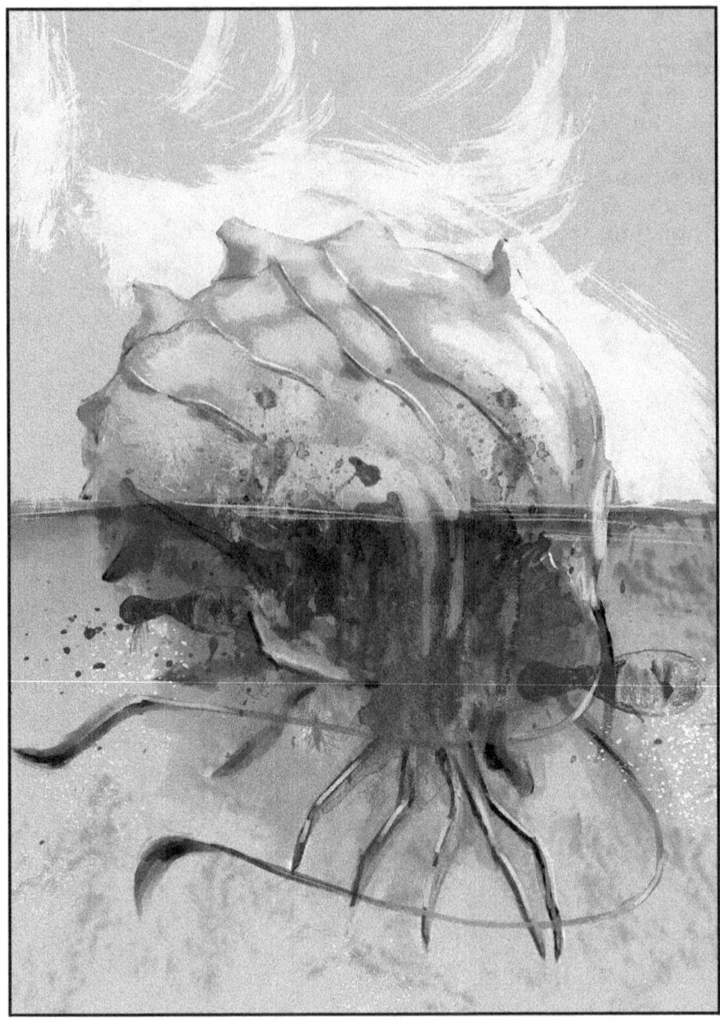

Lithonnites are huge mollusk-like creatures, about one ton in weight, living in subterranean and surface environments. The front of a lithonnite's body is encased in a powerful shell, even to the rock-like eyelids. When the rest of the lithonnite's body is concealed in a grotto or under water, the shell appears like a boulder or other natural rock. It is not possible for the lithonnite to draw its soft body entirely into the shell. In combat, the lithonnite reaches around its shell with two slug-like tentacles to attack. The creature's frontal portion, protected by the shell, can be attacked by any sort of weapon; behind the shell, the soft body is AC 6[13], but cannot be affected by blunt weapons due to its boneless consistency.

— *Author: Matt Finch*

Lithonnite: HD 8; AC 2[17] (frontal shell), 6[13] (body); Atk 2 tentacles (2d6); Move 9; Save 8; AL N; CL/XP 9/1100; Special: Body immune to blunt weapons.

Island in the Stream

Cool water drips from the algae-covered walls of this underground grotto. A river runs through the dark caverns, surging out of the cavern wall before vanishing back underground. The rocky shore is alive with albino crabs and crayfish that crawl over one another in a mad scramble of claws and shells. The clacking of their pinchers is loud in the still room. A massive boulder in the center of the underground river is covered with hundreds more of the crustaceans. The current pushes the body of an elf against the boulder, the rushing water holding the corpse in place against the stone. The crabs scuttle over the body, picking at its flesh. The elf wears waterlogged leather armor.

The boulder is a lithonnite that crawled up from the depths into this cavern. The lithonnite brought a host of albino crabs with it. The lithonnite killed the elf when he waded into the stream to search the rock. The elf carries a pouch on his belt that contains 43 gp, a flat stone with the initials L.C. carved into it, and a small journal he kept about his adventures. A crude map to a lost treasure is drawn inside the cover of the leather journal.

Lizard Samurai

	SAMURAI	SAMURAI CAPTAIN
Hit Dice:	3	6
Armor Class:	3 [16]	2 [17]
Attacks:	1 sword (1d8) or 2 arrows (1d6)	1 sword (1d8) or 2 arrows (1d6)
Saving Throw:	14	11
Special:	Improved saving throw	Improved saving throw
Move:	9	9
Alignment:	Any	Any
Number Encountered:	1d10+20	1
Challenge Level/XP:	3/60	6/400

Lizard samurai come from some unknown race of bipedal lizards, possibly from the spirit world, possibly from another dimension, possibly from far lands. They are only encountered in elaborate armor, bearing sharp swords and sometimes with longbows. Lizard samurai follow a strict code of combat, but consider humans of non-fighting social class to be animals virtually beneath their notice. When venturing into human lands, they are normally formed into well-organized military units, sometimes with members of some other race serving as auxiliary troops. These military units generally consist of at least 20 of the lizard samurai, and are always led by a captain with 6 hit dice. Lizard samurai make all saving throws at +1 (already reflected in the statistics).

— Author: Matt Finch

Lizard Samurai: HD 3; AC 3[16]; Atk 1 sword (1d8) or 2 arrows (1d6); Move 9; Save 14; AL Any; CL/XP 3/60; Special: Improved saving throw.

Lizard Samurai Captain: HD 6; AC 2[17]; Atk 1 sword (1d8) or 2 arrows (1d6); Move 9; Save 11; AL Any; CL/XP 6/400; Special: Improved saving throw.

Warrior Lizards Marching Off to War

The sound of bugles rises through the countryside, and the marching feet of an army on the move can be heard around the bend. But the group that marches into view is not human in the least. Instead, a vanguard of **9 lizard samurai** marches in unison around a massive **ko'haai.** On the massive lizard's back is a howdah where an obese **lizard samurai** lounges on plush cushions as it rides leisurely along.

A line of 20 human and elf slaves are chained to the howdah and march miserably along behind the ko'haai. A female elf slave sits beside the leader lizard, feeding him small white mice from a covered silver bowl. The lizard samurai are marching from a lizardman colony in the Sin Mire Swamp to the Seething Jungle where they plan to beseech the snake-like ophidians for aid against the humans of Mirerest. The slaves following in the lizards' wake are gifts for the snake men. The lizard samurai attack anyone the encounter on the road.

Lizard, Giant

Hit Dice: 3
Armor Class: 5 [14]
Attacks: 1 bite (1d8)
Saving Throw: 14
Special: None
Move: 12
Alignment: Neutrality
Number Encountered: 1d6
Challenge Level/XP: 3/60

Giant lizards (the ones described here, in any case) are about 4ft tall at the shoulder (not quite large enough to ride). Larger specimens could certainly be found – perhaps they continue to grow throughout their long lives, leading to giant lizards of close to saurian dimensions.

Giant Lizard: HD 3; AC 5[14]; Atk 1 bite (1d8); Move 12; Save 14; AL N; CL/XP 3/60; Special: None.

Broad Head, No Tail

A large wriggling tail lies pinned to the ground by four sharp stakes attached to a bent sapling. The spiked tree trap punctures the tail, pinning it to the ground. The spikes are driven deeply into the dirt. Trees and brambles surround the open area. Very little blood dots the ground around the tail, and it appears that the tail pulled cleanly away from whatever it had been attached to. The remains of a half-eaten goat lie on the ground near the tail.

The tail is from a **broad-headed skink giant lizard** that triggered a trap set by hunters. The angry, tailless lizard hides in the brambles. It charges out to attack anyone bothering its old tail.

Lizard, Lightning

Hit Dice: 5
Armor Class: 3 [16]
Attacks: 2 claws (1d4) and 1 bite (1d8) or lightning blast (4d6)
Saving Throw: 12
Special: Lightning blast (4d6)
Move: 12
Alignment: Neutrality
Number Encountered: 1 or 1d4
Challenge Level/XP: 6/400

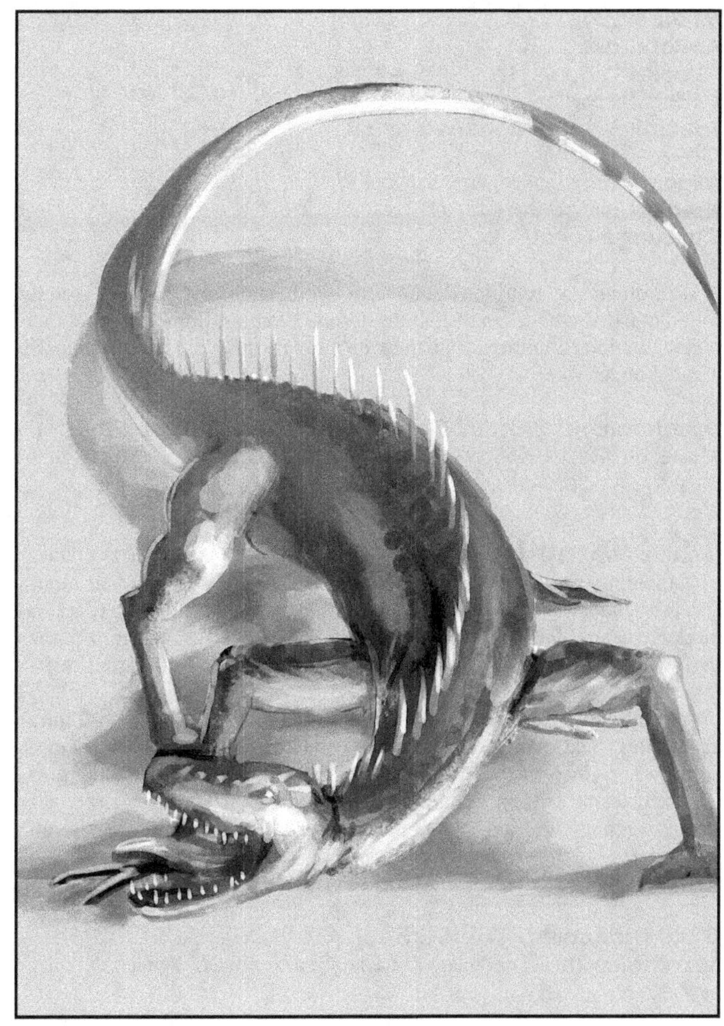

Lightning lizards stand 5ft in height and may reach a length of 14ft. Their scales are a shimmering blue and sparks of lightning constantly crackle around their maw. Lightning lizards have sometimes been used as mounts for powerful orcish chiefs or tribal lords.

A lightning lizard may spew a crackling stream of lightning to assault its foes twice per day. A successful save halves the damage. Lightning lizards are immune to electrical based attacks or spells.

A rare breed of flying lightning lizards are known to exist. They are identical to their earthbound kin with the addition of massive wings which give them a flying movement of 18 (which adjusts the CL/XP to 8/800).

— *Author: Skathros*

Lightning Lizard: HD 5; AC 3[16]; Atk 2 claws (1d4), 1 bite (1d8) or Lighting Blast (4d6); Move 12; Save 12; AL N; CL/XP 6/400; Special: Lightning blast.

Lightning in a Bottleneck

Steep cliffs rise around the tight stone walls of the Khypher Pass. The high walls shroud the rocky trail in deep shadows. Constant storms cover the area, drawn by the high amounts of metal found in the rocks. Lightning blasts out of the black, roiling clouds overhead. Jagged bolts strike the stone with loud resounding booms that echo throughout the canyon. Boulders blasted off the cliffs nearly block the pass, forcing travelers to wind around or climb over them.

The cliffs are home to **6 flying lightning lizards** that launch themselves off the rock walls to descend on potential prey. Travelers using the pass find themselves blasted by streams of lightning as the lizards soar overhead before landing to attack. If the fight goes against the lizards, they climb back up the sheer rock walls to escape. In one of the caves at the top of the cliff is the body of a dead traveler. The dwarf's beard is singed off by electricity, his bald head burned black by the blast. He has a *+2 hammer* hanging from his belt.

301

Lizardman

Hit Dice: 2+1
Armor Class: 5 [14]
Attacks: 2 claws (1d3), 1 bite (1d8)
Saving Throw: 16
Special: Breathe underwater
Move: 6/12 (swimming)
Alignment: Usually Chaos
Number Encountered: 1d10 x4
Challenge Level/XP: 2/30

Lizardmen are reptilian humanoids, both male and female, usually living in tribal villages in the depths of fetid swamps. Some can hold their breath for long durations (an hour or more), while others can actually breathe underwater.

Lizardman: HD 2+1; AC 5[14]; Atk 2 claws (1d3), 1 bite (1d6); Move 6 (Swim 12); Save 16; AL C; CL/XP 2/30; Special: Breathe underwater.

The Swamp Patrol

A mockingbird's call rises above the Sin Mire, the sound echoed and repeated endlessly. Locusts buzz in the tall grass, and dragonflies dart and circle travelers. Frogs munch the swarms of gnats, flies and mosquitoes that rise from the murky waters. Deep splashes signal alligators diving into the marsh.

A band of **12 lizardmen** hunts throughout the Sin Mire with **2 giant crocodiles**. The group moves slowly and methodically as the lizards search every inch of the vast morass. The walking lizards use the grass and mud of the swamp to hide their scaly bodies from the dwarven city of Anvil Plunge built on the edge of the mire. The lizardmen seek a relic lost long ago to the swamp's expanding borders. The silver lizard statue is believed to turn any creature it touches into a lizardman.

Giant Crocodile: HD 6; AC 3[16]; Atk 1 bite (3d6), 1 tail (1d6); Move 9 (Swim 12); Save 11; AL N; CL/XP 6/400; Special: None.

Lobster-Giant

Hit Dice: 10
Armor Class: 2[17]
Attacks: 2 pincers (2d6)
Saving Throw: 5
Special: Grabs
Move: 9/9 (swimming)
Alignment: Chaos
Number Encountered: 1 or 2
Challenge Level/XP: 12/2,000

The Lobster-Giants are strange and rare creatures, living in swamps and remote coastal shallows. They are not related either to giants or to lobsters, save for the fact that they are indeed a bizarre form of intelligent (albeit somewhat stupid) crustaceans. In addition to a pair of large pincers, lobster-giants have a ridge of smaller "arms" along the length of the underbelly, and these smaller limbs are coated with a paralytic poison.

Lobster-Giants attack with their two pincers, and if they succeed in hitting an opponent with both pincers, they have also managed to grab hold and hug the opponent to their chests, where the smaller limbs can scrabble through armor and scratch with the poison. A victim who has been grabbed will suffer an additional 2d6 attacks, and for of these that hits a saving throw is required to avoid being paralyzed for 1d10 turns. A character is allowed to attempt breaking out of the giant's pincer-grip each round, which is done by rolling 4d6. If the resulting number is equal to or lower than the character's strength, the character has escaped.

— *From Black Monastery, detailed by Matt Finch*

Lobster-Giant: HD 10; AC 2[17]; Atk 2 pincers (2d6); Move 9/9 (swimming); Save 5; AL C; CL/XP 12/2000; Special: Grab for 2d6 extra paralysis attacks when hitting with both pincers.

The One That Should Have Gotten Away

Three bodies lie on Bargarsport's waterfront pier. The corpses are crushed into nearly unrecognizable lumps. Blood drains along the wooden planks and into the water below, attracting **4 sharks** into the shallows beneath the pier. Nets hanging along the pier are sliced apart, spilling piles of rotting fish across the dock. One of the large piles shifts slowly, sending fish raining into the water.

A **lobster-giant** came ashore recently, lured by the smell of the day's catch sitting in great nets along the dock. The lobster-giant crushed the morning fishermen, then slashed open nets strung up on the dock containing the catch unloaded that morning by a fishing vessel. The smelly haul dropped atop the lobster-giant. It still sits beneath the fish pile, munching happily on cod and tuna. The lobster-giant bursts out of the pile in a shower of gore, scales and bone to attack PCs.

Lurker, Ceiling

Hit Dice: 10
Armor Class: 6 [13]
Attacks: 1 crush (1d6)
Saving Throw: 5
Special: Smother, surprise
Move: 1/7 (flying)
Alignment: Neutrality
Number Encountered: 1
Challenge Level/XP: 12/2,000

Lurkers resemble floating manta rays, with a rough, stone-like undersurface. They levitate to ceiling-tops and wait for prey to walk underneath, whereupon they drop and enfold the victim in their thick "wings" (to-hit roll). Anyone trapped inside a lurker's clutches takes 1d6 points of damage per round from crushing, and will suffocate within 1d4+1 rounds unless the lurker is killed. There is normally only a 10% chance to detect a lurker's presence visually before it attacks, and it has a 65% chance to gain initiative automatically (unless a "surprise roll" system is being used, in which case the lurker has a 4 in 6 chance to gain surprise).

Ceiling Lurker: HD 10; AC 6[13]; Atk 1 crush (1d6); Move 1 (Fly 7); Save 5; AL N; CL/XP 12/2,000; Special: Smother.

To Kill a King

A wooden throne sits on a dais in the center of this empty and long-unused throne room. Sculpted stone faces adorn the walls. Each head is five foot tall from brow to chin and has a permanent *magic mouth* on it that allows the face to speak a series of programmed phrases. The heads offer motivationally uplifting words meant for royal ears.

A skeleton lies facedown on the floor before the throne. The bones are wrapped in silk clothing and have a long purple robe that leaves just the head and arms exposed. Looking under the robe reveals crushed and broken bones. The body is all that remains of **Mad King Manalcris**, a ruler whose vanity caused his kingdom to crumble until he was left in his empty castle listening to the words of his stone-faced "advisers."

The high ceiling is home to the king's killer: a **ceiling lurker**. The lurker drops on anyone investigating the skeletal remains. It feeds on those who enter the castle looking for forgotten treasures. Its past meals can be found slumped in various parts of the castle. All of their bones are crushed and broken from the lurker's embrace.

LYCANTHROPES

Lycanthropes are were-creatures, particularly those in whom the disease permits assumption of a hybrid form of the human and animal. They cannot be hit by normal weapons: only silver and magical weapons affect them. If anyone is attacked and brought below 50% hit points by a lycanthrope, the person will become a lycanthrope himself.

Lycanthrope, Werebear

Hit Dice: 7+3
Armor Class: 2 [17]
Attacks: 2 claws (1d3), 1 bite (2d4)
Saving Throw: 9
Special: Lycanthropy, hit only by magic or silver weapons. hug
Move: 9
Alignment: Neutrality or Chaos
Number Encountered: 1 or 1d4+1
Challenge Level/XP: 8/800

Werebears are often found in temperate forests. On an attack roll of 18+ (natural roll) with its claws, the werebear grabs its victim and hugs it for an additional 2d8 points of damage.

Werebear: HD 7+3; AC 2[17]; Atk 2 claws (1d3), 1 bite (2d4); Move 9; Save 9; AL N or C; CL/XP 8/800; Special: Lycanthropy.

The Silver Glove

A falling-down wooden shack stands amid a grove of oak trees. The shack's walls are warped, and its flat roof buckles in the middle where a tree branch grows out of the structure. The oak trees support a covered porch that wraps around the building. The bark on the trees is rubbed off and lies in splintered bits on the porch deck. The shack's door is painted bright red. Inside the cabin, an old man sits in a comfortable rocking chair by a large pot-belly stove. His wide grin shows his many teeth as he welcomes visitors. He wraps his tiny frame in a large bearskin blanket for warmth. Candles melting in clay pots provide light.

A magical gauntlet sits on a credenza beside the door. The gauntlet glows with a soft silver light and grants the wearer the ability to see in the dark. It comes with a downside, however, as it turns the wearer into a werebear within a year if he fails a saving throw.

The old man is **Urlak the Great**, the owner – and victim – of the glove. He's a friendly sort unless angered. If someone touches the glove (or gives it too many glances), he throws the bearskin rug away and gets up in the PC's face. His scrawny body doesn't pose much of a threat, but if pushed he changes to his **werebear** form and attacks.

Lycanthrope, Wereboar

Hit Dice: 5+2
Armor Class: 4 [15]
Attacks: Bite (2d6)
Saving Throw: 12
Special: Lycanthropy, hit only by magic or silver weapons
Move: 12
Alignment: Neutrality or Chaos
Number Encountered: 1 or 2d4
Challenge Level/XP: 6/400

Wereboars are often found in the remote wilderness. They can take the form of a boar, a human, or a boar-like biped.

Wereboar: HD 5+2; AC 4[15]; Atk 1 bite (2d6); Move 12; Save 12; AL N or C; CL/XP 6/400; Special: Lycanthropy, hit only by magic or silver weapons

Pig in a Poke

Two shifty looking dwarves struggle down a dark alley in Bargarsport. They carry a large rolled up carpet between them as they stagger into the darkness. The rug struggles weakly in their grasp, causing them to drop it every so often. The pair occasionally beat the rug senseless before picking it up again and moving on.

Kazlach and **Stroog** are slave traders who abduct people off the street and deliver them to the waterfront slave ships. The pair wait in the alleys and ambush passers-by. Kazlach smacks victims over the head, and Stroog catches them in the unrolled rug. Their last victim, however, refuses to get carried off to his fate in peace. The man keeps waking up, threatening to draw attention to the dwarf slavers. Extra beatings aren't helping, and only seem to be making the man madder. The dwarves are ready to abandon their plan and just kill the man unless PCs intervene.

Anyone unrolling the carpet is in for quite a shock. The semiconscious man inside the carpet is Skallec Prieststabber, a **wereboar** mercenary. Skallec transforms into his wereboar self to attack once he fully wakes up in 1d4+1 rounds.

Lycanthrope, Wererat

Hit Dice: 3
Armor Class: 6 [13]
Attacks: Bite (1d3), Weapon (1d6)
Saving Throw: 14
Special: Control rats, lycanthropy, hit only by magic or silver weapons
Move: 12
Alignment: Chaos
Number Encountered: 2d12
Challenge Level/XP: 4/120

Wererats are often found in cities, lurking in shadowy alleyways. Wererats can control rats, and are extremely stealthy, surprising opponents on 1–4 on a d6.

Wererat: HD 3; AC 6[13]; Atk 1 bite (1d3), 1 weapon (1d6); Move 12; Save 14; AL C; CL/XP 4/120; Special: Lycanthropy, control rats, surprise, hit only by magic or silver weapons.

Rat's Revenge

The village of Illmoor sits along a quiet tributary of the Quall River. The farmers are all retired human fighters (the youngest is in his 80s) who found peace in this idyllic village carved out among the plentiful ash trees. Wading birds nest along the slow-moving river, and deer are plentiful in the woods. The warriors hunt and fish to pass the time.

But there's a rat in the village. Or, more specifically, a lot of rats. Illmoor's mayor recently discovered that the communal grain bin near his farm is infested with hundreds of normal rats. The miller found a similar problem: **6 giant rats** moved in overnight to feast on his grain. With winter fast approaching, the rats are eating up food the villagers stored to get them through the coldest months. Residents even complain they are finding rats in their cellars gnawing at their personal supplies.

A recent addition to the town is the root of the problem. **Faragin Gorl** is a **wererat** who discovered that one of the old men slew his pack brother. The vengeful Faragin is taking his revenge on the entire town. He sends the rats on missions to make life miserable, and plans to eventually infect the villagers with lycanthropy to start his own wererat nest. Faragin lives in a small guest house on the mayor's land. The villagers think he is a traveling woodsman looking for work.

Lycanthrope, Weretiger

Hit Dice: 6
Armor Class: 3 [16]
Attacks: 2 claws (1d4), 1 bite (1d10)
Saving Throw: 11
Special: Lycanthropy, hit only by magic or silver weapons
Move: 12
Alignment: Neutrality or Chaos
Number Encountered: 1d2
Challenge Level/XP: 7/600

Weretigers are often found in tropical cities and ancient jungle ruins, but will appear in more temperate climates as well, if tigers live in the surrounding wilderness. These lycanthropes can assume the form of a tiger, a human, or a bipedal, tiger-like hybrid of the two forms.

Weretiger: HD 6; AC 3[16]; Atk 2 claws (1d4), 1 bite (1d10); Move 12; Save 11; AL N or C; CL/XP 7/600; Special: Lycanthropy, hit only by magic or silver weapons.

Hunter Games

Bloody leaves and clawed trees mark the boundary of a deadly six-square-mile hunting ground used by the **rakshasa Tunis el-Cine** and his companion, the **weretiger Mellina Curdil**. The pair abduct people from Bordig's Basin, a river community whose growing presence is depleting the forest's deer population, and bring them to the center of the game preserve. The pair gives the villagers an hour's head start (if they are feeling generous) and then hunt the unfortunate victims through the rugged terrain.

Mellina is a comely woman who uses her charms to lure men into the woods. She wears a silver tiger brooch that contains red lipstick that causes anyone she kisses to fall asleep if they fail a saving throw. Those who fall asleep are taken into the deep woods where they awaken a day later with the vicious hunters standing over them. The skeletons of Tunis and Mellina's victims are scattered throughout the forest. The couple play with their prey as they chase them through the woods. They've also rigged deadfalls and covered pits throughout the forest to make things more interesting. If their prey escapes outside the blood boundary, they can go free (again, if the hunters are feeling generous). No one has lived through the horrible hunt yet.

Lycanthrope, Wereweasel

Hit Dice: 3+2
Armor Class: 4 [15]
Attacks: 1 bite (1d6) and weapon (1d8)
Saving Throw: 14
Special: Drain blood, lycanthropy, +1 initiative, hit only by magical or silver weapons
Move: 15
Alignment: Chaos
Number Encountered: 1 or 1d4+2
Challenge Level/XP: 5/240

Wereweasels tend to be aggressive, cruel and vicious. In their lycanthrope form, they are sleek and quick, biting for 2d4 hit points of damage in addition to any weapons they may wield. They continue to drain blood after a successful bite, inflicting an additional 2d4 points of damage per melee round until slain or until they release their prey. As with other were-creatures, the bite also has a chance to inflict lycanthropy. These lithe creatures are fast, gaining a +1 bonus on initiative rolls. Wereweasels are often found with 1d4 giant weasels, which obey their commands. In human form, wereweasels tend to be thin and wiry, dark of aspect with sharp features.

— Author: John Turcotte

Were-weasel: HD 3+2; AC 4[15]; Atk 1 bite (1d6) and weapon (1d8); Move 15; Save 14; AL C; CL/XP 5/240; Special: Drain blood, lycanthropy, +1 initiative, hit only by magical or silver weapons.

King Weasel

A redwood tree in the Kajaani Forest is hollow, carved out by wood-boring insects that infested the tree before dying off during the harsh winter. The tree contains spacious rooms and corridors that wind randomly up throughout the 80-foot-diameter trunk. Dead beetle husks fill many of the lower chambers like a crunching carpet. Natural knots in the wood allow for easy climbing inside the tree as natural tunnels wind and twist in every direction. The tree's bark is covered in the dry husks of thousands of voracious beetles.

Marley Von Torgen, an eccentric wereweasel, considers himself king of the forest and all of its inhabitants. He dresses in silk robes and wears a platinum crown (100 gp). He addresses visitors from a thick branch 30 feet off the ground. He demands tribute from PCs in the amount of 200 gp per person. If ignored, he orders **8 giant weasels** to attack. The weasels hide inside piles of beetle husks scattered around the base of the tree.

Giant Weasel: HD 3+3; AC 6[13]; Atk 1 bite (2d6 + blood drain); Move 15; Save 14; AL N; CL/XP 4/120; Special: Drain blood.

Lycanthrope, Werewolf

Hit Dice: 4+4
Armor Class: 5 [14]
Attacks: Bite (2d4)
Saving Throw: 13
Special: Lycanthropy, hit only by magic or silver weapons
Move: 12
Alignment: Usually Chaos
Number Encountered: 3d6
Challenge Level/XP: 5/240

Werewolves are the traditional Lycanthropes seen in horror movies. They can turn into a wolf or into a wolf-man. Wolvesbane keeps them at bay.

Werewolf: HD 4+4; AC 5[14]; Atk 1 bite (1d6+1); Move 12; Save 13; AL C; CL/XP 5/240; Special: Lycanthropy, hit only by magic or silver weapons.

Where Wolf?

A 20-foot-tall mirror reflects the black walls of this sloping chamber. Unfinished marble statues stand throughout the room. Each sculpture faces the massive mirror. One statue holding a *crystal ball* in its outstretched hand appears to be trying to drop the ball into a shallow depression atop a 4-foot-tall stone pillar standing at the base of the mirror. Five glowing braziers stand each side of the room.

The mirror reflects the chamber and statues, but anyone making a saving throw realizes there are more statues in the mirror than in the room. If the crystal ball is removed from the statue's hand and placed into the depression, the mirror flickers and the missing statues reappear in the room. Each new statue wears a jeweled necklace and crown. These baubles are worth 2,400 gp total if removed from the statues. The old statues in the room don't have the jewels or crowns.

Besides the statues, the **werewolf Aldus Max** also returns when the statues are summoned. Aldus has been trapped in the mirror world for five years. He wears a *ring of invisibility* that allows him to remain invisible. The werewolf is insane after his years in exile and attacks anyone stealing the jewels from his statue "friends."

If the *crystal ball* is removed from the pillar, anyone in the chamber must make a saving throw or be drawn into the mirror trap and imprisoned. The statue holding the crystal ball is a **stone golem** whose sole task is to retrieve the globe 2d8 rounds after it is removed from its hands.

Stone Golem: HD 15 (60hp); AC 5[14]; Atk 1 fist (3d8); Move 6; Save 3; AL N; CL/XP 16/3200; Special: +1 or better magic weapon to hit, immune to most magic.

Lynx, Giant

Hit Dice: 2
Armor Class: 6 [13]
Attacks: 2 claws (1d2), 1 bite (1d4)
Saving Throw: 16
Special: Rear claws, surprise
Move: 12
Alignment: Neutrality
Number Encountered: 1d4
Challenge Level/XP: 2/30

If a giant lynx hits with both of its front claws, it can make 2 more attacks with its rear claws. These large cats are found in the cold wilderness, where they hide in trees waiting for prey, then leap to the attack. They are highly intelligent, and can communicate with each other when coordinated action is needed. As with the common lynx, giant lynx are well camouflaged, and if waiting in ambush they will surprise opponents (5 in 6 chance).

Giant Lynx: HD 2; AC 6[13]; Atk 2 claws (1d2), 1 bite (1d4); Move 12; Save 16; AL N; CL/XP 2/30; Special: Rear claws, surprise.

Beak and Claw

The dirt covering Farmer Emil Rodger's fields are churned and trampled. Blood puddles around the bodies of 15 emus that have been ripped apart in their fenced-in pen. The giant birds' necks and bodies are shredded and gnawed. Many are missing entire wings. The farmer and his wife are heartbroken. They hatched the birds from eggs, and raised them for years as their children.

The farm sits on land a roaming pride of lynxes visits every couple of years. The giant birds lasted less than a day once the vicious cats converged on the farm. The pride sleeps under a rock overhang in the forest. They return to the farm each night, looking for more easy meals. The **8 lynxes** skulk about the homestead, their bright eyes glittering in the darkness. The farmer and his terrified wife beg for help. They claim that demonic screams arise around the farm each night.

Macaw, Giant

Hit Dice: 5
Armor Class: 5 [14]
Attacks: 1 beak (1d10)
Saving Throw: 12
Special: None
Move: 6/20 (flying)
Alignment: Neutrality
Number Encountered: 1d8
Challenge Level/XP: 6/400

Giant macaws are not predators, but they are highly territorial and very dangerous, being as large as a tall man. They have brilliant green, blue, or red plumage, and are generally found in tropical regions. The giant macaw attacks with a wickedly powerful beak. They are ordinarily found in mated pairs, and their feathers can usually be sold for a tidy sum.

— Author: Matt Finch

Giant Macaw: HD 5; AC 5[14]; Atk 1 beak (1d10); Move 6 (Fly 20); Save 12; AL N; CL/XP 5/240; Special: None.

Polly Really Wants a Cracker

River captain **Tomas Bale** plies the Quall River in the Obsidian Barnacle, a flat boat that has seen its share of trouble. The goodly captain's trade route brings various trade goods to the river cities along the Quall, where he unloads one cargo and loads another for the next stop. He frequently hires deckhands, as his men tire quickly of the mindlessly dull routine trips. He welcomes PCs aboard with a slap on the back and the promise of adventure (his current crew groans after this pronouncement).

The Barnacle's current cargo is crates of dried bread Bale is bringing downriver to Bargarsport. The farmers use the crumbled bread to feed their chickens and to season their soups. A few of the crates split open during as they were loaded, letting the bread grow stale and spill across the shifting boat as it rides the river currents.

The dried bread attracts **4 giant macaws** that swoop out of the trees to get at the tasty treat. The birds attack the crates with beaks and claws, ripping apart the wood to get at the crackers stashed inside. The birds attack anyone getting between them and their prize.

Malcarna

Hit Dice: 5
Armor Class: 3 [16]
Attacks: 1 tail (1d8) and up to 3 weapons (1d8)
Saving Throw: 12
Special: Magic resistance (25%), hit only by magic or silver weapons
Move: 12
Alignment: Chaos
Number Encountered: 1
Challenge Level/XP: 8/800

Malcarnae are female creatures with a four-armed human torso and the lower body of a great, writhing serpent, fifteen feet long. These horrible creatures are one of the many possible teratomorphs that may result from human congress with demons, most commonly an incubus. In some cases they may also be hatched from clutches of eggs laid by Marilith demons following events too hideous to contemplate. When they are born into any but the most depraved human societies they are usually killed at birth, so they are seldom found upon the material planes. Malcarnae generally arm themselves with a shield and three weapons, and can also attack with their lashing tails for 1d8 points of damage. Despite the horrible shape of these creatures, they are obscenely beautiful; creatures of fewer than 4 hit dice cannot attack them, and opponents with 4 or more hit dice must make a saving throw to succeed with any attempted physical attack. They are immune to normal weapons (other than silver ones) and have magic resistance of 25%. The human parentage of the malcarnae prevents them from being turned by a cleric. Some malcarnae may have clerical spell casting ability.

— Author: Matt Finch, first appeared in Footprints magazine

Malcarna: HD 5; AC 3[16]; Atk 1 tail (1d8) and up to 3 weapons (1d8); Move 12; Save 12; AL C; CL/XP 8/800; Special: Magic resistance 25%, hit only by magic or silver weapons.

Forest of the Dead

Deformed trees grow from the briars and brambles of the Redstain Forest, their leafless branches intertwining in a thicket overhead. Trunks grow at twisted angles so that some trees appear bent nearly sideways. Spikes grow naturally from the bark of many of the deformed trees. Impaled on these spikes are decaying torsos, severed heads and the skeletal remains of various humanoids. Squirrels, moles and deer are similarly impaled and gutted. Blood seeps down the trees to soak into the odd-shaped roots.

The forest is home to a colony of malcarnae that hunt the hundreds of square miles they consider their domain. Cast out by their horrified parents, the malcarnae destroy all living things venturing into their territory. Trespassers are guaranteed to meet warbands of **6 malcarnae** who stalk their prey through the dead forest. They pass silently through the deep woods, using owl calls to communicate. Anything caught by the vicious snake-women ends up impaled on the tree spikes. The malcarnae colony is located deep in the forest's interior. It is led by a **marilith** named **Virgris Drees**. Despite the surrounding forest, the village is a place of beauty where flowering plants and climbing vines are molded into artistic creations.

Malformian

Hit Dice: 1+2
Armor Class: 7 [12]
Attacks: 1 weapon (1d6)
Saving Throw: 17
Special: None
Move: 9
Alignment: Usually Chaos
Number Encountered: 1d100
Challenge Level/XP: 1/15

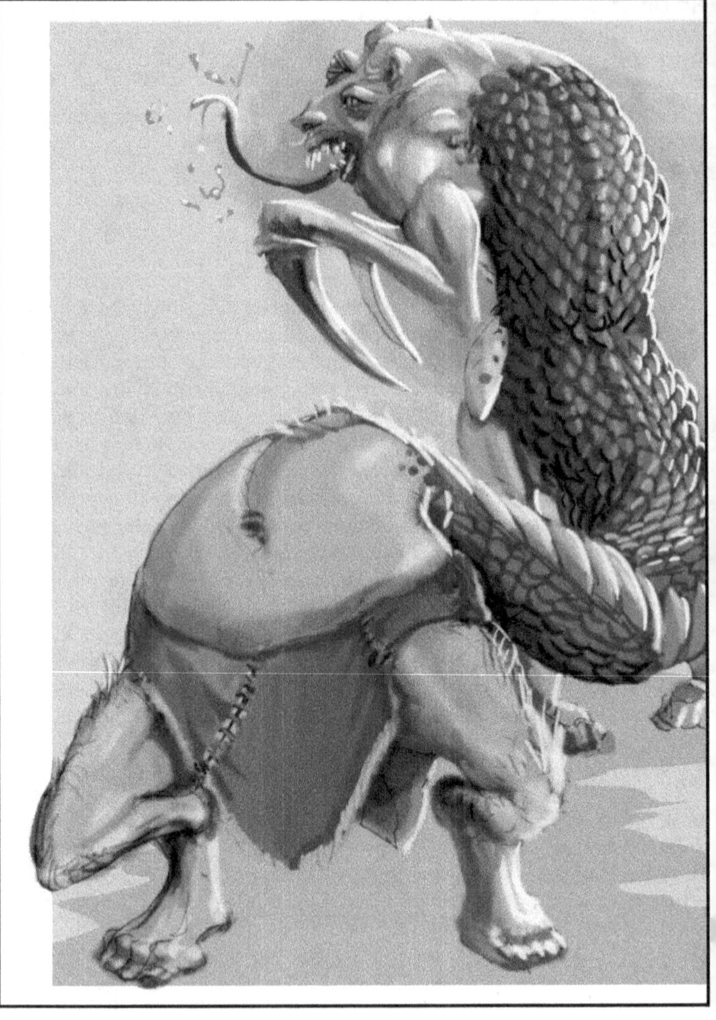

Malformians are the result of magical breeding experiments. They are ugly human-like creatures, often of misshapen proportions, crossbred by insane wizards from humans, goblinoids, animals, and even beings summoned from other worlds. No two malformians look alike; one might be covered in warts and tufts of fur, a second might have useless atrophied wings growing from its back, a third might have eyes and hands of mismatched sizes, and so on. Their various deformities tend to hinder their movement. Any weapons and possessions will be makeshift in nature, such as clubs, staves, crudely stitched cloaks, etc. Gangs of malformians make hideouts in wilderness ruins or subterranean lairs; they do not interact with civilization except as occasional predators and raiders.

— *Author: Scott Wylie Roberts, "Myrystyr"*

Malformian: HD 1+2; AC 7[12]; Atk 1 weapon (1d6); Move 9; Save 17; AL C; CL/XP 1/15; Special: None.

Weight of the Wild

The pelts of various forest animals are staked to trees and wedged into rock piles throughout this stretch of the Kajaani Forest. Pelts hang at all heights throughout the aged trees, but lack any discernible pattern as to their placement. No bones or other remains can be found, although evidence of where the creatures were skinned lies all over the ground.

An oversized scale hangs from the thick bough of a sturdy oak farther into the forest. The scale's two brass plates are supported by vines and ropes rising into the branches overhead. One empty brass plate is suspended three feet off the ground, while the other hovers a foot above the dirt. The lower plate is loaded with skinned animal carcasses. Congealed blood pools in the 10-foot-diameter brass dish. The scale hums with raw magical energy.

The forest is home to a gang of **15 malformians** who protect their "creator." An insane magic-user designed the scale to change enemies into animals. If 100 pounds of dead animals are piled onto one brass plate, the opposite changes the victim into that animal (save avoids). The malformians unfortunately toss every animal they kill and skin onto the scale. Currently, the lowered plate holds 30 pounds of remains, giving the raised plate a 30% chance of changing anyone touching it into a malformian if they fail a saving throw. The malformians are immune to the change, and fight beneath and around the raised brass plate in hopes attackers stumble into the strange device.

Mammoth

Hit Dice: 12
Armor Class: 5 [14]
Attacks: 1 trunk (1d10), 2 gore (1d10+4), and 2 trample (2d6+4)
Saving Throw: 3
Special: None
Move: 12
Alignment: Neutrality
Number Encountered: 1 or 2d6
Challenge Level/XP: 13/2300

Mammoths are huge, shaggy precursors to elephants, larger and more feral, with great, curving tusks. They might be trained as mounts by snow-barbarians. If a lone mammoth is encountered, there is a 50% chance that it is sick or old (no more than 4hp per HD) and a 50% chance that it is a young bull (no fewer than 4hp per HD).

Mammoth: HD 12; AC 5[14]; Atk 1 trunk (1d10), 2 gore (1d10+4), 2 trample (2d6+4); Move 12; Save 3; AL N; CL/XP 13/2300; Special: None.

An Elephant Never Forgets

The longhall is rowdy, with barbarians tossing hunks of meat across the U-shaped wooden table sitting in the center of the room. The men and women wear animal skins and bear furs lie on the ground around the revelers. A roaring fire keeps the room's temperature stifling, pressing back the cold chill that blows through the double doors whenever someone rises to stagger out into the snow. Most of the simple wooden chairs have elk antlers mounted on their high backs, but two seats for the tribe's leader and his wife are much grander. They have wooden slats placed on two sets of giant curved tusks to form giant rocking chairs.

The snow barbarians kill mammoths for meat and decorations. The tusks belonged to a mated pair killed months ago. The remaining **6 mammoths** from the herd remember the attack, however, and track the hunters to their hall. The angry mammoths stomp through the wooden wall, trying to squash anyone using the tusk chairs and eating the mammoth meat.

Manticore

Hit Dice: 6+1
Armor Class: 4 [15]
Attacks: 2 claws (1d3), 1 bite (1d8), 6 tail spikes (1d6)
Saving Throw: 11
Special: Tail spikes
Move: 12/18 (flying)
Alignment: Chaos
Number Encountered: 1d4
Challenge Level/XP: 8/800

This horrid monster has bat wings, the face of a feral human, the body of a lion, and a tail tipped with 24 iron spikes. The manticore can hurl up to 6 of the iron spikes from its tail per round, at a maximum range of 180 ft.

Manticore: HD 6+4; AC 4[15]; Atk 2 claws (1d3), 1 bite (1d8), 6 tail spikes (1d6); Move 12 (Fly 18); Save 11; AL C; CL/XP 8/800; Special: Tail spikes.

Deadly Attraction

A dome of mismatched shields clanks and shudders as it moves slowly down this dirt road. Iron spikes jut from the shields, punching through the metal in places. Wheels can be seen beneath the contraption, and curving slits in the shields reveal a halfling inside pushing the device forward. The halfling inventor Ollie Nematoad is testing his latest creations: manticore attractors and repellants. He has two bottles inside the shields surrounding him. He believes that one attracts manticores (it does) and that the other repels them (it doesn't). He opened the first bottle as he began pushing the mobile shield wall down the road near a known manticore lair.

In 1d4+1 rounds, **2 manticore** arrive, angry and ready for battle. The musky attractor overwhelms the manticores' noses, making them attack with abandon. The spikes on the shields are remnants of Ollie's last encounter with one of the creatures. He didn't get to test the repellant before that creature was killed by passing adventurers. He sprays the second repellent wildly as battle begins around him. Anyone breathing in the second spray must make a saving throw or be overcome by a sneezing fit.

Mantis, Giant Praying

Hit Dice: 8
Armor Class: 3 [16]
Attacks: 1 grab (1d12)
Saving Throw: 8
Special: Bite (1d12)
Move: 9
Alignment: Neutrality
Number Encountered: 1
Challenge Level/XP: 9/1,100

The giant praying mantis is ten feet long, with a bark-like exoskeleton which makes it blend well into forest terrain (desert varieties have chitin with a sand-like texture). The huge insect attacks with blinding speed, usually by surprise, reaching forth with its jointed, serrated front limbs to grab prey. If the mantis hits, and the victim fails a saving throw, the forearms not only do damage but pull the victim close to the mantis' mouth. The victim is held thereafter (not helpless, but unable to pull away) with the mantis doing automatic damage with the serrated forearms and also attacking with its bite for an additional 1d12 points of damage (rolls required to see if the bite hits).

Giant Praying Mantis: HD 8; AC 3[16]; Atk 1 grab (1d12); Move 9; Save 8; AL N; CL/XP 9/1100; Special: Bite (1d12).

Ghostly Prayers

A ring of ghostly figures kneels around a rotting oak tree stump rising out of the ground. The stump is slashed and gouged, and the bark has fallen away so that it vaguely resembles a leering face. The ghostly men, women and children sway to an unheard melody rising from the stump. The ghosts' forms are slashed and battered; three of the figures are missing heads. The sounds of insects are loud in the forest ringing the small clearing. A broken down covered wagon sits on the edge of the clearing. It appears a horse kicked its way out of the harness holding it to the vehicle.

The ghosts are victims of a **giant praying mantis** that killed a family that had stopped to picnic around the stump. Their spirits linger here, unable to move on until the praying mantis is killed. The insect lurks inside the wagon. The insect leaps out to grab fresh meat. The bones of the travelers lie discarded among the tree roots. The wagon contains the family's belongings, including a *+1 dagger* hidden inside a cookie jar rolling around the wooden floor. Two beds are slashed and ripped, their stuffing scattered across the interior.

Marrosian Statue

Hit Dice: 3
Armor Class: 1 [18]
Attacks: 1 stone weapon (1d8)
Saving Throw: 14
Special: Soul chill, slashing/piercing resistance
Move: 12
Alignment: Any
Number Encountered: 1d8
Challenge Level/XP: 5/240

Marrosian Statues are animated statues of human warriors created from a rare, magical marble-like stone frequently used by a lost civilization. Marrosian Statues move with a silent, fluid grace that belies their inorganic nature. Creatures damaged by a Marrosian Statue must make a saving throw or suffer from a deep, soul-chilling cold that radiates outward from the wound. Failure results in a -2 to all subsequent saving throws and combat rolls. This penalty dissipates over the course of the following 24 hours.

Marrosian Statues are partially immune to damage from slashing and piercing weapons, taking only half damage from these sources.

— Author: Andrew Trent

Marrosian Statue: HD 3; AC 1[18]; Atk 1 stone weapon (1d8); Move 12; Save 14; AL Any; CL/XP 5/240; Special: Soul Chill, Slashing/Piercing Resistance.

Game Time

An oversized chessboard stands in the middle of this luxurious garden. The board's dark squares are black dahlias while the lighter squares are white hydrangeas. The marble chess pieces sitting on the board are six feet tall and weigh approximately 500 pounds each. A game appears to be well underway, although the players are nowhere to be found.

The black and white humanoid chess pieces (2 kings, 2 queens, 4 bishops and 4 knights) are **12 Marrosian statues** playing their own game to decide a past squabble between their creators. Each side gets one move per day, with the king moving the "non-living" pieces (pawns and rooks). If the game is interrupted by PCs trying to move pieces, the statues don't react. They return to their spots after PCs leave the board. Once the current game finishes, however, the 12 game pieces track down the offenders. If PCs try to destroy the statues, all 12 animate immediately and attack. They return to their squares once the threat is dealt with.

Maun-Ge

Hit Dice: 1
Armor Class: 9 [10]
Attacks: 1 dagger (1d4)
Saving Throw: 17
Special: Geas
Move: 12
Alignment: Law
Number Encountered: 1
Challenge Level/XP: 3/60

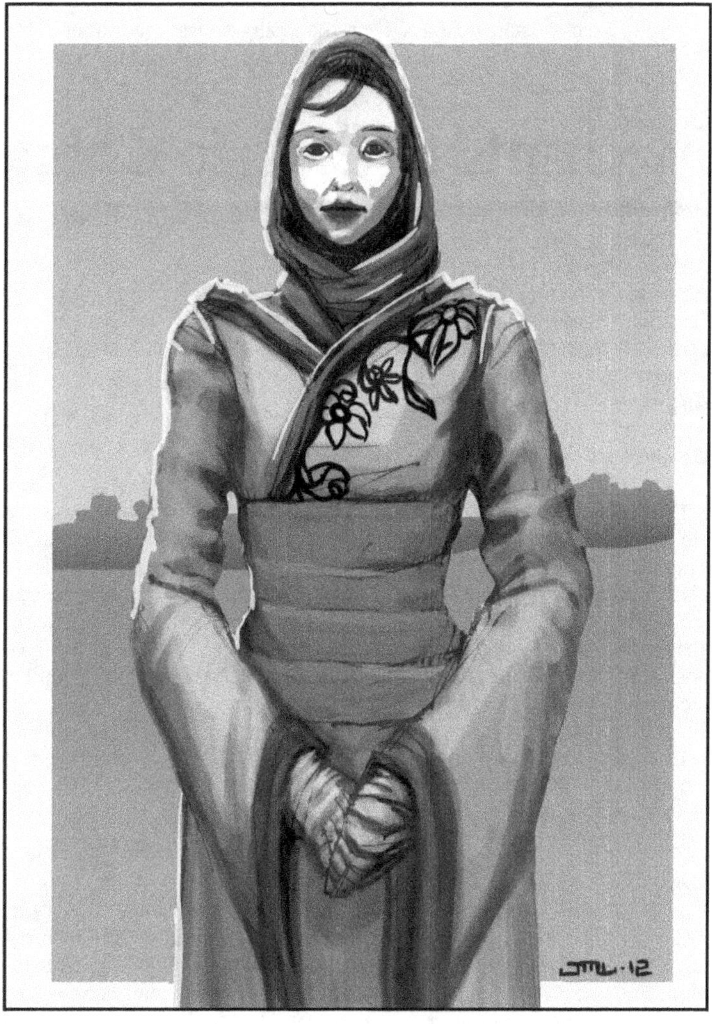

The Maun-Ge are transparent-skinned humanoids. They live alone among humans in remote settlements, usually wearing lacquered wooden masks and an enveloping outer garment that cloaks the entire body. All Maun-Ge are female and will eventually mate with a human male to produce a sole Maun-Ge child. They are able to commune with the spirits of their ancestors who offer guidance, praise and censure to their descendant. With the ability to draw upon the knowledge and experience of their forebears, the Maun-Ge are revered as sages and storytellers. Those who interact with them at length come away feeling somewhat enlightened (+1 wisdom for 2d4 days). The Maun-Ge know the True Names of all men (treat as a Geas Spell), using this knowledge to command humans to play a part in their schemes to increase and perpetuate their bloodline's influence, status and power.

— Author: Sean Wills

Maun-Ge: HD 1; AC 9[10]; Atk dagger (1d4); Move 12; Save 17; AL L; CL/XP 3/60; Special: Geas.

The Ogre Assassin

A lone woman sits in a corner of the Bloke & Dagger Tavern, a beautiful purple quilt decorated with glinting silver thread wrapped around her lithe form. A smaller blanket covers the woman's head, and a porcelain mask hides her features. A small golden harp sits on the table before her, its strings plucking themselves as the instrument plays a mournful dirge. The woman sways to the music. A long stick of smoking incense sits in a glass bowl on the table beside the wondrous harp.

Musun Atanoho is a **maun-ge** fortune-teller. She's on the run from **Ch'talith**, an **ogre mage** whose fortune she told years ago. Upset by her prediction, the angry ogre slew Musun's pseudo-dragon companion. Musun escaped, as she knew she would while the ogre slaughtered her beloved companion. She has seen in a dream that Ch'talith soon shall return to her life, but she also knows that the PCs play a role in her future. She befriends a male PC when they meet, and follows that person, often walking just a few paces behind him, refusing to leave his side once she has singled him out. The ogre mage is indeed close, and attacks when he spies Musun alone. He wears her pseudo-dragon's skin on his armor's spikes. He assumes anyone with her must be her protectors.

Ogre Mage: HD 5+4; AC 4[15]; Atk 1 weapon (1d12); Move 12 (Fly 18); Save 12; AL C; CL/XP 7/600; Special: Magic use.

MECHANISMS

Mechanisms are, effectively, magically-constructed robots. They are not merely animated, for they have a mechanical component to their operations, but these mechanical components require magic in order to function.

Mechanism, Bronze Cobra

Hit Dice: 2
Armor Class: 3 [16]
Attacks: 1 bite (1d2 + poison)
Saving Throw: 16
Special: Non-lethal paralysis poison
Move: 12
Alignment: Neutrality
Number Encountered: 1
Challenge Level/XP: 3/60

Bronze cobras are similar to iron cobras, built in ancient days by powerful spell casters as mechanical servants using powerful magic. These jointed snakes are the size of a normal cobra, and follow commands given to them or programmed into them by their creators. Bronze cobras are not as lethal as iron cobras, being made of softer metal and having a five-dose supply of paralysis poison (3d6 turns) rather than a three-dose supply of lethal poison. They are, however, faster than the similar mechanism created from iron.

Bronze Cobra Mechanism: HD 2; AC 3[16]; Atk 1 bite (1d2 + poison); Move 12; Save 16; AL N; CL/XP 3/60; Special: Non-lethal paralysis poison.

Cobra Commander

A **giant weasel** wearing a bronze collar walks slowly through Ungervilt. The animal has a bronze bracelet wrapped tightly around each of its furry leg. The weasel carries a large, empty bucket in its mouth. A man wearing blood-red robes rides on the weasel's brown back. The man is **Senastys Green**, a corrupt magic-user who relies on his pet, **Tavi**, to help extort gold and jewels from villages he visits as he wanders the countryside. At each stop, he demands that the bucket be filled with gold or he'll let the weasel have its fun with the villagers.

While the weasel is a nasty fighter, Senastys rarely puts his pet in danger. Instead, the bracelets and collar around the weasel's neck and legs detach at the magic-user's command. The **5 bronze cobra mechanisms** slither away from the giant weasel to bite anyone approaching the magic-user or his mount. Senastys and Tavi flee, leaving the bronze cobras to stop anyone trying to follow him.

Giant Weasel: HD 3+3; AC 6[13]; Atk 1 bite (2d6 + blood drain); Move 15; Save 14; AL N; CL/XP 4/120; Special: Drain blood.

Senastys Green, male human magic-user 6: HD 6; HP 21; AC 5[14]; Atk +1 staff (1d6+1); Move 9; Save 10; AL C; CL/XP 7/600; Special: spell use (4/2/2); Equipment: *cloak of displacement, ring of protection +2, wand of slow (3 charges)*

Mechanism, Clockwork Cavalier

Hit Dice: 5
Armor Class: 3 [16]
Attacks: 1 sword (1d8)
Saving Throw: 13
Special: Slows down, immune to sleep, charm, hold, and non-magical piercing weapons, explodes if beheaded
Move: 12
Alignment: Neutrality
Number Encountered: 1
Challenge Level/XP: 5/240

A clockwork cavalier is a metallic humanoid (usually plated with tarnished bronze), elaborately forged to resemble a handsome, mustached gentleman, with a winding mechanism (a key) in its back between the shoulder blades, and armed with a sword extending from its right forearm. Once it has been wound up, the cavalier will wait in place until it can perceive a male humanoid armed with a sword, whom it will challenge to fight a duel to the death. If the opponent declines, the cavalier will accuse him with cowardice, and attack the following round. During combat the Cavalier will mock its opponent with a selection of insults and taunts. Any other combatants striking the Cavalier will also become targets. A Cavalier never flees from a fight.

The cavalier grows slower as it winds down. Each successive round it is in combat it gains a -1 to hit and to its movement rate. Eventually it comes to a complete halt (once movement rate reaches 0, in 12 rounds) and is thereafter totally unable to move or fight (although the insults continue for a further 1d4 rounds). Clockwork cavaliers are immune to Sleep, Charm and Hold, and to all non-magical piercing weapons. Any two-handed sword or axe that hits has a 1 in 6 chance of beheading the Cavalier - which causes it to halt and then explode within the next round (burst radius 20ft, 1d6 damage - a successful saving throw means that a person caught in the blast only takes half damage).

— Author: Sean Wills

Clockwork Cavalier: HD 5; AC 3[16]; Atk: 1 sword (1d8); Move 12; Save 13; AL N; CL/XP 5/240; Special: Slows down, immune to sleep, charm, hold, and non-magical piercing weapons, explodes if beheaded.

The Girl in the Fireplace

An ancient capuchin monkey with a long white beard of untrimmed fur walks slowly down the royally decorated hallway of Pompadour Pointe. The castle is a sprawling complex, but the monkey appears to be the only creature inside it. The monkey drags a heavy silver key down the stone corridor. The central ballroom is an opulent chamber with cream-colored marble tiles on the floor and a majestic staircase rising to a balcony that runs around the entire room. Ten-foot-tall mirrors stand evenly spaced along the walls like windows. The monkey walks slowly across the empty dance floor toward a grandfather clock.

While the room is empty, the mirrors tell a different story: Each shows dancers twirling across the floor, moving to unheard music. A band in the corner provides the tune. The dancers wear large white wigs and paint their faces alabaster. A girl sits in the mirror world's six-foot-tall fireplace, writing with her finger in the ash filling the hearth. Anyone looking in the real fireplace finds the words "Help Us" written there. The monkey climbs a wooden grandfather clock standing off to the side of the room. It inserts the key into a hole in the clock's face. It doesn't turn the key.

The key activates **4 clockwork cavaliers** residing in the mirror realm. If the key is turned, the clockwork cavaliers step out of the mirrors. The mechanisms attack anyone wielding a weapon. If the mirrors are broken, the dancers scream as the shards of glass crash to the floor. In 1d4 rounds, the dancers stagger out of the ashes of the fireplace, returned to the real world from which the clockwork cavaliers abducted them centuries ago.

Mechanism, Giant Robot

Hit Dice: 15
Armor Class: 2 [17]
Attacks: 8 machine gun shots (2d6), mortar (4d6)
Saving Throw: 3
Special: Heat ray
Move: 12
Alignment: Neutrality
Number Encountered: 1
Challenge Level/XP: 19/4,100

Throughout time, every evil genius yearns deep in his heart to create a giant robot armed with a heat ray and machine guns - even (or perhaps especially) in worlds where the height of technology is represented by hammer-pounded iron, waterwheels, and crossbows. With the aid of magic, madness, and perseverance, however, some such evil geniuses succeed in the task against all odds. And then, there might be beings who live in the deserts of Mars, and beyond the dark void of the night sky. One never knows. Giant robots are 13-15 ft. tall. They tend to be sleek in design and most highly advanced. These heavy combat robots have machine guns for hands (each making four attacks per turn), a chest-mounted mortar (damages all in a 5ft radius of the target), and can fire a cone of heat from its head that is 90ft long and 30ft wide at its end, that inflicts hit points equal to the robot's initial hit points (save for half damage).

— Author: Scott Casper

Giant Robot: HD 15; AC 2[17]; Atk 8 machine gun shots (2d6), mortar (4d6); Move 12; Save 3; AL N; CL/XP 19/4100; Special: Heat ray.

The Robot's Hearts

A quarter-mile plane of obsidian sits atop the burning sands of the Kanderi Desert. This featureless plateau reflects the heat of the midday sun, and cools slowly overnight. A 30-foot-tall-by-20-foot-diameter metal cylinder rises in the center of the opaque plane. The metal tube has no doors or windows. A series of numbered dials are attached to the tube's side. The dials cannot be turned by hand, but each begins counting downward if a PC touches the metal cylinder. The tube reacts to the pulse of living beings, and the dials decrease toward zero with each heartbeat. If multiple PCs touch the tube simultaneously, the dials spin toward zero all the faster. The dials continue counting down even if PCs remove their hands from the tube's surface.

When the dials reach zero (in 2d6 rounds), the tube opens with a pneumatic hiss and a blast of scalding steam. A **giant robot mechanism** steps from the enclosure and targets the creatures whose heartbeats released it. The giant robot chases creatures across the desert. Its passage over the desert turns the sand to glass. The robot returns to its tube when the PCs (and their annoying heartbeats) are dead. The robot scoops out the heart of any PC it kills. The hearts are collected in a basket on its back. A number of dried lumps still sit in the basket from past victims.

Mechanism, Iron Cobra

Hit Dice: 3
Armor Class: 1 [18]
Attacks: 1 bite (1d4 + poison)
Saving Throw: 14
Special: Poison
Move: 9
Alignment: Neutrality
Number Encountered: 1
Challenge Level/XP: 4/120

Iron cobras are a type of eldritch mechanism, created by the great wizards of yore using formulae from their legendary spellbooks and tomes of knowledge. They are jointed constructions of iron, the size of a normal cobra, that slither and attack as commanded (perhaps eons in the past) by their makers. The iron cobra contains a reservoir with three doses of lethal venom. Larger specimens might have been built, with an addition venom dose per additional hit die.

Iron Cobra Mechanism: HD 3; AC 1[18]; Atk 1 bite (1d4 + poison); Move 9; Save 14; AL N; CL/XP 4/120; Special: Poison.

Pipe Snakes

Hundreds of iron pipes jut from the earthen walls of this dungeon chamber beneath the wizard Imregar's Iron Tower. The pipes crisscross the room in a metal lattice hovering near the 10-foot-high ceiling. Steam bursts from angled joints in many of the connected pipes, and the sound of water rushing through others is quite loud. Some pipes have frost built up around their outer surface and do 1 hp of damage to anyone touching the metal with exposed skin. Others radiate heat and deal 1 hp of damage.

The pipes carry water into the tower, and waste out of it. The room is protected by **10 iron cobra mechanisms** that hide among the pipes. The iron cobras are difficult to spot (1 in 6 chance) while stationary. They drop onto PCs passing beneath them. A couple of the hollow cobras actually serve as waste pipes. Anyone bitten by them runs the risk of contracting a wasting disease the does 1d4 points of damage each day until cured (save avoids).

Medusa

Hit Dice: 6
Armor Class: 8 [11]
Attacks: Weapon (1d4)
Saving Throw: 11
Special: Gaze turns to stone
Move: 9
Alignment: Chaos
Number Encountered: 1d4
Challenge Level/XP: 8/800

The terrifying medusa has a female face but hair of writhing snakes; it has no legs, but the body of a serpent. The gaze of a medusa turns anyone looking upon it into stone. In addition to the medusa's relatively weak melee-weapon attack, the snake-hair makes one attack per round, causing no damage but inflicting a lethal poison with a successful hit (saving throw applies).

Medusa: HD 6; AC 8[11]; Atk 1 weapon (1d4); Move 9; Save 11; AL C; CL/XP 8/800; Special: Gaze turns to stone, poison.

Snake Oil

The sanctum of this jungle temple contains a 60-foot-wide square pool filled with glistening oil. Seven columns rise out of the pool to support a painted ceiling. Oils winds down the columns into the pool, flowing from spigots high on the columns. Pictures of snakes are painted on the walls around the sanctuary. The pool is surprisingly deep, dropping to a stone floor nearly 40 feet down. The opaque oil makes it difficult to see more than a few feet into the slippery substance.

The oil is not flammable, but it does have one unique property: It allows anyone immersed in it to breathe normally for one hour in any environment (underwater, oil, dirt, etc.). The temple is home to a yellow-and-crimson scaled **medusa** named **Eld'mos-oth Quill**. The creature swims in the pool to keep her scales supple. Any visitors succumbing to her gaze are dropped into the oil. Currently, 9 statues of men, women, dwarves and elves stand on the bottom of the oil pool. The medusa senses the vibrations of people walking about the temple above and bursts out of the oil bath, hoping to surprise people into looking her in the eye.

Melgara

Hit Dice: 3+2
Armor Class: 7 [12]
Attacks: 1 staff (2d4) or wand (1d4 + stun or slow)
Saving Throw: 14
Special: Spells (1 level 1), mentally augmented attack (hold, sleep, or charm), increase speed
Move: 12
Alignment: Neutrality
Number Encountered: 1 or 2d6
Challenge Level/XP: 5/240

The Melgara (singular and plural) are a humanoid race from an alternate world. They appear to be tall, slender, blue-skinned women, dressed in silvery-grey robes and sandals, with long pale hair, and slitted eyes. They have six digits per extremity, plus an extra thumb on the left hand, and live for 200 to 350 years. All members of the Melgara race are mystical and introspective by nature, given to meditating upon philosophy, cosmology, and emotional awareness. They consider most other races to be psychologically impaired, and will communicate with them as condescending parents or teachers to slow or stunted children. The Melgara arm themselves with staffs and wands of a strange, durable crystal found on their world. The staff deals 2d4 damage. The wand, when used as a striking weapon, deals 1d4 damage in addition to 1d4 rounds of a Slowing effect or a Stunning effect (saving throw negates). The Melgara can also channel mental energy through these crystal weapons (3 times per day), causing any one of the following more powerful effects with a successful Attacks: (1) Paralysis for 1 turn, (2) Sleep for 1 hour, or (3) Charm for 1 full day. Each member of the race has spell ability equal to a cleric of level 2, and some have spell casting ability of up to level 5. They do not, however, have the ability to turn undead. In addition to clerical spell casting, all melgara can cast the magic-user spells sleep, shield, blur, and ESP, although these spells take up a clerical spell "slot". Once per day, they can increase their own speed, allowing a bonus of 2 to armor class (AC 5[14]). In any group of melgara, one will possess a crystal pendant or silvery rod of unusual design. These items have no combat function, being ceremonial devices on the Melgaran homeworld.
— *Author: Scott Wylie Roberts, "Myrystyr"*

Melgara: HD 3+2; AC 7[12] or 5[14]; Atk 1 staff (2d4) or wand (1d4 + stun or slow); Save 14; Move 12; AL N; CL/XP 5/240; Special: Spells (1 level 1), mentally augmented attack (hold, sleep, or charm), increase speed.

staff for not following her directions.

No Shoes Allowed

An amethyst gem nearly three feet tall stands upright from a natural rock formation inside a cave hidden in the high peaks of the Hollow Spire Mountains. The amethyst pulses with an inner light, its glow bathing the interior of the cave in purplish colors. A row of sandals sits just inside the cave mouth. Low wooden benches sit along the granite wall. The cave slopes upward into a sanctuary where a 200-foot-long crystal dominates the chamber. Twelve acolytes sit on the floor around the crystal, their eyes turned toward its gleaming depths. They hum in unison, their eyes closed as they meditate. The men and women refuse to move or utter a word.

The cave is home to a tall, blue-skinned woman wearing silvery-grey robes and sandals. Her eyes are slitted, and she has long pale hair. Her name is Queessetumdyn. The **melgara** is teaching her acolytes patience and understanding, and she takes offense to adventurers interrupting the daily meditation. Especially if they don't remove their shoes. Queessetumdyn greets them with staff and wand, and refuses to talk until PCs remove their footwear. Her strikes tend to be against the lower legs to make her point.

Anyone sitting for a month with the melgara gains the ability to divine one question from nature at any point in the next three months. Her patience is short, however, and PCs can expect many whacks from the

Melhukiskata (Snap-Snatcher)

Hit Dice: 2
Armor Class: 7 [12]
Attacks: 1 antler-hand (0), bite (1d6-1)
Saving Throw: 16
Special: Strength-draining poison, holds fast
Move: 9
Alignment: Neutrality
Number Encountered: 1d3
Challenge Level/XP: 4/120

The hunters of the northernmost forests share that terrain with many strange and dangerous beasts. One such predator is the melhukiskata, or "sap snatcher."

So stealthy is the melhukiskata that it is rare for one to be spotted on the move. Those who have seen them report that its body is three feet long, shaped like a weasel or badger, but can walk like a bear. It is covered with shaggy, grey-brown fur all over, down to the tip of its two-foot long tail. Its mouth is elongated and oddly eel-like, while its feet are wickedly taloned. The most unusual features of the beast, though, are its fingers -- for instead of forepaws, the melhukiskata has fingered hands. Odder still, the fingers are long and stiff, and grow out like antlers. The longest of these antler-like fingers yet seen on a melhukiskata were five feet long.

The sap on the hands holds fast anyone touched and also is a weakening contact poison (save vs. poison or lose 1d6 points of strength per round, causing loss of consciousness at 2 strength or lower). Anyone so held can be automatically bitten each round and will be held until the melhukiskata is killed, the adhesive is burned away, or is washed off with vinegar or alcohol. All lost points of strength will be regained in 1d6 hours.

Tracking the melhukiskata is difficult, for when it does travel it often walks backwards, dragging its huge fingers behind it as if to sweep away its trail. Perhaps because of this so many folktales describe the melhukiskata as a clever animal. More likely, such behavior is instinctive. In no other regard does it appear to be smarter than a dog.

—Author: Scott Casper

Melhukiskata: HD 2; AC 7[12]; Atk 1 antler-hand (0), bite (1d6-1); Move 9; Save 16; AL N; CL/XP 4/120; Special: Strength-draining poison, holds fast.

Forest Saps

Piles of orange, red and yellow leaves rest on the ground around maple trees filling this forest. Spigots are tapped into many of the tree trunks, the valves dripping syrup into wooden buckets. Sap also runs from multiple slashes running around the bases of each trunk. The sap is mainly from the trees, but mixed into the syrupy runoff is a contact poison that requires a saving throw vs. poison or the person touching it loses 1 point of strength per round until he loses consciousness at 2 strength.

The trees were slashes by **2 mated melhukiskatas** as they marked their territory. The creatures' sticky hand sap mingled with the sap in the trees to create the contact poison. The sap-snatchers have a lair beneath the roots of a discolored maple tree. The entrance is covered by a pile of multicolored leaves. The sap-snatchers' stick their fingers out of the leaves. The elongated fingers look like gnarled branches sticking out of the leaf pile. Anyone touching the branches is dragged into the root lair and attacked.

MEPHITS

Mephits are minor spirits usually related to fire and heat, that can, from time to time, be loosed on the Material Planes by natural means (such as a volcanic eruption) or by supernatural means (such as being summoned by wizards or sent on errands by demons or devils). All of these creatures have the ability to turn into a (mephitic) bad-smelling gaseous form for 1d6 rounds, once per day.

Mephit, Brimstone & Fire

MEPHIT, BRIMSTONE
Hit Dice: 3
Armor Class: 5 [14]
Attacks: 2 claws (1d3)
Saving Throw: 14
Special: Breathe gas cloud, gaseous form
Move: 12/24 (flying)
Alignment: Chaos
Number Encountered: 1 or 1d6
Challenge Level/XP: 5/240

As with other mephits, brimstone mephits are elemental creatures; they are sly, but not highly intelligent. They spit a reeking cloud of yellowish gas that is 20ft long, by 10ft tall, by 10ft wide. This cloud is choking and caustic, inflicting 2d6 points of damage to anyone caught inside, with a saving throw allowed to reduce the damage to half. The mephit's own gaseous form is not poisonous, although it smells foul. When in gaseous form, the mephit cannot be attacked other than with spells that would affect gas, but it cannot attack, either.

— Author: Matt Finch

Brimstone Mephit: HD 3; AC 5 [14]; Atk 2 claws (1d3); Move 12 (Fly 20); Save 14; AL C; CL/XP 5/240; Special: Breathe gas cloud, gaseous form.

MEPHIT, FIRE
Hit Dice: 3
Armor Class: 5 [14]
Attacks: 2 fiery touches (1d3+1)
Saving Throw: 14
Special: Spit fire, gaseous form
Move: 12/20 (flying)
Alignment: Chaos
Number Encountered: 1 or 1d6
Challenge Level/XP: 5/240

Fire mephits are minor fire imps, cunning, but not terribly intelligent. They are often servitors of more powerful demonic or infernal beings, and may occasionally be found on the material planes under the circumstances described in the general description of mephits, above. A fire mephit can breathe flame for damage of 1d8+1, half if the victim makes a saving throw. The fire has a range of 20ft. When in gaseous form, the mephit is visible and foul-smelling; it cannot be attacked other than with spells that would affect gas, but it also cannot attack.

Fire Mephit: HD 3; AC 5 [14]; Atk 2 fiery touches (1d3+1); Move 12 (Fly 20); Save 14; AL C; CL/XP 5/240; Special: Spit fire, gaseous form.

Flame Bringer

The dwarven forges of Orecrush were abandoned during the Time of Terrible Rains that flooded the lower Mines. The furnaces ceased for the first time in centuries as the dwarves moved their forges aboveground to the city of Anvil Plunge. However, one forge still burns in the deep tunnels. White-hot flames rage in the forge and burning coals pop and sizzle inside the open hearth. A black opal sits amid the coals, white flames ringing its spherical form.

The dwarves left the cursed opal in the burning forge to keep anyone from possessing it. The opal is immersed in flames, and reaching in without protection to grab it does 4d6 points of damage. The opal is worth 500 gp, but possessing it comes at a cost: If the gem is removed from the forge's purifying flames, **1d4+3 fire mephits** immediately leap from the fires to attack. The mephits pursue PCs relentlessly until killed. Furthermore, once per day the opal summons another 1d4+3 fire mephits whenever it is brought within 100 feet of any open flame. The opal belonged to an efreeti who lost it centuries ago to a dwarven thief. The mephits have been seeking the gem for years so they may return it to their master.

Merman

Hit Dice: 1
Armor Class: 7 [12]
Attacks: Weapon (1d6)
Saving Throw: 17
Special: Breathe water
Move: 1/18 (swimming)
Alignment: Any
Number Encountered: 1d6 or 9d20+10
Challenge Level/XP: 1/15

Mermen have the torso of a human and the lower body of a fish. Although the race is called "mermen," there are female members as well.

Merman: HD 1; AC 7[12]; Atk 1 weapon (1d6); Move 1 (Swim 18); Save 17; AL Any; CL/XP 1/15; Special: Breathe water.

Undersea Coup

A dying **merman** struggles through the rough surf, his body bashed and beaten. Blood trails in the water behind him from his missing tail flukes. The waves press him forward, but he is unable to dive into the depths. His skin is burned and peeling from the blazing sun blasting the wave tops. **Agushun** barely escaped a coup in the undersea kingdom of Cnidaria. He has just a short time left unless saved.

The Coral Castle of Cnidaria was recently overthrown by the **sea hag Scombrotix Caryon** and her oktomon and sahuagin minions. She used a spell to charm many of the mermen and turned them into her willing slaves. Teams of **6 mermen** hunt the ocean in all direction, seeking the escaped Agushun before he can summon help. The mermen attack PCs assisting the dying merman, assuming Agushun told them of Cnidaria's plight.

Sea Hag: HD 3; AC 6[13]; Atk 1 bite (1d4); Move 6 (Swim 18); Save 14; AL C; CL/XP 5/240; Special: Death gaze, weakness gaze.

Mimic

Hit Dice: 7
Armor Class: 6 [13]
Attacks: 1 smash (2d6)
Saving Throw: 9
Special: Mimicry, glue
Move: 2
Alignment: Neutrality
Number Encountered: 1
Challenge Level/XP: 8/800

Mimics are formless creatures that imitate surrounding features they have seen. In subterranean settings, they might be disguised as an archway, treasure chest, door, etc. When touched, they glue themselves to the victim with a strong adhesive, while striking with a suddenly-formed tentacle.

Mimic: HD 7; AC 6[13]; Atk 1 smash (2d6); Move 2; Save 9; AL N; CL/XP 8/800; Special: Mimicry, glue.

Not Like the Other

This granite corridor ends in stone blocks that appear to separate in the middle and slide to the sides. The blocks weigh nearly 1 ton apiece, making them nearly impossible to push aside by hand. On the corridor's left wall are six holes situated at waist height. On the right wall are eight holes at the same height. The six holes on the left wall have small handles inside them that can be rotated. The six holes on the right closest to the door contain a recessed button that can be pushed. A PC must put their arm in the hole up to their elbow to find these buttons and levers. If the buttons are pushed and the levers rotated in sequence, the stone blocks slide apart to allow admittance to a small library of ancient scrolls.

The extra two holes on the right wall belong to a **mimic** imitating its surroundings. The holes aren't as deep as the others, and contain no buttons or levers. The holes squeeze tightly around the arms of anyone reaching inside. The mimic detaches itself from the wall to fall atop its trapped victim.

Minotaur

Hit Dice: 6+4
Armor Class: 6 [13]
Attacks: Head butt (2d4), bite (1d3) and weapon (1d8)
Saving Throw: 11
Special: Never get lost in labyrinths
Move: 12
Alignment: Chaos
Challenge Level/XP: 6/400

The minotaur is a man-eating predator, with the head of a bull and the body of a massive human, covered in shaggy hair. Most are not particularly intelligent.

Minotaur: HD 6+4; AC 6[13]; Atk Head butt (2d4), 1 bite (1d3) and 1 weapon (1d8); Move 12; Save 11; AL C; CL/XP 6/400; Special: Never get lost in labyrinths.

The Bull Rushers

A clattering racket rumbles down the cobblestone road as a two-wheeled chariot rolls along. Sixteen nearly naked men and women pull the chariot, each gaunt figure connected to the vehicle with iron chains and leather straps hooked around and through their naked flesh. The reins run back to the chariot, where **2 minotaurs** wielding barbed whips urge the people forward. The minotaurs wear loin-cloths, and one has a white cape fastened around its broad shoulders. Each has bells attached to the tips of their wickedly sharp horns. Leather sacks hang off the sides of the chariot. A pair of giant bull horns adorns the front of the chariot.

The minotaurs ride through the countryside, attacking travelers to add to their slave train. The beasts leap from the chariot to attack. One of the minotaurs wears a *cloak of displacement*. The people chained to the chariot run until they drop, at which point the minotaurs replace them. Three bags hanging from the chariot contain the minotaurs' treasure: 424 gp, a number of gems (357 gp total) and a *chime of opening* the minotaurs use to open villages' locked gates to get at the people inside. Six other bags contain the butchered remains of pullers who died in harness. Among the hands, heads and feet are a pair of *boots of leaping* (with the severed feet still inside).

Mirror Fiend

Hit Dice: 8
Armor Class: 3 [16]
Attacks: 1 mirror weapon (3d4)
Saving Throw: 8
Special: Unaffected by normal weapons, 50% magic resistance
Move: 12
Alignment: Chaos
Number Encountered: 1
Challenge Level/XP: 10/1,400

Mirror fiends inhabit mirrors. They appear as emotionless humans staring out of the reflective surface to the world beyond. If a mirror fiend locks his gaze with someone looking into the mirror, the victim must make a successful saving throw or have his soul sucked into the mirror, while his body remains motionlessly staring at himself in the mirror. While within the mirror, the victim's actions are controlled by his immobilized self as the mirror fiend attacks the victim's mirror-self. The victim's mirror-self suffers -4 to his first attack due to being unfamiliar with the mirror-image environment, but the penalty is reduced by 1 in each subsequent round. Should the immobilized victim's gaze be moved away from his mirror-self, he will no longer be able to control his movements within the mirror, and the mirror-self will become a motionless target for the mirror fiend. Slaying the mirror fiend will restore the victim's soul to his body, but shattering the mirror will forever trap the soul within the mirror. Mirror fiends are immune to attacks from normal weapons, and are 50% resistant to magic. Weapons used from outside will likely shatter the mirror, and spells used from the outside will reflect back upon the caster rather than enter the mirror-realm.

— Author: Skathros

Mirror Fiend: HD 8; AC 3[16]; Atk 1 mirror weapon (3d4); Move 12; Save 8; AL C; CL/XP 10/1400; Special: Unaffected by normal weapons, 50% magic resistance.

To the Victor

The gladiatorial fights held in the Bloke & Dagger Tavern are a sensation in the city of Taharath. The tavern's center floorboards are pushed aside three times each week to reveal a 30-foot-square gladiator pit beneath the building. Competitors are paired up in bouts of skill to face off for the title of champion. Mavis, the kindly owner and coordinator of the fights, awards silver trophies and gold to the winners.

The magic-user Dagnum Corbett was humiliated during a recent bout. The pompous mage thought to use a magic ring to boost his strength, but Mavis caught on to the deception and had her bouncer take the ring. Dagnum's opponent pushed the scrawny mage into the sand-covered floor and sat on him until the man submitted. Dagnum swore to get back at the tavern and its cheering patrons, and devised a deadly scheme.

This week's trophies contain a terrible surprise: Dagnum snared a **mirror fiend** in the reflective surface of the champion's trophy. When Mavis removes the purple cloth covering the traveling trophy, anyone staring into the surface must make a saving throw or be drawn into the mirror-realm to face the deadly mirror fiend.

Mist-Men

Hit Dice: 4
Armor Class: 3 [16]
Attacks: 1 Fist (2d6)
Saving Throw: 13
Special: Exhale mist
Move: 0/18 (flying)
Alignment: Chaos
Number Encountered: 1d8
Challenge Level/XP: 5/240

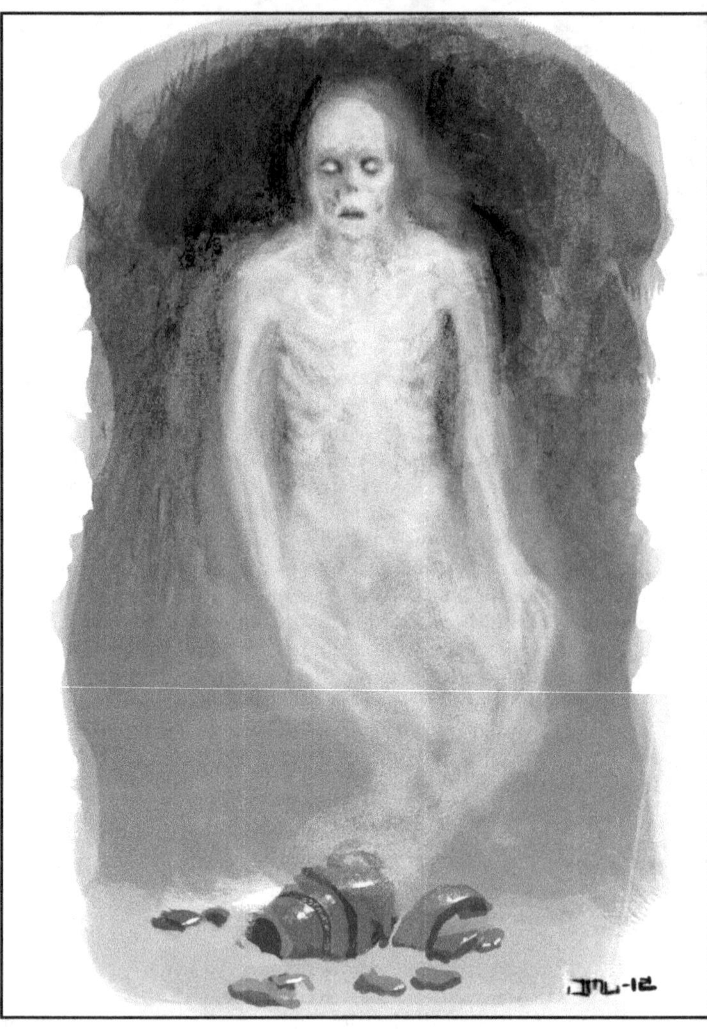

Mist men are humanlike forms summoned from some other plane of existence or dimension, often stored in small containers until they are freed to take their full shape when the container is opened.

Once every four rounds, a mist man can breathe out a heavy cloud of choking mist in a 15 foot cone. Anyone caught in the cone must make a saving throw or be blinded by the noxious fumes for 1d4+1 rounds. The mist persists in an area for 1 full turn.

— *First published in The Black Monastery, adapted by Matt Finch*

Mist Man: HD 4; AC 3[16]; Atk 1 fist (2d6); Move (Fly 18); Save 13; AL C; CL/XP 5/240; Special: Exhale mist.

Misty Mourning

This tomb contains the body of a young woman wearing ceremonial armor. She lies on a silver bier with a clear dome of impenetrable force protecting her remains. Blue mist flowers adorn her dark hair, and a sigil of an eye is painted on her forehead in gray ash. Larisska Malive was a warrior woman killed defending her king during a frost giant attack. Her body was placed here to honor her short life. Paintings on the wall reveal her incredible deeds.

Around the bier are six metal candelabras, each with a delicate framework of silver wire atop the 6-foot-tall pole. The poles are anchored into the stone floor to keep them from falling over. The frame atop each pole contains a head-sized black globe. Light held behind the globes reveals objects inside each one. PCs can make out rings, gems and coins through the dark glass, but can't see details. The globes cannot be removed easily from the wire frames.

If any globe is shattered or broken free of its mounting, the metal frames holding the other globes contract, cracking the remaining spheres simultaneously. Voluminous gray mist billows out of each cracked globe and forms into **6 mist men** within 1d4 rounds. The items inside each globe are generally worthless trinkets worth no more than 20 gp each. There is a 20% chance that a random minor magic item could be mixed into the lot, however. The mist men were placed here to stop grave robbers. The trinkets in the glass were used to trap and contain the mist men.

Mogura-Jin (Cannibal Mole Men)

Hit Dice: 2
Armor Class: 7 [12]
Attacks: 2 claws (1d4)
Saving Throw: 16
Special: Blinded by bright light
Move: 9/9 (burrowing)
Alignment: Chaos
Number Encountered: 2d4 or 1d100
Challenge Level/XP: 2/30

Mogura-Jin are a race of subterranean humanoids, descended from a group of villagers who resorted to cannibalism during a particularly fierce winter and were cursed by the Gods. They are squat beings, between 4 and 5 feet tall with pale skin, small beady red eyes, no body hair, and nails overgrown to claws. Mogura-Jin are always hungry and need to consume human flesh every so often to remain alive. Like their animal namesake (the mole) they are proficient tunnelers and their preferred method of attacking their victims is to tunnel under them and emerge from the ground in a swarm attack to surprise them.

Mogura-Jin can see perfectly well even in total darkness; however their over-sensitive eyes are easily blinded by bright lights.

— *Author: edsan*

Mogura-jin: HD 2; AC 7[12]; Atk 2 claws (1d4); Move 9 (Burrow 9); Save 16; AL C; CL/XP 2/30; Special: Blinded by bright light.

Cannibalistic Humanoid Underground Diggers

The under tunnels of Bargarsport are passages dug through the hardened mud that buried the old city during the great quake brought on by an angry goddess. The tunnels now bore through buried homes and businesses, creating an underground network of interconnected rooms. One cellar still contains casks of old wine. Most of the contents have turned to vinegar, but six casks of fine wine can be salvaged and sold for 200 gp apiece. The wooden racks holding the casks crumble if handled too roughly. Two barrels sound hollow if tapped.

The cellar is located above a tunnel where **8 mogura-jin** hunt. Two of the mole-men tunneled up into the empty barrels and watch PCs holes in the wooden slats. They signal the rest of their group to attack when the PCs are standing amid the racks. The cannibalistic mole-men burst through the dirt floor beneath the rotting racks, causing the casks to tumble and fall about PCs. Anyone failing a saving throw is struck by a casks and takes 1d6 points of damage. The mogura-jin grab PCs and drag them into the lower tunnel to devour.

Mohrg

Hit Dice: 10
Armor Class: 0 [19]
Attacks: 1 fist (1d8) or tongue (paralysis)
Saving Throw: 5
Special: Paralyzing tongue, grabs and holds.
Move: 12
Alignment: Chaos
Number Encountered: 1
Challenge Level/XP: 13/2,300

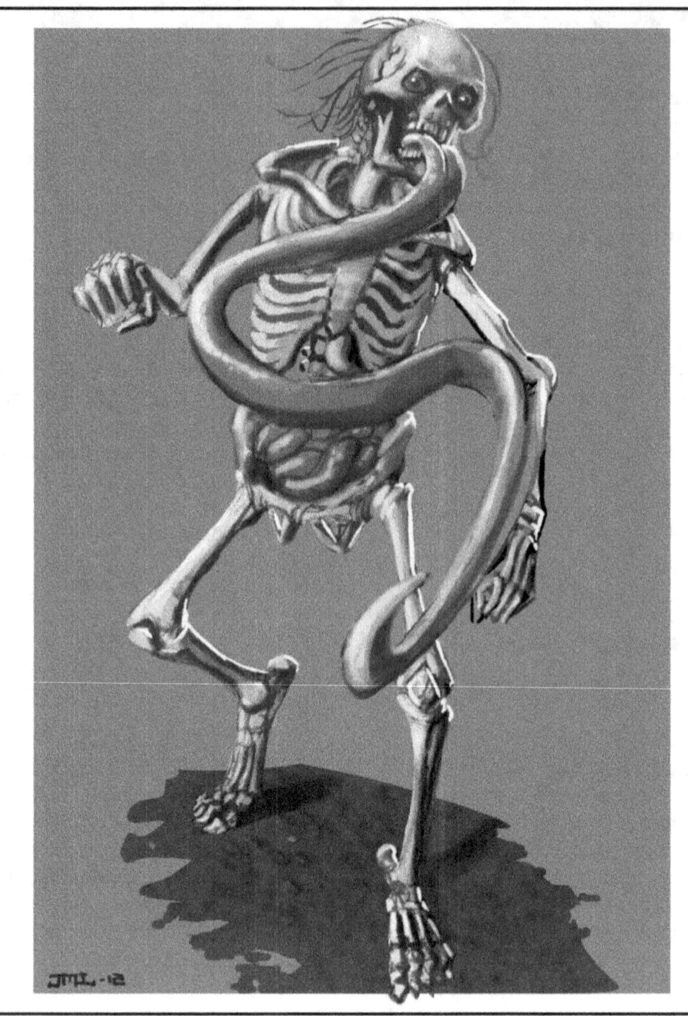

Mohrgs are the animated corpses of mass murderers or similar villains who died without atoning for their crimes. They resemble zombies, but are far more dangerous, being somewhat more intelligent, much faster, and much stronger a zombie.

Due to a mohrg's blinding speed, these monsters will always attack first during a combat round unless squared off against an opponent using some sort of magic that increases the character's own speed of motion (such as *boots of speed*). Mohrgs have two possible methods of attacking. First, the mohrg's tongue extends five feet, and has a paralyzing effect. A saving throw at -2 is permitted to avoid this effect, but victims failing the saving throw are paralyzed for 1d6 turns. The morgh's second option in combat is to strike opponents with its fists. When the mohrg hits with its hands, the strike not only causes damage, but allows the mohrg to hold on if the victim fails a saving throw. A character who is so held cannot attack, and if the mohrg hits with its tongue in a subsequent round, the tongue will hit automatically (although the victim is still allowed a saving throw to avoid paralysis). Any held character may break free with a successful saving throw during the character's attack initiative.

Any character killed by mohrg will rise after 1d4 days as a zombie under the morhg's control. Thus, mohrgs are often found accompanied by 1d6 zombies.

Mohrg: HD 10; AC 0[19]; Atk 1 fist (1d8) or tongue (paralysis); Move 12; Save 5; AL C; CL/XP 13/2,300; Special: paralyzing tongue, grabs and holds.

The Mohrg the Merrier

This wooden house is a patchwork of bright colors. No two walls share the same hues. Even the four square panels in the entry door are different colors. The door is unlocked, and opens onto a gaily decorated foyer filled with circus props and clown mannequins. Streaks of color lining the walls lead into adjoining rooms. Each room is piled with colorful items such as wooden rocking horses, giant blocks with letters and numbers painted on them, and giant fortunetelling cards. Stuffed parrots hang in gilded cages in one room, the birds numbering in the hundreds. One room is not as neat as the others, and contains boxes of stage clothing. The boxes are tossed about the room, their wooden sides clawed and shattered.

The house belonged to a jester named **Katas Polk** who was a vicious killer when he wasn't entertaining people in the bazaar. He lured travelers back to this house, and killed them as they wandered among his many collections. Katas dumped the bodies into a sinkhole behind the house. Katas died accidentally when the heavy boxes of clothing fell on him as he rummaged through his belongings. He rose three nights later as a **mohrg**. The mohrg still wears Katas' jester's motley. Its face is painted white and has tear streaks running down his sunken cheeks, making the creature look like a horrific clown. The mohrg stalks visitors through the house, trying to catch them as they search through the crates and oddities.

Mold, Brown

Hit Dice: n/a
Armor Class: n/a
Attacks: None
Saving Throw: n/a
Special: Drains heat
Move: 0
Alignment: Neutrality
Number Encountered: 1d3
Challenge Level/XP: 4/120

Within 5ft of a patch of brown mold, the mold drains body heat from living creatures (other than creatures which use magical cold or have cold breath weapons, such as a white dragon). Damage from the heat drain is 2d8 hit points per round with no saving throw. If fire comes in contact with the mold, the mold grows to cover an area twice its original size, boiling forth into new areas and beginning to suck heat from them in the following round. Growths of brown mold can only be killed by the use of magical cold.

Brown Mold: HD n/a; AC n/a; Atk none; Move 0; Save n/a; AL N; CL/XP 4/120; Special: Drains heat.

How Do You Like Your Eggs?

A four-foot-diameter fire pit sits in this chamber. Smoldering coals burn brightly in the stone oven, and orange flames dance in the ash. A five-foot-long wooden plank sits over the coals, supported on each side by red adobe bricks. The board is barely a foot above the hot coals, and is charred and darkened by the flames, but refuses to burn. An ovoid depression directly over the flames is carved into the top of the plank.

Sitting on shelves around the room are various colored eggs. The eggs are about a foot long and fit perfectly into the depression carved into the wooden plank. There are 20 eggs total: 10 white, 2 green, 3 pink, 3 spotted and 2 brown. Breaking the eggs does nothing. Heating them produces effects depending on the color of the eggshell:

White: Normal ostrich eggs that pop and burst open. They can be eaten and are quite delicious.

Green: A smelly gas rises into the air and lingers for 1d4+3 rounds. The gas smells like rotten eggs and makes anyone who fails a saving throw violently ill for 1d4 hours.

Pink: A sweet-smelling scent is emitted as the egg burns. The egg dissolves into a puddle within the wooden depression in 1d6 rounds. If the salve is applied to burns or injuries, it heals 1d6+1 points of damage. The pink salve can be collected and stored for a month. There is enough for two applications per egg.

Spotted: These eggs burst in an explosion of fireworks similar to a *pyrotechnics* spell.

Brown: These eggs explode and cover a 15-foot-diameter circle with a **brown mold**.

Mold, Yellow

Hit Dice: n/a
Armor Class: n/a
Attacks: 1d6 damage + spore cloud
Saving Throw: n/a
Special: Poisonous spore cloud, killed by fire
Move: 0
Alignment: Neutrality
Number Encountered: 1d3
Challenge Level/XP: 3/60

Yellow mold is a subterranean fungus; it neither moves nor attacks. However, if it is poked or struck, it may (50% chance) release a cloud of poisonous spores, roughly 10ft in diameter. Failing a saving throw against the spores means that the character dies a rather horrible death. Touching yellow mold causes 1d6 points of acid damage. These growths can be destroyed with fire, but are effectively immune to weapons.

Yellow Mold: HD n/a; AC n/a; Atk 1d6 damage + spore cloud; Move 0; Save n/a; AL N; CL/XP 3/60; Special: Poisonous spore cloud, killed by fire.

Gas Bags

Twelve, three-foot-diameter bags of gas-filled flesh float like pale balloons through this 50-foot-by-50-foot underground cavern. Many have faces, hair, tattoos and even jewelry attached to their bloated forms. Skinned bodies lie on the floor below the floating horrors. Small tubes jutting from the walls have spiked silver nozzles on their ends. A wooden table contains spindles of thread, large needles jammed into the wood, and a paste-like glue.

The gas bags are the creation of a wicked **annis** named **Druella Ga**. She skins her victims, then sews up their flesh. She uses the silver nozzles to inflate the flesh bags with naturally occurring helium. She is unaware that the helium source is tainted with yellow mold spores. Each gas bag is filled with **yellow mold** that grows inside the drifting balloons. Prodding the dried skin has a 1 in 4 chance of causing a flesh bag to burst apart, spraying yellow mold throughout the chamber.

Monstrous Mouth

Hit Dice: 6
Armor Class: 3 [16]
Attacks: 1 bite (4d6) or special
Saving Throw: 11
Special: Slumber rays, inhale
Move: 6
Alignment: Neutrality
Number Encountered: 1d4
Challenge Level/XP: 8/800

A bulbous body twelve feet in diameter, resting atop tiny legs, a monstrous mouth is almost entirely a huge, gaping maw equipped with rows upon rows of sharp, pointed teeth. Atop the strange creature's body, two short eye-stalks allow it to see its prey, even in total darkness. Each of these eye-stalks can discharge a sleep ray, causing potential prey to fall into a deep slumber; this requires a successful attack roll by the monstrous mouth, but no saving throw is permitted. The slumber is identical to that caused by a magic-user's sleep spell, but affects creatures with any number of hit dice. Each eye-stalk can use a sleep ray only once per day.

Another, even stranger, ability is the monstrous mouth's capacity to inhale with such force that a specific target up to 30ft away may be sucked into the creature's toothy maw. A successful attack roll by the monstrous mouth, followed by a failed saving throw on the part of the victim, will result in the victim being "sucked" into the creature's mouth. Once the victim is sucked in, the monstrous mouth constricts its interior to pin the victim, suffocating him in 1d4+2 rounds. A successful saving throw is required to escape. Each round spent trapped within a monstrous mouth will inflict damage equal to 1d6, +1hp if the victim is wearing leather armor, +2 if the victim is wearing metal armor other than plate mail, and +3 if the victim is wearing plate mail.

— Author: Skathros

Monstrous Mouth: HD 6; AC 3[16]; Atk Bite (4d6) or special; Move 6; Save 11; AL N; CL/XP 8/800; Special: Slumber rays, inhale.

Wind Tunnels

Howling, hurricane-like winds roar through this narrow cave opening. The sucking air current creates a banshee-like wail as air whooshes into the cleft between two granite stones marking the cave mouth. The passage slopes downward for 500 feet before splitting into five various-sized tunnels that head deeper into the earth. The floor is smooth, slick stone. The wind is erratic and comes from random directions and tunnel openings.

The wind is caused by a **monstrous mouth** trapped in the lower caverns. The mouth can't climb up the slick stone to get to the surface. When the mouth inhales, the air pulls victims toward its maw, requiring a saving throw to keep from sliding down one of the tunnels because of the slick stone floors. The monstrous mouth cannot climb the sloping passages. The bodies of past victims are strewn throughout the lower cavern. PCs searching the lower tunnels find 274 gp, a collection of ivory chess pieces (150 gp for a complete set) and a silver horseshoe (25 gp).

Mothdog

Hit Dice: 2+2
Armor Class: 8 [11]
Attacks: 1 bite (1d6)
Saving Throw: 16
Special: Moth-scream
Move: 18
Alignment: Neutrality
Number Encountered: 1d8
Challenge Level/XP: 2/30

Feathery and brightly fluttering, the mothdog is, as its name suggests, a magical crossbreed of moth and dog. The head has compound eyes and feelers; otherwise the creature looks like a greenish-feathered dog. Mothdogs can be tamed, due to their canine intelligence. However, these creatures are insects that lay eggs and undergo a larval stage. A mothdog can emit a piercing high-pitched sound, primarily as a warning signal; if maintained for more than one round, it may cause disorientation and temporary deafness to all within a radius of 5ft per mothdog in the group. Some forest folk, particularly nocturnal humanoids, use mothdogs as guard dogs. The combination of canine scent and bat-like echolocation makes the mothdog a superb tracker; some wilderness villages have been known to employ them as tracking beasts.

— *Author: Scott Wylie Roberts, "Myrystyr"*

Mothdog: HD 2+2; AC 8[11]; Atk 1 bite (1d6); Move 18; Save 16; AL N; CL/XP 2/30; Special: Moth-scream.

Dog Daze

Chamomile flowers grow wildly throughout this open field. White petals flutter and green grasses sway as a bracing wind sweeps across the prairie. The strong scent of the flowers rises into the air like an intoxicating brew. Across the field, tall sunflowers shake as unseen creatures flutter among them. Swarms of butterflies wheel through the air.

The field is home to **10 mothdogs** that roll through the highly intoxicating chamomile scent the flowers give off. The mothdogs are wild eyed and erratic, snapping at butterflies and chasing their tails in tight circles through the air. The mothdogs growl and bare their teeth at anyone picking the aromatic flowers. The dogs have a 2 in 6 chance of attacking strangers who approach them. The strong scent clouds their minds, making them unpredictable. Any strong gust of wind (magical or otherwise) blows the scent away and might allow PCs to befriend the capricious creatures.

Mothmere

Hit Dice: 8
Armor Class: 3 [16]
Attacks: 2 foot-talons (1d6)
Saving Throw: 8
Special: Telepathy, mimicry, pyrotechnics, ethereal travel, +1 or better weapon required to hit, magic resistance 30%
Move: 6/24 (flying)
Alignment: Chaos
Number Encountered: 1
Challenge Level/XP: 11/1,700

Little is known about these eerie and malevolent beings. Their appearance in a civilized area is cause for fear and alarm, for they kill humans, sometimes stalking a particular individual, sometimes haunting a specific location such as a crossroads in search of victims. Mothmeres are humanoid in shape, but with great, membranous wings, dark blue-grey skin, and eyes that glow with a faint reddish hue. They have no arms. A mothmere is generally seven feet or so in height, but can be as large as ten feet tall. Mothmeres are most commonly found in the ethereal plane, which may be their natural habitat. They can move into the ethereal plane once per round, becoming immune to any material damage and to all spells other than those with a mental effect. Mothmeres frequently use this ability to enter closed rooms and dismember the inhabitants. A mothmere's faintly glowing eyes cause fear within 30ft, causing any creature of fewer than 4HD to make a saving throw or flee for 3d12 rounds. Mothmeres can carry 300 lbs. weight while flying, and often pick their victims up to drop from great heights. They also have the ability to control fire at will, as per the pyrotechnics spell. It is unknown why these creatures attack (never eating their prey) or why they seem to haunt areas for periods of time and then suddenly leave. Some claim to have been haunted by these creatures for weeks before being found dead or simply never seen again. Mothmeres typically make temporary lairs in old ruined buildings, hidden caves or mines, or in trees, using them as places to rest during the day and to store trophies from their kills.

— Author: M. Ahmed

Mothmere: HD 8; AC 3[16]; Atk 2 foot-talons (1d6); Move 6 (Fly 24); Save 8; AL C; CL/XP 11/1700; Special: Telepathy, mimicry, pyrotechnics, ethereal travel, +1 or better weapon required to hit, magic resistance 30%.

Like a Moth to a Flame

A burned brass lantern hangs from a low tree branch. The magical lantern always remains filled with clear oil, no matter how long it burns. The wick similarly never burns away. The outer surfaces of the lamp are blackened, as if it was pulled from a roaring blaze, but it works just fine.

The lantern was cursed long ago by the witch Granny Hazela when it set her tree house abattoir ablaze. The lamp casts a soft yellow glow in a 60-foot radius around the person holding it when it is lit. It has a 20% chance of attracting a **mothmere** to it the first day it is lit. This chance goes up 5% each day thereafter it is used until one of the creatures appears. The chance drops to 20% after that and rises as described. The mothmere attacks the wielder. The lantern also has a 1% chance any time it is lit of exploding in a fiery explosion that does 6d6 points of damage to anyone within a 30 foot radius (as the witch found out).

Mummy

Hit Dice: 5+1
Armor Class: 3 [16]
Attacks: Fist (1d12)
Saving Throw: 12
Special: Rot, hit only by magic weapons
Move: 6
Alignment: Chaos
Number Encountered: 1d12
Challenge Level/XP: 7/600

Mummies cannot be hit by normal weapons, and even magical weapons cause only half damage. In addition to normal damage, their touch also inflicts a rotting disease which prevents magical healing and causes wounds to heal at one-tenth of the normal rate. A *Cure Disease* spell can increase healing rate to one-half normal, but a *Remove Curse* spell is required to completely lift the mummy's curse.

Mummified kings, pharaohs, priests, or sorcerers might be considerably more powerful than normal mummies.

Mummy: HD 5+1; AC 3[16]; Atk 1 fist (1d12); Move 6; Save 12; AL C; CL/XP 7/600; Special: Rot, hit only by magic weapons.

Unfinished Business

Linen strips hang from the mouth of a stone lion carving serving as a lintel into the room beyond this underground hallway. Torches set into sconces on the wall flicker feebly in the passageway. Creosote darkens the walls and ceiling. The linen strips are soiled and stained, and maggots and other vermin cling tenaciously to the shredded cloth. Anyone touching the bandages must make a saving throw or be afflicted by a rotting disease.

The room beyond is filled with a three-foot-deep layer of sawdust and powdered natron. Clay jars sit on niches along the walls. A stone embalmer's table with a human-body shaped depression is surrounded by the powder. Hooks and other metal implements sit on the table. Six fresh corpses lie partially buried around the table. All of the bodies are slashed and gutted, their insides spilling across the sawdust-covered floor.

Covered by the sawdust and natron are **2 unwrapped mummies**. Each unfinished mummy has various metal hooks jammed into its hands and body that deal an additional 1d4 points of damage with each strike. The mummies appear to be dried zombies. Their wrapping was interrupted and never completed. The embalming table has a false lid that opens to reveal a blood-filled cavity containing a gold crown (200 gp), 657 gp, 3 diamonds (150 gp each) and a jade figure of a cat (240 gp).

Mushroom-Man

Hit Dice: 3, 2, or 1
Armor Class: 5 [14]
Attacks: 1 fist (1d6) or weapon
Saving Throw: 14, 16, or 17
Special: Spores
Move: 12
Alignment: Neutrality
Number Encountered: 1d8
Challenge Level/XP: 5/240, 3/60, or 1/15

Standing 4ft in height, mushroom-men resemble humanoid mushrooms endowed with both arms and legs. Mushroom-men are usually found in natural caves, caverns, and underground passages.

Mushroom-men are initially created by magic. Once given life through magic they reproduce by way of spores. When a mushroom-man dies (0 hit points or less) it releases 1d6 spores which rapidly (within 1d4 rounds) grow into mushroom-men of 1 HD lower than the parent (1 HD mushroom-men do not produce spores upon death). The spores have 2 hit points (before becoming fully formed mushroom-men).

— Author: Skathros

Mushroom-Men (1HD): HD 1; AC 5[14]; Atk Fist (1d6) or weapon; Move 12; Save 17; AL N; CL/XP 1/15; Special: Spores.

Mushroom-Men (2HD): HD 2; AC 5[14]; Atk Fist (1d6) or weapon; Move 12; Save 16; AL N; CL/XP 3/60; Special: Spores.

Mushroom-Men (3HD): HD 3; AC 5[14]; Atk Fist (1d6) or weapon; Move 12; Save 14; AL N; CL/XP 5/240; Special: Spores.

Soft Men

Vines wrap tightly around eight humanoid forms hanging from the rocky ceiling of this wide tunnel leading upward to the Mushroom Grotto, an underground greenhouse of fungi. The bodies hang upside down, their heads swinging just a couple of feet above the stone floor. The vines tighten noticeably like snakes around their charges, causing the bodies to swing and shift. A few of the peoples' heads stick out of the vines. Their mouths gape, and mushrooms grow from their throats. Moss covers their open, unblinking eyes.

The vines are **8 strangle vines** growing from the roof of the tunnel. The vines ignore PCs unless they unwrap or dislodge the victims. Of the eight bodies, two still live, but just barely. **Hannid Everwrought** is an elf maiden who stopped to smell a pretty flower near the Grotto. The other is a dwarf prospector named **Fuglish Ashenchisel** who was mining in the valley when he was abducted by the "soft men." He asks repeatedly if anyone has seen his mule, **Maggard**.

The "soft men" are **16 mushroom-men** who cultivate the fungi growing in the strangle vine incubators. The mushroom-men arrive within 2d4 rounds to investigate disturbances. The dead bodies hanging in the vines all contain mushroom spores. They burst open if struck or if the vines holding them are killed.

Tangle Weed/Strangle Vine: HD 4; AC 6[13]; Atk 4 vines (1d6); Move 0; Save 13; AL N; CL/XP 6/400; Special: Strangulation.

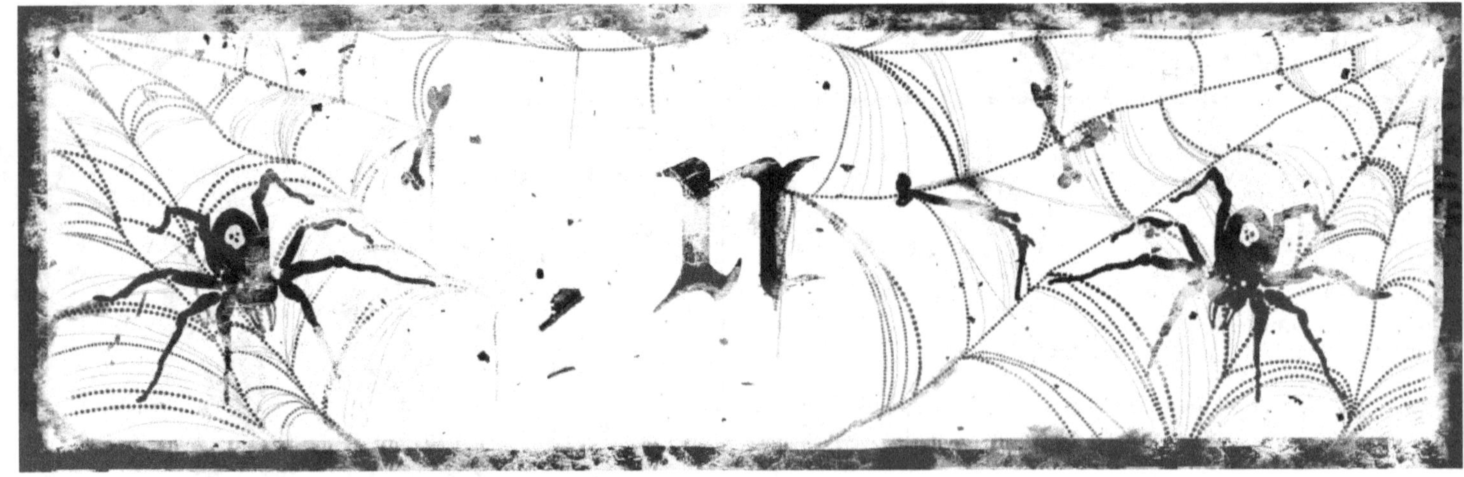

NAGAS

"Naga" is the Sanskrit word for dragon or snake. In mythology, the naga are benevolent and very powerful, equivalent to Asian dragons. The nagas portrayed here are more serpentine and less powerful; all have the body of a snake, although the head is not necessarily that of a serpent. All kinds of interesting abilities may be found in "unusual" nagas designed by the Referee, from breathing fire to moving in and out of strange planes of existence.

Naga, Guardian

Hit Dice: 11
Armor Class: 5 [14]
Attacks: Bite (1d6 + poison)
Saving Throw: 4
Special: Spit poison, constriction, spells.
Move: 18
Number Encountered: 1
Alignment: Law
Challenge Level/XP: 13/2300

The largest and noblest of the naga, guardian nagas are from 20 to 25 feet in length. They do not necessarily have a humanlike head, but some characteristic (a flowing mane of hair, for instance) will immediately set their appearance apart from normal serpents. They can bite or spit with lethal poison, and if they hit with their coils they automatically cause 1d8 points of constriction damage per round thereafter. Guardian nagas cast clerical spells (2/2/1/1). A sample selection of spells for a guardian naga might include: level 1: *Cure light wounds* x2; level 2: *hold person, silence 15-foot radius*; level 3: *cure disease*; level 4: *cure serious wounds*.

Guardian Naga: HD 11; AC 5[14]; Atk 1 bite (1d6 + poison), 1 constrict (1d8), 1 spit (poison); Move 18; Save 4; AL L; CL/XP 13/2300; Special: Poison, constriction, spells.

The Scaled Chapel

In the serpent city of Uroborus, a massive column of rock laced with silver veins rises out of a 30-foot-wide hole cut in a stone terrace located beneath a massive snake sculpture. The stone pillar is 60 feet tall, rising from a below-ground cathedral. Just the pillar's top 15 feet rises above ground level. The pillar is topped by a fist-sized diamond (2,000 gp) that pulses with a red inner light.

Twelve silver manacles are attached to four stout chains that encircle the pillar. The upper torsos of six elves hang from the manacles. Their bodies below the waist are missing. Blood drips from the corpses into the empty expanse beneath them and splashes into a 40-foot-diameter pool around the base of the monstrous pillar.

342

The below-ground cathedral is a 100-foot-square chamber with walls covered in gold-dragon scales. Dragon bones form a throne of sorts. A **guardian naga named Syssastalyx** lives inside the cathedral and is worshipped by the snake men of Uroborus as a goddess. They routinely sacrifice captives and slaves to the naga to slake her blood thirst. The naga curls up the pillar to exit the cathedral. The diamond beats to the rhythm of her heart.

Naga, Hanu-

Hit Dice: 5-6
Armor Class: 5 [14]
Attacks: 1 bite (1d8 + poison) and 1 constrict (1d6)
Saving Throw: 12
Special: Monkey-summoning dance, poison bite, control simians
Move: 12/9 (in treetops)
Alignment: Chaos
Number Encountered: 1d4
Challenge Level/XP: 5HD: 6/400; 6HD: 7/600

Hanu-nagas are a predominantly tropical and subtropical form of naga, less magical than the human-headed variety. Rather than a human-headed giant snake, hanu-nagas have a feral monkey head upon a great serpentine body. These nagas lair in jungles and rainforests, haunting forgotten temples and ancient ruins, where many are worshipped by tribes of wild monkeys and/or apes. The most intelligent of hanu-nagas may have followings of tribesmen or cavemen. The stylized, writhing dance of a hanu-naga allows it to exert a mystic control over apes and monkeys within a radius of 300ft. These controlled creatures will act at the naga's mental command. It is not necessary for the apes to actually see the naga's dance to fall under its control; indeed, when a hanu-naga begins its dance, simian creatures within one mile (to a maximum of 20 apes) will immediately begin moving at top speed to the dancing naga's presence. The naga may dance and attack at the same time. The bite of a hanu-naga is poisonous, and if the naga hits with its constricting attack it will inflict automatic damage of 1d6 per round until killed.

— Author: Matt Finch

Hanu-Naga (5HD): HD 5; AC 5[14]; Atk 1 bite (1d8 + poison) and 1 constrict (1d6); Move 12 (In treetops 9); Save 12; AL C; CL/XP 6/400; Special: Monkey-summoning dance, poison bite, control simians.

Hanu-Naga (6HD): HD 6; AC 5[14]; Atk 1 bite (1d8 + poison) and 1 constrict (1d6); Move 12 (In treetops 9); Save 11; AL C; CL/XP 7/600; Special: Monkey-summoning dance, poison bite, control simians.

The Well-Pit of the Monkey God

Dozens of monkeys sit atop six-foot-tall basalt walls nearly concealed by vines snaking throughout the Seething Jungle. Leering monkey skulls are carved into the tops of the stone barriers. Seven walls rise along the hillside, each about 15 feet farther up the hill than the last. Monkeys sit on the walls, facing outward as if watching the jungle. Their stares are unnerving and direct, and they turn in unison to follow intruders. They make no move to stop people climbing over the walls to the summit, however.

At the top of the hill, a 30-foot-deep stone-lined well descends into the earth. Stones pushed into the wall provide handholds to easily descend the shaft. Monkey skulls sit on many of the handholds and fall with a clatter to the floor below if knocked free. The underground chamber contains hundreds of monkey skeletons. A crude bone-and-vine monkey idol sits atop the broken bones. A tunnel leads into the darkness.

A **hanu-naga** named Tetza'canital sleeps in the darkness of the cave, but rises to attack anyone entering its lair. The hanu-naga dances as it uncurls from its bed. The dance draws **40 monkeys** who sit on the walls outside. They scramble down into the pit to attack intruders. In the cave is a *+1 long sword* with a monkey head engraved in its pommel, 600 gp, an uncut ruby (400 gp), a bronze monkey mask set with emeralds (250 gp) and a silver mirror (30 gp).

Monkey: HD 1d4 hp; AC 7[12]; Atk 2 claws (1d3); Move 15; Save 18; AL N; CL/XP A/5; Special: None.

Naga, Spirit

Hit Dice: 9
Armor Class: 5 [14]
Attacks: Bite (1d3 + poison)
Saving Throw: 6
Special: Poison, charm gaze, spells.
Move: 12
Alignment: Chaos
Number Encountered: 1d3
Challenge Level/XP: 13/2300

Spirit nagas are malicious, evil creatures. Their gaze has the effect of a *Charm Person* spell, their bite is poison, and they cast both Magic-User spells (4/2/1) and Cleric spells (2/1). A sample spell selection for a spirit naga might be: Magic-User spells level 1: *Charm Person* x2, *Magic Missile, Sleep*; level 2: *Mirror Image, Web*; level 3: *Protection from Normal Missiles*. Cleric spells level 1: *Cure Light Wounds* x2; level 2: *Silence 15-foot Radius*. Such nagas are from 10 to 20 feet in length, and have a human head.

Spirit Naga: HD 9; AC 5[14]; Atk 1 bite (1d3 + poison); Move 12; Save 6; AL C; CL/XP 13/2300; Special: Poison, charm gaze, spells.

The Serpent Gems

A golden circlet studded with green emeralds (1,500 gp) sits on a marble bust of a hawk-nosed man in this dark top room atop the Witch's Loft. The abandoned tower stands on a red shale rock promontory deep in the Kanderi Desert where the desert sands bloom in grit-filled geysers. Thick velvet curtains hang from the stone walls of the octagonal chamber. The drapes flutter in the light breezes blowing through the chamber through high iron windows open to the elements. A fine layer of white sand covers the floor.

The circlet is a work of art, with two gold strands twisting around each other. Taking it off the bust releases a **spirit naga** named **Ailyoustis Canebreak** trapped for 500 years in the emeralds. The creature appears in a chamber at the base of the tower and winds her way upward toward the PCs and the circlet. A magic-user trapped the naga in the serpent gems to power a massive iron cobra. Anyone putting on the circlet receives visions of a metal snake body buried under tons of sand. The circlet causes a severe headache in the wearer whenever he faces the direction of the trapped iron cobra. The headache does 1 point of damage per day it is worn.

Naga, Water

Hit Dice: 7
Armor Class: 5 [14]
Attacks: Bite (1d4 + poison)
Saving Throw: 9
Special: Poison, spells
Move: 12/20 (swimming)
Alignment: Any
Number Encountered: 1d3
Challenge Level/XP: 10/1400

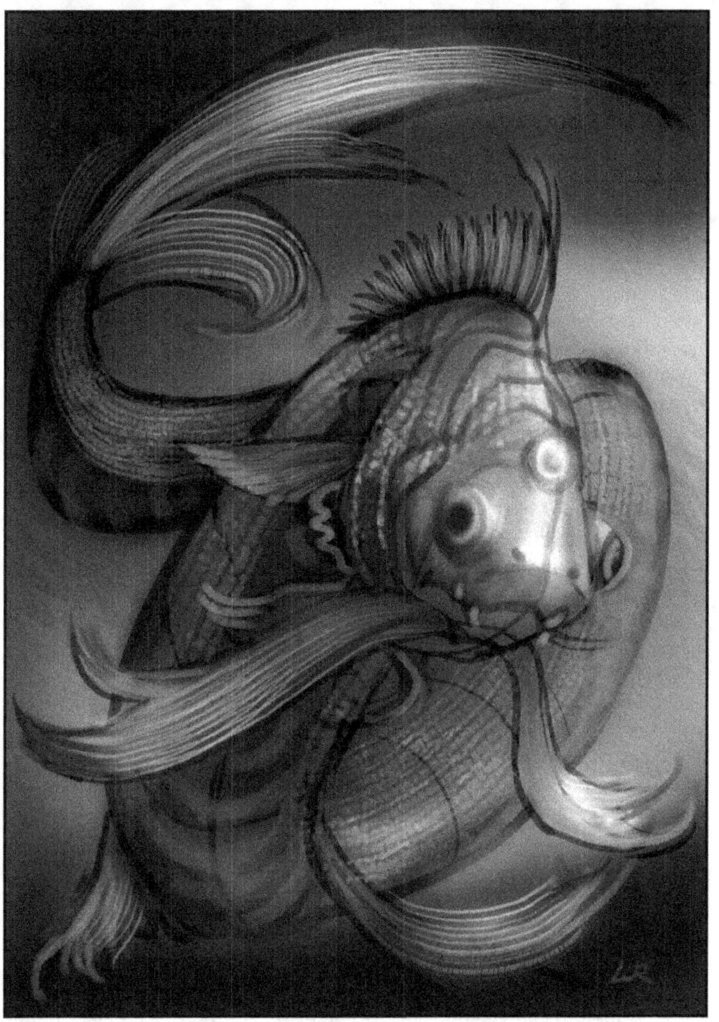

Water nagas might be of any alignment. They do not ordinarily have human heads, but like the guardian nagas they will have some physical attributes separating them clearly from normal serpents. In the case of water nagas, this might be the color of the scales or the presence of flowing beard-like fins, perhaps. Water nagas are from 10 to 15ft long. Water nagas cast magic-user spells (4/2/1). A sample spell selection for a water naga might be: level 1: *charm person* x2, *magic missile, sleep*; level 2: *mirror image, web*; level 3: *protection from normal missiles*.

Water Naga: HD 7; AC 5[14]; Atk 1 bite (1d4 + poison); Move 12 (Swim 20); Save 9; AL Any; CL/XP 10/1400; Special: Poison, spells.

The Whirlpool's Protector

A torrential whirlpool spins rapidly in the middle of the Seris River rushing between the Krait Cliffs. The surging water whips the steep walls, carving its way into the rock to create massive slabs that overhang the circling waters. The whirlpool's funnel twists and spins like a tornado trapped underwater. Floating in the spray above the funnel opening is a glowing blue orb in which a large diamond (2,500 gp) spins at the same speed as the waters below. The gem stays just a few feet above the spray at all times, but moves side to side as the mouth of the whirlpool shifts.

The whirlpool is home to a **water naga** that lives in a cliffside cave beneath the waterline. The water naga is extremely possessive of the whirlpool and the gem that generates it. It rises from the water to attack anyone bothering the gem. The naga has the head of a lion, with a mane of green river weeds. A wand that lowers water (4 charges left) is jammed into a crevice inside the naga's underwater cave.

Neomorphic Twin

Hit Dice: Varies
Armor Class: Varies
Attacks: Varies
Saving Throw: Varies
Special: Psychic link, drain experience
Move: Varies
Alignment: Chaos
Number Encountered: 1
Challenge Level/XP: Varies

A Nemorphis is a non-corporeal entity that absorbs stray memories and thoughts; they are sometimes attracted toward the sudden reassemblance of memories that takes place when a person is raised from the dead. Once a Nemorphis forms a psychic link to its victim (saving throw negates), it drains an experience level per day, using absorbed memories and feelings to become a ghostly duplicate of its victim, a so-called Nemorphic Twin. During the days when the victim is being drained of life energy, he frequently becomes lost in wistful reveries of past times, alternating with vivid nightmares.

Once the victim descends to 1st Level, the Twin becomes corporeal, usually resembling a more youthful version of the victim. The Nemorphic Twin will track the person down the next day and attempt to slay him, having the same stats, skills and spells possessed by the weakened twin. Whichever combatant is victorious "inherits" the drained experience levels, in a rush of sensations that has a 1 in 4 chance of sending the victor into a coma lasting 1d6 hours. If defeated, a Nemorphic Twin disappears, leaving no trace of its short existence. If the Nemorphic Twin wins, it will be drawn to the places and people it "remembers." People interacting with the Nemorphic Twin will find it "wrong" in many ways, for it is still mentally inhuman, whatever its guise.

— Author: Sean Wills, aka "Geordie Racer"

Neomorphic Twin: stats depend on circumstances.

Birds of a Feather

Two large mirrors on opposite walls of this ornate chamber reflect a gilded metal cage standing in the center of the room. The cage is big enough to hold a human if they sit on the small wooden stool placed inside. Angelic figures are fashioned into the cage's gold strands, as are flowers, birds and clouds. Astute PCs may spot that each figure has exactly one twin precisely opposite it on the cage. The door to the cage is closed and latched, but opens easily.

If anyone enters the cage and sits on the stool, a *confusion* spell is triggered that engulfs the entire room. The person inside the cage is immune to the spell effect. As the spell goes off, a **neomorphic twin** is also summoned into the cage with the person inside. The creature escapes with the person in the cage, and then latches onto any PC outside the cage who lost his memory. The creature waits until they regain their memory, then begins usurping their identity.

Night Hag

Hit Dice: 8
Armor Class: 8 [11]
Attacks: 1 bite (2d6)
Saving Throw: 8
Special: Magic resistance (65%), +2 or better magic weapon to hit, magical abilities
Move: 10
Alignment: Chaos
Number Encountered: 1 or 1d4+1
Challenge Level/XP: 12/2,000

Night hags come from beyond the material plane: perhaps from the realms of dream, perhaps from the demonic pits of the underworlds. These creatures prey upon the souls of those who are evil/chaotic: they can cause enchanted sleep once against such individuals (saving throw, affects up to 12th level), or visit the victim's dreams nightly (no saving throw) to leech away a point of constitution per night until the attribute reaches 0 and the hag can steal away the soul. In combat, night hags can magically weaken an opponent to half normal strength (saving throw) three times per day; additionally, they can use a spell that automatically inflicts 2d8 points of damage against a single opponent. Both of these abilities have a range of 100ft. A hag can also also become ethereal and incorporeal at will, summon a demon ally once per day (with only a 50% chance of success), and cannot be hit by weapons with a magical bonus of +2 or less. They are highly resistant to magic, as well.

Night Hag: HD 8; AC 8[11]; Atk 1 bite (2d6); Move 10; Save 8; AL C; CL/XP 12/2000; Special: Magic resistance (65%), +2 or better magic weapon to hit, magical abilities.

Corpse Lights

A twisted redwood deep in the Tanglewood Forest is gnarled and misshapen, its trunk bent over like an old man slouching forward. Its limbs scrape the ground, digging furrows in the dirt when the wind stirs them. Human and animal skulls hang from the branches on vines woven through the eye sockets. Hundreds of jawbones are driven into the redwood's trunk to form a ladder of handholds rising into the upper reaches of the ancient tree.

The tree is the home of **Harig Kwaad, a night hag**. She lives in a small hut sitting on a bent trunk nearly 70 feet in the air. The hag's hut is decorated with animal skins and has a peaked roof of sharpened femurs. The hideous hag has coarse black hair that hangs down around her long, angular face. The skulls of rodents are woven into her black mane. Several corpses cocooned in black hair hang off the trunk beneath her home. She routinely lights them on fire to enjoy the stench of burning flesh. PCs in the forest may see the burning fire flickering in the treetops. Flies and bats swarm around the fiery corpses, some occasionally coming too close and catching fire.

Nightmare

Hit Dice: 7
Armor Class: -4 [23]
Attacks: 1 bite (1d8), 2 hoofs (2d6)
Saving Throw: 9
Special: Breathe smoke, ride between planes/realities
Move: 18/35 (flying)
Alignment: Chaos
Number Encountered: 1 or 1d4+1
Challenge Level/XP: 10/1,400

Nightmares are the steeds of night hags and other demons; black horses with flaming hoofs and mane. Their breath is a cloud of brimstone smoke, which causes any nearby opponent to attack at –2 (saving throw applies). These horrible creatures can become incorporeal and travel between the planes of existence bearing their evil/chaotic riders.

Nightmare: HD 7; AC –4[23]; Atk 1 bite (1d8), 2 hoofs (2d6); Move 18 (Fly 35); Save 9; AL C; CL/XP 10/1400; Special: Breathe smoke, ride between planes/realities.

The Nightmare Carriage

The **night hag Harig Kwaad** is a fickle creature whose presence drains the life from the forest around her home high in a bent and twisted redwood. When the life is sapped from the forest, the night hag transforms the massive redwood into a wooden carriage with a hellish phrase known only to her. As the redwood shrinks and transforms into the thorn-covered carriage, **4 nightmares** also appear to pull the horrible carriage. Two skeletons rise from the many bones entangled in the tree to serve as a driver and coachman.

The nightmares line up in front of the carriage as living vines snake out to serve as harnesses. The animals serve Harig without question, and attack at her bidding.

Night Hag: HD 8; AC 8[11]; Atk 1 bite (2d6); Move 10; Save 8; AL C; CL/XP 11/1700; Special: Magic resistance (65%), +2 or better magic weapon to hit, magical abilities.

Skeleton: HD 1; AC 8[11] or 7[12] with shield; Atk 1 weapon or strike (1d6) or (1d6+1 two-handed); Move 12; Save 17; AL N; CL/XP 1/15; Special: None.

Nixie

Hit Dice: 1d4 hp
Armor Class: 7 [12]
Attacks: Weapon (1d6)
Saving Throw: 18
Special: Charm
Move: 6/12 (swimming)
Alignment: Neutrality
Number Encountered: 1d8 x10
Challenge Level/XP: B/10

Nixies are weak water fey creatures. One in ten of them has the power to cast a powerful *charm person* (-2 penalty to saving throw) that causes the victim to walk into the water and join the nixies as their slave for a year. Casting *dispel magic* against the curse has only a 75% chance of success, and once the victim is actually in the water the chance drops to 25%. Nixies are ordinarily friendly, but they are highly capricious.

Nixie: HD 1d4 hp; AC 7[12]; Atk 1 weapon (1d6); Move 6 (Swim 12); Save 18; AL N; CL/XP 1/15; Special: Charm.

The Water Cult

A group of 16 people — 10 men and six women — stands waist deep in the cool waters of a pond deep in the forest. Their clothing is drenched and their faces are blank. Their hair hangs in limp strands about their slack, doughy faces. White water lilies decorate their hair. Each person holds his hands out before him, allowing fat frogs to squirm and leap from them into the water. The banks of the pond are littered with rusted weapons, inedible rations and rotted parchments. The remnants of a firepit are evident. The skeleton of a pig on a spit sits above the rotted logs.

Living in the pond are **3 nixies**. Two of the fey control five of the people, and one controls six. The people in the water are adventurers who camped beside the pond nearly nine months ago. The nixies took offense to the light, laughter and the adventurers' cursing. When the men slaughtered a wild boar, the angry nixies coaxed the men and women one by one into the water to serve them and the forest they had defiled. PCs that harm the forest or bother the entranced individuals face the same fate. The nixies plan to release their victims after one year serving the forest around them.

Nykoul

Hit Dice: 9
Armor Class: 4 [15]
Attacks: 1 weapon (2d12)
Saving Throw: 6
Special: Undead immunities, confusion, spells
Move: 9
Alignment: Chaos
Number Encountered: 1
Challenge Level/XP: 11/1,700

Nykoul are undead hill giant shamans, driven to continue plaguing the world by dark powers from beyond this world. In addition to being able to cast spells as a 5th level Cleric, Nykoul possess a disorienting gaze attack (as the spell Confusion) that they may use twice per day. One in three Nykoul commands an army of 1-12 Giant Rats.

— *Author: Andrew Trent, "the Venomous Pao"*

Nykoul: HD 9; AC 4[15]; Atk 1 Weapon (2d12); Move 9; Save 6; AL C; CL/XP 11/1700; Special: Spells, Undead immunities, confusion.

Nykoul, Plated

An armor-plated giant crashes through the village gates, swinging a giant club embedded with metal rivets wildly at any creature stupid enough to get in its way. Scrambling around its feet are **8 giant rats** that leap atop those knocked to the ground by the angry giant. The smell wafting off the giant is nauseating, like a dead creature left too long in the hot sun. Anyone looking closely sees that the armor the creature wears is not linked together, but actually sewn into its skin. The monster clanks and creaks as it moves, the plates rubbing and rasping together like continents crashing into one another.

The **nykoul Gergasi Kemation** stomps through the village, smashing things as he walks. The plates make him tougher to hit (giving him AC 2[17]), but cause his spells to fail 20% of the time. A group of malevolent pixies tortured the creature by grafting plates of armor to its skin after it stepped on one of their own.

350

Nymph

Hit Dice: 3
Armor Class: 9 [10]
Attacks: None
Saving Throw: 14
Special: Sight causes blindness or death
Move: 12
Alignment: Neutrality
Number Encountered: 1
Challenge Level/XP: 5/240

Nymphs inhabit the wild and untrammeled places of the earth, spots of beauty and calm. Anyone seeing a nymph naked must make a saving throw or die (or sometimes be transformed into an animal). Even looking upon a nymph causes permanent blindness (saving throw). Nymphs are not powerful in and of themselves, but harming a nymph almost always brings down vengeance of some sort from the gods.

Nymph: HD 3; AC 9[10]; Atk none; Move 12; Save 14; AL N; CL/XP 5/240; Special: Sight causes blindness or death.

Down on the Farm

Orchids, roses and lilies cover the grounds of this pleasant farm set deep in the Fontus Valley. Vines grow greedily over the farmhouse, appearing ready to pull the structure back into the ground if they were given the chance. Pigs run wild through the lush fields. The home is empty and has been for nearly a year. Dust coats the belongings left behind. A pond of crystal blue water sits in the center of the farmstead. A young woman swims naked in the pond, lounging amid the abundant water lilies.

A woman is a **nymph** named **Selmago Grell**. The pigs running free on the farm are all men who looked on the beautiful creature and were transformed into swine. Selmago dislikes weapons of any sort and tosses them into the pond after she deals with their owners. The bottom of the pond is covered in rusting weapons, farm implements (Selmago has a loose definition of weaponry) and even knives and forks. Anyone diving to the bottom of the 20-foot-deep pond has a 10% chance of finding a minor magical weapon amid the rusting clutter. The chance decreases by 1% for each additional attempt (to a 1% chance) as swimming PCs stir up clouds of rust that obscures vision.

Oblivion Wraith

Hit Dice: 12
Armor Class: 1 [18]
Attacks: 1 touch (3d6 + attribute drain)
Saving Throw: 3
Special: Drain attributes, immune to non-magical weapons, disintegrates objects
Move: 15/30 (flying)
Alignment: Chaos
Number Encountered: 1
Challenge Level/XP: 15/2,900

An oblivion wraith appears very much like a wraith, and shares the same immunity to non-magic weapons and cold, but it is not actually undead, being a creature of the void rather than undeath. An oblivion wraith's touch shreds the raw existence of the creature hit, dealing 3d6 points of damage and also permanently draining one point from the target's highest attribute for every natural 5 or 6 rolled on the damage dice. For example, a damage roll of 6, 3, and 5 on 3d6 deals 14 damage and drains 2 points from the target's highest attribute. In addition, if a creature brings any nonliving object (such as a swung weapon) into contact with an oblivion wraith, the object is irrevocably disintegrated (magical objects receive a saving throw). Oddly, oblivion wraiths are unable to actively disintegrate objects by touching them.

— Author: Guy Fullerton

Oblivion Wraith: HD 12; AC 1[18]; Atk 1 touch (3d6 + attribute drain); Move 15/30 (flying); Save 3; AL C; CL/XP 15/2900; Special: Drain attributes, immune to non-magical weapons, disintegrates objects.

Eye of the Beholder

Snowflake-sized particles of ash drift about this gallery of hanging portraits and marble sculptures. Most of the artwork is mundane, depicting aristocrats posing with dead animals or beautiful ladies sitting on coral benches. One disturbing painting stands out among the others, however. The painting's canvas is slathered with an ugly mix of blacks and ochers to create a nauseating splash of anger inside the frame. The four-foot-by-six-foot frame is made of linked leg bones polished to a gleaming white.

The painting is a portal into oblivion created by a deranged magic-user who paid the ultimate price after he made a pact with a demonic princess. His femurs now make up parts of the frame. The painting is mesmerizing, but staring into it activates the portal. Anyone who looks into the portrait must make a saving throw or stand fixated as he tries to make sense of the distorted shapes caught on canvas. An **oblivion wraith** trapped within the painting arrives within 1d4+1 rounds to collect the art lover.

Ochre Jelly

Hit Dice: 6
Armor Class: 8 [11]
Attacks: Acid-laden strike (3d4)
Saving Throw: 11
Special: Lightning divides creature
Move: 3
Alignment: Neutrality
Number Encountered: 1
Challenge Level/XP: 6/400

Ochre jellies are amorphous oozes that damage opponents with their acidic surface. They dissolve any adventurers they kill, making a raise dead spell impossible. The creature divides if struck with lightning (each with half the monster's existing hit points).

Ochre Jelly: HD 6; AC 8[11]; Atk 1 acid-laden strike (3d4); Move 3; Save 11; AL N; CL/XP 6/400; Special: Lightning divides creature.

Jelly Bed

A four-poster bed with a lace canopy draped over it stands in this empty tower room. The chamber is lavishly decorated, but appears to have gone unused for decades. The coverlets on the bed are faded and moldy, and moths have eaten holes in the lace canopy. The mattress has settled into the wooden bedframe. An iron vanity stands against the wall. Matching silver combs and a mirror (100 gp) sit on its green glass top. Dust coats everything in a thick layer. Feathers lie atop the dust, spread across the floor from a rip torn in the down-filled mattress. The mattress is still solid, but sort of spongy to the touch.

An **ochre jelly** crawled under the room's locked door and into the mattress through the rip torn in its side. The ooze's acidic surface ate away at the insides of the mattress, but an outer lining lets the mattress keep its shape. While it appears to be a normal mattress, anyone climbing onto the mattress collapses down into the bed frame and into the middle of the ochre jelly.

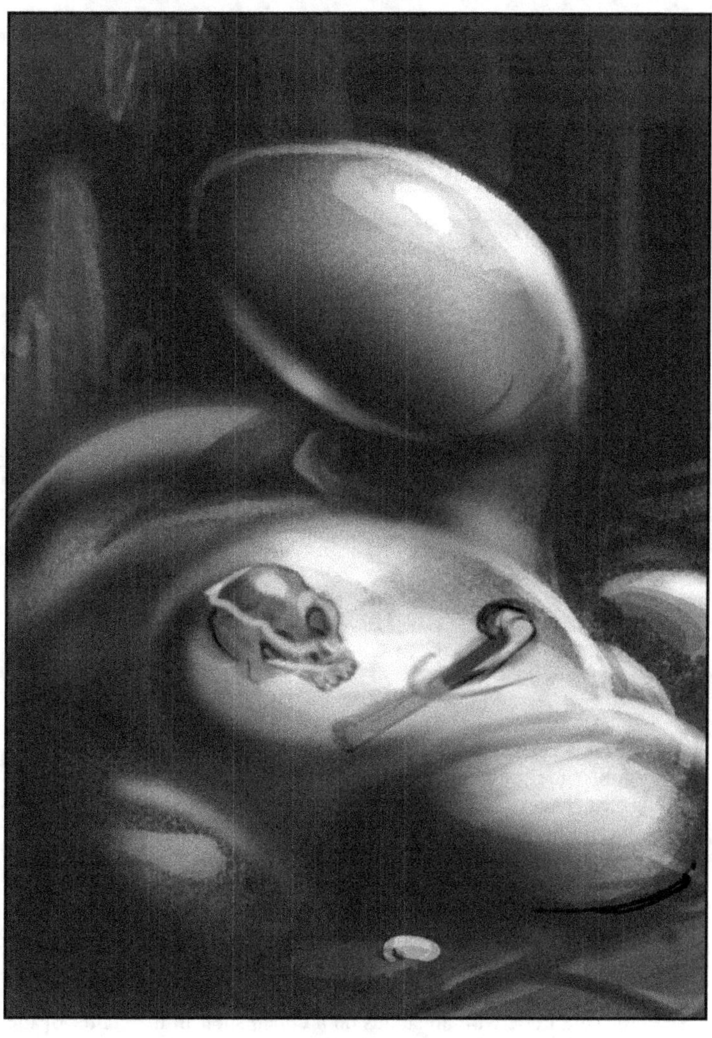

Octopus, Giant

Hit Dice: 4
Armor Class: 7 [12]
Attacks: 8 tentacles (1d3) (see below)
Saving Throw: 13
Special: Jet, Ink, Constriction
Move: 3/9 (swimming)
Alignment: Neutrality
Number Encountered: 1
Challenge Level/XP: 6/400

After a giant octopus hits with a tentacle, it does 1d6 points of damage per round, automatically, instead of the initial 1d3. Also, there is a 25% chance that the tentacle "hit" pinions one of the victim's limbs (roll randomly for left/right arms and legs to see which is immobilized). A giant octopus can jet water out to achieve a movement rate of up to 27, and can also release a huge cloud of ink to obscure its location. Some giant octopi might be able to move onto land for short periods of time. Note: it is occasionally possible to encounter giant octopi that are highly intelligent rather than being no more than a freakishly large animal. These intelligent giant octopi will be followers of Chaos rather than being Neutrally–aligned.

Giant Octopus: HD 4; AC 7[12]; Atk 8 tentacles (1d3); Move 3 (Swim 9); Save 13; AL N or C; CL/XP 6/400; Special: Jet, ink, constriction.

Tentacles and Tridents

A 15-foot-wide gray stone pier extends nearly a quarter mile into the Reaping Sea. The rocks are slick with saltwater washing over the edifice from powerful breakers crashing into the wall. The cobblestone walkway atop the pier is 10 feet above the surface of the sea. During storms, waves easily rise above the walkway, threatening to sweep away anyone walking along the treacherous surface. A 10-foot-tall portico covers the last 50 feet of the pier. Marble pillars spaced every 10 feet hold up a peaked roof. The walkway ends in a 30-foot-diameter gazebo-like structure built at the end of the pier.

A statue of a nude woman stands on a conch shell in the center of the gazebo. Dried seaweed wraps around her body, and live crabs scuttle around her feet. She holds a trident leveled toward the open sea. More tridents line the walls of the temple, each fastened to a stone pillar with silver clamps. Cool, fresh water pours from the conch shell to pool in a basin around the statue of Xeto, the beautiful goddess of sea monsters. The temple is protected by **2 giant octopuses** that pull themselves out of the ocean using the pillars around the temple dedicated to their goddess.

Oculaktis

Hit Dice: 7
Armor Class: 5 [14]
Attacks: Gaze (6d6 or 3d6)
Saving Throw: 9
Special: Heat ray (save for half)
Move: 15 (flying)
Alignment: Neutrality
Number Encountered: 1
Challenge Level/XP: 10/1,400

These spherical monstrosities are essentially gigantic eyeballs that drift through space in some of the more bizarre dimensions of existence. They are used as floating mounts by beings wild and weird. They may transmit their superhuman visual information to riders if desired, as well as make terrifying gaze attacks once per combat round. The concentrated gaze of an oculaktis actually transmits a powerful beam that can cause magnificent explosions, incinerate solid stone, or melt men to puddles of steaming jelly. The heat beam has a range of 100ft and the first time it is used it inflicts 6d6 points of damage (saving throw for half damage) to its target. Thereafter, unless the oculaktis has an hour or more to "recharge," the beam only inflicts 3d6 points of damage (save for half). The oculaktis must make a successful to-hit roll with the heat beam.

— Author: Random

Oculaktis: HD 7; AC 5[14]; Atk Gaze (6d6 or 3d6); Move (Fly 15); Save 9; AL N; CL/XP 10/1400; Special: Heat ray (save for half damage).

The Insane Eye

A crystal ball sits on a golden stand decorated by hundreds of carved eyes. Scintillating colors weave and twist inside the orb. If anyone touches the ball, the colors vanish, replaced by an unblinking eyeball that fills the sphere. The PC touching the globe must make a saving throw or be drawn into the globe. The PC can voluntarily fail the save, if desired. His body vanishes as if winking out of existence.

The PC pulled into the globe finds himself standing atop a gigantic eyeball drifting through a void of flashing colors. The colors each have unique smells. The eyeball is an **oculaktis** drifting randomly around the void. The eyeball occasionally approaches bright points of white light hovering in the colors. Touching a point of light draws the PC back into the real world through another crystal ball. The GM is free to get creative with these destinations.

The eyeball is a transport system the owner of the globe used to get around the world. Up to 10 people can use the crystal ball to arrive on the same oculaktis. However, there is a 10% chance per person (10% chance for one person, 40% chance for four, etc.) that their presence drives the eyeball insane and causes it to attack its riders. Anyone falling off the oculaktis drifts aimlessly in the color-filled void. A PC must make a saving throw to will himself to move in a certain direction. PCs can fight normally while hanging suspended in space.

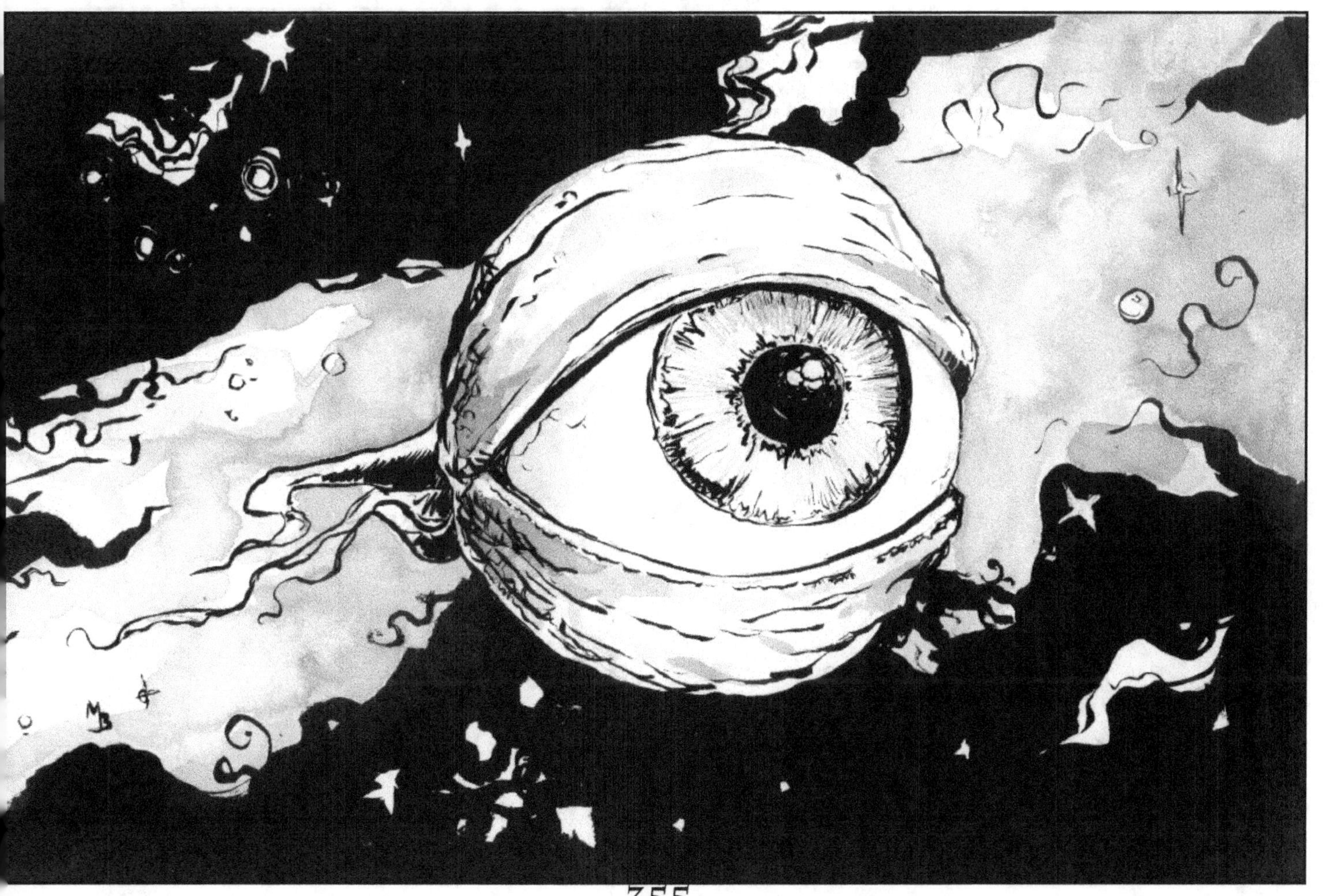

Ogre

Hit Dice: 4+1
Armor Class: 5 [14]
Attacks: Weapon (1d10+1)
Saving Throw: 13
Special: None
Move: 9
Alignment: Chaos
Challenge Level/XP: 4/120

Ogres are normally quite stupid, but more intelligent versions might be encountered here and there.

Ogre: HD 4+1; AC 5[14]; Atk 1 weapon (1d10+1); Move 9; Save 13; AL C; CL/XP 4/120; Special: None.

Whack That Mole

A raucous din rises from beyond a stand of beech trees. Heavy thuds of a club smacking the growl are followed by animal-like growls and grunts. Deep-throated laughter follows each hit. PCs who investigate the sounds find a bizarre sight: Hundreds of iron spikes are driven into the ground, forming a crude 50-foot-diameter circle around the clearing. The area inside the circle is crisscrossed by raised trails of dirt. An **ogre** stands inside the spikes, repeatedly slamming a heavy wooden club into the ground. Dirt clods fly high into the air as the ogre pummels the ground. The ogre growls angrily after each hit, and stomps the ground in frustration.

Sitting on the ground outside the iron spike ring are **3 ogres.** Each one laughs uproariously as the ogre with the club tromps across the clearing. The ogres take turns smashing the club into the ground. The ogres trapped a mole that kept them awake last night, and are trying to beat it to death. The cagey animal weaves across the clearing, trapped by the spikes. The mole can escape whenever it wants, but seems to be playing with the dim-witted ogres. The ogres grab their clubs and attack anyone interrupting their game.

Ogre, Swamp

Hit Dice: 6+1
Armor Class: 4 [15]
Attacks: 2 grabs (submerge opponent), or 2 claws (1d6) and bite (2d6)
Saving Throw: 11
Special: Surprise, grab, swallow whole
Move: 6/12 (swimming)
Alignment: Chaos
Number Encountered: 1d4
Challenge Level/XP: 8/800

Swamp Ogres are larger, semi-aquatic cousins of standard ogres. They range in color from moldy green to burnt yellowish-brown, and they have huge heads that protrude forward from their enormous, hunched shoulders. Their great arms are able to rotate around completely, allowing them to easily reach anywhere on their backs and shoulders. Swamp Ogres are often covered in moss, swamp grass, and mud, which facilitates their favorite mode of Attacks: Surprise. Swamp Ogres sit or lie down in the muck (depending on depth) so that just their great shoulder hump protrudes above the mire; when still, they need to breathe only once each hour. While in this position, a Swamp Ogre waits until someone or something sets foot upon its shoulders, whereupon its arms move with lightning speed to grab its victim and pull it down into the mire to be eaten. If the Swamp Ogre hits with both hands, it drags the opponent completely below the mire to drown in 4-6 rounds. If the Swamp Ogre hits with only one hand, it drags the opponent under on the following round, unless 8 points of damage is dealt to its hand or it is otherwise forced it to loosen its grip. Once its opponent is underneath the mire, the Swamp Ogre uses its conventional claw and bite attacks on the unfortunate victim. If a Swamp Ogre scores a natural 20 with its bite attack against a man-size or smaller opponent, it swallows that opponent whole. A swallowed opponent suffers 1d8 damage each round from stomach acid, can't attack with anything larger than a dagger, and ultimately suffocates in 2d4 rounds.

— *Author: Sean Stone*

Swamp Ogre: HD 6+1; AC 4 [15]; Atk 2 grabs (submerge opponent), or 2 claws (1d6 each) and bite (2d6); Move 6 (Swim12); Save 11; AL C; CL/XP 8/800; Special: Surprise opponents on a 1-5 when hiding in swamp, and swallow whole with bite on a natural 20.

Stay on the Path

A line of slick, flat black stones jut out of the murky waters of the Sin Mire Swamp. The path leads into the center of a thick morass of reeds, red-striped weeds and stagnant water. A twisted banyan tree grows out of the center of the mire at the end of the stone path. Its branches dip into the murky waters around it. Algae cling to its bark, rising up along the trunk in greenish swirls. Moss drapes from the tree's branches, and swamp rats run easily along its broad limbs. A hollow opening in the trunk contains a gleaming gem sitting among a handful of acorns. The gem sparkles in the sunlight.

One of the stones along the path is a **swamp ogre** crouching in the six-foot-deep water. The hungry monster waits for someone to step on its back before grabbing them and holding them underwater. The "gem" is a polished rock the ogre placed in the tree to lure victims. The body of an decomposing elf lies underwater near where the ogre crouches. The elf is dressed in chainmail that weighs the corpse down. A pouch attached to the ogre's belt contains 147 gp, a waterlogged and unreadable journal, and a gold ring (300 gp) engraved with the words "To My Love. Return Always to Me."

Ogre, Tusken

Hit Dice: 5
Armor Class: 4 [15]
Attacks: 1 weapon (1d10+1)
Saving Throw: 12
Special: Mirror image
Move: 12
Alignment: Chaos
Number Encountered: 1d6
Challenge Level/XP: 5/240

Tusken ogres are a race of ogres mid-way between the normal, feral ogre and the magically potent ogre mage. These ogres have a only a pale bluish tint to their skin, and powerful tusks protruding from their mouths. They are somewhat more intelligent than normal ogres, and are often found in the service of an ogre mage. Tusken ogres that are not minions of an ogre mage, encountered in the wild, often inhabit crude but human-like residences. They dress in silk garments taken from victims or merchants, and usually fight with polearms or outsized swords. They are inveterate slavers, and their lairs will often contain human prisoners, especially women. A tusken ogre has one magical ability, which is to create a single mirror image of itself at the beginning of a battle. As with the spell mirror image, the illusory double will disappear when it is hit. Female tusken ogres are encountered only rarely. Asian and European varieties of the tusken ogre are actually quite similar, although the European type would likely not be dressed in silk but in whatever finery might be available.

— Author: Matt Finch

Tusken Ogre: HD 5; AC 4[15]; Atk 1 weapon (1d10+1); Move 12; Save 12; AL C; CL/XP 5/240; Special: Single mirror image.

Tusken Slaver

A large silk tent sits on the desert sands, colorful pennants flying from poles holding the canvas up. A four-foot-tall statue of an elephant sits in front of the tent's entrance flap. Cool water jets into the air from the statue's upraised trunk. The sand around the statue is saturated with the ever-flowing water. A woman wearing silk veils and loose-fitting clothing sits on a red cushion located just inside the tent. She has dark hair and eyes, and her skin is extremely pale. She welcomes visitors and bids them sit on plush cushions thrown around the tent's interior. She offers plump grapes and fresh water to her guests. She claims she is the lost queen of the burning wastes.

The food and water are poisoned with a sleep-inducing agent derived from the venom of a desert scorpion. Anyone eating or drinking the food offered by the woman must make a saving throw or fall asleep for 1d4+2 hours. The tent is the desert home of a **tusken ogre** named **Allatin al-Salk**. The slaver is always looking to add to his collection of slaves. The woman is a loyal companion who sold out her nomadic companions when the ogre attacked. Her friends are chained inside an enclosure buried under the hot sands behind the tent. Inside the slave pen are 4 men and 3 women. All are dehydrated and delirious. The ogre holds slave auctions once a month to sell slaves he captures.

Ogre Mage

Hit Dice: 5+4
Armor Class: 4 [15]
Attacks: Weapon (1d12)
Saving Throw: 12
Special: Magic use (See below), regenerate 1hp/round
Move: 12/18 (flying)
Alignment: Chaos
Number Encountered: 1d6
Challenge Level/XP: 7/600

The ogre mage is an ogre with magic powers, based on Japanese legend. An ogre mage can fly, turn invisible (per the spell), create a 10-foot-radius circle of magical darkness, change into human form, cast *Sleep* and *Charm Person* once per day, and cast a *Cone of Frost* with a range of 60 feet to a base of 30 feet, causing 8d6 damage to any caught within (saving throw applies). Western folklore also contains many examples of shape-shifting, magical ogres (the most famous example being the one in *Puss-in-Boots*), so there might be many different interpretations of magical ogres whether or not they are called "ogre mage."

Ogre Mage: HD 5+4; AC 4[15]; Atk 1 weapon (1d12); Move 12 (Fly 18); Save 12; AL C; CL/XP 7/600; Special: Magic use, regenerate 1hp/round.

Coin Collector

A single gold coin dangles on a silver chain from an oaken crossbeam supporting the roof of a gazebo-like temple standing amid a garden of hyacinths. Four elaborate columns covered with gold leaf hold up the wooden roof. The temple's ceiling is painted with murals of a dragon wrapping around the world, its flaming breath burning the moon and stars into oblivion. The coin is ancient, with the marks of the forgotten kingdom of Kor-Tokeen. One side has a tipping scale, while the other shows a glowing sun rising above a feather.

Anyone taking the gold coin does so at their peril. The coin contains the spirit of an **ogre mage** trapped for nearly 200 years. Removing the coin from the temple allows the ogre mage to reform in 1d4 days within 10 feet of the bearer of the coin. The ogre mage viciously attacks, mistakenly thinking the person with the coin is the person who originally trapped him.

Oktomon

Hit Dice: 3
Armor Class: 6 [13] + shields
Attacks: Up to 4 weapons (damage by weapon type)
Saving Throw: 14
Special: None
Move: 12/18 (swimming)
Alignment: Usually Chaos
Number Encountered: 1d20 or 3d20
Challenge Level/XP: 4/120

Oktomon appear rather like man-sized octopi, but they are actually clever tool and weapon-using "humanoids." They generally live underwater, either fresh or salt, but are fully amphibious and can breathe on land as well as underwater. Oktomon walk on 4 of their eight legs and use the other 4 as arms. In combat, Oktomon use various combinations of four weapons and shields. They do not typically use pulled bows, but may occasionally make use of crossbows. Due to their wide-set eyes and multiple arms, it is virtually impossible to flank an Oktomon or successfully attack one "from behind." Oktomon are attracted to shiny objects and often carry a number of items of jewelry with them as prized possessions. Oktomon are renowned for their mechanical abilities, and an Oktomon lair is typically a very dangerously trapped location. Tales of magic-using Oktomon are often told, but have yet to be verified. Depending on the source, it is also reported that Oktomon are either outright hostile towards or firmly allied with Sea Hags. It is possible, of course, that different groups of Oktomon may have different allegiances.

— Author: Andrew Trent

Oktomon: HD 3; AC without shields 6[13]; Atk Up to 4 weapons (damage by weapon type); Move 12 (Swim 18); Save 14; AL usually C; CL/XP 4/120; Special: None.

The Sea Hag's Entourage

The Coral Castle of Cnidaria rises off the seabed nearly a quarter-mile off Bargarsport's coastline. Delicate coral spires rise above the rolling waves high above the structure. Impaled on these sharp protrusions are dolphins, a mermaid, and various colorful fish. A **great white shark** swims nimbly through the spires, watching for prey. Occasionally, it tears chunks off the hanging corpses. Blood fills the water in dark clouds. The great white has three diamond studs (75 gp each) driven through its dorsal fin.

The castle is an underwater architectural wonder, with arched doorways, sprawling rooms, flying buttresses and floors of smooth pearl. Inside the throne room where giant clams hold the pearl treasures of the undersea kingdom, the **sea hag Scombrotix Caryon** lounges on a throne created from the upper jaws of hundreds of swordfish. She is served by **10 oktomon** and **15 sahuagin**.

Large Shark (8HD): HD 8; AC 6[13]; Atk 1 bite (1d8+4); Move 0 (Swim 24); Save 8; AL N; CL/XP 8/800; Special: Feeding frenzy.

Sahuagin: HD 2+1; AC 5[14]; Atk 1 weapon (1d8); Move 12 (Swim 18); Save 16; AL C; CL/XP 2/30; Special: None.

Sea Hag: HD 3; AC 6[13]; Atk 1 bite (1d4); Move 6 (Swim 18); Save 14; AL C; CL/XP 5/240; Special: Death gaze, weakness gaze.

Old Crawler

Hit Dice: 2
Armor Class: 4 [15]
Attacks: 1 rotting grip (1d8)
Saving Throw: 11
Special: Possible spell casting, good saving throw, continuous damage
Move: 6/12 (scrambling)
Alignment: Neutrality
Number Encountered: 1d2
Challenge Level/XP: 3/60

An "old crawler" is a withered human hand severed at the wrist, black and mummified in appearance. Many think they may originate from the leftovers of a lich. Old crawlers attack by sneaking up on a character and grabbing his or her foot; or they drop from a higher place onto the head, face or shoulder of the poor adventurer. The grip of an old crawler can only be broken with a roll of 1 on a d4 (1-2 if the character has magical or special strength). Any area squeezed by an old crawler is subject to gangrenous rotting, and continues to incur damage until the grip is broken. Once latched on, the old crawler remains so until destroyed or pried loose. Some old crawlers have magical rings that can still cast attacks. While fire would be the most obvious harm to the hand, it poses quite a threat if attached to a victim. Bashing attacks are the most effective. The old crawler can "flee" with a scrambling move when needed at double its normal crawling rate. Note that Old crawlers are extremely resistant to many attacks due to magically improved saving throws left over from their strange origins (included in stats).

— Author: Old Crawler

Old Crawler: HD 2; AC 4[15]; Atk 1 rotting grip (1d8); Move 6 (Scramble 12); Save 11; AL N; CL/XP 3/60; Special: Possible spell casting, good saving throws, continuous damage.

Cool Hand Fluke

A dolphin flies through the waves, leaping from one ocean swell to the next in a dazzling display of agility. The creature hones in on the shore, however, and its headlong flight sends it skidding and tumbling to a stop at PCs' feet on the sandy beach. At a distance, the dolphin was spectacular; close up, it is horrifying. The dolphin's skin is mottled and cankerous, with rotting flesh sloughing down its cadaverous sides. A decayed hand is latched onto the dolphin's tail fluke, the cool fingers grasping firmly into its flesh. Purple welts rise on the fluke under the fingers' pressure.

The hand is an **old crawler** that leaped into the Reaping Sea to escape the pirate ship Red Wolf after the hand strangled the crew and started an oil fire that consumed the ship. The hand latched onto a passing dolphin, and the panicked creature finally brought it to shore. The old crawler attacks anyone investigating the dying dolphin.

Omgoth

Hit Dice: 4
Armor Class: 6 [13]
Attacks: 2 claws (1d6)
Saving Throw: 13
Special: Corruption
Move: 9
Alignment: Chaos
Number Encountered: 1
Challenge Level/XP: 5/240

Omgoths were once holy men who, through betrayal of their faith, now suffer from a curse that has given them a rotting, ghoulish appearance. Indeed, they look so much like ghouls that they are often mistaken for one. Their bodies are in always in a continuous state of decay and they must regularly feed on the living to replenish their lost flesh or the curse will consume them. Omgoths exude an aura of corruption that causes healing magics employed in their presence to damage the intended recipient instead of healing; be they from spells, potions or magical items. Though omgoths may be found in the company of undead creatures, they are not themselves undead and cannot be turned.

— Author: The Lizard of Oz

Omgoth: HD 4; AC 6[13]; Atk 2 claws (1d6); Move 9; Save 13; AL C; CL/XP 5/240; Special: Corruption.

The Unholy Men of Mon-Serreat

A staircase at the top of the Mon-Serreat Cliffs leads downward along the sheer cliff face to a 20-foot-tall recess carved into the rack wall. Carved half-pillars stand on either side of double doors leading into the rock wall to Absence Monastery. Inside the monastery's dark halls, the smell of decay and death rises thickly through the stifling air. Clouds of buzzing flies and biting insects swarm through the stone corridors. A circular central chamber contains a number of wooden pews facing a 2-foot-diameter golden font filled with cool, clear water. Words engraved in the stone floor around the font read "The Health of the World, Flowing from the Mon-Serreat Stones, Drink and be Fulfilled."

The waters once healed all who drank of them. The monastery was taken over years ago by **10 omgoths** that currently live in the ossuary accessed by steep, unlit stairs that descend into the crypts. The presence of the unholy omgoths corrupted the healing waters, so that anyone drinking the liquid takes 2d4+2 points of damage with each sip (save for half). The waters return to normal a few weeks after the omgoths are destroyed. Once restored, the waters heal 1d6+4 points of damage three times per day for a drinker. The water can be stored and carried for up to a month, after which it turns into golden flakes that can be spread on wounds to heal 1d4 points of damage.

Ophidian

	STERILE OPHIDIAN	OPHIDIAN
Hit Dice:	3	3
Armor Class:	4 [15] or 3 [16] with shield	
Attacks:	1 two-handed weapon (1d8+1) or weapon with shield (1d8)	
Saving Throw:	14	14
Special:	None	Reproductive bite
Move:	12	12
Alignment:	Chaos	Chaos
Number Encountered:	1d10 (mixed group) or 2d100 (mixed settlement)	
Challenge Level/XP:	3/60	5/240

Ophidians are an ancient race of snake-beings, with scaly human arms and a somewhat human-looking head. They are denizens of hot climates, deserts and jungles both, often found in forgotten cities or temples from the days when their race held greater sway in the world. Anyone bitten by an ophidian and failing a saving throw will, within 1d4 weeks, produce ophidian children and die in the process. It is in this manner that ophidians reproduce; they are otherwise asexual. The deadly "pregnancy" can be ended by a cure disease spell or similar magics. Lesser, or "sterile," ophidians (a non-breeding caste) are sometimes found – these have no effective bite.

Sterile (Lesser) Ophidian: HD3; AC 4[15] or 3[16] with shield; Atk 1 two-handed weapon (1d8+1) or weapon with shield (1d8); Move 12; Save 14; AL C; CL/XP 3/60; Special: None.

Ophidian: HD3; AC 4[15] or 3[16] with shield; Atk1 two-handed weapon (1d8+1) or weapon with shield (1d8), and bite (0); Move 12; Save 14; AL C; CL/XP 5/240; Special: Reproductive bite.

Breeding Ground

This dank, lightless cellar beneath the dry wastes of the Kanderi Desert stinks of human waste and rotting food. The cellar is barely visible in the desert, and layers of sand hide its presence. A flat wooden door set on the ground may reveal its presence. The door opens into a steep staircase that descends 15 feet below a sand dune. Chained along one cinder-block wall in the desert cellar are four women and three men. Their hands are raised above their heads and held in place by thick manacles driven into the stone behind them. Their feet are free, but their awkward position against the wall doesn't allow them to move. Two of the men's bodies are split from neck to belly, the skin erupting outward in bloody ribbons. Blood trails slither across the ground away from the gore.

The cellar is the breeding ground of **10 ophidians** cast out of the jungle city of Uroborus. The **6 lesser ophidians** scour the desert with a camel-pulled wagon to capture desert nomads. They bring the unlucky victims back to the cellar and chain them to wall to await their fate. The **4 ophidian leaders** visit the cellar at night to bite the sacrifices to spawn a new generation of snake-men. The ophidians live under a massive rock overhang jutting from the desert a quarter-mile to the east. The ophidians hope to start another snake city around the rock. The new city is to be named Pyrrhus. The snake-men attack anyone bothering the cellar.

Orc

Hit Dice: 1
Armor Class: 6 [13]
Attacks: Weapon, usually spear (1d6) or scimitar (1d8)
Saving Throw: 17
Special: None
Move: 9
Alignment: Chaos
Number Encountered: 1d8 or 30d10
Challenge Level/XP: 1/15

Orcs are stupid, brutish humanoids that gather in tribes of hundreds. Most are subterranean dwellers, and fight with a penalty of -1 in sunlight. Occasionally, war-bands or even entire tribes of orcs issue forth from their caverns to raid and pillage by night. Orcish leaders are great brutes with additional hit dice, and magic-using shamans may also be found in the larger tribes. Orcish tribes hate each other, and will fight savagely unless restrained by a powerful and feared commander, such as a Chaotic high priest or an evil sorcerer.

Orc: HD 1; AC 6[13]; Atk 1 by weapon, usually spear (1d6) or scimitar (1d8); Move 9; Save 17; AL C; CL/XP 1/15; Special: None.

Go, Orc, Go

The Karth Badlands contain steep rocky slopes of piled stones that rise nearly 100 feet. The massive slabs of rock lie at all angles, like they were cast about by giants – or something much larger and nastier. Some of the rocks landed to form sloping stone ramps that rise to the tops of the bluffs. Numerous broken wagons sit in the narrow canyon. Most are just piles of rotting wood collapsing on themselves. Some are missing wheels and others look like they smashed into the rock walls at high speeds. A few look like they fell from great heights and smashed to the rocky ground. A few wagons can even be spied sitting atop the bluffs, perched on the cliff like they had stopped just short of going over.

A band of **10 orcs** (all that remain out of 50) from the Chiseled Tusk Clan use the rocky slopes to ambush travelers. The orcs pull stolen wagons to the top of the bluffs, then push them over the side and ride them down upon travelers. The speeding wagons careen wildly down the rocky slopes, bouncing and jumping as they slam into dips in the rock. The orcs ride in the open wagon, hanging on for dear life. Past attempts didn't turn out so well, but the orcs are persistent. PCs should be able to easily get out of the way, and the noise the rolling wagon makes as it flies down the slope eliminates any surprise the orcs might have had. The orcs tumble out of the wagon to attack when the ride stops.

Origami Warrior

Hit Dice: 2
Armor Class: 5[14]
Attacks: 1 spear (1d6)
Saving Throw: 16
Special: Magic resistance 10%, half damage from blunt weapons, immune to piercing weapons, +1 damage from cutting weapons, double damage from fire.
Move: 12
Alignment: Neutral
Number Encountered: 1d10
Challenge Level/XP: 3/60

The origami warrior is a creation made of intricately folded paper, in the shape of a full sized human warrior. They move with lightning speed (accounting for the armor class), and blunt weapons inflict only half damage against them. Piercing weapons pass through the paper construction without causing any damage at all, but cutting weapons inflict +1 damage and fire inflicts double damage. Origami warriors wield normal spears. They are generally found in the service of powerful sorcerers, and have magic resistance of 10%.

— Author: Matt Finch

Origami Warrior: HD 2; AC 5[14]; Atk 1 spear (1d6); Move 12; Save 16; AL N; CL/XP 3/60; Special: Magic resistance 10%, half damage from blunt weapons, immune to piercing weapons, +1 damage from cutting weapons, double damage from fire.

Paper Cuts

This 30-foot-by-40-foot room is filled waist deep with tiny strips of sliced paper. The confetti spills out into the hallway from either oak door when it is opened. Halflings and dwarves entering the chamber find themselves nearly buried in the stuff. Paper lanterns filled with globes of continual light hang from the walls. In the center of the room, a gushing column of wind lifts the confetti from the floor and tosses it out halfway to the 40-foot-high stone ceiling. Tiny strips float down throughout the room like a paper snowstorm. The air column isn't strong enough to lift a person. At the top of the column of air, a fist-size globe of folded paper bobbles near the ceiling.

The room is home to **10 origami warrior** guardians lying flat in the piles of torn paper. The paper-like creatures protect the folded globe, which contains instructions for creating origami warriors. The paper globe is folded tightly from hundreds of sheets of paper, however, and unfolding it may rip the paper so that the process is unusable. Anyone trying to unfold it has a 20% chance of tearing a page as they delicately open it like a flower.

Ostrich, Giant

Hit Dice: 3
Armor Class: 7 [12]
Attacks: 1 bite (1d6)
Saving Throw: 14
Special: None
Move: 18
Alignment: Neutrality
Number Encountered: 1d12
Challenge Level/XP: 3/60

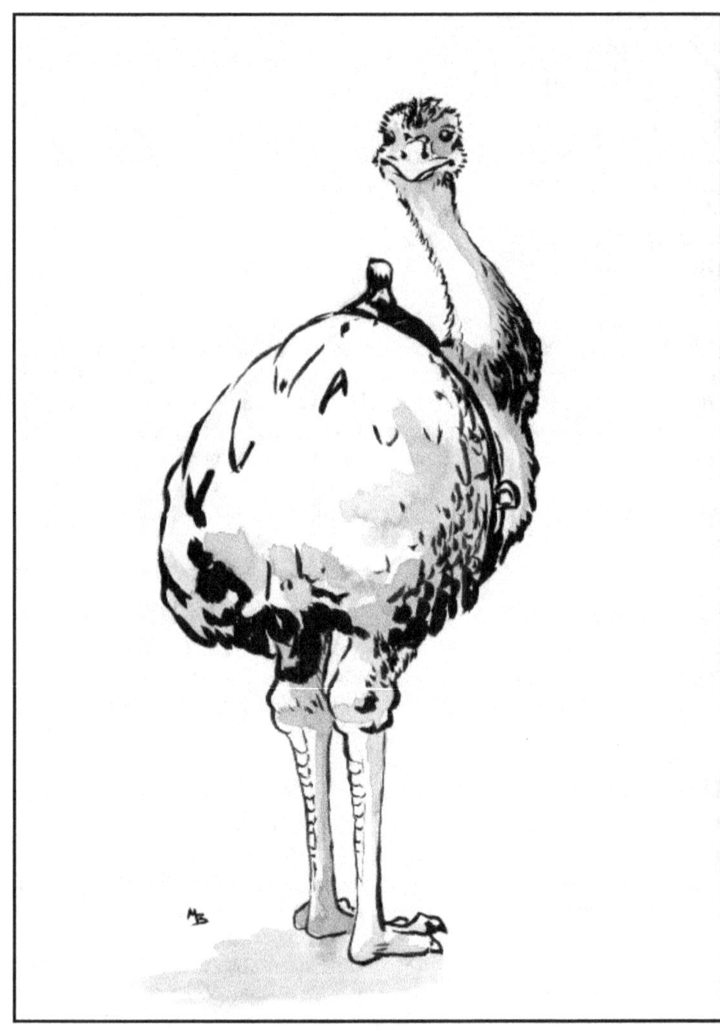

Giant ostriches are large enough to be ridden as mounts, and might be for sale in exotic lands or large cities.

Giant Ostrich: HD 3; AC 7[12]; Atk 1 bite (1d6); Move 18; Save 14; AL N; CL/XP 3/60; Special: None.

Off to the Races

The ostrich races of St. Ruthio draw contestants from around the region for the giant black pearl (200 gp) given as a prize each year. Riders mount the ostriches in a giant holding pen, and drive birds from the pen using leather whips. The ride is bumpy and the birds irritable. Getting the ostrich to move in a specific direction requires leaning and making a successful saving throw to hang on as it fights the order. Anyone who fails a save either tumbles off the bird or it charges off in a random direction.

The birds race out of the enclosure, through the streets, and into the trees along a route that varies each year. This year's course runs through the Camel Hills, where a starving pack of **6 wolves** and **3 worgs** wait to give chase. The wolves work to bring down anyone riding one of the racing ostriches.

Worg: HD 4; AC 6[13]; Atk 1 bite (1d6+1); Move 18; Save 13; AL C; CL/XP 4/120; Special: None.

Wolf: HD 2+2; AC 7[12]; Atk 1 bite (1d4+1); Move 18; Save 16; AL N; CL/XP 2/30; Special: None.

Otyugh

Hit Dice: 7
Armor Class: 3 [16]
Attacks: 2 tentacles (1d8), bite (1d4+1)
Saving Throw: 9
Special: Disease
Move: 6
Alignment: Neutrality
Number Encountered: 1
Challenge Level/XP: 8/800

Otyughs live underground, hiding in piles of refuse, for they are scavengers. These bizarre creatures are slightly larger than a human, a mass of flesh mounted on three squat, elephant-like legs. The otyugh has a sensory-organ stalk, and two rough, bone-ridged tentacles used for attacking enemies. Anyone bitten by an otyugh's mouth has a 90% chance of contracting a fatal disease (death in 3d6 days unless cured). Although they are relatively stupid, otyughs use rudimentary telepathy to communicate with each other (and other telepathic beings, if they are encountered).

Otyugh: HD 7; AC 3[16]; Atk 2 tentacles (1d8), bite (1d4+1); Move 6; Save 9; AL N; CL/XP 8/800; Special: Disease.

Sludge Mutant of the Deep Delve

Raw sewage drips down the sloping walls of this smelly underground vault. The effluence collects in a 30-foot-diameter swill pit that blocks the center of the room. The pit descends 50 feet into side tunnels that connect to another area of the sewer. A mold-covered metal portcullis ripped from the wall lies across half of the swirling brown and green mess to create a makeshift bridge to the other side of the room. Gas bubbles rise to the surface of the sewage and pop, creating broken ripples across the ugly surface. The entire chamber smells of feces and beer.

The sewage pit is home to an **otyugh** mutated by the runoff from an aboveground dwarven bar. The amphibious creature has gills along its sides and webbed feet that allow it to swim easily through the muck. Otherwise, it is the same as its land-dwelling cousins. The otyugh bursts out of the sewage to attack anyone crossing the grate. It chases PCs down the slippery tunnels if they escape its grasping tentacles.

Owlbear

Hit Dice: 5+1
Armor Class: 5 [14]
Attacks: 2 claws (1d6), 1 bite (2d6)
Saving Throw: 12
Special: Hug
Move: 12
Alignment: Neutrality
Number Encountered: 1d2
Challenge Level/XP: 5/240

Owlbears have the body of a bear, but the beak of an owl (with some feathers on the head and places on the body as well). On an attack roll of 18+ (natural roll), the owlbear grabs its victim and hugs it for an additional 2d8 points of damage.

Owlbear: HD 5+1; AC 5[14]; Atk 2 claws (1d6), 1 bite (2d6); Move 12; Save 12; AL N; CL/XP 5/240; Special: hug for additional 2d8 if to-hit roll is 18+.

Feathered Friends

A 20-foot-tall wooden sculpture of an owl stands in this grassy woodland. The owl has large round depressions for eyes. Two fist-sized emeralds (300 gp each) sparkle inside the eyes. Its massive claws stab the ground. Twigs and brush fill the bird of prey's open beak. Chunks of animals lie on the ground around the statue. Bloody streaks mar the statue's lower body.

The statue's open beak contains a twig-and-grass nest made by a **giant owl** that swoops out of the statue at night to hunt for prey in the surrounding forest. The owl is fairly intelligent, and understands Common but cannot speak. The owl lured an **owlbear** to the statue as a protector. The owlbear sleeps in a hole dug beneath one of the claws. At the end of its night of hunting, the giant owl always brings a meal back for the owlbear. The owlbear responds to the owl's screeches, thinking food has arrived. Its lair is lined with feathers molted by the giant owl.

Owl, Giant

Hit Dice: 4
Armor Class: 6 [13]
Attacks: 2 claws (1d8), 1 bite (1d6+1)
Saving Throw: 13
Special: Flies silently, -2 to all die rolls in bright light
Move: 3/20 (flying)
Alignment: Neutrality
Number Encountered: 1
Challenge Level/XP: 5/240

Giant owls are wise, but very predatory – many of them consider humans to be acceptable prey. Their eggs are very valuable on the open market, for if trained from birth, a giant owl can be used as a steed. In bright sunlight, giant owls fight with a penalty of –2 to their die rolls.

Giant Owl: HD 4; AC 6[13]; Atk 2 claws (1d8), 1 bite (1d6+1); Move 3 (Fly 20); Save 13; AL N; CL/XP 5/240; Special: Flies silently, -2 to all die rolls in bright light.

The Great Horned Devil

A birch tree stands tall in Hennis Deep, the ancient trunk surrounded by a man-sized hedge of prickly thorns. Shiny trinkets hang among the thorns. The items include worthless costume jewelry, real brooches, a string of pearls, a horned helmet, and other small baubles. All together, the items bring about 300 gp if collected from the prickly thorns. Anyone doing so takes 1d4 points of damage per hour they search. It takes a minimum of 16 hours to dig through the thick barbs to find all of the treasure.

The thorn hedge contains treasures offered to the Great Horned Devil of the Deep. Villagers in nearby Hennishold speak of this creature as a flying beast that glides on wings as silent as death. They leave the valuables alongside chunks of raw meat so the beast passes over their homes when it glides through the night. The true "beast" is a **giant owl** that cares more for the meat than the trinkets. It casts the worthless items down from its nest in the birch as it dines on the meat.

Panther

Hit Dice: 3
Armor Class: 6 [13]
Attacks: 2 claws (1d3), 1 bite (1d6)
Saving Throw: 14
Special: Additional rear claw attacks when hitting with both front claws
Move: 16
Alignment: Neutrality
Number Encountered: 1
Challenge Level/XP: 4/120

Panthers are large, carnivorous cats. Black leopards, jaguars, and cougars are all called "black panthers," and pale versions of the same cats are all called "white panthers." If a panther hits with both of its front claws, it may draw up its rear legs, raking the victim with these as well (1d3 each).

Panther: HD 3; AC 6[13]; Atk 2 claws (1d3), 1 bite (1d6); Move 16; Save 14; AL N; CL/XP 4/120; Special: Additional rear claw attacks when hitting with both front claws.

Shadow Play

Dark shapes move silently in the inky darkness of the haunted Travyn Core Mines. Most of the shapes are the restless (but harmless) spirits of miners who died choking on coal dust in the dirty tunnels. These shadows flit throughout the tunnels, causing cold winds to whisper across PCs' necks and odd noises to sound around tight corners. Candle flames flicker blue in their presence. The spirits are harmless manifestations that cannot leave the mines where they once worked.

The tunnels and cross corridors are now the hunting grounds of **6 panthers**. Each great cat wears a jeweled collar (120 gp). The panthers are the mine owner's pets. He sets them free each night to roam the mines to keep intruders out. He fears thieves sneaking in to claim the diamond deposits he still hasn't found.

Pegasus

Hit Dice: 4
Armor Class: 6 [13]
Attacks: 2 hooves (1d8)
Saving Throw: 13
Special: None
Move: 24/48 (flying)
Alignment: Law
Number Encountered: 1d12
Challenge Level/XP: 5/240

Pegasi are winged horses. Most have feathered wings, but some might have bat wings and some might be evil—at the Referee's discretion.

Pegasus: HD 4; AC 6[13]; Atk 2 hooves (1d8); Move 24 (Fly 48); Save 13; AL L; CL/XP 5/240; Special: Flying.

The Sound and the Furies

A flutter of beating wings fighting the air erupts over a low ridge as a herd of **8 pegasi** sweeps close to the rocky buttes rising toward the sky. Mesas rise around the columns. The horses fly low, swinging back and forth around the outcroppings. The animals hit the ground running, charging straight for PCs. Sparks scatter as their hooves hit shale. They halt momentarily before PCs, each lowering one wing and dipping a leg to allow PCs to climb aboard. The horses whinny in fear and throw their heads back to look into the air behind them.

A moment later, **2 rocs** soar over the outcropping, chasing the fleeing pegasi. The great birds slam beak-first through the stone columns, their wings sending boulders crashing to the ground. The pegasi wait just a moment longer before taking flight and leaving PCs to their fate with the rocs. If PCs climb aboard, the horses do their best to evade the hungry rocs.

Roc: HD 12; AC 4[15]; Atk 1 bite (3d12), 2 claws (3d6); Move 3 (Fly 30); Save 3; AL N; CL/XP 13/2300; Special: None.

Peryton

Hit Dice: 4
Armor Class: 6 [13]
Attacks: 1 antler gore (2d8)
Saving Throw: 13
Special: Immune to non-magic weapons
Move: 9/24 (flying)
Alignment: Chaos
Number Encountered: 1d8
Challenge Level/XP: 6/400

Perytons have the body of a giant eagle, the head of a stag (but with sharp teeth), and cast the shadow of a man. They eat the hearts of their victims, and lair in high mountain aeries. Perytons are magical creatures (of medieval folklore), and consequently a magical weapon is required to hit them.

Peryton: HD 4; AC 6[13]; Atk 1 antler gore (2d8); Move 9 (Fly 24); Save 13; AL C; CL/XP 6/400; Special: Immune to non-magic weapons.

Strange Shadows

The bodies of eight men and women lie facedown in the thick grasses of the Kajaani Forest, their bodies in various states of decomposition. All are from a nearby village. Pools of blood surround the bodies, and insects wriggle across each mutilated corpse. Some are gored, their entrails spilling around them, while others have bite marks ripping open their necks. All have empty ragged holes where their hearts used to be. One of the dead women wears a cursed brooch around her neck that turns the wearer into a **wight** after death. The woman's eyes snap open and she rises in 1d6+1 rounds to attack anyone investigating the bodies. Another villager has a pouch containing 22 gp and a letter to his daughter.

The villagers were out gathering blueberries when they riled up a nest of **4 perytons** that swooped out of the trees and killed them. The magical creatures descend and attack anyone disturbing their past victims. Their shadows appear to be men falling from the trees as they drop toward PCs.

Wight: HD 3; AC 5[14]; Atk 1 claw (1hp + level drain); Move 9; Save 14; AL C; CL/XP 6/400; Special: Drain 1 level with hit, hit only by magic or silver weapons.

Piercer

Hit Dice: 1 to 4
Armor Class: 3 [16]
Attacks: 1 drop/pierce (1d6 per HD)
Saving Throw: 17, 16, 14, or 13
Special: Drop from ceiling
Move: 1
Alignment: Neutrality
Number Encountered: 3d6 (mixed group)
Challenge Level/XP: 1 HD (1/15), 2 HD (2/30), 3 HD (3/60), 4 HD (4/120)

Piercers resemble stalactites, and drop from cavern ceilings to pierce their victims. After falling (and feeding), they crawl slowly back to the ceiling in order to attack again. Note that the damage inflicted by a piercer is 1d6 per hit die of the creature.

Piercer (1HD): HD 1; AC 3[16]; Atk 1 drop and pierce (1d6); Move 1; Save 17; AL N; CL/XP 1/15; Special: Drop.

Piercer (2HD): HD 2; AC 3[16]; Atk 1 drop and pierce (2d6); Move 1; Save 16; AL N; CL/XP 2/30; Special: Drop.

Piercer (3HD): HD 3; AC 3[16]; Atk 1 drop and pierce (3d6); Move 1; Save 14; AL N; CL/XP 3/60; Special: Drop.

Piercer (4HD): HD 4; AC 3[16]; Atk 1 drop and pierce (4d6); Move 1; Save 13; AL N; CL/XP 4/120; Special: Drop.

Tunnel Run

The ceiling of this 100-foot-long stone corridor is lined by side-by-side tree trunks lying horizontally 20 feet over the floor of the passageway. The stone walls are 20 feet apart. The floor of the tunnel is sandy and pocked by hundreds of depressions. The white sand is a couple of feet deep. Glowing lamps sitting in recesses line the wall. The lamps are spaced every 15 feet down the corridor. Blood mars the white sand in the center of the passage. A skeletal arm lies in the grit.

The log ceiling is an illusion hiding the fact that the tunnel is actually 30 feet higher. Hanging on the real ceiling are **15 piercers**. They are not affected by the illusion below them, and drop onto PCs who cross through the tunnel. Any that miss PCs hit the sand with a thud. The remains of a halfling lie buried in the sand under the blood splotch. A pouch buried in the sand contains a book with a hole punched through it from a piercer hit, 57 gp, a red brick, and a set of salt and pepper shakers (15 gp).

Pixie

Hit Dice: 1d6 hit points
Armor Class: 6 [13]
Attacks: 1 dagger (1d4) or arrow
Saving Throw: 17
Special: Invisibility
Move: 9/18 (flying)
Alignment: Neutrality
Number Encountered: 10d10
Challenge Level/XP: 2/30

Pixies are nasty, treacherous creatures of the fey, resembling small, winged people. They are naturally invisible, and do not become visible when they attack. After one round of attacks, the general location of the pixies may be discerned while they keep fighting, and they may thus be attacked (although with a -4 to the attacker's die rolls to hit them). There may certainly be similar fairies that are more powerful than ordinary pixies – these might have arrows that cause sleep, and attack with a bonus of +4 when using arrows.

Pixie: HD 1d6 hit points; AC 5[14]; Atk 1 dagger (1d4) or arrow; Move 9 (Fly 18); Save 17; AL N; CL/XP 2/30; Special: Invisibility.

Quill Killers

A greenhouse in the Tangled Traces is a steamy paradise of tropical plants unknown in this temperate forest. A single door leads into the humid interior. Vines crawl up wooden trellises, and purple orchids grow in the fertile soil. A massive beehive hangs in the building's upper reaches. A marble fountain gurgles in the center of the steamy room. Pinned to the greenhouse's wooden support beams are **6 dead nixies**. Quills puncture their bodies. Each barb is driven through the small bodies and into the wood behind them. Another nixie lies dead on the edge of the fountain. The dead nixie reaches for the water she'll never touch now. A dead porcupine lies in the damp soil.

The greenhouse is home to **9 pixies** that killed the nixies that once lived in the fountain. The evil fey live in the massive beehive, protected by **2 giant bees**. The pixies use quills from the dead porcupine as arrows. Lying in the fountain's basin are 27 gp, a small diamond (60 gp) and a gold ring (150 gp).

Giant Bee: HD 3; AC 6[13]; Atk 1 sting (1d3 + poison); Move 3/24 (Fly); Save 14; AL N; CL/XP 5/240; Special: Lethal poison sting.

Portal Camel (Sage Beast)

Hit Dice: 2
Armor Class: 7 [12]
Attacks: 2 bites (1hp) and 1 kick (1d4)
Saving Throw: 16
Special: Magical abilities, cooperative *dimension door*
Move: 15
Alignment: Neutrality
Number Encountered: 1d4
Challenge Level/XP: 4/120

The Portal Camel is an intelligent and magical creature. It resembles a normal camel, except that it has three humps and two heads. Though not as ill-tempered as actual camels, it does have a high opinion of itself – which it will loudly voice, being capable of speech. While a portal camel can be used as a pack or riding animal, it will demand a higher level of care and pay than any prospective hirelings might seek. As with its normal kin, a portal camel is herbivorous and capable of storing water for extended periods. They can carry 350 pounds without discomfort.

The left head of a portal camel can cast Protection from Evil and Mirror Image each twice per day. The right head of a portal camel can cast Dispel Magic, Haste and Slow each once per day. Three portal camels acting together can cast Dimension Door, although they may bicker and argue about which one will get to use it. The necks of a portal camel are snake-like in their flexibility, allowing it to turn one head back to face a rider – perhaps to nip him on the knee.

Portal camels collect stories and legends of the lands and dimensions through which they travel, and often become sages on obscure topics. Their lips are almost as dextrous as human fingers, allowing them to manipulate simple objects. They may be convinced to join an adventuring party or merchant caravan if someone offers to act as guide and interpreter.
— *Author: Scott Wylie Roberts, "Myrystyr"*

Portal Camel: HD 2; AC 7[12]; Atk 2 bites (1hp) and 1 kick (1d4); Move 15; Save 16; AL N; CL/XP 4/120; Special: Magical abilities, cooperative dimension door.

The Gatekeeper

A red wooden door appears in a space PCs are sure no door ever existed. The door has a golden knob engraved with two open eyes. The door is unlocked and opens easily. It leads into an extra-dimensional space in a limbo-like realm where fluttering streamers form a spongy corridor that leads off into the distance. Locked doors hover along the banner walls, floating in the space, but all are locked from this side. The corridor leads to a central chamber lined with more random-sized portals. A few windows look into various regions and buildings.

A **portal camel** kneels on a red rug hovering in the center of this open chamber. It smokes from a large hookah floating beside it. The camel can take PCs any place they wish to go by leading them to specific doors and unlocking the portals. However, a **demon-wolf of Braazz** now inhabits the banner corridor between worlds, and the portal camel requires help getting rid of the demon before it can open the correct door to send PCs home.

Demon-wolf of Braazz: HD 5; AC 1[18]; Atk 1 bite (1d10); Move 15; Save 12; AL C; CL/XP 8/800; Special: Blink, invisibility, charm, magic weapon required to hit

Pseudo-Dragon

Hit Dice: 2
Armor Class: 2 [17]
Attacks: 1 bite (1d3), 1 tail sting (1d3 + poison)
Saving Throw: 16
Special: Poison, invisibility, 25% magic resistance
Move: 6/25 (flying)
Alignment: Neutrality
Number Encountered: 1
Challenge Level/XP: 5/240

Pseudo-dragons are tiny relatives of dragons or wyverns, less than 2ft long. Like wyverns, they have a tail stinger: the poison is not lethal in 75% of cases, but it induces catalepsy for 1d4 days (saving throw). When they desire, pseudo-dragons can become almost invisible (80% chance not to be seen). They are somewhat resistant to magic (25%), and this resistance extends to any human touching the creature (if the pseudo-dragon desires).

Pseudo-dragon: HD 2; AC 2[17]; Atk 1 bite (1d3), 1 tail sting (1d3 + poison); Move 6 (Fly 25); Save 16; AL N; CL/XP 5/240; Special: Poison, invisibility, 25% magic resistance.

Sleep Induced

Four prone bodies lie on soft blankets on down mattresses in this abandoned red barn. Three of the people are humans, and one is an elf. Their skin is dried and sunken, and their breathing is shallow and labored. None appears to have moved for days. Three more wooden-frame beds are empty. Washbasins sit on the floor beside each figure, and cold cloths sit on their clammy foreheads.

Each person lying on a bed was stung by a misguided **pseudo-dragon** named Prins. The young dragon was asleep in the hay loft when the adventurers stumbled in after a near-fatal encounter with a rampaging chimera. One of the men said he wished he could just forget all about that (meaning the burning of one of their friends), but the naïve pseudo-dragon misunderstood. She thinks humans (and elves and dwarves and others as well) want to forget all their troubles. She stung the adventurers while they dozed.

The well-meaning pseudo-dragon now watches over them to make sure they aren't eaten by forest animals. She doesn't realize they'll soon die if not awakened. Anyone who lies on one of the empty beds feels the sting of the pseudo-dragon's tail as it tries to "help" him. The dragon releases her charges if PCs convince Prins that she is killing them.

Purple Worm

Hit Dice: 15
Armor Class: 6 [13]
Attacks: Bite (2d12), sting (1d8 + poison)
Saving Throw: 3
Special: Poison sting, swallows whole
Move: 9
Alignment: Neutrality
Number Encountered: 1
Challenge Level/XP: 17/3,500

Purple worms are massive annelids that grow 40 ft and more in length, and sometimes exceed ten feet in width. They are subterranean, chewing tunnels in rock (or through sand, in deserts, where they are a tan color). These beasts swallow their prey whole on a roll 4 higher than the needed number, or if the worm rolls double the number required to hit. They can swallow anything the size of a horse or smaller. In addition to the worm's dreaded bite, it has a poison stinger on its tail, the length of a sword and just as deadly even from the piercing wound it inflicts. In addition, the poison injected by the stinger is lethal if the victim fails a saving throw. What prey the purple worms once hunted with such natural weaponry (or perhaps still do, in deep places), must have been terrifying indeed. Aquatic versions of the purple worm might also exist.

Purple Worm: HD 15; AC 6[13]; Atk 1 bite (2d12), 1 sting (1d8 + poison); Move 9; Save 3; AL N; CL/XP 17/3500; Special: Poison sting, swallow whole.

Rock Worms

A natural dome of black rock rises out of the desert sands to a height of nearly 50 feet at its peak. The rock grows extremely hot in the desert sun, but the underside remains cool throughout the day. Giant troughs of collapsed sand circle around the massive rock, as if it dropped from a massive height and caused great ripples across the desert landscape.

The rock is home to **2 desert purple worms**. The giant annelids sleep under the massive rock during the day, and circle outward through the cooling desert during the night as they search for food. The worms are tan (despite their name), and extremely aggressive. They dive deep into the sand before bursting up around creatures crossing the desert. Under the massive rock are the skeletal remains of past kills digested by the giant worms. Most of the skeletons are desert creatures, but a magic-user still wearing dark robes lies among the broken bones. His finger bone still has a gold ring of mammal control wrapped around it.

Quadricorn

Hit Dice: 6
Armor Class: 4 [15]
Attacks: 4 horns (1d6)
Saving Throw: 11
Special: Magic resistance (25%)
Move: 12
Alignment: Neutrality
Number Encountered: 1
Challenge Level/XP: 8/800

Quadricorns resemble two-headed bulls, although the body is somewhat more massive than that of a normal bull, to accommodate the two heads. Unlike unicorns, with their propensity toward virgins, quadricorns have somewhat the reverse propensity, sometimes charging into villages or towns to find houses of ill-repute, where they batter down walls or doors in an attempt to escape with a captive or two.

In general, quadricorns live in barren wilderness areas, and can even be found making their lairs in caves, although they are not generally found in deeper subterranean catacombs.

— Author: Matt Finch

Quadricorn: HD 6; AC 4[15]; Atk 4 horns (1d6); Move 12; Save 11; AL N; CL/XP 8/800; Special: Magic resistance (25%).

Sitting Bull

The shadiest gambling den in Bargarsport has to be the House of Drudge. Any vice imaginable can be found within its sleazy walls, from gambling to prostitution. Hustlers sit at its grimy tables, and women of the night ply their trade all day long. Ale is watered down and the wine is so cheap it can peel paint, but patrons pay the high prices so they don't anger **Low Gurk**, the dwarven bouncer.

The House of Drudge's most famous attraction is a stuffed bull mounted on an elaborate pulley system in the center of the room. Anyone thinking they can stay on the bull for a 10 seconds can put their money where their mouth is and climb aboard. Patrons yank ropes about the room to spin the bull and try to throw the rider to the hardwood floor. The fake bull is covered in slick and sweaty cow hide.

A **quadricorn** drawn by the scent of the dead cow breaks through the front doors to get at the house of ill repute. It charges anyone wearing red, then attempts to escape with a quatron or one of the working gurls.

Quarn

Hit Dice: 4+4
Armor Class: 3 [16]
Attacks: 2 fists (1d6 + petrification)
Saving Throw: 13
Special: Turn to stone, sink into ground
Move: 0
Alignment: Neutrality
Number Encountered: 1d10
Challenge Level/XP: 6/400

Quarns resemble large boulders, although they do not ordinarily grow much larger than the size of a person. They cannot move other than an ability to rise from or to sink into the stone where they are planted. A quarn does have two arms, which are kept folded against the rest of the body until the quarn attacks. If the quarn hits an opponent, the victim must make a saving throw or begin turning into stone. This process begins immediately with the effects of a *slow* spell, but the process will become complete after 1d4+1 days, at which point the victim will become stone. Until the process is complete, the effects can be reversed with a *remove curse* or *cure disease* spell, but once the transformation is complete, only a *flesh to stone* spell can return the victim to normal. Quarns are slow, and will always attack last in a melee round. Because quarns are immobile, they can cause areas to be hazardous, but colonies of them can be dashed through or bypassed once the nature of the threat is known.

— Author: Matt Finch

Quarn: HD 4+4; AC 3[16]; Atk 2 fists (1d6 + petrification); Move 0; Save 13; AL N; CL/XP 6/400; Special: Turn to stone, sink into ground.

The Stone God

Carved marble columns surround an isolated temple built near the Shadow Peaks. Large boulders stand beside a brick-lined path leading up the rise to the temple's copper gates. Each stone has a woman's face carved into it. The carved images appear to be watching the path winding through the ash trees. Broad steps ring the circular temple and lead upward to an open atrium under a dome ceiling. The temple's floor is ringed with concentric circles of black and gray tiles. Kneeling in the center of the round room are 12 statues of men and women. The prayerful worshippers face inward toward the temple's empty center.

The temple is dedicated to an earth deity named Iolite. Her followers recently discovered a wondrous boulder they planned to add to the collection of stones leading up to the temple. They brought the boulder into the temple to consecrate it, only to discover its true nature. The **quarn** turned the kneeling worshippers to stone, then sank into the temple's floor. It waits until PCs investigate the statues before rising into the temple to attack.

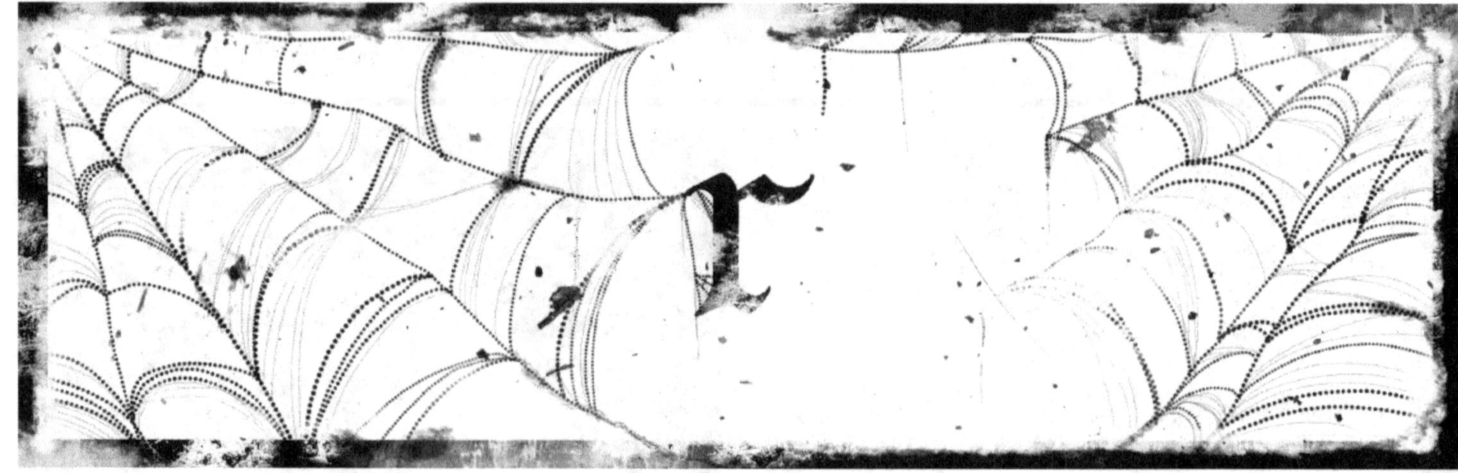

Ragged Craw

Hit Dice: 3
Armor Class: 9 [10]
Attacks: 2 claws (1d4) and beak (1d3) or sleeping darts (1d2+sleep)
Saving Throw: 14
Special: Detect magic, dispel magic (as 4th Level Magic User)
Move: 12
Alignment: Neutrality
Number Encountered: 1d6+6
Challenge Level/XP: 4/120

Ragged Craws are wingless, intelligent bird-people with beaks and clawed hands, who shroud themselves in tattered cowled robes. They tend to be nomadic, often travelling in small groups (1d6+6) in covered wagons. Ragged Craws are fond of carousing and many (1in 10) have alcohol problems, quickly becoming morose and violent. These creatures are inherently magical and have the power to detect and dispel magic. In combat, they use darts coated with a mild poison that causes sleep for 1d6 rounds. The regurgitated food of a Ragged Craw often possesses healing properties when applied as a paste over open wounds (4 in 6 chance of healing 1d4 HP over a day). Ragged Craws have gained notoriety as slavers, gamblers, thieves and wastrels.

— *Author: Sean Wills*

Ragged Craw: HD 3; AC 9[10]; Atk 2 claws (1d4) and beak (1d3) or sleeping darts (1d2+sleep); Move 12; Save 14; AL N; CL/XP 4/120; Special: Detect magic, dispel magic (as 4th Level Magic User).

The Bird Man of Bargarsport

An individual wearing a motley shroud sits on a wooden bench surrounded by a mound of coins inside a crumbling temple to a long-forgotten god in the city of Bargarsport. The figure's odd garment cloaks him from head to foot. Insects curl and crawl across the threadbare cloth, and feathers poke through rips in the fabric. **Three armed warriors** stand at the foot of a staircase rising to the temple floor, their eyes alertly scanning the crowd for trouble. The beleaguered people of the city keep their distance. A young woman chained to the bench laboriously counts the coins, even as the figure randomly tosses new money at her.

Occasionally, a sick or injured resident offers gold and a hunk of fresh meat to one of the warriors. The petitioner is either turned away (giving up his offering) or issued up the steps to meet the healer behind a faded three-fold screen decorated with images of colorful parrots and other birds. The healer is a corrupt **ragged craw** named **Manacis Mudnester** who demands gold in exchange for helping the sick. He chews up the offered food, and then regurgitates a portion of it into the customer's

cupped hands. His guards are loyal as long as he pays them.

The woman is a nobleman's daughter who was cursed by a hag to spread disease. The ragged craw is immune to her curse, but the residents of the cities he visits aren't so lucky. Her presence causes leprosy, plague and other foul diseases to spread rapidly. The ragged craw takes full advantage of the situation to offer his healing salve. Currently, he's made 137 gp from the scared populace as the diseases take hold. The plagues and ailments vanish if the woman leaves town or is cured. If she is healed, her father rewards PCs with 500 gp for returning his beloved daughter.

Human Guards: HD 1; AC 7[12]; Atk 1 weapon (1d8); Move 12; Save 17; AL N; CL/XP 1/15; Special: None.

Rakshasa

Hit Dice: 7
Armor Class: -4 [23]
Attacks: 2 claws (1d3) 1 bite (1d6)
Saving Throw: 9
Special: Illusory appearance, special magic resistance, spells
Move: 15
Alignment: Chaos
Number Encountered: 1
Challenge Level/XP: 12/2,000

Rakshasas are evil spirits from Indian mythology. Their true form is that of a demon with the head of a tiger or other predatory animal, but by magical illusion they always appear to others in a friendly or nonthreatening form. Rakshasas can only be affected by the most powerful of spells (level 8 or 9), and they can only be hit with magical weapons. Crossbow bolts that have been blessed by a Cleric are the bane of the rakshasa – such bolts are treated as +3 weapons against them. Rakshasas are minor spell casters, able to cast Magic-User spells (3/2/1) and Cleric spells (1 Level-1 spell). Typical spells for a rakshasa might be:

Magic-User level 1: *Magic Missile* x3; level 2: *Mirror Image*, *Web*; level 3: *Fly*

Cleric level 1: *Cure Light Wounds*

Rakshasa: HD 7; AC –4[23]; Atk 2 claws (1d3), 1 bite (1d6); Move 15; Save 9; AL N; CL/XP 12/2000; Special: Illusory appearance, special magic resistance, spells.

The Wandering Wastrel

An extremely handsome man sits on a rock in this flower-filled meadow. He plucks long grasses growing around him and weaves them into elaborate headpieces, necklaces and toys. A set of pan pipes hangs from a strand of woven hair around his neck, and his colorful tunic is adorned with freshly snipped flowers. A beagle restlessly paces the grass around the man, sniffing the air and pawing the ground. A small serving table sits beside the man. Dandelion wine and sassafras tea in delicate crystal ewers sit on the table. The man invites guests to drink with him and share stories of the road.

Shasura claims to be a traveling bard seeking fame and fortune, but he is really an evil **rakshasa** seeking servants for his master, a powerful sorcerer from the Seething Jungle. Shasura is never without his companion **Calanasi, a ferocious tiger** cloaked in an illusion of the fawning beagle. The wine and tea are, of course, drugged with a sleep agent to incapacitate those failing a saving throw. Anyone who falls asleep wakes chained in a slave caravan heading for the deep jungle.

Tiger: HD 6; AC 6[13]; Atk 2 claws (1d4+1), 1 bite (1d8); Move 15 (Swim 6); Save 11; AL N; CL/XP 7/600; Special: Rear claws

Ranine

Hit Dice: 2
Armor Class: 4 [15]
Attacks: 2 claws (1d6) and 1 bite (1d4 + paralyzation), or 1 weapon (1d8)
Saving Throw: 16
Special: Breathe water, hop, paralyzing bite
Move: 9/12 (swimming)
Alignment: Chaos
Number Encountered: 1d20 or 5d20
Challenge Level/XP: 4/120

Ranine are degenerate, subterranean creatures who serve the foul frog-demon Tsathoggua. Like their master, the Ranine are of broadly batrachian appearance but possess small bat-like ears in addition to vicious fangs and, in many cases, small horns. They are drawn to underground locations suffused with Chaotic energies, so many also possess chaotic traits of both the major and minor varieties.

Ranine shy away from sunlight and suffer a -1 penalty to their attack rolls and saving throws when they operate aboveground. If given sufficient room in combat, these creatures can hop at enemies, which gives them a +1 bonus to attack and damage rolls. When fighting at close quarters, they try to bite opponents in order to inject them with a paralyzing poison. Failure to save against it results in paralysis for 3d6 turns. Ranine in groups larger than six typically include a leader, who can cast clerical spells as if it were a cleric of the same level as his hit dice.

Precisely how the Ranine reproduce is a mystery, as they appear to be completely asexual. Given that these beings prefer to take opponents prisoner rather than slay them outright, some sages have postulated that the Ranine somehow "convert" their prey into new frog-men to swell their ranks. If true, these creatures pose an even more terrible threat to civilization than is commonly supposed.

— Author: James Maliszewski

Ranine: HD 2; AC 4[15]; Atk 2 claws (1d6) and 1 bite (1d4 + paralyzation), or 1 weapon (1d8); Move 9 (Swim 12); Save 16; AL C; CL/XP 4/120; Special: Breathe water, hop, paralyzing bite.

Flames and Frogs

Six concentric circles of polished green stones surround a six-foot-diameter pit in the wilds of the Seething Jungle. The stones are scratched and streaked with blood. Greenish smoke rises from the central pit, carrying the scent of rendered fat and boiling blood into the winds. Jade flames dance and flicker inside the hole. Thousands of normal frogs hop innocently through the thick vines and heavy palms surrounding the clearing. Their incessant croaking is deafening.

The pit is an unholy shrine to the frog god Tsathogga. Living in the nearby jungle are **12 ranine** that sacrifice people inside the pit to sate their demonic god. Victims are dropped into the 15-foot-deep pit and allowed to burn. The bottom of the pit contains piles of ash and brittle bones.

The jungle frogs croak to alert the aggressive ranine to intruders. The creatures arrive within 1d6 rounds, and leap from the trees to grab potential sacrifices. Anyone thrown into the pit takes 1d6 points of damage per round as the green flames lick at their skin. The sides of the pit are smooth stone, making climbing out difficult without assistance. Occasionally, a sacrifice survives the flames and leaps from the pit as a new ranine to bolster the tribe's ranks.

Ratling

Hit Dice: 1
Armor Class: 9 [10]
Attacks: 1 bite (1d6+disease) or weapon
Saving Throw: 17
Special: Diseased bite
Move: 12
Alignment: Chaos
Number Encountered: 4d6
Challenge Level/XP: 2/30

Standing no taller than 4ft tall, ratlings, as their name implies, resemble humanoid rodents. Although not much of a threat individually, ratlings tend to attack in packs (of 4d6). Ratlings dealing damage via a bite may infect their victims with the same disease that mundane rats do. The chances of passing on the disease are identical to that of their giant-rat kin.

— *Author: Skathros*

Ratling: HD 1; AC 9[10]; Atk 1 bite (1d6+disease) or weapon; Save 17; Move 12; AL C; CL/XP 2/30; Special: Diseased bite.

The Rat Pack

Moldy grain sits in overflowing bins inside this abandoned mill in Torkstill. The grinding wheels still turn slowly, however, as the attached waterwheel spins in the lazy stream flowing past the building. Three large bins are overturned, spilling various grains across the floor. Dead weevils litter the piles. The corn is contaminated with a wasting disease that causes a victim to die slowly over 1d4 weeks unless he makes a saving throw.

The overturned bins hide holes cut through the wooden floorboards. Anyone descending under the mill finds themselves in narrow tunnels dug through the earth. The tunnel rooms are home to **4d6 ratlings** that frequently raid Torkstill for shiny objects, chickens and anything else they can carry off. Their raids have spread disease throughout the village, causing sickness and death in the good people. The residents are unaware of the ratlings, and think they are cursed. Getting rid of the ratlings allows the villagers to recover quickly.

Rat, Giant

Hit Dice: 1d4 hit points
Armor Class: 7 [12]
Attacks: Bite (1d3)
Saving Throw: 18
Special: 5% are diseased
Move: 12
Alignment: Neutrality
Number Encountered: 5d10
Challenge Level/XP: A/5

Giant rats are often found in dungeons, and are about the size of a cat, or perhaps a lynx. The bite of some (1 in 20) giant rats causes disease. A saving throw is allowed (versus poison). The effects of the disease are decided by the Referee.

Giant Rat: HD 1d4hp; AC 7[12]; Atk 1 bite (1d3); Move 12; Save 18; AL N; CL/XP A/5; Special: 5% are diseased.

RAT, GIANT (MONSTROUSLY HUGE)
Hit Dice: 3
Armor Class: 6 [13]
Attacks: 2 claws (1d3), 1 bite (1d6)
Saving Throw: 14
Special: 5% are diseased
Move: 12
Alignment: Neutrality unless intelligent (Chaos)
Number Encountered: 2d6
Challenge Level/XP: 4/120

Giant rats (monstrously huge) are often found in dungeons, and are vicious predators the size of a wolf. The bite of some (1 in 20) giant rats causes disease. A saving throw is allowed (versus poison). The effects of the disease are decided by the Referee.

Monstrously Huge Giant Rat: HD 3; AC 6[13]; Atk 2 claws (1d3), 1 bite (1d6); Move 12; Save 14; AL N; CL/XP 3/120; Special: 5% are diseased.

Rat Trap

Six marble sarcophagi sit in this underground tomb. Each has a sculpted lid depicting the person interred inside. Each sarcophagus has a name engraved along the edge of the heavy lids. The stone containers each have a smaller wooden coffin inside in which a member of a royal elven family killed during a forest fire is laid to rest. Opening the plain wooden lids reveal contorted, burned bodies wrapped in white linen. Each body is buried with a silver pendant of elven royalty (30 gp). Possessing one of the pendants draws the ire of any elves the PC meets. Ragged scratching comes from one of the wooden coffins, like nails raking along the wood.

A **giant rat** gnawed a hole in the base of one sarcophagus and then ate its way through the bottom of the wooden coffin to get to the charred meat inside. The giant rat leaps out of the coffin to attack anyone disturbing its lair.

Rat (Giant Desongnol Rat)

Hit Dice: 1d4 hit points
Armor Class: 7 [12]
Attacks: 1 bite (1d2) and 2 claws (1d3)
Saving Throw: 18
Special: Non-lethal poison +2 to save, effects are up to the referee.
Move: 12
Alignment: Neutrality
Number Encountered: 2d6
Challenge Level/XP: B/10

The Desongnol rat in its larger form, about the size of a cat, is feared by farmer, woodsman and adventurer alike. It has a rather large nose and an extremely nasty temper and bite. When attacking, the Desongnol rat uses its venom to sicken its prey (in humans, a -1 damage penalty or similar effect) and then tears at it with its powerful claws to allow the rat to feed. It has been said to give off pig-like noises and to have a particular stench when in large numbers. These rats are usually found lurking near farms and settlements where food is easy to forage. It is known for constructing complex tunnel systems large enough for a small human/demi-human (halfling sized or smaller) to enter.

— Author: Chgowiz

Giant Desongnol Rat: HD 1d4hp; AC 7[12], Atk 1 bite (1d2) and 2 claws (1d3); Move 12; Save 18; AL N; CL/XP B/10; Special: Non-lethal poison +2 to save.

Running of the Pigs

Squealing pigs charge through the thick weeds rising around the PCs. Six feral pigs and a large **boar** race through the high grasses, their eyes wide with fear. The pigs run past PCs unless they try to stop the sows. The boar rips into PCs with its tusks before running onward. More grunts and squeals follow close behind the fleeing pigs.

The swine are on the run from a swarm of **20 giant desongnol rats** that squeal like another herd of feral pigs. The rats leap and swarm over any creature that gets in their way. The rats live in underground tunnels with openings throughout the high weeds. The pigs blundered into the rats' territory and found themselves surrounded by the vicious creatures. Three dead pigs lie in the weeds near one of the dirt openings.

Wild Boar: HD 3+3; AC 7[12]; Atk 1 gore (3d4); Move 15; Save 14; AL N; CL/XP 4/120; Special: continue attacks 2 rounds after death.

Rat, Wizard's Lab

Hit Dice: 1
Armor Class: 7 [12]
Attacks: 1 bite (1d4)
Saving Throw: 17
Special: Magical effects
Move: 12
Alignment: Neutrality (if intelligent, any)
Number Encountered: 1d8
Challenge Level/XP: 2/30

Wizard's lab rats are giant rats that have been subjected to any number of strange scientific or magical experiments, and have acquired one of a variety of permanent conditions. To determine the condition of a given lab rat, roll once on the magical potion table in the rulebook, with the lab rat gaining the indicated effect as a permanent ability. Ignore poison potions (these rats would have died in the laboratory) and note that a healing potion indicates a number of hit points regenerated per turn. A character bitten by a lab rat has a 5% chance to gain the lab rat's condition for 1d6+1 turns. Any particular lab rat has a 20% chance of possessing human-like intelligence.

— Author: Random

Wizard's Lab Rats: HD 1; AC 7[12]; Atk 1 bite (1d4); Move: 12; Save 17; AL N; CL/XP 2/30; Special: Magical effects.

Strange Brew

A four-foot-tall iron cauldron sits in the center of this dusty laboratory. A thick, green-and-brown brew bubbles inside the pot. Standing around the cauldron are **4 skeleton** in leather apron stands. Each stirs the contents with a five-foot-long wooden paddle. Wooden shelves along each wall rise to the 15-foot-high ceiling. Glass beakers contain dried flakes of all colors, while metal boxes hold dried animal parts. Small cages house mummified rats and other small animals. A wooden table against one wall has leather straps fitted to its surface. Dried blood stains its surface.

The lab was used by a necromancer until his demise at the hands of a sea hag. His skeleton assistants still go about the last command they were given. The lab is also home to another of the necromancer's creations: **6 wizard's lab rats** that live in holes burrowed through the walls. The rats have the following abilities (or roll your own): ethereality, fire resistance, flying, giant strength, invisibility and undead control. The skeletons are under the control of one of the last rat. The rats swarm out of their dens to swarm intruders after the skeletons attack. The stew in the cauldron has a 10% chance of granting a PC who chokes it down a random rat mutation for 1d6+1 turns.

Raven, Giant

Hit Dice: 3
Armor Class: 5 [14]
Attacks: 1 bite (1d8)
Saving Throw: 14
Special: None
Move: 2/20 (flying)
Alignment: Chaos
Number Encountered: 1d3 or 2d10
Challenge Level/XP: 4/120

Intelligent and malign, giant ravens are almost as large as a man. They are ideal servants and scouts for powerful evil sorcerers and other such overlords.

Giant Raven: HD 3; AC 5[14]; Atk 1 bite (1d8); Move 2 (Fly 20); Save 14; AL C; CL/XP 4/120; Special: None.

Raven Seer

A gold perch hangs from the ceiling of this circular chamber. Silver embedded in the walls rises to a solid metal disc at the dome's apex. A metal frame door opens outward halfway up the wall, leading into a dark hallway. The entire room feels like being in a gigantic birdcage. Beneath the perch is a six-foot-square granite altar with a silver platter sitting atop it.

A **giant raven** stands on the perch, watching visitors with a cool eye. The bird cocks its head to stare at PCs, then looks at the altar beneath it. The raven is extremely intelligent, and can predict the future to some small degree. It converses in Common with anyone placing at least 100 gp on the altar as an offering, and answers three questions. The bird is evil, however, and answers just one question honestly. The other answers are twisted lies designed to lead the asker into danger. The crow defends itself if attacked, and curses the PCs before it flies out the open door. Anyone failing a saving throw grows feathers and turns into a giant raven within 1d8+2 days unless cured.

Ray, Giant Manta

Hit Dice: 8
Armor Class: 6 [13]
Attacks: 1 bite (2d6), tail sting (2d10)
Saving Throw: 8
Special: swallow whole, stun
Move: 18 (swimming)
Alignment: Neutrality (or Chaos)
Number Encountered: 1d4
Challenge Level/XP: 10/1,400

Giant manta rays are large enough to swallow most opponents whole (anything smaller than a giant), which they will do if they exceed their needed to-hit number by 3 or more. Anyone swallowed will die in 6 rounds unless the manta is slain (the victim can fight from the inside). A hit by the tail spine stuns the victim for 1d8 rounds (saving throw). Some claim that there is a highly intelligent and evil variety of giant manta rays in the deeper seas.

Giant Manta Ray: HD 8; AC 6[13]; Atk 1 bite (2d6), tail sting (2d10); Move (Swim 18); Save 8; AL N (or C); CL/XP 10/1400; Special: Swallow whole, tail stuns.

Deep Flyer

The sea is turbulent today, the waves rolling across the deep to batter the galleon Melton's Fury as it plies the Reaping Sea. The ship rises and plummets as it rides the waves. The sailors hang on for dear life, speaking in fearful whispers of a monster of the deep that hunts when the winds and rain pummel the sails. They claim the beast from the deep chases ships even as they follow the great whales, ready to strike without warning and swallow men whole in its gaping maw. The last sound you'll hear is the quiet flap of its monstrous wings.

The beast is actually a **giant manta ray** that swallowed a halfling wearing a *ring of flying*. The ring conveys limited flight to the manta, allowing it to soar out of the waves and across the decks of ships in search of prey for 4 rounds. The giant manta uses that time to rise out of the troubled waters and glide across the surface of ships before diving again into the depths. As the beast passes, it stings sailors and swallows others in its way. Anyone who makes a saving throw dives out of the gaping mouth as it swoops down toward them.

Ray, Sting

Hit Dice: 1d6 hit points
Armor Class: 7 [12]
Attacks: 1 sting (1d3 + poison)
Saving Throw: 17
Special: non-lethal poison
Move: 10 (swimming)
Alignment: Neutrality
Number Encountered: 1d6
Challenge Level/XP: 2/30

Sting rays are very difficult to see on the ocean floor. They have a poison sting which they use to defend themselves when danger comes near. Sting ray poison causes paralysis (3d6 turns) and also inflicts 3d6 points of damage. A successful saving throw avoids all effects from the poison.

Sting Ray: HD 1d6hp; AC 7[12]; Atk 1 sting (1d3 + poison); Move (Swim 10); Save 17; AL N; CL/XP 2/30; Special: non-lethal poison.

Love Stings

A sandy beach fills one side of this cavernous underground chamber. An ocean of green-glowing water spreads out across the chamber. The glow comes from algae floating atop the still waters. Splashing fish and dropping rocks create wide ripples that spread in overlapping waves. The sounds echo across the surface. The cave extends for miles over open water, and the underground sea traverses hundreds of miles below ground. A small rowboat sits anchored 500 feet offshore. A warm glow rises around the rowboat from a small lantern sitting on one of its benches.

The water along the shore is home to **12 albino sting rays** that gather here for mating season. The rays are docile unless disturbed (or stepped on). Anyone walking into their midst receives debilitating stings as the startled rays rise up and attack. The rays are nearly invisible in the dark waters. The boat contains a mummified corpse of an ancient dark elf fisherman who was bitten by a sea snake and died atop the waters. The lamp contains a lump of weeds that burns without heat to light the lamp for one month. The dark elf has a belt pouch containing eight more lumps of the mushy weeds. A flint knife on his belt ignites the weeds if they are wrapped around it. If the weeds are set on fire with a normal flame, they produce a noxious gas in a 10-foot-diameter that causes violent vomiting (save avoids).

Razor Wing

Hit Dice: 1
Armor Class: 7 [12]
Attacks: 1 beak (1d4), claw (1d4), or razor wing (1d6)
Saving Throw: 17
Special: Swoop attack
Move: 9/12 (flying)
Alignment: Neutrality
Number Encountered: 1d8
Challenge Level/XP: 2/30

Razor Wings get their name from their razor sharp wings, which they use to bring down potential prey. Razor Wings resemble large crows with shinning steel-like feathers tipping their wings. They attack in groups, swarming over prey from above. Razor Wings will swoop down from above with such swiftness that anyone acting after the bird's initiative is unable to engage it in hand-to-hand combat.

— Author: Skathros

Razor Wings: HD 1; AC 7[12]; Atk 1 beak (1d4), claw (1d4), or razor wing (1d6); Move 9 (Fly 12); Save 17; AL N; CL/XP 2/30; Special: Swoop attack.

Death from Above

A murder of crows pinwheels through the air, the birds riding heated air currents rising off the High Jald Desert. Driven into the burning sands are four 10-foot-tall wooden posts. Strapped to the posts are the bodies of a desert nomad, an ettin and a camel (the nomad's). All of the corpses are dried out and burnt from the glaring sun. The bodies are slashed and torn, and each one is missing its eyes. Blood spatters the sand around the remains. A cackle of **10 desert hyenas** tears at the flesh of the dead, trying to pull the bodies from the posts. The animals watch any approaching PCs warily, baring their teeth and snarling, but the hyenas keep an eye on the sky as well.

The true danger is the flock of **20 razor wings** flying high above. The hyenas drove the angry birds away from their meal, but the flock is circling and reforming to attack the pack. The razor wings descend in a flurry of feathers, claws and beaks to attach anyone near the posts. The hyenas have the sense to run when the birds begin circling lower.

Recurser

Hit Dice: 5+10
Armor Class: 1 [18]
Attacks: Entropic touch (3d6)
Saving Throw: 12
Special: Entropic touch, causes fear, immune to non-magical weapons
Move: 10 (levitating)
Alignment: Chaos
Number Encountered: 1
Challenge Level/XP: 7/600

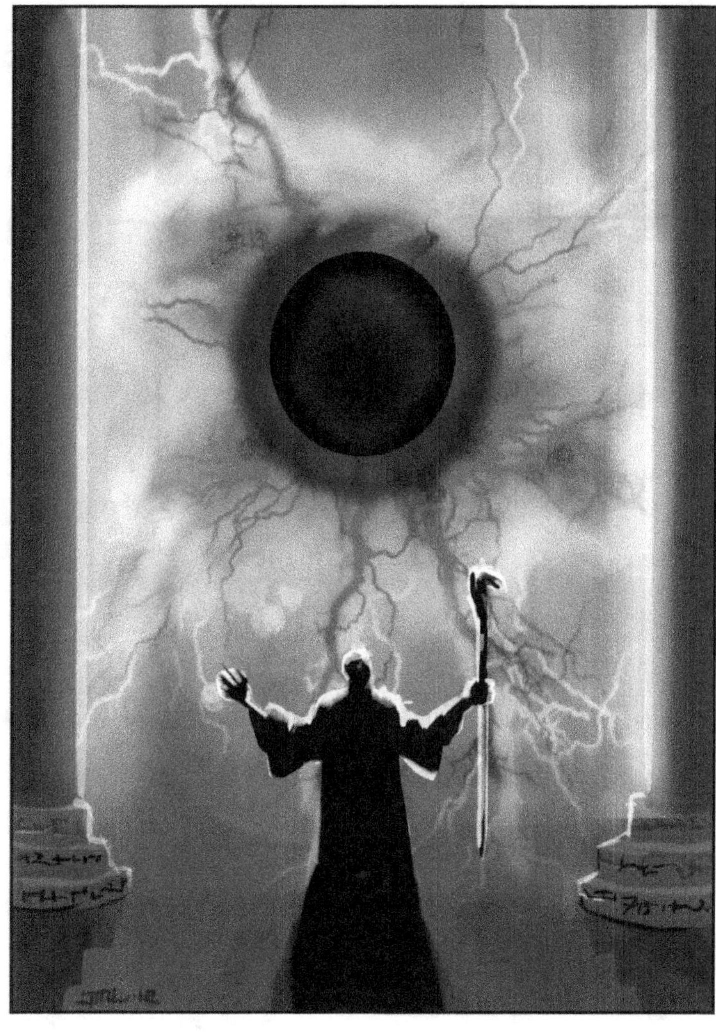

Recursers are intelligent entities from the Plane of Entropy. They are never encountered randomly, but are drawn to the material world by those who try to alter space or time through the use of magic. Recursers appear as shimmering spheres of black electricity, which seem to absorb light rather than emit it. When a recurser appears, it will begin moving towards the one responsible for its appearance immediately, and cannot be diverted. Recursers attack their victims by absorbing them with an entropic touch, which passes through armor or any magical protection as if the target was completely unprotected (AC 9[10]). Recursers can only be hit by magical weapons with a bonus of +1 or better. These creatures - or manifestations - are essentially mindless, and exist purely to destroy anyone or anything that attempts to alter the course of fate. They do not bargain, nor will they surrender. The sight of a recurser is terrifying, and anyone who observes one must make a saving throw or be paralyzed by fear for 1d3 rounds. Recursers do not need food or sleep, and will track the object of their attention tirelessly until they are successful or defeated. There can never be more than one recurser on the Material Plane at any time.

— *Author: Russell Cone*

Recurser: HD 5+10; AC 1[18]; Atk Entropic Touch (3d6); Move (Levitate 10); Save 12; AL C; CL/XP 7/600; Special: Entropic touch, causes fear, immune to non-magical weapons.

The Book of Fate

The Gerdant Library in Taharath contains an ancient tome called the Book of Fate that was written by the Oracle of Destinic long ago. The book contains a single phrase that is said to alter time and fate, allowing the person speaking it to change the course of their life for up to one hour already past. The phrase can be spoken only once in a being's lifetime and saying it again brings about instantaneous, irrevocable death. The entire volume is filled with rules for saying the phrase, before presenting the words themselves on the last of the 275 pages.

In game terms, saying this ancient phrase allows a PC to alter his fate for up to one hour after a single event. If a PC is near death, he can "wish" to be back one hour before he decided to enter the tunnel that led to his doom, for instance. A losing battle can be reversed so a PC gets a "do over." The exact effect is left up to the GM. However, saying the phrase draws a **recurser** after the PC within 1d4 days. The recurser attacks the being who uttered the word. It vanishes if it or the PC dies.

Redwraith

Hit Dice: 5
Armor Class: 3 [16]
Attacks: 1 claw (1d8)
Saving Throw: 12
Special: Drain life energy, silver or magic weapon to hit
Move: 9
Alignment: Chaos
Number Encountered: 1d6
Challenge Level/XP: 8/800

Redwraiths are undead creatures that appear much like wights, although their eyes are red and they are often garbed in crimson, for it is the only color they can perceive, and they take red-colored items from those they kill. Redwraiths are weaker than their kin, the wights and true wraiths, but share many characteristics of this type of undead. If a redwraith hits an opponent, the attack drains 1,000 experience points from the victim as well as inflicting damage. Redwraiths are turned as wights, and take 2d4 points of damage from holy water. If a creature is drained of all life energy by a redwraith, roll d100 to determine the result. 01-40: the creature rises as a weaker redwraith under control of the original one, 41-50: the creature rises as a wight (not under control of the redwraith), 51-00: the creature's body is animated as a zombie under the redwraith's control.

The weaker redwraiths created when a full redwraith drains a victim of all life energy have only 2 hit dice and drain only 400xp with a successful hit. These creatures slowly gain strength over a period of years, eventually becoming full redwraiths that are no longer under the control of the original. For this reason, redwraiths of 3 or 4 hit dice may also be encountered, these being able to drain 200xp per hit die of the creature. These nascent redwraiths have Low intelligence, and can be tricked into attacking a red item such as a prominently-flourished red cloak. Full redwraiths will not be fooled by such tricks, although they are likely to focus their attacks against anyone wearing red.

— *Author: Matt Finch*

Redwraith: HD 5; AC 3[16]; Atk 1 claw (1d8); Move 12; Save 12; AL C; CL/XP 8/800; Special: Drain life energy, silver or magic weapon to hit.

Caught Red Handed

A frail old man sits outside a sealed stone door set into a granite cliff face. The old man's face is scraggly and unshaven, and he appears not to have slept for days. He wears a dirty tunic, and his arms and legs are bone thin. At his feet are a pile of red robes of various sizes. A tear rolls down his wrinkled face as he talks about his wife, Lividia, whose spirit he claims is trapped within the vault by a ghostly entity.

The man is Pebkin, a liar and practicing thief, who discovered that an ancient crown rests within the tomb. Pebkin believes the crown lets its wearer walk through walls (it doesn't). The thief can only dream about the thefts he could pull with such an item. He's tried a couple of times to get the crown, but the tomb's inhabitants stopped him each time. He barely escaped and sealed the vault. Pebkin now sits outside vault, weighing his options and plotting a way to get the crown.

Inside the tomb are **5 redwraiths** that pour out the tomb's stone door if it is unsealed. Pebkin offers each PC one of the red cloaks at his feet. He claims the red material prevents the ghosts inside the tomb from possessing people. The red cloaks actually attract the redwraiths' attention so Pebkin can sneak in (wearing black clothing he hastily puts on) to steal the crown. His plan is to put on the crown then run through the stone wall to escape. That won't go as well as he planned either.

Reef Walker

Hit Dice: 7
Armor Class: 6 [13]
Attacks: 1 arm (1d6 + paralysis)
Saving Throw: 9
Special: Paralysis
Move: 9
Alignment: Neutrality
Number Encountered: 1
Challenge Level/XP: 8/800

Reef walkers are a cluster of anemones with a rudimentary intelligence, shaped into a large bipedal "body" covered all over in the stinging tentacles characteristic of anemones. They walk slowly through coral reefs, stopping often to flatten out into a less threatening shape and wait for schools of fish to approach. Their random meanderings sometimes take them onto land, where they can survive for up to two hours or so, and they continue hunting along the coastline before returning to their reefs. If a reef walker should stumble upon a coastal village, it may return several times to find more prey, for a village full of humans is an excellent hunting ground. If a reef walker hits an opponent, its stinging tentacles inject a paralytic poison (-3 save).

— Author: Thomas Clark

Reef Walker: HD 7; AC 6[13]; Atk 1 arm (1d6+paralysis); Move 9; Save 9; AL N; CL/XP 8/800; Special: Paralyze prey.

Anenomes Among Us

The people of the fishing village of Niborlyn rush to their homes as the sun goes down over the waves, warning visitors not to go near the waterfront at night. They lock their doors and refuse to open them until the sun rises and the morning fog departs. Even the fishermen who make their living on the water make sure they are ashore and in bed when the sun goes down.

Anyone out after dark sees strange men march one by one out of the deep. A cleric of Muir recently marched out to meet the strange, shambling men, but her screams in the night were the last the villagers heard of her. Her holy symbol still lies on the sand beach, but her body was never found. The villagers are afraid to touch the gold medallion for fear that its curse shall affect them.

The "men" marching onto the beach are **4 reef walkers** that sleep in the deep water offshore. They enter the village each night looking for people out after dark. Anyone stung by their poisonous tentacles are dragged into the water to be devoured. What remains of the cleric's bloated body lies tangled in the seaweed off shore.

Remorhaz

Hit Dice: 8-13
Armor Class: 0 [19]
Attacks: 1 bite (5d6)
Saving Throw: By hit die
Special: Melt weapons, swallow whole (10HD+ only)
Move: 12
Alignment: Neutrality
Number Encountered: 1
Challenge Level/XP: 8HD: 9/1,100; 9HD: 10/1,400; 10HD: 12/2,000; 11HD: 13/2,300; 12HD: 14/2,600; 13HD: 15/2,900

Remorhaz live in arctic regions, burrowing tunnels into the snow and ice. They resemble massive centipedes (30ft long), with fan-like rudimentary wings. They generate intense internal heat. Remorhaz with 10 or more hit dice can swallow man-sized prey whole (natural 20 required), and the monster's internal temperature instantly kills anyone swallowed. The top of a remorhaz glows red with heat, and will melt non-magical weapons (also dealing tremendous damage to anyone touching it.

Remorhaz (8HD): HD 8; AC 0[19], head/underside 2 [17]; Atk 1 bite (5d6); Move 12; Save 8; AL N; CL/XP 9/1100; Special: melt weapons.

Remorhaz (9HD): HD 9; AC 0[19], head/underside 2 [17]; Atk 1 bite (5d6); Move 12; Save 6; AL N; CL/XP 10/1400; Special: melt weapons.

Remorhaz (10HD): HD 10; AC 0[19], head/underside 2 [17]; Atk 1 bite (5d6); Move 12; Save 5; AL N; CL/XP 12/2000; Special: swallow whole on natural 20, melt weapons.

Remorhaz (11HD): HD 11; AC 0[19], head/underside 2 [17]; Atk 1 bite (5d6); Move 12; Save 4; AL N; CL/XP 13/2300; Special: swallow whole on natural 20, melt weapons.

Remorhaz (12HD): HD 12; AC 0[19], head/underside 2 [17]; Atk 1 bite (5d6); Move 12; Save 3; AL N; CL/XP 14/2600; Special: swallow whole on natural 20, melt weapons.

Remorhaz (13HD): HD 13; AC 0[19], head/underside 2 [17]; Atk 1 bite (5d6); Move 12; Save 3; AL N; CL/XP 15/2900; Special: swallow whole on natural 20, melt weapons.

Hot and Bothered

The dwarves of the Fire Guzzler Clan stand up to their beards in the deep snow of the Frozen Wastes, their cheeks red and their breath frosting in the air before them. The drifting snow makes moving hard, but the dwarves stick to it. The dwarves carry 40 specially crafted arrows in their heavy packs. The arrows have been blessed and purified by the finest dwarven craftsmen of Anvil Forge, but still must be tempered before they are used. The dwarves haven't been able to complete the task because of the deep snow, but PCs may fit the bill.

To temper them, the arrowheads must be touched to the heated belly of a **remorhaz**. The dwarves tracked one of the beasts to this frozen wasteland, but running up to touch it is beyond their abilities in the thick drifts. If PCs help, the dwarves promise them at least 10 of the magical arrows

If PCs agree to help, they must successfully run up and strike the remorhaz's belly with a grasped arrow. A hit causes the arrowhead to burn red momentarily as the magic takes hold. Each arrow becomes a *+5 arrow*, and automatically slays any creature it strikes on a roll of a natural 20. The remorhaz, however, doesn't take kindly to the stings of the arrows, even if they do just 1 point of damage per hit.

Retriever

Hit Dice: 10
Armor Class: -1 [20]
Attacks: 4 claws (1d8), eye-ray
Saving Throw: 5
Special: Eye rays, crushing damage on natural 20
Move: 9
Alignment: Chaos
Number Encountered: 1
Challenge Level/XP: 13/2,300

Retrievers are massive (20ft tall) spider-mechanisms built of metal. Some claim that these infernal devices are actually built in the hells and underworlds, which is not certain, but the malign intelligence built into them is unquestionably evil and destructive. Every third round, the retriever can shoot a magical ray from its eyes, having one of four effects: fire, cold, or electricity (4d6 hit points, save for half), or flesh-to-stone (save applies). No to-hit roll is required for the rays, but the particular effect each time is random. If one of the retriever's claws hits on a natural roll of 20, it holds the victim and crushes for automatic damage in future rounds.

Retriever: HD 10; AC –1[20]; Atk 4 claws (1d8), eye-ray; Move 9; Save 5; AL C; CL/XP 13/2300; Special: Eye rays, crushing damage on natural 20.

The Invasion Plan

A monstrous black and silver **retriever** moves through the dark underground, its eyes alight with a green glow as it goes on its clanking way. Water gushes from the retriever's joints as it moves. A dark elf raiding party rides atop the creature like angry fleas. The **6 dark elves** attack with arrows and spells as the retriever blasts foes with its eye rays. The dark elves joined forces with the malign retriever to attack the surface city of Endabor. A map of the twisted underground tunnels is carved onto the metal of the giant spider's back. The etching shows the location of an underground city of the dark elves, and various routes to surround the surface city. The city elders reward PCs with 2,000 gp if the dark elves invasion plan is averted. A water-filled compartment on the retriever's back contains the dark elf treasure: 1,798 gp, 16 black diamonds (1,500 gp), an unstopped decanter of endless water, and a medallion of ESP. The drow lost the decanter's stopper and never bothered to find another. The water-filled retriever is slowed to Move 6 because of the weight of the water inside it.

Rhinoceros

Hit Dice: 8
Armor Class: 6 [13]
Attacks: 1 horn (2d6)
Saving Throw: 8
Special: Double damage charge
Move: 12
Alignment: Neutrality
Number Encountered: 1d8
Challenge Level/XP: 8/800

Rhinoceros are aggressive and stupid. They inflict double damage when charging.

Rhinoceros: HD 8; AC 6[13]; Atk 1 horn (2d6); Move 12; Save 8; AL N; CL/XP 8/800; Special: Double damage on charge.

Ground-Shaker Goblins

People line the streets of Taharath's main street to watch a parade of people dressed in gaudy costumes marching through town. The costumed-revelers toss hard candy to the children as they dance and sing along the parade route. The marchers wear medallions with a strange cube engraved into its metal surface. The cultists are harmless worshippers of an ancient cube design found carved throughout the city's ancient ruins. They hold the parade each year to celebrate their religion and hopefully usher new members into their group.

The ground soon shakes and rumbles, and the excitement turns to panic as **3 rhinoceroses** charge through the parade-goers. People jump out of the way of the large beasts, barely escaping the beasts' giant horns and trampling feet. Riding on the backs of the rhinoceroses are **3 goblins**. Each goblin carries a riding whip that he uses to steer the animal (although not very well). The goblins jumped onto the rhinoceroses near the river and guided them into the town. The goblins hope to cause a commotion and eventually leap off and grab some loot before fleeing. The parade was just a happy coincidence.

Goblin: HD 1d6hp; AC 6[13]; Atk 1 weapon (1d6); Move 9; Save 18; AL C; CL/XP B/10; Special: −1 to hit in sunlight.

Rhinoceros, Wooly

Hit Dice: 10
Armor Class: 5 [14]
Attacks: 1 horn (2d6)
Saving Throw: 5
Special: Double damage on charge
Move: 12
Alignment: Neutrality
Number Encountered: 1d6
Challenge Level/XP: 10/1400

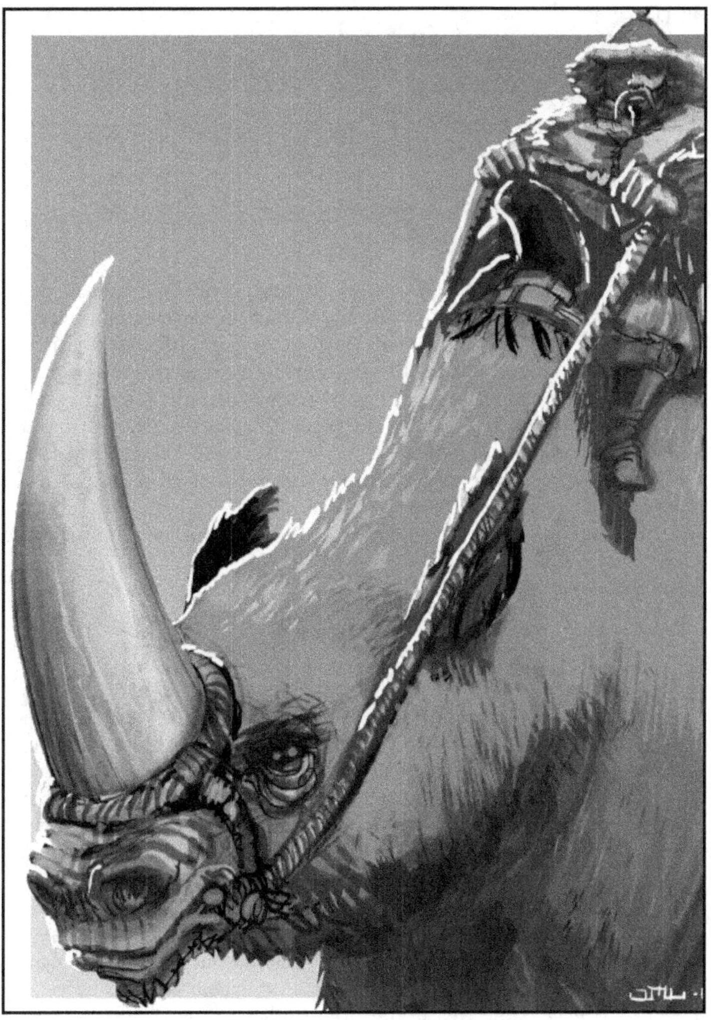

Wooly rhinoceros are Pleistocene beasts, found in the ice ages of strange worlds, and in the cold wastes of the far north. They have extremely long horns and a shaggy coat of hair.

Wooly Rhinoceros: HD 10; AC 5[14]; Atk 1 horn (2d6); Move 12; Save 5; AL N; CL/XP 10/1400; Special: Double damage on charge.

Catch of the Day

Pain-filled screams echo down the icy tunnels cut through the twisting passages winding through the Wailing Glacier. PCs can seek out the wailing or let the sounds come to them. The moans come from seven men and women wailing in agony as they writhe atop the wickedly sharp horns of **2 wooly rhinoceroses**. The horns pierce their bodies through their midsections, and the weight of each person presses down on the others already stuck on the horns.

Walking beside their "pets" are **4 frost giants** out on a snowy hunt through the melting glacier's tunnels. The giants grab prey and push them down onto the rhinoceroses' horns so the rhinos can carry the catch. Any PC caught by the giants faces the same fate. The giant cannibals prefer elf meat, but any flesh is fine to their indiscriminate palates.

Frost Giant: HD 10+3; AC 4[15]; Atk 1 weapon (4d6); Move 12; Save 5; AL C; CL/XP 11/1700; Special: Hurl boulders, immune to cold.

Rock Weasel, Giant

Hit Dice: 4
Armor Class: 2 [17]
Attacks: 1 bite (2d6)
Saving Throw: 13
Special: Stone breath
Move: 9
Alignment: Neutrality
Number Encountered: 1 or 1d4
Challenge Level/XP: 5/240

Rock Weasels are Giant Weasels that have come into contact with potent transmutative magic, becoming attuned to the elemental earths. This magical attunement manifests itself in the form of a breath attack; rock weasels can spit forth a 10ft long cone of rock shards and pebbles, inflicting 8 hit points of damage to all within this area (save negates). Rock Weasels emit low, grumbling vocalizations reminiscent of stone grinding against stone, and their eyes are black as coal. Their earthy nature makes them slower than normal Giant Weasels, but sturdier opponents in close combat.

— Author: Andrew Trent

Rock Weasel: HD 4; AC 2[17]; Atk 1 bite (2d6); Move 9; Save 13; AL N; CL/XP 5/240; Special: Stone breath.

Rock Fall

Thousands of tiny rock shards and small round pebbles cover a 50-foot stretch of a narrow pathway leading upward to a dark cave in the Hollow Spire Mountains. The path winds around the low peaks, ascending to the cave 40 feet above jagged stones in the rocky canyon below. The sound of stones grinding together rises from the dark mouth of the cave. Anyone trying to walk atop the rocky pebbles must make a saving throw to keep from falling off the 10-foot-wide ledge. The bones of three skeletons lie impaled on the rocks below, victims who fell off the ledge.

The cave is the lair of a **giant rock weasel** that hunts within the mountains. The pebbles and rock shards littering the trail to its lair are from the weasel's breath weapon. If PCs approach the cave, they are pelted by pellets as the weasel tries to turn them away. The rock weasel easily sprints along the ledge to attack those who continue. The weasel attempts to grab PCs in its mouth and throw them off the ledge.

Roc

Hit Dice: 12
Armor Class: 4 [15]
Attacks: Bite (3d6), 2 claws (2d6)
Saving Throw: 3
Special: None
Move: 3/30 flying)
Alignment: Neutrality or Law
Number Encountered: 1, or 1d2 and 1d4 fledglings
Challenge Level/XP: 13/2,300

Rocs are the mythological great birds of legend, large enough to prey upon elephants. They can be trained as fledglings to serve as steeds, so roc eggs or fledglings would be a prize indeed, worth great sums of gold. Rocs might grow as large as 18 HD, with commensurately increased statistics.

Roc: HD 12; AC 4[15]; Atk 1 bite (3d6), 2 claws (2d6); Move 3 (Fly 30); Save 3; AL N or L; CL/XP 13/2300; Special: None.

Big Bird, Little Bird

Shattered trees trunks lie across the dry steppes. Pines, firs and elms are splintered and shattered, as if dropped from great heights. Some of the trunks rest at angles atop one another. The land around the trees are gouged by the massive trunks, and PCs can find entire forests where the trees have been pulled from the ground by their roots, leaving deep holes in the dirt. One trunk lays atop three the rear halves of three horses. The horses have been eaten up to the bark pinning their corpses to the ground.

The steppes are the hunting ground of a **roc** and a **giant raven** working together to bring down prey. The raven finds food in the forest, and the roc acts as "hired muscle" to bring down the meal. As the raven watches PCs, the roc rips a tree out of the ground, and carries the huge trunk through the air to drop on them as they cross the steppes. The falling tree does 6d6 points of damage to anyone caught under it (save to jump clear of the falling tree trunk). The roc drops the tree, then swoops away to find another to yank from the ground. The big bird continues softening up PCs until the giant raven gives the signal to attack. The giant raven circles above the PCs at all times, cawing instructions that the roc follows. If the giant raven is killed, the roc eventually loses interest and flies off.

Roper

Hit Dice: 10-12
Armor Class: 0 [19]
Attacks: 1 tentacle (weakness), 1 bite (2d10)
Saving Throw: By hit die
Special: Tentacles grab and cause weakness
Move: 3
Alignment: Neutrality
Number Encountered: 1d3
Challenge Level/XP: 10HD: 11/1,700; 11HD: 12/2,000; 12HD: 13/2,300

Ropers are shapeless but extremely tough-skinned organisms, with about the body mass of a hill giant. They look very much like stone, and can shape themselves to resemble a natural pillar, stalagmite, lump, or any other simple rock formation. To attack, the roper hurls out long tendrils with a range of 50ft (one per round); the roper can use as many as six of these tentacles at a time. If the tentacle hits, it grabs the victim and draws him 10ft per round toward the roper's huge, tooth-filled mouth. The victim must make a saving throw or lose half his strength points due to the secretions on the tentacle (3d6 turns). A human has a 1 in 6 chance per round to break the roper's hold if his strength has been halved, 2 in 6 if his strength remains normal. Ropers are immune to electricity and take only half damage from cold, but they are susceptible to fire, taking +1 damage per hit die inflicted by fires (e.g., a 6 hit die fireball inflicts +6 damage).

Roper (10HD): HD 10; AC 0[19]; Atk 1 tentacle (weakness), 1 bite (2d10); Move 3; Save 5; AL N; CL/XP 11/1700; Special: tentacles grab and cause weakness.

Roper (11HD): HD 11; AC 0[19]; Atk 1 tentacle (weakness), 1 bite (2d10); Move 3; Save 4; AL N; CL/XP 12/2000; Special: tentacles grab and cause weakness.

Roper (12HD): HD 12; AC 0[19]; Atk 1 tentacle (weakness), 1 bite (2d10); Move 3; Save 3; AL N; CL/XP 13/2300; Special: tentacles grab and cause weakness.

Lake Monsters

This underground chamber is filled by a wide lake. The cold, dark water disappears into the darkness as the miles-long cave continues under the earth. Albino fish splash, and glowing green algae cover the stones above the waterline. A wooden pier extends outward from the rocky shore, its planks warped but sturdy. Two rowboats tied to the pier float in the lake. A rope is attached to a post at the end of the pier and leads off across the water to another pole rising out of the murk about 20 yards away. Another rope continues into the darkness in a different direction from the pole. The rope guide weaves between the pointed tops of large rocks sticking out of the lake. The rope continues across the lake.

The boats each have the odd phrase "Adventure's Foray" carved into their sides. The craft were brought here by **Inores Cludding** and **Farg Frensmal**, two enterprising guides who hoped to jumpstart a tour business into the Under Realms. They abandoned the venture after their first boat was attacked and sank by **2 ropers** living in the lake. The ropers lurk underwater with just their heads sticking above the surface. They lash out with their tentacles to pull people into the dark waters.

Rot Grub

Hit Dice: 1 hit point
Armor Class: 9 [10]
Attacks: 1 (burrowing in)
Saving Throw: 18
Special: Burrow to heart
Move: 1
Alignment: Neutrality
Number Encountered: 1d10
Challenge Level/XP: 1/15

Rot grubs are sometimes found, as one might expect from the name, anywhere flesh is left to rot. They are horrid things about an inch long, but they are quite dangerous – any flesh touching them is at great risk, for they bite in and burrow deeply (rolling to hit). For a period of 1d3 turns, rot grubs can be killed by burning (1d6 points of damage will be inflicted per rot grub). Casting Cure Disease will kill all the rot grubs in a person's body. After the 1d3 turns elapse, however, the grub has burrowed too deeply to be affected by spells or fire, and the victim will die within one more turn.

Rot Grub: HD 1hp; AC 9[10]; Atk 1 burrow; Move 1; Save 18; AL N; CL/XP 1/15; Special: Burrows to heart.

Orc Rot

The smell of decay is strong in this torture chamber beneath the curving corridors of Froghell Keep. Six decaying orc bodies are spiked to the walls with iron rods driven through their shoulders and thighs. The orcs died nearly a week ago. Their bloated bodies are purplish and bruised, as if something had chewed them up and spit them out. Tiny frogs sit on their shoulders and heads, croaking noisily at PCs. The orcs wear discolored leather armor. One has a pouch containing 15 broken human teeth, a long braid of silver elf hair, 68 gp and a worthless copper ring.

The orcs are placed over spear traps that burst out of the wall if anyone steps on pressure plates set on the floor in front of the bodies (2 in 6 chance of triggering). The spears burst out of the center of the dead orcs' chests. Each orc body is infested with **6 rot grubs** (36 total) that explode outward with the spear tips. Anyone standing in an area in front of the bodies must make a saving throw of be struck by 1d6 rot grubs as they fly outward. If multiple people are struck, divide the grubs evenly.

Rot Pudding

Hit Dice: 8
Armor Class: 6 [13]
Attacks: 1 (2d8 + disease)
Saving Throw: 8
Special: Disease, immunities
Move: 6
Alignment: Neutral
Number Encountered: 1
Challenge Level/XP: 9/1,100

Rot puddings are nasty subterranean creatures with slug-like bodies made of some viscous substance, looking much like a dark grey jellyfish. These puddings are scavengers in the dark caverns and hallways of underground places. The carrion diet of rot puddings makes them into seething incubators for all kinds of disease, and although they are themselves immune to sickness they are highly contagious host-creatures that can transmit all manner of plagues by the merest touch.

The diseases carried by a rot pudding can be transmitted in various ways during a combat with adventurers. First, if the pudding itself hits a character, the character must make a successful saving throw or be infected. Secondly, if the pudding is hit by a bladed weapon (not a piercing or blunt weapon), the wound will squirt a pus-like substance which will cause the attacker to make a saving throw or contract the disease. There is also a third possibility: if the pudding is burned by a fire larger than a torch, the disease from its surface will temporarily be burned off into a cloud of noxious smoke, which (unless there is some fairly strong source of moving air) will be roughly ten feet in diameter and will drift in a random direction each round at a speed of 1. Anyone in the cloud must make a saving throw or contract the disease. There is one beneficial effect of burning away the surface contagion of a rot pudding, which is that the creature's touch will not cause disease until 3 rounds have passed.

The disease, if a character is infected, has the following effects. The character will immediately be wracked with pains and aches, affected as per a *slow* spell (able to act and move only at half normal speed). After a period of 24 hours, the character must begin making saving throws once every 6 hours. The first failure of such a saving throw causes the character to fall into a comatose state. The second failed saving throw causes death. A cure disease spell will cure a diseased character, and although a neutralize poison spell will not remove the disease it will grant a +1 on all saving throws. A character who is infected with the disease also become contagious, although the contagion is much less virulent than the concentrated effect of an actual rot pudding. Anyone approaching within ten feet of an infected person has a 50% chance to have to make a saving throw against contagion, and if the saving throw fails, the disease is transmitted in the same form as if it had been contracted from the pudding.

Rot puddings are immune to cold and electricity. A *cause disease* spell will cure one half of any damage that has been inflicted upon the creature.

— *Author: Matt Finch*

Rot Pudding: HD 8; AC 6[13]; Atk 1 (2d8 + disease); Move 6; Save 8; AL N; CL/XP 9/1100; Special: Disease, immunities.

Night Terrors

The smell of death hovers over this small village sitting well off the main road. Thick clouds of flies buzz in and out of the empty homes, drawn to the decaying bodies and moldy food contained within. Some corpses lie in the streets, as if they tried to flee the doomed town. Others are curled up in their beds, accepting their fate. All of the bodies have hideous green sores and purple lesions spreading across their skin. Some of the corpses are partially dissolved, their bones and flesh nothing but puddles of gore trailing across the ground. PCs venturing into the village's square hear the sounds of children screaming and see small hands waving from an attic window.

A **rot pudding** crawled into the village well a week ago, poisoning the town's drinking water with contagion. Everyone drinking the contaminated water contracted various diseases that killed them quickly. The only survivors are six children who locked themselves in an attic room before the disease spread to them. They live off rainwater, and eat dry rations their father stored from his adventuring days. The children scream to PCs that the monster "mostly comes out at night." The rot pudding crawls up the well when the sun sets to feed on the dead. The children won't leave the attic room until the pudding is dealt with.

Rothran

Hit Dice: 5
Armor Class: 3 [16]
Attacks: 2 claws (1d6) and bite (1d10)
Saving Throw: 12
Special: Immune to magic weapons, magic resistance (90%)
Move: 9
Alignment: Chaos
Number Encountered: 1
Challenge Level/XP: 8/800

Strange ursine humanoids from the plane of darkness, Rothran often inhabit ruins and dungeons where they seek out magical treasures, which draw them as honey draws earthly bears. Rothran show a strong animosity towards arcane spellcasters. So consumed are they by this vicious hostility that they will seek out magic-users in combat whenever possible, even to the extent of leaving themselves vulnerable to other attackers. Rothran are extraordinarily resistant to magic.

— Author: Andrew Trent, "the Venomous Pao"

Rothran: HD 5; AC 3[16]; Atk 2 claws (1d6), 1 bite (1d10); Move 9; Save 12; AL C; CL/XP 8/800; Special: Immune to magic weapons, magic resistance (90%).

Ursa Major

A 10-foot-diameter totem pole stands in this large underground chamber. The carved pole rises from the floor to touch the 30-foot-high ceiling. The pole is carved so that it has a pile of skulls at its base, a giant bear standing upright in the middle, and leering demonic faces looking down from above. Glowing rubies, diamonds and emeralds decorate the eye sockets. The gems are worth 400 gp if all are pulled out of the wooden carving. The carcasses of four deer, a moose and numerous small rodents are piled in one corner of the cavern.

Sleeping on the tiled floor around the totem pole are **6 grizzly bears**. The bears snore and snuffle in a hibernation-like sleep. Sleeping in the bed of rotting animals is a **rothran** that controls the bears using the bear totem. The rothran rises out of the pile of dead animals, rousing its minions to attack. The grizzlies' eyes glow bright green when they wake.

Grizzly Bear: HD 6; AC 6[13]; Atk 2 claws (1d6), 1 bite (1d10); Move 9; Save 11; AL N; CL/XP 6/400; Special: Hug.

Rottentail

Hit Dice: 3
Armor Class: 6 [13]
Attacks: 2 short swords (1d6) or swordstave (1d8+1)
Saving Throw: 14
Special: Disease, delayed strike, magic resistance (30%).
Move: 14
Alignment: Chaos
Number Encountered: 3d6
Challenge Level/XP: 5/240

Rottentails are carnivorous, man-sized humanoids with rabbit-like heads (floppy ears etc). The rest of their race, which lives on a distant planet, moon, or plane of existence, exiled huge numbers of their kind who carry a horrible disease endemic to the species -- these are the rottentails. Scabby, smelly and forever drooling, the outcasts have survived the plague that caused their exile, but they pass on a weaker strain of it to anyone with whom they come into close proximity (20ft). Anyone coming this close to a rottentail must make a saving throw: if the saving throw fails, the victim's rate of healing is reduced to half normal for the next 2d6 days, and he suffers from frequent vomiting until the disease has run its course. Most rottentail tribes live below ground, and all have excellent low-light vision. The brutal, warlike culture of this species leads many of the rottentail warrens near human civilization to work as mercenaries or scouts when they are hired, and as bandits when they aren't. Rottentails, perhaps because of their otherworldly origins, are somewhat resistant to magic directed at them, but they are unable to cast spells themselves. These scabbed and obviously diseased creatures are far stronger and more vicious than they might appear at first sight, and they are extremely skilled in combat, being exceptionally adept at sizing up an opponent's skills and fighting style. They tend to fight defensively, without attacking, at the outset of most combats, which causes enemies to attack at a -2 penalty to hit; each combat round spent evaluating an opponent in this way gives the rottentail a cumulative bonus of +1 to hit when he eventually decides to strike. (The bonus is only for the one attack, and cannot be made at more than +3). Rumour has it that rottentails often subdue badly outnumbered opponents, in order to feast upon their still-living flesh back in the rottentails' underground warrens. They also have a strong breeding urge, and those who have established a warren are very territorial. Rottentails who fight for a living tend to favour patchwork leather armour and many wield twin short swords, although swordstaves (a two-handed weapon that allows them to reach into the second rank of an enemy formation) are also popular.

— Author: Sean Wills

Rottentail: HD 3; AC 6[13]; Atk 2 short swords (1d6) or swordstave (1d8+1); Move 14; Save 14; AL C; CL/XP 5/240; Special: Disease, delayed strike, magic resistance (30%).

Rabbit-Proof Fence

An eight-foot-tall fence surrounds the prairie village of Auren Glen. Two villagers armed with pitchforks stand at the gate, critically eyeing visitors wanting to enter the town. Rabbit tracks in the dirt are evident around the entire perimeter of the fence. The townsfolk are mostly simple farmers, but the mayor is a talkative and friendly sort who is extremely interested in adventurers. The down-homesy elf introduces himself as Elwood Doud.

Auren Glen is having a little trouble with rabbits. And by a little trouble, it means big trouble with **9 rottentails** that are establishing a warren a mile to the west. The diseased rabbits assault the town each night, trying to wipe out their neighbors. The territorial rottentails even dig tunnels under the walls to get inside, but the vigilant residents are always on alert for trouble. The mayor desperately pleads for the PCs to help end the rabbit infestation. He doesn't let on that the rabbits are giant, carnivorous humanoids infected by virulent plagues until PCs are already marching off to battle.

404

Rusalka (Water Witch)

Hit Dice: 4+3
Armor Class: 3 [16]
Attacks: 1 bite (special)
Saving Throw: 13
Special: Charm, paralyze, drown victims, immune to non-magic weapons, immune to mind-affecting spells, normal undead immunities, create wall of fog
Move: 9/18 (swimming)
Alignment: Chaos
Number Encountered: 1
Challenge Level/XP: 8/800

Rusalka are undead maiden-witches that haunt the cold rivers and lakes in which they drowned. In appearance, rusalka first appear to be comely maidens, clad only in fog. Upon close inspection, however, they are cadaverous with disheveled hair and eyes that shine with evil green fire. Anyone who gazes into the rusalka's eyes must save versus spells or fall under the effect of a charm person spell. The rusalka then leads her charmed individuals under the cold water to drown. Drowning victims will awaken from the charm, but take 2d8 damage first (for the purpose of the Rusalka, drowning inflicts 2d8 points of damage per round). The touch of a rusalka paralyzes for 1–4 turns (saving throw negates). Paralyzed victims are carried down to the monster's underwater lair to drown. When a drowning victim attempts to escape from the rusalka's clutches, there is a base 50% chance that the victim may reach the surface (and air) each round, reduced by 5% for each point of strength below 16, and increased by 5% for each point of strength over 16. Paralyzed victims obviously have no hope of escape on their own and will soon drown. Magic weapons are needed to strike a rusalka, and they are immune to mind-affecting spells as well as other attacks and magic that do not affect undead. Once per day, a rusalka may create a wall of fog. Rusalkas are turned as wraiths. Females slain by a rusalka will themselves rise as rusalkas the next night, and will serve the rusalka who slew them until that rusalka is herself destroyed. Rusalkas are repulsed by holy symbols and by the herb absinth.
— *Author: John A. Turcotte © 2006*

Rusalka: HD 4+3; AC 3[16]; Atk 1 bite (special); Move 9 (Swim 18); Save 13; AL C; CL/XP 8/800; Special: Charm, paralyze, drown victims, immune to non-magic weapons, immune to mind-affecting spells, normal undead immunities, create wall of fog.

The Fog Comes Rolling In

Villagers race through the streets of Niborlyn, running for the stone church in the center of town. Mothers clutch their children tightly to them, screaming for their husbands to hurry. Young families abandon elderly parents as they scramble for safety. A cleric dressed in deep blue robes stands inside a low wall surrounding the church grounds. He exhorts everyone to get inside quickly. The setting sun casts an orange glow over the strange proceedings.

Once everyone is inside, the church doors slam shut, and bolts are thrown to secure the portal from the inside. Shutters are pulled tight to bar the windows. A strong, unpleasant odor similar to sage hangs in the air from clover-like green herbs growing wild on the church grounds. Holy symbols hang on the doors and shutters, and more lie flat on the stone wall surrounding the church.

After the sun sets, a fog rolls slowly off the waterfront and plunges the village into thick mists. Figures move in the darkness, shuffling forward through the streets toward the church. From a distance, it looks like a handful of comely maidens who missed curfew. Closer up, they are revealed to be **6 rusalkas** that terrorize the village each night. The water witches stalk the town, seeking to welcome victims into their watery embrace. The villagers hide in the church after sundown, protected by the

holy symbols and absinth growing around the building. They don't open the doors for any reason until the sun rises and the witches return to their watery lairs. PCs caught out after dark face 6 devious witches intent on prey.

Rust Monster

Hit Dice: 5
Armor Class: 2 [17]
Attacks: 2 antennae (0)
Saving Throw: 12
Special: Cause rusting
Move: 12
Alignment: Neutrality
Number Encountered: 1d2
Challenge Level/XP: 5/240

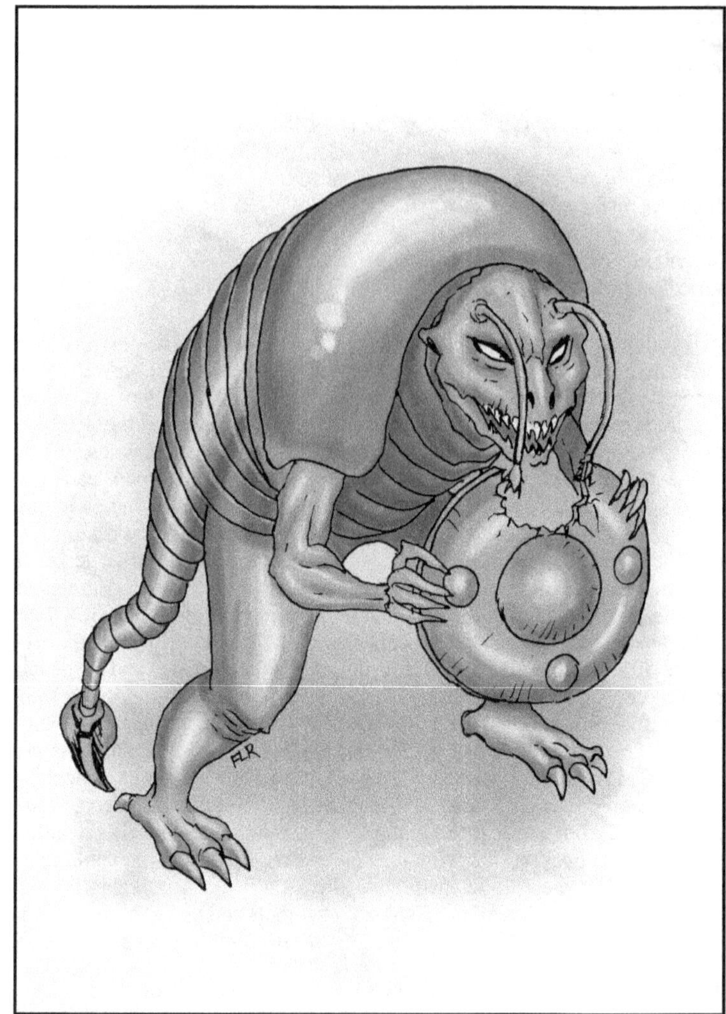

These bizarre creatures are about man-size, and look vaguely like an armadillo; they have armored hide, two antennae, and a long tail with a flanged growth at the end. Rust monsters do not attack people – they turn metal into rust and eat the rust – but they just can't resist trying to eat delicious foods like swords and plate mail, even if they are being attacked. A hit from a rust monster's antennae causes metal to rust into pieces, and the same is true for metal objects striking the rust monster's body. Magical metal has a 10% cumulative chance to avoid rusting per +1 bonus of the armor or weapon.

Rust Monster: HD 5; AC 2[17]; Atk 2 antennae (0); Move 12; Save 12; AL N; CL/XP 5/240; Special: Cause rusting.

The Hall of Trophies

Various stuffed animals and aberrant creatures stand in the foyer and entry room of this vacant manor. The creatures are posed in life-like stances, mounted to appear alive and deadly. PCs find a wyvern, a displacer beast, a giant rat and other odd creatures in the room. One wall contains insectoid antennae sticking from the cracks between the stones. The antennae are dry and brittle, and fall to the floor if disturbed. Piles of rust litter the floor around ugly yellow mannequins standing in the corners.

The antennae are from hundreds of rust monsters killed by the monster hunter Holman Carth. The hunter never returned from his last hunt to find a sea monster in the depths of Loch Brail and nature is slowly reclaiming the empty structure. Already, a storm sent a tree toppling against one corner of the house, shattering a window and allowing to real monsters to climb in among the trophies. Drawn by the scent of the antennae glands, **2 rust monsters** now live amid the trophies, waiting for their next metal meal. The rust monsters are slowly dining on the metal in the house, starting with the armor held up by the dummies in the corners.

Sahuagin

Hit Dice: 2+1
Armor Class: 5 [14]
Attacks: Weapon (1d8)
Saving Throw: 16
Special: None
Move: 12/18 (swimming)
Alignment: Chaos
Number Encountered: 1d6 x10 or 1d10 x10 (lair)
Challenge Level/XP: 2/30

Sahuagin are fish-men with a lamprey's round mouth filled with shark-like teeth. They live in salt water, sometimes at considerable depths, and raid the surface world for plunder and sport. These beings are thoroughly Chaotic and evil. Their society is highly organized, and their lairs are often guarded by sharks. Some sahuagin will have entangling nets used to ensnare opponents. These ferocious raider-predators hate aquatic elves and tritons with an almost insane intensity, and will attack them in preference to any other foe that opposes them in battle. The species has two common mutations: 1 in 100 sahuagin are born with 4 arms, and (raising many questions) 1 in 100 sahuagin are born identical in all respects to a sea elf. Sahuagin leaders can grow to great size, and can have as many as 8 hit dice.

Sahuagin: HD 2+1; AC 5[14]; Atk 1 weapon (1d8); Move 12 (Swim 18); Save 16; AL C; CL/XP 2/30; Special: None.

The Sea Tower of the Sahuagin King

A swirling waterspout of seawater rises 100 feet off the Reaping Sea in a twisting, twining column. The torrent spins ferociously, but retains a squat shape like a liquid tower. Windows and doors remain in place despite the spinning water. The Sea Tower of the Sahuagin King rolls across the waves, moving with the currents. Splintered boards, broken masts and canvas sheets spin in the outer watery wall of the castle. The bodies of unlucky sailors twist in the torrent.

The tower is home to **30 sahuagin** and their king, a **4 HD sahuagin** who wears turtle shell-armor (AC 3[16]) and can cast spells. The tower is surrounded by a "moat" filled with **3 great white sharks** that swim around the twisting tides rising inside the watery structure. The sharks can enter the tower base and swim up and out of the walls. The sahuagin king directs the tower across the ocean to attack ships and coastal cities.

Large Shark (7HD): HD 7; AC 6[13]; Atk 1 bite (1d8+4); Move 0 (Swim 24); Save 9; AL N; CL/XP 7/600; Special: Feeding frenzy.

Sahuagin King: HD 4; AC 3[16]; Atk 1 weapon (1d8+2); Move 12 (Swim 18); Save 13; AL C; CL/XP 4/240; Special: Spells (1—locate animal, purify water; 2—create water)

Salamander

Hit Dice: 7
Armor Class: 5 [14] (torso); 3 [16] (serpent body)
Attacks: Touch and constrict (2d8 + 1d6 heat), 1 weapon (1d6 +1d6 heat)
Saving Throw: 9
Special: Heat, constrict
Move: 9
Alignment: Chaos
Number Encountered: 1d4+1
Challenge Level/XP: 8/800

Salamanders are intelligent creatures of the elemental planes of fire. They have the upper body of a human and the lower body of a snake, and give off tremendous, intense heat. The very touch of a salamander deals 1d6 hit points of fire damage, and they wrap their tails around foes to cause an additional 2d8 points of crushing damage per round as the victim writhes in the deadly heat of the serpentine coils. The salamander's human torso is AC 5 [14], and the armored serpent-tail is AC 3 [16]. Salamanders cannot be enslaved in the same manner djinn and efreet might be.

Salamander: HD 7; AC 5 [14] (torso); 3[16] (serpent body); Atk Touch and constrict (2d8 + 1d6 heat), 1 weapon (1d6 + 1d6 heat); Move 9; Save 9; AL C; CL/XP 8/800; Special: Heat, constrict.

Fire Traps

Five-foot-wide spots in the Kanderi Desert radiate burning heat, the temperatures rising above the hot sands around them. The circles are nearly invisible, but PCs who make a saving throw may spot the circles before they step on one. These spots are rare leftovers from an ancient war between the salamanders and the first elves, when the races fought violent battles across the planes. The salamanders sprinkled the fire spots across sands before the marching elven army, waiting for someone to step on them.

The spheres detonate in an explosive flash of fire doing 3d6 points of damage to anyone stepping on one. The explosion also summons a salamander trapped in stasis since the war with the elves. The salamander immediately attacks, targeting elves over all others. These spots were placed primarily in the deserts, but a few occasionally surface in the oldest forests and most ancient cities. The spot vanishes after the explosion.

Sand Screamer (Ferret Snake)

Hit Dice: 2+2
Armor Class: 4 [15]
Attacks: 1 bite (1d8)
Saving Throw: 16
Special: Sand burrowing
Move: 15/15 (burrowing)
Alignment: Neutrality
Number Encountered: 1d4
Challenge Level/XP: 2/30

The Sand Screamer is a reptilian ferret-like creature the size of a pony, with a long slender body and sandy scales. They can burrow about under the surface of loose sand, leaving a trail like a desert mole, as fast as they dart about when in the open. Sand screamers feed upon tiny creatures hiding from the hot sun, whether in the sand or up a palm tree, and gain their name from the excited hissing noise they make when bursting from the sands. Sand screamers can be trained as mounts for small desert-dwelling humanoids, but they have unpredictable tempers and selective loyalty.

— *Author: Scott Wylie Roberts, "Myrystyr"*

Sand Screamer: HD 2+2; AC 4[15]; Atk 1 bite (1d8); Move 15 (Burrow 15); Save 16; AL N; CL/XP 2/30; Special: Sand burrowing.

Halfling Horsemen

A band of **8 nomadic halflings** stand atop the desert sand, their arms folded flat in front of them. Each wears loose-fitting, white clothing and has a turban wrapped around his head to protect against the blistering desert heat. The halflings stand perfectly still, like statues, but somehow still move closer to anyone crossing the desert. The leader of the group blows short blasts on a silver whistle, and the halflings change direction and separate – all without moving a muscle.

The halflings are desert raiders who travel the Kanderi Desert in search of gold and slaves. The halflings are master riders, capable of doing incredible tricks while on horseback. The desert dwellers don't ride horses, however. Instead, they train **8 sand screamers** that are incredibly loyal to them. The halflings stand atop the backs of the burrowing creatures as they plow through the sand. The halflings wait until the last possible moment before signalling their ferret snake mounts to rise up and attack. The halflings tumble across the burning sand to attack with jambiyas (1d4+1).

Halfling nomads (Fighter 4): HD 4; HP 27; AC 7[12]; Atk 1 jambiya (1d4+1); Move 9; Save 11; AL C; CL/XP 4/120; Special: None

Satyr

Hit Dice: 5
Armor Class: 5 [14]
Attacks: 1 weapon (1d8)
Saving Throw: 12
Special: Magic resistance (50%), pipes, concealment
Move: 18
Alignment: Neutrality
Number Encountered: 1d8
Challenge Level/XP: 6/400

Satyrs are the legendary goat-men of the wilderness, with the legs of a goat, the torso of a man, and horns sprouting from the forehead. Most carry pipes that can be used to cause charm person, sleep, or fear (in each case, a saving throw applies to all hearing the pipes). In woodlands or forest, satyrs are almost invisible unless they wish to be seen (90% chance to avoid notice). Satyrs are well known for their lecherousness, and (to put it delicately) they take great interest in human females. This race is favored of the god Pan (and perhaps also by the powerful Dionysus), which may be the reason why they are resistant to magic (50%).

Satyr: HD 5; AC 5[14]; Atk 1 weapon (1d8); Move 18; Save 12; AL N; CL/XP 6/400; Special: Magic resistance (50%), pipes, concealment.

The Sound of Music

A haunting melody plays through the small hamlet of Janoa. The sound is intoxicating, drawing people to the burg like flies to honey. People wander aimlessly along the single dirt road through town. The sound comes from a pan flute sitting on a rooftop attached to a bellows and small windmill. The turning windmill causes the bellows to pump air through the flute to produce the enchanting melody. Anyone hearing it must make a saving throw or be charmed. Herds of goats run free through the hamlet, grazing on the flowers growing wild throughout the town.

The people of Janoa recently ran a **satyr** named **Grover Hedge** out of town, and the ill-tempered creature swore to get even. He rigged the bellows and pan flute on the rooftop and now claims the town as his own domain. Grover sits inside the town hall on a large chair once used to cut hair. If PCs enter the town without being affected by the charm, he offers to trade goats for any females in the group. He's a lecherous clod who thinks he's above everyone else. If attacked, the villagers rally to his defense.

Scorpion, Giant

Hit Dice: 6
Armor Class: 3 [16]
Attacks: 2 pincers (1d10) and sting (1d4 + poison)
Saving Throw: 11
Special: Lethal poison sting
Move: 12
Alignment: Neutrality
Number Encountered: 1d4
Challenge Level/XP: 7/600

Giant scorpions are the size of a human being, and they are very aggressive.

Giant Scorpion: HD 6; AC 3[16]; Atk 2 pincers (1d10), sting (1d4 + poison); Move 12; Save 11; AL N; CL/XP 7/600; Special: Lethal poison sting.

The Scorpion Curse

A lumbering **zombie titan** shambles across the Galafran Plains, his skin sloughing off his emaciated frame. Bones jut from the skin stretched taut over his enormous body. The haughty titan **Antrapaeus** made the mistake of attacking the god of stinging vermin, and the Vermin Lord cursed injected him with a wasting disease that turned him into a shambling zombie cursed to roam the land. Antrapaeus is a force of nature, blundering through the countryside, destroying everything he encounters. He has no mind and no sense of the damage he is doing. There is no reasoning with the monstrosity.

The titan's blood still burns with the anger of the vermin god. Every 10 points of damage done to the titan causes a drop of blood to splash to the ground. The blood forms into a **giant scorpion** emblazoned with the mark of the Vermin Lord. The scorpion attacks those trying to kill Antrapaeus. The vermin god doesn't want Antrapaeus' suffering to end any time soon.

Zombie Titan: HD 21; AC 2[17]; Atk 1 strike (2d8); Move 17; Save 3; AL N; CL/XP 21/4700; Special: Immune to sleep and charm

Sea Cat

Hit Dice: 5
Armor Class: 4 [15]
Attacks: 2 claws (1d4), 1 bite (1d8)
Saving Throw: 12
Special: None
Move: 3/18 (swimming)
Alignment: Neutrality
Number Encountered: 1d4
Challenge Level/XP: 5/240

Sea cats are aquatic versions of the great cats (lions, leopards, tigers, etc) of the land. Instead of hind legs, they have the tail of a fish. Their scales are tough, and give these creatures a good armor class.

Sea Cat: HD 5; AC 4[15]; Atk 2 claws (1d4), 1 bite (1d8); Move 3 (18 Swim); Save 12; AL N; CL/XP 5/240; Special: None.

Cat Toy

A sailor dressed in rags sits on a large chunk of wood drifting in the middle of the Reaping Sea. The man is burned by the sun, and appears dehydrated. Instead of pleading for rescue, however, he motions any approaching ships away with feeble swipes of his hand. He can't even raise his head to speak. The man is Captain Aldus Hanopar, the captain of a sailing ship that sank within the past week. He has been adrift ever since. The ship was attacked by a giant octopus that rose from the depths to crush its hull. Captain Aldus was the sole survivor.

While the octopus is long gone, the captain is now being toyed with by **2 tritons** named Sigund and Royn and their "pets," **4 white tiger sea cats** that swim around the floating plank. The tritons and sea cats attack any ships approaching the doomed captain. The sea cats grab hold of the wooden sides of ships and claw their way out of the water to attack people on the deck.

Triton: HD 3; AC 5[14]; Atk 1 trident (1d8+1); Move 1 (Swim 18); Save 14; ALN; CL/XP 4/120; Special: Magic resistance 90%.

Sea Horse, Giant

Hit Dice: 3-4
Armor Class: 7 [12]
Attacks: 1 bite (1d6)
Saving Throw: 14 or 13
Special: None
Move: 0/24 (swimming)
Alignment: Neutrality
Number Encountered: 2d10
Challenge Level/XP: 3/60 or 4/120

Giant sea horses can be tamed and ridden as mounts underwater.

Giant Sea Horse (3HD): HD 3; AC 7[12]; Atk 1 bite (1d6); Move 0/24 (swimming); Save 14; AL N; CL/XP 3/60; Special: None.

Giant Sea Horse (4HD): HD 3; AC 7[12]; Atk 1 bite (1d6); Move 0 (Swim 24); Save 13; AL N; CL/XP 4/120; Special: None.

The Sea Horse Tear

A fist-sized bubble of solid glass sits on the sandy shore near the village of Niborlyn. The bauble looks like a teardrop with a tiny seahorse inside. If the teardrop is cast into the ocean, it vanishes under the waves. Within 1d4 rounds, a herd of **wild giant sea horses** rise out of the water. The creatures wait patiently for anyone to mount them. The sea horses swim quickly into the deeps, transporting riders to the undersea coral kingdom of Cnidaria. Bubbles of warm air surround the riders for the length of the journey, protecting them from the icy depths. The sea horses could also transport PCs to anyplace the GM desires.

Sea Lion

Hit Dice: 3
Armor Class: 6 [13]
Attacks: 1 bite (1d8)
Saving Throw: 14
Special: None
Move: 1/24 (swimming)
Alignment: Neutrality
Number Encountered: 1d4
Challenge Level/XP: 3/60

Sea lions resemble huge seals, but are fierce predators with a dangerous bite. Normally, they feed on penguins and fish. Giant versions might be twice the size of a normal sea lion.

Sea Lion: HD 3; AC 6[13]; Atk 1 bite (1d8); Move 1 (Swim 24); Save 14; AL N; CL/XP 3/60; Special: None.

A Day at the Beach Gone Bad

Screams of terror rise from a rocky beach leading down to cold waves crashing ashore near Frumpton. A woman from the nearby village crouches behind a rock, trapped between the pounding water and a colony of sea lions that came ashore to sun themselves on the isolated beach. One oversized blubbery male **sea lion** lounges in the middle of a harem of females gathered tightly around its massive bulk. The male is extremely territorial and attacks anyone crossing the beach. The woman screams for help, unable to move without the male sea lion raising its head to freeze her in place with angry grunts. If PCs try to rescue the woman, the **male** and **3 smaller sea lions** attack.

Sea Monster

Hit Dice: 30
Armor Class: 2 [17]
Attacks: Bite (4d10)
Saving Throw: 3
Special: Swallow whole
Move: 0/18 (swimming)
Alignment: Neutrality
Number Encountered: 1
Challenge Level/XP: 31/7,700

Sea monsters generally resemble bizarre fish, long-necked monsters with seal-like bodies, or massive eels, although virtually all have a hide of incredibly tough scales. In general, their appearance is quite varied, for there does not appear to be a particular "species" of sea monster. Sea monsters swallow their prey whole, like sea serpents: if the attack roll is 4 over the required number (or a natural 20), the victim is swallowed, will die in an hour, and will be fully digested within a day. Sea monsters are not generally venomous. They are generally encountered underwater; unlike sea serpents, they seldom venture to the surface.

Sea Monster: HD 30; AC 2[17]; Atk 1 bite (4d10);
Move 0 (Swim 18); Save 3; AL N; CL/XP 31/7700;
Special: Swallow whole.

Flounder

A small galleon thrashes in the sea. Sailors scream in terror as the ship is tossed about the waves and sometimes goes underwater completely. A huge winch on the galleon secures a chain and leathery tube that extend into the water. The chain and tube connect to an iron sphere with glass windows.

Ollie Nematoad, a halfling inventor, explores the sea's depths inside the rudimentary diving bell. A sea monster snatched Ollie and his diving bell, but the contraption is now lodged in the monster's jaws. The monster thrashes about trying to dislodge the sphere. It is angry and aggressive. If the PCs rescue him, Ollie would gladly reveal the locations of the sunken treasure he has found, absentmindedly neglecting to mention the various dangers.

Sea Serpent

Hit Dice: 15
Armor Class: 6 [13]
Attacks: Bite (2d12)
Saving Throw: 3
Special: Swallow whole
Move: 0/20 (swimming)
Alignment: Neutrality
Number Encountered: 1d4
Challenge Level/XP: 16/3,200

A fully-grown sea serpent is approximately 50 feet in length, and will swallow a person whole on any attack roll in which the die rolled is 4 or more over the required number, and always if the die roll is a 20. Swallowed victims will be dead within an hour, and fully digested within one day. Some sea serpents are also venomous, in which case the CL/XP is 19/4,100.

Sea Serpent: HD 15; AC 6[13]; Atk 1 bite (2d12); Move 0 (Swim 20); Save 3; AL N; CL/XP 16/3200; Special: Swallow whole.

Selfendel's Guardian

The Iron Pillars of Selfendel are eight 100-foot-tall metal posts rising out of the Reaping Sea where the deadly waters touch the glacial runoff of the Wailing Glacier. Layers of rime ice surround the base of each pillar. During the cold months, the ice is thick enough to walk from pillar to pillar without trouble. Each post is smooth and nearly 30 feet in diameter.

Atop each pillar is a small empty brazier that contains a wire frame about the size of a gemstone. If any gem worth at least 1,000 gp is placed in the frame, the brazier lights and burns brightly, consuming the gemstone. Each brazier burns with a different color. If all of the braziers are lighted within one month, the pillars slowly sink into the sea. At the same time, the Tower of Selfendel breaks through the ice to rise in the center of the posts. The tower stands nearly 300 feet tall and contains the tomb of the wizard Selfendel and his last experiments and treasures.

The rising tower releases the tower's guardian: a dormant **sea serpent** trapped beneath the underwater structure for nearly 200 years. The serpent rises to the surface to protect the tower. It wears a golden seal through one its great fins marking it as the property of Selfendel.

Shadow Mastiff

Hit Dice: 3
Armor Class: 6 [13]
Attacks: 1 bite (1d6+1)
Saving Throw: 14
Special: Baying, concealment in shadow
Move: 18
Alignment: Chaos
Number Encountered: 4d4
Challenge Level/XP: 4/120

Shadow mastiffs are large dogs (perhaps originating from another plane of existence) with glossy black coats and powerful jaws. They are hunters of the night, almost invisible in shadowy places (40% likely to disappear from sight after attacking). In bright light, however, their movement rate is reduced to 9 and they immediately lose 1d6 hit points. The baying of shadow mastiffs causes panic in anyone failing a saving throw, causing anyone affected to drop everything and run for 3d6 turns.

Shadow Mastiff: HD 3; AC 6[13]; Atk 1 bite (1d6+1); Move 18; Save 14; AL C; CL/XP 4/120; Special: Baying, concealment in shadow.

Fox Hunt

A fox-like humanoid rushes from the darkness of the Kajaani Forest and falls in the center of the dusty road. He wears tattered and torn clothing and carries a small cane. His backpack is shredded. Whatever it once contained fell out through the large rents. The baying of a hound rises under the new moon, the sound inducing panic in any who hear it and fail a saving throw. The fox monk looks ready to run, but his legs collapse beneath him and he lies still in the dirt. The **fox monk** points toward the trees, just as large creatures crash through the foliage.

Chasing the fox monk are **5 shadow mastiffs**. The large dogs push through the bushes beside the road, their eyes locked on the fox lying on the ground before them. The dogs snarl at PCs, but make no move to attack unless they get between them and their prey. The fox monk caused problems for a local magic-user who finally summoned the shadow mastiffs to deal with the annoying creature.

Fox Monk: HD 2+3; AC 7[12]; Atk 1 bite (1d4) or 1 strike (1d3 + spasms); Move 15; Save 16; AL N; CL/XP 3/60; Special: Spells, monkish strike.

Shadow

Hit Dice: 2+2
Armor Class: 7 [12]
Attacks: 1 touch (1d4 + Str drain)
Saving Throw: 16
Special: Drains 1 Str with hit, can only be hit by magical weapons
Move: 12
Alignment: Chaos
Number Encountered: 2d10
Challenge Level/XP: 4/120

Shadows may or may not be undead creatures: they are immune to *Sleep* and *Charm*, but the Referee may decide whether they are undead creatures subject to turning or whether they are some horrible "other" thing: a manifestation, perhaps, or a creature from another dimension (or gaps in the dimensions). Shadows are dark and resemble actual shadows, though they may be even darker in coloration. They are not corporeal, and can only be harmed with magical weapons or by spells. Their chill touch drains one point of Strength

with a successful hit, and if a victim is brought to a Strength attribute of 0, he or she is transformed into a new shadow. If the person does not come to such a dark ending, then Strength points return after 90 minutes (9 turns).

Shadow: HD 2+2; AC 7[12]; Atk 1 touch (1d4 + strength drain); Move 12; Save 16; AL C; CL/XP 4/120; Special: Drain 1 point str with hit, hit only by magic weapons.

Me and My Shadow

Gleaming onyx tiles line the floor of this long hallway. Twelve brass lanterns hanging on the walls reflect moving patterns that seem to dance across the reflective floor. The hallway leads into a 20-foot-square chamber containing a 10-foot-tall black onyx obelisk made of the same material as the black tiles in the hallway. The floor around the obelisk is pure white, seamless marble. The dividing line between the hall and room is a straight line where black meets white.

Anyone walking down the hallway between the lanterns draws a shadow to their side that replaces their own. The PC is safe as long as he stays in the hallway. Anyone entering the obelisk chamber without first praising Orcus released the **shadow** to rise up and attack. A separate shadow appears for each person who steps across the white marble threshold.

Shambling Mound

Hit Dice: 7 to 12
Armor Class: 1 [18]
Attacks: 2 fists (2d8)
Saving Throw: 9, 8, 6, 5, 4, or 3
Special: Immunities, enfold and suffocate victims.
Move: 6
Alignment: Neutrality
Number Encountered: 1d4
Challenge Level/XP: HD 7 (10/1400); HD 8 (11/1700); HD 9 (12/2000); HD 10 (13/2300); HD 11 (14/2600); HD 12 (15/2900)

Shambling mounds are moving plants, huge masses of slimy vegetation that shamble through swamps and marshes looking for prey. They have a roughly bipedal shape, with two 'legs' and two 'arms.' Shambling mounds are immune to fire because of their slimy, wet bodies. They take only half damage from cold, and half damage from weapons of any kind. Electricity causes a shambling mound to gain one hit die. If a shambling mound hits with both arms, the victim is enfolded into the slimy body and will suffocate in 2d4 melee rounds unless freed.

Shambling Mound (7HD): HD 7; AC 1[18]; Atk 2 fists (2d8); Move 6; Save 9; AL N; CL/XP 10/1400; Special: Damage immunities, enfold and suffocate victims.

Shambling Mound (8HD): HD 8; AC 1[18]; Atk 2 fists (2d8); Move 6; Save 8; AL N; CL/XP 11/1700; Special: Damage immunities, enfold and suffocate victims.

Shambling Mound (9HD): HD 9; AC 1[18]; Atk 2 fists (2d8); Move 6; Save 6; AL N; CL/XP 12/2000; Special: Damage immunities, enfold and suffocate victims.

Shambling Mound (10HD): HD 10; AC 1[18]; Atk 2 fists (2d8); Move 6; Save 5; AL N; CL/XP 13/2300; Special: Damage immunities, enfold and suffocate victims.

Shambling Mound (11HD): HD 11; AC 1[18]; Atk 2 fists (2d8); Move 6; Save 4; AL N; CL/XP 14/2600; Special: Damage immunities, enfold and suffocate victims.

Shambling Mound (12HD): HD 12; AC 1[18]; Atk 2 fists (2d8); Move 6; Save 3; AL N; CL/XP 15/2900; Special: Damage immunities, enfold and suffocate victims.

Plant Life Reborn

A six-foot-tall silver staff is driven into the thick muck of the Sin Mire Swamp. The word "Crokatowa" is engraved along its length. Moss wraps thickly around the staff, and clouds of flies buzz around its length. Affixed to the top of the stake is a small black gem worth 200 gp. Long ago, Crokatowa was an earth elemental that attacked a tribe of halflings living on a swampy island deep in the Sin Mire. The elemental destroyed the village, shouting its name over and over as it tore the halflings apart. Even as their families died around them, a group of halflings enchanted the silver staff to trap and hold the elemental. The last halfling alive sacrificed himself to get close enough to drive the stake into Crokatowa's chest.

Removing the stake from the swamp or pulling the gem free releases the elemental's essence. Trapped for so long in the Sin Mire, the creature's elemental essence merged with the swamp moss. With the staff removed, the creature rises as a **12 HD shambling mound**. Striking the shambling mound with the staff deals 2d4+2 points of damage with each successful hit. The shambling mound focuses its attacks on the staff wielder.

Shark

	Small	Medium	Large
Hit Dice:	3-4	5-6	7-8
Armor Class:	6 [13]	6 [13]	6 [13]
Attacks:	1 bite	1 bite	1 bite
	(1d4+1)	(1d6+2)	(1d8+4)
Saving Throw:	14 or 13	12 or 11	9 or 8

Special: Feeding frenzy
Move: 0/24 (swimming)
Alignment: Neutrality
Number Encountered: 2d6
Challenge Level/XP: 3HD: 3/60; 4HD: 4/120; 5HD: 5/240; 6HD: 6/400; 7HD: 7/600; 8HD: 8/800

When there is blood in the water (say, 6 hit points' worth), more sharks will come to investigate (about 2d6 sharks of any size). All sharks will be attacking madly, and each time a shark attacks there is actually a 1 in 6 chance that it will target another shark instead of a human. Sharks have roughly 1HD per foot of length.

Small Shark (3HD): HD 3; AC 6[13]; Atk 1 bite (1d4+1); Move 0 (Swim 24); Save 14; AL N; CL/XP 3/60; Special: Feeding frenzy.

Small Shark (4HD): HD 4; AC 6[13]; Atk 1 bite (1d4+1); Move 0 (Swim 24); Save 13; AL N; CL/XP 4/120; Special: Feeding frenzy.

Medium Shark (5HD): HD 5; AC 6[13]; Atk 1 bite (1d6+2); Move 0 (Swim 24); Save 12; AL N; CL/XP 5/240; Special: Feeding frenzy.

Medium Shark (6HD): HD 6; AC 6[13]; Atk 1 bite (1d6+2); Move 0 (Swim 24); Save 11; AL N; CL/XP 6/400; Special: Feeding frenzy.

Large Shark (7HD): HD 7; AC 6[13]; Atk 1 bite (1d8+4); Move 0 (Swim 24); Save 9; AL N; CL/XP 7/600; Special: Feeding frenzy.

Large Shark (8HD): HD 8; AC 6[13]; Atk 1 bite (1d8+4); Move 0 (Swim 24); Save 8; AL N; CL/XP 8/800; Special: Feeding frenzy.

GIANT SHARK
Hit Dice: 13
Armor Class: 5 [14]
Attacks: 1 bite (1d10+8)
Saving Throw: 3
Special: Feeding frenzy
Move: 0/18 (swimming)
Alignment: Neutrality
Number Encountered: 1d2
Challenge Level/XP: 13/2,300

Giant sharks are essentially no different than their smaller brethren, other than in their great size. These massive predators are often found cooperating with the evil sahuagin (q.v.).

Giant Shark: HD 13; AC 5[14]; Atk 1 bite (1d10+8); Move 0 (Swim 18); Save 3; AL N; CL/XP 13/2300; Special: Feeding frenzy.

All My Chums

A large inlet of the Reaping Sea rushes between two low cliffs. One cliff slopes upward to a cave entrance blocked by two large boulders. The heavy stones block the entrance, forcing any creature trying to get inside to climb over the slick rocks. Outside the cave, a frame of tree trunks holds six dolphins strung up with sturdy ropes. The dead dolphins are gutted, their entrails spilling out and onto the sloping rocks. A steady flow of blood and gore slides down the slope toward the water. The blood drips over the rocks and falls 20 feet into the sea, creating a blood slick that spreads across the wave tops.

The cave is the home of a **stone giant** named **Granuul Coldstone**. The giant lives a solitary life, catching dolphins for its food. The blood from the dolphins attracts **8 sharks** into the cove to feed. Granuul casts his dolphin leftovers into the waters to feed the predators he now considers his pets. The giant tried eating shark once, but hated the taste. If disturbed, he tries to grab PCs and toss them down the slope into the water for the sharks to take care of. Anyone on the slippery, gore-covered slope must make a saving throw or slide down the hill into the water.

Stone Giant: HD 9+3; AC 0[19]; Atk 1 club (3d6); Move 12; Save 6; AL N; CL/XP 10/1400; Special: Throw boulders.

Shocker Lizard

Hit Dice: 1d6 hit points
Armor Class: 6 [13]
Attacks: 1 bite (1d3)
Saving Throw: 18
Special: Electric shock
Move: 6
Alignment: Neutrality
Number Encountered: 1d6+1
Challenge Level/XP: 1/15

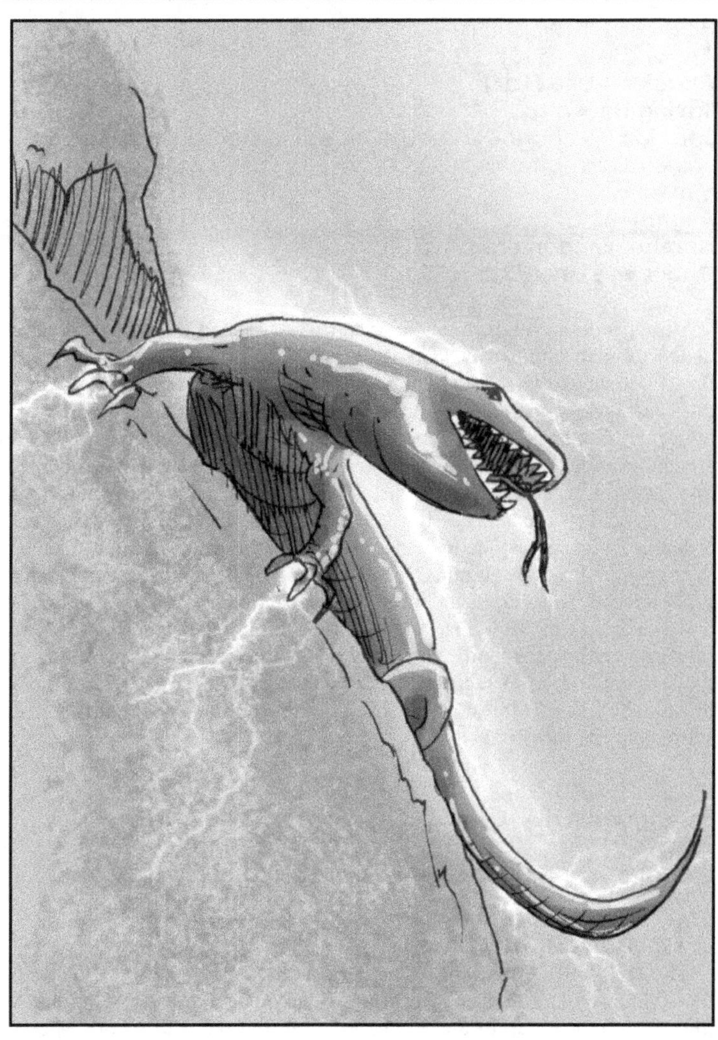

Shocker lizards are large lizards about two feet long and weigh about 25 pounds. They deliver an electrical shock by touch, and anyone hit by the shock must make a saving throw or be stunned for 1d3 rounds. If anyone is hit by two or more shocks in a single round (the lizards hunt in groups), the second shock may cause death as well the chance of stunning.

Shocker Lizard: HD 1d6hp; AC 6 [13]; Atk 1 bite (1d3); Move 6; Save 18; AL N; CL/XP 1/15; Special: Electric shock.

Shock Troops

Two large, sewn-together figures shuffle through the Maze of Xenso the Mad. The **2 flesh golems** carry large bags on their backs that spark, squeal and squirm. The flesh golems converge on intruders, determined to keep them away from the center of the maze where Xenso's Crown of Conundrums sits on the ancient king's abandoned throne. Each golem has a diamond embedded in its forehead worth 300 gp.

The bags contain **12 shocker lizards** (6 per bag). The golems reach over their shoulders and grab one of the lizards and throw the wriggling lizard at intruders. The angry lizards spark like lightning as they arc through the air. While they are in the bag, each lizard heals 1d4 points of damage done to the golem each round (6d4 points total if all are in the bag). The golem can throw one lizard each round.

Flesh Golem: HD 10 (45hp); AC 9[10]; Atk 2 fists (2d8); Move 8; Save 5; AL N; CL/XP 12/2000; Special: Healed by lightning, hit only by magic weapons, slowed by fire and cold, immune to most spells.

Shrangaathi

Hit Dice: 1d6 hit points
Armor Class: 4 [15]
Attacks: 1 bite (1d6)
Saving Throw: 18
Special: 5% chance to cause bleeding damage, limited vulnerability to turning
Move: 9
Alignment: Chaos
Number Encountered: 1d100
Challenge Level/XP: 1/15

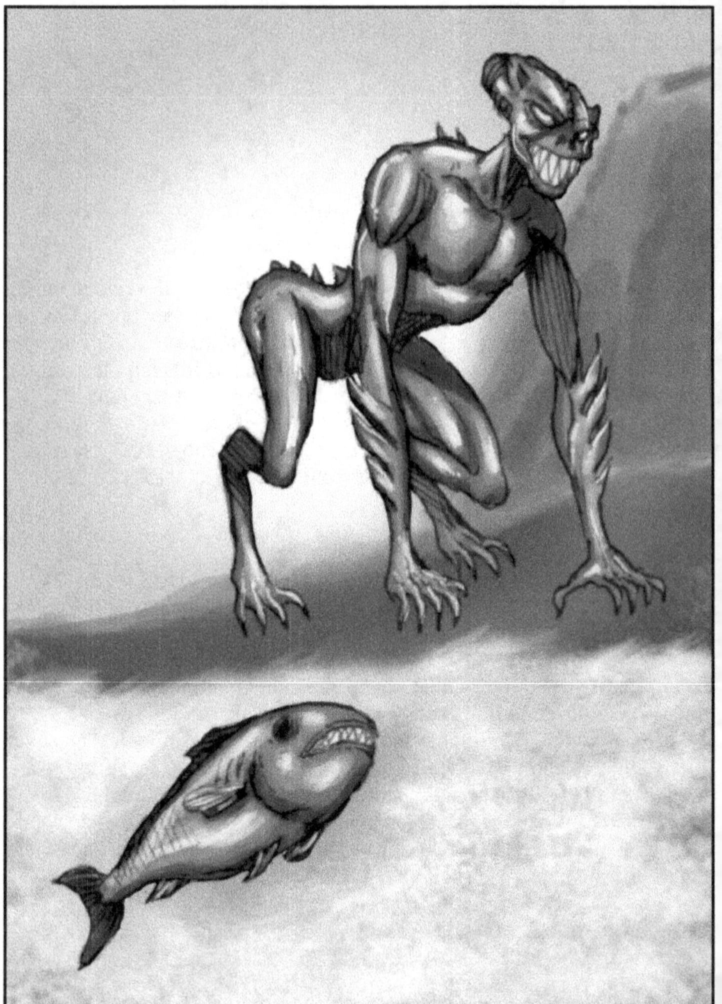

Shrangaathi are malevolent river spirits that spend most of their time in the form of almost transparent river-fish. In this form, they pose no threat. However, when a school of shrangaathi encounters a village that does not have some sort of shrine or spirit to protect it, they will wait until nightfall, change form, and attack the unprotected settlement. When attacking on land, the shrangaathi become small humanoids with white, opalescent skin, needle-like teeth, and spindly limbs. They swarm ashore like a school of predatory fish, often stopping to feed on prey that have fallen in battle against them - a single shrangaathi can devour a human to the bones in 4 rounds and then look for more to eat. A single shrangaathi is not a formidable opponent, but any opponent bitten by a shrangaathi has a 5% chance (1 in 20) to lose 1d4 additional hit points from loss of blood (at a rate of 1hp per round). Shrangaathi are affected by turning, although they are not undead: if successfully turned (as ghouls), up to 1d10 of them must make a saving throw or flee back to the river, never to return to that settlement for 1d6+10 days.

— Author: Matt Finch

Shrangaathi: HD 1d6 hp; AC 4[15]; Atk 1 bite (1d6); Move 9; Save 18; AL C; CL/XP 1/15; Special: 5% chance to cause bleeding damage, limited vulnerability to turning.

The River Horde

The river village of Ransmet is built on a spur of land that juts into the Kisme River. The deep river flows slowly past the wooden buildings that are built right up to the water's edge. A low fence of wooden posts surrounds the village. Each post has a small carved fish atop it. Many more colorful fish swim through the river, providing plenty of food for the fishermen in the village. The normally pleasant village is in an uproar, however, after the precious golden fish idol in the village's center went missing. The good folk blame the theft on a fox monk, and they are correct. They'd go after the thieving creature, but they have bigger fish to fry right now. Like staying alive through the night.

Each night, **40 shrangaathi** rise out of the river to teach the town a lesson for not having a proper shrine. The residents plead for help in finding the missing idol – and the treacherous fox monk. They offer 100 gp (all they have) to anyone who tracks down the fox monk and returns the fish statue. They throw in a basket of fish and pickled eggs if they bring back the fox monk.

Shrieker

Hit Dice: 3
Armor Class: 7 [12]
Attacks: None
Saving Throw: 14
Special: Shriek
Move: 1
Alignment: Neutrality
Number Encountered: 1d8
Challenge Level/XP: 3/60

Shriekers are huge mushrooms with a tough, fibrous body. They do not physically attack, but if light shines on them (within about 30ft) or if anything moves near them (within about 10ft), they emit a high-pitched shrieking noise. This noise causes 1hp damage per round (saving throw applies) to anyone nearby (within about 30ft). The true danger of shriekers is that they tend to summon wandering monsters. If they are attacked with missile weapons, they will attempt to shuffle away, although they do not move very fast.

Shrieker: HD 3; AC 7[12]; Atk None; Move 1; Save 14; AL N; CL/XP 3/60; Special: Shriek.

Breaking Glass

Hundreds of tiny **glass butterflies** rest atop a dozen large mushrooms in this underground cavern. The butterflies sparkle in the light of glowing fungi growing along the walls. Among the giant mushrooms are **6 shriekers**. The butterflies rise off the mushrooms in flashes of colors if approached. The movement causes the shriekers to react. The high-pitched noise causes the glass butterflies to shatter in a twinkle of colored shards. The death of the butterflies sets off a random spell effect (roll 1d6 or choose an effect):

1. Web
2. Fireball
3. Ice Storm
4. Cloudkill
5. Monster Summoning V
6. Reverse Gravity

Shroom

Hit Dice: 6+1
Armor Class: 6 [13]
Attacks: 1 weapon (1d8)
Saving Throw: 11
Special: Spells, control plants, plant growth
Move: 9
Alignment: Chaos
Number Encountered: 1
Challenge Level/XP: 8/800

Shrooms are evil geniuses, toadstool creatures with considerable magical powers. They lurk in the deep places of the earth and in dank forests, plotting ruin against surface dwellers and scheming to gain power for themselves by any means possible. They are highly adept with magic that influences plants, and most of them are knowledgeable in various forms of arcane study of other kinds, such as alchemy. Many, too, will surround themselves with strange minions that they have created, grown, or bred.

Shrooms are highly individual, and the Referee should feel free to invent all kinds of these sinister malefactors. Most will have the spell-casting abilities of at least a fourth level magic user, and all have strange powers to create and shape the plants of their environments (growing and controlling them). Although these powers take time to employ and will not be relevant in combat, they can be used to create a considerably hazardous lair.

The flesh of a Shroom is delectable, but deadly. Any person eating Shroom-flesh must make a saving throw versus poison or be affected as if by a *feeblemind* spell. The condition may be reversed by a *heal* or *restoration* spell. The effects of the toxin can actually turn out to be beneficial in the long run; there is a 5% chance that a feebleminded character who has been healed or restored will permanently gain a point of intelligence from the effects of the Shroom-flesh.

— Author: Matt Finch

Shroom: HD 6+1; AC 6[13]; Atk 1 weapon (1d8); Move 9; Save 11; AL C; CL/XP 8/800; Special: Spells, control plants, plant growth.

My Dinner with Amanita

An idyllic garden hides underground in this quarter-mile sinkhole. Flowering plants grow in abundance, and trees reach for the sky through a hole in the rock above. A group of **3 bugbears** sits on logs around a flat mushroom in the center of the garden. Silver plates sit atop the makeshift table. On the plates is a sumptuous meal of cooked venison topped with sliced mushrooms, white gravy and chilled wine. All of the food is very delicious. The bugbears ate some of the food, but enough remains on the serving platters to feed a small group. The bugbears laugh uproariously, ignoring PCs even if they come right up behind them. The bugbears look at PCs with blank stares, then laugh all the harder.

Anyone eating the mushrooms sliced atop the meat must make a saving throw or be affected by a *feeblemind* spell. An evil **shroom** named Amanita set the table. The vicious shroom sliced off pieces of her body to flavor the meal. She lurks in the trees, hiding among the flowering plants until her poison kicks in. Amanita is accompanied by a **shambling mound** that protects her.

Bugbear: HD 3+1; AC 5[14]; Atk 1 bite (2d4) or weapon (1d8+1); Move 9; Save 14; AL C; CL/XP 3/120; Special: Surprise opponents, 50% chance.

Shambling Mound (8HD): HD 8; AC 1[18]; Atk 2 fists (2d8); Move 6; Save 8; AL N; CL/XP 11/1700; Special: Damage immunities, enfold and suffocate victims.

Silent Knight

Hit Dice: 7
Armor Class: 2 [17]
Attacks: 1 weapon (1d8)
Saving Throw: 9
Special: Silence
Move: 9
Alignment: Chaos
Number Encountered: 1
Challenge Level/XP: 8/800

The silent knight is an undead creature resembling a heavily armored zombie armed with knightly weapons. These rather powerful creatures are quite intelligent in a malign, inhuman way. Their presence is in some way commanding to lesser forms of undead such as skeletons and zombies, and when encountered in tombs or other houses of the dead they are often accompanied by battalions of these creatures that have abandoned their original commands to mindlessly follow the silent knight. The most distinguishing feature of the silent knight, though, is that they radiate utter silence in a huge area, a radius of approximately 200ft. The silence is blocked by stone, but creeps down open corridors, often providing warning of the silent knight's approach with his horde of undead minions. Within the area of the knight's silence, it is impossible to turn undead or to cast most spells due to the absence of sound.

— Author: Matt Finch

Silent Knight: HD 7; AC 2[17]; Atk 1 weapon (1d8); Move 9; Save 9; AL C; CL/XP 8/800; Special: Silence.

Silent Knight, Deadly Knight

Ten suits of polished armor stand along the walls of this throne room, each facing toward a throne sitting at the front of the room before a floor-to-ceiling glass window. The armor stands at the top of three low steps that run around the entire room. Each suit of armor holds a long sword and a shield. Twenty-foot-tall red velvet tapestries hang on the stone walls behind the armor.

In the center of the open room, **20 skeletons** fight one another in bouts of skill. The skeletal combatants dance and spin as they mock fight across the tiled floor. A decaying body sits unmoving on a throne watching the skeletons battle before it. Despite all the swords and shields slamming together, no sounds leave the chamber.

The body on the throne is a dead elf placed there by the true master of the chamber: a **silent knight** that stands disguised as one of the suits of armor along the wall. The undead creature steps out to direct the skeletons if PCs attack the fighting skeletons.

Skeleton: HD 1; AC 8[11] or 7[12] with shield; Atk 1 weapon or strike (1d6) or (1d6+1 two-handed); Move 12; Save 17; AL N; CL/XP 1/15; Special: None.

Skarusoi

Hit Dice: 6
Armor Class: 3 [16]
Attacks: 2 arm-shields (1d8) or 1 weapon (1d8+2)
Saving Throw: 11
Special: Mental powers, 50ft leap
Move: 15
Alignment: Neutrality
Number Encountered: 4d6
Challenge Level/XP: 8/800

The Skarusoi are a race of insectoid bipeds from another world or dimension. Tall and brown, they have shield-like carapaces on their forearms and long feelers sprouting from their heads. They make a muted chittering noise, but seem to communicate with each other through a series of gestures and feeler flicks. Skarusoi attack by buffeting and slashing with their forearm carapace-shields, twice per round, for 1d8 damage each. They may also wield weapons, preferring staves and pole arms, gaining a +2 damage bonus if doing so. A Skarusoi can leap 50ft and attack in the same round.

The Skarusoi also possess strange mental powers. If it foregoes a melee attack, a Skarusoi may cause one of the following effects: (1) Cone of Force, 30ft long x 10ft at end, hurling opponents away and possibly knocking them to the ground (roll lower than strength on a d20); (2) Vortex Leap, whirling the Skarusoi up to 150ft away; (3) Waves of Distress, 15ft radius, causing all creatures drop what they are holding and clutch their heads in agony for 1d4 rounds (saving throw negates); and (4) Blow of Mental Force, causing 4d6 damage to one target within 20ft (save for half). The Skarusoi may use the above mental powers a total of five times per day. In addition, three or more Skarusoi concentrating together can summon an insect swarm (as per the spell).

The Skarusoi are believed to be a mercenary race in a dimensional war that has left countless worlds in ruin. When encountered, they are likely to be upon some mission relating to this war, pursuing tactical objectives incomprehensible to humankind.

— *Author: Scott Wylie Roberts, "Myrystyr"*

Skarusoi: HD 6; AC 3[16]; Atk 2 arm-shields (1d8) or 1 weapon (1d8+2); Move 15; Save 11; AL N; CL/XP 8/800; Special: Mental powers, 50ft leap.

Insect Scouts

A 10-foot-wide pit sits beside the dirt roadway leading into the small farming village of Lessef. A number of dead chickens lie in piles of bloody feathers beside the hole. The hole slopes downward for nearly a mile under the town, where it breaks into an empty circular tomb. A number of doors stand around the door, leading into a circular corridor that surrounds the central chamber. The hole enters the room through the ceiling. One of the doors leading out of the room is broken off its hinges.

An **ankheg** skitters around the outer ring corridor carrying **2 skarusoi** that ride leather saddles affixed to its undulating back. The ankheg attacks intruders while the skarusoi blast PCs with their mental powers. The skarusoi are searching for a missing slab of amber inscribed with the words of the Vermin Lord. Their search has been futile so far.

Ankheg (6HD): HD 6; AC 2[17] underside 4[15]; Atk 1 bite (3d6); Move 12 (burrow 6); Save 11; AL N; CL/XP 7/600XP; Special: Spits acid 5d6 (1/day, save for half)

Skeletal Fury

Hit Dice: 3
Armor Class: 7 [12]
Attacks: 2 claws (1d6) and 1 gore (1d6)
Saving Throw: 14
Special: Immune to sleep, charm, and mind-reading
Move: 12/12 (flying)
Alignment: Neutrality
Number Encountered: 1
Challenge Level/XP: 4/120

The skeletal fury is an undead creature created from the skeleton of a horse, with claws or talons grown from the hooves, horns or antlers grown from the skull, the bones of large bat-like wings grown from the shoulders, and a red glow burning in the eye sockets. Silhouetted against the moon or illuminated by moonlight, faint wispy material seems to line its bones, creating the illusion of ghostly flesh. They are not completely mindless and sometimes display equine mannerisms, such as pawing at the ground or tossing their heads, in a twisted mockery of life. Skeletal furies can be turned by clerics, as ghouls. They are not affected by sleep or charm spells, nor any form of mind reading. Any attempt to read or contact the mind of a skeletal fury that is under the control of a magic-user may result in a brief mental image of the controlling wizard.

— *Author: Scott Wylie Roberts, "Myrystyr"*

Skeletal Fury: HD 3; AC 7[12]; Atk 2 claws (1d6) and 1 gore (1d6); Move 12 (Fly 12); Save 14; AL N; CL/XP 4/120; Special: Immune to sleep, charm, and mind-reading.

The Lich's Wish

A carriage made from the bones of giants thunders down the dirt road, throwing up clouds of dust as it races along. The carriage creaks and shakes ominously, but the bleached bones hold together. Pulling the conveyance are **6 skeletal furies**. The horses have no reins and no driver to guide them, but it stops right beside PCs. The door made from a giant's pelvis opens on its own, but the carriage is empty. The vehicle has plush cushions for seats, and a glass decanter of wine sits in a bucket of ice. A note on one of the cushions reads "An invitation to my peers."

The carriage belongs to the **lich Letor Serane**. The dread lich of the dusty plains wishes to die, but refuses to end his unlife on his own. He seeks adventurers of adequate skill and power who might best him in combat. The skeletal furies are attuned to power, and seek out those who might accomplish the task. If anyone boards the carriage, the horses set off in a gallop for Letor's sand dune castle.

Lich (15HD): HD 15; AC 0[19]; Atk 1 hand (1d10 + automatic paralysis); Move 6; Save 3; AL C; CL/XP 18/3800; Special: Appearance causes paralytic fear, touch causes automatic paralysis, spells.

Skeleton

Hit Dice: 1
Armor Class: 8 [11], with shield 7 [12]
Attacks: Weapon or strike (1d6)
Saving Throw: 17
Special: Immune to sleep and charm spells
Move: 12
Alignment: Neutrality
Number Encountered: 3d10
Challenge Level/XP: 1/15

Skeletons are animated bones of the dead, usually under the control of some evil master.

Skeleton: HD 1; AC 8[11] or 7[12] with shield; Atk 1 weapon or strike (1d6) or (1d6+1 two-handed); Move 12; Save 17; AL N; CL/XP 1/15; Special: Immune to sleep and charm spells.

Blood Curse

Four bone pillars stand about this 30-foot-square ossuary. Each four-foot-diameter pillar is crafted from hundreds of random bits of bones and skulls. A low wall of femurs runs from one pillar to the next. Four skull chalices sit on the wall. Each chalice is filled with steaming blood. Anyone drinking from a chalice must make a saving throw or be cursed so he can only drink blood from that moment onward until cured. If the curse is not reversed within 3 months, the victim becomes a vampire.

If the drinker makes his saving throw, he hears a sibilant word whispering in his mind. If he says the word aloud, jittering bones drop off the pillars and form into **6 skeletons** that serve the PC for one week.

Skeleton, Fossil

Hit Dice: 2
Armor Class: 6 [13]
Attacks: 1 weapon or strike (1d8)
Saving Throw: 16
Special: None
Move: 9
Alignment: Neutrality
Number Encountered: 1d10
Challenge Level/XP: 2/30

Fossilized skeletons are normally found only in underground caverns or complexes that have been left undisturbed for millennia, although they might also be found in inter-dimensional pockets, or in areas where the fossilization has been deliberately induced. In some limestone caverns where the mineralized water is in constant contact with the bones, skeletons might also fossilize relatively quickly – over the course of a hundred years rather than a thousand. Older fossilized skeletons may show pre-human features; fossilized Neanderthal skeletons are not uncommon. Since fossilized skeletons are effectively made of rock rather than bone, they are harder to hit and harder to kill than normal skeletons.

— Author: Matt Finch

Fossil Skeleton: HD 2; AC 6[13]; Atk 1 weapon or strike (1d8); Move 9; Save 16; AL N; CL/XP 2/30; Special: None.

Limestone Lizards

A network of limestone caves exist deep beneath the snake city of Uroborus in the humid depths of the Seething Jungle. Ancient ruins fill these deep tunnels, but the buildings lie crushed beneath boulders of stone amid tons of dirt. PCs must break through limestone stalagmites and thin walls of porous stone to make their way through these twisting corridors. Carvings of snakes, lizardmen and other reptiles cover the exposed buildings and walls.

The caves contain the remains of the first creatures to call the Seething Jungle their home. The native lizardmen died during a natural disaster that collapsed their tunnel homes into the ground around them. The lizardmen's broken bodies merged with the flowing limestone to create **18 skeleton fossils** trapped in the walls. The thin, crusty rock is easy to break, however, and the lizardmen fossils burst outward in a shower of stone to get at those disturbing their rest.

Skullmural

Hit Dice: 3
Armor Class: 6 [13]
Attacks: 1 strike (1d6)
Saving Throw: 16
Special: Drains fluids
Move: 3
Alignment: Neutrality
Number Encountered: 1
Challenge Level/XP: 3/60

The Skullmural appears to be a horrifying skull-like design carved into a wall. It is in fact a bizarre amoeboid creature, suffused with dark mystical power. It may seep slowly along walls, ceilings, and other surfaces, positioning itself for attack, which can cause adventurers to think they have made a mistake in mapping. If anyone touches the skullmural, the creature gains a free attack, at +4 to hit. The skullmural attacks by fastening tiny protoplasmic hooks and suckers into flesh to drink the victim's blood and other juices. Once attached, it drains 1d6 hit points per round and does not stop until killed or driven off with flame, alcohol, or melted butter. If blood is poured out near a skullmural, it will occupy itself with the blood rather than attacking humans. A sated skullmural changes to a reddish colour and bloats slightly, seeping back to its original position.

— *Author: Scott Wylie Roberts, "Myrystyr"*

Skullmural: HD 3; AC 6[13]; Atk 1 strike (1d6); Move 3; Save 16; AL N; CL/XP 3/60; Special: Drains fluids.

Blood Diamonds

This dead-end ossuary is accessed via a long passage filled with bones shoved haphazardly into narrow wall niches. Skulls cover the 15-foot-high walls from floor to ceiling, each staring outward at PCs interrupting their rest. Blood flows from holes in the ceiling and down the walls in a crimson wave that washes over the bones and skulls. The skulls are stained red from the deluge, and congealed blood drips from their jaws. A metal container in the center of the room has a stone lid with the word "Rest" carved into it. The lid weighs about 100 pounds. Inside the stone box are 6 blood-red diamonds worth 200 gp each.

The diamonds are the source of the blood flowing down the wall. Removing them causes the flow of blood to decrease. Returning the diamonds causes the blood flow to increase. If all of the diamonds are removed, the blood stops flowing and the walls move as **4 skullmurals** look for a new food source. The creatures attack any creatures in the room.

Skunk, Giant

Hit Dice: 4
Armor Class: 7 [12]
Attacks: 1 bite (1d6)
Saving Throw: 13
Special: Sprays musk
Move: 9
Alignment: Neutrality
Number Encountered: 1d3
Challenge Level/XP: 5/240

Giant skunks spray a horrible-smelling musk at anyone attacking them, and it is so much more powerful than the musk of normal-sized skunks as to actually be corrosive. The cloud of spray fills a cone 20ft wide at the point, 60ft long, and 60ft wide at the end. Any cloth or unprotected paper in this area dissolves. Leather items have a 20% chance of dissolving. Living creatures are overcome by nausea for 1d6 turns (saving throw), and may also be blinded for 3d6 turns (a second saving throw). The stench remains forever until 1d6 days of washing are completed (washing with tomato juice succeeds on the first or second try, though).

Giant Skunk: HD 4; AC 7[12]; Atk 1 bite (1d6); Move 9; Save 13; AL N; CL/XP 5/240; Special: Sprays musk.

Spray Tan

A partially dissolved suit of leather armor lies outside a three-foot-tall opening that leads into a badger den in the rolling Iron Shale Hills. The grass around the den is dead and yellowed, and a horrible odor hangs over the entire area. A **giant skunk** recently chased off the badger that lived in the den. The skunk also got rid of an exterminator sent to deal with the badger. The skunk's spray melted the man's armor off his body. The skunk charges out of the den to face PCs. Its diet of berries and pumpkins turned its spray a deep orange. The animal's spray stains anyone hit by it a dull orange for 1d4+3 days. Bathing in lemon juice can remove the orange stain and smell.

Sky Worm

Hit Dice: 3+1
Armor Class: 6 [13]
Attacks: 1 bite (1d6) and 1 tail lash (1d4)
Saving Throw: 14
Special: Fly, protect rider
Move: 6/18 (flying)
Alignment: Neutrality
Number Encountered: 1d6
Challenge Level/XP: 4/120

Sky worms, or "worms of the sky," are spiny worms ten feet long, with bat wings sprouting from behind a monstrous head. They are generally dark purple-grey in colour, with red eyes; some have segmented bodies, while others are more rubbery. The sky worm's head is a nightmare catfish-like thing, with long feelers and a gaping maw. Native to distant, cloud-wrapped mountain peaks, sky worms can be captured and trained to serve as aerial mounts.

A worm of the sky may bite for 1d6 damage, and lash with its tail for 1d4 damage. The tail lash is capable of dismounting an enemy rider. Trained worms of the sky can roll in mid-flight to tail-lash a mounted opponent or block their riders from arrows. They are also trained to dive after and catch a falling rider. Trained sky worms develop an empathic bond with their riders, gaining a vicious +2 bonus on attack and damage rolls if the bonded rider is slain or incapacitated. In the wild, they "dance" in thunderstorms.

— Author: Scott Wylie Roberts, "Myrystyr"

Sky Worm: HD 3+1; AC 6 [13]; Atk 1 bite (1d6) and 1 tail lash (1d4); Move 6 (Fly 18); Save 14; AL N; CL/XP 4/120; Special: Fly, protect rider.

Bait and Switch

Coils of chain lie haphazardly across the rocky hillside. One end of the 200-foot-long chain is attached to a large spike driven deeply into the ground. The other end of the chain goes over a drop-off that plunges 30 feet to the angry waves of the Reaping Sea.

A **sky worm** is hooked onto a large metal hook at the end of the chain. The flying worm struggles against the chain holding it to the hillside. It can fly upward in a 400-foot-diameter circle, but cannot escape the chain. The worm usually hunts sea birds flying below the cliff. An inebriated titan looking for the perfect bait to catch a whale placed the hooks here and covered the prongs with chunks of chicken to attract one of the flying sky worms that frequent the area. He was too drunk to remember that the worm could fly. The sky worm soars upward and attacks anyone disturbing the chain.

Skyger

Hit Dice: 9
Armor Class: 4 [15]
Attacks: 2 claws (1d8), 1 bite (2d6+1) and 1 tail (2d6)
Saving Throw: 6
Special: Tail sweep
Move: 6/24 (flying)
Alignment: Neutrality
Number Encountered: 1d2
Challenge Level/XP: 10/1,400

Skygers are furred, serpentine creatures with the head and forepaws of a tiger, fifty feet in length. They fly without visible means of locomotion, slithering through the air like giant snakes. These vicious and indiscriminate predators primarily hunt elephants, small dragons, and rocs; nevertheless, they will swoop to attack any other creatures that look large enough to offer a decent meal, a category that includes humans if the skyger is particularly hungry or in an unusually bad mood.

The attack of a skyger is terrifying to behold. Horses and other normal mounts will bolt as soon as they see the skyger descending. In addition to its claws and bite, the skyger can sweep up to three separate opponents with its long tail (using the same die roll for the three attacks) provided that they are within 10ft of each other.

Skygers can swim at a rate of 120ft and hold their breath for long periods of time; however, most skygers would rather die than be submerged.

— Author: Matt Finch

Skyger: HD 9; AC 4[15]; Atk 2 claws (1d8), 1 bite (2d6+1) and 1 tail (2d6); Move 6 (Fly 24); Save 6; AL N; CL/XP 10/1400; Special: Tail sweep.

Jungle Sacrifice

A terrified elephant struggles against stout ropes holding it in place in this jungle clearing. It trumpets in terror, but the ropes hold it fast. The elephant is a sacrifice offered by a jungle tribe of lizardmen. The lizards fear a monstrous **skyger** that occasionally snatches the lizardmen from the Sunning Rocks where they relax to absorb the morning light. The lizardmen learned that feeding the flying behemoth an elephant twice a month sates its hunger. The skyger arrives within 1d4 rounds. It swoops down from the sky to snatch the elephant off the ground. Anyone in the clearing makes a nice appetizer as the skyger swoops back for another bite to eat.

Slitherat

Hit Dice: 4
Armor Class: 5 [14]
Attacks: 1 bite (1d6+1)
Saving Throw: 13
Special: Slide through crystal, +1 to hit
Move: 12/9 (burrow)/24 (burrow through crystal)
Alignment: Neutrality
Number Encountered: 2d6
Challenge Level/XP: 4/120

Slitherats are a bizarre variant of the giant rat, sometimes found in places with heavy crystalline mineral deposits. These rodents have a long (4ft) snakelike body covered in fur, with four almost vestigial legs on each side. The long body tapers into a ratlike tail at the end, adding another foot to the creature's overall length. The head, although large, is clearly that of a giant rat; but the long front teeth glitter, for they are made of thin, sharp diamond. Because the teeth are so hard and sharp, slitherats attack with a +1 bonus to hit, and inflict 1d6+1 damage. These strange creatures use their teeth to dig through earth and solid rock when they encounter such obstacles, but they pass through crystal as if it were not even present, leaving no trace of their passage. The diamond teeth from a single slitherat are worth 250gp.

Slitherats: HD 4; AC 5[14]; Atk 1 bite (1d6+1); Move 12 (Burrow 9, through crystal 24); Save 13; AL N; CL/XP 4/120; Special: Slide through crystal, +1 to hit.

Crystal Caverns

Giant crystal shards grow randomly throughout this cavernous chamber. Most of the shards are 100 feet long and nearly 40 feet in diameter, but larger and smaller varieties exist. The crystals grow in a multitude of colors, from deep reds to glowing blues and serpentine greens. Three of the largest crystals are nearly a quarter mile long and hundreds of feet in diameter. These shards are rife with tunnels that wind through their facets. Living inside one of the biggest crystals is a colony of **24 slitherats** that are constantly gnawing new passages and nests within the shards. The rats swarm out to attack anyone disturbing their lair. The body of a dead dwarven cleric lies in the largest shard colony. The cleric still holds a *+1 mace* in its hands.

Slithering Tracker

Hit Dice: 4
Armor Class: 5 [14]
Attacks: No normal attack
Saving Throw: 13
Special: Transparent, paralysis, drain fluids
Move: 12
Alignment: Neutrality
Number Encountered: 1
Challenge Level/XP: 6/400

Perhaps the most dangerous of wandering monsters. Slithering trackers are a form of transparent slug, possibly related to gelatinous cubes. They are difficult to see (10% chance for a person to spot it, and he may lose sight of it again in the next round). Unless they are starving, they do not attack moving prey (5% chance to be starving). Instead, they follow the potential prey until it sleeps or camps. They can ooze under doors and through fairly small cracks, so even a barricaded room with a closed door is probably not safe. When it attacks, the victim must make a saving throw or be paralyzed by the slitherer's secretions. A paralyzed victim will be sucked dry of all body fluids in 5 turns (50 minutes), losing 20% of hit points each 10 minutes.

Slithering Tracker: HD 4; AC 5[14]; Atk None; Move 12; Save 13; AL N; CL/XP 6/400; Special: Transparent, paralysis, drain fluids.

The Mummy's Cabin

The smell of dry rot seeps through the walls of this log cabin deep in the forest. The A-frame structure's peak rises nearly 30 feet in the air. The door is boarded up from the inside, and more boards are fastened across the ground-level windows. A cellar door is chained shut. The log-cabin's interior is decorated with stuffed animals such as grizzlies, elk, moose and deer mounted in natural poses. Large bass stuffed with sawdust hang on the walls. Dry rations fill a wooden cupboard. The cellar is mostly empty, although it looks like a party was held recently to celebrate a freshly killed boar. The animal's carcass sits in the middle of a bloody silver dinner platter on a wooden butcher-block table. The leftovers are dried out, but still fresh. Upstairs is a different story. The bodies of six hunters lie in their beds, their bodies wasted away to nothing but papery skin covering their brittle bones. They look like mummies tucked into their bedcovers.

The hunters brought back more than their fresh kill last night. As they made their way home with the boar, **6 slithering trackers** followed them to their cabin's door. The creatures waited until the men were asleep before moving into the unlocked cabin. The trackers killed all of the hunters in their sleep and now rest inside the empty bodies of the stuffed animals displayed in the main room. One camper escaped and was able to chain the doors shut and seal the doors to keep the creatures inside. He died after falling into a freezing stream and getting caught by a grizzly. The slithering trackers attack anyone sleeping in the cabin, or quietly follow PCs to their own campsite.

435

Sloorg (Midden Monster)

Hit Dice: 4
Armor Class: 5 [14]
Attacks: 1 touch (1d8)
Saving Throw: 13
Special: Minimum damage from weapons, immune to missiles, heals by enveloping objects, cause nausea, cause disease
Move: 6
Alignment: Neutrality
Number Encountered: 1
Challenge Level/XP: 6/400

Sloorgs are a form of animate filth. Lumpy brown and oozing constantly, with distended vaguely human-like features at one end, they seem to arise spontaneously from poorly maintained sewers and midden-heaps. Missiles are ineffective against them, adding mass to the body instead of damaging it, and any hand-held weapon striking it may be added to the body if the wielder fails a saving throw. The sloorg gains one hit point for each item accidentally added to it, often making a low rumbling sound like a mockery of laughter when it does so. The sloorg flows through semi-permeable barriers such as gratings, chairs, and hasty barricades, and might pause to spend a round adding the obstacle to its mass. Anyone within 20' must make a saving throw or suffer -2 to all dice rolls from nausea. Anyone coming into contact with it – whether attacking or attacked – must make a saving throw to avoid contracting a non-fatal but debilitating disease. Sloorg take 1d6 points of damage per level of the caster of a Purify Food and Drink, Cure Disease, Neutralise Poison, or Locate Object spell. All physical attacks against a sloorg cause minimum damage.

— Author: Scott Wylie Roberts, "Myrystyr"

Sloorg: HD 4; AC 5[14]; Atk 1 touch (1d8); Move 6; Save 13; AL N; CL/XP 6/400; Special: Minimum damage from weapons, immune to missiles, heals by enveloping objects, cause nausea, cause disease.

Wasting Away

The sewers beneath Bargarsport fill twice a day with seawater as the tide rolls in. When the tide is out, waste from the city above washes into the tunnels for the sea to remove later on. Sometimes, however, the filth catches in the high shafts and broken basements where the sea can't reach. One such tunnel is filled with waste and offal washed down from an aboveground slaughterhouse. The filth formed into a **sloorg** that roams the sewer tunnels. It resembles a wave of diseased mud. The wall of waste and other debris washes easily through the numerous sewer grates that stop adventurers lost in the tunnel. The sloorg knows the tunnels well, and avoids those that might lead it into the cleaner seawater. It tries to pin PCs between sealed portcullises where they can't escape it.

Slug, Giant

Hit Dice: 12
Armor Class: 8 [11]
Attacks: Bite (1d12) or acid
Saving Throw: 3
Special: Spit acid (6d6)
Move: 6
Alignment: Neutrality
Challenge Level/XP: 13/2,300

These tremendously large masses of slimy, rubbery flesh are completely immune to blunt weapons. In addition to their powerful bite,
giant slugs can spit their acidic saliva at one target at a time. The base range for spitting is 60 feet, and within this range the slug's spittle will be 50% likely to hit (no other to-hit roll required). For every additional 10 feet of range, the chance to hit decreases by 10%. On its first spitting attack, the slug only has a 10% chance to hit within 60 feet, and no chance of hitting beyond that range. Some giant slugs might have more or less virulent acidity, thus changing the damage inflicted.

Giant Slug: HD 12; AC 8[11]; Atk 1 bite (1d12) or acid; Move 6; Save 3; AL N; CL/XP 13/2300; Special: Spit acid (6d6).

Sluggish Motivation

A 50-foot-diameter wooden wheel spins slowly on a giant framework holding it aloft in the middle of the Koft Badlands. Massive redwood tree trunks support the rotating structure. Anyone getting close to the wheel hears loud screams of terror coming from within the sealed wooden structure. The wheel is attached to a pulley system that lifts a series of wooden buckets out of a massive sinkhole nearby. Tree trunks are driven into the side of the pit, forming a ladder that descends into the deep earth. The wooden buckets rise out of the pit and dump piles of rock and dirt into a sifter situated over the pit. The sifter works back and forth to separate the dirt and rock. Sitting in the sifter are 16 uncut rubies worth 2,300 gp total.

A cunning group of **4 fire giants** built the wheel to help them mine the depths much easier. To power the wheel, the giants abduct desert nomads and dump them into the enclosed wheel through a small locked door. Currently 20 nomads run inside the wheel. To keep them moving (and to motivate them so they don't stop), the giants also placed a giant slug in the wheel behind the people.

The slug now chases the people around the wheel, its bulk slowly turning the device. If the wheel stops, the slug catches and devours the people inside within 1d4+1 rounds. An outer hatch can be pried open to help the nomads escape, although it also grants the slug its freedom. The giants climb back to the surface within 2d4 rounds to find out what happened to the wheel and to replace the escapees if necessary. PCs are suitable replacements in the giants' eyes.

Fire Giant: HD 11+3; AC 3[16]; Atk 1 weapon (5d6); Move 12; Save 4; AL C; CL/XP 12/2000; Special: Hurl boulders, immune to fire.

Snake

	VIPER	COBRA	PYTHON
Hit Dice:	1d6 hit points	1	2
Armor Class:	5 [14]	5 [14]	6 [13]
Attacks:	1 bite (1hp + poison)	1 bite (1hp + poison)	1 constrict (1d3)
Saving Throw:	18	17	16
Special:	Lethal poison (+2 save)	Lethal poison	Constriction
Move:	18	16	12
Alignment:	Neutrality	Neutrality	Neutrality
Number Encountered:	1d6	1d2	1
Challenge Level/XP:	2/30	3/60	2/30

Normal snakes are not particularly dangerous, with these exceptions. Vipers are highly poisonous, and about a foot or two in length. Their poison is lethal, but the saving throw is at a bonus of +2. Cobras are about four to six feet long, and their poison is lethal with a normal saving throw. Constrictors are not poisonous, but if they hit, they do automatic damage from constriction thereafter. Anacondas and giant pythons are considered "giant" constrictor snakes (q.v.).

Viper: HD 1d6hp; AC 5[14]; Atk 1 bite (1hp + poison); Move 18; Save 18; AL N; CL/XP 2/30; Special: Lethal poison (+2 save).

Cobra: HD 1; AC 5[14]; Atk 1 bite (1hp + poison); Move 16; Save 17; AL N; CL/XP 3/60; Special: Lethal poison.

Python: HD 2; AC 6[13]; Atk 1 constriction (1d3); Move 12; Save 16; AL N; CL/XP 2/30; Special: Constriction.

The Hissing Flute

A silver pan flute sits on the windowsill of the Graymalkin Inn & Tavern. The flute (20 gp) appears to have been left absentmindedly by someone. No one currently in the inn claims it if asked, and some even avert their eyes from the instrument. Playing the flute produces a hissing, sibilant sound no matter how skilled the performer.

The flute is cursed so that whoever blows it attracts snakes of all kinds. The snakes arrive angry and attack the person playing the silver flute. The instrument belongs to the barkeep who died three days ago from the bite of a venomous cobra that popped out of a vat of pickled herrings. The town was overrun by the snakes for months as the barkeep fended off the reptiles, but the cobra was finally too was able to get to the diligent barkeep. The villagers hope the PCs take the flute and leave town, ending the curse they are suffering by association. The villagers left the instrument on the windowsill where the barkeep dropped it when he died. No one was willing to pick up the instrument and suffer the curse themselves.

Snake, Javelin

Hit Dice: 1
Armor Class: 7 [12]
Attacks: 1 impale (1d6)
Saving Throw: 17
Special: Attack as 4HD creature
Move: 6
Alignment: Neutrality
Number Encountered: 2d4
Challenge Level/XP: 2/30

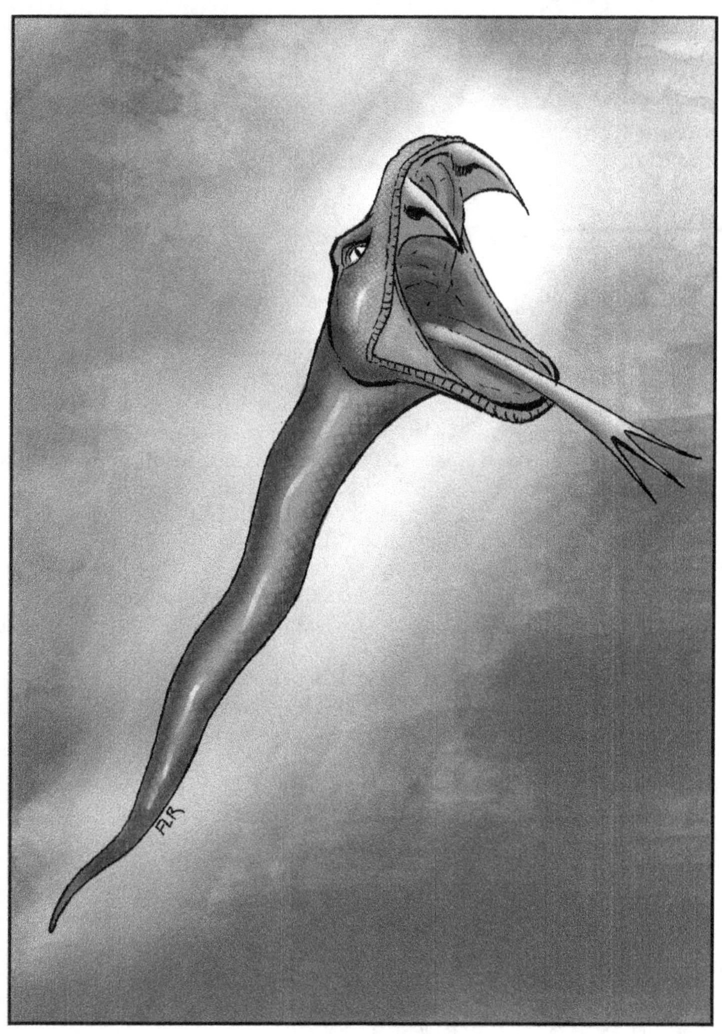

These snakes can be found anywhere that they may obtain a position where they can fall upon their intended victims. They strike as if they were javelins thrown by a 4HD creature, and the points of their heads are very sharp. These snakes are very fond of wine and will go out of their way to obtain some, thus wine merchants are often the targets of their attacks. One of their most distinguishing features is their three-pronged tongue.

— Author: Sean "Stonegiant" Stone

Javelin Snake: HD 1; AC 7[12]; Atk 1 impale (1d6); Move 6; Save 17; AL N; CL/XP 2/30; Special: Attack as 4HD creature.

Wine and Screams

Nearly 100 wine casks sit on their sides in wooden cradles inside this long underground chamber. The chamber is cool and keeps the barrels chilled. Wooden oak beams crisscross the ceiling 40 feet overhead. A few of the casks have taps driven into them. Wooden cups hang by their handles on ivory wall hooks.

The rafters are crawling with **20 javelin snakes**. The snakes are harmless unless a wine cask tap is opened to get a drink. The snakes launch themselves off the rafters at those drinking the intoxicating wine.

Snake, Giant

	GIANT VIPER	GIANT CONSTRICTOR	AMPHISBAENA	GIANT SPITTING
Hit Dice:	4	6	5	4
Armor Class:	5 [14]	5 [14]	5 [14]	5 [14]
Attacks:	1 bite (1d3 + poison)	1 bite (1d3)	1 bite (1d3 + poison)	1 bite (1d3 + poison)
Saving Throw:	13	11	12	11
Special:	Lethal poison	Constriction	Lethal poison	Spit or bite with lethal poison
Move:	12	10	10	13
Alignment:	Neutrality	Neutrality	Neutrality	Neutrality
Number Encountered:	1d4	d4	1d4	1d4
Challenge Level/XP:	6/400	7/600	7/600	6/400

This entry covers four kinds of giant snakes: giant vipers/cobras, giant constrictor snakes, the amphisbaena (which has a head at each end, and the giant spitting snake (similar to the spitting cobra). Giant vipers and cobras are about ten feet long, giant constrictors are twenty to thirty feet long, amphisbaena (two headed snakes) are about seven feet long, and giant spitting snakes are about ten feet long (these are identical to regular giant poisonous snakes, with the exception of the poison spit). The constrictors do automatic constriction damage after hitting, and may also manage to pinion an arm or leg (1 in 6 chance). The spitting snakes have a range of 40ft, aiming at one target with the poison. There are aquatic versions of each of these (except the spitting snake); aquatic varieties swim at 1.5 times the speed noted for land movement.

Giant Viper (or Cobra): HD 4; AC 5[14]; Atk 1 bite (1d3 + poison); Move 12; Save 13; AL N; CL/XP 6/400; Special: Lethal poison.

Giant Constrictor: HD 6; AC 5[14]; Atk 1 bite (1d3), 1 constrict (2d4); Move 10; Save 11; AL N; CL/XP 7/600; Special: Constrict.

Amphisbaena: HD 5; AC 5[14]; Atk 2 bite (1d3 + poison); Move 10; Save 12; AL N; CL/XP 7/600; Special: Lethal Poison.

Giant Spitting Snake: HD 4; AC 5[14]; Atk 1 bite (1d3 + poison) or spit poison; Move 13; Save 11; AL N; CL/XP 6/400; Special: Spit or bite with lethal poison.

Spiked Idol

A golden spike with grooves crushed into its sides rises 60 feet into the gloom within a 30-foot-deep pit inside the jungle city of Uroborus. The snake-like ophidians worship a 30-foot-long giant constrictor that likes to wrap itself around the spike to bask in the sunlight. The snake's head and front half are above ground level, while the majority of its body is still belowground. The constrictor squeezed indentations in the spike over the years, so that it actually appears to be part of the gold metal spike. It sits in the indentations, allowing its body to easy hug the spike. The snake unwinds itself from the spike to attack anyone disturbing it or the ophidians who routinely feed it sacrifices of jungle natives.

Sorcerer Ox

Hit Dice: 4+2
Armor Class: 7 [12]
Attacks: 1 fist (1d6) or weapon (1d8+2)
Saving Throw: 13
Special: Spells as magic-user level 5, catch and destroy weapon (2/day), horoscope bonus (+2 on one roll), charm
Move: 12
Alignment: Law
Number Encountered: 1
Challenge Level/XP: 7/600

A Sorcerer Ox may at first glance be mistaken for a Minotaur. It is a member of a race of humanoid oxen, gifted with magical abilities, clad in an embroidered silken robe, taller than humans, and bearing long curving horns capped with tassels. The clothing and jewellery of a sorcerer ox is worth 200-500 GP, and each has a 25% chance of possessing a minor magical item usable by magic-users. The great size and strength of a sorcerer ox grants it a +2 damage bonus when wielding weapons (usually an ornate staff). All sorcerer oxen have the spell abilities of a magic-user of level 5 (more powerful ones exist as well), and prefer spells with an elemental theme (metal, flame, wind, water, and wood). Twice per day they may catch a weapon aimed at them and cause it to rot or rust away within seconds. Each morning they consult their horoscopes for favourable signs, and so once per day may add a +2 bonus to any one dice roll. However, if they neglect to observe their chosen taboo (not drinking alcoholic beverages, for example, or making an offering of incense to nature spirits) they suffer a -2 penalty to all dice rolls relating to their spells on that day. Lastly, anyone who speaks with a sorcerer ox for more than 1 turn will act as if under a Charm Person spell, although the good-natured sorcerer ox will be loath to exploit this effect of their eloquence and trustworthiness unless in dire circumstances. Having the strength and stamina of an ox, a sorcerer ox is willing to undertake hard work if he should fall upon hard times, and one of them can easily perform the work of three manual laborers.

— Author: Scott Wylie Roberts, "Myrystyr"

Sorcerer Ox: HD 4+2; AC 7[12]; Atk 1 fist (1d6) or weapon (1d8+2); Move 12; Save 13; AL L; CL/XP 7/600; Special: Spells as magic-user level 5, catch and destroy weapon (2/day), horoscope bonus (+2 on one roll), charm.

Minotaur: HD 6+4; AC 6[13]; Atk Head butt (2d4), 1 bite (1d3) and 1 weapon (1d8); Move 12; Save 11; AL C; CL/XP 6/400; Special: Never get lost in labyrinths.

Bull-Headed Ruler

A staff with a carved bull's head atop it is driven into the paving stones in the center of the small village of Callots Mill. Necklaces hang from a small crossbar beneath the bull's head. Most of the necklaces are worthless, but a few are made with real jewels (75 gp worth). The residents of the small timber-cutting community ignore the staff, giving it a wide berth as they go about their daily routines.

The staff belongs to the **sorcerer ox Jantullus Maxilcilus**. The strange creature strode into town nearly a week ago and declared himself the protector of the poor people of Callots Mill. His bodyguards, **3 minotaurs** with bronze-tipped horns, backed up his declaration.

The sorcerer ox now claims the town's feast hall as his own, and the minotaurs use side rooms as barracks. Jantullus hears cases brought before him, and serves as judge and jury on disputes between neighbors. His minotaur minions serve as executioners, although they accept and expect bribes from the condemned to let them escape. Any who come before Jantullus (whether they win or lose their case) are expected to hang a jeweled necklace on the staff to pay for the "privilege" of being judged. The residents of Callots Mill desperately want to be rid of the greedy sorcerer ox, but all fear what the creature might do to those who stand against him.

Sorcery Leech

Hit Dice: 1 hit point
Armor Class: 9 [10]
Attacks: negligible (0)
Saving Throw: 18
Special: Arcane siphoning
Move: 1
Alignment: Neutrality
Number Encountered: 1d6
Challenge Level/XP: 1/15

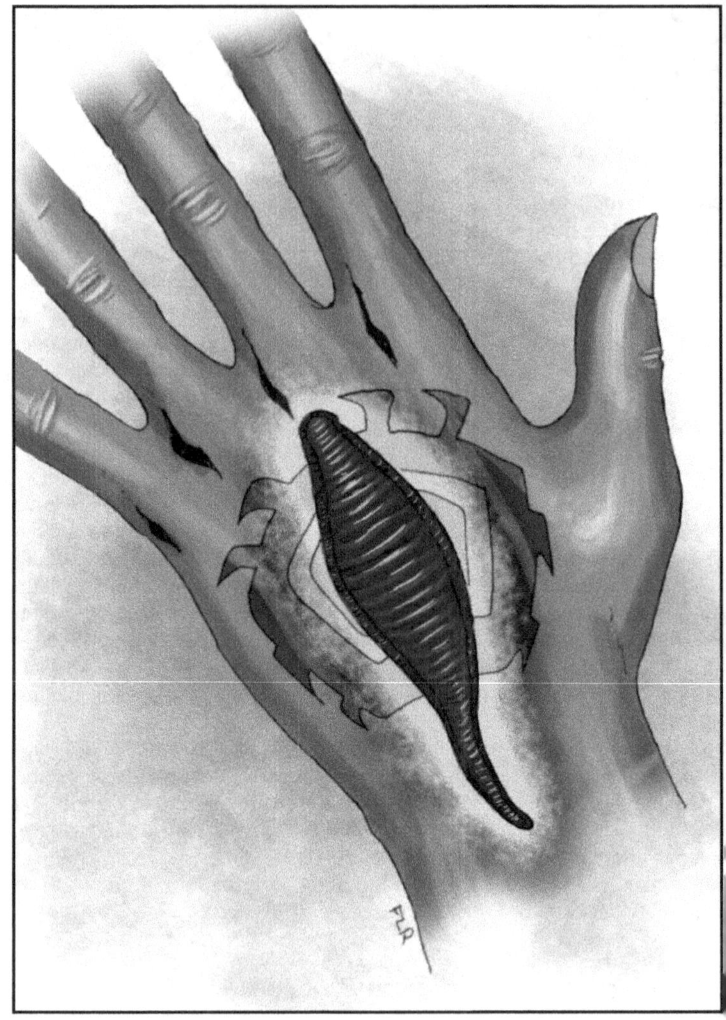

Sorcery Leeches resemble, well…leeches. These tiny critters are often used by Wizards and Mages to subtly deplete an arcane foe's magical arsenal. If a Sorcery Leech attaches itself to someone, it will slowly siphon off the spells pressed into the magic-user's mind. For each round a sorcery leech remains attached to a magic-user, it may deplete 1 level worth of memorized spell (a sorcery leech attached for 3 rounds may siphon a 3rd level spell). The damage inflicted by the leech's siphoning is so negligible that the wizard is usually unaware that something is amiss until he attempts to cast a siphoned spell.

— Author: Skathros

Sorcery Leeches: HD 1 hp; AC 9[10]; Atk negligible (0); Move 1; Save 18; AL N; CL/XP 1/15; Special: Arcane Siphoning.

The Way the Magic Died

A pointed red and green velvet wizard's hat sits on a fake wooden head on a four-foot-tall broom-like stand in front of a full-length silver mirror. The hat has a jaunty, gold-colored brim that wraps around it. The wooden head has a large gash slashed deeply across its face.

A sorcery leech recently laid eggs inside the hat's folded brim. If anyone places the hat on his head, the person's body heat causes 1d4+1 eggs to hatch within 1d6 days. The **sorcery leeches** crawl down the hat and onto the wearer's head, where they attach themselves to draw off spells.

Soulspinner

Hit Dice: 4
Armor Class: 5 [14]
Attacks: 1 bite (1d6 + temporary loss of level)
Saving Throw: 13
Special: Enervating webs, incorporeal, only hit by magic or silver weapons, enervating bite
Move: 12
Alignment: Chaos
Number Encountered: 1d8
Challenge Level/XP: 7/600

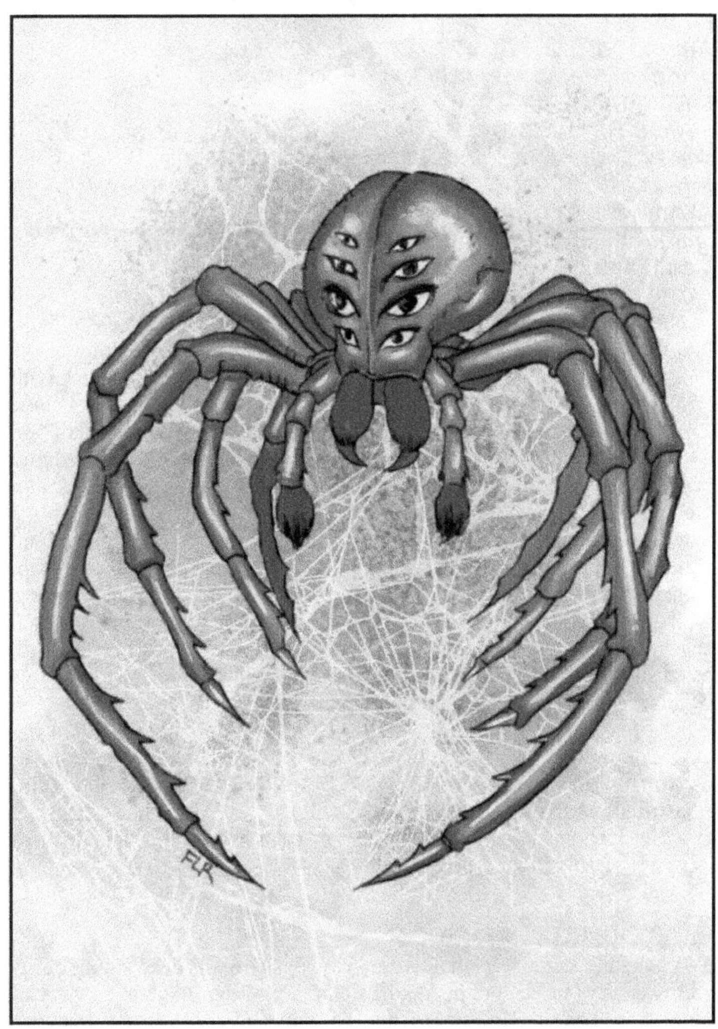

These spirit-creatures inhabit ghostly planes of existence, but often hunt in the material planes - often making their lairs in dark or desolate places. They resemble spiders, but their eight eyes are human rather than insectoid. They are insubstantial, and can only be hit by magical or silver weapons; they are affected normally by spells. The soulspinner spins an incorporeal web, and can shoot these out as a cone 50ft in length and to a width at the end of the cone of 50ft. Anyone entering these webs (which are visible but ghostly) must make a saving throw or become enervated, operating as if at one level of experience lower than normal. Clerical spells cannot be cast through the webs, although magic-user spells operate normally for a webbed character. The webs adhere to anyone entering the webs, but their effects wear off after 1d6 hours. If a soulspinner bites a victim, the victim must make a saving throw or be affected in the same way as if caught in the webs (and the temporary loss of levels is cumulative if a victim is both webbed and bitten). Anyone killed by a soulspinner, if raised from the dead, will have a chaotic alignment unless or until some additional magical remedy is provided, such as remove curse.

Soulspinner: HD 4; AC 5[14]; Atk 1 bite (1d6 + temporary loss of level); Move 12; Save 13; AL C; CL/XP 7/600; Special: Enervating webs, incorporeal, only hit by magic or silver weapons, enervating bite.

The Web of Souls

Silk curtains flutter along a death chute sloping downward beneath the abandoned Kilvyn Gorge Sanitarium. The chute slopes downward at a 20-degree angle. The bodies of those who died in the vile place during a mad wizard's "treatments" were pulled down the slope to a cave opening overlooking Kilvyn chasm. Hired death clerics unceremoniously tossed the bodies into the gorge for wildlife and the flowing river to dispose of. Bloody smears stain the death chute's stone ramp, and the spirits of the dead still wander the halls. These ghostly manifestations are nothing more than memories bound here by the misery they suffered. The ghosts pass through PCs as if they were not there, going about their miserable existence.

The haunted tunnel is now home to a **soulspinner** drawn to the miasma of death and despair gathered about the empty sanitarium. The spirit creature inhabits the death chute, living in the stifling darkness. It spins its webs throughout the tunnel, but seeing them amid the gauzy silk curtains and the pressing darkness requires a successful saving throw. The end of the cave opening is covered in a web to catch anything sliding down the steep chute. The corpse of a halfling thief dangles over the chasm, his rotting leather armor one broken strap from falling off his remains. A pouch dangling from his decaying wrist contains 45 gp, a *+1 ring of protection* and a small knife for paring apples.

Spectral Scavenger

Hit Dice: 8
Armor Class: 2 [17]
Attacks: 1 magic sword (1d8 + bonus)
Saving Throw: 8
Special: Undead immunities, regeneration, lightning bolt, skeletal hands, magical weapon to hit
Move: 12
Alignment: Chaos
Number Encountered: 1
Challenge Level/XP: 11/1,700

The spectral scavenger is an undead creature appears as a dark, billowing, wraith-like creature, with a skull for a head and bony claws for hands. It can attack with its bony claws, but will generally attack with any magical weapons it has, or with its spell-like powers noted below. These creatures can use any magical sword to hurl a Lightning Bolt of 5d6 strength, up to thrice per day. A spectral scavenger can also cause bony hands to erupt from the ground, (twice per day) completely restraining 1d3 targets (range 40ft, saving throw negates). Being of a wraithlike nature, these monsters cannot be damaged by weapons of a non-magical nature. They regenerate at the rate of 2 hit points per round, except from damage caused by holy water, fire, acid, or spells. If one slays an opponent with a magical sword, it additionally regenerates 1d8 hp in that round. A spectral scavenger will possess 1d3 magic items; the first will be a sword. Magical armour will not be possessed, and nor will potions. Any scrolls or wands will be used freely, and rings are especially prized.

— *Author: Scott Wylie Roberts, "Myrystyr"*

Spectral Scavenger: HD 8; AC 2[17]; Atk 1 magic sword (1d8 + bonus); Move 12; Save 8; AL C; CL/XP 11/1700; Special: Undead immunities, regeneration, lightning bolt, skeletal hands, magical weapon to hit.

The Spectre's Blade

A kneeling statue with massive angel wings bows its head and holds its palms upward to visitors inside the Reliquary of the Ancients, a vault of black stone beneath Umbreth Abbey. The statue cries black tears that drip down her tortured marble face. In the angel's upraised palms is a gleaming long sword. A leather scabbard sits alongside the blade. If the sword is removed, the angel's tears cease.

The weapon is a *+2 long sword* that belonged to a deadly **spectral scavenger**. When the spectre was killed years ago, the blade was brought to the abbey to cleanse the weapon. Monks of Muir placed the sword in the statue's hands so their goddess could personally bless the weapon. The sword resisted, however, but eventually the goddesses' will made inroads in redeeming the black blade. The tears the angel cries are drops of concentrated evil sucked straight out of the weapon. If left in the statue's care, the weapon is completely free of evil within five years.

If removed, however, the sword could prove deadly to any PC wielding it. The sword works fine against any living foe, but fighting a member of the undead unlocks the spectral spirit trapped in the blade. Every undead killed by the blade further empowers the spectral scavenger. When the blade kills at least 30 HD total of undead, the **spectral scavenger** reforms and rises to reclaim its weapon.

Spectre

Hit Dice: 6
Armor Class: 2 [17]
Attacks: Spectral weapon or touch (1d8 + level drain)
Saving Throw: 11
Special: Level drain (2 levels) with hit
Move: 15/30 (flying)
Alignment: Chaos
Number Encountered: 1d6
Challenge Level/XP: 9/1,100

Spectres are wraith-like undead creatures without corporeal bodies. When a spectre hits an opponent, with either hand or weapon, the touch drains two levels from the victim. Only magical weapons can damage a spectre. In some cases, these terrifying creatures may be mounted upon living beasts, if the beasts have been trained to tolerate proximity to the undead. Any being killed (or drained below level 0) by a spectre becomes a spectre as well, a pitiful thrall to its creator.

Spectre: HD 6; AC 2[17]; Atk 1 spectral weapon or touch (1d8 + level drain); Move 15 (Fly 30); Save 11; AL C; CL/ XP 9/1100; Special: Drain 2 levels with hit, immune to non-magical weapons.

Death Drum

A large drum sits in the center of this dungeon chamber. Various mallets and drumsticks sit on small shelves around the stone walls. Some drumsticks are made of polished ivory, while others are crudely carved from bone or wood. At least 30 pairs of drumsticks can be found. A few small mallets with leather straps on their handles hang from rusted wall hooks. A gold set of sticks are suspended by fine lines running from the ceiling.

The drum summons spirits if the correct drumsticks are used. The GM is left to decide which pair of drumsticks raises the spirit of a named individual once the drum is played. The spirit speaks the answers to three questions as if a *Speak with the Dead* spell had been cast. If the wrong drumsticks or mallets are used, a **spectre** rises from the drum to attack those offending the dead.

Spectre, Parasitic

Hit Dice: 7
Armor Class: 2 [17]
Attacks: 1 strike (1d8 + possession)
Saving Throw: 9
Special: Possession (saving throw negates)
Move: 15/30 (flying)
Alignment: Chaos
Number Encountered: 1d3
Challenge Level/XP: 9/1,100

Parasitic spectres are like normal spectres, in that they are undead creatures lacking corporeal bodies. Tortured by their insubstantial existence, they hunger to obtain corporeal bodies by possessing humanoid creatures. Possessed creatures are under the total control of the spectre, although they are somehow unable to cause direct harm to themselves. The victim of a parasitic sprectre may (at the player's option) make a new saving throw each round to expel the spectre; success deals 1d8 hit points of damage both to the victim and to the spectre, and expels the spectre. If a possessed creature is slain, the corpse will instantly transform into an undead creature, having abilities identical to those of a wight. If such a "wight" is destroyed, the spectre is expelled, taking 2d8 hit points of damage in the process. Non-magical weapons cannot harm a parasitic spectre. Note that parasitic spectres can possess corpses as well as living beings, and transform them immediately into wight-form, but they cannot possess corpses that have been dead more than a few minutes.

— Author: Random

Parasitic Spectre: HD 7, AC 2 [17], Atk 1 strike (1d8 + possession), Move 15 (Fly 30), Save 9; AL C; CL/XP 9/1100, Special: Possession (saving throw negates).

Wight Knights

Four armored man stride from the depths of this ice cave, long swords raised menacingly before them. Their skin is pale and sunken, but their glowing eyes are filled with malice. Each knight charges PCs, screaming incoherently. The men are all that remain of Lord Mirstol's famed Knights of Insight.

The armored protectors discovered a strange field of heated brass urns inside a cave in the icy Wailing Glacier. They ran afoul of a host of parasitic specters drawn out of the containers by their body heat. The men returned as **4 wights**, still dressed in their once-immaculate armor. Inside the cave, 20 brass urns sit in holes bored into an icy expanse. The tops of 10 of the urns remain sealed, but the knights removed the rest. The open urns contain flecks of glowing green dust.

Each sealed urn still contains a single **parasitic spectre** trapped long ago by clerics of Voard. The ice cave was sealed until a quake reopened it for the knights to discover. The knights opened one urn, releasing a single parasitic spectre that infected their quartermaster. The infection spread rapidly until all of the knights had been possessed. If opened, the parasitic spectres attempt to possess PCs and force them to open the rest of the urns. What happened to the missing 6 wight knights is up to the GM.

Sphinx, Andro-

Hit Dice: 12
Armor Class: 0 [19]
Attacks: 2 claws (2d6)
Saving Throw: 3
Special: Spells, roar
Move: 18/24 (flying)
Alignment: Law
Number Encountered: 1
Challenge Level/XP: 15/2,900

The noble androsphinx has the bearded head of a man, the body of a lion, and the wings of an eagle. The roar of an androsphinx (3/day) is mythic: the first roar causes Fear within 400ft (saving throw), the second roar causes paralysis (saving throw) for 1d4 rounds within 300ft, and the third roar causes the loss of 2d6 points of strength (saving throw), within 200ft,with strength points recovered at a rate of 1 per round. Creatures within 20ft of the third roar must also make a saving throw or be stunned for 2d6 rounds.

Androsphinxes are spell casters, casting clerical spells (2/2/1/1). A common spell list is: level 1: cure light wounds x2; level 2: hold person; level 3: remove curse (or, cure disease).

Androsphinx: HD 12; AC 0[19]; Atk 2 claws (2d6); Move 18 (Fly 24); Save 3; AL L; CL/XP 15/2900; Special: Spells, roar.

The Convocation of Sphinxes

The Convocation of Sphinxes is a once in a lifetime (at least for the sphinxes) gathering of the various elders. The gathering meets in the Desal Vale amid the ruins of a forgotten civilization that only the sphinxes remember. The ruins bear engravings showing men bowing to the wisdom of the sphinxes and receiving the blessings of the gods.

The convocation is convened by the androsphinx Ama-Nemead, but this gathering is fated for disaster unless the Thebian Enigma, a circular puzzle bearing the words of the ancient sphinxes, is recovered. A thief stole the relic after the last convocation (nearly 300 years ago) and divided the relic into four pieces that have since made their way around the world. The golden elements of the Enigma now rest in various locales where the sphinxes cannot retrieve them.

Each sphinx elder brings knowledge of the whereabouts of one piece of the relic, but the convocation requires aid recovering the relics. PCs who accomplish the deed gain the respect of the sphinxes, a promise of aid in times of need, and a king's ransom in gold and jewels.

THE ANDROSPHINX ELDER: The Enigma's central golden ring is worn as a nose ring by an undead lich minotaur who holds court in the Hellhorn Tower.

THE CRIOSPHINX ELDER: One hemisphere of the Enigma's golden globe is lost in the Nest City of Aarock, where rocs fly in deadly formations and the birhaakamen rule with iron claws in towering nest-bastions where men are kept in silver cages as pets.

THE GYNOSPHINX ELDER: The second hemisphere is a golden orb welded to the body of a massive retriever walking the under tunnels. Rumors say the retriever carries a dark elf temple on its broad metal back.

THE HIERACOSPHINX ELDER: The Enigma's outer ring, which is carved with the words of the ancients, is used as a bracelet by the wife of the storm giant **King Jorgas Shunurtilas**. The golden circlet never leaves the queen's wrist and is said to speak to her of the deceit of man.

Any PCs who undertake the deadly trials of the sphinxes is assured a place among legends. Any who seek to betray the convocation face the wrath of the deadly creatures and their sphinx brethren.

Sphinx, Crio-

Hit Dice: 10
Armor Class: 2 [17]
Attacks: 2 claws (1d8), head butt (2d6)
Saving Throw: 5
Special: None
Move: 18/24 (flying)
Alignment: Neutrality
Number Encountered: 1
Challenge Level/XP: 11/1,700

The criosphinx has the head of a ram, the body of a lion, and the wings of an eagle. This variety of sphinx is neutral with regard to human affairs, and they have a tendency to create impromptu toll-roads and other such obstacles.

Criosphinx: HD 10; AC 2[17]; Atk 2 claws (1d8), head butt (2d6); Move 18 (Fly 24); Save 5; AL N; CL/XP 11/1700; Special: None.

Sphinx, Gyno-

Hit Dice: 8
Armor Class: 1 [18]
Attacks: 2 claws (1d8)
Saving Throw: 8
Special: Divination, dispel magic at 8th level (3/day)
Move: 18/24 (flying)
Alignment: Neutrality
Number Encountered: 1
Challenge Level/XP: 11/1,700

A gynosphinx has the head and upper torso of a woman, the body of a lion, and the wings of an eagle. The female human arms become lion legs by the point of the forearm. Gynosphinxes are probably smarter than other varieties of sphinx (enjoying riddles), but they are quite willing to consider humans as prey. The gynosphinx can cast dispel magic (at 8th level) three times per day. They also have considerable powers of divination, being able to answer most questions posed to them – but for a hefty price.

Gynosphinx: HD 8; AC 1[18]; Atk 2 claws (1d8); Move 18 (Fly 24); Save 8; AL N; CL/XP 11/1700; Special: Divination, Dispel Magic at 8th level (3/day).

Sphinx, Hieraco-

Hit Dice: 9
Armor Class: 3 [16]
Attacks: 2 claws (1d6+1), 1 bite (1d10)
Saving Throw: 7
Special: None
Move: 9/30 (flying)
Alignment: Chaos
Number Encountered: 1
Challenge Level/XP: 10/1,400

The hieracosphinx has the head and forelegs of a hawk, with the hindquarters of a lion. This variety of sphinx is decidedly malevolent, evil, and/or chaotic in temperament.

Hieracosphinx: HD 9; AC 3[16]; Atk 2 claws (1d6+1), 1 bite (1d10); Move 9 (Fly 30); Save 7; AL C; CL/XP 10/1400; Special: None.

Spider, Giant

SPIDER, GIANT (SMALLER)
Hit Dice: 1+1
Armor Class: 8 [11]
Attacks: Bite (1 hp) + poison
Saving Throw: 17
Special: Poison (+2 save or die)
Move: 9
Alignment: Neutrality
Number Encountered: 2d10
Challenge Level/XP: 3/60

Giant spiders are aggressive hunters. The smaller variety pounces on prey and does not spin webs.

Giant Spider (1ft diameter): HD 1+1; AC 8[11]; Atk 1 bite (1hp + poison); Move 9; Save 17; AL N; CL/XP 3/60; Special: lethal poison (+2 saving throw).

SPIDER, GIANT (MAN-SIZED, 4-FOOT DIAMETER)
Hit Dice: 2+2
Armor Class: 6 [13]
Attacks: Bite (1d6) + poison
Saving Throw: 16
Special: Poison (+1 save or die), surprise
Move: 18
Alignment: Neutrality unless intelligent (Chaos)
Number Encountered: 1d12
Challenge Level/XP: 5/240

Man-sized giant spiders surprise on a roll of 1–5 on a d6, being able to hide well in shadows. Most are not web-spinners.

Giant Spider (4ft diameter): HD 2+2; AC 6[13]; Atk 1 bite (1d6 + poison); Move 18; Save 16; AL N; CL/XP 5/240; Special: lethal poison, 5 in 6 chance to surprise prey.

SPIDER, GIANT (GREATER, 6-FOOT DIAMETER)
Hit Dice: 4+2
Armor Class: 4 [15]
Attacks: Bite (1d6+2) + poison
Saving Throw: 13
Special: Poison (save or die), webs
Move: 4
Alignment: Chaos
Number Encountered: 2d8
Challenge Level/XP: 7/600

The greater giant spiders are all web builders. Webs spun by giant spiders require a saving throw to avoid becoming stuck. Those who make a saving throw can fight in and move (5 ft per round) through the webs. The webs are flammable.

Giant Spider (6ft diameter): HD 4+2; AC 4[15]; Atk 1 bite (1d6+2 + poison); Move 4; Save 13; AL C; CL/XP 7/600; Special: lethal poison, webs.

Step Into My Parlor

Webs cover this grove of trees deep in the Kajaani Forest. The strands are so thick that they weigh the tree branches down. Gauzy sheets of webbing spread through the leaves, trapping birds and insects. Normal spiders move through the webs, scurrying for the smaller bugs, while **12 giant spiders** stalk the thick strands to get at larger meals. The webbing starts near the base of one tree to form a doorway of sorts that leads inside

the tent of webs.

The spiders' nest is the home of a nasty **annis** named Dreenis Mal. Spiders crawl about her giant frame, and she sits in a throne made from bones held together by spider webs. She is always found in the company of **2 giant phase spiders**, and can command the spiders of the nest to do her bidding. Dreenis wears a silver crown that is shaped like a spider. It allows her to communicate and control the arachnids. The crown grants this ability to any who wear it, but has a 20% chance per month of infesting their body with thousands of spiders that burst forth from their skin, doing 2d6 points of damage.

Annis: HD 8; AC 1[18]; Atk 2 claws (2d8), 1 bite (1d8); Move 12; Save 8; AL C; CL/XP 10/1400; Special: Hug and rend, polymorph, call mists.

Spider, Giant Invisible & Phase

SPIDER, GIANT, INVISIBLE
Hit Dice: 4+2
Armor Class: 4 [15]
Attacks: 1 bite (1d6 + 2 + poison)
Saving Throw: 13
Special: Slow-acting lethal poison, webs, invisibility
Move: 4
Alignment: Neutrality
Number Encountered: 1d8
Challenge Level/XP: 8/800

Giant invisible spiders are similar in most respects to the largest type of giant spider, but they are invisible and so are their webs. Their poison is slower-acting: if the victim fails a saving throw, the poison paralyzes for 3d6 rounds before the victim dies, and also turns the victim invisible. If the spider successfully paralyzes its prey, it will try to haul it up into its ceiling lair, waiting for any other dangerous adventurers to give up the search and leave.

— Author: Matt Finch

Giant Spider, Invisible (6ft diameter): HD 4+2; AC 4[15]; Atk 1 bite (1d6 + 2 + poison); Move 4; Save 13; AL N; CL/XP 8/800; Special: Slow-acting lethal poison, webs, invisibility.

SPIDER, PHASE
Hit Dice: 2+2
Armor Class: 6 [13]
Attacks: Bite (1d6) + poison
Saving Throw: 16
Special: Poison (+1 save or die), phase shifting
Move: 18
Alignment: Neutrality
Number Encountered: 1d4
Challenge Level/XP: 6/400

Phase spiders can shift out of phase with their surroundings (so they can be attacked only be ethereal creatures), only to come back into phase later for an attack.

Giant Phase Spider: HD 2+2; AC 6[13]; Atk 1 bite (1d6 + poison); Move 18; Save 16; AL N; CL/XP 6/400; Special: lethal poison (+1 save or die), dimension phasing.

Waldon Canary, male human (Thief 6): HD 6; HP 23; AC 4[15]; Atk 1 short sword (1d6+1); Move 9; Save 10; AL C; CL/XP 6/400; Equipment: +2 leather armor, +1 short sword, +1 ring of protection

Where's Waldon?

A flamboyant thief named Waldon Canary thrives in the mean streets of Bargarsport. He openly flaunts the law and even works against the thieves' guild that runs the town. The brazen Waldon steals from the rich, the poor, fellow thieves and even orphans. He is a sneak thief who wears striped white and red clothing that makes him extremely easy to spot. But so far, he's been impossible to catch. Local thieves following the man claim he just vanishes into thin air, even when being watched closely. They suspect the thief uses magic to pull off his capers and then escape.

Waldon is indeed a thief, and a good one, but he's got help in his vanishing act. Waldon was badly bitten by a nest of spiders as a child and is immune to spider venom. As an adult, he stole a small fortune and paid a druid handsomely for the secrets to controlling one of the larger breeds. When Waldon met his **giant invisible spider** Hugo, it was love at first sight. Sort of. Waldon spent years teaching Hugo, and now the pair are working together in Bargarsport's mean streets to make a little profit. Waldon steals items and then flees to where he knows Hugo waits. The thief simply runs into Hugo's webs, and the spider pulls the invisible man to safety. Anyone else caught in the webs meets the spider's venomous fangs.

Spider, Flagstone

Hit Dice: 1d4 hit points
Armor Class: 3 [16]
Attacks: 2 claws (1d2) and 1 bite (0hp + poison)
Saving Throw: 18
Special: Poisonous bite (+4 save or die), surprise on 1-3 on d6
Move: 15
Alignment: Neutrality
Number Encountered: 1d10
Challenge Level/XP: 1/15

This race of spiders has completely adapted to living in dungeon and dungeon-like environments. Its central body appears to be nothing more than a flagstone with 6 chitinous legs sprouting from the edges of either side. It has a mouth with fangs, two eyestalks, and two front legs ending with hook-like appendages. All of its legs can be retracted into the stone-like exoskeleton. The hooked front legs are used to pry flagstones loose, allowing the spider to hide as part of a stone floor, but they are also used for attack and defence. The flagstone spider's bite is poisonous (save at +4 or die). When waiting for prey, the spider is undistinguishable from other flagstones 90% of the time (with any adjustments the referee deems appropriate). If potential victims fail to notice them, they will attack with surprise 50% off the time (1-3 on d6). Some adventurers have reported entire hallways floored with these vermin.

— Author: Sean Stone

Flagstone Spider: HD 1d4 hp; AC 3[16]; Atk 2 claws (1d2) and 1 bite (0hp + poison); Move 15; Save 18; AL N; CL/XP 1/15; Special: Poisonous bite (+4 save or die), surprise on 1-3 on d6.

Put'Em in the Pit!

A flagstone corridor slopes down into darkness, running for nearly 300 feet. At its midway point is a 15-foot-deep concealed pit (1 in 6 chance to spot; dwarves 2 in 6). Anyone stepping on the pit must make a saving throw or be dumped into a 10-foot-by-10-foot room beneath the upper hallway. The pit resets and locks for 1d4+1 rounds after it is triggered. It can be forced open by breaking the trap's hinges.

The pit has a flagstone floor, although four of the stones are loose and are push atop other stones. Three mummified bodies lie on the floor. Each wears leather armor and a short sword lies nearby. The pit is home to **4 giant flagstone spiders** that kill anyone caught in the trap. The spiders pried out the flagstones and took their place. They attack anyone stepping on them as they look to escape the hole. The three bodies are fighters who discovered the pits and couldn't get out before the spiders got them.

Spiderweed

Hit Dice: 2
Armor Class: 7 [12]
Attacks: 2 thorn slashes (1d4 + sap)
Saving Throw: 16
Special: Sap
Move: 6
Alignment: Neutrality
Number Encountered: 1d8
Challenge Level/XP: 2/30

Spiderweed is an ambulatory plant that has adapted to mimic the appearance of giant spiders as a means of defense. A single spiderweed is usually about the size of a dog, although they can grow much larger in the wild. In conditions of poor light, such as in a dungeon or a dense forest, one will appear to be a giant spider. If it is attacked, spiderweed responds by lashing out with two of its thorny appendages. These cause 1d4 damage, and secrete a sticky, poisonous sap. This sap will stick to flesh and clothing, unless thoroughly washed off. It inflicts no damage, but causes a very painful rash for 4d4 hours that causes a penalty of -2 to all die rolls (saving throw negates). Goblins are immune to spiderweed rash.

— Author: Scott Wylie Roberts, "Myrystyr"

Spiderweed: HD 2; AC 7[12]; Atk 2 thorn slashes (1d4 + sap); Move 6; Save 16; AL N; CL/XP 2/30; Special: Sap.

Monkey See, Monkey Die

A struggling monkey lies bound tightly in green-and-yellow weeds on the floor of the Seething Jungle. Sticky sap coats the monkey's fur. Three other dead monkeys lie in the dense vegetation off the main trail. The weed-wrapped monkeys fight against the vines holding them, but are unable to escape. Spidery weeds hang down from the banyan trees about this small clearing.

The monkeys stumbled into a patch of spiderweed clinging to the tree branches. The weeds wrapped around the monkeys, causing the primates to fall heavily to the ground. There are **6 patches of spiderweed** still hanging from the trees, and **4 spiderweeds** on the ground (including the one wrapped around the struggling monkey). If the monkey is rescued, it has a 20% chance of staying with its protector if it is given food.

Spine Rat

Hit Dice: 1d4 hit points
Armor Class: 6 [13]
Attacks: 1 bite (1d3) or spine (1d3 + poison)
Saving Throw: 18
Special: Diseased spines
Move: 12
Alignment: Neutrality
Number Encountered: 4d6
Challenge Level/XP: A/5

Spine rats are as long as a human's arm, red-eyed, and covered in spiny overlapping scales; they appear to be the product of some sort of crossbreeding between rats and lizards. A ridge of spines along the back runs from neck to tail. Due to the muck and slime of their habitat, the ridge-spines of a spine rat are likely to be tainted with soiled material. Anyone jabbed by a spine must make a saving throw or contract a disease that leaves them bed-ridden and fevered for 3d6 days. The bite of a spine rat is not especially dangerous, and only leads to the risk of infection if the wound is not cleaned.

Rare varieties of spine rats are able to shake spines from their backs like tiny darts; and extremely rare large specimens may be able to walk in semi-bipedal fashion and craft crude tools and weapons.

— *Author: Scott Wylie Roberts, "Myrystyr"*

Spine Rat: HD 1d4hp; AC 6[13]; Atk 1 bite (1d3) or spine (1d3 + poison); Move 12; Save 18; AL N; CL/XP A/5; Special: Diseased spines.

You Dirty Rats

A pair of outhouses behind the Grinning Troll Tavern are connected to the inn via a wooden walkway obviously added to the tavern long after it was built. The hall is just six feet wide, and slopes 30 feet down the hill behind the tavern to where two outhouses stand. The hallway is open at the end nearest the outhouses, allowing the elements to get inside. The hallway's roof extends outward over the privies to block the worst of the elements, however. Both outhouses are the same inside and out.

The raised floor of the hallway add-on is a breeding ground for **30 spine rats**. The rats can't get into the tavern, since it is built on a stone foundation, but they are free to scurry beneath the wooden hallway and outhouses. The rain seeping into the poorly built hallway rotted the floorboards, so that anyone using the hallway must make a saving throw or step through a rotten board and onto a spine rat beneath the flooring. The spine rats swarm out of the hole and attack those disturbing their nest. The rats are covered with waste from the outhouses, and anyone struck by a spine must make a saving throw or contract a debilitating disease.

Spire Monkey

Hit Dice: 2
Armor Class: 7 [12]
Attacks: 3 claws (1d3)
Saving Throw: 16
Special: None
Move: 15
Alignment: Neutrality
Number Encountered: 3d6
Challenge Level/XP: 2/30

The Spire Monkey is a two-headed, six-armed monkey that lives on roofs (spires and minarets are preferred) and high in the treetops. In some tropical countries they are tolerated in cities as messengers of the gods, and roam temples with impunity. Omnivorous and foul-tempered, they race from rooftop to rooftop and steal food (and occasionally loose coins or trinkets) from the streets below. Spire monkeys attack by clawing, as well as by throwing rocks or other small objects (such as roof tiles), and can divide their attacks between two opponents. They can climb as fast as they can run, and leap from tree to tree or building to building.

— Author: Scott Wylie Roberts, "Myrystyr"

Spire Monkey: HD 2; AC 7[12]; Atk 3 claws (1d3); Move 15; Save 16; AL N; CL/XP 2/30; Special: None.

The Pickpockets' Melody

An elderly peddler shuffles slowly through the city streets. He holds a faded music box in his wrinkled hands and turns a crank on the side of the box. The musicbox plays a tinny melody that echoes through the streets and alleys. A mule pulls a cart of hay behind him, the animal plodding along slowly behind its master.

The man is Torgus Bright, a crafty (and actually quite young) thief who is particularly adept at makeup and controlling animals. Torgus makes a living by walking through various cities dressed as an old man, kindly accepting the charity people offer him. With him are **4 trained spire monkeys** that sleep in the cart his faithful mule pulls. The spire monkeys leap from the wagon as they approach cities and make their own way inside, then scamper along the rooftops looking for open windows. The monkeys toss trinkets they find into the hay-filled wagon as it moves slowly through the streets below them. When Torgus feels the time is right, he walks slowly out of the gates and the monkeys follow.

If PCs are staying in an inn with open shutters, they can expect a visit from the thieving spire monkeys whenever Torgus is in town. Any stolen belongings are taken to Torgus' home in a shaded valley outside Bargarsport where he trains the monkeys and other exotic animals.

Squid, Giant

Hit Dice: 6
Armor Class: 3 [16] (body shell), 7 [12] tentacles and front
Attacks: 10 tentacles (1d3)
Saving Throw: 11
Special: Jet, Ink, Constrict
Move: 9 (swimming)
Alignment: Neutrality
Number Encountered: 1
Challenge Level/XP: 9/1100

Giant squid are one of the more feared sort of sea monster; they can sink small vessels and occasionally try to pick prey off the decks even of large ships. These creatures are often mistaken for a true kraken, but they are not intelligent. After a giant squid hits with a tentacle, it does 1d6 points of damage per round, automatically, instead of the initial 1d3. Also, there is a 25% chance that the tentacle "hit" pinions one of the victim's limbs (roll randomly for left/right arms and legs to see which is immobilized). A giant squid can jet water out to achieve a movement rate of up to 27, and can also release a huge cloud of ink to obscure its location. If a giant squid wraps its tentacles around a ship, the ship will be crushed in 10 rounds, taking damage throughout that time.

Giant Squid: HD 6; AC 7[12] head and tentacles; 3[16] body; Atk 10 tentacles (1d3); Move 0 (Swim 9); Save 11; AL N; CL/XP 9/1,100; Special: Jet, ink, constrict.

It Came from the Deep

Ships sailing out of the port of Duresteen north of the Shallow Glades are finding themselves under attack from the deep. Three ships sank within the past week, and all of the sailors aboard were lost at sea. Broken bits of ships are occasionally spotted floating atop the waves, but rescuers never find any remains; sharks and other maritime dangers fee quickly on unfortunate sailors splashing in the water. A rare few of the biggest ships limped back to port, their hulls cracked, their masts split, but the ships somehow still afloat. The fearful sailors claimed the sea erupted around them as the ship began tearing itself apart. Sailors were smashed across the deck, but nothing was seen.

An experiment recently escaped from the undersea kingdom of Cnidaria and swims the deep waters as it searches for prey. A **giant squid** was made permanently invisible by the triton rulers who planned to use the sea beast as a weapon against the surface world. The sea monster strikes ships from below, wrapping its invisible tentacles tightly around their hulls. Despite its invisible nature, the creature is easy to spot from the damage it does and the explosion of water around the ship.

Squid, Giant Aerial

Hit Dice: 12
Armor Class: 7 [12] (head and tentacles); 3 [16] (body)
Attacks: 8 tentacles (1d8+1), 1 beak (5d4)
Saving Throw: 3
Special: Constrict
Move: 0/20 (flying)
Alignment: Neutrality
Number Encountered: 1d2
Challenge Level/XP: 16/3,200

Giant aerial squids are cousins of the normal giant squid, but their bodies are filled with lighter-than-air gases that allow them to float in the air. In general, they are found in mountains, where they pick mountain goats and goblins off the slopes as food. Giant aerial squid can grow up to 60ft in length. The squid's tentacles constrict for 1d8+1 points of damage after the first hit, and they are used to pull food to the sharp beak. When a tentacle hits, roll 1d6: 1= both arms pinned, 2= right arm pinned, 3= left arm pinned, 4-6= arms are not pinned. The tentacles can take 10hp of damage before being severed, but attacking tentacles does not affect the squid's actual hit point total – only attacks to the body and head affect the squid's true hit points. These creatures are not good mounts, for they have a tendency to reach back and eat their riders.

— Author: Matt Finch

Giant Aerial Squid: HD 12; AC 7[12] head and tentacles; 3[16] body; Atk 8 tentacles (1d8+1), 1 beak (5d4); Move 0 (Fly 20); Save 3; AL N; CL/XP 16/3200; Special: Constrict.

Goat Meat Surprise

The rocky crags of the Hollow Spire Mountains are a strange and deadly place, with monsters that roam the high peaks looking for prey. As the PCs climb along the high trails and through the rocky passes, a herd of mountain goats scampers past, the animals desperate to get away from something following close behind them. Some of the animals have weird sucker welts burned across their backs and flanks. A few limp, falling behind the scampering herd.

A **giant aerial squid** floats over the rocky crest of the ridge, its tentacles swinging wildly as it reaches for the delicious goats. PCs are the next best thing for the floating predator. A number of dead goats are still clutched in its swaying tentacles.

Stag, Giant

Hit Dice: 4
Armor Class: 7 [12]
Attacks: 2 antlers (2d6)
Saving Throw: 13
Special: None
Move: 20
Alignment: Neutrality
Number Encountered: 1d8
Challenge Level/XP: 4/120

The Pleistocene stag stands 8-9ft at the shoulder, and has antlers spreading 10ft across. Giant stags might also be magical rather than prehistoric, in which case they might be very intelligent or even have additional magical abilities. Such creatures, due to their intelligence, might be of any alignment.

Giant Stag: HD 4; AC 7[12]; Atk 2 antlers (2d6); Move 20; Save 13; AL N; CL/XP 4/120; Special: None.

Hunter and Prey

A portal of swirling colors opens above any fire burning in the southern edges of the Kajaani Forest. The portal expands until it is nearly 10 feet in diameter. The colors swirl together into a single point of bright light that expands rapidly outward to fill the circle. A **giant albino stag** leaps from the portal, landing with a crash in the brush around the campsite. One of the animal's legs is bent awkwardly and blood runs down the creature's flanks. The stag breathes heavily, its sides rising and falling. Sweat glistens across its body.

A wolf's howl rises from inside the glowing portal, and **2 demon-wolves of Braazz** leap through soon after in pursuit of their prey. The stag is incredibly intelligent, and can magically open glowing portals to cover miles of ground with a single bound. The stag grants this ability for three days to anyone who assists it against the demonic wolves.

Demon-wolf of Braazz: HD 5; AC 1[18; Atk 1 bite (1d10); Move 12; Save 12; AL C; CL/XP 8/800; Special: Blink, invisibility, charm, magic weapons to hit

Star-Mouthed Worm

Hit Dice: 10
Armor Class: 4 [15]
Attacks: 3 mouths (1d10)
Saving Throw: 5
Special: Swallow whole on 19 or 20
Move: 9
Alignment: Neutrality
Number Encountered: 1d3
Challenge Level/XP: 11/1,700

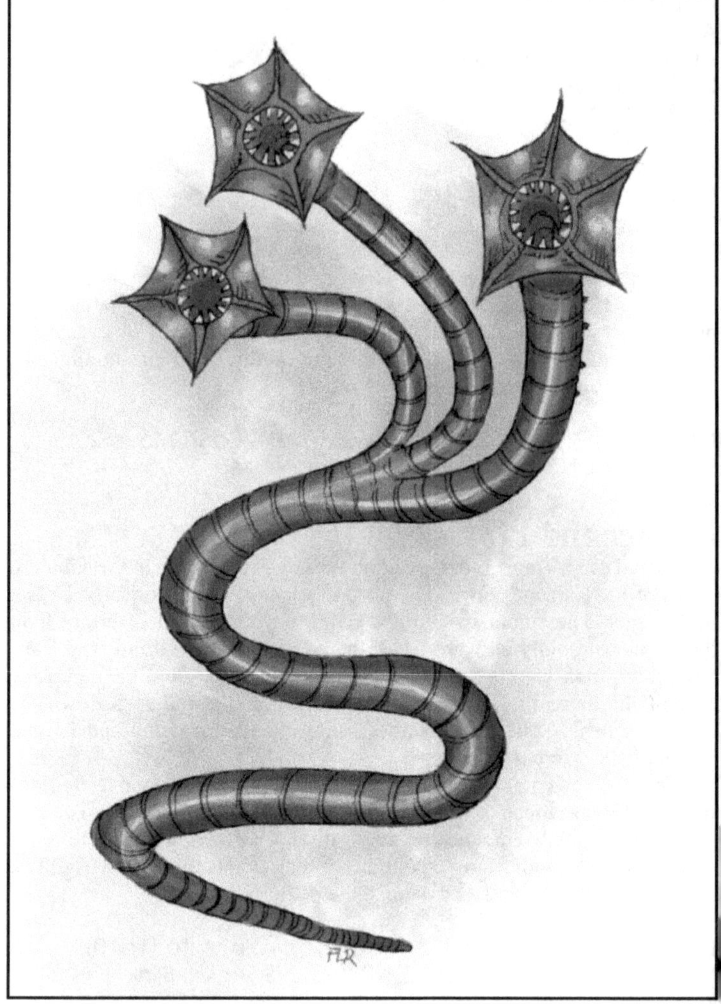

The star-mouthed worm is a horrendous creature 20ft in length, a massive segmented worm. The front of the worm's body trifurcates into three parts, each with a swallowing mouth surrounded by a membranous fan of skin. In combat, the worm bites with its mouths, the membranes around each mouth flailing and contracting to grab and pull prey inside. If the worm hits with a natural attack roll of 19 or 20, man-sized or smaller prey will be swallowed whole. Being swallowed whole inflicts an automatic 1d8 points of damage per round from digestive juices; one can, however, attack the worm from within, using a dagger-sized weapon against the worm's internal armor class of 9[10]. Star-mouthed worms cannot swallow more than two man-sized meals, and will generally seek to retreat peacefully once they have filled themselves. If they accidentally swallow a third person, they will choke and die in 1d4 rounds.

— Author: Matt Finch

Star-Mouthed Worm: HD 10; AC 4[15]; Atk 3 mouths (1d10); Move 9; Save 5; AL N; CL/XP 11/1700; Special: Swallow whole on 19 or 20.

It's Full of Stars

Star-shaped tunnels lead off from the points of a star-shaped room under Mims Observatory on a barren hill near the Colter Flats. The observatory is a round dome with a massive set of lenses focused through a glass window on the sky above. The dome turns slowly as it follows the stars across the sky. The observatory was built by a brilliant but star-obsessed magic-user named **Ferric Noccult**. The observatory still functions, although deciphering Ferric's shorthand for zooming in on particular stars takes years to understand. The tunnels beneath the observatory contain thousands of moving gears and pulleys that rotate the dome.

In the underground passages is a strange menagerie of dead animals. The dried body of a monkey with a star-shaped white patch on its fur lies in a glass cage. A desiccated bull with a white star on its forehead kneels inside a sturdy pen. Other dead animals have star markings on their bodies. The menagerie's star attraction, however, and Ferric's favorite beast before it ate him, is missing. The **star-mouthed worm** attacked its owner when the tipsy mage – celebrating a successful acquisition of star-shaped flowers – accidentally left the creature's cage open. The worm now roams freely through the tunnels as it looks for food. It ate the few animals it could get to, while the others starved in their glass pens.

Stirge

Hit Dice: 1+1
Armor Class: 7 [12]
Attacks: "Sting" (1d3 + blood drain)
Saving Throw: 17
Special: Drain blood 1d4/round,+2 bonus to hit
Move: 3/18 (when flying)
Alignment: Neutrality
Number Encountered: 3d10
Challenge Level/XP: 2/30

Resembling small, feathered, bat-winged anteaters, stirges have a proboscis which they jab into their prey to drain blood. After a stirge's first hit, it drains blood automatically at a rate of 1d4 hp per round.

Stirge: HD 1+1; AC 7[12]; Atk 1 proboscis (1d3); Move 3 (Fly 18); Save 17; AL N; CL/XP 2/30; Special: blood drain (1d4), +2 to hit bonus.

Best Bloods

The wizard Nanwar Dukelt never cared for his familiar, a hideous-looking **stirge** named Mung. The neglected stirge stuck by its master, however, occasionally draining the many servants who failed the wizard in his quest to find the Silver Tooth of Bodacki. Nanwar eventually found the relic, but the vampire servants of the tooth killed him.

Mung waited patiently for the hour when his master awoke as a **vampire**. The pair have a symbiotic relationship now, with Mung attaching himself freely to Nanwar's withered corpse. Holes from Mung's proboscis mar Nanwar's face, torso and arms. Most often, Mung hangs on Nanwar's back, drawing blood from the vampire as it feeds. At times, the stirge flaps free to attack juicy meals on its own. Mung knows where Nanwar's coffin is buried in an abandoned basement and returns there if Nanwar is defeated to await the vampire's reawakening.

Vampire (7HD): HD 7; AC 2[17]; Atk 1 bite (1d10 + level drain); Move 12 (Fly 18); Save 9; AL C; CL/XP 10/1400; Special: See description.

Stoneflower

Hit Dice: 3
Armor Class: 1 [18]
Attacks: 1d6 hurled stones (1d3)
Saving Throw: 14
Special: Magnetic, moves through stone
Move: 9
Alignment: Neutrality
Number Encountered: 1d6
Challenge Level/XP: 5/240

A stoneflower resembles a pile of rock about five feet in diameter, covered with exquisitely realized carved flowers. In actuality, these beasts are from some other dimension, or possibly the elemental plane of earth. The whole growth, including the rock, is a sentient predator that can morph through stone walls, flowing along quite rapidly as long as it is touching stone. They cannot cross water or wooden surfaces. The flowers of the growth are its weapons; they can eject rocks at very high speeds, causing 1d3 points of damage. In any combat round, the stoneflower can eject 1d6 such missiles. The growth is also extremely magnetic; any metal weapon touching the stoneflower will stick to it until the creature is killed (unless the wielder has a strength of 15+).

— *Author: Matt Finch*

Stoneflower: HD 3; AC 1[18]; Atk 1d6 hurled stones (1d3 each); Move 9; Save 14; AL N; CL/XP 5/240; Special: Magnetic, moves through stone.

Rock Garden

A five-foot-tall boulder sits in the middle of a 30-foot-diameter sandbox surrounded by white stone globes. Ripples crisscross the sand, creating strange patterns across the surface. A low wooden wall of pointed posts surrounds the sand and rock globes to keep the grit off the room's tiled floor. Colorful flowers bloom on the gray boulder. The bright petals are the only splash of color in the otherwise drab room. A gleaming sword leans against the rock. The point of the blade is stuck into the sand.

The boulder is a **stoneflower** that wanders back and forth across the sand pit to create patterns in the sand. The globes are magical wards to keep the creature contained in the circle. Removing the globes allows the stoneflower to eventually get close enough to the wooden posts to knock them down and escape. The weapon is a *+1 long sword* stuck to the rock by a strong adhesive. The sword moves with the rock, digging furrows behind the stone. The creature attacks anyone stepping into the sand or trying to get the sword.

Sumatran Rat-Ghoul

Hit Dice: 1d6 hit points
Armor Class: 6 [13]
Attacks: 1 bite (1d4)
Saving Throw: 18
Special: Paralytic bite (+2 save)
Move: 9
Alignment: Chaos
Number Encountered: 2d10
Challenge Level/XP: 1/15

These horrid undead creatures are not much larger than a giant rat; they resemble tiny humans but with twisted, feral features, grey skin, and no hair other than a line of rat-fur down their backs. They obviously have never been human; they are carrion eaters of the grave, an undead vermin whose horrid similarity to human beings is (one hopes) a twisted coincidence. Sumatran rat-ghouls travel with packs of giant rats, raiding graves and tombs for their abominable food. Their bite causes paralysis, much like that of a normal ghoul, but the effect lasts only 2d6 combat rounds (a saving throw will negate the effect, and the saving throw is made at +2). Like ghouls, they are immune to sleep spells.

— Author: Matt Finch

Sumatran rat-ghoul: HD 1d6hp; AC 6[13]; Atk 1 bite (1d4); Move 9; Save 18; AL C; CL/XP 1/15; Special: Paralytic bite (+2 save).

Thieves in the Night

Ancient graves ring the hill leading up to Poverty's Bethel, a small temple to Freya in the dying village of Fessel. Most of the gravesites are ancient, but a few of the newer graves appear to have been dug up. Clods of dark dirt and clumps of weeds are tossed out among the stones. The tracks of scavengers weave throughout the dirt. A shredded chicken lies on a weathered stone slab, and white puffs of loose feathers flutter across the grounds. The elderly **Almery Burgand**, a priest of Freya, often hears strange skittering noises at night, and fears going outside after the sun sets.

A pack of **20 Sumatran rat-ghouls** is ripping up graves to feast on the bodies of the dead. The rat-ghouls supplement their meals by killing chickens that run free throughout the village. The rat-ghouls come out at night, climbing out of holes that can be found throughout the graveyard. The rat-sized holes burrow deep into the hillside to the forgotten tomb of Akruel Rathamon. The rat-ghouls run through the tomb's circular halls during the day, tormenting the ghouls that live within the tomb.

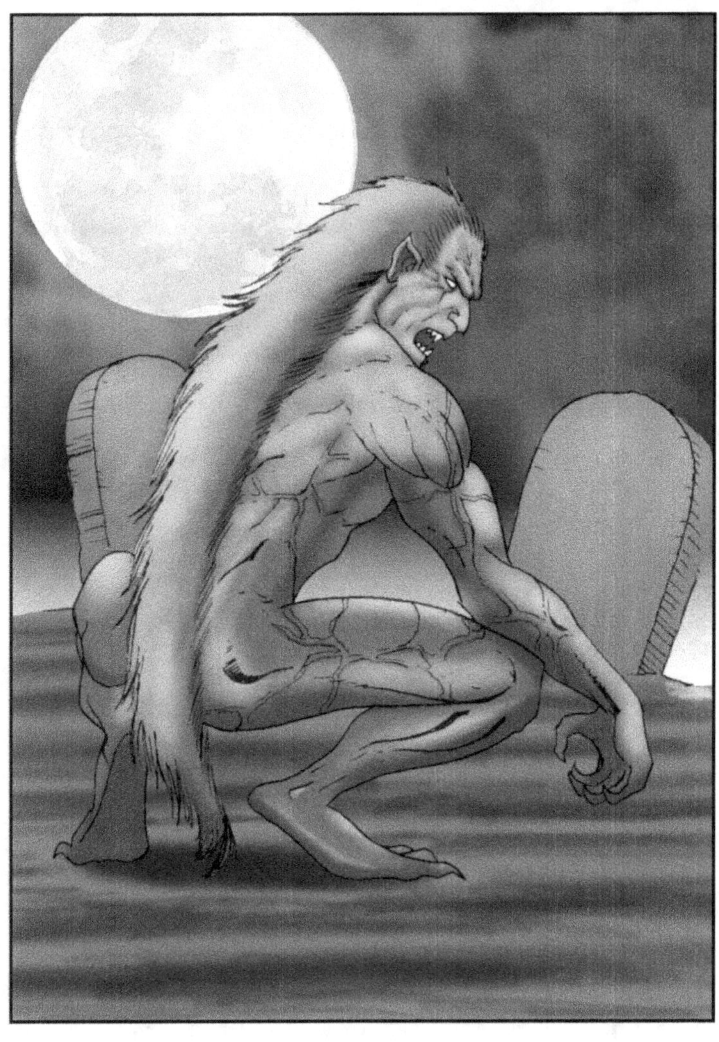

Syanngg

Hit Dice: 8+20hp
Armor Class: 2 [17]
Attacks: up to 6 bites (1d4)
Saving Throw: 7
Special: Slow, lightning bolt, dispel magic, petrify, paralysis, charm, 25% magic resistance
Move: 6
Alignment: Chaos
Number Encountered: 1
Challenge Level/XP: 14/2600

The syanngg is a radially-symmetrical creature a bit like a starfish, with six backbones running upward through its central body to form six serpentine necks above the body and six reptilian tentacles below. The bottom tentacles are connected by a circular fan of leathery skin that runs approximately halfway down the length of the tentacle, giving the creature a strangely cone-like shape. It has 6 heads, and can bring 1d4 heads to point toward any given 90-degree quarter around itself. Each head has a different type of magic that can be projected from its eyes, as follows:

1 — *slow* (range 40ft)
2 — *lightning bolt* (5d6 damage, range 60ft)
3 — *dispel magic* (level 12, range 40ft)
4 — *turn to stone* (range 30ft)
5 — *paralysis* (range 30ft, duration 3d6 turns)
6 — *charm* (range 20ft)

Syanngs are ferocious creatures, dedicated to accumulating power and treasure by whatever means they can contrive. They are quite intelligent, and it is not uncommon for a syanngg to be found as the tyrannical mastermind behind the activities of weaker minions. Their plans are not devilishly intricate, reflecting the single-minded brutality of the syanngg mindset, but they are usually well considered and practical. In particular, syanngs do not hesitate to risk themselves in battle, since they glory in victorious slaughter just as much as they lust after gold and power.

— Author: Matt Finch

Syanngg: HD 8+20; AC 2[17]; Atk up to 6 bites (1d4); Move 6; Save 7; AL C; CL/XP 14/2600; Special: Slow, lightning bolt, dispel magic, petrify, paralysis, charm, 25% magic resistance.

No Mercy

Rock benches rise up around a 200-foot-wide sand-filled pit inside this deep underground chamber. Bloodstains splatter across the cold sands, and skeletal remains rise out of the arena's patchy floor. This forsaken arena was once used by dark elves to prove their skills against men and monsters from the world above. The vicious dark elves killed all those who entered the pit with them. But finally, the games moved on, and the arena was left empty as the dark elves sought new vices and dangers.

But the empty stands and sand pit didn't remain empty for long. A **syanngg** moved into the pit, and now has a small lair in an underground stockade where fighters prepared for battle. The syanngg revels in combat. Anyone stepping onto the bloody sand is fair game for the aggressive starfish-shaped creature as it strides out of a tunnel in the side wall, ready for battle. The beast hasn't lost yet. It asks for no mercy and gives none in return.

Sycorex (Archæopteryx Potens)

Hit Dice: 5
Armor Class: 2 [17]
Attacks: 2 claws (1d4), 1 bite (2d8)
Saving Throw: 12
Special: Shriek
Move: 9/24 (flying)
Alignment: Neutrality
Number Encountered: 1d6
Challenge Level/XP: 6/400

The Sycorex is a quasi-prehistoric flying, feathered lizard, vast in size, which prefers warmer climates and is a voracious carnivore. Sycorex are only slightly smaller than Black Dragons, but they are not related to dragon-kind, having a long, straight beak with sharp teeth, and feathers rather than hard scales. They have an ear-piercing shriek that is typically heard as they enter a hawk-like dive from out of the sun, deafening their prey and relying on the sunlight to partially blind them as well. The shriek of a Sycorex functions as a Hold Person spell. It is rumored that men in far-off lands may have tamed the Sycorex, and ride them into battle. (Author: Michael Kotschi).

Sycorex: HD 5; AC 2[17]; Atk 2 claws (1d4), 1 bite (2d8); Move 9 (Fly 24); Save 12; AL N; CL/XP 6/400; Special: Shriek.

Treehouse of Terror

A sprawling, multi-room tree house sits high in the branches of a stout oak. The house has thatched roofs and a broad porch that wraps around the entire wooden structure. A railing wrapped with discoloured red ribbon keeps people on the porch from falling. A staircase wraps around the tree trunk as it rises up to the house's front door.

The tree house belonged to an eccentric diamond miner who built the structure to protect his family. He didn't realize that the forest was home to a number of giant birds and other opportunistic creatures looking for pre-built nests to claim. Currently, a monstrous **sycorex** nests inside the shattered home. The flying lizard ripped off part of the structure's roof, and now soars in and out through the gaping hole. It leaps from the roof and descends on anyone climbing up the staircase. It sweeps past, trying to knock them off the stairs. Anyone stunned by the creature's deafening shriek must make a saving throw or fall from the steps.

Tangle Weed / Strangle Vine

Hit Dice: 4
Armor Class: 6 [13]
Attacks: 4 vines (1d6)
Saving Throw: 13
Special: Strangulation
Move: 0
Alignment: Neutrality
Number Encountered: 1d3
Challenge Level/XP: 6/400

Tangle Weeds and Strangle Vines are essentially the same creature, the only difference being that the Tangle Weed attacks its victims from below, while the Strangle Vine attacks from above. In appearance, they resemble a mass of weeds or vines, their animate nature only becoming apparent during an attack.

On a successful attack, the animate plant has a 2 in 6 chance of entangling its foe, immobilizing its prey and slowly strangling the life out of him. Each round, the victim will suffer 1d6 points of damage due to the strangulation. A successful save is required to break free of the immobilizing, strangling grasp.

— *Author: Skathros*

Tangle Weed/Strangle Vine: HD 4; AC 6[13]; Atk 4 vines (1d6); Move 0; Save 13; AL N; CL/XP 6/400; Special: Strangulation.

Grapes of Wrath

Rows of oak trellises stand in Lord Arnsworth Du Vaine's fertile hillside garden, each wooden support wrapped in thick vines. Succulent grapes hang in clusters from the drooping vines. A narrow dirt path meanders through the garden, winding around and under the trellises. Sections of the path are covered by arched open-roof gazebos from which hanging vines dangle. The vineyard has seen better days, much like the manor house falling into disrepair on the hill above. Weeds are slowly choking all of the paths, and no one appears to be pruning the spreading vines.

One of the gazebo trellis' is home to **3 strangle vines**, while **4 tangle weeds** grow along the paths. The deadly vines attempt to grab passers-by and drag them into the grape vines to strangle and consume. The bones of the gardener lie under a patch of tomato plants. A rake lies near his body on the path.

Tatzelworm

Hit Dice: 1d6 hit points
Armor Class: 6 [13]
Attacks: 1 bite (1d3hp + lethal poison)
Saving Throw: 18
Special: Lethal poison, leap (+1 to hit), partial resistance to cold.
Move: 12
Alignment: Neutrality
Number Encountered: 1d10
Challenge Level/XP: 2/30

These curious creatures inhabit cold alpine peaks. In appearance, they look like silvery fat-bodied lizards lacking hind legs. They can move surprisingly fast, slithering on their stomachs, and can leap up to 10ft. They are notoriously aggressive and will not hesitate to attack larger creatures that intrude upon their territory. When leaping to the attack, they gain a +1 bonus to hit. The bite of a tatzelworm is deadly, and a victim must successfully save versus poison or die.

These cold-loving reptiles save at +1 against cold-based attacked, and such damage against them is reduced by 1 hit point per die. They save versus fire normally.

— *Author: John Turcotte*

Tatzelworm: HD 1d6hp; AC 6[13]; Atk 1 bite (1d3hp + lethal poison); Move 12; Save 18; AL N; CL/XP 2/30; Special: Lethal poison, leap (+1 to hit), partial resistance to cold.

Lost in the Snow

Deep snows surround a caravan of seven highly gaily painted wagons drawn into a circle on a frozen plateau overlooking a forest valley more than a mile down a steep cliff. One wagon has the words Donner Circus painted in flowing letters across its high wooden sides. Seven enormous elephants slump in the deepening snow. Each elephant stands in wooden yokes connecting them to the wagons. Snowdrifts rise to the bottom of each wagon. The elephants' massive legs are lost in the white powder. The wagons' doors and windows are shut tight against the cold, and fur and cloth are pushed through openings to keep the freezing mountain air out. The remains of a firepit sit in the center of the caravan, although the deepening snow has nearly wiped it away.

The caravan met an unfortunate end after the lead elephant crushed a tatzelworm hiding under a snowbank. When the caravan stopped for the night, **9 tatzelworms** attacked the elephants, killing all of the beasts by burrowing up into their bellies from beneath the snow piles. The men and women were left stranded — easy pickings for the aggressive reptiles. One tatzelworm hides beneath each wagon, while the remaining two feast on the undersides of two of the elephants. They attack anyone stopping to investigate the lost caravan.

Tendriculos

Hit Dice: 8
Armor Class: 4 [15]
Attacks: 2 tendrils (1d6), 1 bite (2d6)
Saving Throw: 8
Special: Swallow whole.
Move: 9
Alignment: Neutrality
Number Encountered: 1d2
Challenge Level/XP: 9/1,100

A tendriculos is a plant creature resembling a hillock or haystack, but it is a voracious predator that uses tendrils and a powerful bite to kill and digest prey. If the tendriculos hits with both tendrils, the victim must make a saving throw or be swallowed whole. Each round spent within the plant's body automatically inflicts 1d6 hit points of acid damage and necessitates a saving throw to avoid being paralyzed for 1d4+1 rounds.

Tendriculos: HD 8; AC 4[15]; Atk 2 tendrils (1d6), 1 bite (2d6); Move 9; Save 8; AL N; CL/XP 9/1100; Special: Swallow whole.

Hay Horror

This two-story wooden barn has seen better days. The tangled trees of the Kajaani Forest press tightly against its sides, probably the only thing keeping it standing. Warped slats buckle and split along its walls, and its oversized double doors hang askew, leaving the interior open to vermin and thieves. Hooks on the walls where farm tools once hung are empty. Nine stalls are empty but could be used to board horses for the night if needed. A rotting leather bridle lies on the dirty straw floor. Mice skitter noisily through the rotting hay. A creaky wooden ladder ascends 15 feet upward to a partial loft that overlooks the stalls. Twelve rolled hay bales sit in the loft, each broken apart and spilling molding straw across the wooden rafters.

One of the stacks is a **tendriculos** that hunts throughout the area by night. Anyone climbing into its loft is fair game for the creature's deadly tentacles and bite. Lying under one of the bales are the bodies of two young elf lovers killed by the monster. If the bones are discovered and not properly buried, the female rises in 2d4 days as a **banshee** that hunts down the PCs.

Banshee: HD 7; AC 0[19]; Atk 1 claw (1d8); Move (Fly 12); Save 9; AL C; CL/XP 11/1700; Special: Magic or silver to hit; magic resistance 49%; shriek of death; Immune to enchantments

Thugtoad

Hit Dice: 1
Armor Class: 6[13]
Attacks: 1 weapon (1d6)
Saving Throw: 17
Special: Camouflage, hop
Move: 4/15 (swimming)
Alignment: Chaos
Number Encountered: 3d6 or 1d100
Challenge Level/XP: 2/30

Thugtoads are bipedal toad-men, normally about 4ft tall, but with some growing as large as 6ft. Thugtoads can hop as far as 30ft to attack, adding +1 to hit and inflicting double damage when they do so. Because their skin color changes to match their surroundings, they have a 75% chance not to be noticed when waiting in ambush.

Thugtoad: HD 1; AC 6[13]; Atk 1 weapon (1d6); Move 4 (Swim 15); Save 17; AL C; CL/XP 2/30; Special: Camouflage, hop.

Frog Pond

The Anuran Cliffs are green nephrite jade overhangs containing numerous cave mouths rising up a steep bluff. A deep pool of algae-covered water sits at the base of the cliff. A waterfall steps down the rock face to splash into the pool of water at the base. Logs roll lazily in the current kicked up by the falling water. Eight jade sculptures of giant frogs sit at some of the cave entrances. Each statue has greenstone gems (50 gp) for eyes that sparkle in the sunlight. Thick banyan trees grow around the pool.

The caves are the homes of **10 thugtoads**. The thugtoads leap from their cliffs into the deep water below. They splash down in an explosion of water. Four of the creatures emerge immediately riding on **4 trained large giant frogs** that help defend the pond. The other thugtoads clamber out of the pool to attack.

Giant Frog (large): HD 3; AC 7[12]; Atk 1 bite (1d8); Move 3 (or 100ft leap); Save 14; AL N; CL/XP 4/120; Special: Leap, swallow whole.

Thylacine

Hit Dice: 2+1
Armor Class: 7 [12]
Attacks: 1 bite (1d6+1)
Saving Throw: 16
Special: None
Move: 12
Alignment: Neutrality
Number Encountered: 2d4
Challenge Level/XP: 2/30

Commonly known as the "Lemurian Wolf" or "Ekaru," Thylacines are carnivorous marsupials with a body somewhat like a wolf's, although they are not related to wolves or dogs. Thylacines are found in all climates, but prefer forested hills to open areas. Hunters have killed Thylacines that measured seven and a half feet from the tip of the nose to end of the tail. The thylacine's most dangerous attribute is a large powerful jaw that can be overextended for a disproportionately large bite. They hunt at night in groups similar to wolf packs. When agitated a Thylacine will rear up on its hind legs and secrete a musky odor before leaping on the intended victim. Though they have a poor sense of smell their eyesight is very sharp. Their keen intellect and pack hunting instincts see them employed as guards in certain nobles' or wizards' gardens.

— Author: Michael Kotschi

Thylacine: HD 2+1; AC 7[12]; Atk 1 bite (1d6+1); Move 12; Save 16; AL N; CL/XP 2/30; Special: None.

The Capistran Wolves

The royal hedgemaze of the Capistran family fills a mile-square wooded game preserve. Animals roam freely in through the nine-foot-tall hedges. The maze is filled with dead-ends and vine-covered tunnels. A redwood growing in the center of the maze has a winding staircase cut into its outer bark. A magnificent treehouse stands in the high branches and allows those getting to the center of the maze an amazing view of the whole preserve spread out below them. Comfortable divans inside the treehouse let people lounge in comfort and watch those below them lost in the hedge. Dress-up jewelry (real diamonds worth 400 gp) is kept in the treehouse, and crystal drinking glasses (120 gp total) sit on shelves. A magnificent spyglass (300 gp) lets people get a closer look at the garden's sculptures.

At night, **10 thylacine** are set loose to protect the garden and its treehouse treasures from intruders. The wolves hound people into dead-ends before converging on them.

Tick, Giant

Hit Dice: 3
Armor Class: 4 [15]
Attacks: Bite (1d4)
Saving Throw: 14
Special: Drains blood, disease
Move: 3
Alignment: Neutrality
Number Encountered: 3d4
Challenge Level/XP: 4/120

Giant ticks drain blood at a rate of 4 hit points per round after a successful hit. Their bite causes disease, which will kill the victim in 2d4 days. (*cure disease* spells will remove the infection.) A giant tick can be forced off a victim by fire or by simply killing it.

Giant Tick: HD 3; AC 4[15]; Atk 1 bite (1d4); Move 3; Save 14; AL N; CL/XP 4/120; Special: Drain blood, disease.

Yak Attack

A dozen dead yaks lie on their sides in the high grasses of the Gorst Steppes. The animals appear to have collapsed where they walked, falling face first into the thick sawgrass. A bloated reddish bag the size of a small calf lies in the middle of the yaks, its head buried in the neck of one of the bovines. The massive bloated **tick** can barely move and is easy to kill by simply puncturing its taut skin. It bursts in a shower of yak blood, splashing anyone in a 10 foot radius. Rooting for blood among the dead yaks are **6 giant ticks** that crawl out to attack. They go for anyone coated in the thick yak blood.

Tiger

Hit Dice: 6
Armor Class: 6 [13]
Attacks: 2 claws (1d4+1), 1 bite (1d8)
Saving Throw: 11
Special: Rear claws
Move: 15/6 (swimming)
Alignment: Neutrality
Number Encountered: 1d4
Challenge Level/XP: 7/600

If a tiger hits the same target with both fore claws, it can rake with its rear claws as well, gaining two more claw attacks. Yes, tigers swim, which can be a nasty surprise for fleeing adventurers.

Tiger: HD 6; AC 6[13]; Atk 2 claws (1d4+1), 1 bite (1d8); Move 15 (Swim 6); Save 11; AL N; CL/XP 7/600; Special: Rear claws.

Cat's Eye

A ziggurat of worn and broken stone rises through the choking tree canopy in the Seething Jungle. Stone steps rise along one side of the stair-step structure. Engravings of snakes curl down the sides of the massive temple, and carved squat skeletons hold up each of the six stairstep levels. A bloodstained slide drops from the very top of the pyramid alongside the stairs into a deep pit filled with thousands of brittle bones. The rib cages are split and broken on the many skeletons dumped into the pit. A three-foot-tall golden apatite gem (300 gp) stands in a golden frame atop the ziggurat. The gem looks down on the jungle spread around it like a giant cat's eye.

The ziggurat is home to 8 tigers that sleep inside chambers accessed via recessed doorways near the top of the temple. Sloping ramps lead into the stone rooms. The tigers drag kills back to their rooms to devour. The bodies of monkeys, jungle natives, and a gorilla lie inside the chambers.

Tiger, Sabre-Tooth

Hit Dice: 7
Armor Class: 6 [13]
Attacks: 2 claws (1d4+1), 1 bite (2d6)
Saving Throw: 10
Special: Rear claws
Move: 12/6 (swimming)
Alignment: Neutrality
Number Encountered: 1d2
Challenge Level/XP: 8/800

Sabre-tooth tigers are larger than normal tigers and have huge, curving, front fangs. Like normal tigers, if they hit with both fore claws, they can pull up to rake with their rear claws (2 additional attacks).

Sabre-tooth Tiger: HD 7; AC 6[13]; Atk 2 claws (1d4+1), 1 bite (2d6); Move 12 (Swim 6); Save 10; AL N; CL/XP 8/800; Special: Rear claws.

The Mountain Cabin

A small mountain shack in the frozen wastes invites frost-bitten travelers with a golden glow showing through the frozen shutters. The shack is built on raised platforms that lift it above the ice and drifting snow. Boards seal the crawlspace away from the drifting snow. An iron furnace in the middle of the shack is empty, but nevertheless generates a warming heat and soft glow that fills the room. Blankets cut from mammoth fur lie on wooden-plank beds set against the wall, and more of the blankets are scrunched into a pile in the corner. The doors of a cupboard are broken and shattered, and dried foodstuffs are scattered about the room. Bags of dried fruit are sliced apart. The beds, blankets and walls smell heavily of cat urine.

A **sabre-tooth tiger** recently claimed the cabin. It tore a hole in the planks beneath the cabin from the outside to sleep under the magical furnace. When it got hungry, the great cat broke through the floor and climbed into the cabin to ransack the shelves. It marked its territory, and then climbed back into the hole to curl up out of the cold. As it descended back under the hut, it dragged some of the blankets with it to sleep on. A few of the heavy hides got caught in the hole in the floor and block the opening. The tiger tears through the hide to get into the cabin if it hears PCs wandering about in its territory.

473

Titan

Hit Dice: 16 HD+1d6 HD
Armor Class: 2 [17] to –3 [22]
Attacks: Weapon (7d6)
Saving Throw: 3
Special: Spells
Move: 21
Alignment: Any
Challenge Level/XP: 17 HD (19/4,100), 18+ HD (Add 1 challenge level and 300 XP per additional HD over 17. Add 1 additional challenge level when the Armor Class CL -1[20])

Titans are mythological creatures, almost as powerful as gods. A titan has 2 Magic-User spells of each spell level from 1st-level spells to 7th-level spells, and 2 Cleric spells of each spell level from 1st to 7th. The Referee might choose to substitute other magical abilities for spells— these creatures vary considerably in powers and personalities from one to the next.

One possible spell list for a titan might include the following Magic-User and Cleric spells:

Magic-User: *Charm Person* (1), *Sleep* (1), *Invisibility* (2), *Mirror Image* (2), *Fireball* (3), *Fly* (3), *Polymorph Other* (4), *Confusion* (4), *Conjure Elemental* (5), Feeblemind (5), *Anti-magic Shell* (6), *Stone to Flesh* (6), *Limited Wish* (7), *Power Word Stun* (7).

Cleric: *Light* (1), *Protection From Evil* (1), *Hold Person* (2), *Speak with Animals* (2), *Cure Disease* (3), *Dispel Magic* (3), *Cure Serious Wounds* (4), *Neutralize Poison* (4), *Finger of Death* (5), *Quest* (5), *Blade Barrier* (6), *Word of Recall* (6), *Earthquake* (7), *Resurrection (Raise Dead Fully)* (7).

Titan (17HD): HD 17; AC 2[17]; Atk 1 weapon (7d6); Move 21; Save 3; AL Any; CL/XP 19/4100; Special: Spells.

Titan (18HD): HD 18; AC 1[18]; Atk 1 weapon (7d6); Move 21; Save 3; AL Any; CL/XP 20/4400; Special: Spells.

Titan (19HD): HD 19; AC 0[19]; Atk 1 weapon (7d6); Move 21; Save 3; AL Any; CL/XP 21/4700; Special: Spells.

Titan (20HD): HD 20; AC –1[20]; Atk 1 weapon (7d6); Move 21; Save 3; AL Any; CL/XP 23/5300; Special: Spells.

Titan (21HD): HD 21; AC –2[21]; Atk 1 weapon (7d6); Move 21; Save 3; AL Any; CL/XP 24/5600; Special: Spells.

Titan (22HD): HD 22; AC –3[22]; Atk 1 weapon (7d6); Move 21; Save 3; AL Any; CL/XP 25/5900; Special: Spells.

TITAN, CURSED
Hit Dice: 17 HD
Armor Class: 2 [17]
Attacks: Weapon (7d6)
Saving Throw: 3
Special: Magic resistance (50%), immune to non-magical weapons
Move: 21
Alignment: Chaos
Challenge Level/XP: 19/4,100

There are some acts so heinous and foul that the Gods – and fellow Titans themselves – may banish and curse one of the titans to an eternity of horrific toil. Now in a form no longer comely, but appalling and demonic, its powers twisted, these extremely rare creatures will be found forever attending to the geas placed upon them. In one case, such a titan was set as a guardian to slay the endless stream of creatures that emerged through a rift in space and time. Legends tell, too, of a cursed titan doomed to guard a treasure so coveted that all manner of beings would seek to take it…

A cursed titan does not have the controlled spellcasting ability of a normal titan; its magical powers are still very much in evidence, but in a wilder, more feral form. Each of these beings is highly unique, and their powers will vary.

Aura and Surroundings

The area around a cursed titan is dangerous to a radius of 10ft. The exact nature of the danger may be one of the following: (1) fire, (2) frost, (3) whirlwind, (4) attacking tentacles, (5) caustic air, (6) lightning. The damage from entering this area will generally be 3d6, with a saving throw allowed to take only half damage. Fire will burn flammable items, frost will paralyze anyone failing a saving throw, whirlwinds will throw people 30ft (saving throw allowed), tentacles will entangle people (saving throw allowed similar to a web spell), caustic air will cause additional 1d4 damage with no saving throw, and lightning will stun for 1d3 rounds and throw 20ft (saving throw allowed).

Bodily Powers

A cursed titan will have two of the following three additional abilities: bellow, persuade, or summon. Each of the titan's two abilities may be used only twice per day. Bellowing causes fear (saving throw allowed) to anyone in hearing. Persuasion causes paralysis as all victims within hearing drop all items and kowtow to the creature (saving throw allowed). Summoning brings 1d4 creatures of CL 5 to the cursed titan's assistance. These might include (1) 4HD ankhegs, (2) chalkeion hoplites, (3) formian warriors, (4) hell hounds, (5) jackals of darkness, (6) kurok-spirits, (7) owlbears, (8) wights.

Magical Powers

In addition to the above, a cursed titan will have one beneficial power and one malevolent power. The Benevolent powers are (1) Reincarnate, (2) Remove Curse/Neutralize Poison, (3) Flesh to Stone, (4) Restoration. Malevolent powers include (1) Stone to Flesh, (2) Earthquake, (3) Creeping Doom, (4) Finger of Death.

— Author: Erol Otus

Cursed Titan: HD 16; AC 2[17]; Atk 1 weapon (7d6); Move 21; Save 3; AL C; CL/XP 19/4100; Special: Magic resistance (50%), immune to non-magical weapons, special abilities.

The Titan's Curse

An angry bellow resounds through the towering oaks. Trees crash to the ground and the entire forest shakes under an assault. Birds and animals flee before the destruction. A number of the scared animals are various shades of green. Verdant bears lumber along, while jade and emerald birds soar through the branches.

An angry **titan** named Leoburn stomps through the trees, uprooting the massive trunks with his bare hands. His skin is a bright lime green caused by eating berries tainted by a magical curse. The berries also affected his mind, making him paranoid and hostile. He can be reasoned with, but anyone pointing out his skin condition (or worse still, laughing at the odd color) finds himself staring down one angry titan. Worse still, the color spreads automatically to any creature within 150 feet of the titan within 1d6 rounds (saving throw avoids). The color can be washed off by bathing in lemon juice. Anyone helping the titan remove the color wins his eternal gratitude, but finding enough juice is a challenge.

Toad, Giant

Hit Dice: 3
Armor Class: 6 [13]
Attacks: 1 bite (1d8)
Saving Throw: 14
Special: Hop
Move: 6 (hop 30ft)
Alignment: Neutrality
Number Encountered: 2d6
Challenge Level/XP: 3/60

Giant toads are about the size and weight of a human. They are predators, willing to attack creatures as large as men. Giant toads can attack at the end of a hop, which is in addition to the toad's normal move.

Giant Toad: HD 3; AC 6[13]; Atk 1 bite (1d8); Move 6 (Hop 30ft); Save 14; AL N; CL/XP 3/60; Special: Hop.

Catching Flies

A dead cow on the side of the road attracts fist-sized flies that buzz noisily around the carcass. Maggots squirm and writhe on the dead animal. The stench is horrible. Another dead cow floats in the water of a small stagnant pond just off the dirt path. A wooden fence surrounds the field around the dead animals. Each cows wears a silver bell (10 gp) on a frayed rope around its neck. Mosquitoes buzz in thick clouds over the water.

The pond is home to a **giant toad** that killed the cows and is feeding on the flies. It leaps from the water with a splash to get at creatures bothering its food supply.

Toad, Giant Horned

Hit Dice: 4+4
Armor Class: 4 [15]
Attacks: 1 bite (1d8)
Saving Throw: 13
Special: Squirt blood
Move: 6
Alignment: Neutrality
Challenge Level/XP: 5/240

These lizard-looking creatures are as large as wolves, and are armored with a thick, knobbly hide. The head of a giant horned toad is wedge-shaped, with short, thick horns protruding from the sides. Twice per day, these monsters can squirt a jet of blood from their eyes, directed at a single target within 50ft. The target must make a successful saving throw or take full damage from the caustic blood (4d6 hit points); a successful saving throw results in only half damage. Giant horned toads are normally found only in dry regions such as deserts or badlands.

— Author: Matt Finch

Giant Horned Toad: HD 4+4; AC 4[15]; Atk 1 bite (1d8); Move 6; Save 13; AL N; CL/XP 5/240; Special: Squirt blood.

Blood Brothers

Two elf corpses sit beside a partially buried boulder in the rock badlands. One of the elves is partially buried, while the other slumps face down on the red sand. The face of the corpse sitting against the boulder is gone, burned down to the bone. Blood stains the sand around the body, and his leather armor is soaked. The second corpse has a hole burned through its chest. A leather backpack lies near the bodies and contains a change of clothes, matching gold combs from their mother (30 gp each) and 75 gp (their spending money).

The brothers were traveling through the badlands seeking a lost relic known as the Fire Shroud of the Ancient Brethren. The boulder sitting near the bodies is actually a sleeping **giant horned toad** partially covered by layers of blowing sand. It squirts caustic blood on anyone rummaging through the backpack or disturbing the elven corpses.

Toad, Giant Ice

Hit Dice: 5
Armor Class: 5 [14]
Attacks: 1 bite (1d10+2)
Saving Throw: 12
Special: Radiates cold
Move: 9 (hop 10ft)
Alignment: Neutrality (occasionally Chaos)
Number Encountered: 1d8 or 4d100
Challenge Level/XP: 6/400

These bizarre creatures are as intelligent as men (perhaps more so), and use their long, unwebbed fore-toes to carve structures and tunnels in the ice. They use tools, but do not bother with weapons, for their toothy mouths are quite deadly. An ice toad can radiate intense, damaging cold (10ft) once every second melee round, causing 2d6 points of damage. They can also hop to attack, as giant toads do. In the wilds of the arctic regions, in the deserts of snow and ice, there may be entire cities of these unusual beings, perhaps even civilizations remaining from times before known history.

Giant Ice Toad: HD 5; AC 5[14]; Atk 1 bite (1d10+2); Move 9 (Hop 10ft); Save 12; AL N; CL/XP 6/400; Special: Radiate cold.

The Toad King

A 12-foot-tall ice sculpture of a giant frog holding down a struggling man stands at the entrance to this frozen chamber inside the Wailing Glacier. Giant boulder peek out of the ice walls and are engraved with carvings of giant frogs leaping atop men and ripping their heads off. One carving shows a frog sitting on a squat throne built atop a mound of humanoid bodies. The floor is cloudy, scuffed ice.

The room sits atop a tunnel from a lower passage that wraps beneath it. The lower passage is the hunting ground of **2 giant ice toads**. The floor is strong enough to support the weight of a normal man, but weak enough that the toads can leap upward through it. The highly intelligent toads work together to catch intruders in the blasts of their icy breath.

Toad, Giant Poisonous

Hit Dice: 2
Armor Class: 7 [12]
Attacks: 1 bite (1d6 + poison)
Saving Throw: 16
Special: Poison skin and bite
Move: 6 (hop 30ft)
Alignment: Neutrality
Number Encountered: 1d8
Challenge Level/XP: 4/120

Giant poisonous toads bite with lethal poison, and their skin is also poisonous to the touch. They are about the size of a large dog, and can attack at the end of a hop, just as non-poisonous giant toads do. These toads can sometimes be brightly colored in vibrant reds and greens.

Giant Poisonous Toad: HD 2; AC 7[12]; Atk 1 bite (1d6 + poison); Move 6 (Hop 30ft); Save 16; AL N; CL/XP 4/120; Special: Poison skin and bite.

The Pleasure Garden of Xanis II

A magnificent garden of elaborate topiary and sculptures fills the grounds behind the chateau of King Xanis II. Stone fountains burble quietly into wide marble basins, and birds sing a chirping melody through the fruit-filled trees. Water lilies, hydrangeas, geraniums and rare orchids grow on the well-maintained grounds.

But not all is right in the garden of Xanis II. The gardener recently went missing, and three servants sent into the garden to find him haven't returned. The luxuriant garden attracted **6 giant poisonous toads** that hop through the wildflowers as they chase the three-foot-wide butterflies Xanis raises. The gardener was the first to die after he pushed one of the toads away from a prized orchid. The servants met similar fates. Their bodies are hidden under various plants throughout the garden.

Toad-Hydra

Hit Dice: 6
Armor Class: 7 [12]
Attacks: 4-6 bites (1d6+3) and/or tongues (grab)
Saving Throw: 11
Special: Regeneration 2hp/round, tongues grab
Move: 6/12 (swimming)
Alignment: Neutrality
Challenge Level/XP: 8/800 + 300 per head over 4.

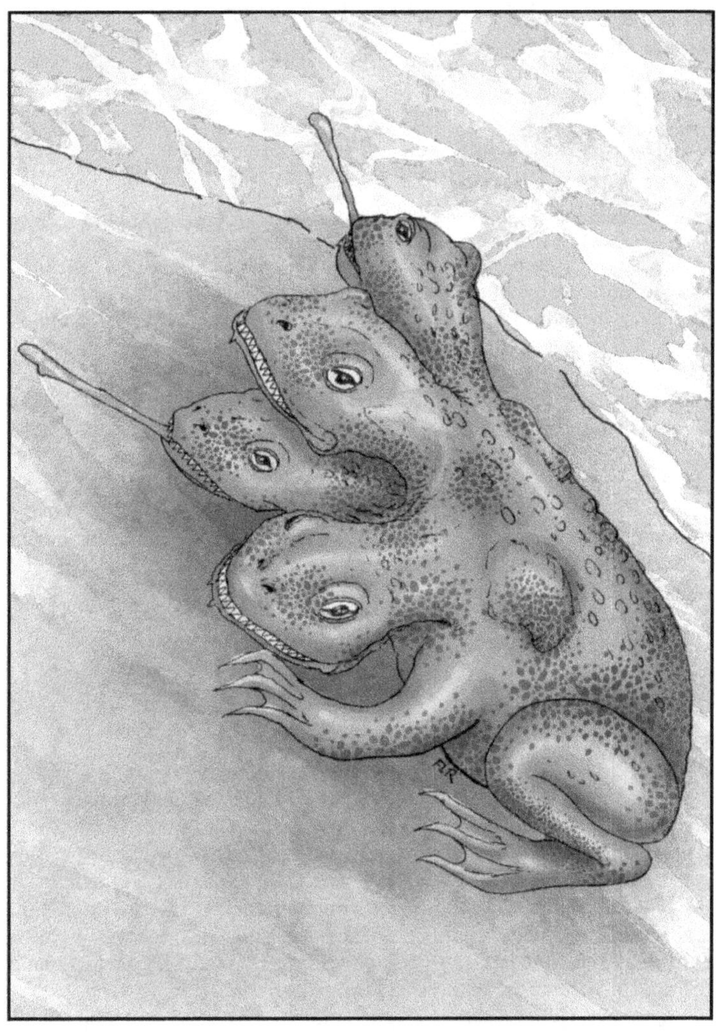

Toad-Hydrae resemble giant toads with multiple heads (usually 4-6), although the body is somewhat longer than that of a toad, and the mouths of a toad-hydra are filled with nasty, sharp teeth. These creatures have one attack per head. Each head can attack either by biting or by flicking out its long tongue in attempt to grab (and later swallow) prey. A toad-hydra will not usually attack with more than two of its tongues; if attacking with three tongues, *all* of the tongue attacks are made at -1, if with four tongues, all the attacks are at -2, etc. If, however, the toad-hydra hits with one of its tongues, the victim is immobilized and the hydra may begin trying to gulp it down in the next round. Gulping attempts are treated as attacks, but rather than dealing damage in hit points, success means the victim is swallowed whole and will die in 1d4+3 rounds. Immobilized opponents can attempt to break free (successful saving throw at -5).

— Author: Matt Finch

Toad Hydra (4 heads): HD 6; AC 7[12]; Atk up to 4 bites (1d6+3) and/or up to 4 tongues (grab); Move 6/12 (swimming); Save 11; AL N; CL/XP 8/800; Special: Tongues grab, regeneration 2hp/round.

A Light in the Darkness

A scream pierces the darkness, the sound rolling over the bayou. Off in the night, a lantern bobs and shakes unnaturally 10 feet off the ground. Another agonized scream comes from the direction of the bobbing light. The whipping light creates arcs of red and orange through the inky blackness.

A none-too-bright elven fighter named **Nelion Brightwave** was making his way through the bayou by night when he stumbled upon a larger-than-normal **toad-hydra**. The toad grabbed Nelion in two of its six mouths and holds him by his legs and torso. The lantern he trusted to get him through the swamp swings wildly as the toad-hydra heads fight over the treat that blundered into their path.

Toad-Men

Hit Dice: 3
Armor Class: 6[13]
Attacks: 1 weapon (1d8)
Saving Throw: 14
Special: None
Move: 9/12 (swimming)
Alignment: Chaotic (usually)
Challenge Level/XP: 3/60

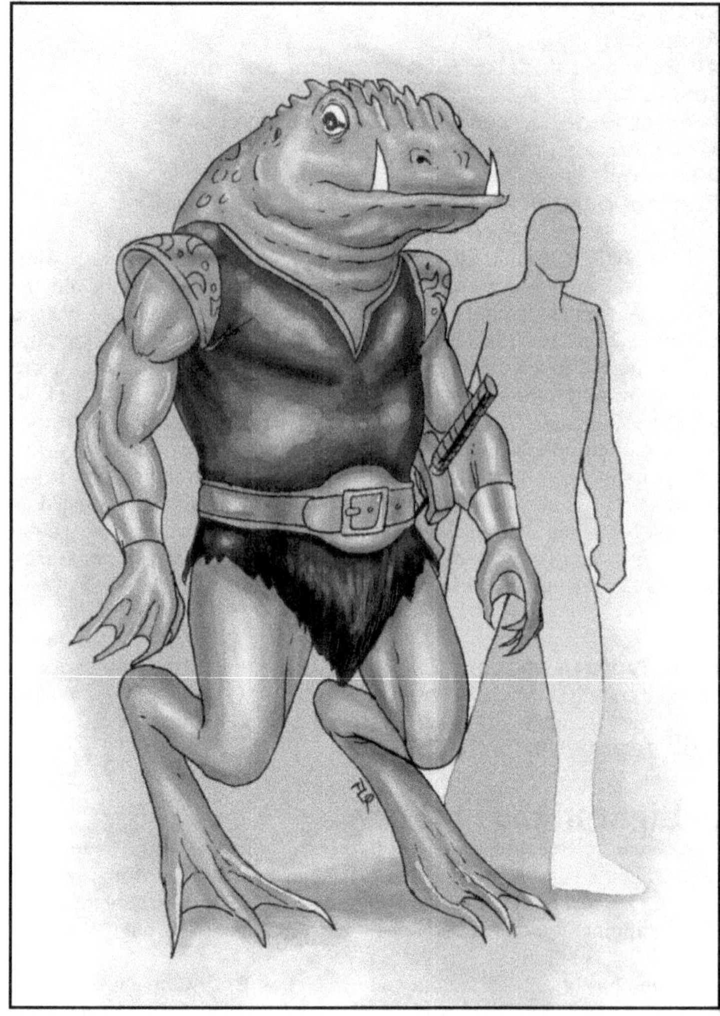

Toad-men resemble bipedal toads, with warty skin and webbed feet. However, they have blunt horned ridges at the top of the head, and tusk-like teeth jutting upward from the lower jaw. The creatures stand almost seven feet tall, and they are bulkier than humans. The civilization of toad-men can range from that of brutish cavemen all the way to highly cultivated societies with refined arts (the latter are more likely to be of Neutral or Lawful alignment, although this is not always the case).

In some cases, Toad-Men will be found as the ruling class or as war leaders for tribes of thugtoads. These batrachian species do not appear to be related unless the connection lies at some point in the very distant past, but each of the two races can roughly understand the speech of the other.

For the most part, toad-men are a subterranean species, especially the more brutish varieties, but they incur no penalties for fighting in sunlight.

Toad-Men: HD 3; AC 6[13]; Atk 1 weapon (1d8); Move 9 (Swim 12); Save 14; AL C; CL/XP 3/60; Special: None.

Clever Old Toads

The sounds of digging fill this downward sloping tunnel in the Legene Mines. Clumps of glowing moss are rolled into two-foot-diameter balls and staked to the walls with iron spikes. Each moss-ball provides a feeble yellow light but no heat. Two lines of nearly naked men and dwarves stand along the walls. They are all chained one to the next via lengths of iron chains running through shackles on their ankles. The slaves are thin and starving. Each has a pick that he swings against the rock wall. A mine car containing gold ore (200 gp) and a few diamonds (300 gp total) sits in the tunnel between the two rows of miners.

Standing on ledges overlooking the miners are **6 toad-men** and their **3 giant toad pets**. Each of the toad-men carries a whip and a longsword. The giant toads leap down to attack, not caring if they grab a slave or an intruder.

Giant Toad: HD 3; AC 6[13]; Atk 1 bite (1d8); Move 6 (Hop 30ft); Save 14; AL N; CL/XP 3/60; Special: Hop

Todawan Master

Hit Dice: 8
Armor Class: 1 [18]
Attacks: 2 staff (1d6) or 1 kick (2d6 + special)
Saving Throw: 8
Special: Leaping kick, block missiles (75%), half damage from fire and cold, immune to mental control and illusion, mental suggestion (1/day)
Move: 12
Alignment: Law
Number Encountered: 1
Challenge Level/XP: 11/1,400

Todawan masters are an enigmatic race of solitary giant toads that have achieved mystic enlightenment. They wear robes and carry a staff. Living solitary lives in the depths of dangerous swamps, todawan masters do not accept students but occasionally answer questions about the future when worthy individuals seek them out. Unfortunately, some todawan masters go bad. These subtle servants of chaos and ruin may assemble bands of thugtoads or other minions, and begin to act as evil masterminds. Such chaotic todawan masters do not often leave their swamps, but their influence can be felt far and wide through the use of assassins, spies, and soldiery. Any todawan master (lawful or chaotic) is a formidable foe. In combat, provided they have at least 40ft for the jump, they can leap into battle and deliver a tremendously powerful kick with their hind legs for 2d6 points of damage; the victim must make a saving throw or be hurled back ten feet to lie prone on the ground, stunned for 1d4 rounds. Todawan masters can block missile weapons with their whirling staffs, with a 75% chance to deflect incoming missiles before the to-hit roll is even made. Their mental discipline is such that they take only half damage from fire and cold. They are immune to all forms of mental control and illusion. Once per day, a todawan master can make a powerful mental attack, suggesting that the victim not follow some course of action. If the victim fails a saving throw (made at -4), he will become unable to force himself to follow whatever course of action the todawan master has prohibited. The skin of a todawan master is coated in an extremely hallucinogenic substance.

— Author: Matt Finch

Todawan Master: HD 8; AC 1[18]; Atk 2 staff (1d6) or 1 kick (2d6 + special); Move 12; Save 8; AL L; CL/XP 11/1400; Special: Leaping kick, block missiles (75%), half damage from fire and cold, immune to mental control and illusion, mental suggestion (1/day).

8/800 + 1,300 per head over 4; Special: Regeneration 2hp/round

So Croaks the Master

A tall wooden tower stands in the Sin Mire Swamp. The structure reaches nearly 40 feet into the air. Fireflies flit about the tower, and dragonflies dart back and forth in lazy circles. A series of switchback stairs lead upward to a small platform atop the tower. Waxy white-and-red candles sit on the various landings and provide a weak glow. More candles sit on the landing.

A **todawan master** wearing red robes sits in a lotus position in a small hut atop the tower. His head is bowed and he holds a quarterstaff across his lap. The todawan's name is **Inhoep Gress**. He truthfully answers one question for anyone who climbs his tower and seeks his assistance, provided they bring his favorite delicacy: the forelimbs of a giant praying mantis. He is accompanied by **2 toad-men** initiates who sit on stools behind him. Inhoep carries a bone whistle that summons a **toad-hydra** from the bayou to his side. He sometimes rides the beast to get around the swamp. Inhoep croaks out his pronouncements in scratchy Common.

Toad-hydra: HD 6; AC 7[12]; Atk 4-6 bites (1d6+3) and/or tongues (grab); Move 6 (Swim 12); Save 11; AL N; CL/XP

Torthri

Hit Dice: 2+3
Armor Class: 6 [13]
Attacks: 2 claws (1d2) and 1 bite (1d6) or 1 weapon (1d6) and 1 bite (1d6)
Saving Throw: 16
Special: Charm gaze
Move: 15 (6 when standing)
Alignment: Chaos
Number Encountered: 1 or 1d4 (family)
Challenge Level/XP: 3/60

At first glance, a Torthri may be mistaken for a well-fed leopard or jaguar. While they are related to large feline predators, they are semi-bipedal and of near-human intelligence. In some lands they are venerated as nature spirits and pass freely through humanoid villages. A torthri is capable of walking on all fours, but it can also rise up on its hind legs, and the elongated forepaws are capable of grasping tools, opening containers, etc. When semi-erect, a torthri moves at a reduced movement rate. To run, it must drop to all fours. A torthri can exert a magical Charm upon humans and humanoids by meeting their gaze and concentrating for one round. The saving throw against a torthri's charm is at a penalty of -2, and those charmed become the creature's willing slaves and worshippers. Whole villages have been known to come under the sway of a Torthri, constructing shrines in which to offer up food and treasure. Although charmed villagers will tell outsiders that their "spirit cat" is like an overgrown pet, no domestic cats will be found in the village, for the Torthri will slay or drive out all other felines.

If forced into combat, the Torthri can defend itself with claws and bite. However, the claws are weaker than those of its feline kin, and its hands are clumsy; it cannot use missile weapons or complex devices, although it can handle simple weapons such as the spear, staff, club, and axe. It may thus attack with a weapon and bite, and will do so if its true nature is discovered. The Torthri is intelligent enough to realise the value of magical weapons and shields, but cannot utter command words or wear armour. Any treasure possessed by a Torthri will be stored in a village shrine or hidden cave. There persist tales of Torthri speaking through their charmed slaves by telepathy, and of whole villages starving to feed their greedy idols.

— *Author: Scott Wylie Roberts, "Myrystyr"*

Torthri: HD 2+3; AC 6[13]; Atk 2 claws (1d2) and 1 bite (1d6) or 1 weapon (1d6) and 1 bite (1d6); Move 15 (6 when standing); Save 16; AL C; CL/XP 3/60; Special: Charm gaze.

Reign of the Cat

The villagers of Rytsyrym scramble for their homes when the sun sets. Shutters are hastily fastened, animals are corralled, and doors are locked well before the sun touches the horizon. The village goes silent after sundown with the residents afraid to make even the slightest sound lest they attract the demon cat. They won't venture out until the sun rises. Anyone pounding on closed doors gets quiet whispers telling them to go away.

Soon after sunset, a troupe of **16 humans, elves and dwarves** walks into town from the forest. They immediately begin work on a wood-and-stone building in the center of town. The workers move clumsily but steadily as they convert the former temple to Muir into a shrine. Images carved into the outer walls depict a cat walking among men who bow down to worship at its clawed paws. The charmed villagers make no moves against PCs. The dazed individuals direct PCs to the Great Spirit if they try to talk to them.

Inside the temple, rows of newly built ledges rise into the open rafters. Golden cat idols (100 gp each) stand in the room's four corners. Nailed to a small altar at the front of the temple are the bodies of several dead housecats. A **torthri** lounges on the altar, awaiting supplicants. A massive **human warrior** wearing a cat mask and armed with a wicked scythe serves as the cat's protector. The cat mask lets the warrior see in the dark.

Human warrior: HD 3; AC 5[14]; Atk 1 scythe (1d6+1); Move 12; Save 15; AL C; CL/XP 3/60; Special: None.

Trapper Beast

Hit Dice: 10-12
Armor Class: 3 [16]
Attacks: 1 Enfold
Saving Throw: 5, 4, or 3
Special: Enfold and suffocate prey
Move: 1
Alignment: Neutrality
Number Encountered: 1
Challenge Level/XP: 10HD: 11/1,700; 11HD: 12/2,000; 12HD: 13/2,300

Trapper-beasts are manta-like creatures resembling the stone floors of the subterranean areas where they live. When prey steps onto the trapper's body, it whips up its wings to enfold and smother its victims (to a maximum of four). Death occurs in 7 melee rounds. Cold does not damage them, and fire inflicts only half damage.

Trapper Beast (10HD): HD 10; AC 3[16]; Atk 1 Enfold; Move 1; Save 5; AL N; CL/XP 11/1700; Special: Enfold and suffocate prey.

Trapper Beast (11HD): HD 11; AC 3[16]; Atk 1 Enfold; Move 1; Save 4; AL N; CL/XP 12/2000; Special: Enfold and suffocate prey.

Trapper Beast (12HD): HD 12; AC 3[16]; Atk 1 Enfold; Move 1; Save 3; AL N; CL/XP 13/2300; Special: Enfold and suffocate prey.

Roll With It

A stone incline at the end of this rectangular chamber leads upward to a stone balcony 20 feet above floor level. The balcony runs around the entire room, and has polished oak railings. An oak banister runs up the ramp. A dark idol of a winged bat sits at the far end of the balcony. The idol's metal exterior glows red with intense heat and it head swivels back and forth as it surveys the room. Red velvet curtains tied with golden tassels hang from the ceiling, blocking passages leading away from the balcony. The room is stuffy and several degrees warmer than the corridors leading into it.

The idol is a cleverly constructed furnace with a swiveling head that directs heat throughout the room. The true danger in the room is a **trapper beast** lying in wait near the top of the ramp to the balcony. The beast closes tightly over anyone who walks across it. When it does, the monster rolls like a giant ball down the ramp with the trapped prey caught inside it.

Treacherous Treasure

Hit Dice: 7
Armor Class: 3 [16]
Attacks: 1 slam (3d6)
Saving Throw: 9
Special: Surprise (40%)
Move: 6
Alignment: Neutrality
Number Encountered: 1
Challenge Level/XP: 7/600

At first glance, a treacherous treasure appears to be an envious pile of riches. In reality, a treacherous treasure is a large, slime-like creature that exudes a sticky film from its pores. Throughout its life span, the slimy critter gathers up various coins, gems, and riches found within most dungeons. These objects stick to the slime's adhesive secretion, giving it the appearance of a pile of treasure. Once the slimy beast is slain, it will take 1d4 weeks for the adhesive film to lose its bonding properties. Only then may the adventurers claim the slime-beast's hoard.

A treacherous treasure that remains motionless may surprise its foes (40%).

— Author: Skathros

Treacherous Treasure: HD 7; AC 3[16]; Atk 1 slam (3d6); Move 6; Save 9; AL N; CL/XP 7/600; Special: Surprises foes (40%).

Window Pain

Loose coins and jewels (300 gp total) are stuck fast to the floor, walls and ceiling of this dank corridor. Each is coated with sticky glue that holds them in place. The coins form a rough trail that winds drunkenly through the hall into 20-foot-high chamber beyond. A mound of treasure sits in the center of the room. Six golden lanterns (60 gp each) hanging on the walls glow warmly, making the coins and gems sparkle.

The pile of coins and jewels (1,500 gp total) is a **treacherous treasure** spread across a 10-foot-diameter glass window looking down into a lower chamber. The treacherous treasure completely covers the glass, hiding the fact that the lower room exists. Anyone attacking the sticky treasure pile has a 1 in 6 chance of shattering the glass and dumping the attacker and the treacherous treasure 20 feet down onto the lower room's stone tile floor.

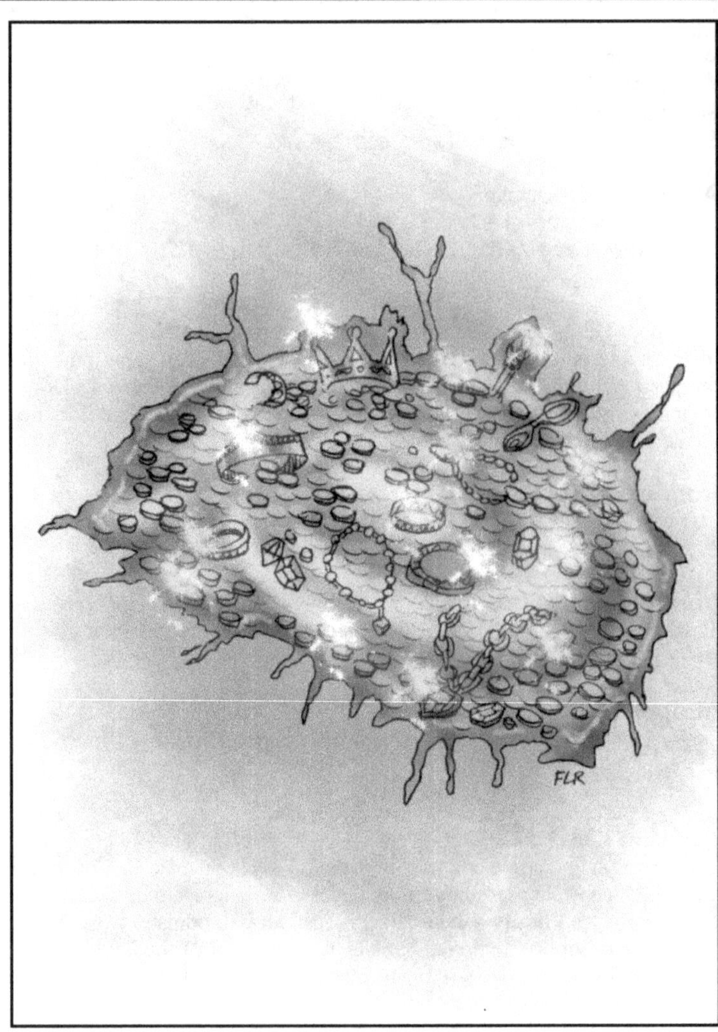

Treant

Hit Dice: 6 HD + 1d6 HD
Armor Class: 2 [17]
Attacks: 2 strikes (2d6, 3d6, or 4d6)
Saving Throw: 9, 8, 6, 5, 4, or 3
Special: Control trees
Move: 12
Alignment: Law
Number Encountered: 1
Challenge Level/XP: 7 HD (7/600), 8 HD (8/800), 9 HD (9/1,100), 10 HD (10/1,400), 11 HD (11/1,700) 12 HD (12/2,000)

Treants are tree-like protectors and "shepherds" of forest trees. Depending upon their size, they have different hit dice and do different amounts of damage: treants of 7 to 8 hit dice inflict 2d6 points of damage with each strike of their branch-like hands, treants of 9–10 hit dice inflict 3d6 points, and treants of 11–12 hit dice inflict 4d6 points. All treants can "wake" trees within 60 ft, allowing them to walk at a rate of 3, and possibly to attack. (No more than two trees at a time can be awake at the behest of a single treant.)

Treant (7HD): HD 7; AC 2[17]; Atk 2 strikes (2d6); Move 6; Save 9; AL L; CL/XP 7/600; Special: Control trees.

Treant (8HD): HD 8; AC 2[17]; Atk 2 strikes (2d6); Move 6; Save 8; AL L; CL/XP 8/800; Special: Control trees.

Treant (9HD): HD 9; AC 2[17]; Atk 2 strikes (3d6); Move 6; Save 6; AL L; CL/XP 9/1100; Special: Control trees.

Treant (10HD): HD 10; AC 2[17]; Atk 2 strikes (3d6); Move 6; Save 5; AL L; CL/XP 10/1400; Special: Control trees.

Treant (11HD): HD 11; AC 2[17]; Atk 2 strikes (4d6); Move 6; Save 4; AL L; CL/XP 11/1700; Special: Control trees.

Treant (12HD): HD 12; AC 2[17]; Atk 2 strikes (4d6); Move 6; Save 3; AL L; CL/XP 12/2000; Special: Control trees.

The Swinging Ship

A caravel hangs suspended above the river by pulleys and sturdy ropes strung up into two mighty oak trees. The ship's crew swarms over the sides and deck of the ship as it hangs in the makeshift drydock. The sailors hang from ropes as they rush to fix a hole punched through the wooden hull. The ship is the Stalwart Corsair. It has a large winged masthead riding high on its prow. Captain Terrance Capstand commands his crew as they chop down nearby trees to make repairs.

The sailors picked the wrong spot to make their repairs after they slammed into an underwater shoal. They don't know that the region is under the protection of a **treant**. The sound of chopping wood brings the treant in 1d4+2 rounds to investigate. It immediately awakens the two trees holding the Stalwart Corsair to join it as it attacks the sailors. The trees swing the ship wildly as they pull free of the ropes wrapped around their branches.

Tree Ghost

Hit Dice: 3
Armor Class: 6 [13]
Attacks: 2 claws (1d3) or thorns (0)
Saving Throw: 14
Special: Charisma drain, insect plague, animate wood, immune to normal weapons, cold, electricity, acid, and non-magical fire
Move: 12
Alignment: Chaos
Number Encountered: 1
Challenge Level/XP: 10/1,400

Tree ghosts are the undead form of a Dryad who was killed by a wraith, vampire, or other such undead creature. They are gaunt and emaciated ghostly horrors, with fingers ending in thorn-like claws, reeking of rotting plant matter. Vines of thorn and briar grow from a tree ghost's body, writhing around her like snakes. Tree ghosts are partially incorporeal, and are invisible until they attack. In close combat, a tree ghost uses her claws to tear at victims, but she can also hurl a spray of thorns from her serpentine thorn-vines to attack a single opponent at a distance of up to 60ft. Both the thorns and the tree ghost's claws carry a virulent sap; anyone hit by one of the tree ghost's attacks must make a saving throw or become ill with a strange delirium that drains away his willpower. The victim loses 1d4 points of charisma per hour, and once his charisma reaches 0 he becomes a servant of the Tree Ghost's will. He will follow her back to the Corpse Tree and begin sprouting runners and twigs, becoming absorbed into the Corpse Tree (the victim loses 1d4 constitution points per day, and upon reaching a constitution of 0 becomes part of the tree). The process is very painful and foul to look upon. If the Corpse Tree or the Tree Ghost is killed, anyone under the tree ghost's power who has not started the absorption process will regain lost charisma points at a rate of 1d4 per hour, and will suffer no other effects. Those that have already started to become absorbed into a corpse tree do not fare as well: all constitution loss is permanent, and cannot be reversed without the use of powerful magic. In addition to her poisonous claws and thorns, tree ghosts can exhale an Insect Plague (per the spell) once per day. They can also animate any wooden objects, plants, and other vegetation within 50ft; these animated things can attack and ensnare anyone in the area. Tree Ghosts are immune to normal weapons and can only be harmed by silver and magical weapons. Magic fire affects them, but ice, electricity, and acid have no effect, nor does normal fire. If a tree ghost is killed, but her corpse tree is not, the tree ghost will be reborn 24 hours after being killed.
— *Author: Sean Stone*

Tree Ghost: HD 3; AC 6[13]; Atk: 2 claws (1d3) or thorns (0); Move 12; Save 14; AL C; CL/XP: 10/1400; Special: Charisma drain, Insect Plague, animate wood, immune to normal weapons, cold, electricity, acid, and non-magical fire.

The Willow's Lullaby

An ethereal voice sings a children's lullaby quietly beneath a willow tree in the Kajaani Forest. The tree's drooping branches hang lifeless like a withered shroud about the clearing. Under the tree's canopy, six headstones arranged in a circle mark the graves of children who died in a horrible mill fire hundreds of years ago. A ghostly woman wearing a shawl of leaves sits on the ground amid the graves. Her beautiful golden hair flows around her lithe body, and clinging vines hug her form. She sings quietly to the headstones, and touches the earth sadly.

The pale woman is a **dryad** named Melene slain years ago by the vampire Valmont De Shade as he traveled the countryside seeking a permanent lair. Melene is a tormented spirit leading a double life. Within the circle of graves (which she used to sing to each night to ease the troubled spirits of the children), she appears as she did in life. Outside the circle, she changes into a hideous **tree ghost**. The willow overhanging the area is a **corpse tree** that changes along with the dryad. Melene is unaware of the transformations that overcome her when she leaves or enters the grave circle. A desire to protect the children always draws her back to the circle after nights of horrible rampages through the forest.

Corpse Tree: HD 5+2; AC 4[15]; Atk 2 fists (1d8); Move 0; Save 12; AL C; CL/XP 7/600; Special: if both fists hit the victim is "bear" hugged for an additional 2d6 damage.

Triton and Triton, Dark

Hit Dice: 3
Armor Class: 5 [14]
Attacks: 1 trident (1d8+1)
Saving Throw: 14
Special: Magic resistance (90%), leaders summon sea-creatures
Move: 1/18 (swimming)
Alignment: Law
Number Encountered: 1d6+1 or 1d6 x10
Challenge Level/XP: 5/240

Tritons are almost indistinguishable from mermen, but for their nobler appearance. They are, however, a much more magical race entirely. They are, for instance, almost entirely resistant to magic (90%). Their leaders carry conch horns that summon giant sea horses and panic normal sea animals aiding enemies of the tritons. Many triton leaders also have spell casting powers.

Triton: HD 3; AC 5[14]; Atk 1 trident (1d8+1); Move 1 (Swim 18); Save 14; AL L; CL/XP 4/120; Special: Magic resistance 90%.

TRITON, DARK
Hit Dice: 3
Armor Class: 5 [14]
Attacks: 1 trrident (1d8+1)
Saving Throw: 14
Special: Magic resistance (75%), leaders summon sea-creatures
Move: 1/18 (swimming)
Alignment: Chaos
Number Encountered: 1d6x10
Challenge Level/XP: 5/240

Dark tritons resemble their more benevolent cousins, the normal tritons, but they are malevolent creatures. Just as the normal tritons are rumored to be servants of a sea god, the dark tritons are servants of oceanic demons of various types, most commonly the demon-prince Thalasskoptis (q.v.). Dark tritons have tentacle rather than the fish-like "legs" of normal tritons, and often ride giant moray eels as mounts when traveling in the dark depths of the sea where their make their castle-like lairs on the sea floor.

For every 10 dark tritons, either in their lairs or in hunting parties, there will be a leader with 5 hit dice, and for every 20 there will be another leader with 7 hit dice. If a group with 50 or more is encountered there will also be a chief with 9 hit dice. Dark tritons do not have magic-users as many normal triton bands do, but for each 10 dark tritons encountered there is a non-cumulative 15% chance that the band will include a cleric of level 1d6 (check separately for each set of 10 dark tritons; there is a chance that the band will include more than one cleric).

As with normal tritons, the leaders of the dark tritons (5HD+) are capable of summoning aquatic beasts to do their bidding. Once per day, a dark triton leader may summon sea-creatures, with the following results (1d6):

1. 1d3 giant octopi
2. 3d10 sharks
3. 1 sea serpent (q.v.)
4. 3d6 aquatic ghouls
5. 1d4 aquatic trolls
6. 1 sea-wight (an aquatic wight with normal abilities but swimming) leading 1d6+2 aquatic ghouls

Summoning creatures, even if there are multiple leaders in the dark triton band, is not possible multiple times; all nearby creatures will already have responded to the first call.

— Author: Matt Finch

Dark Triton: HD 3; AC 5[14]; Atk 1 trident (1d8+1); Move 1 (Swim 18); Save 14; AL C; CL/XP 4/120; Special: Magic resistance 75%.

Depths of Betrayal

A foot-long conch shell lies in the gray sands of Kullk Beach. Black streaks and minute cracks wrap around the shell, but it is otherwise intact. The shell tapers to a pointed opening on one end and has a wide opening on the other, much like a trumpet. Blowing into the shell produces a deep note that echoes across the water and causes a 10-foot-wide path to open through the waves. The corridor descends along the seabed until it enters a tunnel surrounded entirely by seawater. The passage leads a mile offshore to a round water chamber nearly 100 feet beneath the surface.

Tied to an open oyster shell with wiry seaweed is a **triton**. The triton breathes shallowly and appears to have been tortured recently. Open wounds cover his face and arms, and whip scars mark his torso. He is barely alive. Untying the triton causes the watery corridor to collapse, starting from the beach outward to the circular chamber. A giant pearl (200 gp) lies in the open shell. The circular chamber remains open with breathable air despite the passage back to the land vanishing.

Lin-Talishan is a **triton** prince of the undersea kingdom of Effervelt.

He was recently tricked by a **dark triton** named **Yennel Scald** who tortured him to learn the secrets of the triton king. Lin-Talishan tossed his conch shell into the waves as he was taken, where it floated to the surface and onto the beach. **Scald** arrives in 1d4 rounds with **2 sharks** and **3 aquatic ghouls** to halt any rescuers.

If rescued and nursed back to health, Lin-Talishan gives PCs a small coral statue depicting of white and black tritons locked in combat. Submerging the statue in water gives the PC the ability to breathe for one day underwater. Lin-Talishan had planned to give the statue to Scald as a token of brotherhood until the dark triton betrayed him.

Large Shark (7HD): HD 7; AC 6[13]; Atk 1 bite (1d8+4); Move 0 (Swim 24); Save 9; AL N; CL/XP 7/600; Special: Feeding frenzy.

Ghoul: HD 2; AC 6[13]; Atk 2 claws (1d3), 1 bite (1d4); Move 9 (Swim 12); Save 16; AL C; CL/XP 3/60; Special: Immunities, paralyzing touch.

Troglodyte

Hit Dice: 2
Armor Class: 4 [15]
Attacks: 2 claws (1d3), bite (1d4+1) or by weapon with shield (1d8)
Saving Throw: 16
Special: Stench, chameleon skin
Move: 12
Alignment: Chaos
Number Encountered: 1d10 or 1d10x10
Challenge Level/XP: 3/60

Troglodytes are subterranean reptile-people. In battle, they emit a horrible smell that weakens most other races. Failing a saving throw against the smell causes the victim to lose 1 point of strength per round for 1d6 rounds, with the loss persisting for another 10 rounds thereafter. Troglodyte skin is slightly chameleon-like, which allows them to mount very effective ambushes. Troglodytes despise the civilized races and seek to annihilate them, but different clans do not ordinarily work well together. Troglodyte bands are often led by strong specimens, which can be 3 or 4 hit dice monsters.

Troglodyte: HD 2; AC 4[15]; Atk 2 claws (1d3), Bite (1d4+1) or by weapon with shield (1d8); Move 12; Save 16; AL C; CL/XP 3/60; Special: Stench, chameleon skin.

Water Torture

The smell of rotten eggs wafts over a waterway filling the center of this 500-foot-long tubular tunnel. The brackish water is a couple of feet deep and flows steadily out of the tunnel toward a grate that empties into the sea along a steep cliff face. Flowing water rushes out of a small opening broken through a wooden door smeared with grease and oil that blocks a side passage.

The main tunnel is the hunting ground of **5 troglodytes**. The creatures reside in rooms above the tunnel and watch intruders through concealed murder holes. When PCs near the wooden door, the troglodytes drop a solid metal portcullis down the passageway behind the PCs to trap them in the tunnel between the portcullis and the locked door. Once PCs are trapped in the sealed tunnel, the troglodytes open the wooden door via a series of levers and wheels in the upper chambers to release a torrential surge of water. The passage quickly fills with water in 2d4+1 rounds. The troglodytes drop into the chamber via a secret door in the ceiling to get at drowning PCs.

Troll

Hit Dice: 6+3
Armor Class: 4 [15]
Attacks: 2 claws (1d4), 1 bite (1d8)
Saving Throw: 11
Special: Regenerates
Move: 12
Alignment: Chaos
Number Encountered: 2d6
Challenge Level/XP: 8/800

Trolls are as tall as ogres, and just as strong. Unlike ogres, however, they attack with claws and teeth instead of weapons. Trolls regenerate, which is to say that any damage inflicted upon them heals within minutes (3 hit points per round). The only way to utterly kill a troll is to submerse it in acid or burn it. Trolls can even re-grow lopped-off heads and limbs.

Troll: HD 6+3; AC 4[15]; Atk 2 claws (1d4), 1 bite (1d8); Move 12; Save 11; AL C; CL/XP 8/800; Special: Regenerate 3hp/round.

Parts is Parts

A four-foot-tall pile of rubbery limbs, legs and even heads lies in the center of this 15-foot-wide stone hallway. The body parts are all from a troll, and most have decayed into putrid piles. The smell in the corridor is intolerable. At the opposite end of the hallway is a stone shelf jutting off the wall where the tunnel dead-ends. A sparkling diamond (400 gp) sits on the shelf. A hovering halo of green fire dances above the gemstone.

The limbs and heads belong to a **troll** named **Craqjaw**. The troll wants the diamond at the end of the hall, but a whirling blade trap constantly slices off any body part the troll sticks in the blades' path. The blades are located halfway down the hall, and slice out of the ceiling, floors and walls simultaneously to deal 6d6 points of damage (save for half). Craqjaw hides under the pile of his body parts and leaps out if discovered. Otherwise, the troll waits until PCs are killed by the blades or grab the diamond before making his presence known.

The green halo of fire is a protective spell cast over the gem. It slices off a finger of anyone reaching for the gem unless they make a saving throw.

Tsalakian

Hit Dice: 2+2
Armor Class: -4 [23]
Attacks: 4 weapon attacks (1d4)
Saving Throw: 16
Special: Incorporeal/teleport movement, perceive secret and hidden things, immune to spells affecting a "person," saving throw against all magic, reduced damage from spells, immune to restraint, detect good, magic and evil, sense emotions (empathy)
Move: Infinite
Alignment: Chaos
Number Encountered: 1d3
Challenge Level/XP: 7/600

Tsalakians exist outside of normal space. It is said that they have no individual wills of their own, but are instead the fearful servitors of some greater malign power. They eternally scheme against, and are in turn defied by, another trans-dimensional race called the Kzaddich (q.v.). Tsalakians appear as tall men, completely enshrouded in cowled cloaks. Although capable of speaking with any sentient being (an innate form of tongues), their voices float bizarrely around them, as though through a ventriloquism spell with a random range and direction. They rarely allow their true forms to be seen, for they are difficult to comprehend. When uncloaked, they have been described as a blurry whirl of teeth forming a rough approximation of a man-like form.

Tsalakians can bend and fold themselves through space, and are therefore extraordinarily difficult to successfully strike (thereby accounting for their high armor class). Moreover, they are fearsome in combat as they have the spell-like ability to blink at will. Their multiple attacks represent their ability to strike from several directions at once. A Tsalakian may divide its attacks among opponents within 20' of itself. They may move any distance in any given round, ignoring physical or magic obstacles in their path. This functions as an innate form of teleport without error. They can even enter concealed or hidden areas, as they do not perceive space as others do, and can see "around" walls, floors and ceilings. Thus, they can disregard held portals, walls of force and the like. Secret, concealed and hidden doors and traps are always exposed to their weird senses, as are hidden people. Note that they are, however, subject to illusions and cannot perceive invisible, out of phase, ethereal or astral objects or creatures; nevertheless, they are virtually impossible to take by surprise. They are immune to "person" affecting spells, such as charm person. Tsalakians are allowed saving throws against all spells of any kind, take no damage from damage-causing spells on a successful saving throw, and take only half damage if they save successfully. They cannot be restrained by any impediment and act as if wearing rings of free action at all times.

Tsalakians possess the mental power to detect good, evil, and magic at will, to cause fear (saving throw negates), and can sense the exact emotions of any being within 100ft. Tsalakians are usually found in the act of planning or carrying out some great ill, for they perpetually strive to bend all other sentient beings to the will of their dread master. They prefer to work through others, themselves remaining out of the fray if possible, revealing their fearsome abilities only if pressed. Their hatred of the Kzaddich knows no bounds and they will always attack these creatures on sight.

Tsalakian: HD 2+2; AC -4 [23]; Atk 4 weapon attacks (1d4); Move Infinite; Save 16; AL C; CL/XP: 7/600; Special: Incorporeal/teleport movement, perceive secret and hidden things, immune to spells affecting a "person," saving throw against all magic, reduced damage from spells, immune to restraint, detect good, magic and evil, sense emotions (empathy).

The Head That Wears the Crown

An elaborate throne sits on a raised dais in this magnificent reception hall. Tapestries that hung over the stone-block walls are now crumpled on the floor. The doors are open and unguarded. Scratches across the tile floor are the only evidence that the room is used. An unmoving skeleton wearing vestments of royalty sits on the throne. It wears two gold rings (60 gp each) on its finger bones and a jeweled crown (300 gp) on its brow. Slumped against the wall and hidden beneath fallen tapestries are 16 skeletons of guards and servants. Their clothing is torn and ripped.

Anyone touching the crown must make a saving throw or be tempted to place it on their head. Once the crown is firmly in place, the wearer freezes and a **tsalakian** appears in the center of the chamber. The tsalakian viciously attacks everyone in the room except the frozen crown wearer. The crown is a portal that summons the vicious creature, but only when it is worn by a sentient being. The tsalakian can exist only so long as the creature lives. Once the wearer dies (usually of starvation), the tsalakian is banished again. Removing the crown requires a remove curse spell. The crown can be destroyed by dipping it into a heated forge of blue flames.

Tunnel Prawn

Hit Dice: 1
Armor Class: 4 [15]
Attacks: 2 pincers (1d2)
Saving Throw: 17
Special: Climbing
Move: 6
Alignment: Neutrality
Number Encountered: 2d6
Challenge Level/XP: 1/15

Tunnel prawns are scavengers resembling very large lobsters, with a hard, rocklike shell. These creatures wander through subterranean caverns eating bugs and fungi from the wall, floor, and ceiling. A tunnel prawn can scale walls and move along ceilings with no more difficulty than walking along a floor. These dungeon vermin are easily antagonized, and will attack any living beings venturing near. One tunnel prawn can provide the equivalent of a day's rations. The meat is tough and very chewy, and keeps for only one day, but is actually quite delicious. Some taverns, usually those located near dungeon entrances, serve tunnel prawn as an item on the bill of fare, and will pay up to 3 gps for a fresh tunnel prawn. The prawns weigh about 20 lbs each.

— Author: Matt Finch

Tunnel Prawn: HD 1; AC 4[15]; Atk 2 pincers (1d2); Move 6; Save 17; AL N; CL/XP: 1/15; Special: Climbing.

Catch of the Day

A skittering rustle slides across the darkness of the ceiling of this 20-foot-wide-by-30-foot-long chamber. The ceiling rises 30 feet above a red brick floor. Anyone stepping into the room has a 2 in 6 chance of triggering an ancient trap.

If the trap is set off, a rotting cargo net spread across the ceiling drops to the floor. Its strands are frayed and torn, and thousands of worms and insects burrow through the knotted strands. The rope was designed to lift intruders into the air and hold them until the fire giant who designed it could retrieve his catch. The trap fell into disrepair after the giant's death at the hands of a pack of feral trolls. Now, the net simply falls flat atop PCs.

The ceiling is alive with **30 tunnel prawn** feasting on the bugs and insects infesting the heavy strands of rope. The tunnel prawns charge down the walls to attack PCs stealing their meal.

Turtle, Giant Sea

Hit Dice: 15
Armor Class: 3 [16] (shell), 5 [14] head/flippers
Attacks: 1 bite (4d6)
Saving Throw: 3
Special: None
Move: 3/12 (swimming)
Alignment: Neutrality
Number Encountered: 1d4
Challenge Level/XP: 15/2,900

Giant sea turtles do not hunt humans, but they are aggressive in their territory, and are large enough to capsize small ships (15 foot diameter shell). Obviously, the size and hit dice of individual specimens will vary; these stats are for an average adult turtle.

Giant Sea Turtle: HD 15; AC 3[16] shell, 5[14] head/flippers; Atk 1 bite (4d6); Move 3/12 (swimming); Save 3; AL N; CL/XP 15/2900; Special: None.

The Old Man and the Sea Turtle

An old man sits on the surface of the ocean, the rolling waves lapping around him. He has a long beard and wears ragged clothing bleached by the sun. The man's scrawny body is burned from overexposure, but he sits serenely as he stares toward the empty horizon. He rises and falls easily on the waves.

The old man is Santiago, a druid who became lost at sea weeks ago when his boat was attacked by a **giant sea turtle**. Santiago somewhat befriended beast. The turtle doesn't attack him when he's in the water — and even lets him ride atop its shell as it swims — but it won't let him leave, either. Santiago has survived so far by eating a dead marlin he caught. The giant sea turtle dumps Santiago into the waves to attack any ships approaching the old man.

Turtle, Giant Snapping

Hit Dice: 8-10
Armor Class: 1[18] shell, 5[14] head/limbs
Attacks: 1 bite (4d6)
Saving Throw: 8, 6, or 5
Special: None
Move: 4/9 (swimming)
Alignment: Neutrality
Number Encountered: 1d4
Challenge Level/XP: 8HD: 8/800; 9HD: 9/1,100; 10HD: 10/1,400

Giant snapping turtles are massive, having a shell with the same diameter in feet as the creature's hit dice. Their incredibly thick shells make them almost invulnerable to attacks that are not targeted at the head or limbs.

Giant Snapping Turtle (8HD): HD 8; AC 2[17] shell, 5[14] head/limbs; Atk 1 bite (4d6); Move 4 (Swim 9); Save 8; AL N; CL/XP 8/800; Special: None.

Giant Snapping Turtle (9HD): HD 9; AC 2[17] shell, 5[14] head/limbs; Atk 1 bite (4d6); Move 4 (Swim 9); Save 6; AL N; CL/XP 9/1100; Special: None.

Giant Snapping Turtle (10HD): HD 10; AC 2[17] shell, 5[14] head/limbs; Atk 1 bite (4d6); Move 44 (Swim 9); Save 5; AL N; CL/XP 10/1400; Special: None.

What Lies Beneath

Six barrels tied together by ropes bob on the surface of Altsheel Lake. A rope tied to the barrels dips into the water, the line taut. The barrels are slightly submerged, as if something below is pulling them down. Each of the containers is empty, although sealed with wax to keep them afloat. Wooden debris floats around the barrels. A gnoll's waterlogged body floats facedown in the lake.

A group of crafty gnolls tied the barrels together to bring up their preferred prey: **giant snapping turtles** that live in the lake. The gnolls' strategy was to harpoon a turtle's thick shell, and then loop the rope through a hook attached to the roped-together barrels. They let the turtle struggle against the barrels until it wore itself out and surfaced where they could finish it off. During the last fishing trip, the turtle snapped the rope on an underwater branch and turned back to attack the gnolls in the small skiff. The turtle made short work of the gnolls as they splashed about in the lake. The tired turtle is still underwater, but surfaces to attack anyone approaching the gnoll or the barrels.

Unicorn

Hit Dice: 4
Armor Class: 2 [17]
Attacks: 2 hoofs (1d8), 1 horn (1d8)
Saving Throw: 13
Special: Magic resistance (25%), double damage for charge, teleport
Move: 24
Alignment: Law
Number Encountered: 1d4+1
Challenge Level/XP: 5/240

Unicorns are generally shy and benevolent creatures, who will allow only a chaste maiden to approach them. They can teleport once per day to a distance of 360 ft, with a rider. The unicorn's horn has healing properties, according to legend. (The details of this, if any, are left to the Referee). There is considerable room to create variant sorts of unicorns: evil ones, flying ones, etc.

Unicorn: HD 4; AC 2[17]; Atk 2 hoofs (1d8), 1 horn (1d8); Move 24; Save 13; AL L; CL/XP 5/240; Special: double damage for charge, 25% magic resistance, teleport.

The Bounty Hunter

At the crest of the hill is an apple tree with fruit hanging on the dipping branches. The sound of an angry horse kicking and snorting can be heard coming from under the tree. A deep voice laughs at every sound the horse makes. Anyone investigating finds a **hill giant** sitting with its back against the apple tree's trunk. The giant has a broken branch of apples in its hand and casually nibbles apples from the leaves. A **unicorn** with its head bent low stands beside the relaxing giant. A massive club lies on the ground by the giant's leg.

Kurg is a bounty hunter employed to find unicorn horns for an evil magic-user. The dimwitted giant somehow discovered one of the creatures, but couldn't bring himself to kill the beautiful creature. Instead, he's determined to drag the horse back to the wizard alive and collect his reward. Kurg has a unique strategy to keep the unicorn from getting away when he sleeps or rests: He slams the (slightly dazed) animal's head into trees, letting its own horn hold it fast. The animal bucks and kicks, but is unable to pull itself free. Kurg fights anyone trying to free the unicorn, thinking they are looking to collect the bounty from the mage themselves.

Urrslumber

Hit Dice: 5
Armor Class: 4 [15]
Attacks: 1 grapple in plant form (1d6 + sleep poison), or 1 claw or bite in bear form (2d6)
Saving Throw: 12
Special: Surprise on 1-4 in plant form, gaze attack (blindness) in bear form, bear form is blind.
Move: 9
Alignment: Chaos
Number Encountered: 1
Challenge Level/XP: 6/400

By day, the urrslumber is a lurching heap of leafy vegetation, roughly in the shape of a headless bear, with tangled masses of thorny limb-vines extending from a twisted clump of pliable abdominal roots; when stationary, it is nearly indistinguishable from normal plant life. It hunts by ambush, sensing the vibrations of passersby and lunging forth to grapple with its thorny limbs. Its thorns secrete a sleep-inducing poison with effects that last for 1d6 hours, possibly less, depending on size and constitution of the victim. The urrslumber drags sleeping prey back to its lair (often within the root base of an enormous tree), binds the prey, and awaits nightfall. At sunset, the urrslumber transforms into a jet-black bear with red, sightless eyes. In this form, it hungrily devours the captured prey and then falls asleep, transforming back into plant form at sunrise. While in bear form, the urrslumber's gaze causes blindness for 1d6 rounds (saving throw negates). If it is killed while in plant form, the urrslumber regenerates completely from its remains (even burnt ashes) on the next new moon. Urrslumbers killed in bear form are permanently dead.

— *Author: Guy Fullerton*

Urrslumber: HD 5; AC 4[15]; Atk 1 grapple in plant form (1d6 + sleep poison), or 1 claw or bite in bear form (2d6); Move 9; Save 12; AL C; CL/XP 6/400; Special: Surprise opponents on a 1-4 in plant form, gaze attack (blindness) in bear form, and the bear form itself is blind.

Sleepaway Camp

A small cabin sits in this clearing in the deep woods. It has six wooden bunk beds for travellers and a small porcelain wash basin. A chunk of lye soap lies inside the basin. A small porch wraps around the wooden structure. Six rickety but usable chairs sit outside for anyone wanting to enjoy the night air. A 5-foot-wide shallow firepit filled with thick ash sits in a dirt clearing outside the cabin's door. Someone recently used the firepit to stoke up a small bonfire. Grass is scorched in a 15-foot-wide circle around the ring of stones surrounding the ash pit. The low-hanging leaves hanging over the area are singed and curled. A burnt axe handle rests in a clump of wildflowers.

A group of loggers burned an **urrslumber** in the firepit. They tossed the leafy creature into the flames and kept it there with their axes. They cremated the creature, stoking the fires higher to burn its body completely. The loggers departed the next day, satisfied they'd killed the forest demon. They didn't know the creature would rise on the next full moon. The urrslumber rises out of the firepit in the moonlight, reforming into a jet-black bear with red eyes to devour anyone camping in the cabin.

Uruak (Scrap Gnoll)

Hit Dice: 2
Armor Class: 5 [14]
Attacks: 1 weapon (1d10)
Saving Throw: 16
Special: May possess explosives or firearms
Move: 12
Alignment: Chaos
Number Encountered: 4d10
Challenge Level/XP: 2/30

Uruak, or "scrap gnolls" are a race of hyena-like humanoids from an alternate reality, similar to gnolls in appearance but much more intelligent. They are intelligent, civilised, and fanatically obsessed with mechanical devices and inventions. The culture of their world is equivalent to the Bronze Age. Scrap gnolls managed to survive magical cataclysms and inhospitable wastelands by combining their scavenging and tool-using skills. Although their world is now believed destroyed, they have somehow spread across the multiverse. Wherever they go, the landscape is littered with smashed sand ships, exploded steam engines, and rusting piles of scrap left behind their evolving technological skills.

Scrap gnolls spend most of their time creating and testing tools and devices, for they are instinctively gifted artificers. Many scrap gnolls are skilled in alchemy, clockwork, mining and smithing, and they may possess crude explosives (3d6 damage in 10' radius, must be thrown, may have a timing device of up to 3 rounds) or arquebus-type 'smoke-powder' weapons (1d10 damage, backfire and be unusable until repaired on an attack roll of 1). Any weapons they make will be finely crafted and lovingly cared for. In a group of 6 or more scrap gnolls, there will be a leader with magic-user spells and the vision to direct the gnolls in working together towards a major task, as well as a pet snake or scorpion as their mascot. For every male actively inventing, scrounging, or repairing, there will be a female of close kin seeing to the more mundane domestic tasks. All scrap gnolls yearn to regain the expertise of building ornithopters and battle-automata.

— Author: Scott Wylie Roberts, "Myrystyr"

Uruak (Scrap Gnoll): HD 2; AC 5[14]; Atk 1 weapon (1d10); Move 12; Save 16; AL C; CL/XP 2/30; Special: May possess explosives or firearms.

mandibles (1d4), 1 sting (1 + non-lethal poison); Move 12; Save 14; AL L; CL/XP 4/120; Special: Non-lethal poison sting (2d4 damage, save for half).

The Watched Clock

In the Urlick Wastes, a massive 40-foot-diameter metal clock face juts halfway out of the shifting sands. Half of the clock rises 20 feet above the ground, with the rest buried. Giant metal hands move sluggishly through the clogging sand. A door in the side of the frame enters a nightmare of copper pipes, bent metal struts and other bits of strange metals. Gears and pulleys whir and click around curious intruders. Metal circular stairs lead downward into a shaft descending 90 feet under the sand.

A lost colony of **20 uruak** lives inside the clock tower. They have been here a long time (before the desert was even named), waiting for the clock to strike a specific time foretold in their myths. The uruak are peaceful, looking only to maintain their clock and to keep it winding forward. What happens when the clock strikes the appointed hour is left to the Game Referee.

Despite their isolation, the uruak are under constant attack by an army of **15 formian scavengers (10 workers** and **5 warriors)** that are constantly trying to dismantle the clock and carry off its inner workings. Any help stopping the formians puts PCs in the uruaks' good graces.

Formian Worker: HD 1; AC 3[16]; Atk 1 bite (1d4); Move 15; Save 17; AL L; CL/XP 1/15; Special: None.

Formian Warrior: HD 3; AC 2[17]; Atk 1 bite (1d6), 2

Vampire Tree (Jubokko)

Hit Dice: 4
Armor Class: 6 [13]
Attacks: 4 branches (1d6)
Saving Throw: 13
Special: Immobilization
Move: 0
Alignment: Neutrality
Number Encountered: 1d3
Challenge Level/XP: 6/400

The Jubokko grow on battlefields or other scenes of bloody carnage, where so much human blood may be shed on the ground that it is sucked up in great quantities by the roots of nearby trees. These trees grow up nourished by this blood, and knowing no other sustenance, they begin to thirst for the blood of human beings. They will await motionless, appearing as a normal tree, until some unsuspecting person passing beneath is snatched up by its branches and murdered, the trees then feast upon their victims blood. If the Jubokko hits with 2 of its branches against a single victim, that victim becomes immobilized and cannot fight or cast spells until freed by his companions. Such a victim becomes AC 9[10] for further attacks by the Jubokko.

Vampire Tree/Jubokko: HD 4; AC 6[13]; Atk 4 branches (1d6); Move 0; Save 13; AL N; CL/XP 6/400; Special: Immobilization.

Up a Tree

The broken body of a fighter in plate mail is slumped against the bloody roots of a tall cedar tree. The man's plate mail is crushed around his limp form, making his arms and legs jut out in unnatural directions. A crumpled shield lies in the thick grasses. The metal has been bent nearly in half. The branches and limbs above the man shake and shudder as if something large hides among the leaf canopy.

Tung Antonfeld was a knight off to war who decided — unfortunately, it turned out — to rest beneath the cedar tree's quiet leaves and contemplate his existence. The massive oak is a **Jubokko** that grabbed Tung and crushed him to death as soon as the man fell asleep. Tung's trusty warhorse Oakstaff didn't fare much better. The tree grabbed the animal and pulled it in the high branches to consume. The dying animal kicks the branches around it with its hooves. The branches shake under the weakening assault. The jubokko drops the horse to get at PCs investigating the dead knight. Oakstaff falls through the high branches, bouncing back and forth before striking the ground.

Vampire

Hit Dice: 7–9
Armor Class: 2 [17]
Attacks: Bite (1d10 + level drain)
Saving Throw: 9, 8, or 6
Special: See below
Move: 12/18 (flying)
Alignment: Chaos
Number Encountered: 1d4
Challenge Level/XP: 7 HD (9/1,100), 8 HD (10/1,400), 9 HD (11/1,700)

Vampires are some of the most powerful of undead creatures. They can only be hit with magic weapons, and when "killed" in this way they turn into a gaseous form, returning to their coffins. They regenerate at a rate of 3 hit points per round, can turn into a gaseous form or into a giant bat at will, and can summon a horde of bats or 3d6 wolves out from the night. Looking into a vampire's eyes necessitates a saving throw at -2, or the character is charmed (per the *Charm Person* spell). Most terrifyingly, a vampire's bite drains two levels from the victim. Fortunately, vampires have some weaknesses. They can be killed (though these are the only known methods) by immersing them in running water, exposing them to sunlight, or driving a wooden stake through the heart. They retreat from the smell of garlic, the sight of a mirror, or the sight of "good" holy symbols. Any human killed by a vampire becomes a vampire under the control of its creator.

This description will be recognized easily as the "Dracula" type of vampire. Many other possibilities for vampires exist in folklore: Chinese vampires, for instance, and blood-drinkers more feral than intelligent. Plus, other cultural templates with different attributes could be created— how about an ancient Egyptian mummified vampire, or an Aztec vampire?

Vampire (7HD): HD 7; AC 2[17]; Atk 1 bite (1d10 + level drain); Move 12 (Fly 18); Save 9; AL C; CL/XP 10/1400; Special: Immune to non-magic weapons, only killed in coffin, regenerate (3/round), gaseous form, shapeshift, summon rats or wolves, charm gaze, drain 2 levels with hit.

Vampire (8HD): HD 8; AC 2[17]; Atk 1 bite (1d10 + level drain); Move 12 (Fly 18); Save 8; AL C; CL/XP 11/1700; Special: Immune to non-magic weapons, only killed in coffin, regenerate (3/round), gaseous form, shapeshift, summon rats or wolves, charm gaze, drain 2 levels with hit.

Vampire (9HD): HD 9; AC 2[17]; Atk 1 bite (1d10 + level drain); Move 12 (Fly 18); Save 6; AL C; CL/XP 12/2000; Special: Immune to non-magic weapons, only killed in coffin, regenerate (3/round), gaseous form, shapeshift, summon rats or wolves, charm gaze, drain 2 levels with hit.

The Patient Handmaiden

This immaculate chamber is decorated in finery usually reserved for royalty. Flickering wall sconces provide golden light that fills the windowless room. Liquid-filled ornate flasks sit on shelves all about the room. Purple cushions rest on a plush red carpet and a low silver divan stands before a gold-leaf bathtub. Plush folded towels sit on the divan. Long white curtains hanging from the ceiling obscure the tub. A woman lounges in the tub, her form obvious but her features hidden by the curtains. A handmaiden dressed in a white robe kneels outside the curtained bathing area, awaiting the woman's command.

The woman in the tub is a recently slain adventurer named Regina Bont. Her blood fills the tub, freshly drained out of slits cut into her arms, legs and neck. The handmaiden is a **vampire** named **Helene Sendriss** who drains beautiful maidens and then stores their blood in flasks sitting on the shelves around the room. She keeps the blood for a "rainy day."

Vapor Crane

	LARGE ADULT	SMALL ADULT	FLEDGLING
Hit Dice:	6	3	2
Armor Class: 4[15]			
Attacks:	1 bite (1d4+5)	1 bite (1d4+2)	1 bite (1d4+1)
Saving Throw:	12	16	17
Special: Scalding to touch, steam cloud (1d6+1/ hit die) in cone or 15ft radius			
Move: 5/12 (flying)			
Alignment: Neutrality			
Number Encountered: 1d6 (mixed group)			
Challenge Level/XP:	7/600	4/120	3/60

Vapor Cranes make their homes where geysers spews and hot springs make great boiling pools, arranging their rock nests so that they fill with boiling water. Strangely, they do not eat, but draw their sustenance from the steaming waters they inhabit. They will attempt to fly away if they are endangered but they will fight to the death if cornered.

Touching a Vapor Crane without the proper precautions can be deadly, for their bodies are boiling hot (1d6+1 hp/hit die). They are also able to spew clouds of steam from their nostrils as both an offensive and a defensive measure and will use this ability to flee, unless guarding a nest. The steam cloud can be used in one of two ways (3 times per day total): if the crane is attacking, it blows the steam in a cone 30ft long to a width of 30ft, inflicting 1d6 + 1/ hit die. When used defensively, the crane surrounds itself with the cloud in a radius of 15ft, which not only inflicts damage but also obscures the bird from sight. In normal combat, a vapor crane attacks with its beak, which is filled with needle-sharp teeth.

— Author: Russell Cone

Large Adult Vapor Crane: HD 6; AC 4[15]; Atk 1 bite (1d4+5); Move 5 (Fly 12); Save 12; AL N; CL/XP 7/600; Special: Scalding to touch, steam cloud (1d6+1/ hit die) in cone or 15ft radius.

Small Adult Vapor Crane: HD 3; AC 4[15]; Atk 1 bite (1d4+2); Move 5 (Fly 12); Save 16; AL N; CL/XP 4/120; Special: Scalding to touch, steam cloud (1d6+1/ hit die) in cone or 15ft radius.

Fledgling Vapor Crane: HD 2; AC 4[15]; Atk 1 bite (1d4+1); Move 5 (Fly 6); Save 17; AL N; CL/XP 3/60; Special: Scalding to touch, steam cloud (1d6+1/ hit die) in cone or 15ft radius.

The Angry Statue

A 20-foot-tall idol carved from volcanic rock sits amid banyan trees in the jungle. The giant idol has large eyes, flaring nostrils and vicious fangs like a monstrous tiki idol. Curls of steam rise from vents in the idol's wide base, and wisps blast periodically out of the nostrils. Ten-foot-wide hot springs are located in the clearing around the statue; A small geyser erupts every few minutes through the statue's hollow center. The water jet blasts upward and causes trickles of dark water to wind down the creases and curves of the idol's horrid face. A low basalt altar sits beneath the idol's face, its crystal top stained with blood and bits of gore. Grasses around the altar are blasted and withered.

A **vapor crane** makes its nest inside the statue's left nostril. The bird shoots its steam cloud outward at anyone looking into the nostril, and the rock channels the blast into the intruder. The altar normally takes the brunt of the blasts when the bird is startled.

Vargouille

Hit Dice: 1
Armor Class: 8 [11]
Attacks: 1 bite (1d4)
Saving Throw: 17
Special: Permanent hp loss
Move: 0/12 (flying)
Alignment: Chaos
Number Encountered: 1d20
Challenge Level/XP: 3/60

Vargouilles are demonic creatures, a horrid head, bearded with small, writhing tentacles, with bat wings protruding from the back. Their bite is deadly, causing permanent hit point loss (saving throw).

Vargouille: HD 1; AC 8[11]; Atk 1 bite (1d4); Move 0 (Fly 12); Save 17; AL C; CL/XP 3/60; Special: permanent hit point loss.

Trophy Room

Nearly 40 severed heads of dwarves, elves, humans and even orcs hang from rusting chains in this dark dungeon room. Their eyes and mouths are open, and many still show the terror of their last moments. Dried blood coats the floor beneath the ugly trophies. The wide splotches mar the tile floor. A few of the heads swing slightly in undetectable air currents moving through the chamber. The room smells of decay. Hundreds of chains with empty hooks on the end dangle among the heads. The bodies are nowhere to be found.

One of the heads is a **vargouille** that sits on a small swinging platform beneath a rusty chain. The demonic head keeps its wings curled behind it until it rises up to attack. The heads are its trophies from its nightly forays.

Varn (Eternal Gladiator)

Hit Dice: 5
Armor Class: 2 [17]
Attacks: 1 +1 weapon (1d10+1)
Saving Throw: 12
Special: Undead immunities, takes double damage from fire
Move: 9
Alignment: Neutrality
Number Encountered: 1
Challenge Level/XP: 5/240

These are the restless spirits of dead fighters and warriors whose armor continues to fight long after they are gone. The armor stands six feet tall (sometimes taller), and is usually of the plate mail type. Varn carry enchanted weapons, usually a +1 sword or axe. Because it is an animated suit of armor, it has immunity to *charm, sleep,* and *cold* spells. However, fire spells do +1 additional damage to eternal gladiators. Varn are typically not used to guard locations, as they will attack anyone who gets near them on sight. They can be found in dungeons, or at the locations of large battles.

A weapon that has been used by an eternal gladiator will be cursed forever after; attempts to remove the curse will simply cause it to collapse into rust. A varn may be turned as a wight.

Varn: HD 5; AC 2[17]; Atk 1 +1 weapon (1d10+1); Move 9; Save 12; AL N; CL/XP 5/240; Special: Undead immunities, takes double damage from fire.

The Warden's Tomb

A 10-foot-tall iron fence cuts through the forest, vines and weeds growing up around it. Beyond the fence is a weed-covered clearing. One-foot-square grave markers set into the ground are aligned in perfect rows. Each bears a single, unknown number.

Dunkire Prison is lost to memory, but its cemetery remains. The graveyard is nearly a mile square, but overrun by the forest it was hidden within. Hundreds of bodies are buried here, each nothing more than a prisoner number. These were the worst of the worst who died within the prison's walls.

A stone mausoleum in the center of the graveyard is the only structure within the clearing. Cherry trees surround the stone building. Four carved caryatids hold the roof. A weathered name on a marker over the door is illegible, but the words "beloved warden" can be made out.

Inside the structure is a sarcophagus set into the tiled floor. It is carved to resemble the man buried within. Standing before the grave is the warden's guardian, a Varn who fell in battle protecting the body from those who would defile it, and continues to do so after death.

Vierd

Hit Dice: 2+4
Armor Class: 6 [13]
Attacks: 2 claws (1d3 + paralysis), 2 bites (1d4 + disease)
Saving Throw: 16
Special: Paralysis, disease, immunities
Move: 9
Alignment: Chaos
Number Encountered: 1d6+1
Challenge Level/XP: 4/120

Vierds are creepy, two-headed cousins to ghouls, standing only 3ft tall. They are nocturnal albinos with pink eyes, yellow claws and dirty fangs. Like their kin, they are immune to charm and sleep spells. A vierd has a paralyzing touch on a failed save (2d6 turns), and if bitten, the victim must make a saving throw or contract a disease. The diseased spot must be purified (burning, amputation, holy water, etc.) in order to arrest the spread of the disease.

— Author: Oldcrawler

Vierd: HD 2+4; AC 6[13]; Atk 2 claws (1d3 + paralysis), 2 bites (1d4 + disease); Move 9; Save 16; AL C; CL/XP 4/120; Special: Paralysis, disease, immunities.

The Leper's Curse

Disease struck the hamlet of Pyrot's Grove many months ago. The residents of the small town walk around dazed and confused. All have painful red sores that are spreading over their bodies. Men sit on doorsteps, too beaten down by cancers burning within them to move. Women and children cough up bloody bits from deep in their lungs. Animals slink along the streets behind their masters, the heads drooping. No one is immune to the horrible wasting disease. The townsfolk believe the gods are punishing them for turning away a leper who sought safe haven from ruffians on the road. Worse still, some of the villagers are missing. They vanished right out of their homes a couple of nights ago. The remaining people are frightened and fearful of strangers.

The true culprits are **5 vierds** living in a cemetery outside town. Weeds cover most of the headstones, and all but one mausoleum has crumbled. The vierds paralyze victims and drag them into the mausoleum to devour at their leisure. Their forays into the hamlet contaminated the town with the many diseases they carry. Getting rid of the creatures prevents more outbreaks and allows the villagers to be cured.

Walking Slime

Hit Dice: 2
Armor Class: 9 [11]
Attacks: 1 (1d6 + turn to slime)
Saving Throw: 16
Special: Transform to slime
Move: 6
Alignment: Neutrality
Number Encountered: 1
Challenge Level/XP: 4/120

These vaguely humanoid monsters slop their way through underground passages in search of living flesh to "eat." They attack by smacking prey with their large oozing fists, attempting to cover them and turn them into living slimes as well (on a natural roll of 15+, the victim must make a saving throw or begin transforming into a walking slime).

— *Author: Random*

Walking Slime: HD 2; AC 9[11]; Atk 1 (1d6 + turn to slime); Move 6; Save 16; AL N; CL/XP 4/120; Special: Transform to slime.

Glowing Goop

Goopy footprints lead down the flagstones of this stone passage. Each step glows a ghastly green in the darkness. A phosphorescent handprint occasionally appears on a wall or door, although these are few and far between. The prints eventually lead through an arched doorway carved to resemble a demon's face. A 12-foot-wide flowering plant spreads across the floor beneath the archway, its fronds arching like a low canopy. Giant tendrils flow across the stone floor, some winding through the broken stones where the plant pushed its way out of the earth. The petals glow the same nauseating green as the footsteps.

The plant is harmless, a mutant variety thriving in the nutrient-rich earth beneath the stone hallway. It gives off fragrant pollen that smells like rotting meat. The room's true danger is a **walking slime** that sleeps beneath the plant's protective leaves. The creature is coated in the plant's phosphorescent pollen, which makes it glow in the dark.

Wandering Hole

Hit Dice: 5
Armor Class: 1 [18]
Attacks: 1 special
Saving Throw: 12
Special: Surprise, constrict
Move: 12
Alignment: Neutrality
Number Encountered: 1
Challenge Level/XP: 7/600

A wandering hole is a creature that exists in a different dimension but extends into the normal world as a living emptiness, a hole in space. In its expanded form, it resembles a 10ft x 10ft hole running 20ft to 50ft deep (1d4+1 x10). The creature possesses the capacity to constrict its anti-mass to a 1/4 inch square. Contracting itself from a 10ft x 10ft square to a 1/4in x 1/4in square takes 1d4+1 rounds. Expanding its form back to 10ft x 10ft takes only 1 round. The most common tactic used by wandering holes is to constrict themselves to their smallest size, then, as an adventurer walks above, the wandering hole expands, sending the victim plummeting down its depth. The wandering hole then compresses itself anew to crush the hapless victim. Victims of this tactic always run the risk of being surprised (50%).

Victims who find themselves within the depths of a wandering hole have but 1d4+1 rounds to get themselves out before the contracting critter crushes them: on the last round, the constricting wandering hole crushes the victim to death.

Wandering holes may be damaged, but only by spells or magic weapons and items. When it dies, a wandering hole returns to its expanded size of 10ft x 10ft, but as a normal, nonliving hole in the ground.

— Author: Skathros

Wandering Hole: HD 5; AC 1[18]; Atk 1 special; Move 12; Save 12; AL N; CL/XP 7/600; Special: Surprise, Constrict.

Garbage Disposal

Piles of refuse cover the floor of this cavernous room. Bone mounds, bodies and animal carcasses rot amid the stalagmites and stone columns. The smell is horrible. A slanted granite slab leans against the 30-foot-tall wall. A dazed elf lies on a pile of gnoll bodies. He moans feebly, and rolls across the bloody bodies beneath him. He doesn't appear to know where he is.

Standing before the stone slab are **3 hill giants.** The giants take turns tossing refuse into a 10-foot-diameter hole cut into the stone. The giants hoot and holler gleefully as they chuck bodies and half-eaten meals into the pit. The giants continue shoveling things into the pit unless stopped. They'll eventually reach the poor elf.

If PCs intervene, the giants attack with wooden clubs. They also try to grab PCs and throw them into the pit. Anyone thrown or knocked into the hole lands amid a heap of dead bodies, bones and smelly garbage. That PC also learns the secret of the pit that made the hill giants so happy: It's actually a **wandering hole** lying on the slanted wall. The hole constricts to crush the garbage the giants toss into it, but prefers warm flesh.

Tovalit Greene is an elf from a noble family. He sought to prove himself by taking down the hill giant clan that was ransacking elven villages along the High Cavelis River. He was taken out with one hit from a giant's club and tossed into the pile of dead gnolls. Tovalit doesn't remember who he is, but his family pays 300 gp for his safe return (if PCs can figure out where to take the poor elf).

Hill Giant: HD 8+2; AC 4[15]; Atk 1 weapon (2d8); Move 12; Save 8; AL C; CL/XP 9/1100; Special: Throw boulders.

Wasp, Giant

Hit Dice: 4
Armor Class: 4 [15]
Attacks: 1 sting (1d4 + poison), 1 bite (1d8)
Saving Throw: 13
Special: Paralyzing poison, larvae
Move: 1/20 (flying)
Alignment: Neutrality
Number Encountered: 1d20
Challenge Level/XP: 6/400

Giant wasps are as large as humans, and are incredibly aggressive. Their sting paralyzes (saving throw) for 1d4+1 days (at the end of which time, wasp larvae eat the victim from the inside out). Cure disease will kill the larvae. The wasp wings are paper-thin, and flammable.

Giant Wasp: HD 4; AC 4[15]; Atk 1 sting (1d4 + poison), 1 bite (1d8); Move 1 (Fly 20); Save 13; AL N; CL/XP 6/400; Special: Paralyzing poison, larvae.

Ground Assault

A prospector's body lies next to the bloated carcass of his mule. Both are barely recognizable from numerous ragged and bloody holes puncturing their dead bodies. The mule's distended belly pulses as larvae crawl beneath its skin. Both have been dead for days.

A buzzing reverberates through the stone canyon if PCs disturb the bodies. The low hum echoes off the rocks and seems to come from deep underground. The buzzing grows louder until **8 giant wasps** launch themselves into the air from rocky tunnels that lead underground to a nest built into the canyon wall. The aggressive wasps attack anyone in the canyon. The prospector carries a pickaxe, a coil of rope and rations for a few days. The mule has a saddle, a pouch containing a lock of golden hair, and a journal with women's names written into it. A strap wrapped around the miner's belt holds four gemstones worth 200 gp each.

Weasel, Giant

Hit Dice: 3+3
Armor Class: 6 [13]
Attacks: 1 bite (2d6+blood drain)
Saving Throw: 14
Special: Drain blood
Move: 15
Alignment: Neutrality
Number Encountered: 1d8
Challenge Level/XP: 4/120

These ferocious predators are often found in dungeon complexes, for they lair in caves. When a giant weasel hits an opponent, it clamps its jaws and sucks blood, automatically inflicting 2d6 points of damage per round. Giant weasels can be trained as guard animals; although they cannot be trained to warn of intruders, they are far more deadly than guard dogs. Their pelts sell for 1d6x100gp each.

Giant Weasel: HD 3+3; AC 6[13]; Atk 1 bite (2d6 + blood drain); Move 15; Save 14; AL N; CL/XP 4/120; Special: Drain blood.

Pop Goes the Giant Weasel

Giant ferns and flowering plants fill this magnificent garden paradise in the Crimson Vale. Scarlet-hued birds of paradise flit swoop through the trees, and squawking parrots sit on twisting branches. Thick grasses sway in the summer breezes. Butterflies flit from flower to flower in long ribbons of color.

The picturesque garden is the hunting ground of a **giant weasel**. The weasel sleeps in a cave in the center of the garden, but hunts for many miles around its den. The animal stalks prey by staying beneath the plant life, then pops up out of the ferns and flowers to grab a victim in its teeth. It tries to carry prey off to devour in peace. Its lair contains a dead warhorse (with a chewed leather saddle containing 60 gp, a ruby-encrusted chalice (100 gp) and a set of silverware (30 gp).

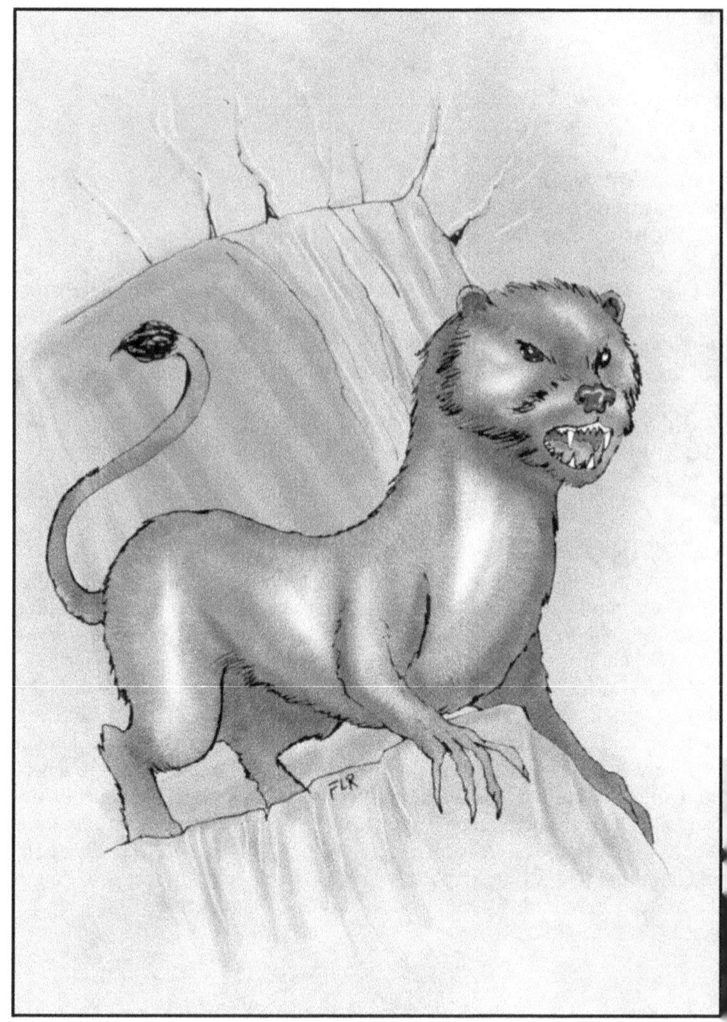

Were-Mist

Hit Dice: 3+3
Armor Class: 4 [15]
Attacks: 1 enfold (special)
Saving Throw: 14
Special: Immune to non-magic weapons, transform and enslave
Move: 9
Alignment: Chaos
Number Encountered: 1
Challenge Level/XP: 6/400

Despite its name, a were-mist is not a form of true lycanthropy, but is a monster than can inflict involuntary shapechanging upon other creatures. The were-mist attacks by enveloping and attempting to transform an opponent. The creature surrounded by the were-mist must make a saving throw or be transformed into a ravening beast (similar in appearance to a werewolf) that will attack at the were-mist's directions. The were-mist remains wrapped around the victim, but it can be attacked independently without risk to the controlled creature. The were-mist itself can only be harmed by silver or magical weapons (or with spells), but the beast-form of its slaves may be damaged normally.

When the were-mist's slave is weakened by combat, the mist will attempt to move on to a new victim. As soon as it departs from a victim, the spell is broken and the slave returns to normal shape and self-control. In battle, the were-mist will attempt to move from victim to victim, causing them to attack their allies, and discarding one puppet when it becomes weak, moving to the next strongest potential victim.

Were-mists are solitary due to their rarity, rather than due to an unwillingness to congregate; in rare instances there might be lairs containing more than one of these creatures. Since they do not appear to reproduce, such better-populated lairs might exist closer to whatever "source" creates the mists.

— Author: Matt Finch

Were-mist: HD 3+3; AC 4[15]; Atk 1 enfold (special); Move 9; Save 14; AL C; CL/XP 6/400; Special: Immune to non-magic weapons, transform and enslave.

Source of Confusion

A green tapered bottle with a large cork stuck in its end sits on a four-foot-tall stone pedestal in this 60-foot-diameter circular chamber. Pinkish mists bubble and roll fluidly inside the glass. Two doors lead out of the room. Crumpled on the floor are eight skeletons. The skeletons appear to have been ripped and torn apart. Clothing and bits of bone are cast throughout the chamber.

The roiling contents of the bottle is a **were-mist**. Removing the bottle from the shelf causes two portcullises to clank closed over the exits. The gates are sturdy, but can be lifted by a couple of PCs and pushed up into the door frame to lock them in place again.

The were-mist appears to be contained by the cork in the bottle neck, but appearances are deceiving. The were-mist can flow easily through pores in the old cork to escape its container. It waits until a PC is holding the bottle before flowing out to engulf him. The skeletons are a group of adventurers who were torn apart by one of their own when the mist changed him into a feral beast. PCs looting the corpses can find 67 gp, an onyx ring (50 gp), a calendar with nights of the eclipses marked, and a gold key.

Whale, Killer

Hit Dice: 12
Armor Class: 4 [15]
Attacks: 1 bite (3d10)
Saving Throw: 3
Special: None
Move: 24 (swimming)
Alignment: Neutrality
Number Encountered: 2d6
Challenge Level/XP: 12/2,000

Killer whales might be found as the allies of any intelligent underwater species, chaotic or lawful, good or evil. Some killer whales are as intelligent as humans, others are not.

Killer Whale: HD 12; AC 4[15]; Atk 1 bite (3d10); Move (Swim 24); Save 3; AL N; CL/XP 12/2000; Special: None.

Revenge Served Cold

A fisherman wearing thick seal skin lies sprawled on an ice floe surrounded by the freezing waters of the Icefringe Sea. He appears unconscious, lying face down on the ice. A spear lies beside his gloved hand. The wicked barb at the end of the spear is bloody and has a chunk of blubber hanging from it.

No'lan Frostreacher fishes the bitterly cold waves to feed his family. He recently killed a young orca, however, and did not honor the kill. Its mother rose from the depths to take revenge.

The large **killer whale** tracked the fisherman to his home on the ice and battered its way upward until it erupted inside the couple's igloo. No'lan's wife disappeared beneath the cold waters. No'lan escaped onto a floating sheet of ice but now suffers from exposure to the harsh elements. The mother whale swims beneath the ice floe, pushing it forward and out to sea. She leaps from the water to attack anyone helping the doomed fisherman. Her weight causes the massive ice block to tip precariously, dumping PCs who fail a saving throw and No'lan into the frigid waves.

Whale, Sperm

Hit Dice: 36
Armor Class: 4 [15]
Attacks: 1 bite (4d10), 1 tail (4d10)
Saving Throw: 3
Special: Swallow whole
Move: 18 (swimming)
Alignment: Neutrality
Number Encountered: 1
Challenge Level/XP: 37/7,400

Sperm whales can swallow small ships whole, and automatically swallow whole any human-sized prey they hit with an attack. Blows from their tails destroy boats and might also destroy ships, or damage them terribly. Some sperm whales are intelligent (and often malevolent).

Sperm Whale: HD 36; AC 4[15]; Atk 1 bite (4d10), 1 tail (4d10); Move (Swim 18); Save 3; AL N; CL/XP 37/7400; Special: Swallow whole.

Whalers' Lament

A whaling ship glides across the ocean; its colorful sails tattered and bleached by the sun. Sailors slump over the rails or hang motionless in the tangled rigging. Blankets cover bodies stacked like cordwood on the deck. The ship's captain stands resolutely at the wheel, eyes forward, refusing to turn his ship. A few seamen on deck beckon passing ships closer, some looking as if they might jump into the deep to escape the ship of the dead and dying.

The Lionfish angered a great **sperm whale** and the crew is paying the price. The whale was struck by three harpoons, but broke free of the ropes. It now follows the ship's wake. When the Lionfish turns toward land, the whale nudges it back into open water. When another ship sails near the vessel, the whale sinks it. The sailors have been at sea for weeks now, and their food is nearly gone. Many aboard died from sunstroke, dehydration or starvation. The men refuse to throw the dead overboard to spite the wicked whale.

Wight

Hit Dice: 3
Armor Class: 5 [14]
Attacks: 1 claw (1hp + level drain)
Saving Throw: 14
Special: Drain 1 level with hit, hit only by magic or silver weapons
Move: 9
Alignment: Chaos
Number Encountered: 2d8
Challenge Level/XP: 6/400

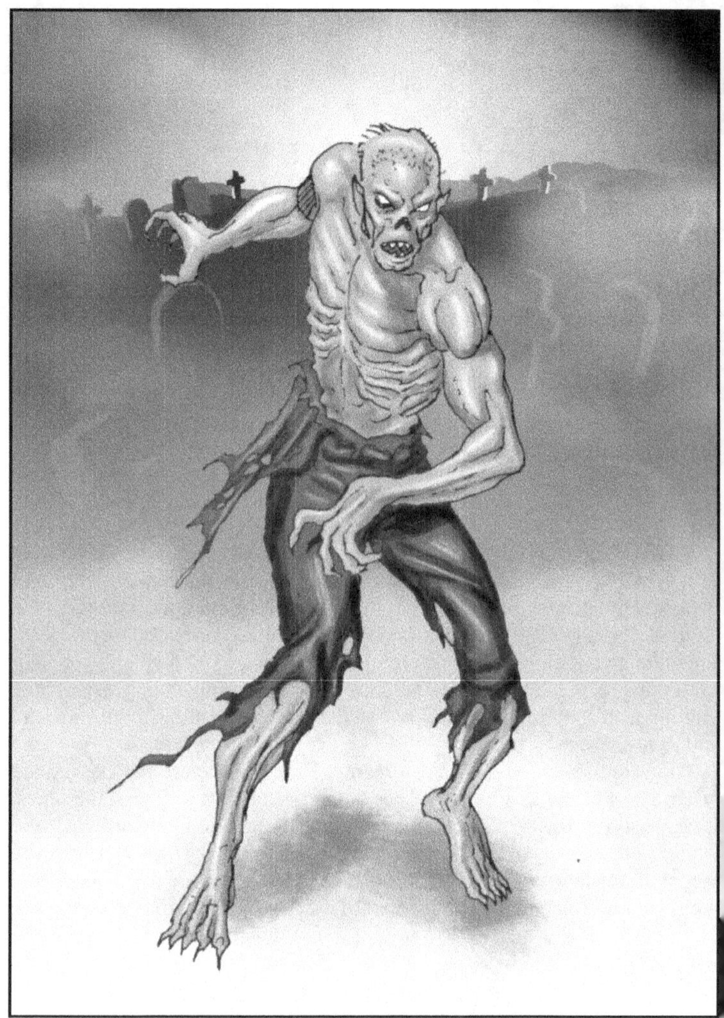

Wights live in tombs, graveyards, and burial mounds (barrows). They are undead, and thus not affected by sleep or charm spells. Wights are immune to all non-magical weapons, with the exception of silver weapons. Any human killed or completely drained of levels by a wight becomes a wight.

Wight: HD 3; AC 5[14]; Atk 1 claw (1hp + level drain); Move 9; Save 14; AL C; CL/XP 6/400; Special: Drain 1 level with hit, hit only by magic or silver weapons.

Digging Out

Frantic villagers dig at the ruins of a collapsed house, pulling beams and walls free. Others scoop dirt and debris up with their hands and buckets. The people's voices are frantic as they dig. A wooden roof lies at an angle over the broken masonry pushed out beneath it. The people pause to listen occasionally, and the sounds of digging coming up through the rubble can be heard. The villagers have no idea why the building fell in upon itself, but they believe the owner, a moneylender named Castor Wainwright, is trapped inside.

The paranoid banker feared thieves breaking into his home to steal his fortunes. He rigged the entire house with traps to protect himself and his gold. Unfortunately, those same traps turned out to be a little too effective when Castor heard a noise in the night. He pulled a lever to seal off the rooms, but instead everything came crashing down around him and his two bodyguards. The intruders turned out to be **2 wights** that climbed in through an open window and became trapped with the three men. The wights made short work of the injured banker and his guards. When rescuers break through the rubble, **5 wights** are eagerly digging out to meet them.

Wight, Sea

Hit Dice: 4+3
Armor Class: 4 [15]
Attacks: 1 touch (level drain)
Special: Energy drain, silver or magic weapon to hit, command other undead
Move: 12/9 (swimming)
Saving Throw: 13
Alignment: Chaos
Number Encountered: 1 or 2d10
Challenge Level/XP: 7/600

Sea-wights are highly similar to normal wights, originating from bodies in ocean-flooded tombs, bodies that were consigned to the depths of the ocean, or from individuals – usually those of some power – who perished beneath the dark waves. They have a more bloated appearance than normal wights, and their skins are crusted with barnacles or other sea-growths, giving them a somewhat better armor class than a land-wight. In the course of transforming into a sea-wight, the hands and feet become webbed, allowing the creatures to swim at a rate of 90ft.

Sea-wights have a greater tendency than normal wights to associate with and command other undead creatures. Although some sea-wights are solitary, many sea-wight lairs are found in ship graveyards, forest-beds of deep seaweed, and other places that may have a strong evil animus. In this case, the lair will ordinarily contain the following:

1d4+4 Additional **sea-wights**
1d4 **giant zombie sharks** (50% chance)
2d10 **giant zombie piranhas** (q.v.) (75% chance)
1d10 **human zombies** (80% chance)
1 **giant zombie octopus** (10% chance)

All of the zombie creatures in a sea-wight lair will be under the control of the strongest sea-wight. If this wight is killed, 2 rounds will be required for the next strongest sea-wight to establish dominance over the creatures.

Giant zombie sharks and giant zombie octopi have an armor class inferior by 1 point to the normal AC of the living creature, but have an additional hit die. They are otherwise identical to the living form of the creature, but will attack last in any melee round.

As with normal wights, a successful attack by a sea-wight drains one level of experience from the victim, and a fully-drained victim rises as a sea-wight of half normal strength under the command of its killer.

— *Author: Matt Finch*

Sea-Wight: HD 4+3; AC 4[15]; Atk 1 touch (level drain); Move 12 (Swim 9); Save 13; AL C; CL/XP 7/600; Special: Drain 1 level with hit, hit only by magic or silver weapons, command other undead.

Giant Octopus Zombie: HD 7; AC 8[11]; Atk 8 tentacles (1d3); Move 2 (Swim 6); Save 9; AL N; CL/XP 10/1400; Special: Immune to sleep and charm.

Wight Water

Destiny's Traveler lies under 50 feet of water, its hull split by a jagged hole running along the wooden side. Seaweed-wrapped bodies lie on the sandy bottom around the vessel, items cast off the sinking ship buried alongside them. The broken vessel lies on a sharp rock, which further split the ship into two empty halves. Fish swim in and out of the open ends of the wreckage. Gold coins (1,000 gp total), 30 gems (2,000 gp total) and a statue of a sea god with tentacles for a face (400 gp) are scattered around the site.

Two of the seaweed-wrapped bodies are sea-wights that sunk the ship. Hiding in the ship's halves are their companions, **2 giant zombie sharks** and a **giant zombie octopus**.

Giant Shark Zombie: HD 13; AC 7[12]; Atk 1 bite (1d10+8); Move 0 (Swim 12); Save 3; AL N; CL/XP 13/2300; Special: Immune to sleep and charm.

Will-o'-the-Wisp

Hit Dice: 9
Armor Class: -8 [27]
Attacks: 1 shock (2d6)
Saving Throw: 6
Special: Lights
Move: 18
Alignment: Chaos
Number Encountered: 1
Challenge Level/XP: 10/1,400

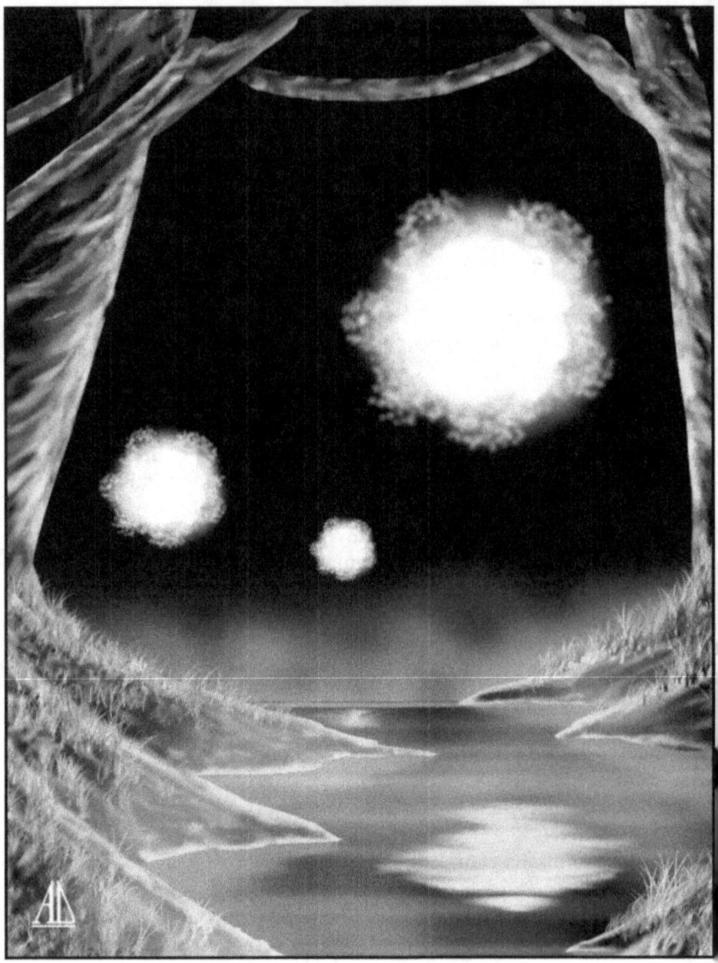

Will o' the wisps are phantom-like shapes of eerie light, creatures that live in dangerous places and try to lure travelers into quicksand, off the edges of cliffs, etc. They usually inhabit swamps or high moors. They can brighten or dim their own luminescence, and change their shapes as well, to appear as a group of lights, a wisp of light, or in the glowing wraithlike shape of a human (often female). They will generally depart if the attempt to lead victims into danger fails, but if they are attacked they can defend themselves with violent shocks of lightning-like power. These creatures are intelligent, and can be forced to reveal the location of their treasure hoards.

Will-o-the-wisp: HD 9; AC –8[27]; Atk 1 shock (2d6); Move 18; Save 6; AL C; CL/XP 10/1400; Special: Lights.

Lightning Lasses

Marsh gases rise around a 60-foot-tall rock promontory jutting out over the Sin Mire Swamp. Standing around the edges of the cliff are six detailed crystal statues of women. Each has flowing hair and delicate features, and holds her hands before her, palms upward. Resting in each woman's hands is a silver page inscribed with delicate flowering writing. The pages tell the story of a young woman sacrificed to protect her village from the Lord of Lightning. Touching one of the silver pages causes a glowing ball of light to rise up through that woman's statue. The golden light expands and brightens as long as the page is touched. The light fades if the page is released. If two pages are touched at the same time, the lights inside both statues brighten.

The lights rising inside the hollow statues are actually **6 will-o'-the-wisps** that live in the swamp below. The creatures rise up through openings in the rock that once channeled water into the statues. The wisps use their lights to trick curious visitors into setting off the plateau's trap: If four of the silver pages are touched at the same time, a lightning bolt blasts out of the sky and strikes the plateau. The bolt does 5d6 points of damage (save for half) to anyone standing near the statues.

Wolf

Hit Dice: 2+2
Armor Class: 7 [12]
Attacks: Bite (1d4+1)
Saving Throw: 16
Special: None
Move: 18
Alignment: Neutrality
Number Encountered: 2d10
Challenge Level/XP: 2/30

Wolves are pack hunters, and may be found in large numbers. Male wolves weigh from 80 to 100 pounds.

Wolf: HD 2+2; AC 7[12]; Atk 1 bite (1d4+1); Move 18; Save 16; AL N; CL/XP 2/30; Special: None.

Backwoods Cabin

A cabin in the woods is empty, but appears to be used seasonally by deer hunters. The cabin has a single locked door and a window with a closed shutter. The door and shutter open with a loud creak on rusty hinges. A locked cabinet contains dried foodstuffs, and a couple of folded blankets sit on a white shelf against one wall. A blanket is thrown across a mattress stuffed with goose feathers. The bed appears to have been slept in recently. A small fireplace in one corner contains embers from a recent fire. Sitting in the fireplace is a charred caribou antler.

The creaking of the door draws the attention of **10 wolves** that sleep in a nearby den. The wolves killed the last hunters to use the cabin then dragged their bodies to their den. One of the bodies has a pouch containing 5 gold nuggets worth 250 gp total.

Wolf, Winter

Hit Dice: 5
Armor Class: 5 [14]
Attacks: 1 bite (1d6+1)
Saving Throw: 12
Special: Breathe frost
Move: 18
Alignment: Neutrality
Number Encountered: 2d4
Challenge Level/XP: 6/400

Winter wolves are as intelligent as humans, and many packs or their leaders are not friendly to humankind. Some, indeed, are actively malevolent and hostile, hunting humans as prey and stalking arctic villages for lone victims. Winter wolves can breathe frost at a range of 10ft, blasting anything in front of them in a wide area for 4d6 points of damage (save for half). This ability can only be used once per turn (10 rounds). Winter wolf pelts are very valuable (1d4+2 x1000gp).

Winter Wolf: HD 5; AC 5[14]; Atk 1 bite (1d6+1); Move 18; Save 12; AL N; CL/XP 6/400; Special: Breathe frost.

Cold Cuts

A dogsled sits frozen to the tundra, its wooden runners caught in inches of thick ice. Bloody splotches dot the white snow around it. Bits of dog fur and gnawed bones cover the ground. A shredded backpack lies by the sled. A rolled blanket is dumped on the ice, and 42 sp are frozen to the ground. They must be heated to be removed.

The sled dogs and their driver were attacked by **4 winter wolves** as they crossed the open tundra. The driver released the dogs, thinking they could escape, but the wolves killed the animals before they could run far. The driver didn't last much longer. The wolves attack anyone investigating the sled. The driver's bloody body is in the wolves' underground den. His body is cut and torn, the skin shredded by the hungry wolves and their pups.

Wolf, Worg

Hit Dice: 4
Armor Class: 6 [13]
Attacks: Bite (1d6+1)
Saving Throw: 13
Special: None
Move: 18
Alignment: Chaos
Number Encountered: 3d4
Challenge Level/XP: 4/120

Worgs are large, intelligent, and evil wolves. They are believed by many to be normal wolves that are inhabited by malevolent spirits, gaining size and strength accordingly. Others simply believe that worgs are an intelligent species of great wolves.

Worg: HD 4; AC 6[13]; Atk 1 bite (1d6+1); Move 18; Save 13; AL C; CL/XP 4/120; Special: None.

Demon of the Wastes

A path of gray paving stones is the only access to a small island sitting in an inlet of the Icefringe Sea. A fantastic ice castle stands in the center the island. Towering snow drifts push against the castle's walls, allowing a nimble PC to climb right up the deep snow to the top of the castle's frozen walls. The bodies of two bodies of ice nomads hang from the walls, ice spikes driven through their midsections. Their hands and feet are frozen into the ice wall.

The castle is home to Namacki, a **grimlek demon** that escaped its masters and now lives out its days freely on the frozen wastes. The grimlek commands **5 worgs** that wander the castle and the lands around it. The worgs attack anyone trying to gain entrance without Namacki's approval. The worgs work together to bring down prey. They occasionally herd living victims to Namacki for the demon to deal with.

Grimlek: HD 5+3; AC 5[14]; Atk 1 bite (2d6); Move 24; Save 12; AL C; CL/XP 7/600; Special: Disease, continuous damage.

Wolverine

Hit Dice: 3
Armor Class: 6 [13]
Attacks: 1 bite (1d6+3)
Saving Throw: 14
Special: Musk, +4 to hit bonus
Move: 12
Alignment: Neutrality
Number Encountered: 1
Challenge Level/XP: 4/120

Wolverines are vicious and tough, living in arctic and tundra (taiga) regions of the world. Its musk is not dangerous, but the smell remains for days, and it spoils food. They attack with a +4 to-hit bonus for their ferocity.

Wolverine: HD 3; AC 6[13]; Atk 1 bite/claw (1d6+3); Move 12; Save 14; AL N; CL/XP 4/120; Special: Musk, +4 to hit bonus.

Trapped

A **wolverine** struggles in a trap anchored to one of the few arctic trees growing from the frozen ground. The trap snapped shut around the creature's tail and holds it fast. The wolverine's mate watches from the tree branches. Anyone helping the poor creature (and who can talk to animals) may gain two loyal companions that follow him around and can be taught simple commands. The wolverines can squeeze through small spaces and can even carry small items. The free wolverine leaps down and attacks if PCs attempt to harm the trapped wolverine.

Wolverine, Giant

Hit Dice: 6
Armor Class: 5 [14]
Attacks: 2 claws (1d4) and 1 bite (1d6)
Saving Throw: 11
Special: Musk, +4 to hit
Move: 12
Alignment: Neutral (or Chaotic)
Number Encountered: 1
Challenge Level/XP: 7/600

Giant wolverines are larger than their normal cousins, and some of them may be possessed of a malign intelligence. They attack with a +4 to-hit bonus for their ferocity.

Giant Wolverine: HD 6; AC 5[14]; Atk 2 claws (1d4), 1 bite (1d6); Move 12; Save 11; CL/XP 7/600; Special: Musk, +4 to hit.

Scent of Danger

A dead yak lies on the cold ground, its body smelling heavily of musk. The yak's throat is ripped out, and blood spatters the ground in front of it where the beast bled out. Two of the yak's legs are missing, each bitten off just above the knee. A **giant wolverine** is curled in a den dug down into mound of dirt near its kill. The angry creature erupts from the dirt to attack anyone examining the yak. The yak's fur is coated in the wolverine's musk to mark its territory.

Wraith

Hit Dice: 4
Armor Class: 3 [16]
Attacks: Touch (1d6 + level drain)
Saving Throw: 13
Special: Level drain (1 level) with hit, magic or silver weapon to hit
Move: 9/24 (flying)
Alignment: Chaos
Number Encountered: 2d6
Challenge Level/XP: 8/800

Wraiths are powerful wights, immune to all non-magical weapons other than silver ones (which inflict only half damage). Arrows are particularly ineffective against them, for even magical and silver arrows inflict only one hit point of damage per hit. Wraiths can be found riding well-trained battle steeds or more unusual mounts that will tolerate their presence. Just as wights do, wraiths drain a level of experience from those they hit.

Wraith: HD 4; AC 3[16]; Atk 1 touch (1d6+ level drain); Move 9 (Fly 24); Save 13; AL C; CL/XP 8/800; Special: drain 1 level with hit, magic or silver weapon to hit.

Portraits of the Damned

Six-foot-tall portraits line the staircase leading up to the second floor of this empty chateau. The pictures show members of the Corliss family, well-known, but unscrupulous, winemakers in the village of Orlen. All of the paintings show the family in various stages of decay, with their bodies burned, hacked apart or poisoned. The family members suffered their horrible fates after a witch cursed the family for selling her diluted wine. The paintings – made long before the curse – showed the thieving family members how they would die before their usually violent ends.

Two portraits hide the souls of Lady Ketyh and Sir Mahli Corliss. They died together in the house, the last members of the family to own it. Their bodies are still upstairs, one dead in a bathtub from a snakebite and the other crushed under a chandelier. The pair returned as **2 vengeful wraiths** to exact revenge on the living. The wraiths leap through the portraits at anyone examining the portraits.

Wyvern

Hit Dice: 8
Armor Class: 3 [16]
Attacks: Bite (2d8) or sting (1d6 + poison)
Saving Throw: 8
Special: Poison sting
Move: 6/24 (flying)
Alignment: Neutrality
Number Encountered: 1d6
Challenge Level/XP: 10/1,400

A wyvern is a two-legged form of dragon. These creatures are smaller and less intelligent than true four-legged dragons, not to mention that they do not have a breath weapon. Each wyvern has a poisonous sting at the end of its tail. However, they are not coordinated enough to attack with both bite and sting in a single round. In any given round, a wyvern is 60% likely to use its tail, which can lash out to the creature's front even farther than its head can reach.

Wyvern: HD 8; AC 3[16]; Atk 1 bite (2d8) or 1 sting (1d6+poison); Move 6 (Fly 24); Save 8; AL N; CL/XP 10/1400; Special: Poison sting.

The Knight Errant

A warhorse charges through the forest, its eyes wide and sweat coating its sides. It froths from the mouth and its breathing is labored. The animal races ahead, refusing to stop. From the direction the horse came, a man screams for help. His shrieks are loud in the stillness of the dark forest.

The obese knight **Fergut the Brash** decided over a dinner of roast lamb and potatoes that he was meant to be a dragonslayer. He handcrafted thick (and expansive) armor to withstand the creatures' claws and gnashing teeth, and insulated it with a magical cloth to withstand the elements. He can barely move in the weighty metal armor, however, and relied on his horse (which wasn't too happy about carrying the "knight") to help him get to and from the wyrms he dreamed of chasing. He didn't expect the horse to bolt at the first sign of trouble.

Fergut lies on his back in the middle of the trees, trying desperately to turn himself over or raise his sword. His armor is dented and battered. He shouts for help if he sees PCs. Fergut's first battle wasn't with a dragon; instead a **wyvern** spooked the warhorse and left Fergut on the ground like a helpless turtle. The wyvern soars in to protect its meal from anyone approaching the helpless knight. The wyvern turns its stinger – which has proven ineffectual against Fergut's armor – on PCs. Fergut rewards his rescuers with a small cask of wine (but not the good stuff) from his cellar if PCs get him back home intact. He regales them with his conquests the entire way, and steps in to defend them from anyone they meet, although he usually ends up making situations worse.

Xole

Hit Dice: 8+4
Armor Class: 2 [17]
Attacks: 1 two-handed mace (1d10+5) and tail (2d6)
Saving Throw: 8
Special: Constriction, immune to fire and cold
Move: 12
Alignment: Chaos
Number Encountered: 1d6
Challenge Level/XP: 10/1,400

Xoles bear a close physical resemblance to the salamanders of the elemental plane of fire, having a somewhat human head, human arms, and a serpentine body. Rather than being creatures of fire, however, the xoles are creatures of stone, being native to the elemental plane of earth. As such, they are immune to fire and cold, and can be affected by *protection from evil*.

A xole is only slightly larger than a salamander; the torso of a xole is equivalent to that of a seven-foot tall, but massive, person. The tail is almost ten feet in length, which is the reason xoles are categorized as "Large" size. Xoles generally carry heavy stone maces as weapons; even xoles can only wield these weapons two-handed, and they cannot be lifted by any creature not from the elemental plane of earth. If one of the weapons is dropped to the ground, it will dissolve into the stone after a period of a year and one day. If a xole hits successfully with its tail, it inflicts automatic constriction damage thereafter.

Xoles can move through solid rock or earth, although it takes a full round to enter solid stone.

There is no allegiance between xoles and xorns beyond the fact that both types of creatures are native to the elemental plane of earth. Xoles, obviously, are more organized than xorns, and are generally found on the prime material plane in the service of some evil purpose, as contrasted to the neutral and relatively purposeless wanderings of the xorns.

— *Author: Matt Finch*

Xole: HD 8+4; AC 2[17]; Atk 1 two-handed mace (1d10+5) and tail (2d6); Move 12; Save 8; AL C; CL/XP 10/1400; Special: Constriction, immune to fire and cold.

There's a Xole in the Middle of the Sea

The Isle of Echoes is a three-mile-wide rocky island of volcanic rock rising from the Reaping Sea. Little vegetation grows on the barren outcropping of rock, and sailors who pass the strange place whisper of the grinding crash of stones slamming together. Rocky bluffs and crags hide the island's interior, and any who land on the boulder-covered beaches never return.

Twenty curling stone columns rise 30 feet into the air in the center of a flat plateau at the island's heart. The pillars stand in a wide circle. Around them are hundreds of stone weapons resting unattended on the rocky ground. Most of the weapons are large maces, but a few spears, swords and clubs can also be found. Three four-foot-tall, flat-top blocks of black stone surround a 12-foot-wide circular cauldron filled with bubbling magma. Working the primitive forge are **3 xoles**, each busy crafting stone weapons for an unknown reason. The xoles attack anyone interrupting their work.

Xorn

Hit Dice: 7
Armor Class: -2 [21]
Attacks: 3 claws (1d3), 1 bite (4d6)
Saving Throw: 9
Special: Immune to fire and cold, half damage from electricity, travel through stone
Move: 9
Alignment: Neutrality
Number Encountered: 1d4
Challenge Level/XP: 9/1,100

Xorn are bizarre creatures, originally from the elemental planes of earth, which eat precious metals and other minerals. They have a rock-like consistency, granting an extremely good armor class, and appear to be made of stone. Xorn have a barrel-shaped body, radially symmetrical with three eyes, three arms, three stubby legs, and a powerful mouth set in the top of the creature's body. The stone-like appearance grants the xorn a tremendously good chance of surprising its enemies.

These creatures are immune to fire and cold damage, and take only half damage from electrical attacks (no damage when saving throws are successful). A xorn can swim through stone, but requires a full melee round to enter solid rock, during which time it cannot attack. Phase Door spells will utterly destroy a xorn that is traveling through rock or readjusting its composition.

Xorn are particularly vulnerable to spells that affect earth and stone. Move Earth spells may be used to hurl a xorn backwards 30ft and stun them for a full round. Stone to flesh and rock to mud spells weaken the xorn's elemental structure, increasing the creature's AC to 8 [11] until the xorn concentrates for a full round to readjust its composition. Passwall spells inflict 1d10+10 points of damage with no saving throw.

Xorn: HD 7; AC –2[21]; Atk 3 claws (1d3), 1 bite (4d6); Move 9; Save 9; AL N; CL/XP 9/1100; Special: Immune to fire and cold, half damage from electricity, travel through stone.

The Halfling's Carriage

An upright metal box sits in the middle of the Thresheel Woods, its sides gleaming silver in the little sunlight that penetrates the thick leaves rustling overhead. The box is six feet tall and barely four feet wide. The walls are beaten and scratched. A door in one side opens to reveal a cramped interior with just enough room for one person to squeeze inside (two if they really try). A word engraved in Common on the inside wall reads "Onward."

Halfling inventor Ollie Nematoad created the box to convey him through the mountains rather than over them. Stepping inside, closing the door and speaking the command causes the box to jerk downward suddenly and disappear into the ground. Connected to the box via a heavy chain are **2 xorn.** The box gains the xorns' swim through stone ability when in motion. The xorn cannot break free of the magical chain binding them to the box. Once the command word is spoken, however, the person inside the box can't control the box's path (a definite design flaw) and the imprisoned xorn gain free will to act. The creatures charge into the ground, then circle back to attack the box and the person inside. Ollie escaped using a special ring he keeps for just such an emergency. The box immediately returns to the surface if the cabin is empty, pulling the xorn with it and returning them to magical stasis until the command word is spoken again.

Yaruga

Hit Dice: 3
Armor Class: 5 [14]
Attacks: 1 kick (1d6)
Saving Throw: 14
Special: Blinding flatulence, running kick
Move: 18
Alignment: Neutrality
Number Encountered: 1d2 or 2d4
Challenge Level/XP: 3/60

Named after their distinctive call, Yaruga are agile, hammerheaded lizards, 10ft in height, which walk on two long bird-like legs. Yaruga graze on plants and grasses by day, but become vicious hunters by night. During the day Yaruga are skittish and scare easily. They excrete a foul-smelling gas if approached within 50 ft, then run away; the gas blinds anyone within 10ft of the Yaruga for 1d4 rounds (saving throw applies). At night, Yaruga become extremely dangerous and aggressive, chasing their prey down and kicking them to death before feasting on them. When they make the initial charge, a yaruga's running kick inflicts double damage on a successful hit. Anyone sprayed by Yaruga-gas during the day becomes the main target of the savage lizards by night. In the wild, Yaruga are usually encountered in pairs, day or night, but there may be 2d4 together during mating season.

— *Author: Sean Wills*

Yaruga: HD 3; AC 5 [14]; Atk 1 kick (1d6); Move 18; Save 14; AL N; CL/XP 3/60; Special: Blinding flatulence, running kick.

Coconut Gas

Coconuts hang from oversized palm trees growing wild throughout the Seething Jungle. The coconuts are part of a defensive perimeter set up around the village of Cata'Anar to keep beasts out. Jungle vines crisscrossing the weed-covered ground rise into the trees to connect to some hollowed-out coconuts rigged to fall on creatures tripping the trap. The Cata'Anar natives drill holes into the coconuts to empty them out. They then refill the coconuts with chopped up yaruga glands.

The coconuts split open when they strike the ground (or unlucky PCs). The glands explode in a 10-foot-radius, covering unwanted visitors in the smelly chunks and the foul-smelling yaruga gas. The gas blinds anyone for 1d4 rounds unless they make a saving throw. Animals approaching Cata'Anar are driven away by the nauseating gas and glands. The chunks can be picked off, but the smell of the gas takes 1d4 days to wash away. The villagers use a mixture of crushed coconut, vinegar and turtle blood. They'll sell the goopy concoction to PCs for 300 gp.

The jungle is home to **8 yaruga** that roam the area, drawn by the scent of the glands. They gather in force at night to attack anyone struck by one of the coconut traps and coated in the foul-smelling gas.

Yeti

Hit Dice: 5
Armor Class: 6 [13]
Attacks: 2 fists (1d6)
Saving Throw: 12
Special: Hug, fear, immune to cold
Move: 14
Alignment: Neutrality or Chaos
Number Encountered: 1d6 or 2d12
Challenge Level/XP: 7/600

Yetis are the "Bigfoot" of the arctic and the high mountains. If a yeti strikes the same opponent with both fists, it bear-hugs for an additional 2d6 points of damage. Anyone caught in the yeti's arms like this must make a saving throw or be paralyzed with fear for 1d3 rounds (during which time the yeti hits automatically). Yetis are very intelligent, and can be quite malevolent. They are immune to magical cold.

Yeti: HD 5; AC 6[13]; Atk 2 fists (1d6); Move 14; Save 12; AL N or C; CL/XP 7/600; Special: Immune to cold, hug, fear.

Winter Green

A mammoth lies on its side in the field of deep snow beneath an overhanging ice ridge, its furry body a brown lump marring the pristine white expanse. Its curving tusks jut from the snowfield like massive ribs. A massive icicle-like spear juts from the mammoth's side. Frozen blood stains the white snow in arcs around it. Many more sharp icicles hang like teeth from the icy promontory rising above the dead mammoth. Small green humanoids slash at the mammoth's body, ripping into its flesh. Snow drifts surround the vicious creatures as they hack at the dead animal's body.

The icy ridge is the "kingdom" of a **yeti** and his servants, **8 clawed fiends**. The clawed fiends wear polar bear skins to protect themselves from the biting cold. They are loyal to the yeti, which keeps them fed in the harsh environment by occasionally bringing down some of the larger animals. The yeti hides as one of the snow drifts away from the clawed fiends and mammoth. It lets its servants attack first before it rises up to surprise PCs. The massive yeti throws icicle spears (2d4 points of damage) at foes before charging into combat.

Ygg (Gallows Tree)

Hit Dice: 8
Armor Class: 2 [17]
Attacks: 1d6 impalements (1d6+1 each)
Saving Throw: 8
Special: Immune to cold, spore cloud.
Move: 6
Alignment: Neutrality
Number Encountered: 1
Challenge Level/XP: 10/1,400

Ygg (commonly called 'Gallows Trees') are ancient, tree-like predators that impale both beast and man on the thorn-covered bark of their snaking branches. An Ygg's branches can whip out to a distance of 30ft to seize prey, who must make a successful saving throw to avoid being caught (the Ygg can use 1d6 of these branches in any given combat round). Once impaled upon the massive thorns, the life force and nutrients of the victim is drained at the rate of 1 hit point per round, leaving the empty husks to slough off in the fullness of time. Any man-sized creature has a 1 in 6 chance per round of pulling free of the branch. Reeking of putrefaction and festooned with corpses, Ygg roam the countryside in search of flesh, producing a cloud of spores (60ft radius) that draws creatures to them. Prey within the sporecloud must make a saving throw (each round) or be drawn closer to the Ygg. Once the Ygg attacks, these victims come to their senses, but it may be too late. Ygg have no visual organs but can detect any creatures within 60ft using sound, scent, and vibration. They are immune to cold, but are susceptible to fire (+1 damage per hit die). Folklore suggests that the peach-like fruit Ygg produce has magical life-enhancing properties.

— Author: Sean Wills

Ygg: HD 8; AC 2[17]; Atk 1d6 impalements (1d6+1 each); Move 6; Save 8; AL N; CL/XP 10/1400; Special: Immune to cold, spore cloud.

Thorny Decision

A hedge of wickedly sharp three-foot-long thorns surrounds the Bauxile Precipice, a 100-foot-tall slab of black rock rising into the storm-filled sky. Steps cut into the black rock ring the slender stone. The bodies of men and beasts are impaled on the thorns, their desiccated remains scratched and torn by the fast-growing and decidedly deadly hedge. A wall of bleached bones lies at the base of the hedge, and skeletal remains hang precariously in the thorns.

Two golden bowls containing peach-like fruits sit on a red-stone altar atop the rock. One bowl of fruit heals 2d8 points of damage, while the other instills an overwhelming desire to jump from the precipice. Falling bodies slam into the piercing thorns. Standing in the hedge are **2 ygg.** The trees are bound to the rock and cannot leave the area. The trees don't stop visitors from climbing the stairs, but they do prevent them from leaving without making a choice once they reach the top.

Yienhool

Hit Dice: 1d6hp
Armor Class: 8 [11]
Attacks: 1 claw (1d4)
Saving Throw: 18
Special: grab and pin arms, swarm over the top of battle lines.
Move: 9
Alignment: Chaos
Number Encountered: 3d10+3 or 2d10x5
Challenge Level/XP: 1/15

Yienhools are pale humanoids with long, thin arms and elongated, clawed hands. Their bulging, white eyes are well adapted to dim light, but they are virtually blind in sunlight and never emerge from below ground unless forced to do so. They are deep-dwellers of the underground, but small groups of them are occasionally found in the upper reaches of the subterranean world. Yienhools are more intelligent than animals, but barely so - they can communicate and follow orders, and in packs they can hunt with considerable cunning, but their ability to act independently of a pack or a strong leader is very weak. Yienhool packs swarm their prey, the first ranks grabbing, clutching, and immobilizing to allow their total numbers to swarm over the foe and bring them down. If a yienhool hits, it has grabbed successfully at one of the foe's arms, rendering weapon or shield unusable as the yienhool clings on, regardless of danger (such attacks are made at -1 to hit). While holding on, the yienhool can make more attempts to grab the other arm as well. Yienhool can swarm over the backs of their fighting brethren to climb past front ranks and into the rear ranks of their opponents. If a yienhool is not already holding an enemy, and chooses not to make grabbing attacks, it can attack with its claws. These creatures are usually encountered in large numbers, for they do not divide into packs of fewer than 6.

Yienhool packs are often led by unusually large and vicious specimens of the race who are much more intelligent – or, at least more cunning – than the average member of the species. These leaders are normally of 3HD, but some can be as large as trolls, with 5-7 hit dice.

— *Author: Matt Finch*

Yienhool: HD 1d6; AC 8[11]; Atk 1 claw (1d4); Move 9; Save 18; AL C; CL/XP 1/15; Special: grab and pin arms, swarm over the top of battle lines.

One Note or Two?

A silver whistle (100 gp) sits on a jade gargoyle head protruding from the rock wall of this water-filled cave. The whistle is four inches long and has two openings cut along its length. The whistle produces a high-pitched sound humans can't hear. The noise causes considerable pain to animals, however. Covering the first hole and blowing a note summons **1d4 war dogs** to serve the PC for 2d6 hours. This note can be blown once per week to summon the dogs. Covering both holes and blowing causes **3d4+4 yienhools** to converge on the instrument. The yienhools mercilessly attack the whistle's wielder. They steal the offending instrument if possible and destroy it.

Guard Dog: HD 2; AC 7[12]; Atk 1 bite (1d6); Move 14; Save 16; AL N; CL/XP 2/30; Special: None.

Yith, Hound of

Hit Dice: 3
Armor Class: 1 [18]
Attacks: 1 bite (1d6+1)
Saving Throw: 14
Special: Baying, harmed only by magic/silver weapons, magic resistance 10%
Move: 18/25 (flying)
Alignment: Chaos
Number Encountered: 1 or 2d4
Challenge Level/XP: 7/600

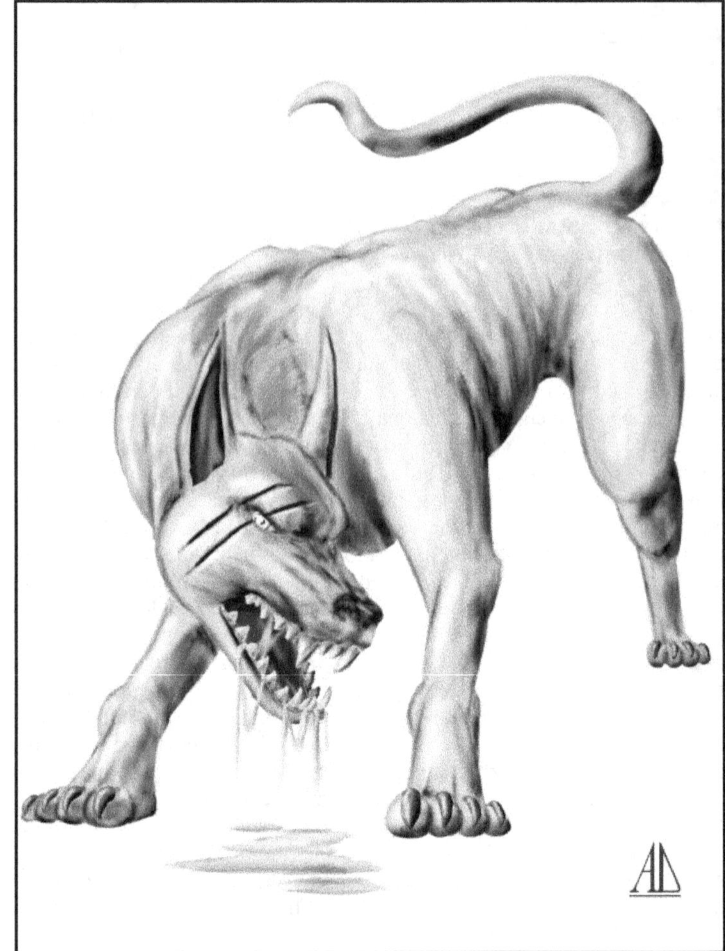

Hounds of Yith are supernatural creatures of the night, resembling large dogs (most say). They are, perhaps, originally denizens of another plane of existence, and they are summoned to the hunt by powerful and malign beings. The baying of the hounds causes fear within 100ft (per the spell). Normal weapons do not damage the hounds of Yith: silver weapons inflict only 1hp damage per hit, and magical weapons inflict 1hp per point of to-hit bonus. The hounds have 10% resistance to magic.

Hound of Yith: HD 3; AC 1[18]; Atk 1 bite (1d6+1); Move 18 (Fly 25); Save 14; AL C; CL/XP 7/600; Special: Baying, harmed only by magic/silver weapons, magic resistance 10%.

Hounds of Hell

The villagers of the small hamlet of Appenzell each wear a studded leather strap around their necks. They watch visitors nervously, and none dares approach outsiders. The tavern owner grudgingly serves one drink, but won't rent rooms for the night. Emelda, a young serving girl, quietly warns PCs to leave immediately.

An evil wizard named Traywick cursed the town after the constable slew his favorite mastiffs for nearly killing a small child. Traywick made a deal with a demon lord to punish the villagers. Nearly a year ago, demonic servants quietly wrapped leather collars around the necks of everyone in town — including Traywick's.

Every full moon, two random villagers turn into **2 hounds of Yith** and wreak havoc through the countryside. The villagers long ago learned to identify which of their number would change each month, and lock the two chosen in a large barn outside town. The rest hide in their homes hoping the hounds don't escape and come looking for them. The scent of new blood in the village draws the hounds to PCs.

The curse can be broken by killing Traywick and burning the leather collar he wears. Traywick attempted to magically remove the strap soon after he awoke with it. The effort cost him his head, and turned him permanently into a **headless hound** that now wanders the valley about his vacant manor home.

Headless Hound: HD 6; AC 5[14]; Atk 1 bite (2d6); Move 18 (Fly 6); Save 11; AL N; CL/XP 7/600; Special: Bite passes through armor (only dex bonus modifies AC), half normal healing rate from wounds, pack-howl causes fear.

Yurmp (Toad Robber)

Hit Dice: 5+3
Armor Class: 4 [15]
Attacks: 1 polearm (1d8)
Saving Throw: 12
Special: Backstab, unarmed grapple with hit 4+ over number needed
Move: 12
Alignment: Neutrality
Number Encountered: 3d6 or 6d10
Challenge Level/XP: 5/240

Fat and ugly toad-like humanoids, the Yurmp are bandits and scroungers. Though of fine material, such as silk, their clothes are torn and soiled. Any armour is mismatched and poorly maintained, held together by rusty buckles and double-wrapped cords. Yurmp have sour expressions and grumpy attitudes, often becoming impatient and bored while waiting beside a road or path for someone to ambush. Their weapons are generally polearms looted from battle sites. If yurmp are able to coordinate an ambush, they have an increased chance of surprising their opponents (1-3 on 1d6). In villages that tolerate their presence they are usually part of any organised crime; in areas where they are not tolerated, yurmp live by "finding" dropped items and digging through the garbage of other races, bemoaning their poor luck all the while. For every 5 yurmp in a group there is a cumulative 2 in 6 chance that a wrestler yurmp will be present. These grossly fat yurmps disdain weapons and armour, and strike for 1d6 damage in unarmed combat. If the unarmed attack succeeds by four or more points, the wrestler has a firm hold on the foe and can throw him to the ground, disarm him, prevent attacks, or inflict continuous strangling damage (1d6 per round). Wrestler yurmps have an effective Strength score of 18, and usually enjoy challenging humans to arm wrestling contests. The rest of the yurmp enjoy gambling on these contests. If yurmp are able to attack by stealth or surprise from behind, they gain +4 on the attack and inflict double normal damage.

— *Author: Scott Wylie Roberts, "Myrystyr"*

Yurmp: HD 5+3; AC 4[15]; Atk 1 polearm (1d8); Move 12; Save 12; AL N; CL/XP 5/240; Special: Backstab.

Wrestler Yurmp: HD 5+3; AC 6[13]; Atk 1 unarmed (1d6); Move 12; Save 12; AL N; CL/XP 6/400; Special: Backstab, unarmed grapple with hit 4+ over number needed.

An Offer You Can't Refuse

A dilapidated carriage waits in the middle of the road as PCs to approach. Trash litters the ground around the expensive vehicle, and a fat, toad-like creature sits on the driver's bench. Instead of horses, the thing is pulled by a team of **3 giant horned toads**. The toads sit peacefully, snatching flies from the air. A grossly obese hand holds a silk handkerchief out the carriage's window, waving PCs over. Standing behind and atop the carriage are more toad creatures, each armed with crossbows. The carriage is the conveyance of a fat blobby toad creature named Dung Vianco, a fastidious **yurmp**. He is protected by **5 yurmps**.

Dung's prize, a **wrestler yurmp named Rouss**, ate tainted berries that drove him mad. The crazed giant of a yurmp hides off the road in a nearby cornfield. Dung wants his fighter returned so they can feed him an antidote. He asks PCs to do this favor for him. If they don't, he turns the giant horned toads and his lackeys loose on them. It's their choice, after all.

Giant Horned Toad: HD 4+4; AC 4[15]; Atk 1 bite (1d8); Move 9; Save 13; AL N; CL/XP 5/240; Special: Squirt blood.

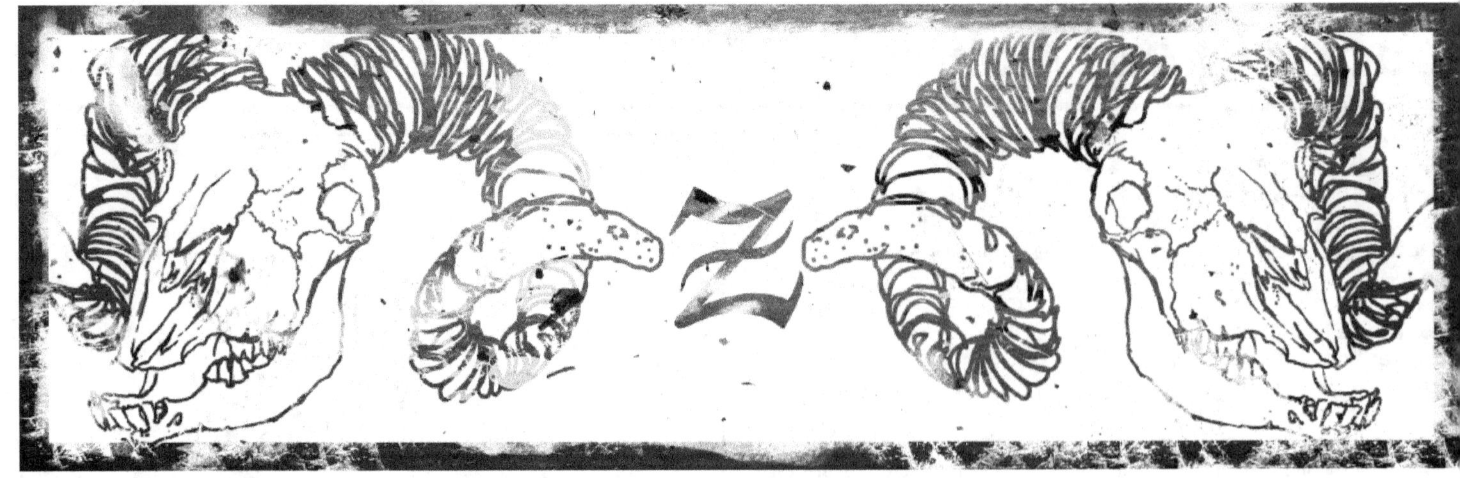

Zetan

Hit Dice: 1
Armor Class: 9 [10]
Attacks: 1 weapon (1d4)
Saving Throw: 17
Special: +1 or better weapon to hit, fear aura
Move: 6
Alignment: Neutrality
Number Encountered: 3d10 x3
Challenge Level/XP: 3/60

Zetans are a grey skinned collective-intelligence race originally hailing from somewhere beyond the material plane. Workers are about four feet tall, and leaders are as tall as six feet. All zetans have thin arms and legs, oversized heads and eyes, and extremely long fingers. They are encountered most frequently on the Ethereal and Astral planes. Their purpose in visiting the Material Plane is a mystery, although they have been known to abduct mortals or livestock, sometimes in broad daylight. Zetans have an aura which causes Fear (as per the spell, saving throw negates), and they are immune to non-magical weapons. It is believed that Zetans are not truly evil, but merely inscrutable and totally alien in motivation; individuals that have met the Zetans will have wildly different stories to tell about them. Smaller Zetans seem to function most often as workers; the taller leader-types are conjectured to have more independence, but still serve the collective. Zetans travel in a thought conveyance which is only temporarily physical, glows various unearthly colors, and is able to become invisible (by entering the Ethereal Plane) at will. For every fifteen Zetans there will always be at least one leader type. A leader must be present for transport of any mortals or livestock. If a Zetan is killed on the prime material plane it is dispatched back to the collective unless its leader is killed as well, in which case it is dispersed. More permanent Zetan fortresses may exist under some of the more inaccessible desert areas of the world; nomads speak of the sound of great machines beneath the sands.

— Author: Michael Kotschi

Zetan (Worker): HD 1; AC 9[10]; Atk 1 Weapon (1d4); Move 6; Save 17; AL N; CL/XP 3/60 Special: +1 or better weapon to hit, Fear aura.

Zetan (Leader): HD 3; AC 7[12]; Atk Weapon (1d8); Move 9; Save 14; AL N; CL/XP 5/240; Special: +1 or better weapon to hit, Fear aura, Ethereal Travel.

Little Gray Men

The Exetyr Inn & Tavern is a bustling place, with a lively clientele dancing, singing and, of course, drinking the night away. The party never seems to stop. The tavern is run by **Endril Mackeal**, a female barbarian from the frozen north strand. Endril always takes part in the drinking and dancing, and sometimes shares stories of her days adventuring. She has faced dragons and demons, and killed grizzlies with her bare hands. A bear-skin rug she killed and skinned herself rests on the floor in the middle of the tavern.

But Endril's newest challenge is vexing her to no end: Guests are vanishing from the inn's upper attic rooms. Three people are missing now, and Endril has no answer as to where they might be. She's stumped, and worried more people might vanish. She fears her business will suffer if word gets out that it's dangerous to stay at the Exetyr. She's offering a 20 gp reward for anyone who'll stay the night in the upper rooms and bring her an answer. The local patrons know better; they've heard the stories of bright flashing lights swirling around the attic windows and they've seen the carved up and bloodless cattle in the fields the next morning.

Anyone staying on the upper floor awakens to find 10 grey-skinned creatures scurrying about the room and surveying the PC with their long, black eyes. A larger creature stands to the side, directing the unknown actions. The creatures are **10 Zetan workers** and **1 Zetan leader**. They attempt to take one PC captive to experiment upon. Kidnapped villagers are never seen again.

Zombie

Hit Dice: 2
Armor Class: 8 [11], or 7 [12] with shield
Attacks: Weapon or strike (1d8)
Saving Throw: 16
Special: Immune to sleep and charm spells
Move: 6
Alignment: Neutrality
Number Encountered: 4d6
Challenge Level/XP: 2/30

Zombies are mindless creatures, the walking dead. (These are merely animated corpses, not carriers of any sort of undead contagion as are ghouls.) If their Undeath is contagious, they should be worth a few more experience points than described here, and if a single hit from a zombie causes contagion or any other sort of disease, they should be worth considerably more experience. However, the standard zombie is simply a corpse animated to do its creator's bidding.

Zombie: HD 2; AC 8[11] or with shield 7[12]; Atk 1 weapon or strike (1d8); Move 6; Save 16; AL N; CL/XP 2/30; Special: Immune to sleep and charm.

Waterlogged

This stone hallway slopes down into a large chamber filled nearly to the ceiling with brackish water. Blubbery balls of bloated flesh and bits of gore float atop the water. A dead gnoll floats face down in the water, its wet fur smelling heavily of rot. A treasure chest on the floor of the flooded chamber contains 129 gp, a gold swan statue (50 gp) and a magical wand of the Referee's choosing.

The floating balls of flesh are **8 bloated zombies**. The zombies' bodies make them incredibly buoyant so that they float freely in the water. They splash awkwardly to get to PCs in the water.

Zombie, Brain-Eating

Hit Dice: 3
Armor Class: 8 [11]
Attacks: 1 strike (1d8)
Saving Throw: 14
Special: Absorbs spells
Move: 6
Alignment: Chaos
Number Encountered: 3d6
Challenge Level/XP: 5/240

Brain-eaters are a rare variety of zombie, appearing as bloated, swollen-headed walking corpses. These semi-intelligent monsters hunger for the brains of intelligent creatures, especially those with the ability to cast spells. Brain-eaters are capable of absorbing the energy of magical spells cast near them, negating any effect they might have had. A brain-eater may absorb up to 2d4 spell levels, its head growing ever larger during the process. When its capacity is reached, the brain-eater's head violently explodes. A brain-eater regains the ability to absorb an additional spell level with each fresh brain it eats.

— Author: Random

Brain-eating Zombie: HD 3; AC 8 [11]; Atk 1 strike (1d8); Move: 6; Save 14; AL C; CL/XP 5/240; Special: Absorbs spells.

Bobble-Headed Bodyguards

Dozens of decomposing bodies lie on the stone floor inside this foul-smelling chamber. Most of the corpses are missing the tops of their skulls, and their brains have been scooped out. Blood spatters the stone floor and pools in congealed lumps. Other bodies are bloated beyond belief, their heads swollen to humongous dimensions. The brain-less bodies belong to villagers who were kidnapped and locked in this room to feed **10 brain-eating zombies**. The bloated bodies are the zombies, each with a massive head from absorbing spells cast at their death-worshipping cleric master, **Lonan Cur**.

Lonan uses the zombies as undead shields to absorb spells cast at him. He walks inside a circle of the undead as he ransacks small villages and hamlets around the region. As he leaves with the village's gold, he grabs a few villagers to feed the engorged zombies.

Zombie, Leper

Hit Dice: 1
Armor Class: 6 [13]
Attacks: 1 claw or bite (1d6)
Saving Throw: 17
Special: Disease, victims are re-animated
Move: 9
Alignment: Neutrality
Number Encountered: 1d6
Challenge Level/XP: 3/60

Leper zombies are clearly undead, afflicted with a horrific disease resembling a form of leprosy, more agile than other types of zombies, and far more deadly: any who battle them must save vs disease at the end of the fight or contract Zombie Leprosy (die in 3 days and return as a Leper Zombie). Leper zombies may be turned by clerics as ghouls, and they are immune to sleep and charm spells. Anyone slain by a Leper Zombie reanimates as a leper zombie in 1d6 rounds. Carrying equipment, arms or armor of one slain by a leper zombie or used to destroy a leper zombie carries a risk to the bearer, they must save vs disease at +4 each day or contract Zombie Leprosy. Holy water, remove curse and other methods of cleansing may render the gear safe again.

— Author: JD Jarvis

Leper Zombie: HD 1; AC 6[13]; Atk 1 claw or bite (1d6); Move 9; Save 17; AL N; CL/XP 3/60; Special: Disease, victims animate as leper zombies.

Death Warmed Over

A lone figure sits bundled in blankets before the ashes of a campfire along the banks of a pristine pond. A large cooking pot sits atop the flames, still half-filled with water. A wagon waits in the trees, bodies in the back huddled under blankets.

The figure in front of the fire is a woman with bright red hair. Her arms are marred by sores, and her throat is scratched open. Her legs are burned and blackened. She's been dead less than a day. The woman and her companions drank from the tainted pond and turned into **8 leper zombies**. The undead leap from the wagon to attack passers-by. The zombies killed their mounts after they turned. The animals' bodies lay a slight ravine down a steep rocky slope behind the wagon. The wagon contains the group's belongings, including 60 sp, a large rocking chair, six ivory drinking horns (60 gp), and various items of clothing. All of the clothes are tainted with leprosy that turns someone wearing them into a leper zombie if they fail a saving throw.

Zombie, Pyre

Hit Dice: 2
Armor Class: 8[11] or with shield 7[12]
Attacks: 1 weapon or strike (1d8)
Saving Throw: 16
Special: Immune to sleep and charm, immolation
Move: 6
Alignment: Neutrality
Number Encountered: 1d3
Challenge Level/XP: 3/60

These undead creatures are weirdly enchanted with some sort of necromancy. When hit by a melee weapon, they burst violently into flame, inflicting 1d6 points of damage to anyone within 5ft. Only the bones remain after this conflagration: the remaining skeleton fights as a skeleton rather than as a zombie (including the lower hit points). The flesh regrows rapidly, and the creature will fight as a zombie again in 10 combat rounds, including the restored ability to immolate itself.

— *Author: Scott Casper*

Pyre Zombie: HD 2; AC 8[11] or with shield 7[12]; Atk 1 weapon or strike (1d8); Move 6; Save 16; AL N; CL/XP 3/60; Special: Immune to sleep and charm, immolation.

Road Flares

Shambling down the road toward PCs are 10 rotting soldiers, each armed with swords and shields. Each zombie wears a golden helmet emblazoned with a fiery eagle. Emblazoned on their shields are large sun emblems. The undead are **10 pyre zombies** fulfilling their last mission: Raze the city of Dalstrak. Unfortunately, the city was destroyed hundreds of years ago during the Battle of the Four Winds. The soldiers died quickly in an earthquake as they were swallowed by the ground. Dark energies recently awoke the warriors and they crawled from their unmarked grave to march again on the long-forgotten city.

Zombie Raven

Hit Dice: 1d6 hit points
Armor Class: 8 [11]
Attacks: 1 bite (1d3)
Saving Throw: 18
Special: Immune to sleep and cold
Move: 1/6 (flying)
Alignment: Neutrality
Number Encountered: 4d6
Challenge Level/XP: 1/15

Zombie Ravens are the rotting, undead bodies of ravens. As with other zombies, they have no independent intellect and move very slowly.

— *Author: Matt Finch*

Zombie Raven: HD 1d6hp; AC 8[11]; Atk 1 bite (1d3); Move 1 (Fly 6); Save 18; AL N; CL/XP 1/15; Special: Immune to sleep and cold.

Death from Above

A massive flock of raven's blocks out the sun, turning the day to night as they fly high overhead. The birds caw and wheel through the sky. A slower flock trails the main body of birds. This secondary flock appears to be chasing the lead birds. The lead birds bank and swerve trying to keep away from the second flock. The trailing flock is made up of **40 zombie ravens** hunting the living birds. The decomposing birds barely flap through the air, but turn and dive on PCs.

Monsters by Challenge Level

Challenge Level A

Cliessid	Jackal	Spine Rat
Flying Squirrel, Carnivorous	Kobold	
Glass Butterfly	Rat, Giant	

Challenge Level B

Cat, Feral Undead	Goblin	Rat (Giant Desongnol Rat)
Centipede, Giant (Small, Non-lethal)	Human, Normal	
Gillmonkey	Nixie	

Challenge Level 1

Animated Objects	Goblin, Redcap (Chaos Goblin)	Rot Grub
Baboon	Hobgoblin	Shocker Lizard
Barracuda	Human, Bandits	Shrangaathi
Beetle, Giant Fire	Human, Soldier	Skeleton
Centipede, Giant (Small, Lethal)	Hyena	Sorcery Leech
Dog, Pet or Wild	Lamprey, Lightning	Spider, Flagstone
Dwarf	Malformian	Sumatran Rat-Ghoul
Elf	Merman	Tunnel Prawn
Formian, Worker	Mushroom-Man (1HD)	Yienhool
Frog, Giant (Small)	Orc	Zombie Raven
Goblin, Oni-Aka (Asian Red Goblin)	Piercer (1HD)	

Challenge Level 2

Ant, Giant (worker)	Goblin, Belfry	Ray, Sting
Baboon, Alpha	Goblin, Oni-Kage (Asian Shadow Goblin)	Razor Wing
Bag of Teeth	Goblin, Oni-Yama (Asian Mountain Goblin)	Sahuagin
Beetle, Giant Huhu	Horses, Riding	Sand Screamer (Ferret Snake)
Birhaakaman	Human, Berserkers	Skeleton, Fossil
Camel	Jack-in-the-Box	Snake, Javelin
Cave Eel	Koi Folk	Snake, Python
Clawed Fiend	Leaping Maw	Snake, Viper
Crab Man	Leech, Giant (Freshwater, 1HD)	Spiderweed
Darkmantle	Lizardman	Spire Monkey
Demon, Manes	Lynx, Giant	Stirge
Dog, Guard or War	Mogura-Jin (Cannibal Mole Men)	Tatzelworm
Dolphin	Mothdog	Thugtoad
Exoskeleton, Giant (Ant)	Piercer (2HD)	Thylacine
Frog, Giant (Medium)	Pixie	Uruak (Scrap Gnoll)
Frog, Giant Killer	Ratling	Wolf
Gnoll	Rat, Wizardís Lab	Zombie

Challenge Level 3

Azer
Baboon, Giant
Badger, Giant
Cattle
Centipede, Giant (Man-sized)
Crab, Giant
Crocodile, Normal
Crumbler
Dark Creeper
Demon-Stirge
Degenue (Wall Wench)
Draug (Wolf-Bear Folk)
Dryad
Duergar
Exploding Bones
Fox Monk
Ghoul
Goat, Giant

Gravebird
Hawktoad
Head-Stealer
Homonculus
Horses, War
Human, Sergeant-at-Arms
Leech, Giant (Freshwater, 2HD)
Leapord
Lizard Samurai
Lizard, Giant
Maun-Ge
Mechanism, Bronze Cobra
Mold, Yellow
Mushroom-Man (2HD)
Old Crawler
Ophidian, Sterile
Origami Warrior
Ostrich, Giant

Piercer (3HD)
Sea Horse, Giant (3HD)
Sea Lion
Shark, Small (3HD)
Shrieker
Skullmural
Snake, Cobra
Spider, Giant (1 ft diameter)
Toad, Giant
Toad-Men
Torthri
Troglodyte
Vapor Crane, Fledgling
Vargouille
Yaruga
Zetan
Zombie, Leper
Zombie, Pyre

Challenge Level 4

Air Gust
Amphorons of Yothri, Worker
Ankheg (HD3)
Ant, Giant (Warrior)
Ape, Gorilla (and Ape, Carnivorous)
Bear, Black
Boar, Wild
Borsin (Ape Centaur)
Bugbear
Centaur
Centipede Nest (Swarm)
Demon, Lemures
Eel, Giant
Flowershroud
Flytrap Shambler
Frog, Giant (Large)
Fungal Creeper
Fungi, Violet
Gas Spore

Goblin, Belfry (Vampiric)
Grick
Growling Shadow
Harpy
Hippocampus
Hippogriff
Koíhaai
Komodo Dragon
Leech, Giant (Freshwater, 3HD)
Lycanthrope, Wererat
Mechanism, Iron Cobra
Melhukiskata (Snap-Snatcher)
Mold, Brown
Ogre
Oktomon
Panther
Piercer (4HD)
Portal Camel (Sage Beast)
Ragged Craw

Ranine
Rat, Giant (Monstrously Huge)
Raven, Giant
Sea Horse, Giant (4HD)
Shadow Mastiff
Shadow
Shark, Small (4HD)
Skeletal Fury
Sky Worm
Slitherat
Stag, Giant
Tick, Giant
Toad, Giant Poisonous
Vapor Crane, Small Adult
Vierd
Walking Slime
Weasel, Giant
Wolf, Worg
Wolverine

Challenge Level 5

Ankheg (HD4)
Aqueous Orb
Arcanix, Minor
Astral Moth
Baboon, Giant Alpha
Bat, Giant
Bee, Giant
Beetle, Giant (Normal)
Blink Dog
Chalkeion (hoplite)
Crabnipede
Crystal Growth
Crystaline
Dhezik
Doppleganger
Drow
Dwelver

Eagle, Giant
Formian, Warrior
Gelatinous Cube
Ghast
Glurm (Zen Frog)
Grey Ooze
Gump
Hag, Sea
Hellhound (4HD)
Hound of Chronos
Hyena, Giant
Igniguana
Inner Child
Jackal of Darkness
Jackalwere
Jellyfish, Hypnotic
Kurok-Spirit

Lamprey, Giant
Leech, Giant (Freshwater, 4HD)
Leech, Giant (Sea)
Leprechaun
Lichenthrope
Lion
Lycanthrope, Wereweasel
Lycanthrope, Werewolf
Marrosian Statue
Mechanism, Clockwork Cavalier
Melgara
Mephit, Brimstone
Mephit, Fire
Mist-Men
Mushroom-Man (3HD)
Nymph
Ogre, Tusken

Challenge Level 5 (continued)

Omgoth
Ophidian
Owlbear
Owl, Giant
Pegasus
Pseudo-Dragon
Rock Weasel, Giant

Rottentail
Rust Monster
Sea Cat
Shark, Medium (5HD)
Skunk, Giant
Spider, Giant (4 ft diameter)
Stoneflower

Toad, Giant Horned
Triton
Triton, Dark
Unicorn
Varn (Eternal Gladiator)
Yurmp (Toad Robber)
Zombie, Brain-Eating

Challenge Level 6

Ankheg (HD5)
Ape, Flying
Basilisk, Desert
Bear, Grizzly
Centipede, Giant (Large, 20 ft long)
Chalkeion (sergeant)
Crocodile, Giant
Demon, Dretch
Ettercap
Ferec (Foxtaur)
Gargoyle
Ghoul, Ao-Nyobo (Blue Wife)
Ghoul, Crimson
Gibbering Mouther
Golem, Wax
Green Brain

Hellhound (5HD)
Imp
Kzaddich
Leech, Giant (Freshwater, 5HD)
Leucrota
Lizard Samurai, Captain
Lizard, Lightning
Lycanthrope, Wereboar
Macaw, Giant
Minotaur
Naga, Hanu- (5HD)
Ochre Jelly
Octopus, Giant
Peryton
Quarn
Satyr

Shark, Medium (6HD)
Slithering Tracker
Sloorg (Midden Monster)
Snake, Giant (Spitting)
Snake, Giant (Viper)
Spider, Phase
Sycorex (Archaeopteryx Potens)
Tangle Weed / Strangle Vine
Toad, Giant Ice
Urrslumber
Vampire Tree (Jubokko)
Wasp, Giant
Were-Mist
Wight
Wolf, Winter
Yurmp (Toad Robber), Wrestler

Challenge Level 7

Allip
Ankheg (HD6)
Aranea
Bear, Cave or Polar
Beetle, Giant Arcane
Brainstorm
Carrion Fly
Chalkeion (lieutenant)
Corpse Tree
Demon, Grimlek
Demon, Quasit
Dinosaur, Elasmosaurus
Dragon, White (Adult, 5HD)
Exoskeleton, Giant (Beetle)
Flowerchild
Gargoyle, Maggog

Ghost, Strangling
Hag, Mountain (Yama-Uba)
Hellhound (6HD)
Hippopotamus
Hydra (5 headed)
Inaed
Komodo Dragon, Giant
Leech, Giant (Freshwater, 6HD)
Lycanthrope, Weretiger
Mummy
Naga, Hanu- (6HD)
Ogre Mage
Recurser
Scorpion, Giant
Shark, Large (7HD)
Snake, Giant (Amphisbaena)

Snake, Giant (Constrictor)
Sorcerer Ox
Soulspinner
Spider, Giant (6 ft diameter)
Tiger
Treacherous Treasure
Treant (7HD)
Tsalakian
Vapor Crane, Large Adult
Wandering Hole
Wight, Sea
Wolverine, Giant
Yeti
Yith, Hound of

Challenge Level 8

Amphorons of Yothri, Warrior
Ankheg (HD7)
Arcanix, Major
Archer Tree
Assassin Vine
Basilisk
Catoblepas
Cloaker
Cockatrice
Coral Clamper

Dark Stalker
Demon-Wolf of Braazz
Dragon, Black (Adult, 6HD)
Dragon, Brass (Adult, 6HD)
Dragon, White (Adult, 6HD)
Exoskeleton, Giant (Crab)
Formian, Taskmaster
Froglum
Glimmer
Griffon

Headless Hound
Hellhound (7HD)
Hieroglyphicroc
Hydra (6 headed)
Kheph, Warrior
Lephane
Lycanthrope, Werebear
Malcarna
Manticore
Medusa

Challenge Level 8 (continued)

Mimic	Rothran	Tiger, Sabre-Tooth
Monstrous Mouth	Rusalka (Water Witch)	Toad-Hydra (4 headed)
Ogre, Swamp	Salamander	Treant (8HD)
Otyugh	Shark, Large (8HD)	Troll
Quadricorn	Shroom	Turtle, Giant Snapping (8HD)
Redwraith	Silent Knight	Wraith
Reef Walker	Skarusoi	
Rhinoceros	Spider, Giant Invisible	

Challenge Level 9

Aaztar-Ghola	Dragon, White (Adult, 7HD)	Lammasu
Ankheg (HD8)	Drider	Linnorm
Bat Monster	Elemental, Air (8HD)	Lithonnite
Bulette (HD 7)	Elemental, Earth (8HD)	Mantis, Giant Praying
Demon, Achaierai	Elemental, Fire (8HD)	Remorhaz (8HD)
Demonvessel	Elemental, Water (8HD)	Rot Pudding
Dertesha	Flenser	Spectre
Dinosaur, Ankylosaurus	Formian, Male	Spectre, Parasitic
Djinni	Giant, Hill	Squid, Giant
Dragon, Black (Adult, 7HD)	Hellcat	Tendriculos
Dragon, Brass (Adult, 7HD)	Hydra (7 headed)	Treant (9HD)
Dragon, Copper (Adult, 7HD)	Invisible Stalker	Turtle, Giant Snapping (9HD)
Dragon, Green (Adult, 7HD)	Janni	Xorn

Challenge Level 10

Ant, Giant (Queen)	Felikaur	Shambling Mound (7HD)
Bulette (HD 8)	Giant, Stone	Skyger
Demon, Erinyes	Gorgon	Sphinx, Hieraco-
Dragon, Black (Adult, 8HD)	Hag, Annis	Treant (10HD)
Dragon, Blue (Adult, 8HD)	Hydra (8 headed)	Tree Ghost
Dragon, Brass (Adult, 8HD)	Mirror Fiend	Turtle, Giant Snapping (10HD)
Dragon, Bronze (Adult, 8HD)	Naga, Water	Vampire (7HD)
Dragon, Copper (Adult, 8HD)	Nightmare	Will-oí-the-Wisp
Dragon, Green (Adult, 8HD)	Oculaktis	Wyvern
Dragonne	Ray, Giant Manta	Xole
Ethereal Shade	Remorhaz (9HD)	Ygg (Gallows Tree)
Ettin	Rhinoceros, Wooly	

Challenge Level 11

Aardvark, Giant	Dragon, Blue (Adult, 9HD)	Mothmere
Banshee	Dragon, Bronze (Adult, 9HD)	Nykoul
Brainosaurian	Dragon, Copper (Adult, 9HD)	Roper (10HD)
Bulette (HD 9)	Dragon, Green (Adult, 9HD)	Shambling Mound (8HD)
Chalkeion (captain)	Dragon, Red (Adult, 9HD)	Spectral Scavenger
Chimera	Dragon, Silver (Adult, 9HD)	Sphinx, Crio-
Couatl	Elephant	Sphinx, Gyno-
Darakel	Giant, Frost	Star-Mouthed Worm
Deasic (Ice Creeper)	Giant, Khmornian (Male)	Todawan Master
Demon, Arauk (First-Category Demon)	Giant Slug of PíNahk	Trapper Beast (10HD)
Demon, Hezrou (Second-Category Demon)	Grue (Type 2)	Treant (11HD)
Demon, Vrock (First-Category Demon)	Hydra (9 headed)	Vampire (8HD)

Challenge Level 12

Aboleth
Black Pudding
Bone Mound
Bulette (HD 10)
Demon, Nalfeshnee (Fourth-Category Demon)
Demon, Yildra
Dragolem
Dragon, Blue (Adult, 10HD)
Dragon, Bronze (Adult, 10HD)
Dragon, Red (Adult, 10HD)
Dragon, Silver (Adult, 10HD)
Efreeti

Eyeless Filcher
Falshantog-Yoth (Fal-Yoth, the ìHungering Vineî)
Giant, Fire
Giant, Khmornian (Female)
Golem, Flesh
Golem, Glass
Grue (Type 1)
Gwurrum (Mists of Faerie Vengeance)
Hydra (10 headed)
Keeper of the Well
Kheph, Priest

Lamia
Lobster-Giant
Lurker, Ceiling
Night Hag
Rakshasa
Remorhaz (10HD)
Roper (11HD)
Shambling Mound (9HD)
Trapper Beast (11HD)
Treant (12HD)
Vampire (9HD)
Whale, Killer

Challenge Level 13

Amphorons of Yothri, Juggernaut
Behir
Demon, Khavorr (Third-Category Demon)
Demon, Larvaxu (Second-Category Demon)
Demon, Marilith (Fifth-Category Demon)
Denizen of Leng
Dragon, Gold (Adult, 10HD)
Dragon, Red (Adult, 11HD)
Dragon, Silver (Adult, 11HD)
Dragon Turtle (11HD)
Elemental, Air (12HD)

Elemental, Earth (12HD)
Elemental, Fire (12HD)
Elemental, Water (12HD)
Giant, Cloud
Glitterskull
Hydra (11 headed)
Kheph, Mage
Khryll
Mammot
Mohrg
Naga, Guardian

Naga, Spirit
Remorhaz (11HD)
Retriever
Roc
Roper (12HD)
Shambling Mound (10HD)
Shark, Giant
Slug, Giant
Trapper Beast (12HD)

Challenge Level 14

Arcanix, Greater
Artificers of Yothri
Chaos Knight
Dragon, Gold (Adult, 11HD)

Dragon Turtle (12HD)
Golem, Clay
Hydra (12 headed)
Remorhaz (12HD)

Shambling Mound (11HD)
Syanngg

Challenge Level 15

Athatch
Demon, Coral
Demon, Darkswimmer
Demon, Glabrezu (Third-Category Demon)
Demon, Shaavazi (Fourth-Category Demon)

Dragon, Gold (Adult, 12HD)
Dragon Turtle (13HD)
Giant, Daimyo
Kheph, Elder
Lich (12HD)

Oblivion Wraith
Remorhaz (13HD)
Shambling Mound (12HD)
Sphinx, Andro-
Turtle, Giant Sea

Challenge Level 16+

Demon, Baalroch (Balor), (Sixth-Category Demon) (CL 17)
Demon Prince, Isclaadra (CL 30)
Demon Prince, Kharkazax (CL 38)
Demon Prince, Orcus (CL 40)
Demon Princess, Teratashia (CL 42)
Demon Prince, Thalasskoptis (CL 39)
Demon Prince, Yildraathu (CL 40)
Dinosaur, Brontosaurus (CL 30)
Dinosaur, Stegosaurus (CL 17)
Dinosaur, Triceratops (CL 17)
Dinosaur, Tyrannosaurus (CL 19)
Dragon Turtle (14HD) (CL 16)
Elemental, Air (16HD) (CL 17)
Elemental, Earth (16HD) (CL 17)
Elemental, Fire (16HD) (CL 17)
Elemental, Water (16HD) (CL 17)
Flying Jellyfish, Giant (CL 19)
Furious Fountain (CL 18)
Giant, Storm (CL 16)
Golem, Iron (CL 17)
Golem, Stone (CL 16)
Great Lantern Worm (CL 30)
Ki-rin (CL 18)
Kraken (CL 24)
Lich (13HD) (CL 16)
Lich (14HD) (CL 17)
Lich (15HD) (CL 18)
Lich (16HD) (CL 19)
Lich (17HD) (CL 20)
Lich (18HD) (CL 21)
Mechanism, Giant Robot (CL 19)
Purple Worm (CL 17)
Sea Monster (CL 31)
Sea Serpent (CL 16)
Squid, Giant Aerial (CL 16)
Titan (17HD) (CL 19)
Titan (18HD) (CL 20)
Titan (19HD) (CL 21)
Titan (20HD) (CL 23)
Titan (21HD) (CL 24)
Titan (22HD) (CL 25)
Titan, Cursed (CL 19)
Whale, Sperm (CL 37)

Creating New Monsters

Monsters are not player characters, and their abilities are not at all determined by the rules for player characters – not even the stats for races that can have player characters, such as dwarves. The Game Master decides a monster's abilities, and he doesn't have to follow any rules about this! Feel free to add wings, breath weapons, extra hit dice, wounded versions, or whatever suits your adventure and your campaign. Toggle and tweak, imagine and invent! The rules aren't responsible for the quality of the swords and sorcery in your game, you are! So don't try to create monsters according to any sort of power formula. Create monsters based on how they feel and how they play at the gaming table. Create challenges for the players, not headaches for yourself. Your job is to imagine and create, not to slave at rulebooks finding out what you're "allowed" to do.

Attacks and Saving Throws

To determine a monster's saving throws and to-hit bonuses (if using the ascending AC system), use the table below.

Monster Attack and Saving Throw Table		
Monster Hit Dice	Base To Hit Bonus (Ascending AC system)	Saving Throw Target Number
Less than 1	+0	18
1	+1	17
2	+2	16
3	+3	14
4	+4	13
5	+5	12
6	+6	11
7	+7	9
8	+8	8
9	+9	6
10	+10	5
11	+11	4
12+	+12, etc.	3 (remains at 3)

To help you with determining Challenge Levels and experience point values for monsters, the table below may be helpful. "Challenge Level" determines the experience point value for a monster. To determine a monster's challenge level, take its hit dice and then add to that number if the monster has special abilities that make it harder to kill, or more dangerous to the characters. The first table shows the XP values for challenge levels. The second table contains guidelines for how many additional challenge levels to add to a monster's hit dice, based on special abilities.

Experience Point Value of Monsters

Challenge Level (see below)	XP Value
A (1d4 hit points or less)	5
B (1d6 hit points)	10
1	15
2	30
3	60
4	120
5	240
6	400
7	600
8	800
9	1100
10	1400
11	1700
12	2000
13	2300
14	2600
15	2900
16	3200
17	3500
18	3800
19	4100
20+	+300 per additional HD level

Challenge Level Modifications

Challenge Level Modifications (see special note on Undead)	
4+ attacks per round (minimum d6 or saving throw each)	+1 HD value
AC 20 or higher	+1 HD value
Automatic damage after hit	+1 HD value
Breath weapon 25 points max or below	+1 HD value
Breath Weapon 26 points max or more	+1 HD value
Disease	+1 HD value
Drains level with no save	+3 HD value
Drains level with save	+2 HD value
Flies, or breathes water	+1 HD value
Greater than human intelligence	+1 HD value
Immune to blunt/piercing (including half damage)	+1 HD value
Immune to energy type (acid, fire, etc)	+1 HD value
Immune to non-magic weapons	+1 HD value
Magic resistance 50% or below	+1 HD value
Magic resistance higher than 50%	+2 HD value
Massive attack for 20+ hps	+1 HD value
Paralysis, swallows whole, immobilizes enemies (web, etc)	+1 HD value
Petrifaction, poison, or death magic	+2 HD value
Regenerates	+1 HD value
Undead (subject to banishment but immune to sleep, charm, hold)	+0 HD value, net
Uses a spell-like power level 3 equivalent or above	+2 HD value
Uses multiple spells level 2 or lower	+1 HD value
Uses multiple spells level 3 or above	+2 HD value
Uses multiple spells level 5 or higher	+3 HD value
Poison	+1 HD value
Miscellaneous other	+1 HD value

Generating Encounters

At each "Level," whether it's how deep into a dungeon or how far into a forest they've gone, the players ought to know they're moving into an area where there's a somewhat predictable level of risk and reward. The first thing to keep in mind is that a monster's challenge level isn't the same as the "level" on which it's found: challenge level is really about calculating experience points. The table below gives you an idea of what might be found in a particular "level" of a dungeon or forest. The table is NOT a rule; it's a guideline. Use your judgment.

Level One has the lowest level of risk, and the lowest level of treasure. Players are never guaranteed that every encounter is beatable at a particular level, though. Survival depends on knowing when to run and when to get tricky; assuming that every encounter is designed to fit the party's combat capabilities is a sure way to die.

Die Roll	Level 1	Level 2	Level 3	Level 4	Level 5
1	3d8 CL A creatures	6d8 CL A creatures	12d8 CL A creatures	2d100 CL A creatures	3d100 CL A creatures
2	3d6 CL B creatures	6d6 CL B creatures	12d6 CL B creatures	1d100 CL B creatures	2d100 CL B creatures
3	2d6 CL 1 creatures	4d6 CL 1 creatures	8d6 CL 1 creatures	16d6 CL 1 creatures	32d6 CL 1 creatures
4	1d6 CL 2 creatures	2d6 CL 2 creatures	4d6 CL 2 creatures	8d6 CL 2 creatures	16d6 CL 2 creatures
5	1 CL 3 creature	1d6 CL 3 creatures	2d6 CL 3 creatures	4d6 CL 3 creatures	8d6 CL 3 creatures
6	1 CL 4 creature	1 CL 4 creature	1d6 CL 4 creatures	2d6 CL 4 creatures	4d6 CL 4 creatures
7		1 CL 5 creature	1 CL 5 creature	1d6 CL 5 creatures	2d6 CL 5 creatures
8		Roll again	1 CL 6 creature	1 CL 6 creature	1 CL 6 creature
9				1 CL 7 creature	1 CL 7 creature
10				Roll again	Roll again

Die Roll	Level 6	Level 7	Level 8	Level 9	Level 10
1	16d6 CL 3 creatures	16d6 CL 4 creatures	16d6 CL 5 creatures	16d6 CL 6 creature	16d6 CL 7 creature
2	8d6 CL 4 creatures	8d6 CL 5 creatures	8d6 CL 6 creature	8d6 CL 7 creature	8d6 CL 8 creature
3	4d6 CL 5 creatures	4d6 CL 6 creature	4d6 CL 7 creature	4d6 CL 8 creature	4d6 CL 9 creature
4	2d6 CL 6 creature	2d6 CL 7 creature	2d6 CL 8 creature	2d6 CL 9 creature	2d6 CL 10 creature
5	1d6 CL 7 creature	1d6 CL 8 creature	1d6 CL 9 creature	1d6 CL 10 creature	1d6 CL 11 creature
6	1 CL 8 creature	1 CL 9 creature	1 CL 10 creature	1 CL 11 creature	1 CL 12+ creature

Resource Tables

It was a difficult decision whether or not to include any wilderness encounter tables or terrain-type breakdown of monsters in this book, because this sort of world-specific detail can feel restrictive, especially if it's included in the monster's actual description. However, this sort of table is also a very useful tool for allowing the referee to organize his thoughts around a large number of monsters, and if you're playing a "sandbox" type game where the players may roam their characters all over the place, random tables can be a real necessity for handling that sort of thing on a moment's notice.

The first set of tables is one possible arrangement of monsters by the terrain types in which they might be encountered. Each terrain type has a basic table, showing a relatively intuitive set of monsters that might live in that climate. The second table, labeled "Weirder," contains the book's more unusual monsters, or monsters that could be placed into the terrain/climate if they were slightly modified. The "weirder" table is a good tool for referees who want to avoid too normal a feel in outdoor adventuring.

The second set of tables are random encounter tables using 3d6 to determine the nature of the encounter. The random encounter tables do not cover all the monsters identified as being found in that terrain type; there is plenty of scope for referees to design their own tables using different monsters.

Here goes.

Aquatic, Basic Table

Aboleth (CL 12)	Ghoul (CL 3)	Ray, Giant Manta (CL 10)
Aqueous Orb (CL 5)	Giant Crab (CL 3)	Ray, Sting (CL 3)
Barracuda (CL 1)	Giant, Storm (CL 16)	Reef Walker (CL 8)
Cliessid (CL A)	Gillmonkey (CL B)	Rusalka (CL 8)
Crabmen (CL 3)	Hag, Sea (CL 5)	Sahuagin (CL 2)
Crocodile, Giant (CL 6)	Hippocampus (CL 4)	Sea Cats (CL 5)
Crocodile, Normal (CL 3)	Lamprey, giant (CL 5)	Sea Horse (CL 3-4)
Darakel (CL 11)	Leech, giant (CL 2-7)	Sea Lion (CL 3)
Dinosaur, Elasmosaurus (CL 15)	Lizardman (CL 2)	Shark, Medium (CL 5-6)
Dragon Turtle (CL 13)	Merman (CL 1)	Shark, Small (CL 3-4)
Dolphin (CL 2)	Naga, water (CL 10)	Snake, Giant Amphisbaena (CL 7)
Eel, giant electric (CL 4)	Nixie (CL 1)	Snake, Giant Constrictor (CL 7)
Eel, giant moray (CL 4)	Nymph (CL 5)	Snake, Giant Viper (CL 6)
Elemental, Water (CL 8, 12, 16)	Octopus, Giant (CL 10)	Whale, Killer (CL 12)
Ghast (CL 5)	Oktomon (CL 4)	Whale, Sperm (CL 37)

Aquatic, Weirder Subtable

Centipede, giant (Large) (CL 6)	Gelatinous Cube (CL 5)	Shark, Large (CL 7-8)
Centipede, giant (Man-sized) (CL 4)	Golem, Stone (CL 16)	Shrangaathi (CL B)
Centipede, giant (Small, Lethal) (CL 2)	Grick (CL 4)	Squid, Giant (CL 14)
Coral Clamper (CL 8)	Hydra (CL 7-15)	Titan (CL 17-22)
Crabnipede (CL 5)	Lephane (CL 8)	Triton (CL 4)
Dertesha (CL 9)	Mimic (CL 8)	Turtles, Giant Sea (CL 15)
Exoskeleton, giant (crab) (CL 8)	Sea Serpent (CL 30)	Turtles, Giant Snapping (CL 8-10)
Gargoyle, aquatic (CL 6)	Shark, Giant (CL 13)	

Arctic, Basic Table

Air Gusts (CL 4)	Linnorm (CL 10)	Stag, Giant (CL 4)
Bear, Polar (CL 7)	Lycanthrope, Werebear (CL 8)	Tiger, Sabre-Tooth (CL 8)
Dragon, White (CL varies)	Lynx, Giant (CL 2)	Wolverines (CL 4)
Ettin (CL 10)	Mammoth (CL 13)	Wolves (CL 2)
Giant, Frost (CL 11)	Owl, Giant (CL 5)	Yeti (CL 7)
Giant, Storm (CL 16)	Remorhaz (CL 10-15)	
Human, Berserkers (CL 2)	Rhinoceros, Wooly (CL 10)	

Arctic, Weirder Subtable

Allip (CL 7)
Centaur (CL 5)
Chalkeions (CL 5-11)
Clawed Fiend (CL 3)
Deasic (CL 10)
Draug (CL 3)
Fox monk (CL 3)
Ghast (CL 5)
Ghoul (CL 3)
Glurm (CL 4)
Gnoll (CL 2)
Goblins (CL B)
Golem, flesh (CL 12)

Headless Hound (CL 7)
Hounds of Chronos (CL 5)
Lycanthrope, wereweasel (CL 5)
Lycanthrope, werewolf (CL 5)
Malformians (CL 1)
Melhukiskata (CL 4)
Minotaur (CL 6)
Oblivion Wraith (CL 14)
Ogre (CL 4)
Owlbear (CL 5)
Silent Knight (CL 8)
Sorcerer Ox (CL 7)
Tatzelworm (CL 3)

Titan (CL 17-22)
Toad, Giant Ice (CL 6)
Vampire (CL 10-12)
Wight (CL 5)
Will-o-Wisp (CL 10)
Wolverines, Giant (CL 7)
Wolves, Winter (CL 6)
Wolves, Worg (CL 4)
Wraith (CL 6)
Wyvern (CL 10)
Yith, hounds of (CL 7)
Zombie, Raven (CL B)

Desert, Basic Table

Air Gusts (CL 4)
Androsphinx (CL 15)
Ant, giant (CL 2, 4, 8)
Beetle, Giant (CL 4)
Camel (CL 2)
Centipede Swarm (CL 1)
Centipede, giant (Large) (CL 6)
Centipede, giant (Man-sized) (CL 4)
Centipede, giant (Small, Lethal) (CL 2)
Centipede, giant (Small, Nonlethal) (CL 1)
Criosphinx (CL 10)
Djinni (CL 9)
Dragonne (CL 10)

Eagle, giant (CL 4)
Efreeti (CL 12)
Elemental, Air (CL 9, 13, 17)
Elemental, Fire (CL 9, 13, 17)
Ghoul (CL 3)
Goblins, Oni-Aka (CL 1)
Gorgon (CL 10)
Gravebird (CL 3)
Gynosphinx (CL 9)
Hieracosphinx (CL 9)
Human, bandits (CL 1)
Human, patrol (CL 1)
Igniguana (CL 6)

Lamia (CL 12)
Lizard, giant (CL 3)
Ophidian (CL 5 or 3)
Sand Screamer (CL 2)
Shocker Lizard (CL 2)
Snake, Cobra (CL 3)
Snake, Giant Amphisbaena (CL 7)
Snake, Giant Spitting (CL 6)
Snake, Giant Viper (CL 6)
Snake, Viper (CL 2)
Spider, Giant (1 ft. diameter) (CL 3)
Spider, Giant (4 ft. diameter) (CL 5)
Wyvern (CL 10)

Desert, Weirder Subtable

Allip (CL 7)
Azer (CL 2)
Basilisk, Desert (CL 6)
Beetle, giant fire (CL 1)
Carrion Fly (CL 7)
Centaur (CL 5)
Chalkeions (CL 5-11)
Exoskeleton (giant ant) (CL 2)
Exoskeleton (giant beetle) (CL 5)
Formian male (CL 9)
Formian taskmaster (CL 8)
Formian warrior (CL 5)
Formian worker (CL 1)
Fungi, violet (CL 4)
Ghast (CL 5)

Ghoul, Ao-nyobo (blue wife) (CL 6)
Goblins (CL B)
Golem, Clay (CL 14)
Golem, Stone (CL 16)
Headless Hound (CL 7)
Hounds of Chronos (CL 5)
Human, berserkers (CL 2)
Leucrota (CL 6)
Lizard, lightning (CL 7)
Malcarna (CL 8)
Malformians (CL 1)
Maun-Ge (CL 3)
Oblivion Wraith (CL 14)
Omgoth (CL 5)
Owl, Giant (CL 5)

Ragged Craw (CL 3)
Scorpion, Giant (CL 8)
Spider, Giant (6 ft. diameter) (CL 7)
Stirges (CL 1)
Sycorex (CL 7)
Tiger, Sabre-Tooth (CL 8)
Vampire (CL 10-12)
Vargouille (CL 4)
Wasps, Giant (CL 6)
Wight (CL 5)
Yaruga (CL 3)
Zetan (CL 3, 5)
Zombie, Pyre (CL 3)

Dimensions, Basic Table

Air Gusts (CL 4)
Arcanix (CL 4, 8, 14)
Athatch (CL 15)
Azer (CL 2)
Chalkeions (CL 5-11)
Chaos Knight (CL 14)
Chimera (CL 11)
Cloud Giant (CL 13)
Demon, Achaierai (CL 8)
Demon, Baalroch (CL 13)
Demon, Dretch (CL 6)
Demon, Erinyes (CL 9)
Demon, Glabrezu (CL 11)
Demon, Grimlek (CL 7)
Demon, Hezrou (CL 11)
Demon, Lemures (CL 4)
Demon, Manes (CL 2)
Demon, Marilith (CL 13)
Demon, Nalfeshnee (CL 13)
Demon, Quasit (CL 7)
Demon, Vrock (CL 9)
Djinni (CL 9)
Efreeti (CL 12)

Elemental, Air (CL 9, 13, 17)
Elemental, Earth (CL 8, 13, 17)
Elemental, Fire (CL 9, 13, 17)
Elemental, Water (CL 9, 13, 17)
Ethereal Shade (CL 10)
Formian male (CL 9)
Formian taskmaster (CL 8)
Formian warrior (CL 5)
Formian worker (CL 1)
Frog, giant killer (CL 2)
Froglum (CL 8)
Fungi, violet (CL 4)
Gargoyle (CL 6)
Gargoyle, Maggog (CL 7)
Gelatinous Cube (CL 5)
Ghast (CL 5)
Giant Phase Spider (CL 6)
Giant, Storm (CL 16)
Gibbering Mouther (CL 6)
Glass Butterfly (CL A)
Goblins, Oni-Aka (CL 1)
Goblins, Redcap (CL 1)
Golem, Clay (CL 14)

Golem, Iron (CL 18)
Grey Ooze (CL 5)
Grick (CL 4)
Hell Hound (CL 5-8)
Hounds of Chronos (CL 5)
Imp (CL 6)
Invisible Stalker (CL 9)
Malcarna (CL 8)
Mothdog (CL 2)
Night Hag (CL 11)
Nightmare (CL 10)
Oblivion Wraith (CL 14)
Shadow (CL 4)
Shadow Mastiff (CL 5)
Sorcery Leech (CL 1)
Stoneflower (CL 5)
Vargouille (CL 4)
Wight (CL 5)
Wraith (CL 6)
Xorn (CL 8)
Yith, hounds of (CL 7)
Zetan (CL 5)

Dimensions, Weirder Subtable

Amphorons of Yothri (CL 4, 8, 13)
Artificer of Yothri (CL 14)
Beetle, Giant Arcane (CL 7)
Centipede, giant (Large) (CL 6)
Clawed Fiend (CL 3)
Couatl (CL 11)
Crystal Growth (CL 5)
Crystaline (CL 5)
Fox monk (CL 3)
Furious fountain (CL 18)
Glitterskull (CL 13)
Glurm (CL 4)
Goblins, Belfry (CL 3)

Great Lantern Worm (CL 30)
Grue (CL 10 or 11)
Hawktoad (CL 3)
Igniguana (CL 6)
Leaping Maw (CL 2)
Lich (CL 15-21)
Marrosian Statue (CL 5)
Mechanism, Giant Robot (CL 19)
Melgara (CL 5)
Mimic (CL 8)
Mothmere (CL 11)
Oculaktis (CL 10)
Origami Warrior (CL 2)

Retriever (CL 12)
Rothran (CL 7)
Salamander (CL 8)
Shocker Lizard (CL 2)
Silent Knight (CL 8)
Sorcerer Ox (CL 7)
Titan (CL 19-24)
Tsalakian (CL 7)
Vierd (CL 4)
Wandering Hole (CL 7)
Will-o-Wisp (CL 10)

Dungeons, Basic Table

Aboleth (CL 12)
Air Gusts (CL 4)
Allip (CL 7)
Animated Objects (CL 1+)
Ant, giant (CL 2, 4, 8)
Aranea (CL 7)
Athatch (CL 15)
Azer (CL 2)
Badger, Giant (CL 3)
Basilisk (CL 8)
Beetle, Giant (CL 4)
Beetle, Giant Arcane (CL 7)
Beetle, Giant Fire (CL 1)
Black Hunter (CL 3)
Black Pudding (CL 11)
Bugbear (CL 3)
Cave Eel (CL 2)

Centipede Swarm (CL 1)
Centipede, giant (Large) (CL 6)
Centipede, giant (Man-sized) (CL 4)
Centipede, giant (Small, Lethal) (CL 2)
Centipede, giant (Small, Nonlethal) (CL 1)
Chalkeions (CL 5-11)
Chaos Knight (CL 14)
Chimera (CL 11)
Clawed Fiend (CL 3)
Cloud Giant (CL 13)
Cockatrice (CL 7)
Crabmen (CL 3)
Crocodile, giant (CL 6)
Crocodile, normal (CL 3)
Crumbler (CL 2)
Darkmantle (CL 2)
Demon, Dretch (CL 6)

Demon, Lemures (CL 4)
Demon, Manes (CL 2)
Demon, Marilith (CL 13)
Demon, Quasit (CL 7)
Demon, Vrock (CL 9)
Doppelganger (CL 5)
Dragon, Black (CL varies)
Dragon, Blue (CL varies)
Dragon, Green (CL varies)
Dragon, Red (CL varies)
Dragon, White (CL varies)
Drider (CL 9)
Dwarf (CL 1)
Efreeti (CL 12)
Elemental, Air (CL 9, 13, 17)
Elemental, Earth (CL 8, 13, 17)
Elemental, Fire (CL 9, 13, 17)

Dungeons, Basic Table Continued

Elemental, Water (CL 8, 12, 16)
Elf (CL 1)
Ethereal Shade (CL 10)
Ettercap (CL 6)
Ettin (CL 10)
Fire Giant (CL 12)
Frog, giant (large) (CL 4)
Frog, giant (medium) (CL 2)
Frog, giant (small) (CL1)
Frog, giant killer (CL 2)
Fungal Creeper (CL 4)
Fungi, violet (CL 4)
Furious fountain (CL 18)
Gargoyle (CL 6)
Gargoyle, Maggog (CL 7)
Gelatinous Cube (CL 5)
Ghast (CL 5)
Ghoul (CL 3)
Ghoul, Ao-nyobo (blue wife) (CL 6)
Giant Crab (CL 3)
Giant, Hill (CL 9)
Giant, Stone (CL 10)
Gibbering Mouther (CL 6)
Glass Butterfly (CL A)
Glitterskull (CL 13)
Gnoll (CL 2)
Goblins (CL B)
Goblins, Oni-Aka (CL 1)
Goblins, Oni-Kage (CL 2)
Goblins, Oni-Yama (CL 2)
Goblins, Redcap (CL 1)
Golem, Clay (CL 14)
Golem, Flesh (CL 12)
Golem, Iron (CL 18)
Golem, Stone (CL 16)
Golem, Wax (CL 7)
Gorgon (CL 10)
Green Slime (no CL)
Grey Ooze (CL 5)
Grick (CL 4)

Grue (CL 10 or 11)
Gump (CL 5)
Hag, Annis (CL 10)
Headless Hound (CL 7)
Hieroglyphicroc (CL 8)
Human, bandits (CL 1)
Human, berserkers (CL 2)
Hydra (CL 7-15)
Igniguana (CL 6)
Imp (CL 6)
Leech, giant (CL 2-7)
Lich (CL 15-21)
Linnorm (CL 10)
Lithonnite (CL 9)
Lizard, giant (CL 3)
Lizard, lightning (CL 7)
Lizardman (CL 2)
Lurker, Ceiling (CL 10)
Lycanthrope, were-rat (CL 4)
Lycanthrope, wereweasel (CL 5)
Lycanthrope, werewolf (CL 5)
Malcarna (CL 8)
Malformian (CL 1)
Manticore (CL 8)
Mechanism, Bronze Cobra (CL 3)
Mechanism, Iron Cobra (CL 5)
Medusa (CL 8)
Mimic (CL 8)
Minotaur (CL 6)
Mold, Brown (CL 4)
Mold, Yellow (CL 3)
Monstrous Mouth (CL 8)
Mummy (CL 7)
Naga, Guardian (CL 13)
Naga, Spirit (CL 13)
Oblivion Wraith (CL 14)
Ogre (CL 4)
Ogre Mage (CL 7)
Ogre, Tusken (CL 5)
Ophidian (CL 5 or 3)

Orc (CL 1)
Otyugh (CL 8)
Owlbear (CL 5)
Piercer (CL 1-4)
Pseudo-dragon (CL 5)
Purple Worm (CL 17)
Rat, Giant (CL A)
Rat, Giant Desongnol (CL 1)
Rat, Giant, monstrously huge (CL 3)
Ratling (CL 2)
Roper (CL 11-13)
Rot Grub (CL 1)
Rust Monster (CL 5)
Shadow (CL 4)
Shadow Mastiff (CL 5)
Shocker Lizard (CL 2)
Shrieker (CL 3)
Silent Knight (CL 8)
Sorcery Leech (CL 1)
Spectre (CL 9)
Spider, Giant, Flagstone (CL 1)
Spiderweed (CL 2)
Spine Rat (CL A)
Stirges (CL 1)
Stoneflower (CL 5)
Sumatran Rat-ghouls (CL 1)
Thugtoads (CL 2)
Ticks, Giant (CL 3)
Troglodyte (CL 3)
Troll (CL 8)
Tunnel Prawn (CL 1)
Vampire (CL 10-12)
Vargouille (CL 4)
Walking Slimes (CL 4)
Weasels, Giant (CL 5)
Wight (CL 5)
Wraith (CL 6)
Xorn (CL 8)
Yurmp (CL 5)
Zombie (CL 2)

Dungeons, Weirder Subtable

Amphorons of Yothri (CL 4, 8, 13)
Androsphinx (CL 15)
Arcanix (CL 4, 8, 14)
Bag of Teeth (CL 1)
Beetle, Giant Arcane (CL 7)
Bone Mound (CL 12)
Carrion Fly (CL 7)
Criosphinx (CL 10)
Crystal Growth (CL 5)
Crystaline (CL 5)
Dergenue (CL 3)
Dhezik (CL 5)
Dragolem (CL 11)
Exoskeleton (giant ant) (CL 2)
Exoskeleton (giant beetle) (CL 5)
Exploding Bones (CL 3)
Flying squirrel, carnivorous (CL B)
Formian male (CL 9)

Formian taskmaster (CL 8)
Formian warrior (CL 5)
Formian worker (CL 1)
Froglum (CL 8)
Glurm (CL 4)
Goblins, Belfry (CL 3)
Great Lantern Worm (CL 30)
Gynosphinx (CL 9)
Harpy (CL 4)
Hawktoad (CL 3)
Head Stealer (CL 3)
Headless Hound (CL 7)
Hieracosphinx (CL 9)
Hounds of Chronos (CL 5)
Iounifier (CL varies)
Lamia (CL 12)
Leaping Maw (CL 2)
Lizard Samurai (CL 3)

Marrosian Statue (CL 5)
Mechanism, Clockwork Cavalier (CL 5)
Melgara (CL 5)
Mirror Fiend (CL 12)
Mushroom-men (CL 5,3,1)
Oblivion Wraith (CL 14)
Ogre Mage (CL 7)
Ogre, Tusken (CL 5)
Old Crawler (CL 3)
Omgoth (CL 5)
Origami Warrior (CL 2)
Ragged Craw (CL 3)
Ranine (CL 4)
Rat, Wizard's Lab (CL 2)
Rock Weasel, Giant (CL 5)
Rothran (CL 7)
Rottentail (CL 4)
Skullmural (CL 3)

Dungeons, Weirder Subtable Continued

Slitherat (CL 4)
Slithering Tracker (CL 6)
Sloorg (CL 6)
Slug, Giant (CL 13)
Sorcerer Ox (CL 7)
Spectral Scavenger (CL 11)
Spider, Giant, Invisible (CL 8)

Star-Mouthed Worm (CL 12)
Trapper Beast (CL 11-13)
Treacherous Treasure (CL 7)
Tsalakian (CL 7)
Vampire (CL 10-12)
Vierd (CL 4)
Will-o-Wisp (CL 10)

Yienhools (CL 1)
Yith, hounds of (CL 7)
Zombie, Brain-Eating (CL 5)
Zombie, Leper (CL 3)
Zombie, Pyre (CL 3)

Forests, Basic Table

Ankheg (CL 4-9)
Ant, giant (CL 2, 4, 8)
Aranea (CL 7)
Archer Tree (CL 8)
Assassin Vine (CL 8)
Badger, Giant (CL 3)
Bear, Cave (CL 7)
Bear, Grizzly (CL 6)
Beetle, Giant (CL 4)
Birhaakamen (CL 2)
Boar, Wild (CL 4)
Bugbear (CL 3)
Catoblepas (CL 8)
Centaur (CL 5)
Centipede Swarm (CL 1)
Centipede, giant (Man-sized) (CL 4)
Centipede, giant (Small, Lethal) (CL 2)
Centipede, giant (Small, Nonlethal) (CL 1)
Chimera (CL 11)
Clawed Fiend (CL 3)
Cockatrice (CL 7)
Draug (CL 3)
Druid (CL 6, 10, 14)
Dryad (CL 3)
Elf (CL 1)
Ettercap (CL 6)
Ettin (CL 10)
Ferec (CL 6)

Flying squirrel, carnivorous (CL B)
Fox monk (CL 3)
Frog, giant (large) (CL 4)
Frog, giant (medium) (CL 2)
Frog, giant (small) (CL 1)
Fungi, violet (CL 4)
Gnoll (CL 2)
Goblins (CL B)
Goblins, Belfry (CL 3)
Goblins, Redcap (CL 1)
Gwurrum (CL 10)
Hag, Annis (CL 10)
Harpy (CL 4)
Headless Hound (CL 7)
Human, Bandits (CL 1)
Human, Berserkers (CL 2)
Human, Patrol (CL 1)
Lamia (CL 12)
Leprechaun (CL 5)
Linnorm (CL 10)
Lizard, giant (CL 3)
Lycanthrope, werebear (CL 8)
Lycanthrope, wereboar (CL 6)
Lycanthrope, were-rat (CL 4)
Lycanthrope, wereweasel (CL 5)
Lycanthrope, werewolf (CL 5)
Lynx, giant (CL 2)
Manticore (CL 8)

Mantis, Giant Praying (CL 9)
Ogre (CL 4)
Ogre Mage (CL 7)
Ogre, Tusken (CL 5)
Owl, Giant (CL 5)
Owlbear (CL 5)
Pixie (CL 5)
Raven, Giant (CL 4)
Skunk, Giant (CL 6)
Snake, Constrictor (CL 2)
Snake, Javelin (CL 2)
Snake, Viper (CL 2)
Spider, Giant (1 ft. diameter) (CL 3)
Spider, Giant (4 ft. diameter) (CL 5)
Spider, Giant (6 ft. diameter) (CL 7)
Spiderweed (CL 2)
Spire Monkey (CL 2)
Stag, Giant (CL 4)
Stirge (CL 1)
Thylacine (CL 2)
Ticks, Giant (CL 3)
Tigers, Giant (CL 7)
Unicorn (CL 6)
Vargouille (CL 4)
Wasps, Giant (CL 6)
Wolves (CL 2)
Wolves, Worg (CL 4)

Forests, Weirder Subtable

Allip (CL 7)
Athatch (CL 15)
Blink dog (CL 4)
Borsin (CL 4)
Carrion Fly (CL 7)
Centipede, giant (Large) (CL 6)
Chaos Knight (CL 14)
Corpse Tree (CL 7)
Couatl (CL 11)
Dinosaur, Ankylosaurus (CL 8)
Dinosaur, Brontosaurus (CL 25)
Dinosaur, Stegosaurus (CL 15)
Dinosaur, Triceratops (CL 15)
Dinosaur, Tyrannosaurus (CL 19)
Exoskeleton (giant ant) (CL 2)
Exoskeleton (giant beetle) (CL 5)
Formian male (CL 9)
Formian taskmaster (CL 8)
Formian warrior (CL 5)

Formian worker (CL 1)
Frog, giant killer (CL 2)
Ghoul, Ao-nyobo (blue wife) (CL 6)
Giant, Hill (CL 9)
Gibbering Mouther (CL 6)
Glurm (CL 4)
Goblins, Oni-Aka (CL 1)
Gravebird (CL 3)
Gump (CL 5)
Hawktoad (CL 3)
Head Stealer (CL 3)
Hydra (CL 7-15)
Leech, giant (CL 2-7)
Leucrota (CL 6)
Lizard Samurai (CL 3)
Lizardman (CL 2)
Macaw, giant (CL 5)
Malcarna (CL 8)
Malformians (CL 1)

Maun-Ge (CL 3)
Medusa (CL 8)
Melgara (CL 5)
Melhukiskata (CL 4)
Mothdog (CL 2)
Mothmere (CL 11)
Mushroom-men (CL 5,3,1)
Omgoth (CL 5)
Ophidian (CL 5 or 3)
Ragged Craw (CL 3)
Razor Wing (CL 2)
Satyr (CL 6)
Shadow (CL 4)
Shadow Mastiff (CL 5)
Shocker Lizard (CL 2)
Snake, Giant Constrictor (CL 7)
Snake, Giant Viper (CL 6)
Sorcerer Ox (CL 7)
Spider, Giant, Invisible (CL 8)

Forests, Weirder Subtable Continued

Tangle Weed/Strangle Vine (CL 6)
Tendriculos (CL 9)
Tiger, Giant (CL 7)
Tiger, Sabre-Tooth (CL 8)
Treant (CL 7-12)

Tree Ghost (CL 10)
Urslumber (CL 6)
Vampire Trees (CL 6)
Wight (CL 5)
Wraith (CL 6)

Ygg (CL 10)
Yith, hounds of (CL 7)
Yurmp (CL 5)

Grasslands, Basic Table

Aardvark, giant (CL 11)
Air Gusts (CL 4)
Ankheg (CL 4-9)
Ant, giant (CL 2, 4, 8)
Birhaakamen (CL 2)
Blink dog (CL 4)
Boar, wild (CL 4)
Borsin (CL 4)
Bullette (CL 11)
Catoblepas (CL 8)
Cattle (CL 3)
Centaur (CL 5)
Centipede, giant (Small, Lethal) (CL 2)
Centipede, giant (Small, Nonlethal) (CL 1)
Chalkeions (CL 5-11)
Chimera (CL 11)
Cockatrice (CL 7)
Dragonne (CL 10)
Druid (CL 6, 10, 14)

Eagle, giant (CL 4)
Elephant (CL 11)
Fox monk (CL 3)
Frog, giant (large) (CL 4)
Frog, giant (medium) (CL 2)
Frog, giant (small) (CL 1)
Fungi, violet (CL 4)
Gnoll (CL 2)
Goat, giant (CL 3)
Gorgon (CL 10)
Gwurrum (CL 10)
Hippogriff (CL 4)
Human, bandits (CL 1)
Human, patrol (CL 1)
Hyena (CL 1)
Hyena, giant (CL 5)
Lamia (CL 12)
Lion (CL 5)
Lycanthrope, wereboar (CL 6)

Lycanthrope, were-rat (CL 4)
Lycanthrope, weretiger (CL 7)
Lycanthrope, werewolf (CL 5)
Ogre (CL 4)
Ostrich, Giant (CL 3)
Pixie (CL 5)
Ragged Craw (CL 3)
Raven, Giant (CL 4)
Skunk, Giant (CL 6)
Snake, Viper (CL 2)
Spider, Giant (1 ft. diameter) (CL 3)
Stag, Giant (CL 4)
Thugtoads (CL 2)
Tiger, Giant (CL 7)
Toads, Giant (CL 3)
Unicorn (CL 6)
Wasps, Giant (CL 6)
Wolves (CL 2)
Wolves, Worg (CL 4)

Grasslands, Weirder Subtable

Baboon (CL 2)
Baboon, Giant (CL 4)
Carrion Fly (CL 7)
Centipede, giant (Large) (CL 6)
Centipede, giant (Man-sized) (CL 4)
Chaos Knight (CL 14)
Crocodile, giant (CL 6)
Crocodile, normal (CL 3)
Dinosaur, Ankylosaurus (CL 8)
Dinosaur, Brontosaurus (CL 25)
Dinosaur, Stegosaurus (CL 15)
Dinosaur, Triceratops (CL 15)
Dinosaur, Tyrannosaurus (CL 19)
Draug (CL 3)
Exoskeleton (giant ant) (CL 2)
Exoskeleton (giant beetle) (CL 5)
Felikaur (CL 9)
Ferec (CL 6)
Formian male (CL 9)
Formian taskmaster (CL 8)
Formian warrior (CL 5)
Formian worker (CL 1)
Frog, giant killer (CL 2)
Ghoul, Ao-nyobo (blue wife) (CL 6)

Glurm (CL 4)
Goblins (CL B)
Harpy (CL 4)
Head Stealer (CL 3)
Headless Hound (CL 7)
Hieroglyphicroc (CL 8)
Human, patrol (CL 1)
Igniguana (CL 6)
Leucrota (CL 6)
Lizard Samurai (CL 3)
Lizard, giant (CL 3)
Lycanthrope, wereweasel (CL 5)
Malcarna (CL 8)
Malformians (CL 1)
Mammoth (CL 13)
Maun-Ge (CL 3)
Melgara (CL 5)
Mothdog (CL 2)
Mothmere (CL 11)
Mushroom-men (CL 5,3,1)
Night Hag (CL 11)
Nightmare (CL 10)
Ogre Mage (CL 7)
Ogre, Tusken (CL 5)

Omgoth (CL 5)
Pegasus (CL 4)
Razor Wing (CL 2)
Rhinoceros (CL 8)
Snake, Giant Spitting (CL 6)
Snake, Giant Viper (CL 6)
Sorcerer Ox (CL 7)
Spider, Giant (4 ft. diameter) (CL 5)
Spider, Giant (6 ft. diameter) (CL 7)
Sycorex (CL 7)
Tangle Weed/Strangle Vine (CL 6)
Tendriculos (CL 9)
Tiger, Sabre-Tooth (CL 8)
Toad, Giant Poisonous (CL 4)
Torthri (CL 3)
Tsalakians (CL 7)
Urslumber (CL 6)
Vampire Trees (CL 6)
Wight (CL 5)
Yaruga (CL 3)
Yith, hounds of (CL 7)
Yurmp (CL 5)

Hills, Basic Table

Aardvark, giant (CL 11)
Air Gusts (CL 4)
Androsphinx (CL 15)
Ankheg (CL 4-9)
Ant, giant (CL 2, 4, 8)
Archer Tree (CL 8)
Assassin Vine (CL 8)
Badger, Giant (CL 3)
Bear, Cave (CL 7)
Birhaakamen (CL 2)
Blink dog (CL 4)
Bugbear (CL 3)
Bulette (CL 11)
Centaur (CL 5)
Centipede Swarm (CL 1)
Centipede, giant (Large) (CL 6)
Centipede, giant (Man-sized) (CL 4)
Centipede, giant (Small, Lethal) (CL 2)
Centipede, giant (Small, Nonlethal) (CL 1)
Chalkeions (CL 5-11)
Chimera (CL 11)
Clawed Fiend (CL 3)
Cloud Giant (CL 13)
Cockatrice (CL 7)
Couatl (CL 11)
Criosphinx (CL 10)
Dragon, Blue (CL varies)
Dragonne (CL 10)
Druid (CL 6, 10, 14)
Dwarf (CL 1)
Eagle, giant (CL 4)
Elemental, Air (CL 9, 13, 17)
Elemental, Earth (CL 8, 13, 17)
Elephant (CL 11)
Ettercap (CL 6)
Ettin (CL 10)
Flying squirrel, carnivorous (CL B)

Fox monk (CL 3)
Fungi, violet (CL 4)
Gargoyle (CL 6)
Ghoul, Ao-nyobo (blue wife) (CL 6)
Giant, Hill (CL 9)
Giant, Stone (CL 10)
Giant, Storm (CL 16)
Gnoll (CL 2)
Goat, giant (CL 3)
Goblins (CL B)
Goblins, Oni-Aka (CL 1)
Goblins, Oni-Yama (CL 2)
Goblins, Redcap (CL 1)
Gorgon (CL 10)
Griffon (CL 8)
Gynosphinx (CL 9)
Hag, Annis (CL 10)
Harpy (CL 4)
Headless Hound (CL 7)
Hieracosphinx (CL 9)
Hippogriff (CL 4)
Human, bandits (CL 1)
Human, Berserkers (CL 2)
Human, Patrol (CL 1)
Hydra (CL 7-15)
Hyena (CL 1)
Hyena, Giant (CL 5)
Igniguana (CL 6)
Lamia (CL 12)
Leucrota (CL 6)
Linnorm (CL 10)
Lion (CL 5)
Lizard, giant (CL 3)
Lycanthrope, werebear (CL 8)
Lycanthrope, wereboar (CL 6)
Lycanthrope, were-rat (CL 4)
Lycanthrope, weretiger (CL 7)

Lycanthrope, werewolf (CL 5)
Lynx, giant (CL 2)
Malformians (CL 1)
Manticore (CL 8)
Medusa (CL 8)
Minotaur (CL 6)
Naga, Guardian (CL 13)
Naga, Spirit (CL 13)
Ogre (CL 4)
Ogre Mage (CL 7)
Ogre, Tusken (CL 5)
Ophidian (CL 5 or 3)
Orc (CL 1)
Owl, Giant (CL 5)
Owlbear (CL 5)
Pegasus (CL 4)
Peryton (CL 6)
Pixie (CL 5)
Pseudo-dragon (CL 5)
Ragged Craw (CL 3)
Raven, Giant (CL 4)
Shadow (CL 4)
Shocker Lizard (CL 2)
Skunk, Giant (CL 6)
Sorcerer Ox (CL 7)
Spider, Giant (1 ft. diameter) (CL 3)
Spider, Giant (4 ft. diameter) (CL 5)
Spider, Giant (6 ft. diameter) (CL 7)
Stag, Giant (CL 4)
Thylacine (CL 2)
Unicorn (CL 6)
Wasps, Giant (CL 6)
Wight (CL 5)
Wolves (CL 2)
Wolves, Worg (CL 4)
Wyvern (CL 10)

Hills, Weirder Subtable

Athatch (CL 15)
Banshee (CL 11)
Behir (CL 13)
Blink Dog (CL 4)
Carrion Fly (CL 7)
Chaos Knight (CL 14)
Corpse Tree (CL 7)
Draug (CL 3)
Drider (CL 9)
Ethereal Shade (CL 10)
Exoskeleton (giant ant) (CL 2)
Exoskeleton (giant beetle) (CL 5)
Felikaur (CL 9)
Ferec (CL 6)
Flying Jellyfish (CL 19)
Formian male (CL 9)
Formian taskmaster (CL 8)
Formian warrior (CL 5)
Formian worker (CL 1)
Frog, giant killer (CL 2)
Ghast (CL 5)
Ghoul (CL 3)

Glurm (CL 4)
Goblins, Belfry (CL 3)
Golem, Iron (CL 18)
Gravebird (CL 3)
Grey Ooze (CL 5)
Gwurrum (CL 10)
Hag, Mountain (Yama-Uba) (CL 7)
Headless Hound (CL 7)
Hounds of Chronos (CL 5)
Leopard (CL 4)
Lich (CL 15-21)
Lizard Samurai (CL 3)
Lizard, lightning (CL 7)
Lycanthrope, wereweasel (CL 5)
Malcarna (CL 8)
Mammoth (CL 13)
Maun-Ge (CL 3)
Mechanism, Giant Robot (CL 19)
Melgara (CL 5)
Mogura-jin (CL 2)
Mothdog (CL 2)
Mothmere (CL 11)

Mushroom-men (CL 5,3,1)
Night Hag (CL 11)
Nightmare (CL 10)
Nykoul (CL 11)
Omgoth (CL 5)
Razor Wing (CL 2)
Rock Weasel, Giant (CL 5)
Shocker Lizard (CL 2)
Silent Knight (CL 8)
Skeletal Fury (CL 3)
Stirges (CL 1)
Sumatran Rat-ghouls (CL 1)
Tiger, Giant (CL 7)
Tiger, Sabre-Tooth (CL 8)
Toad. Giant Poisonous (CL 4)
Troll (CL 8)
Tsalakians (CL 7)
Uruak (scrap gnolls) (CL 2)
Vampire Trees (CL 6)
Vapor Crane (CL 2,3,6)
Vargouille (CL 4)
Yith, hounds of (CL 7)

Jungle, Basic Table

Ape, flying (CL 6)
Ape, gorilla (CL 4)
Aranea (CL 7)
Assassin Vine (CL 8)
Athatch (CL 15)
Baboon, Giant (CL 4)
Baboon, Normal (CL 3)
Bat Monster (CL 9)
Bat, Giant (CL 5)
Bear, Black (CL 4)
Bear, Cave (CL 7)
Beetle, Giant (CL 4)
Beetle, Giant Fire (CL 1)
Beetle, Giant Huhu (CL 2)
Boar, Wild (CL 4)
Borsin (CL 4)
Carrion Fly (CL 7)
Catoblepas (CL 8)
Centipede Swarm (CL 1)
Centipede, giant (Large) (CL 6)
Centipede, giant (Man-sized) (CL 4)
Centipede, giant (Small, Lethal) (CL 2)
Centipede, giant (Small, Nonlethal) (CL 1)

Clawed Fiend (CL 3)
Couatl (CL 11)
Crabmen (CL 3)
Crocodile, giant (CL 6)
Crocodile, normal (CL 3)
Elephant (CL 11)
Ettercap (CL 6)
Ettin (CL 10)
Frog, giant (large) (CL 4)
Frog, giant (medium) (CL 2)
Frog, giant (small) (CL1)
Frog, giant killer (CL 2)
Fungi, violet (CL 4)
Ghast (CL 5)
Ghoul (CL 3)
Green Slime (no CL)
Grey Ooze (CL 5)
Grick (CL 4)
Gump (CL 5)
Harpy (CL 4)
Hieroglyphicroc (CL 8)
Hippopotamus (CL 7)
Human, Berserkers (CL 2)

Human, Patrol (CL 1)
Hydra (CL 7-15)
Leech, giant (CL 2-7)
Leopard (CL 4)
Lizard, giant (CL 3)
Lizardman (CL 2)
Lycanthrope, were-rat (CL 4)
Lycanthrope, weretiger (CL 7)
Macaw, giant (CL 5)
Mantis, Giant Praying (CL 9)
Medusa (CL 8)
Naga, Guardian (CL 13)
Naga, Hanu- (CL 6)
Naga, Spirit (CL 13)
Ochre Jelly (CL 6)
Ophidian (CL 5 or 3)
Shadow (CL 4)
Spider, Giant (1 ft. diameter) (CL 3)
Spider, Giant (4 ft. diameter) (CL 5)
Spider, Giant (6 ft. diameter) (CL 7)
Vampire Trees (CL 6)
Zombie, Brain-Eating (CL 5)

Jungle, Weirder Subtable

Banshee (CL 11)
Bugbear (CL 3)
Cloud Giant (CL 13)
Crabnipede (CL 5)
Dinosaur, Ankylosaurus (CL 8)
Dinosaur, Brontosaurus (CL 25)
Dinosaur, Stegosaurus (CL 15)
Dinosaur, Triceratops (CL 15)
Dinosaur, Tyrannosaurus (CL 19)
Exoskeleton (giant ant) (CL 2)
Exoskeleton (giant beetle) (CL 5)
Felikaur (CL 9)
Formian male (CL 9)
Formian taskmaster (CL 8)
Formian warrior (CL 5)
Formian worker (CL 1)

Giant, Storm (CL 16)
Gibbering Mouther (CL 6)
Glurm (CL 4)
Goblins (CL B)
Goblins, Belfry (CL 3)
Goblins, Oni-Aka (CL 1)
Goblins, Oni-Kage (CL 2)
Goblins, Redcap (CL 1)
Golem, Stone (CL 16)
Gravebird (CL 3)
Hag, Annis (CL 10)
Hawktoad (CL 3)
Lephane (CL 8)
Lich (CL 15-21)
Malcarna (CL 8)
Malformians (CL 1)

Manticore (CL 8)
Mushroom-men (CL 5,3,1)
Ogre (CL 4)
Ogre Mage (CL 7)
Ogre, Tusken (CL 5)
Omgoth (CL 5)
Shadow Mastiff (CL 5)
Shocker Lizard (CL 2)
Sycorex (CL 7)
Torthri (CL 3)
Vargouille (CL 4)
Wight (CL 5)
Yith, hounds of (CL 7)
Yurmp (CL 5)

Mountains, Basic Table

Air Gusts (CL 4)
Androsphinx (CL 15)
Ant, Giant (CL 2, 4, 8)
Athatch (CL 15)
Bear, Grizzly (CL 6)
Bugbear (CL 3)
Centipede, giant (Large) (CL 6)
Centipede, giant (Man-sized) (CL 4)
Centipede, giant (Small, Lethal) (CL 2)
Centipede, giant (Small, Nonlethal) (CL 1)
Chimera (CL 11)
Cloud Giant (CL 13)
Criosphinx (CL 10)
Dragon, blue
Dragon, red
Dragonne (CL 10)
Druid (CL 6, 10, 14)
Dwarf (CL 1)
Eagle, giant (CL 4)
Elemental, Air (CL 9, 13, 17)
Elemental, Earth (CL 8, 13, 17)
Elemental, Fire (CL 9, 13, 17)
Ettin (CL 10)
Fire Giant (CL 12)
Gargoyle (CL 6)

Giant, Stone (CL 10)
Giant, Storm (CL 16)
Goat, giant (CL 3)
Goblins (CL B)
Goblins, Oni-Aka (CL 1)
Goblins, Oni-Yama (CL 2)
Goblins, Redcap (CL 1)
Golem, Iron (CL 18)
Gorgon (CL 10)
Griffon (CL 8)
Gynosphinx (CL 9)
Hag, Annis (CL 10)
Harpy (CL 4)
Hieracosphinx (CL 9)
Hippogriff (CL 4)
Igniguana (CL 6)
Leucrota (CL 6)
Linnorm (CL 10)
Lycanthrope, werewolf (CL 5)
Lynx, giant (CL 2)
Manticore (CL 8)
Medusa (CL 8)
Minotaur (CL 6)
Ogre (CL 4)
Ogre Mage (CL 7)

Ogre, Tusken (CL 5)
Orc (CL 1)
Owl, Giant (CL 5)
Owlbear (CL 5)
Pegasus (CL 4)
Peryton (CL 6)
Roc (CL 12)
Shocker Lizard (CL 2)
Skyworms (CL 4)
Sorcerer Ox (CL 7)
Spider, Giant (1 ft. diameter) (CL 3)
Spider, Giant (4 ft. diameter) (CL 5)
Spider, Giant (6 ft. diameter) (CL 7)
Tatzelworm (CL 3)
Tiger, Sabre-Tooth (CL 8)
Vapor Crane (CL 2,3,6)
Weasels, Giant (CL 5)
Will-o-Wisp (CL 10)
Wolves (CL 2)
Wolves, Winter (CL 6)
Wolves, Worg (CL 4)
Wraith (CL 6)
Wyvern (CL 10)
Yeti (CL 7)

Mountains, Weirder Subtable

Amphorons of Yothri (CL 4, 8, 13)
Azer (CL 2)
Behir (CL 13)
Crumbler (CL 2)
Darkmantle (CL 2)
Drider (CL 9)
Exoskeleton (giant ant) (CL 2)
Felikaur (CL 9)
Flying Jellyfish (CL 19)
Formian male (CL 9)
Formian taskmaster (CL 8)
Formian warrior (CL 5)
Formian worker (CL 1)

Glurm (CL 4)
Hag, Mountain (Yama-Uba) (CL 7)
Lightning lamprey (CL 1)
Lizard, lightning (CL 7)
Malcarna (CL 8)
Malformians (CL 1)
Maun-Ge (CL 3)
Mothmere (CL 11)
Night Hag (CL 11)
Nightmare (CL 10)
Oblivion Wraith (CL 14)
Rock Weasel, Giant (CL 5)
Rothran (CL 7)

Shadow (CL 4)
Shocker Lizard (CL 2)
Slitherat (CL 4)
Squid, Giant Aerial (CL 14)
Stoneflower (CL 5)
Sycorex (CL 7)
Titan (CL 17-22)
Troll (CL 8)
Uruak (scrap gnolls) (CL 2)
Xorn (CL 8)
Yith, hounds of (CL 7)

Swamp, Basic Table

Allip (CL 7)
Aqueous Orb (CL 5)
Assassin Vine (CL 8)
Athatch (CL 15)
Banshee (CL 11)
Basilisk (CL 8)
Bat, Giant (CL 5)
Bear, Black (CL 4)
Boar, Wild (CL 4)
Catoblepas (CL 8)
Centipede Swarm (CL 1)
Centipede, giant (Large) (CL 6)
Centipede, giant (Man-sized) (CL 4)
Centipede, giant (Small, Lethal) (CL 2)
Centipede, giant (Small, Nonlethal) (CL 1)
Crabmen (CL 3)
Crocodile, giant (CL 6)
Crocodile, normal (CL 3)
Dragon Turtle (CL 13)
Dragon, Black (CL varies)
Dragon, Green (CL varies)
Elemental, Water (CL 8, 12, 16)
Ettercap (CL 6)

Ettin (CL 10)
Frog, giant (large) (CL 4)
Frog, giant (medium) (CL 2)
Frog, giant (small) (CL 1)
Frog, giant killer (CL 2)
Fungi, violet (CL 4)
Ghast (CL 5)
Ghoul (CL 3)
Ghoul, Ao-nyobo (blue wife) (CL 6)
Gillmonkey (CL B)
Glurm (CL 4)
Goblins, Oni-Kage (CL 2)
Gravebird (CL 3)
Green Slime (no CL)
Grey Ooze (CL 5)
Grick (CL 4)
Gump (CL 5)
Hag, Annis (CL 10)
Harpy (CL 4)
Hawktoad (CL 3)
Hippopotamus (CL 7)
Human, Patrol (CL 1)
Hydra (CL 7-15)

Leech, giant (CL 2-7)
Lephane (CL 8)
Lizard, giant (CL 3)
Lizardman (CL 2)
Lycanthrope, were-rat (CL 4)
Macaw, giant (CL 5)
Medusa (CL 8)
Ogre (CL 4)
Raven, Giant (CL 4)
Snake, Constrictor (CL 2)
Snake, Viper (CL 2)
Spider, Giant (1 ft. diameter) (CL 3)
Spider, Giant (4 ft. diameter) (CL 5)
Spider, Giant (6 ft. diameter) (CL 7)
Spiderweed (CL 2)
Spine Rat (CL A)
Stirges (CL 1)
Thugtoads (CL 2)
Toad. Giant Poisonous (CL 4)
Toad, Giant (CL 3)
Will-o-Wisp (CL 10)
Zombie (CL 2)
Zombie, Brain-Eating (CL 5)

Swamp, Weirder Subtable

Ape, flying (CL 6)
Bat Monster (CL 9)
Bat, giant (CL 5)
Behir (CL 13)
Carrion Fly (CL 7)
Couatl (CL 11)
Crabnipede (CL 5)
Dragon Turtle (CL 13)
Exoskeleton (giant beetle) (CL 5)
Giant Crab (CL 3)
Gibbering Mouther (CL 6)
Goblins (CL B)
Goblins, Belfry (CL 3)
Goblins, Redcap (CL 1)
Head Stealer (CL 3)

Hieroglyphicroc (CL 8)
Malcarna (CL 8)
Malformians (CL 1)
Maun-Ge (CL 3)
Mushroom-men (CL 5,3,1)
Naga, Guardian (CL 13)
Naga, Hanu- (CL 6)
Naga, Spirit (CL 13)
Naga, Water (CL 10)
Ochre Jelly (CL 6)
Ogre Mage (CL 7)
Ogre, Tusken (CL 5)
Oktomon (CL 4)
Omgoth (CL 5)
Ophidian (CL 5 or 3)

Shadow (CL 4)
Shadow Mastiff (CL 5)
Shambling Mound (CL 10-15)
Slug, Giant (CL 13)
Sorcery Leech (CL 1)
Tangle Weed/Strangle Vine (CL 6)
Tendriculos (CL 9)
Todawan Master (CL 11)
Torthri (CL 3)
Urslumber (CL 6)
Vargouille (CL 4)
Wight (CL 5)
Ygg (CL 10)
Yurmp (CL 5)

Aquatic River

Die Roll (3d6)	Monster
3	Dragon Turtle (CL 13)
4	Yurmp (CL 5)
5	Aqueous Orb (CL 5)
6	Naga, Water (CL 10)
7	Crabmen (CL 3)
8	Thugtoads (CL 2)
9	Crocodile, Normal (CL 3)
10	Lizardman (CL 2)
11	Frog, giant (large) (CL 4)
12	Toad, Giant (CL 3)
13	Barracuda (CL 1)
14	Nymph (CL 5)
15	Crocodile, Giant (CL 6)
16	Nixie (CL 1)
17	Cliessid (CL A)
18	Hag, Sea (CL 5)

Arctic

Die Roll (3d6)	Monster
3	Wight (CL 5)
4	Mammoth (CL 13)
5	Rhinoceros, Wooly (CL 10)
6	Toad, Giant Ice (CL 6)
7	Wolverine (CL 4)
8	Yeti (CL 7)
9	Bear, Polar (CL 7)
10	Wolf (CL 2)
11	Lynx, Giant (CL 2)
12	Human, Berserkers (CL 2)
13	Giant, Frost (CL 11)
14	Dragon, White (CL varies)
15	Wolf, Winter (CL 6)
16	Deasic (CL 10)
17	Ettin (CL 10)
18	Remorhaz (CL 10-15)

Aquatic, Lake or Sea

Die Roll (3d6)	Monster
3	Dragon Turtle (CL 13)
4	Nixie (CL 1)
5	Ray, Giant Manta (CL 10)
6	Sahuagin (CL 2)
7	Whale, Killer (CL 12)
8	Ray, Sting (CL 3)
9	Barracuda (CL 1)
10	Sea Horse (CL 3-4)
11	Dolphin (CL 2)
12	Shark, Medium (CL 5-6)
13	Shark, Small (CL 3-4)
14	Sea Lion (CL 3)
15	Triton (CL 4)
16	Hag, Sea (CL 5)
17	Dinosaur, Elasmosaurus (CL 15)
18	Sea Serpent (CL 30)

Desert

Die Roll (3d6)	Monster
3	Dragonne (CL 10)
4	Elemental, Air (CL 9, 13, 17) or Djinni (CL 9)
5	Centipede, giant (Man-sized) (CL 4)
6	Camel, wild (CL 2)
7	Sphinx (any type)
8	Centipede, giant (Small, Lethal) (CL 2)
9	Human, bandits or tribesmen (CL 1)
10	Lizard, giant (CL 3)
11	Ant, giant (CL 2, 4, 8)
12	Snake, Giant Spitting (CL 6)
13	Snake, Giant Viper (CL 6)
14	Snake, Viper (CL 2)
15	Sand Screamer (CL 2)
16	Scorpion, Giant (CL 8)
17	Malformians (CL 1)
18	Efreeti (CL 12)

Forest

Die Roll (3d6)	Monster
3	Lynx, giant (CL 2)
4	Lycanthrope, wereboar (CL 6)
5	Wolves (CL 2)
6	Ogre (CL 4)
7	Ant, giant (CL 2, 4, 8)
8	Human, Bandits (CL 1)
9	Giant Spider (CL 3-5)
10	Boar, Wild (CL 4)
11	Elf (CL 1)
12	Bear, Grizzly (CL 6)
13	Bugbear (CL 3)
14	Stag, Giant (CL 4)
15	Owl, Giant (CL 5)
16	Archer Tree (CL 8)
17	Assassin Vine (CL 8)
18	Druid (CL 6, 10, 14)

Hills

Die Roll (3d6)	Monster
3	Wyvern (CL 10)
4	Hippogriff (CL 4) or Manticore (CL 8)
5	Troll (CL 8)
6	Human, bandits (CL 1)
7	Harpy (CL 4)
8	Giant, Hill (CL 9)
9	Bugbear (CL 3)
10	Goat, giant (CL 3)
11	Orc (CL 1)
12	Goblins (CL B)
13	Ogre (CL 4)
14	Stirges (CL 1)
15	Gnoll (CL 2)
16	Dwarf (CL 1)
17	Dragon (red, blue, or green)
18	Chimera (CL 11)

Grasslands

Die Roll (3d6)	Monster
3	Sorcerer Ox (CL 7)
4	Snake, Viper (CL 2)
5	Boar, wild (CL 4)
6	Cattle (CL 3)
7	Lycanthrope, weretiger (CL 7)
8	Centaur (CL 5)
9	Human, bandits (CL 1)
10	Human, patrol (CL 1)
11	Ankheg (CL 4-9)
12	Gnoll (CL 2)
13	Lion (CL 5)
14	Hyena (CL 1) or Hyena, giant (CL 5)
15	Wolves (CL 2)
16	Ostrich, Giant (CL 3)
17	Tiger, Sabre-Tooth (CL 8)
18	Bullette (CL 11)

Jungles

Die Roll (3d6)	Monster
3	Hydra (CL 7-15)
4	Zombie, Brain-Eating (CL 5)
5	Ape, flying (CL 6)
6	Leech, giant (CL 2-7)
7	Centipede, giant (Large) (CL 6)
8	Leopard (CL 4)
9	Ape, gorilla (CL 4)
10	Baboon, Giant (CL 4) or Baboon, Normal (CL 3)
11	Beetle, Giant (CL 4)
12	Lizardman (CL 2)
13	Crocodile, giant (CL 6)
14	Giant Spider (CL 3, 5, or 7)
15	Human, tribesmen (CL 1)
16	Ophidian (CL 5 or 3)
17	Naga, Hanu- (CL 6)
18	Couatl (CL 11)

Mountains

Die Roll (3d6)	Monster
3	Chimera (CL 11)
4	Giant, Storm (CL 16)
5	Hag, Annis (CL 10)
6	Eagle, giant (CL 4)
7	Troll (CL 8)
8	Dragon (red or blue)
9	Bear, Grizzly (CL 6)
10	Ogre (CL 4) or Ettin (CL 10)
11	Centipede, giant (Large) (CL 6)
12	Goblins (CL B) or Orc (CL 1)
13	Griffon (CL 8)
14	Giant, Stone (CL 10)
15	Dwarf (CL 1)
16	Hag, Mountain (Yama-Uba) (CL 7)
17	Minotaur (CL 6)
18	Roc (CL 12)

Swamp

Die Roll (3d6)	Monster
3	Dragon, Black (CL varies) or Dragon Turtle (CL 13)
4	Will-o-Wisp (CL 10)
5	Thugtoads (CL 2)
6	Toad. Giant Poisonous (CL 4)
7	Hippopotamus (CL 7)
8	Crocodile, giant (CL 6)
9	Crocodile, normal (CL 3)
10	Leech, giant (CL 2-7)
11	Lizardman (CL 2)
12	Frog, giant (any type)
13	Spider, Giant (6 ft. diameter) (CL 7)
14	Snake, Constrictor (CL 2)
15	Hydra (CL 7-15)
16	Medusa (CL 8)
17	Shambling Mound (CL 10-15)
18	Banshee (CL 11)

9 781943 067343